Chapter 1

Oh, Jesus. I slam the pillow over my head and reach my hand out from the bed to feel around for the goddamn alarm clock. Why, why, why do I live like this? I am not a morning person. Not now, not ever.

Shit. I throw my sheet off and get up quick, grabbing the stupid alarm clock and pushing in the button that'll stop that godawful beeping. Oooooh, I feel like I've been run over by ten fire trucks. I rub my face hard as I sit on the edge of the bed, and I'm sorely tempted to crawl back under the covers. It's a physical craving, this urge to go back to sleep, as bad as wanting coffee or sex.

Well, wanting something doesn't mean that's what I'm getting. I stand up and slap my cheeks a little to get into the day. *Come on, Ruth,* I tell myself as I head into the bathroom. *The hardest part's over.* At least that goddamn alarm has shut up its racket.

Takes me about five minutes to pee, brush my teeth, and throw on some shorts and a T-shirt. That's the upside of not caring so much about the way you look – gives you a lot of time to fill up with better things. Things like what I'm doing right now – tiptoeing into Hope's room so I can actually look at her for more than two seconds without her whining, 'Ruuuth, stop loo-ooking at me.' She's a big girl now. Turning twelve years old this very day, in fact. Doesn't like me looking at her anymore or hugging

1

her or calling her cutesy little nicknames like buttercup and baby doll. Could be that she has a point about buttercup; I just might grant her that.

I'm standing over my little girl's bed, watching her chest rise and fall, rise and fall, as she sleeps. My little girl. I've been raising her since she was a week old, so I guess I can think of her as mine. Besides, I'd lay odds that Sara Lynn thinks of Hope as *her* little girl. Not that she doesn't have the right after all this time, but I'm not about to let old Sara Lynn get ahead of me, especially when it comes to my own niece.

I smooth my fingers over Hope's dark mop of curly hair and bend down to kiss her warm cheek. 'Happy birthday, baby doll,' I whisper, and she whimpers a little as she rolls over onto her side. 'See you at lunchtime.' She doesn't hear me, just clutches her pillow and makes little smacking noises with her mouth. I could cry from happiness just watching her settle back into sleep, but all I do is shake my head in wonder as I turn and start downstairs. I surely haven't done anything in my life to deserve such joy.

I let myself out of the house just after five, and my car starting in the quiet of the morning sounds like gunfire. I about jump out of my skin at the noise, scared to death I'm going to wake the world. My mother's smug voice pipes up from inside me, jeering that my jitters are nothing but a guilty conscience talking. *Ah, shut up, Ma,* I tell her. *Just go play your harp or whatever the hell else you do in heaven.*

See, Ma would believe my conscience is giving me a hint or two because I'm driving over to see Jack. Jack's my boss; he's the owner of the diner where I waitress. He's also my lover, although I hate that word like anything. Sounds like fingernails scratching down a blackboard to me. Makes me think of porn movies, with a big-breasted blondie and a muscleman with a full head of hair going at it. Ha! I'm a flat-chested, short-haired brunette, and Jack is flabby, bald, and pushing sixty. Plus, our lovemaking is nothing like what you see in those movies. For one thing, there are times when we sort of fumble around, trying to watch out for

Raising Hope

Raising Hope

Katie Willard

PIATKUS

♋ Visit the Piatkus website!

Piatkus publishes a wide range of best-selling fiction and non-fiction, including books on health, mind, body & spirit, sex, self-help, cookery, biography and the paranormal.

If you want to:
- read descriptions of our popular titles
- buy our books over the internet
- take advantage of our special offers
- enter our monthly competition
- learn more about your favourite Piatkus authors

VISIT OUR WEBSITE AT: **www.piatkus.co.uk**

Copyright © 2005 by Katie Willard

First published in Great Britain in 2005 by
Piatkus Books Ltd of
5 Windmill Street, London W1T 2JA
email: info@piatkus.co.uk

This edition published 2005

First published in the United States in 2005 by
Time Warner Book Group,
New York

The moral right of the author has been asserted

A catalogue record for this book is available from the British Library

ISBN 0 7499 0784 3

Set in Garamond by
Action Publishing Technology Ltd, Gloucester

Printed and bound in Great Britain by
Biddles Ltd, Kings Lynn, Norfolk

To John and Zoë with love

his bad back and my skinny rear end. For another thing, I don't imagine porn star lovers ever have any mess to clean up afterward or times when the sex is okay but doesn't really rock their world, if you know what I mean.

I yawn and flick on my blinker, heading south to Jack's house. I'm like a homing pigeon; I could make this drive blindfolded, that's how long I've been doing it. Down Morning Glory Lane. Left on Ritter Avenue. Right on Lark Street. Left to Main Street. Left on Spruce and a quick right on Pine. Twelve minutes door-to-door. I stretch my aching, sleep-deprived back before I hop out of the car, trot up the back steps, and unlock the door. *Just going over some accounts.* That's what I'd tell anybody who happened to see my car outside. At five in the morning? *Well,* I'd say with a straight face, *Mr. Pignoli is a very busy man.*

I kick off my sneakers and leave them on the doormat, and then I tiptoe through the kitchen and down the narrow hall to Jack's bedroom. I throw my T-shirt over my head and pull down my shorts, and then off come my bra and panties. I feel like a natural woman, just like in the song.

'Hi, sweetie,' Jack groans from the bed, and I hop in next to him.

'Damn,' I say, elbowing him. 'I was wanting to surprise you.'

'You always surprise me,' he tells me, rolling over to hug me. 'You're the nicest surprise. My angel.'

I can barely keep back my smile. Because I'm pleased, sure, but also because everyone in this town would die laughing if they knew Jack and I were sleeping together. And they'd really split a gut if they knew Jack calls me his angel. His angel! I'm more likely than not headed to hell with a red tail and horns.

'That's me.' I bury my face in his chest hair and laugh. 'I'm your angel.'

'Why don't you ever spend the night?' he complains, running his hands all over my body and giving me goose bumps. He asks me this at least once a week. 'I miss you every night.'

3

'We've been through all that,' I say between kisses. 'I don't want to set a bad example for Hope.'

'Well then, marry me,' he murmurs, rolling me over onto my back and climbing on top of me. 'Marry me, my angel.'

Being otherwise occupied, if you know what I mean, I can't answer him right away. But when we're finished, lying side by side, I ask, 'Say, did you just ask me to marry you?'

He leans over and traces designs on my stomach with his finger. 'Stop that—' I laugh, grabbing his hand. 'Tickles.'

'You know I asked you to marry me.' He smiles. 'I've been asking you for the past two years.'

'Just checking.' I reach up and wiggle my ears. 'Just making sure my ears are still working properly.'

It's a game of ours. He asks me to marry him, and I act like it's the first time, like he's taking me by surprise. And, in a way, it *is* a surprise, every time. I'll just never get used to being the one who's wanted instead of the one on the outside trying to push my way in.

'Why don't you?' he asks. 'I mean it, Ruth. I want to marry you and be with you all the time, out in the open.'

'You're beating a dead horse, Jack.' I laugh, rolling away from him. 'Sara Lynn and I are both guardians of Hope. Even-steven. That's by law. I can't move out on her, and I can't take her with me if I go.'

'Can't we at least date?' He puts his hand on my lower back. 'I'm tired of us being a secret.'

'For crying out loud.' I shake off his hand and sit up in bed. He's just crossed the line from funny to annoying. 'We've been a secret for three years. It's been working fine as it is; why change it? I for one don't want the whole town squawking about us. And I'm busy, Jack.' I kick off the sheets and get up to take a shower. As I turn on the water, I yell, 'I'm busy raising a child. I don't have time to date.'

I scrub myself clean, annoyed at how men don't ever understand that women have other responsibilities besides screwing them whenever they feel like it. As I rinse the shampoo from my hair, a thought comes to me from deep inside, in a little girl's timid voice: *Maybe he just really loves you, Ruth.*

Bah! I step out of the shower and rub a towel hard on my head to get all that water out. I'm nothing but a sap. I stick my tongue out in the mirror and make fun of myself. 'Maybe he just really loves you, Ruth,' I say in a high, fluttery whisper. Sure. They love you today and throw you away in front of the whole town tomorrow. At least when he dumps me now, I'll be the only one who knows about it.

I dry off and slap on some deodorant. Nothing like a day at the diner to make you smell. I walk back into Jack's room and fish around for a clean uniform in the bureau drawer I claim as mine.

'You're mighty pretty, Ruth.' Jack's lying in bed with his arms behind his head, smiling like the cat that ate the canary. I swear, men get a little action and they feel all macho and sexy, like they're James Bond. Well, I sure as hell am not looking like a Bond girl right now. No Pussy Galore; just plain old Ruth Teller.

'And you're mighty blind,' I snap. I get dressed quick, my back to him. 'Damn,' I mutter, struggling with my zipper.

Jack gets out of bed and zips me up the back, giving me a little spank on the bottom when he's through. 'I love you, I love you, I love you,' he sings like a lullaby, pulling me to him for a hug.

I can't help but hug him back because I'm so glad he knows not to take my nastiness personally. Just ignores me and goes on singing me songs and telling me he loves me. 'Yeah, yeah,' I say, slapping his hands away from my bottom. 'Now, would you please let me go so I can open up your diner?'

'Promise me you'll think about it.' He holds me tight, not letting me squirm out of his hold.

I sigh. 'About what?'

'About marrying me.'

'How many times do I have to tell you I've got Hope to think about!' I finally break free of his grip, which is starting to feel too damn tight. He's hanging on to this idea today like a dog gnawing at a bone. 'You don't understand, Jack. She's . . . she's this

5

fragile little creature who's mine.' I point at my bony chest and start talking fast and loud, probably to drown out the firecracker-loud sound of my heart beating. I gotta make him see, gotta get it through his head that this marriage thing we talk about is just a sweet little joke. Hell, he doesn't really want to marry me anyway. It's just that his brain gets addled after sex. That's all it is. And even if he really was serious, I've got responsibilities to Hope. And, dammit, I'm going to be there for her. Going to see my job through. 'Listen to me – my whole life, I've never had squat. And then one day I had this little baby girl handed to me to raise. I . . . she's everything to me. I worry about her all the time. What if something happens to her? What if she can't handle all the crap this world is going to throw at her? I need to be there for her. I need to make sure she's all right.'

'Ruth,' Jack says, 'she's a beautiful little girl. What could possibly happen?' His eyes are real sad, like he's sorry for me, like he knows the worry I put myself through. He's being so nice that I have to blink hard to keep back tears, tears of sheer relief that someone in my life can look at me and say, 'You feel like shit, Ruth, and that's okay.'

'Can you just quit being nice to me and let me blow my nose?' I wipe my eyes and try to laugh.

He rubs my back and chuckles. 'Angel, do you think you're the only one who's ever worried over a kid? When Donna and Paulie were babies, there were times I'd wake up in the middle of the night and go into their bedrooms just to be sure they were still breathing. Then when they were a little older, I was convinced they were going to kill themselves on their skateboards and bikes. And when they were teenagers' – he rolls his eyes – 'oh, boy. Diane and I would sit up nights waiting for them to come in. We'd watch the clock and worry and get no sleep at all until they were in their beds. Safe.' He pauses, and his voice thickens. 'And then when their mother died, there was nothing I could do for them. I couldn't protect them from feeling sad. . . .'

His voice trails off, and I hug him as tight as I can because there aren't any words to make that hurt better.

'Listen,' he says, his face in my hair. 'Share your worry with me. Marry me, and we can tear our hair out worrying about Hope together.'

'Be careful what you wish for, Jack,' I say as I twist out of his arms. 'You've got little enough hair left to lose.'

He laughs, and I'm glad I lightened his mood. I kiss him and run out the back door, hollering, 'See you at three! Don't be late! I've got a million things to do for Hope's birthday today!'

I started working for Jack twelve years ago, right at the end of the summer straight from hell. See, Ma died in early June that year; then, about three weeks later, my brother Bobby's wife died in childbirth; then Bobby just plain took off, too grief-stricken to stay and look after his baby daughter. Everything happened at once that crazy summer. It was like a goddamn soap opera, it truly was. I walked through it like a sleepwalker, just putting one foot in front of the other with no clear idea of where I was going. But one good thing did come out of all the crap, all the sorrow: I got Hope. Sara Lynn and I did, that is. Bobby gave her to both of us, and we decided between us that I'd move in with Sara Lynn because her house was bigger and she had her mother to look after. Hell, I didn't mind. It had been only Ma and me living in her little house on South Street. Bobby and his wife, Sandra, had been up in Maine for a little less than a year, and my other brother, Tim, had already gone off to Montana to find himself. You know, it's something, it really is – all the men in my family who have felt the need to run off and find themselves. It's my opinion they'd have been better off squinting real hard to locate themselves right where they were.

Once I moved in with Sara Lynn, I thought I'd continue to clean the houses Ma and I had been doing together. My friend

Gina Logan said, a little jealously, as is her way, 'Oh, I guess you won't be needing to work now that you'll be living high off the hog over at the Hoffmans' mansion.'

I looked her hard in the eye and said, 'I have no idea where you're getting your information. I am not a charity case. This is a business arrangement between me and Sara Lynn Hoffman regarding what's best for little Hope. Nothing more. Nothing less. I'm going to keep up the cleaning business Ma and I worked so hard to build.'

But I couldn't do it. I was tired from being up nights with Hope. I missed her every second of the day I was away from her. And I hate to admit this, but I was damn mad about the fact that Sara Lynn was getting more time than I was with my own niece. She'd taken a leave from her magazine job and was just pleased as punch about it. 'The magazine has a maternity leave policy, and I talked them into applying it to my situation,' she explained. I just nodded and smiled, trying to act thrilled for her, trying not to mind that she was cooing over Hope while I was out vacuuming and dusting and polishing. I was so afraid Sara Lynn would win Hope over to her, that she'd gain Hope's love as easily as she'd gained everything else in her life, and that, as always, I'd be left with the short end of the stick.

There was also the fact that I saw Ma in every nook and cranny of the houses we'd cleaned together for so many years. I knew I had to find another way to make a living when Mrs. Oliver set out her silver set of 120 pieces for polishing, including fish knives and asparagus tongs and other nonsensical items. I burst into tears when I saw those pieces lying on the dining room table, and it wasn't because I dreaded the way my arms would ache after polishing them. No, I cried because I was remembering the last time Ma and I had cleaned that silver and she had held up a serving spoon with flowers twirling up the side. 'Oh, Ruth,' she'd said softly, 'look how lovely this is. Sometimes I wish I had something like this.'

I'd felt a lump in my throat when she'd said that, thinking of everything in her life that she'd probably wanted and had never got. 'Oh, Ma,' I'd scoffed, 'you'd hate having this dumb old silver set. Think of how the boys would come over on holidays and eat with it and scratch it up.'

'You're right.' And she'd laughed, gently setting the spoon down. 'Besides, getting to keep all these pretty things in order is the next best thing to owning them for myself. I'm awfully lucky, Ruth.'

Well, not me. As I cried over Mrs. Oliver's silver after Ma's death, I knew I couldn't spend the rest of my life looking at other people's pretty things and thinking I was living. After work that day, I drove right down to the diner, where I'd seen the HELP WANTED sign in the window for the past month.

I parked my car, got my courage up, and walked into the diner and right up to Jack. 'I'm inquiring about the job,' I told him. I knew Jack because everyone in this town knows everybody else, although I didn't know him well because he was so much older.

'You're the Teller girl, right?'

'Ruth,' I said, sticking out my hand. 'Ruth Teller.'

'I was sorry to hear about your mother,' he said, and he really did sound sorry, so I had to narrow my eyes and clear my throat to prevent myself from crying. He told me years later that he'd decided to hire me right then. He always was a soft touch.

'So,' he said. 'Let's sit down and talk.' He led me to a booth, sat me down, and asked about my waitressing experience – a big fat zero – and my requirements. I remembered how Sara Lynn had told her magazine what she would and would not do now that a child had been dropped in her lap, so I took a chance and decided to do the same.

'Well,' I said, sitting up straight and trying to sound self-assured like Sara Lynn, 'you may have heard that I'm taking care of my brother's baby girl. I'd like to see her as much as possible, so I'd prefer to work out some flexible hours.'

'Hmm,' said Jack, drumming his fingers on the table and thinking.

'Or not,' I said, filling the silence. I started talking a mile a minute. 'I mean, I don't really care. All I know is that I'm desperate to get out of cleaning. It makes me think of my mother, and I'm not getting to spend any time with Hope, and I'm going crazy for wanting a change. It's all right for every member of my family who feels like it to take off for California or Montana or God knows where, but I need to stay right here. I have responsibilities now. I have this child to think of. So what I'm telling you is that I really need a new job, and this job sounds tailor-made for me. I'm friendly and I work hard and I'll do whatever you say. And just forget all about my need for flexible hours.'

He looked at me like he was trying to hold back from smiling. 'You got it,' he said. 'Job's yours. And we can work out the hours that make sense for you and your baby.'

'Really?' My face must have lit up like a neon sign; that's how happy I was. Not only did I get the job, but he'd also called Hope my baby. It was the first time anyone had acknowledged Hope as mine, as my little girl.

'Absolutely,' he said.

'Thank you. Thanks from me and from . . . from my baby.'

My baby . . . God, she's twelve today. I shake my head to imagine it; it was truly yesterday that she came to me and I started working for Jack. It's like I blinked my eyes and suddenly she's twelve. Better watch it – I'll blink again and she'll be thirty-two.

Dammit! I squint hard and shake my head to get rid of the tears misting up my vision. Sweet Jesus, it must be the menopause coming on early. Ma's revenge from up in heaven, I think as I rub my eyes hard. But how can I not be sad for Sandra, who didn't live to raise her own daughter? Or for Bobby, who ran away from his heartbreak and left his little girl behind? There's a flip side to my happiness at having Hope to love as my own child, and that's the losses that led to her becoming mine.

'She's doing great, Sandra,' I say out loud as I pull into the

10

back lot of the diner. I'm crazy as a loon, talking to a dead person as if she's sitting beside me, but I don't care. Sandra died and her baby was born twelve years ago today. That's important. 'Thank you,' I whisper to her. 'Thanks for having Hope.'

I park the car and roll up the windows – the goddamn AC's on the blink again – and I wonder about Bobby for a minute. The last letter from him came, oh, four or five years ago, postmarked California, no return address. It just said, 'Hi, Ruth. Things are good. Give my little girl a kiss for me. Bobby.' That was it. I haven't heard from him since, but I don't doubt I will one of these days. That's Bobby, sort of breezing in when you least expect him.

I lock up my shitbox car out of habit and then unlock it again, hoping God will see fit to have someone steal the damn thing. I wonder if Bobby doesn't come back because he doesn't want to face Sara Lynn. She hurt him real bad when she broke up with him. Not that I thought it was a great idea for those two to be carrying on together. But he did love her in his own weird way, and she broke his heart when she told him good-bye. Of course, if Sara Lynn hadn't broken up with Bobby, Bobby wouldn't have got together with Sandra and made Hope. Poor kid! I shake my head. So much trouble and sorrow bound up in her coming into the world.

Well, there's no trouble now. I narrow my eyes as I walk up the cement step to the diner. No more goddamn trouble on my watch.

Jesus! I straighten up and look around, hoping nobody's watching me nod and mutter in a public place like a crazy person.

Oh, hell, I'm just being paranoid. It's six-thirty in the morning, for Christ's sake, and I'm standing here alone in the teeny back lot of the diner. I laugh out loud as I turn my key in the door and punch in the alarm code. That's what I like best about getting up a little on the early side – no one's around to see me acting like the lunatic I surely am. I laugh again, and the sound echoes in the empty diner. I whistle as I get the coffee started.

Chapter 2

$\mathcal{S}$ara Lynn tries to hold my hand as we cross Main Street to go to the diner. She actually grabs on to my hand like I'm a baby who might get hit by a car, for crying out loud. I just pull away from her as fast as I can and walk a little ahead. She's so clueless. I'm twelve years old today, which is practically being a teenager. I don't need my hand held to cross the street.

I walk up the stone step to Ruth's diner and scuff my sneakered toe in the worn spot in the middle. As I open the door, the smell of hamburger grease makes my mouth water. Yum! I think no matter where I end up in this world, I'll get a whiff of this particular smell and it'll bring me right back here, to Ruth's diner.

Well, technically it's not Ruth's diner. But even though Mr. Pignoli owns it, he's always saying how Ruth is his right-hand woman, how there wouldn't even be a diner without her. Whenever I come in and he's working, he always yells, 'Ruth, get this little lady a huge chocolate sundae. My right-hand woman's niece deserves the royal treatment.'

'What about the right-hand woman herself, Jack?' Ruth will snort.

'Oh, you,' Mr. Pignoli will say, waving his hands like he's shooing her away. 'Hmm. I'll figure out your royal treatment later.'

I try to catch Ruth's attention as Sara Lynn and I slide into the red vinyl seats of the last free booth, but she's busy pouring coffee for a table, laughing as one of the men points to his cup and says, 'Load me up with some more of that diesel fuel, too.'

'This is the best diesel fuel in town, I'll have you know,' Ruth says back as she pours.

She sees me when she walks behind the counter to put the coffeepot back. She wipes her hands on her apron as she comes back from around the counter, and she grins wide so all her teeth are showing.

'Hi, birthday girl.' She bends down to squeeze my shoulders and kiss the top of my head. 'Have you had a good day so far? You were fast asleep when I looked in on you before I left.'

'*I* was still sleeping when you left,' says Sara Lynn.

'Yeah, well.' Ruth shrugs. 'I like to get up early, have a little time to myself before the craziness here starts.'

'Can we order?' I ask. 'I'm starving.'

'You wouldn't be so hungry if you'd eaten a good breakfast,' Sara Lynn says, looking up from her menu. She thinks I don't eat right just because I won't wolf down two eggs and a side of bacon every morning. She keeps telling me how a growing girl needs more than just a piece of toast to start the day. She's even shown me studies proving that kids who eat a full breakfast get better grades in school. So go raise one of those kids. That's what I feel like telling her.

'I want a cheeseburger and fries and a Coke,' I tell Ruth. 'Please,' I remember to add.

'I'm assuming you want that medium-well,' Ruth says matter-of-factly, looking at Sara Lynn. Sara Lynn strongly disapproves of undercooked meat; she says it can cause a host of evils.

Sara Lynn nods, then points to the menu. 'I'll have a BLT dry on white toast, and a seltzer water, please.'

'Okay, girls, let me go put that order in and I'll come back and talk for a minute.'

Ruth hustles away in her red waitress uniform with a white

apron tied around her waist. She looks like Olive Oyl, her bony knees and elbows sticking out as she scurries off behind the counter to the kitchen. I look like her – tall and thin and dark – but I hope I'm not quite so Olive Oyl-ish as she is. For one thing, I'm only just starting to develop my figure. I hold out hope that my boobs will be bigger than Ruth's. Lots bigger, please God. For another thing, her brown hair is a little darker and straighter than mine, and she wears it real short, even though Sara Lynn is always suggesting that a nice shoulder-length cut would be very flattering.

'Who am I trying to impress, Sara Lynn?' Ruth will hoot when Sara Lynn brings up ways Ruth could improve her appearance. 'You? Hope?'

I sink into my seat and think about how good my cheeseburger is going to taste. Chet, the cook, always makes me extra-big ones and piles on the fries. When Ruth comes back to our booth, she slides in next to me.

'You look different,' says, looking me up and down and pretending to be serious. 'Older. More . . . mysterious. Are you by any chance . . . *twelve* today?'

I laugh at her silliness, and Sara Lynn leans forward to say, 'I can't believe she's turning twelve. Ruth, we're old.'

'Speak for yourself,' Ruth says, grinning.

I lower my voice and say, 'Listen! Do you want to hear something funny that Mamie said to me today?' Mamie is Sara Lynn's mother, who lives with us. She's like my grandmother, except I'm not related to her by blood.

I clear my throat, pausing a little for dramatic effect. 'She asked me if, since I was twelve years old, I had got "the curse" yet.'

'The curse?' Ruth laughs, slapping her palm to her forehead. 'She called it the curse?'

'At least she gave it a name.' Sara Lynn rolls her eyes. 'When I was growing up, it wasn't even mentioned.'

I'm getting that warm, satisfied feeling that comes over me when I've made Ruth and Sara Lynn laugh. I just laugh along with them, acting like it's nothing but a big, fat joke. Little do they know how much I'm dying to get my period, how I keep checking my underpants every chance I get, just waiting to see blood.

'Hey, Ruth,' Jim McPherson calls from a counter stool. 'Can I settle up with you here? I gotta get back to work.'

'I'm coming.' Ruth hauls herself out of the booth and hustles over to the counter. 'Keep your pants on.'

Ruth is busy today. She rings the cash register for Mr. McPherson, telling him not to spend all his change in one place. Then she serves cherry pie to two police officers sitting at the booth closest to the door. When our food comes up, she brings it over. It seems she never gets a rest from wiping tables, taking orders, and bringing out food.

When we're ready to leave, Ruth won't take Sara Lynn's money for lunch. It's a little dance they do, where Sara Lynn puts down money to pay and Ruth ends up practically throwing it back at her.

'You're being ridiculous,' Sara Lynn says as she shakes her head and puts her money back in her purse.

'I've always thought of you as the ridiculous one,' Ruth shoots back. She wipes her forehead with the back of her hand and asks me, 'What's on the agenda for this afternoon?'

'Swimming at the club,' I tell her.

'No mall?' Ruth asks, throwing up her hands and acting like she's amazed.

'Nah.' I wrinkle my nose. 'It's such a nice day that I want to be outside.'

'Sara Lynn, she looks just like you when she does that, when she squinches up her nose.' Ruth touches Sara Lynn's arm.

Sara Lynn smiles slowly, her eyes widening, like Ruth just gave her a present. Now, it's obvious to anyone with eyes that I look like Ruth. But it makes me so happy that Sara Lynn would want for me to look like her and that Ruth tries to make Sara Lynn feel good. It makes me feel like my heart is growing big inside me, and I want everything to stop right here so I'll always be just this happy and bighearted. I want to burst out with all my love for Ruth and Sara Lynn, but that would be beyond stupid, so I just say, 'See you at home for my party tonight, and don't forget I want yellow cake with chocolate icing.'

⌐

Yellow cake with chocolate icing; yellow cake with chocolate icing. I'm humming a little birthday tune in my head as Sara Lynn and I walk into the country club. I'd skip if I weren't too old. That's how much I love my birthday.

'I want you to wait a half hour before you swim, Hope,' Sara Lynn reminds me, shifting her tennis bag on her shoulder. 'You did just eat.'

I sort of nod and shake my head at the same time, my way of getting her off my back but really saying, 'I'll do what I want, thanks anyhow.' I'm going to jump in the pool the second she takes her eyes off me and goes over to the tennis courts. What does she think, that I'm going to drown on my birthday?

When we get to the locker room, I shimmy out of my shorts – as much as a person can shimmy when they don't have any hips – and I happen to look over at Sara Lynn. As she's pulling her sundress over her head, my eyes can't help but notice how her body curves so softly and prettily in just the right places. I step into my red tank swimsuit and wish the bottom weren't pilling so much.

'Put your sunscreen on,' Sara Lynn orders. She's standing in front of her locker in her white tennis dress, rubbing thick, gooey lotion onto her arms.

'I don't know where mine is,' I lie, picturing it in the third drawer of my bathroom cabinet at home. 'And besides, I'm tanning.'

'Here.' She squeezes some of her lotion onto her fingers and rubs it into my cheeks, like I'm a little kid.

'I'll do it.' I scowl, grabbing the bottle from her hand and half-

16

heartedly rubbing the sunscreen into my skin. 'Satisfied?' I ask as I hand the bottle back to her.

'You'll thank me when you're older,' she tells me, putting the sunscreen in her locker and shutting the door firmly.

I guess.

When we walk out to the pool, Sara Lynn disappears behind the row of high shrubs dividing the pool from the tennis courts. I make sure she's gone and then run to the pool's edge, hold my nose, and jump in. Ow! It's cold as I hit the water, but that's the only way to do it. None of this sticking in a toe, and then a foot, and then an ankle. I come up to the surface and, still chilly, swim the length of the pool.

When I hop out, I wrap myself in one of the club's fluffy white towels and lay myself out on a lounge chair, closing my eyes. I shiver deliciously because I know it'll only be a minute before the sun warms me up. I'm sort of thinking about nothing, only that thinking about nothing is one of the finest feelings there is, and also that being really cold and then lying out in the hot sun must feel like being a slice of bread slowly getting cooked in the toaster.

'Hey, Hope.' I crack open an eye and raise a hand to my forehead to shade out the sun. Pop! Toast is up!

'Ginny!' I scramble up so I'm sitting, still holding the towel around my shoulders. It's Ginny Stevens, my friend from school. Well, to be honest, she's more like just my summer friend because she's popular in school and I'm just regular. Since none of the popular girls from my class belong to the country club, though, she's stuck with me. Sometimes I feel kind of like an understudy in a show, waiting for my big break. If I act cool enough around Ginny in the summer, then maybe I'll move up from regular to popular in the fall. I'm not exactly holding my breath waiting for this, though, because I've been the understudy for lots of summers and here I am. Still not a star. Still the same old me.

Ginny sits on the chaise longue beside me, smoothing the little pink skirt of her bikini as she stretches her legs out in front of her.

17

'You want to swim?' I ask. Even when the water's freezing, it always feels warmer when there's someone to swim with.

Ginny gets this little smile on her face, looking like a Mona Lisa wannabe. 'Can't,' she says, all mysterious.

'Why not?'

'Cramps,' she says under her breath, barely stopping herself from jumping up and down about it. 'I have my period.'

'Oh.' I try to nod like I know exactly what she's talking about, when inside I just feel left behind, like she's on a train speeding down the track and I'm at the station holding a sign that reads, 'Have a Nice Trip.'

She sighs and stretches her arms over her head. 'I really wish I could take a swim today.' If she weren't so popular, I'd tell her exactly how annoying she's being, bragging and sticking out her puny chest like she has something to show.

'So just wear a tampon,' I say, trying to be cool.

'I'm scared to,' she says. She leans in close to me and whispers, 'Don't you have to have had, like, sex to use those?'

'No,' I scoff, bluffing a little but pretty sure I'm right on this one. 'That's a myth.'

'Are you sure?' Ginny asks. She's looking at me like I'm the one on the train to womanhood now and she's the one saying sayonara. It sure feels good to be the one sitting up high and going somewhere.

'Positive. Cross my heart. They just slide right up there. Really.' I swear, at this rate I'll be the *leader* of the popular girls.

Ginny looks at me wide-eyed. 'Do you use them?'

'Sure,' I say. Oh, I'm riding that train right out of the station. Pretty soon Ginny's just going to be a little speck receding in the distance. 'I use them all the time.'

'Can you bring one of yours to show me sometime?' she asks, twirling a strand of her long brown hair. 'My mom is so lame; she won't let me or my sister use them, and I just want to look at one and see if I could dare to put it in.'

18

'Actually,' I say slowly, watching my fantasy train crash right off the track, 'I used them all up last time. I don't have any more.'

Ginny puckers her lips together in a puzzled frown. 'Well, you'll need some for next time, right?'

'Uh, yeah. Yeah, I guess I need to get some more.' The bug bites on my legs are suddenly pretty interesting to me, and I bend over and scratch them. 'These mosquito bites are killing me,' I say, standing up quick. 'I gotta go in the pool to make them stop itching.' I walk to the pool's edge and jump in and under the water. The understudy is under the water. Ha! Story of my life. I hold my breath until I feel ready to burst, swimming underwater practically all the way across the length of the pool. When I can't stand it another second, I swim up and break through the blue surface to gulp in a few big breaths.

By the time I swim back over to Ginny, Kim Anderson and Kelly Jacobs are putting their swim bags down, sliding off their sandals, and sitting on *my* chaise. Ick. Double ick, in fact. Kelly and Kim are a grade ahead of Ginny and me. They think they're so great just because they're thirteen and real teenagers. They're sometimes nice to Ginny, even though she's a whole year younger, just because she's popular. They don't give me the time of day.

I swim over to them, gritting my teeth through a fake, plastered-on smile. Did I mention that Kim and Kelly are best friends and call themselves the KKs? Yes, that's right – the KKs. As in, 'KK, do you want to swim?' 'No, KK, I'd rather sit out just now.' Add their special nicknames for each other to the fact that they dress alike, talk alike, and look alike, and it's no wonder that, in my head, I don't call them the KKs; I call them the psycho twins from hell.

I hoist myself up at the pool's edge and climb out, looking down at the wet footprints I make as I walk back to *my* seat. Ginny and the KKs are in the middle of talking about something, and I shake my head back and forth, flicking water from my wet hair on them.

'Ick!'

'Gross!'

'You're not a dog, Hope.'

'Yes, she is.'

'Ha, ha,' I say, plopping down in a chair a little bit separate from the huddle the other girls are in. Looking in from the outside, you might not think I'm so far apart, but trust me, from where I'm sitting, I am.

'Anyway,' Kim says to Ginny, 'my mom can pick you up at six-thirty. KK and I have been sooo dying to see this movie.'

Ginny bites her lip and glances at me before turning back to Kim and Kelly. She says, 'Maybe Hope would like to come, too?' She says it all tentative, like she needs their permission.

Well, I don't need the KKs' permission to do anything. Besides, I have a birthday party to go to tonight. 'I have plans,' I say from my chair just outside the circle.

'Plans?' Kelly sneers. 'What kind of plans do *you* have?'

'There's a party for my birthday,' I say, sticking out my chin. 'My family's counting on my being home for it.'

Kelly leans back on the chaise, using her feet to practically push Kim off. 'What's the story with your family, anyhow?' she asks, and her eyes look glittery and mean. 'I mean, you don't really have one, right? Like, you don't have a mom and dad.'

Everybody's looking at me, waiting for an answer. Ginny finally puts her head down to pick at her fingernail polish.

'My mother is dead,' I say in a tiny voice. There's a lonely, hollowed-out feeling that starts in my heart and spreads up to my throat and down to my stomach, and it takes me by surprise. I mean, my mother's been dead forever. I never even knew her, for crying out loud, so what's the big deal? I mean, sure, I feel sad about it sometimes. But not like this, not like I'm going to put my head between my knees and cry.

'And isn't your father an alcoholic who can't take care of you?' presses Kim. She pushes Kelly's legs out of the way and scoots back up on the chaise.

'Cut it out!' Kelly snaps.

'My father?' It's funny how those two words can barely squeeze out of my throat. The whole idea of him hurts so bad that I have to make up a story on the spot, just to try to put a Band-Aid on the pain. I sit up straight and flip my wet hair back over my shoulders. I squint at the pool as I say, 'He's in California because of his job. But he talks to me all the time on the phone and writes me the nicest letters. Ruth and Sara Lynn just take care of me for him.'

'Are they lezzies?' asks Kelly, and she and Kim and even Ginny giggle at the thought of Sara Lynn and Ruth being intimate. It feels like they're drawing their chairs in closer and closer just with the words they say and the looks they give one another. I may as well be on another continent. Greenland, maybe. Oh, that's a country. Antarctica, then. I may as well be in Antarctica.

I push back my chair and stand up. Exiling myself even farther into the Arctic tundra, I smile meanly and say, 'Actually, there are all these rumors that you two are hot and heavy with each other. Same clothes, same hair, all those sleepovers at each other's houses, your special little pet names for each other . . . everyone's talking about it.'

'Bitch,' they hiss.

As I walk away, I hear them ask Ginny in their squealing little popular-girl voices, 'Ohmygod, who's saying that about us?'

Don't cry, Hope, I warn myself, taking big steps toward the locker room. *Don't let them see you cry. Think birthday, presents, yellow cake with chocolate frosting.* But thinking about happy things just makes me sadder.

I barely make it to the locker room before my shoulders start shaking and my eyes spill over. I run to a bathroom stall, lock the door, and plop down on the closed toilet seat, drowning in my tears and wondering how my life would have turned out if my mother hadn't died and my father hadn't left, running away from me as fast and as far as he could.

Chapter 3

*H*ope is chattering away as we drive home from the club, her voice a pleasant hum in my ear. My goodness, that girl's moods are changeable. A prelude of the teen years ahead of us, I suppose. Not that I know a thing about being a normal teenager. I didn't rebel until my twenties, and even then my mother reined me in with a firm hand.

Hope was all smiles when we arrived at the club this afternoon, but it wasn't an hour later that she stomped over to the tennis courts insisting we go home. Are you sick? I asked her. No, she sulked. Just bored. Now, I couldn't very well walk out in the middle of a tennis match just because Hope was having a mood swing, so I told her to wait a while, that we'd leave soon. Ten minutes later, there she was, hitting balls over on court two with the new club pro, laughing and talking to beat the band.

And you wouldn't mind it, but she hates tennis; she simply hates it. I've been trying to get her to take it up for years. It's such a social sport, you know. Just a good skill to have. But she's never wanted anything to do with it. It's too hot out on the courts, she's said; she can't hit the ball; it's not any fun. Well, she certainly was doing a marvelous impression of enjoying it out there today; she was swinging that racket like she was having the time of her life.

'What do I owe you for the lesson?' I asked the pro when I finished my match and went over to fetch Hope.

'Nothing.' He smiled. 'Call it a birthday present for Hope.'

A birthday present! That's Hope for you – announcing her birthday to someone she's only just met.

'Sam says I could really be good,' she tells me from the passenger seat. She's hugging her knees to her chest and has her feet up on the car seat.

'Hmm?' I ask, turning my head to glance at her. 'Is your seat belt on?' I brush her knees aside to make sure.

'I *said*,' she announces, 'Sam says I could really be good.'

'Who's Sam?'

Hope takes a big breath and holds it, her cheeks full of air. As she exhales, she says, 'Do you listen to anything?'

'Well, I do have other things on my mind besides you,' I point out. God, the self-centeredness of children! She sounds like Bobby. My lips start to form a smile in spite of myself. 'You know' – I laugh – 'someone I once knew used to tell me I was visiting places in my mind instead of listening. He'd be in the middle of a story, and I'd have this look on my face, I guess, and he'd say, 'You're not hearing a word, are you. You're visiting places in your mind again.''

'Who?'

'Who what?'

'Who used to tell you that?'

'Oh, no one you'd know.' *Just your father.* I put my hand up to my face and fumble with my sunglasses, and then I say brightly, 'Now. I'm listening. Who's Sam?'

'Sam's the tennis pro. You know, the new guy at the club? He's so nice, Sara Lynn. I mean, he just saw me sitting there bored out of my skull, waiting forever for you to be finished—'

'Sorry,' I interject wryly.

'—and he says, "Hey, want to hit a little while you wait for your baby-sitter?"' Her voice deepens when she says his words, like she's onstage playing a role.

23

'Your baby-sitter?' I laugh. 'He thought I was your baby-sitter?'

'That's what *I* said. I said, "Listen, it's my birthday today, and I'm twelve years old. I don't have baby-sitters anymore."'

I smile, imagining Hope taking the poor man's head off.

'And then,' she continues, 'he sort of shakes his head, like how could he be so dumb, right? And he says, "I'm sorry. Of course you're too old to have a baby-sitter." So I forgive him, because he's being so nice, and he says, "Come on. I'll give you a free lesson, seeing as it's your birthday."'

'It looked like you were having fun,' I say, turning the car onto our street.

'Oh, I was. And he thinks I'm good. Or that I could be if I practice.'

'Well, that's great. I'm happy to practice with you anytime you'd like.' I decide to be gracious and omit the 'I told you you'd like tennis if only you gave it a chance' speech that's on the tip of my tongue. It is her birthday, after all.

'Um . . . I was thinking . . .'

I glance over to see Hope chewing the inside of her cheek.

'I was thinking that I kind of want to take lessons. At the club. From Sam.'

'Oh, no . . .' I laugh. Goodness, she thinks she can talk me into anything. 'No, no, no. Remember a mere six months ago when you convinced me you wanted to be a skater? And I bought you the skates, the costumes, the ice time? How many lessons did you take before you decided skating was not for you?'

'Well, that was different!'

'How many lessons?' It's my lawyer's training. I haven't practiced law in years, but my skills aren't so rusty that I'll let a wily twelve-year-old distract me from the issue.

She sighs. 'Three.'

'Three. And those skates were not inexpensive.'

'I know. And I've already said I was sorry. It wasn't really my fault, though. How was I supposed to know it'd be, like, below

24

zero on that ice rink? I was going to catch pneumonia or something if I kept skating! But that won't happen in tennis. It's not cold on a tennis court.'

'What if gets too hot out there?' I shoot back.

'Then I'll drink some water and take a break.'

'Hmmm.' That's a pretty good answer. Maybe *she* should study law.

'Please?' she begs. 'Pretty pretty please?'

Oh, for heaven's sake. I can't even recall how many times I've been down this road with Hope. Before skating, it was ballet. Before ballet, it was gymnastics. She throws herself into whatever her current passion is and then quits when she discovers she's going to have to work at it if she wants to be any good. Honestly, I worry about her work ethic sometimes. I take a deep breath and say, 'Do you promise you won't give up the second you get frustrated? Because tennis isn't easy, you know. You'll have to work very hard to become competent, never mind proficient, at it.'

'Duh!' she says, a syllable she uses that drives me batty. 'I was practicing today, wasn't I? With Sam?'

'I'm only saying—'

'Yeah, yeah,' she interrupts. 'I won't quit; I'll listen to Sam; I'll practice a lot. Come on, Sara Lynn. You're always saying how great a sport tennis would be for me, and now I really want to do it!'

I sigh. We do belong to the club, after all; we might as well use the facilities there. 'All right.'

'Yay!' Hope cheers. 'Maybe I'll get so good we can enter the family doubles tournament this year.'

'Maybe,' I say, trying to mask my skepticism.

We're pulling up the driveway now, and Hope bounces in her seat. 'Ruth's home!' she cries, spotting Ruth's blue car. 'I wonder if she's baking my cake.'

'I would bet she is.' I can't help but smile. Even if Hope is almost a teenager, she's still a kid who loves birthday cake. These days, she's been reminding me of herself at five, when she proudly paraded through the house in my high heels and Mama's old fur stole. 'I'm a big lady,' she used to tell us, utterly oblivious to the skinned knees and gapped baby teeth that gave her away. And now, at twelve, she's trying on being a young woman. She reads teen magazines with articles like 'How to Impress That Special Boy!' and 'Dressing Right for Your Body Type!' She sneaks my lipstick sometimes, putting on a lopsided clown mouth she thinks I don't notice. And she's picky about her clothes these days, flatly refusing to wear outfits she herself chose just a few months ago. But in spite of all this, she's still, in many ways, a little girl. As I slide my keys into my purse, my heart lurches out toward her, toward my sunny, stormy, changeable daughter.

My daughter. She's not. Of course she's not. But, oh, in my heart, she is. My Hope.

'Honey, look how beautiful the front gardens are.' I point out the gardens lining the pathway as we walk from the driveway to the front door – yellow snapdragons and purple salvia mixed with pink dianthus and white sweet alyssum. Anything to distract myself, anything to dilute this frightening feeling that overtakes me at times, this feeling of intense love for Hope that wraps itself around me and squeezes so tightly, I can't breathe.

'Yeah, yeah,' Hope says, rolling her eyes. She jumps up the steps, opens the door, and runs in the house, calling, 'Ruth! Ruth! Are you making my cake?'

I follow Hope to the back of the house, where my mother is sitting on the screened-in porch adjacent to the kitchen. She likes to sit there in her rocker while Ruth cooks dinner, so they can visit.

'Goodness, Hope, hasn't Sara Lynn taught you not to yell in the house?' Mama's eyes glitter as she looks up from her book, taking in Hope and me.

'Actually,' I say in a low voice as I pass by Ruth, busy at the stove, 'I've encouraged Hope to yell in the house. I'm hoping she throws a screaming fit so all the neighbors hear.'

Ruth snorts out a laugh as she holds on to her pot handle with one hand and stirs with the other.

'Hi, Mama,' I say, speaking with a brightness I don't feel as I walk onto the porch.

Her soft white curls appear to float as she shakes her head at me. 'Hope's yelling and carrying on like it's Judgment Day.' Her smile softens her words, though, and she chuckles a little as Hope bends down to hug her. 'Well, well,' she tells Hope, patting her on the back. 'Here you are at last.'

Hope springs away from Mama and skips past me over to the kitchen counter, her wild curls sticking out from her head in every direction. She must not have combed her hair out after swimming, though I've told her times too numerous to count that it'll snarl right up if she doesn't rinse and comb it immediately after she gets out of the pool.

'Are you making my cake?' she teases Ruth.

'Cake's done. I'm just whipping up the frosting now,' Ruth says, looking down at her pot and whistling.

'It's chocolate, right?' Hope asks.

'Your frosting?' Ruth replies, her shoulders freezing for a second. 'Uh-oh – I thought you wanted vanilla.'

'Oh no,' Hope wails as if it'll be the end of the world if she eats white instead of dark frosting.

Ruth turns around, her eyes twinkling, and points her spoon at Hope. 'Ha! Fooled you! Of course it's chocolate.'

'Ru-uth,' whines Hope, stomping her foot halfheartedly.

'Boy, I'm good!' Ruth brags, turning back to the stove. 'When you're good, you're good, and I am good!'

Hope sticks her tongue out at Ruth's back, then smiles as she jumps up and down. 'Yum!' she says to all of us. 'I love Ruth's chocolate frosting.'

I turn from her and look out the porch screen to the meadow and woodland gardens. I'm hearing that siren call that woos me out there, and I can't resist it when it comes. My gardens are speaking to me, telling me to be with them for a while, to leave the people in my life behind. I can feel the slight weight of my cutting scissors in my hand, smell the sweetness of the blooming roses. I rise on my toes and lean toward the outside.

'I'm going out to work in the garden for a bit,' I say. I whirl around to see my mother looking at the backyard as well, perhaps lost in a siren call of her own. After all, these were her gardens before they were mine.

She nods, still gazing outside. 'Good to keep up on the outdoor work.'

'Just be done in time for supper,' Ruth says. 'We're having steak, potatoes, and veggies.'

'I'll be on time,' I promise, and I head out the porch door, letting it slap behind me as I walk down the wooden steps. I cross the terrace and check the potted plants as I walk by. They're plenty wet – that summer storm yesterday did wonders for them. I deadhead a few petunias and scaevola, but I save the real nitty-gritty work on the terrace for another day. The sun's at my back, warming my shoulders as I walk down the hill. I'm walking farther and farther away from the house, and my breathing is slower and deeper as I settle into the person I am when I'm alone. Bobby was right: I do visit places in my mind. And when I'm alone, I can give myself over to those visits, can play over the whole keyboard of my thoughts.

I laugh softly as I find my pruning scissors in the little shed hidden by the bottlebrush buckeye shrubs. Who would have thought, way back when, that I'd become a recluse? I *tsk* my tongue at my exaggerating tendencies; really, I'm absolutely over-stating the case. After all, a person's not a recluse if she holds down a job. And I do work, even if I don't go to an office.

You write articles, I remind myself. *You write articles about gardens. That hardly requires people skills.*

Well, I'm raising a child, I argue back. *Which does, in fact, require people skills.*

I enter the woodland garden and stand among the viburnum, spicebushes, and rhododendron that cluster underneath the large pines and maples in this corner of the yard. In a little clearing

28

made long before my time sits a gray stone birdbath – three little cherubs holding up a flat bowl that fills with rainwater. I pull a soggy maple leaf from the birdbath, then turn from the woodland corner, my feet crunching lightly on the gravel path that leads to the meadow garden.

The butterflies and finches are crisscrossing the meadow's sunflowers and phlox and buddleia. Oh, the garden is lovely at this time of day, aglow in the mellow rays of the late afternoon sun. The flowers move in this meadow, even when – as today – there isn't any breeze. It's the birds, I think, and even the lightest of the butterflies. They land on a flower, stay for a moment, and then – *whoosh* – they're gone, jumping off their perch and leaving it slightly vibrating.

The small parcel of land that bridges the meadow and woodland gardens is planted thickly with pink and white roses edged with blue scabiosa. I bend to the first rosebush and smell the sweet, honeylike odor of the fullest blooms. I reach into the bush, gently, gently, so as not to be pricked by a thorn, and look for the faded blossoms. I clip them off without compunction, leaving the dead flowers where they fall to fertilize the earth. As I cut away the old to make room for the new, I croon, 'Beautiful,' at the buds starting to open. In a week's time, they'll have faded, too, and I'll be cutting them away. I won't forget they were beautiful once, though. I treat the dead flowers as tenderly as I do the blooming ones. It gives me comfort that the earth will take them in and use them to create still more beauty.

As I gently pull back a branch full of just blooming roses, I startle, for I see a bright green on top of the duller, darker green of a leaf. It's a tiny frog sunning himself, and I crouch down to watch. His eyes blink now and again, but otherwise he's perfectly still. The green on green is stunning, and it's moments like this that make me love gardening, moments when I can be amazed at the variations that exist in the simple color green.

I didn't use to notice anything about colors or textures or the way the rain was needed to make the flowers grow. I was going to be a lawyer like my father, and lawyers don't care about anything except twisting words to win their cases. I was the talk of the town when I went to Wellesley College, and then again when I went to Harvard Law School. 'Everyone's talking about you,' Mama used to say proudly. 'They're so excited to see what you'll do next.'

What I was supposed to do next was practice law for a few years, marry a nice young man from a good family, have a couple of children – a boy and a girl, naturally – and then gracefully retire from my brilliant career to raise them. It was all headed that way until I tripped off the fast track and never managed to get back on.

~~~~~

I received nine job offers during my last year of law school. That was two more than Frank Doblinski, the smartest person in our class. I was raised to play the game, you see, intuiting exactly what I needed to say and who I needed to be to make those lawyers leaning back in their leather chairs feel smart and powerful. They fired their interview questions at me, ostensibly to gauge whether or not I'd be an asset to their law firm, but what they really wanted to talk about was themselves. They were just dying for someone to bring the conversation around to them, and I – wearing my blue interview suit from Saks and the strand of pearls my parents had given me for my twenty-first birthday – was happy to oblige.

I took my time in deciding which law firm would get me. I let Harrison, Miller, and Hogan take me to dinner at a little restaurant overlooking the Boston Public Garden. I went to tea at the Ritz with Townshend and Black. Coleman and Dempsey gave me symphony tickets, and I heard a lovely program of Brahms and Beethoven.

I called my mother after each of these occasions and told her everything. 'Mama,' I said, 'you would not believe how fancy this tea was! Someone was playing a harp in the corner, and we weren't even allowed to pour our own tea. A waiter came over to do it for us. And we each had a little silver teapot and all of these gorgeous little pastries on a silver tray.'

'What did you wear, Sara Lynn?' asked Mama, holding her breath.

'My red silk dress. With my pearls.'

My mother sighed as though she'd reached the promised land. Then my father got on the line and asked if I needed any money.

My parents had me late in their lives. My father was a highly regarded lawyer in Ridley Falls and, indeed, all of New Hampshire. My mother taught school as a way of making herself useful until she found someone to marry. She met my father when he came to speak to her sixth-graders on careers in the law, and she became his wife six months later. She didn't teach school after that, as she was determined to settle right down to the business of having children of her own.

But there was a slight problem, a small glitch in the master plan. No children came. Indeed, it was seventeen years before I arrived on the scene. For seventeen years, my mother must have made my father his dry toast and black coffee for breakfast, tidied up our big house in the old, nice section of Ridley Falls, had a little lunch with some of her lady friends, cooked dinner for my father, asked him politely how he'd spent his day, and waited to see whether or not menstrual blood would stain her white cotton underpants.

She must have cried bitterly each month when she ran cold water in the sink to soak her panties and popped an aspirin to help the cramps. She must have lain beside my father each night they tried to have me and prayed. Please let it happen this time, she must have pleaded, picturing a tiny tadpole sperm penetrating the egg she had put out specially for the occasion.

She must have gardened as though her life depended upon it, because surely it did. She must have wanted so badly to create

31

something beautiful, and if she couldn't make a child in her womb, at least she could make flowers bloom in the dirt.

Of course, I really don't know any of this because I've never dared to ask. Oh, I've tap-danced around the issue, saying things like 'I must have been quite a surprise to you when I showed up so many years after you were married.' But I've always been too frightened to look my mother in the eye and ask, 'How did you feel when you kept trying and trying? Were you sad? Did you despair?' I've simply never had it in me to force her to relive her pain in the name of finding my own truth.

'You were a wonderful surprise,' she used to say, and she'd beam so brightly that it was hard to imagine she'd ever once given up hope of having me during those years she couldn't conceive.

Ow! I bring the cut on my thumb up to my mouth and suck it, hard. I wasn't paying close attention and I got pricked. I back away from the roses, my thumb still smarting, and begin to deadhead the scabiosa flowers growing beneath them. My mother loved me until I failed her. I think about this as I clip off the scabiosa seed heads, making room for new flowers. Was it really love, then? Did she really love me at all, or was she loving only the reflection of herself I worked so hard to shine back at her?

I'm cutting dead flower after dead flower, but still the plants don't seem at all bare. The harder you cut back scabiosa, the more vigorously it blooms. Cruel to be kind, you know. I'm fond of these blue flowers – pincushion flowers, Mama calls them, for they look like the tiny cushions a seamstress might use to store her pins. The pincushion flower's not a showy perennial, but neither does it ask for much. I like that in a plant.

Now, the delphinium – that's a different story altogether. As I glance over at the tall, proud, luminously blue flowers sitting in their own patch down a bit from the roses, I put my hands on my hips for a moment and say, 'Hmmph!' Delphinium. Too much sun, too much shade, too wet, too dry – they're never happy. Some gardeners say they grow better in the cooler, wetter climates of the Pacific Northwest, but I don't believe it for a second. They're likely fussy things everywhere. Even if they're blooming tall, straight, and the blue of the bluest sky, and you think that finally you've got it right – you know how to cultivate delphinium – well, they'll wither up and die on you one day just because they feel like it. I still grow them every summer, just because we always have, but I don't trust them one little bit.

Not like my scabiosa, and I run my finger over one of the blossoms the bees aren't climbing all over. Ruth is like a scabiosa. I picture her at the stove, waving her spoon in the air and joking with Hope about her frosting. Ruth doesn't need much of anything to keep smiling and laughing her way through life. A little sun, a little rain – it's all the same to her. Mama, on the other hand, is definitely a delphinium. A real pain in the ass, to use a choice term of Ruth's. I draw my back up straight, surprised at my own vehemence. She's just getting old, I tell myself. She wasn't always that way.

Oh, yes, she was. I pull up some weeds in the beds and tell myself the truth. She's always been fussy about things, demanding and demanding from me ever since I was a little girl. Sara Lynn, wear your hair this way. Sara Lynn, I hope you're staying at the top of your class. Sara Lynn, I don't want you wearing the tacky clothes other girls wear. Sara Lynn, you don't really feel sad; you're a happy, happy, happy girl. Yes, Mama is a delphinium, for sure.

If Ruth is a scabiosa and my mother a delphinium, then what am I? Nothing living in the garden, I think. Maybe part of the hardscape. Maybe a rock.

33

Chapter 4

*K*eep your hands out of the cake!' Ruth slaps at my hand as she spreads the frosting in a thick layer.

'She's got eyes in the back of her head,' Mamie calls from the porch rocking chair. 'Best to be careful around that one, Hope.'

'Tell it, Mamie!' says Ruth. 'I'm bad!'

Mamie chuckles. 'Stay out of trouble, Hope. Come sit by me and tell me about your day.'

I walk out to the porch and sit at the foot of her rocker. 'I played tennis,' I tell her, picking at a callus on my heel that's been there forever and doesn't show any sign of going away.

'Stop that picking, now,' Mamie says as she pats the top of my head with her old hand.

'Tennis?' Ruth calls from the kitchen. 'I thought you hated tennis. Isn't Sara Lynn always trying to get you to take it up? Sport for life, and all that?'

I swear, you express an opinion one time, and people hold you to it forever. 'Actually, I love tennis,' I call back.

'Hmmph.' Ruth sounds skeptical. 'Who'd you play with?'

'The new club pro. His name is Sam. Sam Johnson.'

'Did you beat him?' asks Ruth.

'Duh!' I laugh, picking at my heel again. 'He's the pro.'

'Will you stop it? You'll make it bleed,' Mamie says, clucking.

I roll my eyes and call in to Ruth, 'Can I lick the frosting bowl?'

'Sure,' Ruth says at the same time Mamie corrects, '*May* I lick the frosting bowl?'

'May or can, it's all going down her gullet,' jokes Ruth, and Mamie laughs at that one. I scramble up from the porch floor and go into the kitchen to grab the frosting bowl.

'Take two spoons,' Ruth says as she opens the silverware drawer and hands them to me. 'Share with Mamie.'

Mamie doesn't object to that. I give her a spoon, and she winks at me like we're partners in crime. 'Mmm-mmm-mmm!' she says, dipping her spoon in and putting it to her mouth. She looks like a kid sucking on a lollypop, and I laugh at her as I run my spoon around the inside of the bowl.

'Go on upstairs and shower, Hope,' calls Ruth. 'Dinner's in half an hour.'

'Sara Lynn hasn't showered yet,' I argue, licking my spoon. 'She's still fussing with her flowers.'

'Oh, don't worry about Miss Clean.' Ruth laughs. 'She wouldn't think of eating dinner after an afternoon at the club without showering first.' Ruth says 'the club' in a fake snooty voice. It's not really her kind of place.

I sigh. 'Okay.' Mamie and I have licked the frosting bowl clean anyway.

'And don't forget to comb out that mop of hair!' Mamie says as I get up and head inside.

⌒

It doesn't take me any time at all to shower. It's combing out my beastly hair that's the problem. I frown into the bathroom mirror, throw my comb on the sink, and walk into my bedroom. I flop on the bed and lie flat on my back, looking up at the ceiling and jiggling my feet. Then this lonesome feeling starts gnawing at me, and I turn onto my stomach and reach under the bed to get my *Diary of Anne Frank* book. I look at Anne's face on the cover, and for like the thousandth time, I feel a pain inside that always comes from looking at her. I love Anne so much. It's my special secret, something I can't tell a single soul because they'd think I was stupid. Heck, even *I* think I'm stupid. She's dead, for crying out loud. That's what I yell at myself in my head whenever I start thinking about Anne like she's a living person. But then I just quiet that mean voice inside and imagine she's right here with me, my best friend.

The thing is, we would be best friends if she were here right now. We wouldn't care about being popular because we'd have each other. I'd tell her everything, and she'd understand. I touch her face on the book cover and wish hard for what can never be.

Even though I've read the book about fifty times, I still can't believe she dies. I mean, of course she dies! God! I knew that even before I first read it. That was, like, the whole point of having to read the book for school. 'Class,' said Mrs. Wilson, 'this is a very sad book about a young girl who died in the Holocaust.' But here's the funny thing: Every time I read the book, every single time, I get to the end and I cry and cry because there's no more Anne and my mind just can't take it in.

When I first read the book, I tried to wear my hair like Anne's. Since my hair's a lot curlier than hers, it was a big, ugly failure. I tried keeping a diary, too, but that lasted only about a week. I even asked Sara Lynn and Ruth if I could become Jewish, but Sara Lynn said we were Episcopalians, and that was that. Ruth told me later that maybe when I was older and knew my own mind more, I could look into it. Then she asked me if maybe I was getting a little too attached to Anne Frank.

'What do you mean?' I asked her, practically shaking from embarrassment.

'Well,' she said, and it was killing me because she was trying so hard to be nice, like she was talking to a baby or a crazy person, for crying out loud, 'you read that book an awful lot. You carry it with you wherever you go. Now, I'm not saying there's anything wrong with that. But maybe it's time to read something else.'

I tried to act like I had no idea what she was talking about, like it didn't want to make me sink into the ground that she suspected how much I loved Anne Frank. 'It's no big deal,' I snapped, deciding right then that I'd hide the book under my bed so nobody would ever see me with it again. 'I'd think you'd be glad I'm at least a little bit interested in history.'

History. They taught us in school that if you don't learn from the past, you're doomed to repeat it. Sometimes that scares me so much, it makes my heart stop for a second. I mean, the Holocaust was so horrible that it just can't happen again. But, of course, I know it could. See, people don't like people who are different. Look at me. No mother, no father. That's why the KKs were so mean to me today. Because I'm different.

I put my head on the pillow and close my eyes for a minute, wondering what it would be like — what I'd be like — if I had my mother and father. It's not that I don't love Ruth and Sara Lynn, because I do. But what would it be like to have my mother tell me what it was like to have me growing inside her? What would it be like to have my father take me to the seventh-grade father/daughter dance, shaking his head as he looks at me all dressed up, saying, 'Hope, you're getting so pretty. You're the spitting image of your mom.'

'Hope! Dinner!'

They're calling me. I shove my Anne Frank book back under my bed and leap up, shouting, 'Coming! Coming already!'

⁓

'Happy birthday, dear Hope, happy birthday to you!'

The dining room table is set with Mamie's best china — the white plates with blue and pink flowers all over them. We're using the good silver, too, with the curly 'H' etched in each of the pieces. Sara Lynn dimmed the chandelier lights as Ruth brought out my cake, so the room is dusky as I take a deep breath and blow out all twelve of the little pink-and-white twisted birthday candles on top of my cake. I think of a bunch of wishes, but at the last minute I can't decide which one I want most, so my wish is a jumble of 'Anne Frank, parents, popular, period.' All spelled out, what I wish is: 'I wish Anne Frank were here; I wish I had my parents; I hope I get to be popular; I hope I get my period.'

'Hooray!' Ruth, Sara Lynn, and Mamie cheer, and Sara Lynn slides out of her chair to adjust the lighting. I blink at the brightness, and Ruth hands me a knife.

'Go ahead and cut,' she says, and I place the knife into the cake slowly and carefully, so as to cut a nice, even slice.

The dining room is quiet until I finally slice a piece, and then they all sigh happily when I get it onto the plate Ruth has set next to the cake. I smile as I reach across the table and put the plate of cake at Mamie's place. She's sitting up straight and prim in her yellow sundress, and she says, 'Age before beauty.' We all laugh, even though we've heard her say this a million times, whenever any of us serves her first.

Then I cut another piece, and I'm more confident this time because everyone knows that cutting the first piece is hardest by far. I slide this plate over to Ruth, since she's the cook. 'Don't mind if I do try my own creation here,' she says, rubbing her hands over the plate like she can't wait to dig in.

Sara Lynn's piece comes next. 'Just a sliver, Hope,' she says as I lift the knife again. Her hair is still damp from her shower and falling straight and blond down her back. She's wearing a white sundress and no shoes. I can smell her honeysuckle body lotion.

I slice off a huge hunk for myself. 'Too much sugar,' Sara Lynn objects.

'Well, it is her birthday,' Ruth points out.

'All right,' Sara Lynn says, giving in with a sigh. 'But that's it.'

We pick up our forks and eat in silence until we're done. The cake tastes too good for us to bother making conversation; we just shovel it in until it's gone. 'Uuuhhh,' I groan, finishing the last bite. 'I'm so full.'

'I should say so,' says Sara Lynn.

'Too full to open presents?' Ruth asks, leaning back in her chair and patting her stomach.

'I'll clear the table,' says Sara Lynn, rising as she gently stacks up the plates – 'Careful with that china,' Mamie reminds her – 'then Hope can open her presents.'

Ruth jumps up to help, and Sara Lynn says, 'Ruth, sit. You've been on your feet all day.'

'If you insist.' Ruth plops back down in her chair and stretches her arms to the ceiling. 'Mmm-mmm, that was good, if I don't say so myself!' She puts her elbows on the table and leans toward me. 'So, what do you think you're getting?' she asks, nodding at the presents piled up in the corner.

'A makeover,' I say right away. I've been teasing Ruth and Sara Lynn about it for a month, arguing that I'm old enough to wear makeup. I get a tingly feeling all over when I picture myself at school, pulling out my makeup bag in the girls' room and casually putting on a little blush as I study myself in the mirror. I'd better be getting a makeover; it'll really stink if I'm the only seventh-grader still wearing just plain old ChapStick.

'Hmm,' teases Ruth, 'you're awfully sure about that. How do you know you're not getting a dollhouse instead?'

'My sister Julia Rae and I had the most beautiful dollhouse when we were girls,' says Mamie. I roll my eyes at Ruth. We've all heard about the dollhouse a million times. The little dining room table with little chairs, the little beds, the little cradle that really rocked, the miniature pots and pans. 'You know, everything was tiny,' Mamie says as if she's remembering this for the first time in sixty years.

Ruth and I just listen politely until Sara Lynn glides back in and claps her hands together. 'Now,' she says, 'let's get to those presents.' She picks up the pile sitting on a chair in the corner and brings them over to me.

I look at the wrapped gifts with bows and ribbons hanging off them – there's no doubt that Sara Lynn wrapped these – and hesitate. I wave my hands over the pile and say, 'Oooh, I don't know which one to pick!' Finally, I grab the biggest box and shake it. It's not very heavy, and from the way something in there moves back and forth, making rustling sounds, I can tell it's clothes.

'Don't you want to save the nice paper?' Mamie asks as I tear open the pink paper with little white polka dots. Well, I could care less about the wrapping paper, so I just keep ripping.

When I open the box and pull away layers of pink tissue paper, I take out the most beautiful sundress. It's light purple, my favorite color, with spaghetti straps that cross over in the back and a floaty, flared skirt. It's the one I admired at the mall a few weeks ago, and I smile widely as I picture myself in it, beautiful and grown-up, the purple skirt fluttering as I walk. 'I love it!' I say, holding it up to myself and then tossing it to one side.

The next package I pick up is flat and square, and sure enough, when I tear off the paper, there are three CDs of music I like. 'Thanks,' I say, and I set them down on top of my new dress and grab the next present, a small rectangular one that feels light.

'This one is something you might be interested in,' Ruth says. I rip the paper fast, open the box, and – yay! – it's a gift certificate for a makeover at Hallon's Department Store.

'I knew it!' I scream, jumping up and down. 'My makeover!' I run around the table to hug Ruth, Sara Lynn, and Mamie.

'Beth Connors is going to do it,' Sara Lynn tells me, reaching up to pat my arms around her neck. 'Ruth told her we want a natural look for a young girl.'

'A little light blush and lipstick,' says Ruth.

'Don't you think she's a bit young yet for all that?' Mamie asks.

'The girls all wear it,' Ruth explains as I dance around, holding my little piece of paper that's a ticket to the new me. All I can think about is how pretty I'm going to be, so pretty that no one will even know me, so pretty that anything in the world will be possible.

At 11:37, I slide out of bed and walk over to my bedroom window that overlooks the backyard. My birthday is almost over, and I'm just not sleepy. Plus, I'm driving myself half-crazy by watching the numbers on my digital clock turn. There's a big old half-moon out my window and lots of stars. I can see Ruth sitting on the terrace, her long legs stretched out in front of her, looking up at the night sky, too.

Whenever I think of Ruth, I always picture her moving in lots of different directions all at once. In my mind, I see her cooking something on the stove, putting dishes in the dishwasher, peeling carrots over the sink, and visiting with Mamie – all at the same time, in perpetual motion. But here she is just sitting, looking up at the sky and not doing a thing. There's a funny little knot in the pit of my stomach when I see her like this – not scared, exactly, but the dreading feeling I get right before I get scared, the 'uh-oh, here it comes' feeling. I don't like people to be different from the way they are in my mind. It makes me feel like they've changed all the rules without bothering to fill me in on it. I jump up from the window and run out of my room. I want to go ask her, 'Hey, remember me?' I want her to stop this lonely feeling creeping up inside me.

I run down the back stairs and through the darkened kitchen – just the little light on over the stove – and step onto the porch. The wooden planks of the porch floor are cool on my bare feet. The screen door to the outside creaks as I open it, and Ruth turns at the sound.

'Aren't you supposed to be in bed?' she whispers.

I run down the steps and scoot in next to her, saying, 'Can't sleep.' She puts an arm around my shoulders and I lay my head against her. I put my arms around her waist and hug her tightly, like I haven't done in a long time, like I don't ever want to let her go.

41

'What's the trouble?' she murmurs, rubbing my back. My eyes blur as I look up at the sky, and I shrug.

'Sometimes there's a letdown after a big day like today,' she suggests.

I nod, not wanting to talk in case I start bawling like a baby. No use, though; tears are spilling down my face. I'm feeling sad for a lot of different reasons, but they sound so stupid that I can't possibly say them. I've been so busy being happy about turning twelve that I haven't noticed until this minute that I'm sad about growing up, too. I'm sad Ruth and Sara Lynn are getting older; and if I'm a year older, does that mean Mamie is a year closer to dying? I'm sad, too, because Anne Frank died for no reason at all, only because people were stupid and hating. I'm sad because I'll always be an understudy and never a star, not even in my new purple dress. I'm sad that I'll never know my parents because my mom is dead and my dad, well, he just doesn't care about me. It's not fair. The whole world just seems unbearably unfair.

'What's the matter, kid?' Ruth asks again, and my mind is so confused that I can tell her only one of the reasons, the one that sounds clearest to me.

'Why doesn't my father want to see me?' I wail. 'He's your brother. Do you know?'

'Shh,' she says, putting her arms around me and squeezing tight. She's quiet a minute and then says, 'You know what I think? I think he's afraid if he sees you, he'll never want to let you go.'

'That's dumb,' I protest, pulling away from her and wiping my eyes. 'He wouldn't have to let me go. He's my father.'

She doesn't say anything, just rubs my back and tells me to 'shh' once in a while.

'Doesn't he care about me at all?' My shoulders shake even more and I'm crying real hard, and some of this is about my father and the rest of it is about things too hard to put into words. 'I don't know who I am, Ruth. My mother is dead and my father doesn't want me. I don't know who I am.'

Ruth smooths my hair and rocks me back and forth until I cry myself out. She chuckles. 'Just like when you were a baby. I'd rock you and rock you until you got sick of crying. I'd make deals with you. I'd say, "Listen here, Hope. If you shut up that screaming, I'll take you for a walk in the carriage first thing in the morning." It never worked, though. You'd just cry and cry, and I'd rock you until you fell asleep.'

I smile a little, and she goes on. 'And then Sara Lynn would come on the scene and take her turn rocking you.' Ruth snorts out a laugh and shakes her head. 'She'd put her lips tight together in that way she has, you know? And she'd say, "It's astonishing to me that a baby can make all this noise."'

I smile at the thought of Sara Lynn being befuddled by a little old baby, and I breathe a long, shaky sigh and wipe my eyes.

Ruth tilts her head back and squints up at the stars. 'We loved you, Hope,' she says, her voice all quivery and funny. 'We loved you the best we could, and we love you now.'

I hug her, whispering, 'I'm sorry.'

She lets me go and jumps up, clearing her throat. 'Dammit to hell!' she says. 'Too much sugar running around our systems after all that cake!'

She leaps up the porch steps and says, 'You coming? I'm going to pop up some popcorn. The only cure for too much sugar is a dose of butter and salt.'

I walk up the steps after her, wiping my nose with the back of my hand. The kitchen brightens as Ruth flicks on all the lights and slams cabinets, gathering the corn and butter and salt.

'Shhh.' Sara Lynn strides into the kitchen in her nightgown, holding a book at her side, her finger marking her place. 'Hope's sleeping.'

Ruth points to me sitting at the table as she pours popcorn kernels into a pan on the stove.

Sara Lynn looks at my red eyes and then back at Ruth. 'What's wrong?' she asks, frowning and folding her arms over her chest. 'You've both been crying.'

'She was crying worse than I was,' Ruth says, pointing her chin at me. She sounds so mad about it that Sara Lynn and I laugh.

'What happened?' Sara Lynn asks.

'Oh, it's nothing but Bobby,' Ruth says, shaking the pan over the stove.

'Bobby?!' Sara Lynn's eyes pop wide open and her hand flies up to her throat. 'What about Bobby?'

'She was just wondering why he doesn't come around.'

'Oh, Hope.' Sara Lynn sits next to me at the table and sighs.

Ruth adds, 'She says she doesn't know who she is. On account of not having any parents.'

'Honestly, Hope, that's absolutely ridiculous – Ruth and I are your parents,' Sara Lynn protests. 'Think of the poor children who don't have anyone to take care of them.'

I set my elbows on the table and put my chin in my hands. I swear, if I lost a leg, Sara Lynn would tell me to buck up, at least I still had one left.

We're all quiet now. Sara Lynn puckers her forehead, Ruth scowls at the stove as the popcorn begins to pop, and I roll the edges of my place mat until Sara Lynn puts her hand over mine to make me stop. I listen to the popcorn popping faster and faster, and I wonder what Sara Lynn and Ruth are thinking right now. I can hear the clock on the wall tick when Ruth takes the pan off the stove.

I take a deep breath as Ruth slams down the bowl of popcorn on the table and pulls out a chair to sit with us. 'It's not that I don't love you,' I try to explain, 'but you're not my real mother and father. Other kids can say, 'Oh, I have my mother's eyes,' or, 'I'm good at art like my dad.' I throw up my hands. 'How am I ever supposed to find out who I take after, or even who I am?'

'You take after us,' Sara Lynn says. She purses her lips together and nods her head up and down. 'You're the spitting image of Ruth and me.'

'Well,' Ruth says, taking a handful of popcorn, 'you do look a lot like me.'

'And you like to dress up and keep yourself looking nice like I do,' adds Sara Lynn.

'You can get up on your high horse sometimes, like her,' says Ruth, jerking her head at Sara Lynn and twisting one side of her mouth up into a smile.

'And you sometimes forget your manners the way Ruth does,' Sara Lynn finishes, tossing her head.

Ruth snorts out a laugh and pushes the popcorn bowl toward us. 'Eat,' she commands.

Sara Lynn chews her popcorn with intention, like she's thinking hard about something. When she swallows, she says slowly, 'Listen, here's the thing: You don't have any of my genes in you, and you have Ruth's only indirectly, but you have our stories running through your veins. That's what makes you ours.'

'What do you mean?' I ask, not understanding. Ruth is looking at Sara Lynn as if she could use a little explanation, too.

'Well, we raised you. You've been living with us since you were a baby, for twelve years now. You know our ways and our mannerisms and our stories. Our stories of who we are have rubbed off on you. They've gone into making you who you are – Hope Teller.'

'Ha!' I say, slapping my hand on the table. 'You never tell me any stories about you.' It's a sore spot with me, and I'm glad to have a chance to bring it up. 'I always ask what you were like when you were my age, about the things that happened to you, and you both just say, "Oh, water over the dam" or "I don't remember."'

Sara Lynn presses her hands to her heart. 'Doesn't matter. You know in here.'

'Hmmph,' I say, thinking about it as I take some more popcorn.

Ruth flicks a kernel of popcorn at Sara Lynn and says, 'You know, I am beginning to believe my mother was correct all those times she told me you were a genius.'

Sara Lynn laughs. 'Your mother said that?'

'Only every goddamn day!' Ruth looks up at the ceiling and says, 'Ma, you were right.' Then she looks at Sara Lynn and says, 'Oh, Jesus, Ma's so happy I finally admitted she was right about something that she's doing a little dance with Saint Peter.'

Those two start laughing, and I can't help but laugh with them, even if I don't really get the joke. I mean, what's so hilarious about Ruth's dead mother — my grandmother, I might add — dancing in heaven?

Chapter 5

Oh man, I'm tired. It's the crack of dawn and I'm driving to Jack's. Five hours of sleep just won't do it for me these days, although it used to be just fine. I'm damned if I can keep my eyes open lately. Having a little drama fest with Hope last night didn't help matters much. Goddamn Bobby, anyway! I shake my head and drum my fingers on the steering wheel as I stop at the red light. Stupid to be parked here at a light when there's no one else on the road at this hour, but it'd be just my luck to get caught and have to pay a big, fat ticket.

God, Hope about broke my heart last night. What in hell am I supposed to tell a twelve-year-old kid about her father who took off when she was a week old and never came back? The line I fed her about how he's just scared was pretty good. Pulled that one out of the old hat. But, man, that's all it was – a line I pulled out to help my little girl feel better. 'We're all scared, Bobby,' I say out loud, narrowing my eyes. That's just what I'd tell him if he was sitting here next to me in my little shitbox car. I'd say that we're all freakin' terrified every day of our lives, but we still get up in the morning and put one foot in front of the other like the world is a certain place.

Christ, I sound like Ma. God helps him who helps himself! When the going gets tough, the tough get going! Got to play with the hand you've been dealt! I dreamed about her last night, and it was a bad one. Probably part of the reason I'm about to drop off to sleep over my steering wheel. It's not exactly restful to dream about your dead mother screaming at you. And that's what I dreamed. We were cleaning a house and she was yelling over the noise of the vacuum cleaner I was running. 'You're not doing it right, Ruth. You're just a big failure.' And then I hollered back, 'I'm trying my best.' 'Well, your best never was good enough,' she said back to me, and as she walked away, I chased her, yelling, 'Ma! Come back!'

Sick! Sick, sick, sick! What's going on in my head that would make me have a crazy dream like that? I don't like to remember the bad stuff; I just like to block out those years Ma and I didn't see eye-to-eye. Oh hell, I'm being like Sara Lynn, hiding what's true behind pretty words. I should say, those years when Ma and I couldn't stand each other, those years when all we did was fight, those years when we wondered what kind of a twisted God had ever thought it was a good idea to put us together in the same family.

⁓

Four days after I graduated from high school, Ma decided it was time to put me to work. I was taking it easy that morning, sitting with my bare legs hanging over the arm of the La-Z-Boy chair and chomping on a bowl of Cocoa Puffs as I watched a talk show. Ma stomped in with her usual storm cloud hovering above her gray, permed hair helmet, pulling on the shades fiercely and letting go so they raced up to the roller with a *crack*! Then she cleared the boys' breakfast dishes from the table right next to the La-Z-Boy where I sat, clanking the bowls and spoons and sighing all the while. Didn't even say 'Good morning, Ruth' or grunt a little 'Hey' in my direction.

Well, I was damned if I was going to say hi to her. She was in a bad mood, as usual, with poison instead of blood flowing through her veins. It was just like Ma to get up on the wrong side of the bed every day of her life and take it out on me. She sighed again, and I watched her from the family room as she stomped into the kitchen and grabbed the loaf of Wonder bread sitting out on the counter. She yanked out two slices and stuffed them in the toaster, sighing yet again as she slammed down the toaster lever.

'Ruth!' she snapped.

That was Ma all over. Not content to sit in her own toxic waste; had to spill it over onto me, too. I was eating my last mouthful of Cocoa Puffs, and I took my sweet time answering. She said again, real mean, 'Ruth! I'm talking to you.'

'Ma! For God's sake, I'm right here.' I brought the bowl up to my mouth and slurped the last of the milk in there. Then I rattled the spoon in the bowl and set it down on the rug next to the chair. I knew what Ma was thinking. I could see her glaring at me all red in the face and breathing hard like her head was going to pop off. She was thinking, Why can't you get up and put that bowl in the dishwasher, Miss Lazy? Would it kill you to help out around here? Well, I'd put my bowl in the dishwasher when I damn well felt like it. She could just go to hell and back waiting for me to do it. I looked hard at the TV, hoping she'd leave and never come back.

'What're you doing today?' Ma asked, and it wasn't at all nice the way she said it. It wasn't like 'Ruth, dear, do you have plans that will be fun today?' No, it was more like 'You little shit, what evil schemes do you have up your sleeve today?'

Goddammit, couldn't she be even a little bit nice to me? I hadn't bothered her at all this morning. Just sat and minded my own business, and here she was trying to cause trouble. I squinted hard at her and asked, 'Why do you want to know?'

'Watch it,' she said. 'Your face'll stay like that. You look just like your father when you do that with your mean little eyes.'

Me looking like my father was about the worst insult she could think of, seeing as she hated the man with her whole heart. It was always that way – you look just like your father; your disposition is exactly like your father's; you're the spitting image of that man. So, what were you, Ma? Just the unlucky incubator of your husband's child?

'What's the issue, Ma?' I said, sighing. It sure as hell wasn't me looking like my father or not picking up my cereal bowl right away. It was something else, and Ma could never just spit it out. Dammit! She never could just say what she meant. 'What exactly is your problem?'

'My problem?' Ma said. Her toast popped up and she started attacking it with a butter knife. 'My problem is you!'

Oh, that's right – I'd forgotten. If only I'd been born different, Ma's life would be just dandy. She'd been shoveling that load of shit on me for years. I picked up the remote and aimed it at the TV, pressing the volume button so it got louder and louder, drowning out Ma's nasty voice. She marched over and turned it off, stuffing toast into her mouth all the while.

'I have the remote,' I said, aiming it at the TV again and turning up the sound. Ma thought she was so smart. Couldn't even figure out that turning off the television was pointless if someone else held the remote control.

'Big deal,' she said as she stomped back into the kitchen, and I snickered because I knew she couldn't think of anything else to say. I kept my eyes glued to the TV, but I could hear her banging her dishes around, pouring herself a glass of orange juice, and gulping it down like there was no tomorrow.

She slammed her glass on the counter and walked back over to the TV set to turn it off. Then she wiped her mouth with the back of her hand and stood in front of the TV so the remote wouldn't work. Her eyes glittered at me. 'Who was the damn fool who ever thought daughters were a good idea? Tim and Bobby together don't give me the hassles you do.'

'Oh, right,' I snorted. 'Tim getting arrested for pot and Bobby drinking all the time don't bother you a bit.'

Her face reddened, and she said, 'That's not what I'm talking about, you spiteful little witch, and you know it. No matter what the boys do, they don't give me the attitude you do; they don't look at me like they're going to spit in my eye.' Ma's curly hair stood out from her head, and I wondered idly if she'd stuck her finger in a socket when she got up.

'Don't you have anything to say for yourself?' she asked me.

I sighed. 'Not really. What do you want me to say?'

'Look at your cereal bowl,' she said, pointing to the bowl and spoon on the rug next to the chair. 'Why don't you say something about that? Something like – Gee, Ma, I know you're going out to clean other people's houses all day. It's the least I can do to *get off my lazy ass, pick up my own dishes, and put them in the dishwasher.*'

'Everything always has to be on your time,' I yelled right back at her. 'It's your way or the highway.'

'You're damn right,' she said, her voice rising with every word she spoke. 'It is my way when you're living under my roof.' She got quiet then and walked up to me and stuck her finger in my face. 'You listen here, missy . . .'

'My name's not "missy,"' I said, looking right into her crazy-lady eyes.

She stepped back a little, like she was afraid she might hit me if she got too close. 'I'm done with you hanging around here being lazy. Time for you to get to work.'

Jesus H. Christ! I'd only been home four days. Four crummy days and she was saying I didn't do anything except hang around. I threw up my hands and banged my head back on the chair. 'What do you want me to do, Ma?' I hollered. I swear, that woman would drive anyone to booze. No wonder my father had left. 'I put in applications everywhere. Is it my fault that no one's hiring? God! You blame me if the sun doesn't shine.'

'Listen,' she said, 'you and I both know you're not going to get any of the jobs you applied for. You got through high school by the skin of your teeth, and no one with any common sense is going to hire you.'

'Thanks, Ma,' I said. She didn't even care that she was hurting

51

me, didn't even care that she was being so mean. 'That's a real nice way to talk about your own daughter.'

'Facts are facts,' she replied. 'The sooner you wake up and smell the coffee, the better off you'll be.'

I stood up then, still in my big T-shirt I'd worn to bed last night, and I folded my long, skinny arms across my chest. I stared right at her and asked, 'What in hell is your point?'

'My point is that you're coming to work for me.' She twisted her mouth into a spiteful smile. She had laid down her trump card and was waiting for my move. *What do you say to that, missy?* I knew exactly what she was thinking.

I just laughed, a short bark of a sound, and said, 'I'm not cleaning up other people's shit.'

I got nervous right after I said it; I knew I'd stepped way over the line. 'You listen here,' Ma hollered, coming up close to my face. 'My cleaning houses has kept a roof over your head and food in your mouth. And seeing as you've got no better prospects, you'll get off your sorry ass and help me.'

'What if I don't want to?' I wasn't willing to give up yet. It wasn't in me to back down from a fight so easily.

'What if I don't want to keep feeding you and housing you?' she shot back. 'It's grown-up time, time you start contributing. Besides, I could use the help.'

The only sound I heard then was Ma breathing hard through her nose. She backed away from me a little and lowered her voice, her tone almost gentle for a change. 'Listen,' she said, 'you damn well have to do something with your life, and it looks like I'm your only option. Get dressed and come on. You're starting today. We have three houses to do.'

Now, I knew this could go one of two ways. I could say, 'Are you fucking crazy, you lunatic bitch?' or I could say, 'Okay. You're right. I don't know what the hell I'm going to do with my life, and cleaning seems as good a job as any.' I compromised by rolling my eyes to the ceiling and saying, 'Just so you know, I'm only doing this until a *real* job comes through.'

'Save your threats and promises, and go on and get dressed.'

'Jesus Christ,' I muttered, striding to my bedroom. I looked through the piles of clothes on the floor until I found my favorite denim shorts and Black Sabbath T-shirt. Ma hated my concert T-shirts; she always scowled and said, 'Why do you have to wear those shirts with creepy-looking weirdos on them?' Just because I was helping her at work didn't mean I had to dress to please her, though. She could just look at me in my concert T-shirt all day. I hoped it drove her crazy and she ended up in the loony bin.

I came back into the kitchen and stared at Ma without saying anything, following her as she headed for the door. As she plopped herself into the driver's seat of her car, she sighed as loudly as she could, acting all put-upon even after I'd agreed to go to work with her.

'What now, Ma?' I asked, throwing up my hands. 'What are you huffing about, acting like a martyr?'

'I don't know what you're talking about,' she replied, starting the car.

'Huuuuuhhhhhh!' I imitated her sigh and glared at her. 'That's what I'm talking about! What the hell did I do now to set you off?'

Ma just put her lips together tight, like she was afraid if she opened her mouth, she'd never stop screaming about how I disappointed her every day of my life.

Neither of us spoke a word until we were pulling up a long, hilly driveway practically the length of a road. 'You've got to be kidding me,' I said. I couldn't believe she would do this to me.

'What?' asked Ma, all innocent, like she didn't know. She turned off the ignition and slid the keys into her brown suede shoulder bag. As she heaved herself out of the car, I thought about sitting there and pouting, but I knew it wouldn't get me anywhere. So I got out of the car and followed her up the stone walk lined with flowers of every goddamn pastel color ever invented.

It was so typical of Ma to drag me to clean the Hoffmans'

house on my very first day working for her. I hated Sara Lynn Hoffman. I hated her prissy little mouth that never smiled at me, her cool blue eyes that looked right through me, and her blond hair that shone so prettily in the sunlight. I dragged my sneakers as I walked, making a scuffing sound. I was trapped, but I wouldn't act like I was happy about it.

'You mind your manners,' Ma said, and I could tell she was just bursting with happiness over me having to clean the Hoffmans' house. 'I don't care how jealous you are of Sara Lynn. This is a job, and you'll do it well.'

'Ma, I'd rather get rabies shots than be cleaning Sara Lynn Hoffman's house.'

I stood there with Ma at the Hoffmans' dark green front door, looking at the freshly painted gray steps and the big black urns with pink and purple flowers pouring out of them. A perfect house for a perfect family, I thought bitterly, and I twisted off a flower hanging out of an urn and twirled it between my finger and thumb.

'Don't pick Mrs. Hoffman's flowers!' Ma was hissing like a cat in heat. 'Sweet Jesus, I can't take you anywhere.'

I gave her a mean look and stuffed the flower in my shorts pocket. I scratched my cheek where it felt like a bug was crawling and tapped my foot on the porch floor.

'And stop fidgeting,' Ma hissed again.

'Oh, for Christ's sake, Ma . . .' She was driving me crazy. I was about to tell her to go to hell when I heard footsteps tapping toward the door and Ma gave me a sharp nudge.

'Why, Mary! How nice to see you!' Mrs. Hoffman, queen of the phony rich people in town, opened the door. I just stared at her as if I were looking at a Barbie doll come to life. She was all dressed up to the nines, wearing a pink dress printed with green frogs and lily pads. I looked down to rest my eyes from the bright colors of her getup and saw her little coral-painted toes sticking out of white sandals. I brought my eyes back up and noticed she wore pearls. Who the hell wore pearls at nine in the morning?

But there she was, her long fingers playing at her neck, fiddling with those pearls. 'And Ruth! Are you here to help your mother today?'

'Yes, Ruth is here to help me,' Ma said in her fake 'we're a perfect family' voice.

'Sara Lynn'll be home soon, Ruth,' Mrs. Hoffman offered brightly, like she was telling me some good news. 'She's just out for a run right now.'

'What do I care?' I felt like saying, but I just smiled and nodded as I followed her and my mother into the hallway of the house. It was cool in there, not like our heat box of a house. Maybe the high ceilings made it cooler, I thought, and I lifted my head to get the full effect. There was an archway in the hall that led into a huge living room. I had never seen such a big room. And it wasn't cluttered, either, not like the rooms at our house, so cluttered that my junk was mixed up with everybody else's and we felt like we were drowning in stuff. There was a large white sofa facing a marble fireplace and two plush coral chairs on either side of the fireplace. There was a piano about the size of my bedroom sitting in the corner of that room, and I just stood there looking at the whole scene until Ma jerked me along back to the kitchen, where Mrs. Hoffman kept the cleaning supplies.

'Well, I'll just go along into the garden, then,' said Mrs. Hoffman. She smiled at us as she put on a straw hat with black ribbons hanging down the back. 'You call me if you need anything.'

'Thank you, Mrs. Hoffman,' Ma simpered, and I wanted to throw up.

'How many times must I remind you to call me Aimee?' Mrs. Hoffman said lightly. 'Haven't we known each other since before our daughters were born?'

Well, Ma about went through the roof with pleasure on that comment. She giggled and blushed and said, 'Oh, gosh, okay, Aimee.'

I had to clamp my mouth shut for fear I might open it and say something I might regret, something like 'How did I happen to get such a damn fool for a mother?'

Ma wiped the smile off her face the second Mrs. Hoffman closed the back door behind her, and then she turned to me briskly. 'Okay,' she said, handing me a bucket of cleaning supplies. 'I'm going to let you start on the kitchen while I dust the living room and dining room. Wash the counters and appliances. Don't forget to scrub the sink. When you're finished, I'll look at what you've done.'

'What about letting me dust, Ma, and you do the kitchen?'

'That's the great thing about being your boss,' she said, smiling in a way that wasn't a smile at all. 'I can give you the dirty work.'

Great, I thought. I just get out of school where my whole life teachers have told me what to do, and now Ma's got it into her head that she's going to take over where they left off. 'Ruth Teller, have you come in without your homework again?' 'Ruth Teller, are you as dumb as you appear to be?' 'Miss Teller, I can tell you spent about a second studying for this test. Don't you care about your future?' I had hated school; I shuddered just to recall it as I wiped down Mrs. Hoffman's stone countertops. I was no good at school – that was that – but every damn day of my life, teachers would act like this was news to them, like they really were surprised when I didn't do my homework and study for tests. If they were so smart, shouldn't they have figured out I wasn't ever going to be any good at learning? It was just stupid – thinking I was going to change overnight and come in one day raising my hand like Sara Lynn Hoffman.

Sara Lynn . . . ugh. I hit the refrigerator with my cloth and thought of how many A+ papers Mrs. Hoffman must have tacked up to this fridge. Sara Lynn was so smart, she was valedictorian of our class. She got to make a little speech and all at graduation, and I tell you, I didn't understand half of what she was yammering about. The future . . . blah, blah. The past . . . blah, blah. Who the hell could figure? She'd always been about as boring as

56

the limp cleaning rag I held in my hand. She used to just saunter by me at school, looking above my head like she was checking for birds or something. Never said hi or anything. Wouldn't be caught dead talking to the daughter of her mother's cleaning lady.

They were all like that, those rich kids. Just kept to themselves and acted like we were the plague. Although I slept with one of them once – Jeff Barnes. I wasn't a slut; he was the only guy I ever slept with. Besides, I didn't want to get on to thinking about that. Just put it out of your mind – that's what Ma told me to do whenever I thought about something bad.

Anyhow, Ma wasn't crazy about any of the rich kids, either, except – you guessed it – Sara Lynn Hoffman. Of course, her precious Mrs. Hoffman's daughter could do no wrong. When we were growing up, it was always 'Sara Lynn Hoffman this' and 'Sara Lynn Hoffman that.' 'That child is so bright!' she'd tell me. 'And her manners! Such a polite little thing. You'd do well to be friendly with her, Ruth; never mind that tarty Gina Logan you hang around with.' I'd nudge Bobby, crossing my eyes and sticking my tongue out to make him laugh, and she'd say, 'It's a shame all you two can do is laugh at someone who's gifted and nice.' We'd just crack up more and say, 'We're not laughing at her, Ma, we're laughing at you,' and then she'd get in a huff and mutter about how some people just weren't lucky when it came to the children God decided to give them.

I cleaned the stove next, scrubbing down beneath the burners. Not much dirt was coming up. Either Mrs. Hoffman never cooked or she cleaned up after herself. Maybe that's why Ma loved Mrs. Hoffman so much – because she wasn't a slob like some of the other ladies. Ma could tell you stories that would make your hair curl about the filthy habits some people had. Habits like not cleaning the sink after they spit into it or leaving their used tampons lying on top of the trash for anybody to see. Yuck! At least Mrs. Hoffman wasn't gross. I was hoping to find something disgusting about Sara Lynn, though, something that would turn my stomach. I laughed, imagining finding a floppy, smelly used condom under her bed. Wouldn't that be something to show Ma? 'Look what your perfect Sara Lynn has been up to,' I'd say.

The sink was easy to clean, too. I remembered not to forget the base of the faucet, and sure enough, I got a little crud out of that. It pleased me, so I scrubbed out the drain and got some more. Cleaning was sort of like detective work. You guessed where you'd find the dirt and then you went in and took care of it. I did the dishwasher next, and then I took a dry cloth and wiped down the white-painted cabinets. I stood back to look at my work, and I nodded. I hadn't done a half-bad job.

'Ma!' I hollered. Then I remembered I was in someone else's house, so I clapped my hand over my mouth and went into the living room to find her. She wasn't in there, so I walked across the hall into the dining room. She was on her knees, dusting the legs of one of the ten dining room chairs. They weren't just legs, either. They were curlicued, fancy legs with designs cut into them. Poor Ma had to dust in all the cracks and crevices of the designs. 'Ma . . .' I walked up to her, my footsteps muffled by the large blue-and-red rug, and tapped her shoulder.

'Oh, my sweet Jesus!' she exclaimed, jumping up. 'You scared me.' She placed her hand on her chest. 'Whew! I get so used to having my mind go off on its own when I'm working . . . I wasn't expecting you.'

'I'm done in the kitchen,' I said, and I tried not to sound as eager as I was for her to see it. I thought I'd done a good job; I'd surprised myself with how thorough I'd been.

'Okay,' she replied, and she stretched her arms over her head and leaned to one side to crack her back as she threw down her dust rag and walked toward the kitchen.

'Ewww,' I said, following her. I hated when she cracked her back – it was disgusting. All the little bones up and down her spine taking their turn snapping, like someone playing an out-of-tune piano.

'Ewww back to you,' she said as she stepped into the kitchen and looked around. She examined the countertops, getting down at their level and squinting her eyes to see that I had got all the crumbs. She looked at the appliances and the cabinets. 'Hmm,' she said, and I could tell she was pleasantly surprised. 'This isn't bad, Ruth. You forgot to wipe off the handles on the cabinets and' – she opened the refrigerator door and pointed to the white, accordionlike plastic folds that sealed the door shut – 'you'll want to wipe down right here. Other than that' – she shrugged – 'you're ready to wash the floor.'

I wiped those cabinet handles until they shone, and then I cleaned every last white fold in the refrigerator seal. When I was done with all that, I scrubbed the floor on my hands and knees until I practically could see my reflection in it.

'Done,' I said triumphantly to Ma as I poked my head back in on her doing the vacuuming. She held up her hand for me to wait a minute, and then, when she had finished, she turned off the vacuum and followed me into the kitchen. I sure was proud of the job I had done. Ma thought I was lazy, I knew, but that wasn't true. I just hated doing things I wasn't very good at. I was good at this – I knew I was – and it made me want to do it right.

'Hmmph!' said Ma, putting her hands on her hips and looking around the room. She nodded her head and looked at me, pleased, like she was seeing something new in me. 'Not bad at all.'

That was high praise from Ma, and I basked in it like a cat rolling around in a patch of sunlight. I must have done a good job, because she started to treat me a little more like a co-worker trying to get the job done and a little less like a rotten tag-along kid she needed to keep her eye on.

'Time to move upstairs,' said Ma. She hefted the vacuum cleaner, and I moved to help her with it. She grunted appreciatively and said, 'Fair is fair. I'll do the bathrooms up here and you can do the tidying and dusting and vacuuming.'

'What do you mean – bathrooms?' I asked. 'How many do they have?'

'Four,' replied Ma.

'Four?!'

'Yep. One in Mr. and Mrs. Hoffman's room, one in Sara Lynn's room, one in each of the guest rooms.'

'So there's a bathroom for everyone, plus one to spare,' I said, shaking my head in disgust. 'It's not fair.'

'Life's not fair, Ruth,' Ma replied briskly. She loved telling me this, as if I couldn't see it with my own two eyes. 'Nobody ever said it would be.'

We stopped at the top of the stairs, and Ma pointed down the hall. 'Door at the end,' she said. 'We'll start with Mr. and Mrs. Hoffman's room.'

'Don't you mean "Eliot and Aimee's room"?' I teased.

'Just get to work, smart mouth,' she said, but her lips were twisting up into a smile as she pushed the vacuum down the hall and into the Hoffmans' bedroom.

'God, Ma!' I gasped. Sara Lynn's parents' room was about as big as our whole kitchen and family room area, no lie. It was also neat as a pin. The bed was even made! I chuckled, thinking that there was no way in hell I'd make my bed on the day I knew a cleaning lady was coming over.

'It's beautiful, isn't it?' Ma walked across the floor and went into the bathroom. She sounded sort of sad, and I wanted to kick the wallpapered wall and leave a scuffmark because Mrs. Hoffman had so much and Ma didn't have hardly anything at all. The windows faced the backyard, and I peered through the gauzy curtains to see Mrs. Hoffman below, cutting flowers and placing them into a basket.

I frowned and figured I'd better get on with it. I dusted the carved four-poster bed, wondering why in the name of God Mrs. Hoffman had such a liking for carved things. I dusted the bedside tables stacked with books and photos, and the high bureau that opened like a closet, with doors in front. I wiped down the baseboards and windowsills and then vacuumed the rug and washed down the surrounding wood floor. I looked around, pleased, and went into the bathroom to find Ma.

'Ma?' I called over the running water. Ma was on her knees, cleaning the tub.

'Yeah?' she said back, and she looked old to me right then, her face haggard underneath her graying, Brillo-pad hair.

'Done,' I said. 'You can check if you want to, but I'm sure I did a good job.'

She looked at me a moment and said, 'I don't need to check. If you say it's good, then it's good.'

Now, I bet my brothers' lives on the fact that the minute I hightailed it out of there, she nosed around to make sure my work was up to snuff. But still, I thought it was nice of her to act like she trusted me.

'We'll work our way down the hall,' she said. 'The two guest rooms won't need much, so start in there. The last room on the other end of the hall is Sara Lynn's.'

Ma was right: It wasn't anything to clean rooms that nobody used. We zipped right along, Ma a little bit behind me because the bathrooms took longer to do. When I came to Sara Lynn's room, I growled under my breath. 'Bitch,' I muttered as I opened the door.

I walked in and looked around. It was all different shades of white. Now, I had gone along in my life thinking white is white, but leave it to Sara Lynn to show me I was mistaken. The walls were cream, the bedspread was white, and the lampshade was somewhere in between. The bed was white-painted iron, and the curtains matched the lampshade. The only nonwhite item in that room was the bureau, which was a dark wood. There was an oval mirror hung up over the bureau with a wire hidden by a large white ribbon. The one picture on the wall was a blown-up black-and-white photograph of Sara Lynn's profile, her hair blowing back from her face. In case she forgets what she looks like, I sneered. In case she can't remember how goddamn beautiful she is.

I got to work with the dusting, asking myself just who in the world would slap a picture of herself on her bedroom wall. I'd scare the bejesus out of myself if I woke up to a picture of myself, I can tell you that. Of course, Sara Lynn was so in love with herself that it probably started her day just right to open her eyes and see her mug on the wall.

When it was time to dust the bureau, I picked up the little music box that sat in the middle of it and dusted that. Then I ran my cloth over the top of the bureau and gently replaced the music box. I began to move my cloth down the sides of the bureau and, I couldn't help myself, I got the biggest itch to find out what was inside those drawers. I glanced at the door real quick and slid the top drawer open. Just underpants and bras and socks. I fished around to see if she had anything hidden underneath those things but found nothing. I closed it and opened the next drawer – it held piles of shirts folded neatly on top of one another. I felt at the back of that drawer, too. Nothing. As I slid open the bottom drawer, I jumped a mile as I heard a voice say, 'What do you think you're doing?'

Sara Lynn stood at her bedroom door, breathing hard and bending over a bit, her hand pressed to her stomach. Her long blond hair was pulled back in a ponytail, and she was wearing blue running shorts, a white T-shirt, and sneakers. Her eyebrows were raised practically up to her hairline, and her mouth was set in a hard line.

'I asked you what you were doing,' she said again, and she wasn't the least uncomfortable watching me ferret through her bureau drawers. That's what I'd always hated about her, the way she didn't ever look afraid or upset or caught off guard.

'I'm helping my mother clean your house,' I offered, trying to sound like putting my hands into her bureau drawers was all part of the job.

'Does your mother look through my private things, too? Or just you?' Sara Lynn put her hands on her hips and tilted her head. She didn't even sound mad, just curious.

'I was just cleaning,' I said breezily. Lie and deny, as Bobby always said. Just lie and deny.

'Oh, really? You need to open my bureau drawers and look inside them when you're cleaning? Maybe I should ask your mother if that's the way she recommends cleaning my bedroom. I'll just go ask her right now.' Sara Lynn made a move to turn around and walk out of the bedroom.

'No!' I cried. Shit. The jig was up. 'Listen, I'm sorry, Sara Lynn. I won't do it again.'

'So you admit that you were going through my things when you shouldn't have been?'

'Well, I didn't mean to,' I protested. 'I didn't come in here and say, "Hmm, I'm going to spy on Sara Lynn's things."'

'But you did it, didn't you?' she insisted.

'Yeah, I guess,' I finally said. Then I added quickly, 'But I won't do it again!'

'And I should believe you because . . .' She stood there looking at me coldly, drumming her fingers on the doorway's woodwork.

'Because I'm telling you I won't,' I cried. I was getting mighty tired of her little lawyer act. 'God, Sara Lynn, you're so prissy sometimes.'

Sara Lynn smiled smugly and turned away, her blond ponytail flying behind her.

'Wait!' My heart pounded in my throat. Here I was finally doing something that pleased Ma, and Sara Lynn was going to ruin it all. 'Don't tell my mother, okay? I'm sorry I looked through your stuff; I'm sorry I called you prissy. I'm asking you, please, as a favor, not to tell my mother. I promise I won't do it again. Okay?' I hated that my voice quavered on the last word.

Sara Lynn wrinkled her nose and tilted her head as if she were surprised. She said, 'I wasn't going to tell your mother.'

I felt like an idiot, standing there looking at her with pleading eyes, and then she added, 'But I will next time if I catch you doing anything you're not supposed to be doing.'

I dug my nails into my arms to stop myself from opening my mouth. When I heard Sara Lynn's sneakered feet tap lightly down the stairs, I took a deep breath of relief and sat on the rug. My hands were trembling, and I just sat there trying to look anywhere but at the damn picture of Sara Lynn.

As my relief faded away, I wanted to tear up that picture. 'How about this?' I'd yell at her as she found me smashing the picture frame and ripping apart the photo. 'Is this cleaning your house the way you like it?'

I hated her. I'd hated her ever since I could remember. Little Miss Perfect with her clothes from Boston and her long blond hair that never tangled and all her school awards. Had her own car, too – a brand-new convertible she got just for turning sixteen. It wasn't fair. And it sure didn't help that Ma thought she was so great, either.

'Why can't you be friends with Sara Lynn Hoffman?' Ma would carp. 'She'd be a good influence on you.'

'I hate Sara Lynn, Ma,' I'd reply. 'She's a priss ass.'

Sara Lynn played the piano so beautifully. Sara Lynn didn't talk back to her mother. Sara Lynn got all A's on her last report card. Sara Lynn was going to horseback-riding camp. Ick! It's all I ever heard, how Mrs. Hoffman's daughter was so smart and nice and talented.

'What're you doing sitting here parked on your rear end?' Ma said. I looked up and saw her standing at the doorway. Ma looked at me skeptically, as if I were showing my true colors after all.

I scrambled up and said, 'I'd be done already if Sara Lynn hadn't been in here bothering me.'

Ma smiled this goofy smile. 'Oh, did Sara Lynn come up to say hello? That was nice of her.'

I wanted to scream, but I just shrugged and said, 'Yeah, because she's a nice girl. I should be half as nice.'

Disappointment clouded Ma's eyes, and my back stiffened as I turned away and got back to work. Once a screwup, always a screwup. I knew that was exactly what she was thinking. Well, I was damned if I cared. Ma could march right downstairs and kiss Sara Lynn Hoffman's ass, because hell would freeze over before I'd do it.

I'm pulling into Jack's driveway, and I sit in the car for a sec and close my eyes. Ma was a tough old bird, that's for sure. But I don't want to think about her right now – hurts too damn much. Besides, it's hotter than hell in my stinking car, so I turn off the ignition and slide out of the driver's seat. On my way up the back walk, I fumble in my purse for the key. I sigh as I unlock the door because the cool of the house feels so good to my tired self. I pour a glass of cold water at the kitchen sink and drink it in a gulp, and then I walk to the bedroom, where Jack is lying on his back, looking up at the ceiling.

'Hi, angel,' he says, smiling at me. 'I heard your car driving up.'

I snort. 'Who didn't hear it? It needs a new muffler, I'm sure. Though why I keep throwing money at it is a mystery to me.'

I kick off my shoes and sit on the bed, and Jack rolls toward me and starts rubbing my back. 'Why don't you let me buy you a new car?' he asks.

'Why do you think?' I reply, lying down next to him. 'What am I supposed to tell people – that I just happened to have enough dough socked away to buy myself something that big? Besides, I don't want to be beholden to you.'

'Beholden to me?' Jack stops rubbing my back. 'Ruth, I love you. You need a new car, and I can afford to give you one. It's as simple as that.'

'Keep rubbing,' I say, pointing to my back. 'It felt good.'

'Aren't you afraid you'll be beholden to me if you let me rub your back?'

I laugh. 'No, because I've rubbed you enough, that's for sure.'

He laughs with me and pulls me in to him. 'Yeah, you have.' He starts touching my nonexistent breasts, and I take his hands away.

'Can we not do this today?' I ask. 'I'm so tired.'

'Are you okay?'

'Yeah, I'm fine. It's my old age,' I tell him. 'I'm just not as young as I used to be.'

'Jesus,' he says, 'if you're getting old, what does that make me?'

I laugh and snuggle into him. 'Just wake me when it's time to get up, okay?'

'Why don't you sleep in today? Take the day off.'

'Who's going to run your damn diner?' I say sleepily.

'I can handle it, angel. You sleep today.'

It sounds so tempting that I almost say yes, but I jerk myself out of the sleep I'm heading toward and say, 'No! I want to work today. Promise you'll wake me up.'

'Okay, darling,' he says, rubbing the back of my neck gently. 'Just rest for now.'

It takes me about a minute to close my eyes and drift back into the world of sleep, where, God willing, I won't dream about anything this time. My mind'll be blank as a freshly scrubbed white countertop, and nothing will hurt me, just for a little while.

Chapter 6

*N*ow, you remember how we went over the difference between a forehand and a backhand, right?'

'Umm-hmm.' I look out the car window, trying to tune out Sara Lynn's annoying voice. I'm on my way to my first tennis lesson, and I'm a little nervous, because what if I totally stink? What if I make a fool out of myself in front of everybody? It'd be just so typical. A picture floats into my mind of me tripping over a tennis ball and falling into the net with everyone looking at me in horror. Ugh! I shudder and chew at my pinky nail.

'Stop that biting,' Sara Lynn says automatically. And without hardly taking a breath, she quizzes, 'What's the scoring system in tennis? Do you remember?' She doesn't even give me a chance before she prompts, 'Love, fifteen . . .'

'Thirty, forty, game,' I recite, still looking out the window at the houses and trees whizzing by.

'What about ad in and ad out points?' she asks.

I shrug. I'm losing interest in this conversation real quick.

'If the game's at deuce, that means you're tied forty-forty. Then, if—'

'Sara Lynn!' I interrupt, whipping my head around to glare at her. 'Can't I just have the fun of taking a lesson?'

I could swear her eyes get soft and hurt-looking before they turn all hard and glittery. 'What's that supposed to mean?' she asks.

'It means that you don't have to cram everything into my head. The whole point of taking a lesson is to learn stuff you don't know! God!'

'Don't say "God,"' she says, braking for a red light. 'And besides' – she sniffs, tapping her pink-painted fingernails on the leather steering wheel – 'it never hurts to be prepared.'

I slump down in my seat and duck my head so my hair covers my face. 'Well, it's not helping right now, so why don't you just be quiet?' I mutter.

'What?' she asks, accelerating the car and emphasizing the 't' part of the word. 'What did you say?'

'Sorry,' I mumble, still not looking at her.

'Watch yourself, Hope. I mean it,' she warns.

Oooh, I'm shaking in my sneakers. That's what goes through my mind, but I don't say it. I just sigh and think how much I hate Sara Lynn sometimes. I hate her; I hate her; I hate her. I really do.

When we get to the club, she acts like we're all lovey-dovey, like that little scene in the car never happened. 'Oh, I'm so proud of you!' she coos, putting her arm around me and squeezing my shoulders as we walk toward the courts. 'Just look at you in your little tennis outfit!'

I wrinkle my nose. It was her idea to buy me a new tennis dress, but I wouldn't let her get me the one she wanted to buy me. The one she liked had pink rickrack trim on the skirt, for crying out loud. Can you imagine? 'Oh, it's so darling,' she kept saying, holding up that darn dress.

'No way, Sara Lynn,' I told her, clutching the plain dress I'd picked out. 'It's this dress or forget it – I'll just wear shorts.'

'All right,' she said, sighing. But even when we were at the cash register, she kept asking, 'Are you sure you don't want to try on the other dress? It would look so cute on you.'

Just thinking about it makes my blood boil, and I shrug off her arm like I'm shaking off an annoying bug. She gets the picture, because she just pats my back real quick and then stops touching me.

When we arrive at the tennis courts, she takes an elastic out of her purse. 'Here,' she says, grabbing my hair and starting to tie it up in a ponytail.

'Ow!' I say, jerking my head away from her. 'I don't want it up.'

'Of course you do,' she hisses, pulling at my hair again. 'It'll get in your face otherwise.'

'I don't care!' I almost stamp my foot; that's how mad I feel. Why does she have to embarrass me all the time?

'Hi, ladies!' Oh, no. It's Sam, the tennis pro, jogging up to us. He gives me a wave, then puts his hand out to Sara Lynn and says, 'Hi, I'm Sam Johnson. We met last week, on Hope's birthday.'

'How nice to see you again,' Sara Lynn replies. 'Hope is just sooo excited to start lessons!' Oh, I could throw up. She's acting like a Hostess cupcake – all fake, sugary sweet.

She puts her hand up to her forehead to block out the sun and says, 'I've just been telling Hope she should put her hair back. Don't you think so, too? I wouldn't want her to trip and fall because her hair's in her eyes.'

Get a life, Sara Lynn! Get a life so you can get out of mine! I know I can't say it to her, but I'm sending her my thoughts, and they aren't pretty.

Sam takes a quick look at me, standing there with my arms crossed over my chest and shooting Sara Lynn the evil eye; then he looks back at Sara Lynn, her blond hair falling straight and shiny over her shoulders and her baby blue eyes blinking up at him. 'Why don't we let her start whichever way she's comfortable?' he says, smiling right back at her. 'I'm sure once she gets going, she'll figure out the best way to wear her hair.'

Ha! I uncross my arms and put them on my hips. *What do you think about that, Miss Know-it-all?*

Sara Lynn's smile fades for a split second, but then she puts it right back on. 'I suppose you're right,' she says cheerily. She turns

to me. 'Here's the elastic just in case you want it,' she says, handing me the elastic band. 'Oh, and don't forget your racket.' She
hands that over, too.

'It's one of my old ones,' she tells Sam, motioning at the racket.
'It's a tad big for her, but I think it'll do.' She looks doubtful all
of a sudden, and then she frowns as she peers at the racket in my
hand. 'Hmm. Well.' She shakes her head. 'You know, I take that
back. Actually, she's going to need a new racket. Looking at it in
her hand, I think it's much too big for her. Gosh, I don't know
what I was thinking.' She tries to take the racket away from me,
but I hold on tight. Still tugging at it, she says to Sam, 'Maybe
we should run up to the pro shop right now and find her something suitable. You could let her try some demos to see what
works best. She's so excited, and I'd hate for her to lose interest
just because she's using a racket that's not sized properly. I think
it's important she gets a good start.'

I finally manage to pull the racket away from her, saying between my gritted teeth, 'It's fine!'

Sam sort of half smiles, like he's getting a kick out of this
ridiculous scene Sara Lynn's causing. 'We'll figure it out,' he tells
her. He says it like he's going to pat her on the head and say,
'There, there – everything will be okay.'

'Maybe one of the new Wilson junior rackets,' she says, twisting her mouth and squinting as if she's thinking hard. 'No, perhaps a Prince racket. Something that'll give her some power
without losing too much control.'

God. I just roll my eyes and inch away from her. She's so clueless, she doesn't even see that Sam's laughing at her.

'Sara Lynn?' Sam says gently.

'Hmm?' Her eyes flicker as she comes back to earth and looks
at him.

'We'll figure it out. We're just going to have some fun today,
get loosened up and all. There's plenty of time for Hope to try a
bunch of rackets and see what she likes. Don't worry.'

'Worry! Worry!' She throws up her hands and laughs, and her

little silver teardrop earrings shake back and forth. 'That's my middle name!'

'It's okay,' Sam tells her, his eyes twinkling. 'It's all good.'

She shakes her head sweetly and says, 'I'm sorry. I can get a little, well, carried away.'

Ooh, she makes me so mad. She's just trying to be nice to him so he'll agree with her that I should wear my hair up or get a new racket or do whatever other crazy thing she says I should do. 'You can go now,' I say, and I don't mean it to sound as rude as it comes out. I feel a little prickle of shame when I see her forehead pucker and her mouth scrunch up for a minute like I've hurt her.

She loses the soft, laughing look she had just a second ago, and she turns away quickly so that her hair flies out behind her. 'Okay, then,' she says.

'Ready?' I ask Sam.

'Sure,' he says, and we walk toward the courts together.

'Hope!' My back stiffens, and before I can even turn around, Sara Lynn is calling, 'Don't forget to drink lots of water! It's hot today!'

'Okay,' I say back.

Then, in another second, she calls again, 'I'll pick you up at two! Eat a decent lunch and don't forget to wait a half hour after you eat before you swim.'

'Oooohhhh,' I mutter through gritted teeth as Sam and I walk to the court together. 'She's driving me nuts!'

'It's what moms do,' he says, laughing. 'I'm twenty-nine, and my mom still drives me nuts.'

'She's *not* my mother,' I say. God! I don't want him to imagine for one second that I'm related to her, especially since she was acting like such an idiot. Of course, he thought she was my babysitter the other day, and I told him she wasn't that, either. I frown and sneak a peek up at him to see if he's looking at me like I have four heads, which is the way most people look when stuff starts to come up about my crazy family. He just looks down at me with

71

patient eyes like he's interested, like he's waiting to hear what I have to say.

'Sara Lynn's my guardian. Well, she and my aunt Ruth are. See, my mother died when I was born.'

'Oh, I'm sorry,' Sam says, and his eyes get soft and sad, like he's sorry for me.

'Don't be.' I shrug, trying to show off how brave I am. 'I never knew her.'

I'm on a roll, so I keep going. 'And my father's in the CIA,' I lie.

Sam raises his eyebrows. 'The CIA?'

I nod. 'He's, like, a really important secret agent, so he can't raise me. That's why I live with Sara Lynn and Ruth.'

Oh, no. My stomach flips over as I remember the KKs teasing me about Ruth and Sara Lynn being a romantic couple. 'You know,' I say, trying to be casual, 'Ruth and Sara Lynn are just friends.' I emphasize the word *friends,* so he won't misunderstand me.

'Is that so?' Sam asks, and his eyes are twinkling like he wants to laugh. God! I always say the wrong thing. So what do I do? Like an idiot, I keep talking. And talking. And talking.

'Yeah.' I nod. 'I mean, they'd both like to get married some-day. To guys, I mean. Well, at least Sara Lynn would. She won't do it until she meets the right person, though. At least, that's what she tells me when I ask her about it. She says, "Hope, I'd rather be alone for the rest of my life than with the wrong guy."' I can't seem to shut up. My mouth is flapping and flapping, and all these words are gushing out. 'And Ruth, ha! Ruth says she's too stubborn to get married. Says she'd drive any man to booze.'

Sam throws back his head and laughs, but I get the feeling he's laughing with me and not at me, so I smile, too. 'Hope,' he says, smiling down at me, 'I can tell that you and I are going to have some fun together. What do you say we get started?'

'Sure.' I shrug and unzip my racket case and hold my racket out in front of me.

'Okay,' he says. 'We'll start with a basic forehand grip.'

'Sara Lynn told me about the forehand,' I say. I fumble with the racket handle, trying to keep straight in my mind what I'm supposed to do with my thumb. Does it go over my fingers? Above them?

'Here,' Sam says, arranging my fingers on the racket handle. 'Try this. It might feel a little weird, but trust me, this grip will be automatic to you after a few lessons.'

One thing I notice with Sam so close to me, touching my hand and all, is that he has a man's smell. Well, he is a man. Duh. But, see, not having a dad or even an uncle, I'm not around men very much, and they smell different to me. Not bad different. Not at all. I kind of like Sam standing so close that I can smell him. He smells like soap and sweat and something else . . . moss, I think. I mean, I don't know if moss even has a smell. But, see, women smell the way I imagine little flowers in the woods smell – sort of sweet when you get up close. And Sam, well, to me he smells the way I imagine moss smells – all fresh in a deep, soft, green kind of way.

God! I hope he doesn't see me sniffing him. I jerk away and hold up my racket, using the grip he showed me. 'Okay,' I tell him. 'I think I've got it.'

We play for a half hour, and you know what? I think I'm improving. In fact, I know I am. I'm actually hitting the ball in the court about half the time. The other half of the time, it goes way wild or I miss it altogether. But, as Sam keeps telling me when I get frustrated, you can't expect to play tennis without missing some shots.

I'm out of breath at the end of my lesson. My hair is frizzing like crazy, and I pull it back and tie it up with the elastic Sara Lynn gave me.

'You okay?' Sam asks, putting his hand on my shoulder as I gasp for breath.

I nod. 'Uh-huh.'

'It's getting warm,' he says, glancing up at the sky. 'High

73

noon.' He grins at me. 'Want to grab a quick sandwich at the snack bar? You ran me around the court so much, I need a break.'

'Sure,' I say. I can't believe he likes me enough to want to eat with me, and a warm feeling uncurls in my stomach and spreads all over my body. That nice feeling fades pretty fast, though, because I get all tongue-tied as we walk over to the snack bar together. I can't think of a thing to say, and that's very unlike me. I keep willing him to talk, but he doesn't, and it doesn't seem to bother him, either. He just lopes along next to me, whistling a little bit.

When we get our sandwiches, we sit at a table by the pool. It's not until we start eating that Sam leans his chair back on two legs and asks, 'So what grade are you going into?'

'Seventh,' I tell him. I don't want him to think I'm a big baby, so I add, 'I feel a lot older than twelve, though.'

'Really?' He leans toward me and draws his eyebrows together. 'How so?'

'Hmm . . .' I scrape some of the goopy mayonnaise off my sandwich and curse my big mouth. Think before you speak — that's what Sara Lynn always says. Unfortunately, the motto I seem to live by is 'Speak before you think.' Time and time again, I just go ahead and say any old thing that comes into my head, even if I have no idea what I'm talking about.

'Well, I just like older people,' I say lamely. 'I mean, I've never lived with anyone my age. I don't have any brothers or sisters.' He doesn't say anything, and I wonder if he sees what a fraud I am, just shooting off my mouth without knowing a thing about what I'm saying. I take a deep breath. In for a penny, in for a pound. That's what Ruth says. It means that once you've made a little bit of an idiot out of yourself, why not go ahead and take it all the way. I try to sound wise as I say, 'Besides, it doesn't matter how old a person is. It's all about what you're like inside.'

'That's true,' he says, nodding.

Phew! I pulled it off — sounding smarter than I am, that is. But now my stomach is sinking, because what if he thinks I'm a big loser who hangs out with older people because nobody my age will give me the time of day? What if he thinks I'm not popular?

'Look, see those girls?' I point at Ginny and the KKs, who are in the pool trying not to stare at me eating lunch with Sam. 'They're my friends from school. I have lots of friends.'

'That's nice,' he says, smiling. 'It's good to have friends.'

We keep eating, silent for a minute, and then I ask, 'Do you . . . I mean . . . who are your friends?' I wonder if he has any friends who are younger, like my age.

'Nobody you'd know.' He smiles. 'My friends are down in Boston. That's where I live.'

Huh? Then who's sitting across from me? His evil twin? 'But you moved here now, right?'

'Just for the summer,' he says. 'I have to go back to my teaching job in Boston in the fall.'

'But you could keep teaching tennis here,' I say, trying to persuade him. I mean, it's so typical. The first interesting person I meet in years, and he's only passing through.

'I don't teach tennis in Boston,' he says. 'I teach art.'

Okay. No wonder he didn't bat an eyelash when I told him about my family. His life's even more confusing than mine. 'What?' I ask.

He laughs. 'I'm a painter,' he says. 'I also teach art at a private high school outside of Boston.'

'So what are you doing here?' I mean, it's not like Ridley Falls is the vacation capital of the world.

'I'm filling in for the regular pro, Pete Dempsey. Do you know him?'

I nod. I don't really know him, but I know who he is.

'He's a buddy of mine. He broke his arm a few weeks ago, believe it or not, so he's up in Maine with his family, relaxing. He asked me to take over for him here.'

'That was nice of you to help out,' I say.

He shrugs. 'He'd do the same for me. Besides' – he flashes me a smile – 'I'm living in his house on the lake. The light's amazing out there. Great for my painting.'

I nod. The lake is really pretty. I can see why he likes living there. 'Boy, it sure must be different from Boston,' I say. I've only been to Boston a few times, once on a school trip and the other times with Sara Lynn to see a ballet or play. It's filled with people and cars and noise and huge buildings – totally the opposite of Ridley Falls.

'Yeah,' he says. 'It's very different.'

I poke at my sandwich for a minute, and then, because I can't think of anything to say, I burst out with, 'Sara Lynn went to college and law school in Boston.' Now, isn't that a conversation opener. Dumb, dumb, dumb.

But Sam doesn't seem to think it's as dumb as I do. He tilts his chin up and asks, 'Oh, is Sara Lynn a lawyer?'

'No.' I shake my head. 'She used to be. But she gave it up. Too bad, too, because I bet she was pretty good at it. She sure can argue.'

He laughs, and I laugh with him. Ha! He thinks I'm funny!

'She writes for a magazine now,' I offer, crunching a potato chip. 'She writes about gardens for this magazine called *New England Gardening*. I think she likes it better than being a lawyer because nobody can talk back to her.'

Hello? Ha, ha? He doesn't laugh at this joke, just says, 'Gardening, huh?'

'Oh, yeah.' I nod, rolling my eyes. 'Just ask her about it; she'll tell you anything you want to know and then some.'

'Good to know,' he says in his easy way, and then he stands up quickly and smiles at me. 'Listen, I've got another lesson; I've got to go. You did great today. I'll see you Thursday, okay?'

I nod. Sara Lynn decided I should take two lessons a week, so that I'd progress faster. 'You'll see me before then because I'll be coming here to practice and swim and stuff.'

'All right, then,' he says. 'Thanks for the company. It was nice to have a meal with somebody.'

76

'Bye,' I call out as he strides away.

Before I can even take a sip of my lemonade, Ginny and the KKs jump out of the pool and come rushing over to my table.

'You guys,' I say, pretending to be annoyed, 'you're dripping water all over the place.'

'What were you doing with him?' Kelly asks, her eyes big and excited.

'Just having lunch.' I shrug, trying not to show how happy I am they're making a fuss over me.

'Just having lunch? Ohmygod! Ohmygod!' they shriek.

'It was no big deal,' I say.

'Oh, he's so cute.' Ginny sighs. 'That blond hair and those blue eyes!'

'And that bod,' Kim chimes in. As if she even knows what she's talking about.

'Tell. Us. Everything.' Kelly leans across the table and puts her hand on my arm.

I think about how I could make them pay for being mean to me on my birthday. I could just walk away and say, 'Who needs you? I'm busy making new friends, like Sam, who appreciate me.' But I don't do this at all. I tell them what I know about Sam, how he's really an artist and lives in Boston, how he's an amazing tennis player, and how he's super nice. My cool quotient is skyrocketing.

Sara Lynn always says not to burn your bridges, and I think she's right. Even if these girls aren't so nice to me sometimes, I don't see the harm in spending the afternoon swimming with them and sitting on towels listening to the radio and looking through Kelly's *Seventeen* magazine at clothes. I don't see the harm in that at all, especially when a song comes on the radio that I love and Kim says, 'Oh, this song is awesome,' and I sing right along with her. I can't believe it, but she's smiling at me like she likes me, like for once in my life I belong, like the understudy inside me is finally getting her big break.

Chapter 7

$\mathcal{S}$o I'll be going over to Vermont to look at Langley's Lovely Lavender Gardens.' I tuck the phone between my ear and shoulder and take a sip of my iced tea. 'Is it just me, or is the name a little precious?'

Margaret laughs. 'The name's a tad much. But the garden is beautiful. It'll make for a great piece.'

I'm finishing up on the phone with Margaret Harnett, my editor at *New England Gardening*. We've gone over the edits to the long piece I sent in about designing a mixed border, and now we're reviewing my assignments for the month. I curl my toes around a chair rung and smile. One thing I love about my job is that I can take meetings sitting barefoot at my kitchen table. It feels so . . . subversive to me. I roll my eyes at my own inanity. Really, my life is beyond tame when going barefoot counts as deviant behavior.

I leaf through tear sheets of the lavender garden photos Margaret sent me last week. 'You're right. I'm looking forward to seeing it in person.'

'And next week you're in Boston to interview Irene Luger about her Beacon Hill garden.'

I flip my date book ahead. 'Yes.' I pencil a check mark next to the appropriate date. 'I've made those arrangements.'

There's a pause, a companionable silence, and then Margaret says, 'So how *are* you, Sara Lynn?'

'Well, I'm fine,' I reply, a little taken aback by the seriousness with which she asks her question. 'How are you?'

'Oh, you know. The kids. Mike. The dog. Life is good.'

'Yes,' I say. 'It is.'

'Next time you're in Portland, I've got someone I want you to meet.'

I force myself to smile so that what I have to say will come out of a happy mouth, not one that's prim and old-maidish. 'I'm fine as I am, Margaret.'

'Oh, pooh, don't you want to be swept off your feet by some-one?'

My eyes narrow at the time on the stove. 'Look at the time! I told Hope I'd pick her up at two. Gotta go! And no, I have ab-solutely zero desire to be swept anywhere by anyone.'

'All right.' Margaret laughs. 'Forgive me for trying. I'll talk to you next week.'

I press the end button on the phone and get up from the table, sliding into my sandals. As I grab my purse from the mudroom bench and head for the car, I can feel a red flush creeping up my face. I *tsk* my tongue in annoyance. My God, does Margaret think I'm a charity case? That my life is so barren, I'm desperate for her to find me a man?

I'm not the slightest bit lonely. Actually, my life is very full. Overflowing, even. Hope, Ruth, Mama . . . I'm certainly not lacking for companionship. And as for the sex part of things, well, who needs it? It's my experience that it only complicates matters, makes things messy.

My life is in perfect balance right now – family, career, time for my garden. I'm absolutely not interested in changing a thing. I'm annoyed at Margaret; I really am. I know she was only trying to be kind, but that's precisely the point. I don't need kindness – not from her, not from anybody.

I shudder even to imagine the man she's got on the hook for

me. Probably some divorced milquetoast eager to find wife number two. Well, it won't be me. Not by a long shot.

I shake my head as I start the car, and then I flick on the radio to take my mind off this ridiculous folly of Margaret's. 'Swept off my feet indeed. I prefer my feet flat on the ground, thank you very much. . . .' I realize I'm talking to myself, so I close my mouth with a click.

<hr/>

It's exactly two o'clock as I pull into the driveway of the country club. Right on time, I think as I slide my car into a parking spot near the pool. I reluctantly leave the air-conditioning, push the lock button on my key chain, and place my keys in my purse. Then I hear a low, gravelly voice say, 'Hi, Sara Lynn.'

I whirl around, surprised. 'Oh, hello,' I say. It's that tennis pro who teaches Hope. Sam. My eyes widen as I see how handsome he is. Where in the world was my head at that I didn't notice his looks this morning? He's tall, and his body is lean and muscled. He's got blond, wavy hair over a tanned face with blue, blue eyes. He's smiling the most dazzling smile at me, and my hand inadvertently goes to my throat.

I collect myself, drawing my back up straight. Ridiculous, to be so shaken by a good-looking man. I'm certainly not looking to find anyone, contrary to what Margaret might wish for me. Sam is just Hope's tennis teacher, for heaven's sake. 'How was Hope's lesson?' I ask.

'Terrific,' he says. 'She's got some natural ability. Like you.'

'Like me?' I don't know when he would have seen me play.

'Yeah.' He nods. 'I've seen you out on the courts. You're good.'

'Thank you,' I say automatically. Then, just as I'm about to excuse myself, he leans against the hood of my car and says, 'Listen, I hear you're a garden writer.'

Now, how in the world does he know that? He certainly doesn't seem the kind of person who'd be an avid reader of *New*

80

England Gardening. Well, chatterbox Hope must have filled him in. 'Yes,' I say, adjusting my sunglasses up higher on my nose. 'That's so.'

'Well, if it wouldn't be too much trouble, would you mind showing me some gardens around here?'

'You're a gardener?' I ask, raising an eyebrow and crossing my arms over my chest. He certainly doesn't look like a gardener.

He laughs and shakes his head. 'No – I can't even keep a houseplant alive. I'm a painter.'

'A painter?' Well! I wouldn't have called that one. What does he paint – houses? I glance at my watch, hoping he'll take the hint that I need to end this conversation. He's obviously in no hurry, however, or else he chooses to ignore the fact that I am. So typical of a good-looking man – thinks women are just swooning at his feet.

'Yeah. My work is primarily abstract, but I use nature as a theme. When Hope told me you were a garden expert, I thought you might recommend some gardens I should take a look at.'

The photographs Margaret sent me of Langley's Lovely Lavender Gardens flash into my mind, and I get excited, thinking about how a painter could drown in all that purple. 'Oh, my gosh,' I say, and without even thinking, I touch his arm. 'There's this wonderful lavender garden in Vermont I'll be visiting for the magazine. The pictures indicate it's breathtaking.'

'Great.' A smile lights up his face, and I realize I'm touching this man I barely know, this man who's probably an egomaniacal idiot. I take my hand back. Stupid, stupid to have become so excited over the silly lavender garden. 'Do you mind if I tag along with you?'

The heat of a blush floods my cheeks, and I have to restrain myself from putting my hands to my face. 'I'm happy to just give you the contact information,' I say, shifting my purse firmly onto my shoulder. 'That way you won't be tied down by my schedule.' I certainly didn't mean to sound like I was angling for us to do something together. Honestly, that conversation with Margaret threw me off my game, and I haven't recovered.

'Oh, I'd really like to go with *you*,' he says easily.

With me? I look at him through my sunglasses, and his eyes are warm and shiny. I could swear he's flirting with me, and I'm a sucker for it – I feel pretty and young under his admiring gaze. It's been a long time since an attractive man has looked at me like this, and I wish I'd put on a little lipstick before I left the house.

Oh, for God's sake! It's embarrassing to be thinking about Hope's tennis teacher in this way. He's – what? – in his twenties? And I'm a settled woman caring for a young child and an aging mother. Of course he isn't interested in me. He's probably got nubile twenty-one-year-olds just lining up for him. And here I am rounding the bend into middle age – well, early middle age, anyhow – with my pathetic little fantasies. Hope suddenly pops into my mind and gives me that disgusted look she's perfecting: *Get a clue, Sara Lynn. You're old. O-l-d. Like, get over yourself already.*

Well, wait a minute, I argue back. *Why wouldn't a man like Sam be interested in me? I'm attractive and smart and kind. Right?* Yes, and I'm also thirty-seven years old.

Looking on the bright side, maybe he's intrigued by my age. Perhaps he imagines that I'm terribly sexually experienced. An older and wiser woman. My mouth twists into a smile at that thought, and he must think it's a smile meant for him because he smiles back at me. At me! I toss my hair back and tilt my chin up.

'So when were you planning on going?' he asks.

Going? Where are we going? Oh, the garden. 'Um, Friday. I was planning on Friday.'

'That works,' he says, nodding. 'I can reschedule any lessons I have.'

'Great!' I say brightly. Too brightly? Why isn't he saying anything back? Am I supposed to keep talking? I'm terribly rusty at this whole flirtation thing, if that's even what this is.

Finally he asks, 'You want me to pick you up?'

'No!' Mama's disapproving face flashes into my head, and I cringe to imagine him arriving at my doorstep on Friday. 'I'll pick you up. You know, the magazine reimburses me gas and mileage. It just makes more sense.'

'That's cool,' he says.

Cool? It's 'cool'?! Nobody my age talks like that. God, I'm all aflutter over a man who likely was in high school when I started raising Hope. He grew up with different music, different defining political events. Our reference points don't match up at all. I'm being utterly ridiculous in even imagining he could see me as anything other than a garden guide.

'Want me to give you directions to my house?' he offers.

'Um . . .' I have to get out of here. Right now, before I do something silly, like say, 'Are you attracted to me? Because it seems like you might be, and, well, I'm a lot older than you. Not that I don't find you terribly attractive, too, but, you know, the age difference and all . . .' Oh, the horror. I shake my head to rid myself of that vision and say hastily, 'Just e-mail me.' I dig into my bag and pull out a business card. 'I really need to go get Hope now,' I say apologetically as I practically run from his side.

My head clears a bit as I walk up the path to the pool area. I can breathe again, and I think maybe the sun just got to me out there in the parking lot. Good Lord, I'm thirty-seven years old! Years beyond getting weak in the knees over anybody, let alone some devastatingly handsome kid! I scan the pool and see Hope sitting on her towel with some girls from school. As I walk over to them, I recognize Ginny, but not the other two. It looks like Hope's having fun, laughing about something with her friends. 'Hi, girls,' I say.

'Hi,' they all mumble back, not looking at me. I feel brittle and old all of a sudden, and there's a bad taste in my mouth. Am I so dour that I can shut up a pack of twelve-year-old girls just by showing up? Ruth's voice echoes inside me – *Jesus H. Christ, Sara Lynn, do you have to take things so goddamn personally?*

83

'Time to go,' I say, and I try to smile, willing myself to grow a thicker skin right here, right now.

'Okay.' Hope gets up and grabs her swim bag, dragging her feet behind her as if I've asked her to make a great sacrifice. 'Bye,' she calls back to her friends mournfully.

'You can come back tomorrow.' I put my arm around her and give her a quick squeeze as we walk to the car. Honestly, everything is so dramatic at this age.

'Really?' she says eagerly. 'Great, because I want to practice my tennis and hang out with my friends.'

'Who were those girls? Besides Ginny, I mean.'

'KK and KK.'

'Pardon me?'

She sighs and slowly says, as though I've asked her to explain the alphabet, 'Kelly Jacobs and Kim Anderson. They're going into eighth grade.'

I look around the parking lot as I unlock my car. I know who I'm looking for – Sam. Despite my better judgment, I was anticipating seeing him again, and I feel as if the sun's gone behind a cloud. Dammit! Haven't I learned my lesson? I'm angry at myself as I get in the car and turn the key. *Just stop! Stop thinking about anybody in that way.* My mother's voice speaks from inside me, railing against my tendency to pursue inappropriate men. *I'm not pursuing anybody,* I respond firmly to her voice, *not anybody at all.*

<hr>

After I quit my job at the law firm and came home for good, I alternated between walking about the house restlessly and sulking in my room. Mama gamely ignored the desperation seeping out of me. She was certain that all I needed was 'a little rest,' and then I'd join Daddy's law practice until I married a nice man and raised children right here in Ridley Falls. When I refused to smile and agree with her, she decided to take matters into her own hands. 'God helps those who help themselves,' I could imagine her muttering as she pulled out her blue leather address book and made some phone calls.

At dinner one evening, Daddy had just remarked about the warm autumn we'd been having when Mama said, 'Sara Lynn, I have the most wonderful news. Edith Jergens from my garden club is close friends with Marilyn Hanson. Marilyn's son is that nice Ray Hanson from your class in high school.'

'He wasn't in my class, Mama,' I told her through gritted teeth. Was it so difficult for her to see that I didn't have it in me to discuss her friends and their children and all the other nonsense she insisted on prattling about? 'He was probably about five classes ahead of me.'

'Now, let me finish,' she replied gaily, cutting her steak. 'Ray knows you're back in town, and guess what?' She paused and then, as if she were reading the week's winning lottery numbers, announced, 'He'd like to take you out to dinner!' She patted her mouth with her napkin and wriggled in her chair with delight. 'He's working at his father's bank, you know. He'll take it all over when Ray senior retires. Ooh, it's just too exciting.'

'Exciting?' I dropped my fork onto my plate so it made a loud clink. 'Exciting for whom, exactly?'

She looked at me with wide eyes and said, 'Honey, I'm only trying to help.'

I grabbed my napkin off my lap and threw it on the table. 'Excuse me, please,' I said to my father as I pushed back my chair and stood up. 'I've lost my appetite.'

I retreated to my bedroom, barely restraining myself from slamming the door. Instead, I shut it gently with a precise click and whirled around to catch sight of myself in the mirror hanging over my bureau. I moved closer, drawn in by steely blue eyes, high cheekbones flushed an angry red, and full pink lips. I stared at myself as I twisted my hair up and put it on top of my head and then let it fly loose around my shoulders again. For the first time, I saw myself as a troubled, passionate woman rather than a sweetly pretty girl. I was beautiful in my complexity, and a reckless urge rose up in me to strip naked and show myself to a man. *Look at me,* my brain howled to the phantom man. *Look at me.*

'Bobby Teller,' I said to my reflection, and his image replaced that of my ghost admirer as his name crashed through my mind. I remembered how he'd made me feel in high school, when we'd pass each other in the halls. We hadn't spoken, but we'd looked at each other with a frankness that had scared and thrilled me. I hadn't come anywhere close to acting on that attraction between us, because girls like me didn't even think about boys like him; but now I was hurtling toward it, my body tingling with a jittery excitement. I pictured myself driving with him, fast, with all the car windows rolled down. I was throwing my head back and laughing so that my throat was exposed, and he was pulling me close with his hand that wasn't on the wheel. I bet it would hurt a little to be pulled close by Bobby Teller. I opened my bureau drawers and began throwing clothes on the floor, trying to find something to wear that night when I went out to track him down.

I knew he'd be at O'Malley's. It had always been the hangout for people like him – people who'd never left town to go to college, people who worked menial jobs that paid minimum wage, people I'd not spoken twice to in high school. When I walked in the doorway of the bar, my bravado surrounded me like an electric field. I saw him right away, leaning over the pool table with his cue poised behind the ball. He missed his shot, stood up and shrugged, then said something that made his opponent laugh. He looked toward the door then, and his eyes locked with mine. As I started to smile, he turned back to the pool table without acknowledging me, and I felt as if I'd been kicked in the stomach.

'God!' sneered a girl trying to walk past me into the bar. 'Figure out what you're doing! Are you going in or coming out?'

'Oh!' I said, startled. 'I'm . . . I'm . . .' I stared at her dumbly for a moment. 'I'm going in. I'm in,' I told her, and my words decided it for me.

I held my head high as I walked into the smoky dimness, trying not to jump out of my skin with the uncertainty of what I'd do next. I hoped I wasn't looking frantic as I scanned the room, looking for someone to talk to, someone to make me look like a confident young woman out on the town as opposed to a lonely failure desperate to connect with her bad-boy high school crush at last.

Ah! Finally. I spied Ruth Teller with a group of girls in the corner. She was Bobby's sister, but she also had cleaned my mother's house for years. I'd seen her over my vacations from school when she'd come to clean. I knew her. It was perfectly plausible that I walk up to her and talk. Thank God, I thought, my knees buckling a little. Thank God there is one person here I know well enough to approach.

I walked across the room and said, 'Hi, Ruth.'

'What?' Ruth yelled over the loud music, her eyes glaring at me.

I cleared my throat and spoke over the music. 'It's nice to see you.'

My words hung between us, and I was beginning to doubt that she'd respond when, finally, she sort of grunted. My warm feeling toward her faded as I realized she wasn't going to make this easy for me.

I took a deep breath and said loudly, 'I love your outfit. It's great.' I was lying, of course. She was wearing a halter top and jeans that did little to flatter her tall, lanky frame.

She stared at me as if to say, 'Shut up right now,' so I turned to the other girls and smiled my party smile. 'Hello,' I said, including all four of them in my greeting. 'I'm Sara Lynn Hoffman.'

'We know who you are,' said a stocky girl with blond hair in bangs that stuck straight up from her forehead.

'Oh!' I said, feigning surprise. Well, of course they knew who I was. Hadn't I been valedictorian and class vice president and best dressed and popular? It would have shocked me if they had looked at me and said, 'Who are you?'

'Well,' I said, 'I'm afraid my memory for names has failed me. I've been down in Boston, you know. For college and law school and work.'

They didn't bat an eyelash; it was as if I hadn't spoken. *Ask them about themselves,* Mama's voice prodded me. *Get out of my head,* I told my mother, and then I smiled and asked, 'And what do you do?'

They didn't answer, just looked at me as if I were an alien trying to make conversation with them in an entirely different language. I stood my ground, though, smiling all the while.

The music changed to a slow song, and Ruth and her friends began glancing around, straightening their clothes and flipping their hair. Sure enough, some boys trickled over from the bar and pool table. They didn't even ask, 'Would you like to dance?' They just came over and claimed the girls they wanted. How barbaric, I sneered inwardly. I'd never let a man just gesture to me and expect me to go with him.

My superiority plummeted into terror as everyone continued to pair up. I felt as if I were in a biblical scene, where all the animals were boarding the ark and I was going to be left behind to drown because I didn't have a partner. Finally, only Ruth, the girl with blond bangs, and I were left standing on the outskirts of the dance floor. I put on a bored, indifferent look to hide the panic that was overtaking me. I tossed my hair and looked at my watch, and when I looked up from checking the time, there was Bobby striding over from the pool table. He was just as handsome as I'd remembered, with his broad shoulders and his dark, curly hair. He still had that power he'd had over me in high school, the power to make my stomach flip and my skin tingle. I held my breath as he approached me, and when he touched my arm I went with him onto the dance floor and swallowed a few times to open up my closed throat.

I was absolutely light-headed being so close to him, and I

feared if I opened my mouth, I'd utter nothing but giddy nonsense words. *Talk, Sara Lynn,* I lectured myself. *Talk.* 'Well,' I finally said, and my voice was brittle and high-pitched, but not as foolish-sounding as it might have been. 'Fancy meeting you here.'

He didn't say anything for a moment, and I wondered if I'd only imagined saying something. That's how being around him affected me: I wasn't even certain whether or not I'd spoken. Finally, he raised a corner of his mouth in a half smile and said, 'Shouldn't I be saying that to you?'

'Why?' I asked, tossing back my hair and looking up at him. 'Why is it so surprising to see me here?'

'Because you actually got the hell out of this town. Why would you come back to nothing?'

My back stiffened, and I tried to sound casual as I said, 'Oh, I don't know that I'll stay. I just got tired of Boston. Maybe I'll try New York next.'

'Must be nice just to be able to go anywhere you want whenever you feel like it.' His dark eyes smirked at me, almost as if he knew I was just a scared little girl who'd never get out of Ridley Falls again.

'Maybe that's why Ridley Falls doesn't feel so suffocating to me,' I said, trying to lighten the defensiveness creeping into my voice. 'Because I can leave anytime I want.'

He shrugged, and then he pulled me closer. His arms were strong, and his back, where I touched it, was hard and muscular. I could feel his breath moving little strands of my hair.

'So what have you been doing since you got back?' he said into my ear.

'Nothing at all,' I said, my heart pounding because here was my opening, my chance. 'I'm so bored I could scream. I'd forgotten how dull this town is.'

He laughed. 'I don't know how you could have forgotten that.'

'At least it's really pretty here outdoors. Down in Boston, it was just tall buildings and dirty sidewalks and air pollution.' *It's now or never,* I told myself. *Be brave. For once in your ridiculous life, be brave.* At least I didn't have to look at him when I asked, 'Do you ever hike or anything like that?'

'No,' he replied. 'Can't say that I do.'

I swallowed hard as the music ended and our bodies broke apart. I looked at him then and asked, 'Well, would you ever like to?'

He flashed me that half smile again and said, 'Are you asking me on a date?'

Oh God, I'd blown the whole thing to pieces. Stupid, stupid, I chided myself. He'll tell everyone, and they'll all laugh at me for even thinking someone like Bobby Teller would look at me. 'Don't flatter yourself,' I said in a bored voice. 'It came up in conversation and I was simply being polite by asking if you wanted to come along.'

He shrugged and said, 'Yeah, I'll go. Nothing else to do around here anyway.'

'Fine,' I said, flooded with relief followed by a twinge of disappointment. What had I expected, for heaven's sake? For him to fall at my feet, saying, 'Sara Lynn, I've worshipped you all these years. Thank God you're back so we can finally consummate our great passion for each other'? Right. I shook my head a little as if to clear the stars from my eyes. I looked up at him, and he was giving me that sly, knowing half smile again, as if he could read my mind.

'Well, why don't you call me sometime?' he asked.

Me? Call him? Oh, no, no, no. This wasn't the way things were supposed to go. I could tell he was going to bolt back over to the pool table any minute and just leave things like this, so I pulled my last card from my hand and said, 'I have to go now. Would you mind walking me to my car?'

His eyes looked puzzled for a minute, but then he smiled and said, 'Sure.' He ran one hand through his dark, curly hair. 'No problem.'

As we walked out of the bar, I sighed heavily, breathing in the clean night air. 'God,' I said, 'it was smoky and loud in there. Isn't it peaceful out here?' I breathed again, moving my arms from my side and holding them out from my body to take in a big gulp of air.

'You always were strange, Sara Lynn Hoffman,' he said, but he didn't say it meanly.

'You were always strange to me, too, Bobby Teller,' I replied, and it sounded like a promise I was saying back to him.

'This is me,' I said when we arrived at my car.

He patted the hood of my jazzy little car. 'Sweet wheels,' he said.

'You can drive it when we go on our hike,' I told him.

'Isn't the point of a hike to walk?' he asked.

'Well, I thought we might drive over to the nature preserve in Hadley and walk through there.'

'Planned it all out, have you?' he said, and there was that smile again, quick and mocking.

'What's that supposed to mean?' I crossed my arms over my chest, and he gently uncrossed them.

'Nothing,' he said as he pulled me into his arms. 'Nothing at all.' He kissed me then, and I lost my breath. I just kept kissing him until my lips went past hurting and became numb, until my insides were aching with wanting him. We were splayed out on the hood of my car, him on top of me, when we heard a voice in the night.

'Bobby, what in hell are you doing?' It was Ruth, standing in the alley watching us.

'Shit,' he muttered. 'Get out of here,' he yelled to her. 'Just go.'

He got up off me and I slid off the car, and we stood looking at each other, panting hard. 'Sorry,' he finally said, his voice soft. He touched my nose and kissed me hard before he turned away. 'Come back tomorrow night. Maybe I'll see you.'

I see him in my mind right now like I could reach out and touch him. I see his dark eyes glimmering and that half smile, two thirds mocking and one third sweet, that I used to trace with my finger.

'Sara Lynn!' I hear Hope's voice speaking to me, and I realize I'm leaning over the steering wheel, gripping it hard.

'Yes?' I say jumpily.

'I've been trying to tell you about a million times that I saw some clothes I want for school. Kelly had a *Seventeen* magazine, and we were looking through it, and . . .'

I nod and smile, trying to respond appropriately. I'm not with Hope in this car, though. I'm someplace else, a place where ghosts surround me, pulling at the corners of my heart. I need to get out and work in my garden. There's weeding to be done, and watering, and every little chore I can possibly do to take myself away from the regret and yearning that would choke me if I let it, would strangle me like the bittersweet vine I hack away in my garden year after year, getting rid of it all only to have it come back, again and again.

Chapter 8

ow was your day?' Ruth asks, serving me a breast of chicken, rice, and spinach.

'It was awesome.' I slide into my chair and pick up my knife and fork. 'Oops,' I say, remembering to put my napkin in my lap. 'It was the best. I had my tennis lesson today, and I loved it. I did really good.'

'Well,' corrects Sara Lynn. 'You did very well.'

'Sara Lynn was always quite accomplished at tennis,' Mamie says, patting her mouth gently with her napkin. 'She reminded me so of that cute Chris Evert.'

Sara Lynn rolls her eyes and says, 'I'm okay at tennis, Mama. Hardly Chris Evert material.'

Mamie acts like she hasn't heard Sara Lynn. 'Oh, she was such a sweet thing, with her hair pulled back in a long braid. So graceful on the court.' She turns to Sara Lynn then and says, 'You really were graceful, dear. You could have been a prima ballerina.'

'My goodness,' says Sara Lynn, her voice sounding brittle. She's cutting her chicken into tiny pieces, moving her knife over the chicken like it'll get up and run away from her if she doesn't show it who's boss. 'Chris Evert! A prima ballerina! Is there anything I couldn't have been?'

Mamie sets her mouth hard and gives her head a quick, impa-

93

tient shake. 'Now, what did I say that possibly could have upset you?' she asks, a forkful of rice poised in the air. 'I was only complimenting you on how talented you were.' She turns to Ruth and me. 'Talented at anything she set her mind to.'

Sara Lynn doesn't say anything, just keeps spearing her food and bringing it to her mouth. Her eyes look a little bright, and that line she gets between her eyebrows when she's upset appears.

I glance at Ruth, and she gives me a look that says, 'Here we go again – the old invisible wall.' Actually, the 'invisible wall' is my name for it, for this barrier between Sara Lynn and Mamie. It's like there's a wall of ice that separates them, a wall where they can look through and see each other, but there's no way they can touch. Sometimes we all forget the wall is there until one of them says or does something to set the other one off. Then there it is, this wall between them that they hide behind, one on each side.

'You want to play Scrabble or something after dinner?' I ask Mamie. I've found it's best to take everyone's mind off the wall when it appears. Just change the subject and get them on to something else.

'Fine,' Mamie says, in a stiff voice like she's still hurt. But then she turns to me and tries to smile. 'That would be lovely.'

So here I am. A promise is a promise, after all, and I did say I'd play Scrabble with Mamie, even though it's as boring as all get-out because I never, ever win. It's my turn, and I'm fooling around with my letter tiles, trying to figure out how to make a Scrabble word with seven consonants. I don't think it's possible. Mamie is sitting across from me, drumming her fingers on the card table I've set up between the two wing chairs in her bedroom.

'Just give me a second,' I say, squinting hard at the letters, trying to will a vowel to appear. Mamie's on this hot streak tonight, getting triple word scores practically every turn, when it's all I can do to put 'cat' or 'dog' on the board.

'Dang,' I finally say. I put back my L and my M and pull up two letters. I don't want to put back the X and the J I have. Big points if I can use them. Okay, I have a U now, at least. Hmmm.

Mamie puts down 'zephyr,' and I groan. 'Double word score, too,' she points out modestly. I write her score and look at my letters, wondering if 'pux' is a word. Maybe it's kind of like 'pox.' I glance at Mamie, wondering if she'll challenge me.

'P-u-x,' I say, adding the U and the X to the P Mamie just put down on the board. 'Pux.'

'Pux?' Mamie raises an eyebrow. She looks just like Sara Lynn when she does that. 'Did you really think I wouldn't challenge, Hope?'

'Oh, fine,' I grumble, taking the letters off. Technically, I should lose a turn, but Mamie usually lets me try again if I try to pull a fast one on her.

I sigh as I look at my loser letters. 'You know what? I can't make a word. And I'm so far behind that it's not fun anymore. Let's just call it and say you won.'

'Are you sure you don't want to keep going?' she asks. 'The game's not over until it's over.'

'Oh, it's over all right,' I say.

'All right, then,' says Mamie. 'Would you like to play some rummy?'

I drum my fingers on the card table and think a minute. 'No. You know what I really want to do?'

'Crazy eights?'

'Try on your rings.'

She chuckles, a smile widening across her little wrinkled face. 'Sweet girl. You haven't wanted to do that in some time.' She slides her diamond engagement ring and wedding band off her left hand and places them into my palm. I put them onto my right index finger and hold them up so the big round diamond shines in the lamplight.

'Look at me,' I say in an affected voice. 'I'm rich.'

'Don't go talking about your money like you're common trash,' Mamie says, grinning. This is an old game of ours. She tugs slowly at the ring on her right hand; it's what she calls her dinner ring, and it's my favorite, a wide band with six small square diamonds set into it. I don't in the least see what all those diamonds have to do with dinner, but Mamie says she cherishes it because it was her mother's from back home in St. Louis.

She reaches over to give it to me, and I place it on my middle finger, next to her wedding rings. 'Now I'm really rich,' I say, waving my hand in the air.

'Tacky,' she snorts, shaking her head. 'Wearing them all on the same hand.'

'I like them all together.' I look at my jeweled hand for a while, and then I tip my right hand upside down into my left, and the rings fall off. I hand them back to Mamie.

'My, my,' she says, shaking her head as she slides her rings back on the fingers where they belong. 'That brings back memories. When you were little, you were like a monkey, always climbing up on my lap wanting to try on my rings.'

I laugh from the pleasure of recalling cuddling with Mamie and playing with her jewelry, but a little pang of sorrow hits me, too. I'm coming to realize that as you get older, remembering things is half-happy and half-sad. When you're little it's all happy, because the things you remember – like Santa coming, for example – will all happen again. But when you get older, you realize that some happy things go away forever and that's it – they're gone for good. You're glad you have the memory of those things, but you're also sad because that's all you have – the memory and never again the thing itself.

Mamie's in a remembering mood tonight. She shakes her head and *tsk*s her tongue, saying, "My Lord, it seems like yesterday you came here as a baby. Sara Lynn just came bursting through the door one day and said, 'Mama, Bobby Teller has made his sister, Ruth, and me guardians of his baby girl, and I'm going to do it.'"

'How did my father come to choose Sara Lynn?' I ask, even though I can already guess what she'll say.

Mamie's mouth puckers, and she says, 'Oh, Sara Lynn and Ruth were always friends. Classmates, you know, all through school. Your father likely knew Sara Lynn would help do what needed to be done regarding you.' Mamie's voice trails off, and she looks over my head as if she's seeing something.

'Mamie.' I'm sitting on the edge of my chair. 'Go on with the story.' I'm forever trying to get them all to tell me how I came to live here. None of them tells it the same, or even the same way twice, and I keep hoping that someday I'll put all the versions together to find the truth.

'Patience, child,' Mamie says, still looking at something I can't see. 'Patience is a virtue.'

I sigh. Grown-ups are so lame. They take their sweet time telling you the things you want to know, and when they finally do get around to talking, you just know you're getting the *Reader's Digest* condensed version.

Mamie yawns delicately, putting her fingers up to her mouth. 'My goodness,' she says, coming back from wherever she was in her head. She looks at me surprised, as if she's half forgotten I'm in the room. 'I'm a bit sleepy. This has been a lovely visit, dear, but I think I'd better get a little rest.'

'Love you, Mamie,' I say, standing up and walking over to her chair. I put my arms around her neck and wait for her kiss on my cheek.

'Good night, dear Hope,' she says.

I close her bedroom door behind me and walk down the quiet hallway. Sara Lynn and Ruth are likely downstairs, probably reading or watching TV, but I don't feel like being with them right now.

When I reach my bedroom and flick on the light, my eyes happen to fall on my desk. Now, I never, and I mean never, use my desk during the summer. My desk gives me the heebie-jeebies, in fact, because it reminds me of homework and school and how the

97

clock is tick-tocking double time in summer. But it's like I'm under a spell or something – I pull out my desk chair and sit, and then I rummage through my desk drawer for paper and a pen. I think it was talking to Mamie about how I came to live here that put this idea into my head, but I must have been storing up the right words for a long time because I'm not even hesitating a little bit. I just write without stopping, as if I know exactly what to say.

Dear Dad,

It's your daughter Hope. I'm twelve now, and I've been wondering a lot about you. Ruth has some pictures of you when you were little, and I think I look like you. I've been wondering about my mother, too. Maybe I look somewhat like her, too, but I wouldn't know because I don't have a picture of her. Do you have a picture of her? If you do, I would like to see it. Ruth says she was nice.

It's not that I'm not happy with Ruth and Sara Lynn. I really am, and I love them a lot, even though they do drive me crazy sometimes, especially Sara Lynn.

I wonder what you're like. It's hit me lately that maybe you're married to someone else and have other kids. That would be okay. I just want to know how you are and maybe a little bit about the time that you left. I know my mother had just died and all, but I wonder a lot about that time in your life. In my life, too, I guess, although I don't remember any of it.

I am growing up to be a person I think you would like. I'm getting prettier, and I'm smart in school, and I think I have a good personality. At least, Ruth and Sara Lynn say I do. I'm not sure what I want to be when I grow up, but Mamie says isn't it wonderful how girls can be anything they want these days. What are you? I mean, what job do you do?

What did you feel like when you met my mother? I just

wonder how you knew you were in love, how you knew she was the right person for you. Did you know right away? Did she?

Do you think about me sometimes? I think about you.

These are some of the questions I have for you. I would really, really like it if you would write back and answer some of them. It's hard not knowing these things. You could call me if you're not much of a letter writer. This is my address and my telephone number:

Hope Teller
24 Morning Glory Lane
Ridley Falls, New Hampshire 03577
(603) 665-9987

Love,
Hope

I fold the piece of paper and slide it into my desk drawer. Then I get up from my desk, turn out the light, and feel my way over to my bed. I pull off the covers and lie flat on my back, looking up at the dark ceiling. The air in my bedroom stills suddenly, and then my mother is there with me, outside my body and in it at the same time. I've felt her spirit a couple of times before, always when I'm alone and don't expect her. I lie perfectly still, and I can taste salt from the tears running into my mouth.

I miss you, I tell her without words.

I know you do, she says back. *I know.*

Chapter 9

Ah! The most delightful part of the day for me – putting my head on the pillow and sailing into sleep. Well, I don't sail so much these days. It takes a bit when a body is as old as mine.

I chuckle remembering Hope trying on my rings this evening. Such a dear, dear girl with that mop of curls and those dark eyes. Doesn't look a bit like Sara Lynn, but then why would she? She's not ours by blood, only by heart. Oh, I wish my sister Julia Rae were alive to know her. She'd like Hope. Indeed she would.

I miss Julia Rae. I miss all the old folks – Baby Caroline, Brother, Mama, and Daddy. I'm the last one of my family. Whoever would have thought it? It seems to me the older I get, the closer I feel to being that young girl again, whispering secrets with Julia Rae and rocking with my mama on our porch swing, smelling the night jasmine. It's Mama I miss most of all. I miss her more than I miss my own husband, I'm ashamed to say. Now, I loved Eliot. Love him still, even with him gone these thirteen years. Couldn't have asked for a better, kinder husband. But there's a hole in my heart no one but my mother ever could fill.

A girl needs her mother. That's just the way it is. But not my daughter. No. She and I don't sit side by side on a porch swing, talking without words. Instead, we holler at each other across a canyon deep and wide just to be heard. This distance between us would break my heart if I let it. It surely would.

⁓

Sara Lynn didn't give me a lick of trouble until she quit her lawyering job and came on home to live. Now, it would have been fine if she had quit because she got married and decided to start a family. But no, she left with absolutely no prospects of doing anything else, and after all that education, too. It bored her to tears, she said, all those men storming around so convinced they were right. She just didn't care to take part in that anymore, so she up and left on a whim one day. That is when I began to think I may have spoiled her, her being an only child I had all but given up hope of having.

'What about Daddy?' I asked her. Her own father was a lawyer, so if she was saying that lawyers were too lowly for her to associate with, what was she saying about her father? 'Are you telling me Daddy's not the most honorable, kindest man you've ever known in your whole life?'

'I am not saying one word about Daddy,' she replied crossly, 'and I don't appreciate you trying to put a guilt trip on me.'

Guilt trip? I wasn't trying to take her on any kind of a trip; I was only trying to see where on earth she had put her mind.

She didn't do a blessed thing when she came home. Wasn't interested, she said. Needed a rest. Well, she didn't *have* to work, that was for certain. But still, couldn't she have found some volunteer project to keep her occupied? I suggested she work down at the hospital as a greeter. 'You might meet a nice doctor,' I told her.

'I don't want to meet a nice doctor,' she said. 'You think finding a husband solves every little problem. Well, it doesn't.'

'Who said anything about getting married?' I asked her. 'I'm just talking about going out in the evenings, getting out of the house for a little enjoyment.'

'Well, mind your own business,' she said.

'Sara Lynn!' I gasped. She had never spoken to me so freshly before.

'Sorry, Mama,' she replied, 'but you're driving me crazy.'

There was nobody on this earth with whom I could discuss my only child's erratic behavior. I had prided myself on raising a perfect daughter. Through the years, my friends had marveled at Sara Lynn's accomplishments. She'd always had top grades and played flawless pieces in the yearly piano recitals. She was so pretty, too, with her long blond hair and her sweet smile she flashed on everyone who came to the house.

'She's such an angel, Aimee,' my friends would say longingly. 'I wish mine could be like her.'

I must admit I had preened under their praise. But pride goeth before a fall, and there I was, rubbing my skinned knees.

'We're so happy she's home,' I told my friends cheerfully. 'They worked her to the bone at that law firm. It was, well, a bit dull for her as well. She's so creative, you know.'

'What will she do now?' they'd ask me. 'Whatever is she going to do now?'

I was so used to having something to tell them about what Sara Lynn was up to – whether it was winning the state essay contest on why she was proud to be an American or where she was going to college or how she was planning on being a lawyer – that I was at a loss as to how to respond. 'She's thinking over her options,' I told them. 'She has so many that it takes time to think them through.'

She overheard me once on the telephone having just this conversation, and she rushed into my bedroom after I'd hung up the phone, hissing, 'Stop talking about me! Why can't you let me lead my own life without always shaping it to be what you want?'

'I'm just saving your face,' I told her, my patience wearing thin. 'What would you have me tell them?'

'Tell them the truth,' she said. 'Tell them you don't know the first thing about me.'

Now, wasn't that a crazy thing to say! She grew inside me for nine months, and then out she came. I fed her and loved her and kept her clothed and warm and happy for the whole of her life, giving her absolutely everything she wanted. I didn't know the first thing about her? I knew everything about her. I knew things she didn't know about herself.

I referred to her behavior obliquely once to Mary Teller, who'd been my cleaning lady forever. 'Mary,' I said, 'do you find that things can get, well, testy with your adult children?' Mary had a girl just Sara Lynn's age and two older boys. They were always in trouble, and I suppose I wanted to hear about how horrid they were so as to put my own little problem into perspective.

Mary threw her dust cloth onto the table and howled with laughter. 'We're certainly not the Waltons,' she said. 'You have no idea.' She picked up her cloth and started dusting again, and I stood at the dining room entryway, fiddling with my pearls, a nervous habit of mine.

'Why?' Mary asked. 'Is Sara Lynn going through a hard time just now?'

'No, no,' I protested, twisting those pearls. 'She's just seeking her independence, and I'm having a hard time letting go.'

Mary laughed again. 'The grass is always greener,' she said. 'Here I am trying to get mine out from underfoot. They could use a little more independence. Always asking me for money and whining to me about this and that.'

'Ma, stop complaining about us.' Mary's daughter, Ruth, poked her head in from the hallway. Ruth had been helping her mother clean since she graduated from high school with Sara Lynn.

'I'll do as I like,' Mary replied, laughing.

'You always have,' Ruth told her.

Those two cackled like a couple of geese and then went on with their work. I felt alone in my own house, and I went up to my room to read a bit and try to put Sara Lynn out of my mind.

Then came the night she went out to O'Malley's, where no re-spectable lady ever would think to go.

103

'I'm going out,' she said. 'I'm as bored as anything in this house.'

Eliot and I were listening to Mozart on the record player, and I was needlepointing while he read some new case law. We looked up at her, startled. It was ten at night, for heaven's sake.

'Where are you going?' I asked, and I ignored the look Eliot was giving me. He believed Sara Lynn was an adult woman who needed time and space to find her own way in the world. 'Time and space' — that's exactly what he said. He was getting to be as new agey as Sara Lynn herself. I half expected him to tell me I was putting a 'guilt trip' on him next time I asked him to take out the trash.

'Out,' she said. She was wearing jeans with a tight-fitting top she must have bought down in Boston, because I knew I hadn't bought it for her when she lived in this house.

'Where?' I persisted.

'Now, Aimee,' Eliot said.

'O'Malley's,' she said.

'O'Malley's?' Eliot asked, surprised. Ha! I thought. What do you think of that, Mr. Liberal Thinker?

'Oh, Daddy,' she said, turning on all her charm for him. My hands shook with anger as I kept poking that needle into my canvas again and again. 'All the girls go there. It's the place to go to meet other people. There's nothing else to do in this town. I'm just going in to have a drink, see who's there, and then come home.'

'Have a drink?' I asked, my voice sounding like acid corroding metal.

'I'm of age, Mama,' Sara Lynn replied, enunciating the words as if I were dull-normal in the head. 'You're always telling me to make friends, and then when I take one little step toward doing so, you want to hold me back. It's always been like this.'

'Just what is that supposed to mean?' I asked, throwing down my needlepoint and glaring at her. She'd lately been insinuating that she'd had a terrible childhood at my ignorant hands, and I

104

wanted to stop all this dancing around and just get it out on the table.

'I never had real friends like other children,' she said, her eyes snapping at me. 'I always had to take music lessons and dance lessons and win writing contests and make the best grades in school. You wanted me to be perfect. A little dancing bear.'

I looked at her as if she were changing into a stranger before my eyes. 'That is not true,' I replied. 'You loved your lessons and you loved winning things and you loved being perfect.'

'You loved me being perfect!' Her voice was mean and accusing.

'Now, hold on,' said Eliot. 'What's all this "perfect" talk? Sara Lynn is a lovely girl, but she's not the risen Christ.'

'Sacrilegious!' I snapped at him. I turned to Sara Lynn, truly puzzled as to where her ideas were coming from. 'You think I pushed you into doing well at things? I only tried to encourage you, to show you I was interested in whatever you were doing.'

She sighed. 'Fine, Mama. Just forget I said anything. Can I go now?'

'*May* I go,' I corrected automatically.

'See?' she said, appealing to her father. 'See? This is what she has been like since the day I was born.'

'Go along, honey,' Eliot told her without even a reprimand about hurting her mother like she was doing. 'Have fun and be careful.'

'Thanks, Daddy,' she said to him. To me she said nothing at all.

When she shut the door and we heard her car back out of the driveway, I picked up my needlepoint and started stabbing the needle into the canvas again. I could hardly see straight, and I said, 'Well, thank you very much, Mr. Concerned Father. Thank you for helping to turn my own daughter against me.'

'Aimee,' he said in his lawyer's voice that told me I was a hysterical woman who needed calming, 'be reasonable.'

'That's right,' I said, needlepointing away furiously. 'I'm not reasonable at all. It's a good thing you and Sara Lynn are back living together in this house again so that you can commiserate about how reasonable you two are and how horrible I am.'

'We just need to give her a little rope.'

'Why, so she can hang herself?' I slid my needle into the canvas to store it and rolled up the silly needlework — a rooster, it was; I was needlepointing a rooster while my life was falling apart. I stood up and said, 'What I like is how you remained utterly uninvolved all throughout her growing-up years and only now have decided to give me the benefit of your parenting expertise. Why don't you write a book, Dr. Spock?'

I stormed upstairs, ran myself a hot bath, and soaked in it for a good half hour. Then I read a bit before Eliot came upstairs. When I heard his footsteps, I shut off the light and pretended I was asleep. Sara Lynn wasn't home yet, and I knew I wouldn't be getting any rest until she saw fit to grace us with her presence once again.

Oh, that was a horrible time in our lives. I don't know, truly, whether or not we've ever recovered from it.

Back home in St. Louis, when I was young, Mama had a beautiful platter with a blue-and-white design of a bridge and trees and people walking. How she loved that platter! She cried and cried when Brother accidentally broke it from playing ball in the kitchen with Baby Caroline. 'Silly!' she kept saying, wiping her eyes and trying to smile at us. 'Silly of me to make such a fuss over a platter!'

Julia Rae patted Mama's shoulders, saying, 'Don't worry. Aimee has steady fingers, and she and I'll put it back together again.' Then she shooed everyone out of the kitchen except me, and she sat me down at the table. She bent down and found every last piece of the platter and placed them before me with some glue. 'Now, Sister,' she said, 'you just glue these pieces back together the best you can. We'll save Mama's platter. Make it as good as new.'

I glued and glued, fitting each piece together like I was doing a jigsaw puzzle, Julia Rae beside me, saying, 'That piece doesn't go there; better try this one.' We worked together for close to an hour, and when it was done we let it dry, calling Mama in to look at it.

'My girls!' she said, putting her hand to her chest in amazement. 'It looks beautiful!'

'Let it dry overnight, Mama,' said Julia Rae. 'Then nobody will ever know.'

I always knew, though. Whenever I looked at that platter, my eyes followed the minuscule cracks that broke up the picture of the people and the bridge and the trees. I never saw it whole again, never was able to look at it sitting on the shelf without my breath catching for fear it would disintegrate into little bits.

That's how I feel about Sara Lynn and me. We broke something between us, and on the surface it looks mended. But we both can see the cracks, and we know not to push too hard on the bond between us, lest it give way and the whole thing fall to the ground in pieces.

Chapter 10

$\mathcal{S}$hit on a stick, I think I'm pregnant. I'm careful as careful can be, and still I'm up shit's creek without a paddle here. Dammit, dammit, dammit. Well, Ma always said she was like a rabbit – just had to look at my father and along we all came. So I'm following right along in the Teller tradition.

Now, I'm not like Sara Lynn. I've seen the calendar she keeps on the kitchen desk, and I know she keeps a perfect record of the dates her period comes. No reason – she probably just likes to know that every cycle of the moon her body's going to do what it's supposed to. Every twenty-eight days, there's a little circle around the date's number. 'Hello, friend,' she probably says with a smile as she draws her circle. I'm surprised she doesn't color-code it in red ink.

I don't keep any sort of track. It comes when it comes, the achy cramps and the disposition from hell, and I'm damned if I could tell you when it last was here. It's been a while, though. Longer than usual. Shit.

I'm finishing up the last of the lunches here at the diner, and I've finally got a second to think. I'll drive to the drugstore and get one of those pregnancy tests, that's what I'll do. Can't get it here in town – that blabbermouth Mary Beth Casey will tell everyone. Anyone who buys personal items from Casey's Pharmacy is crazy, with that busybody running the place. I'll drive over to Hadley, where nobody knows me.

'Chet, I'm leaving a little early today,' I say, glancing at the clock. Two-thirty. I don't want to face Jack again today. I locked myself in his bathroom this morning and did the Q-tip test – stuck a Q-tip inside me to check for any blood that might be a little sluggish up there. Nothing. Not one speck of red. I must've looked like I'd seen a ghost when I came out of that bathroom. I numbly said my good-byes and got myself to work, where I wouldn't have to think. 'Just tell Jack I had something I had to do.' I pick up my purse and sling it over my shoulder as I'm leaving.

'You okay, Ruth?'

'Yeah, yeah, I'm fine. See you tomorrow.'

I step into the heat and my stomach sort of turns over. I haven't been feeling great lately. Tired and . . . off. Food tastes funny to me. I sigh and hop into my shitbox car. Hotter than hell. I pump the gas a few times to get the damn thing to start, and my stomach turns over again. It's flipping and flopping inside me, and I swallow a few times. Could just be the heat. Not likely, though, not with my luck. I wish Ma were here. Dammit, I miss that old witch something awful sometimes. Know what I'd ask her if she were here? I'd ask her if I was worth it.

'Worth what?' she'd say.

Worth having. Worth keeping and raising. 'Look,' I'd say, 'you've only told me about a million times how I was a big surprise – but did you want me after you had me? Did you love me right when you saw me, or did I sort of grow on you?'

'Yeah,' she'd say. 'Like a fungus.'

I'm laughing like a crazy person in my ninety-degree car, and I have to pull over because I can't stop myself. I just keep laughing and laughing, and I swear I'm going to pee my pants if I can't get it together. I pull into the Stop & Shop parking lot and stop the car, and then I put my head on the wheel and laugh as loud as I can. It's damn strange, that's what it is: The sounds coming

109

out of my mouth are hoots of laughter, but there are tears running down the steering wheel.

～

When Ma was dying, it was the prettiest month of the year, and I thought that was a damn shame. She'd never liked the other months in New Hampshire – the long, snowy winters, the mud-season springs, the hot summers when the grass burned out and the mosquitoes swarmed. Even in the fall, when leaf peepers came from all over to take a look at the trees, she just sniffed and said autumn was nothing but decaying things all dressed up. So that left June, and here she was dying just as her favorite month began.

As I walked up the hospital steps for the third time that June day, I said a general 'hey' to the patients in their hospital gowns holding on to their IV poles and smoking by the scraggly bushes at the front entrance. They looked pretty bad, all pale and skinny and desperate, puffing on those cigarettes like it was their last chance for happiness, but they raised their heads and mumbled their hellos back. It drove Ma crazy, these people who insisted on smoking even as it was killing them, but I didn't have any problem with them taking their happiness where they found it.

I walked past the front desk and nodded to Cassie MacBrien, who sat there doodling on a pad of paper as she manned the phones. She looked up and cracked her gum, waving her hand at me halfheartedly, but she didn't stop me or anything. Nobody made me check in anymore; that's how often I was at the hospital.

I passed the gift shop and wondered for a second if I should go in and get Ma something, but I knew every last piece of goods they sold in there and decided against it. Nothing but blue and pink teddy bears, mugs with 'Get well soon at Ridley Falls Hospital!' written on them, and stunted carnations dyed different colors sitting in a beat-up refrigerator at the back of the shop. Ma was past wanting a magazine or a stick of gum, and besides, I had

110

to pee like a racehorse, so I kept going, heading for the ladies' room across from the elevator.

I swung open the ladies' room door and hustled into a stall, practically jumping up and down from holding my pee so long. I was just coming back from my last cleaning job of the day, and I hadn't bothered to stop home before driving to the hospital. I jammed the stall's lock shut, spread some toilet paper out on the seat, and unzipped my shorts. I sat down, sighed with relief to finally let all that pee out, and pressed the mute button on my thoughts. I was so tired that I rested my elbows on my knees and put my chin in my hands, just sitting there even after I had done my business. I stared at the graffiti on the door in front of me — 'Tim loves Dee'; 'R.L. + H.T.'; 'For a good time, call Mark' — though I wasn't reading the words as much as I was just looking at the letters I'd looked at a million times before. Then I heard the ladies' room door swing open and some footsteps, so I woke myself up from my open-eyed nap and wiped and flushed before letting myself out of the stall. Washing my hands, I chanced to look at myself in the mirror. I looked terrible. My skin was all splotchy, probably from getting too many meals at the hospital vending machines, and there were dark circles under my eyes. I rubbed at the circles as if I could erase them, but of course it didn't do any good. Ugly, I thought, and then I asked myself who really cared anyhow.

I opened the bathroom door and crossed to the elevator bank, then pressed the button and tapped my foot while I waited for the elevator that was older than dirt. I could hear it lurching its way down slowly and loudly, rumbling and jerking to a stop as the bell dinged and the door opened. I stepped in and punched 3, and then the elevator decided to have one of its seizures, its bell dinging and its door half shutting and then opening, again and again. It sounded like that stuttering Mr. Parsons at the garage, I thought as I pressed hard on the Door Close button. Just kept repeating the same jerky sound over and over. 'You're in need of an oil ch———, an oil ch———, an oil ch———.'

An oil change! I screamed inwardly as I jabbed that Door Close button again and again. The elevator groaned shut and finally began to lumber its way up.

That's not nice, I reproached myself. Mr. Parsons can't help it if he talks funny. I felt ashamed of myself then, and a smug little voice inside my head said, *Maybe if you weren't so mean, your mother wouldn't be dying.* Then another voice inside that I call 'the referee' piped up and said, *Time out. It's not your fault Ma is sick.*

I'm going crazy, I thought grimly. I've got voices in my head that talk to each other and another voice that shuts them all up.

Damn! I rubbed my goose-bumped arms. I had left my hospital sweater in the backseat of the car. It was nothing but a ratty old black cardigan that used to be Ma's about a hundred years ago, but it kept me warm when I was visiting. I supposed I could head back down and grab it, but I probably would have a screaming fit if I had to fight that demon-possessed elevator again.

They kept it so damn freezing in the hospital. Ma and me used to joke about it when I'd drag her in for chemo. God, she'd complain every step of the way. 'I hate the way it makes me feel, Ruth.' 'It's not doing any good.' 'I don't think those doctors know their asses from their elbows.'

'Come on, Ma,' I'd say to her. 'We're going for your chemo and that is that.'

When we'd get to the chemo ward on the fifth floor, I'd tell her to keep her winter coat on, that we were back in Alaska. She'd always crack a little smile when I said this, even though it wasn't that funny a joke. 'Here you go, dear,' one of the nurses would say as they covered her with a heated blanket where she lay shivering on her gurney in nothing but her hospital gown and thick socks from home. I'd wait for the nurse to hitch up Ma's IV and flick the tube a few times to make sure the medicine was pouring into her vein the way it was supposed to. As the nurse walked away, I'd bend down and whisper to Ma, 'Why don't they just turn the damn heat up? It'd save them the trouble of heating their linens.'

No chemo anymore, though. I hadn't been up to the fifth floor since April, when they'd opened Ma up and then closed her again, saying there was nothing they could do. I had been so hopeful before that last surgery, yammering my big mouth about how this was it – they'd cut out the cancer that the chemo surely had shrunk and Ma would be cured. I had called Bobby and Sandra to tell them that Ma would soon be well enough to go up to Maine and help Sandra before their new baby came. I had been so sure Ma would live to see her grandchild.

But if pride came before a fall, then I guess hope appeared before a letdown. Ma had kept shaking her head, saying, 'Don't count your chickens before they're hatched, Ruth. Stop telling everyone I'm going to get better.' And she'd been right.

I thought back to her telling me last September that she had cancer. 'C,' she'd called it; she couldn't even say the word. We'd been cleaning the Olivers' house, and I'd about jumped out of my skin when Ma tapped me on the arm as I was swinging the vacuum cleaner back and forth over the dining room rug.

'What?' I had yelled without stopping work, expecting her to holler, 'You missed a spot,' or, 'Move those chairs out, Ruth; don't just vacuum around them.'

She'd motioned for me to turn off the vacuum, and when I had, she'd said, 'Ruth, I need to tell you something I thought I wasn't going to tell anybody for a while. But it's just sitting in me itching to get out and I need to tell you.'

'Let me guess,' I had wisecracked. 'You're pregnant.' I'd give anything if I could take that back. My big, smart mouth.

'No,' Ma had said, wiping her hands on her apron. 'I'm dying.'

'Ma, cut it out. What is it really?'

'That's it. Really. I've got . . .' She lowered her voice. 'Well, I've got "C."'

'Oh, Ma,' I had said, stepping over the vacuum cord to hug her.

Ma had just patted my shoulder and said, 'I meant to spare you this for as long as possible.'

113

'Spare me?' I had said to her. 'For Christ's sake, Ma, I'm your daughter.'

'Yeah, well, nobody else knows, so don't tell the others until I decide it's time.'

The elevator finally got me to the third floor in one piece. Wouldn't that be a fine kettle of fish if it broke off its shaky old cables and dropped to the ground, killing me before Ma was taken? I smiled to think of Ma coming up to heaven to find me already sitting there with St. Peter. 'You just had to beat me here, didn't you, Ruth,' she'd say. 'Here I was hoping for a rest from you, and I've got you yipping at my ear up here, too.' But she'd be grinning as she said it.

'Hey, Christine,' I said, waving to Ma's nurse at the nurses' station. She was at the computer, scowling at the screen. 'What's wrong?'

'Just the damn computer,' she replied. She was about Ma's age, and she was always telling me that computers were the worst things to hit the hospital. 'I'm a nurse, for God's sake, not a computer scientist,' she'd say.

'Give it a good kick,' I advised her. 'That'll show it who's boss.'

Christine laughed and looked up at me. 'How're you doing, honey?'

I shrugged and said, 'Okay.'

'I'll come in and check on your mom in a little bit. If she needs anything before I get to her, just buzz for me, all right?'

I nodded and said, 'Thanks,' and I walked down to room 305. The woman in the bed closer to the door was sleeping. She was an elderly woman, nothing but papery skin covering a skeleton. Mrs. Harris. I crept by her bed and peeked behind the curtain separating her side of the room from my mother's.

I couldn't tell if Ma was sleeping or not. She lay in bed with her eyes closed, but she was grimacing and lifting her head a little bit as if she were in pain. I went in and sat on the blue vinyl-covered visitors' chair pushed up beside her bed. 'Hi, Ma,' I said. 'It's me, Ruth.'

'Ruth, Ruth,' Ma mumbled as if her mouth were full of pebbles that she had to talk around. I reached over and brushed one of her wispy strands of hair out of her face. Her face was all puffy and shiny from the drugs they gave her, and for a minute she opened her eyes, set little and glittery in her doughy face. She looked at me pleadingly, and I steeled myself to not look away from her. I can't do anything for you, Ma, I thought, but I can look at you. I won't leave you alone with all of this.

'Hurt,' she whimpered. She lifted a hand and let it drop back to the bed.

'Where do you hurt, Ma?' I asked loudly. Jesus Christ, why was I talking so loud? Ma was dying, not deaf. 'Where do you hurt?' I asked in my regular voice.

Ma opened her mouth to speak but just smacked her dry lips together and closed her eyes.

'Do you need more pain meds?' I asked, my voice rising again. *Will you cut it out?* I warned myself. *She doesn't need you screaming in her ear.*

'More pain meds?' I asked again, touching her hand.

She shook her head and swallowed hard, then croaked, 'Doesn't help.'

'Here,' I said, and I lifted Ma's head gently with one hand and fluffed the pillows with the other. 'Better?'

Ma didn't answer, only breathed shallowly with her eyes closed.

Why didn't anyone tell you what dying was really like? That's what I wanted to know. You went to the movies and they made you think that someone just passes on to the next life as nicely as you please, all prettied up and ready to go. They didn't tell you about the streams of shit and the vomiting up of blood and the wild eyes that looked at you as if you were the Judas in all of this, as if you could have prevented this from happening. They didn't tell you about the waiting around and the endless cups of coffee from the vending machine and the hoping in spite of yourself that your mother would just get it over with and die already. Die so she wouldn't be suffering anymore, but also, selfishly, so you

115

could be done with the whole business, so you could finally stop worrying over what life would be like when she was gone and just *live* it, for God's sake.

I seethed as I watched my mother struggle for a moment of comfort as she tried to die. It just wasn't goddamn fair.

Life's not fair, Ruth. That was one of Ma's favorite sayings. If I came home whining about how it wasn't fair I didn't get picked for softball or invited to a party, Ma would jump right at me and say, 'Life's not fair, Ruth, and the quicker you learn that, the better off you'll be.' It was her voice echoing in my head now, telling me to get a grip and shut up about expecting anything in the world to be fair. Still, I said it out loud, defying her even as she was dying. 'It's not fair,' I whispered, just because I wanted to say it out to the air, to put myself on record as believing that life was too damn hard. I wanted to take any little stand I could now.

I patted Ma's bony arm. Nothing but bones, I thought, and then a saying popped into my head about how 'they have counted all my bones.' The Bible, I thought; it came from the Bible, when Jesus died. They have counted all Ma's bones. The words kept repeating in my head.

'You're too mean to die, Ma.' It's what I used to tell her when she got scared, and she'd laugh. 'I guess I am,' she'd say, but we were both wrong. Mean or not, she was heading out the door of this earth. I made a mental note to myself to call Tim and Bobby. My brothers weren't here, Tim because he was in Montana and too chicken to come. At least that was my take on the situation. As for Bobby, well, Sandra was due to have the baby real soon, and seeing as she didn't have any family, Bobby didn't want to leave her by herself. I could see that. Ma would have been first to agree, too.

I remembered when Bobby and Sandra had got married, just last year when Sandra got pregnant. 'You treat her well, son,' Ma had said to him the morning of the wedding, holding his face in her two hands and looking right into his eyes. None of us knew Sandra very well, but Ma had said she seemed like a nice girl who was making Bobby happy and that was all that mattered. She had wanted them to be happy.

My eyes teared up, and I rubbed them angrily. She wouldn't get to see her first grandchild, I thought, and I wanted to shake my fist at God and tell Him to goddamn Himself. What had my mother ever done to deserve this? Just minded her own business and worked herself to the bone to take care of all of us after my dad left. I wondered for a second if I should call him. Ha! I didn't even know how to get in touch with him. Besides, he didn't deserve to know anything about her. I was certain of that.

Her breathing was ragged, like it hurt, and I wished so much that it didn't hurt her. *Give some of that pain to me,* I told God. *She's had enough of it. I'll take it for her, okay?* There wasn't any answer except the sound of Ma trying to get air.

Then Ma's eyes opened, and I sat forward on my chair, trying to be ready to give her what she'd need. But she was focused on something across the room, and then she took in a huge gasp of breath. When she let the breath out, she was gone.

'I love you, Ma,' I said, touching her bony hand that was still warm. I couldn't remember the last time I'd said those words out loud to her. We just didn't go in for that in my family, and I thought about what a damn stupid shame that had been. 'I love you,' I said again, hoping she could hear me somehow, wherever she was. I just sat with her, holding on to her hand while I could still feel warmth in it. I imagined I'd sit there forever, that this would be a fine way to live out my days, just sitting beside Ma, keeping her company. I guess I couldn't stand to let her go.

After a while, I heard footsteps coming into the room and then a rustling of the curtain. 'How're we doing?' Christine asked me quietly.

'She's fine,' I replied. 'She died about ten minutes ago.'

'Oh,' Christine said sympathetically, coming over to touch one hand to me and one to Ma. She looked me right in the eyes and said, 'She was a lovely person,' and that was when I began to cry and cry. It's not fair, it's not fair, it's not fair, I thought; and I was mostly thinking it wasn't fair that my mother had to up and die for me to see that I'd miss her every remaining day of my own life.

⁓

'Okay,' I say, lifting my head from the steering wheel and wiping my swollen eyes hard. 'Okay, pity party's over.' Looks like I'm going to have to talk myself through this little scene I'm throwing. First thing I'm going to do is turn around and go home. I don't need a damn pregnancy kit to tell me the obvious. Don't need to pee on a stick to know that something's going on in my body. I'll need a doctor, though. Someone who can deliver the damn baby when it's ready to pop out.

'You're not having the baby, Ruth,' I say aloud as I turn the key and pump the gas pedal. 'Look at the facts.'

The facts . . . I drum my fingers on the steering wheel as I wait to turn onto the highway from the shopping center parking lot. The facts are that I'm in no position to be a single mother. What in hell would I tell Hope, and Sara Lynn, and Mamie, for God's sake? By the way, I'll be bringing a baby into the household we all share, and never mind how I happened to come by it. Ha! That'd go over well.

A little, timid voice inside me speaks up – *What about Jack?* – and I shout it down. What about him? He doesn't want a baby. He's going on sixty! Hasn't he always said how much responsibility it was raising Paulie and Donna? And what would he tell them? That he's having a kid younger than his grandchildren? No, he wouldn't want to have to deal with that mess. And I won't make him, either. I can handle this myself.

Haven't I always handled everything myself? Watching Ma die. Raising Hope. Well, there's Sara Lynn involved in Hope's up-bringing, too. I do give credit where credit is due. Something in my heart moves just thinking about Sara Lynn, and I wish so badly I could tell her about the jam I'm in. But there's still a part of her that thinks she's better than me, just like back in high school, and I don't want to prove her right. Ruth the loser; Ruth the slut. I'll be able to see it in her eyes, and I won't be able to stand it.

The car behind me honks, and I jump out of my skin. 'Fine, fine,' I mutter, raising my hand in apology when I see the green light. Nothing else to do now except turn out of the parking lot toward home.

Chapter 11

$\mathcal{I}$'m riding my bike to the library so I can use the computer there. Not that I told anyone at my house what I'm up to. Are you kidding? That would have started a game of twenty questions: 'Why can't you use the computer at home?' 'Why do you need the computer, anyhow? It's summer; you don't have homework.' 'I hope you're not using those weird chat rooms to talk to strangers. Are you?'

It's always like this. Absolutely no privacy whatsoever. I know just how Anne Frank felt living in that attic with her family breathing down her throat. She complains about it a lot in her diary, and I always nod and think, Amen to that.

When I got up this morning, the coast was pretty clear. Ruth was at work, and Sara Lynn was off looking at some garden for her magazine. So I sat with Mamie on the porch while she read the paper, and then I sort of casually yawned and stretched. 'I guess I'll ride my bike down to the library this morning,' I told her. 'I want to find a book to read.'

'That's fine, dear,' she said, turning a page of her paper. 'Are you looking for anything special?'

See? Even going to the library under the pretense of taking out a book gets me the third degree. How many pages do you think your book will be? Are you in the mood for a made-up story or something true? Who is the author? Do you think she's a decent person?

I gritted my teeth and said, 'No. Just looking.'

'Well, be careful, and wear—'

'My helmet,' I finished, scrambling up from the porch floor. 'I know. I always wear my helmet.'

'Would you mind picking me up one of the books I like? Mrs. Shelton likely will have set aside a new one for me.'

'Sure,' I told her. 'Not a problem.'

I giggle now as I turn my bike onto the library sidewalk. Mamie always refers to 'the books she likes' instead of just spitting out clearly what she means. 'The books she likes' are cheesy romances, the kind that have a lady with a big chest and dazed expression on the cover, a lady who is sort of swooning into the arms of some guy who looks like a pirate. Not that he's wearing an eye patch or carrying a sword or anything, but he always looks the way I imagine a pirate would look without his costume – a little sinister.

Sara Lynn *tsk*s her tongue whenever she catches Mamie reading one of these books – 'bodice rippers' is what Sara Lynn calls them. 'Reading another bodice ripper, Mama?' she'll ask, raising an eyebrow.

'I'm only passing the time,' Mamie will reply, her lips pursing and her eyes flashing. 'A person's world gets a lot narrower when she's older and hasn't as much to keep her busy.'

'Hmmph,' Sara Lynn will say skeptically.

'Oh, Mamie, you're the spring chicken out of all of us,' Ruth will chime in hastily, trying to keep the peace. 'You've got more romance going on in your books than any of the rest of us has in real life. Keeps you young, right?'

I park my bike in the bike rack and run up the stone steps of the library with my backpack slung over one shoulder. When I pull open the heavy wooden door, the air-conditioning makes the hairs on my arms stand up. I walk over to the computer area, where I sit down and take a deep breath. I'm sick of sitting around waiting for things to happen in my life; I'm finally going to make them happen. So I've made a plan. I'm going to look for my father on the Internet, find his address, and send him the letter I wrote. All I get when I ask Ruth or Sara Lynn about him are the same dumb answers. 'Why do you want to know?' 'Why are you asking?' 'It was a long time ago.' 'I don't know.' Well, if they don't care to tell me anything about him, that's their problem. I'm his daughter, and I want to know. I want to know right now.

⌐⌐⌐⌐

Okay. Have you ever noticed how when you make a plan to do something, you're all excited? You keep patting yourself on the back for your sheer genius, telling yourself it's too bad your talents are being wasted in this backwater town.

Then you start to put your plan to work, and you're still feeling good. You're thinking, Boy, not only can I think up a really cool plan, but I can make it happen, too. Look at me go!

Then everything starts going wrong. Way wrong. Like the fact that you didn't count on there being tons of Robert Tellers on the Internet. Like the fact that all you know about your father is his name. Could he be the Robert Teller who won the Boonetown, Iowa, big-pumpkin contest? (Lord, I hope not.) Could he be the Robert Teller who's the owner of a chain of department stores down south? (That would be nice.) Could he be the Robert Teller who competed in the National Spelling Bee? (No, because it's for darn sure my father's not in fifth grade.)

Aaargghh! I throw my pencil down and bury my face in my hands to rub my eyes. Here I thought I'd just waltz right in and find him; little did I know I'd be a fool looking for a needle in a haystack.

'Hey.' I hear a voice, and I look up. There's a boy about my age sitting at a computer a couple of desks down from me. He's got the reddest hair I've ever seen and braces that glint in the overhead library lights.

'Yeah?' I say, trying to sound cool.

'Are you okay?'

'Why wouldn't I be?'

'You kind of had your face in your hands, and you were all bent over. I didn't know if you were going to faint or something.'

Great. He's basically telling me I looked like a big dork. 'No,' I say coldly. I narrow my eyes and raise my chin. 'I wasn't going to faint.'

His face gets as red as his hair, and he shrugs. 'Jeez, forget it. I was only wondering if you needed any help.'

I stare real hard at my computer screen and swallow a few times. I didn't mean to sound like such a jerk. I thought he was making fun of me. I didn't know he was just trying to be nice. And now I'm the one who's been mean and made him feel bad. Ugh. Sometimes I think I should just live in my closet and not speak at all.

I take a deep breath and turn to him. He's back on the computer, biting his lower lip as he types. 'Hey,' I whisper. He doesn't hear me, so I say it again a little louder. 'Hey!'

He looks up like he's worried I'm going to tear into him again, like he's feeling a little uncomfortable around me. 'Yeah?' he asks.

'I'm sorry. I didn't mean to sound like that. You know, all snotty and mean.'

'It's okay.' He shrugs. 'No big deal.'

'I'm . . . I'm kind of under a lot of pressure with this, um, project I'm doing. I'm not usually a mean person.'

'What are you working on?' he asks.

'Um . . .' What the heck am I supposed to tell him? Oh, I'm just looking for my father who hasn't wanted to see me since I was born? I settle for saying, 'It's kind of a long story.'

'Oh,' he says. He doesn't turn back to his computer. He just looks at me. I look away, sort of embarrassed, because I can't help but think it seems like he might think I'm pretty. Maybe. I mean, he's not covering his eyes and saying, 'Ick. I can't look at that dog face anymore.'

'What are you working on?' I ask him hastily, trying to make my embarrassed feeling go away.

'Nothing,' he says. His voice sounds kind of sad and mad, and I don't know whether I said the wrong thing. Then he explains, 'I just moved here. So I don't have any friends to hang out with or anything. I just come here and surf the Net.'

'Don't you have a computer at your house?'

'Yeah. I mean, we will when our stuff gets here and we unpack all the boxes.'

'Where'd you move from?'

'New Jersey.'

I nod and try to look like I've been all over, like being from New Jersey doesn't sound so exotic to me.

He sighs and says, 'So what is there to do around here?'

I laugh. 'Not much.'

Mrs. Shelton bustles over to us, her plaid skirt stretched tight across her wide hips. 'Shhh!' She has her finger to her lips and shakes her head at us. 'No talking in the library.'

I roll my eyes at the new boy and shrug. I turn back to my computer screen when I hear, 'Psst!'

I sneak a glance over at him. We're really not supposed to be talking, and I don't want to get in trouble again.

'Do you want to go someplace?'

I don't know that I've heard him right. I mouth, 'What?'

'Do you want to get out of here so we can talk?'

I nod like it's no big deal, but my heart sort of clenches up all excited and nervous. This is the first time a boy has ever asked me to do anything. I focus real hard on the computer screen, pushing the buttons that will get me back to the library's main page. I wish my hands weren't trembling as I slide my notebook off the desk and put it into my backpack.

'Ready?' he asks. He's pretty tall for a boy about my age. Most

124

of them are shorter than I am. 'How's the weather up there?' the boys in my class tease. 'That's original,' I say back, rolling my eyes and acting like they're not hurting my feelings.

'Okay,' I whisper.

We walk out of the library, our sneakers squeaking on the waxed marble floor. Then we're outside, and we look at each other kind of shyly.

'No talking in the library,' he finally says, mimicking Mrs. Shelton's crisp, prim voice.

I laugh at him, and he grins like he's happy I'm laughing.

'You want to just sit here and talk?' he says, flopping down on one of the stone steps.

I'm a little disappointed because I thought he was going to ask me to do something with him, maybe get a soda at the diner or something. It's not like I like him or anything; it's just that it would have been nice to be asked. I shrug. 'Sure,' I say, and I sit next to him.

'I'm Dan,' he tells me, putting his elbows back on the step behind him and looking out at the street. 'Dan Quinn.'

'I'm Hope Teller,' I reply.

'You're the first kid I've met here,' he says.

'How . . . how old are you?' I ask.

'Thirteen. How 'bout you?'

'Twelve. I'm going into seventh grade.'

'At the middle school?'

I nod. 'Mmm-hmm.'

'Me too. Eighth grade.' He sounds really glum about it.

'The middle school's okay,' I reassure him. 'It's really not that bad.'

He doesn't say anything, and I say, 'You'll make new friends, you know. You'll really like it.'

He turns and smiles a little, his braces shining in the sun. 'Thanks, Hope.'

We're quiet for a minute, and then I ask, 'Where do you live?'

'Easton Street.'

'Hey, that's right near my house!'

'Yeah?' he asks.

'Yeah, you kind of pass my street if you're heading from here to Easton.'

He stands up and puts his hands in his shorts pockets. 'Well, I'll walk you back that way,' he says. 'I should probably get home pretty soon. I'm supposed to be helping my stupid dad with the yardwork.'

'I have my bike,' I say, 'but I'll walk it.'

'Okay,' he says. He kicks a little rock with his sneaker as I grab my bike from the rack and wheel it alongside him.

'What kind of yardwork do you have to do?'

Dan snorts and grimaces. 'Who knows? My dad's all into fixing up the landscaping. Putting in more shrubs along the side of the house. And guess who has to do most of it? Me. My dad's an idiot.'

'At least you have a dad.' It pops out of my mouth before I can stop it.

He looks sideways at me and says, 'Sorry. I didn't know. Your dad . . . died?'

I shake my head.

'Divorced from your mom?' he asks.

I shake my head again, looking down so my hair covers my cheeks.

'Well, what's the story?' he asks.

I don't say anything, and he says, 'I mean, if you don't want to talk about it, that's cool.'

I take a breath and look up, shaking my curls off my face. 'No, it's okay.' I quickly look at him and then at the ground again. As I walk my bike, the wheels make a clicking sound as they spin around and around. I listen to the *click-click-click* for a minute, and then I say all in one breath, 'My mother died when I was born, and my father left. I haven't seen him since I was, like, a week old; and I don't know where he is.'

126

'No kidding?' he asks like I'm telling him a tall tale or some-thing. As if.

'Do you think I could make up something like that?' I ask flatly. He's annoying me all of a sudden, and I wish I hadn't told him. I wish I could put the truth about my family right back in-side me.

'No, no,' he says. 'Sorry. I mean, I've just never known a real orphan before.'

I stop my bike and glare at him. 'I am *not* an orphan. An or-phan is someone who doesn't have any parents. I have a father. It's just that I don't know where he is.'

I start walking again, and I focus on the *click-click-click* of my bike wheels to stop myself from crying or screaming in frustra-tion.

'So who do you live with?' he asks.

'Never mind,' I say, my voice all tight.

Now he stops walking and turns to me. 'Look, I'm sorry if I'm not saying the right thing.'

'Do you promise you won't tell anyone?' It's what comes out of my mouth, all in a rush.

He looks puzzled. 'Tell anyone what?'

'About my father.' I'm pleading with him.

'Whoa,' he says. 'You're weirding out on me. Don't people know that your father's gone?'

'Yeah, yeah,' I say impatiently. 'Of course they do. But I've sort of . . . I've kind of led them to believe that I know where he is. That he, you know, calls me up and writes me letters and stuff.'

He still looks puzzled, his eyes squinched up like he's trying to figure things out. 'Why would you do that?'

I stamp my foot on the pavement and half shout, 'Oh, never mind *why* I did it. Just don't tell anyone, okay?'

'Okay, okay.' He pulls his hands out of his pockets and puts them up like he's showing me he's innocent of everything I might be accusing him of.

My heart's beating fast as I start walking my bike again. 'That was what I was doing today,' I say in a low voice. 'Trying to find him on the Internet.'

'Jeez,' Dan says. 'Like, you have no idea where he is?'

Why are boys so stupid? I swear, Ruth's right when she says God was just practicing on Adam and didn't get it right till he made Eve. 'Ri-ight,' I say exaggeratedly, nodding and trying to get it through his thick head. *I have no idea where he is.*

'Jeez,' he says. Then a minute later he shakes his head and says it again. 'Jeez.'

'Are you just going to keep saying 'Jeez'?' I ask.

'No,' he replies, sounding hurt. 'Jeez.'

I can't help it. I laugh. I shake my head and look up at the blue sky and laugh. Hopeless. He's absolutely hopeless. It's Hope and Hopeless walking up Main Street here. I have to stop and wipe my eyes from laughing so hard.

'Sorry,' I gasp. 'I'm not laughing at you. I'm just—'

'Go ahead and laugh,' he says, waving his hand. 'I don't mind.'

'Really?' I ask, stealing a peek at his face. I get so mad when someone laughs at me, but he's just looking all peaceful, like I haven't totally been making fun of him.

'Can I help you find him?' he asks. 'Not to sound stupid or anything, but I kind of like mysteries.'

I think about it for a second. 'Okay,' I tell him. He doesn't seem so bad. Besides, I'm not exactly progressing very far on my own. 'Yeah, you can help me.'

Chapter 12

$\mathcal{M}$y stomach's in my throat, where it never is. Where it shouldn't be. I swallow hard and remind myself that this is nothing more than a work arrangement. Sam Johnson just wants to see the lavender garden for his painting, and I'm living in a fantasy world if I believe he's the slightest bit interested in me. Or I in him, for that matter.

So why is my stomach in my throat as I'm driving to pick him up for our little garden visit? Why are my hands on the steering wheel practically trembling? I squeeze my fingers tightly around the wheel and remind myself that he's not even my type, although I admit he's handsome in his lanky, blond, open way. My type is broad-shouldered, dark, and aloof. My type is Bobby.

Right, Sara Lynn. I shake my head and *tsk* my tongue. *Your type is Bobby. Well, then why aren't you with him now?* I'll tell you why, I lecture myself. *Because we were too different, about as unlikely a pair as one could imagine.* Almost as unlikely a couple as Sam and I would make.

I can't help it: Thinking about Sam, even in the abstract, causes an image of him to float through my mind. His blue eyes, his easy grin, the way he raked his fingers through his hair when he asked if he could go to the garden with me. I shiver a little, then frown, reminding myself to show some of the common sense for which I'm known.

Oh, if Mama only knew the way I've been thinking about that man, the fantasies he's been headlining in my mind ever since I made the plan to take him to Langley's Lovely Lavender Gardens (what an idiotic name) with me. 'That's your problem, Sara Lynn,' she'd say, and she'd be looking me up and down while she shook her head. 'You fall head over teakettles for the most inappropriate men.'

Well, for goodness' sake. I'm not falling head over teakettles for anyone. So what if I think he's good-looking? So what if I've been counting the days until today? It doesn't mean a darn thing. Just a little last hurrah, I suppose, before everything shuts down and I ride into the sunset, leading my sensible, no-nonsense life till the end. I might not have made it as a big-time lawyer, but, dammit, at least I'm sensible. I laugh, more bitterly than I intend to.

Darn it all, I've finally made it across town over to Lake Road, and I'm supposed to be taking a left right here, across from the gas station. I don't see any lefts, though, just a narrow driveway. Well, there's nothing to do but drive up it, so I put on my blinker and turn slowly onto a dirt road full of stones and potholes. Take it nice and easy, now; don't wreck the Mercedes. I smile a little, thinking of my father and how he taught me to drive on some of these dusty dirt roads on the outskirts of town.

Dad. Now there was a sensible man. 'You'll want to have your oil checked every three months, Sara Lynn.' 'In the winter, always keep your tank at least a quarter full.' 'Don't drive over the speed limit; nothing's so important that you need to get yourself killed trying to get there.' My father taught me about automobiles; my mother taught me about sex. His information was more useful by far.

As I reach the end of the narrow road, I spy a little gray-shingled cottage, and there's Sam, sitting out on the peeling, sagging steps, squinting at the sun reflecting on the lake. His hands twist in his lap as if they don't like being still, as if they're used to swinging a racket or holding a paintbrush. He leaps up and grabs his backpack in one motion, smiling like he's glad to see me. It's breathtaking, really, the way that man moves. But I'm not going to think about that right now. Everything'll get terribly muddled if I start thinking about that.

When he gets into the car, he says, 'Did you find the place okay?'

'Yes,' I lie, turning the car around so I don't have to back straight out of that narrow road. 'No problem.'

We're back on Lake Road and then through town and then on the highway. He's looking out the car window, and it's not until we've been driving a bit that he speaks. 'I brought my camera. Will it be all right if I take some pictures?'

'Of what?' I ask, and then I could kick myself. What, did I think he wanted to take a picture of me? 'The garden, of course,' I say hastily. 'Yes, I'm sure it'll be fine.' I take one hand off the wheel and gesture toward the backseat. 'There are some tear sheets of photos taken by the magazine's photographers in that folder back there. Go ahead and look at them if you'd like.'

He reaches an arm back, and it brushes against my shoulder. 'Sorry,' he says, and I blink my eyes fast behind my sunglasses.

As he looks through the photos, he says, 'Wow. This is beautiful.'

'It is interesting, isn't it.' I relax my shoulders a little. If there's one thing I can talk about – with anybody – it's gardens.

'Mmm. It's a composition about purpleness, you know what I mean?'

I nod. 'Yes, I do. There aren't any other notes in the garden – no whites to cool it down or reds to heat it up. It's just purple. So you find yourself really seeing how pure and, and . . . purply . . . purple is.'

He laughs and reaches over the seat to replace the folder. 'It's hard to put into words. I guess that's why I paint. Because it's the only way I know how to show the purpleness of purple.'

I turn to look at him for a second before returning my eyes to the road. 'That's why I garden, too. It's a way of communicating something I don't know how to say, something about color and harmony and beauty.'

'Oh, I think gardening is very much like painting,' he agrees. 'Only it's braver, in a way, because it's an ephemeral art form. Once a canvas is done, it stays the same. But gardens change.'

'Yes!' I'm surprised he understands this about what I do. 'When you're creating a garden, you have to take into account when plants will bloom, how big they'll get, what they'll look like in different seasons – all sorts of variables. It's one of the biggest challenges of planning a garden – the fact that its composition is constantly changing.'

'Tell me about your garden at home.' He leans back in his seat and waits for my answer, adding, 'Hope told me it's beautiful.'

'She did? Really?'

'Yeah. She's a cute kid. She likes to chat as much as she likes tennis.'

'She's a talkative child.' I shake my head and smile, thinking about Hope prattling on and on.

'So . . . ?'

'Hmm?' I take my eyes off the road and look at him.

'Your garden.' He smiles. 'You were going to tell me about your garden.'

'My garden.' I smile back at him. You know, Hope's right the way she raves about Sam. He's really quite nice. All that anxiety I felt driving over here is dissipating, and I'm starting to enjoy being with him. 'Well, it's . . . hmm . . . it's actually several gardens. There's the woodland garden, where it's shady and cool and quiet. Then there's the meadow garden, which is sunny and, well, full of color and life. I've . . . I've got perennial beds in the front. They look different each season. Right now, they're sort of like a Monet painting – lots of color, one blending into the next.' I laugh. 'Listen to me, going on. Ask a gardener about her gardens, though, and that's what you get.'

'Tell me more.'

'Only if you tell me about your paintings.' I'm not flirting with him. This doesn't feel like flirting to me. We're just talking, and it feels very comfortable.

'I aim for my paintings to be just the way you described your perennial beds – lots of color, one blending into the next.'

'Hmm . . . what colors do you like?'

'I'm in a green phase right now.' He laughs and shakes his head. 'That sounded very pseudoartiste.'

'I like green, too,' I reassure him. 'You should see my woodland garden. Standing in the middle of it is like being in an ocean of different shades of green.'

'I'd like that. Could I see it sometime?'

I can feel my telltale blush creeping up my cheeks again. Just when I was starting to lose my self-consciousness, too. 'Sure,' I say cautiously. 'That would be fine.'

Mrs. Langley is a delightful interviewee, chatty and well versed about gardening. I'm terribly glad I have a tape recorder with me, though, because I'm taking in one out of every three words she utters. My mind is elsewhere – on Sam, if I'm honest. I just can't wait for the ride home with him so we can continue our conversation. But at the same time, I'm dreading it because I'm liking him more and more and, oh, it's just stupid and silly when there's no way he thinks of me as more than a friend. A nice, older friend at that.

Finally I'm through, and I switch off my tape recorder, thank Mrs. Langley, and walk through endless billowy mounds of purple lavender over to where Sam sits on a bench, sketching. He grins at me and tilts up his notebook so I can see.

'Oh, it's beautiful!' I say, leaning over to look at the sketch he's done of one branch of lavender. I trace my finger over the tiny leaves and flowers, each drawn with immense care and detail.

He stands up. 'How'd the interview go?'

'Oh, fine,' I say. 'I'm through whenever you're ready.'

'Do you need to get back right away?' he asks. Maybe he wants to keep working. Or perhaps he's not as eager as I am to resume talking the way we were on the ride over here.

'I mean,' he explains, 'we could grab some coffee in town, walk around, and explore a little bit.'

Well. Does this mean he likes me? I thought he might, the day he asked about coming here to the garden with me. But today he acted more like a friend or colleague. Oh, for goodness' sake, I'm sure I'm mistaking his friendliness for something else. But what if I'm not? What if . . . My mind is whirling in a million different directions, and my face feels frozen, like a Halloween mask. What do I say? I can't . . . I want . . .

'Why?' I blurt out, confused. Dear Lord, have I completely forgotten how to act, how to be around people? 'I mean 'yes.' Yes,' I say hastily, shaking my head as if to dismiss my silly question.

'Yes?' he asks, ducking his head to look at me. His eyes look confused, and why wouldn't they? God! I could kick myself for being such an idiot.

'Sure,' I say, looking up to meet his gaze, and I give a little shrug and smile apologetically. It's either smile or run away, and I'm thinking that smiling is the better option. And, it's so funny, but once I smile, my mask thaws and I feel all this . . . well, possibility surrounding me. I feel the way I do on the first nice day of spring, when the sun is finally out and I'm raking my perennial beds. I rub my arms just to feel my tingling body that's been asleep for more than a decade.

'Cold?' Sam asks.

'No.' Still smiling, I shake my head. 'Not at all.'

My father died the winter after I came home from the law firm. He had a heart attack while he was reading over some legal briefs. It was a lovely death, really. It was quick, and he was doing what he most loved. But my mother was beside herself. She aged ten years in a month. I don't think she realized how much she had depended on him. She had developed a rhythm with him wherein he was the background music and she was the lead vocal. She hadn't realized how important that background music was until it was gone.

My father's death is intertwined in my memory with Bobby Teller. I was sleeping with Bobby. Of course I was. There wasn't an option to involve myself halfway, not when I went home after that first night at O'Malley's with my mouth sore and bruised and my insides unsettled and yearning from all that kissing.

We had sex everywhere – in my car, in his car, in his friend's apartment, in the storeroom of O'Malley's, in a motel outside Hadley where no one knew us. I thought about him constantly, the way he gasped and held me tightly when he came, the way I pushed my hips against him, again and again, faster and faster, until I was practically crying as I came, too. 'God, you're beautiful,' he'd say when we were finished. He'd smooth my hair back from my face and look at me, shaking his head slowly. 'I can't believe I'm lying here with Sara Lynn Hoffman,' he'd say.

Being with him was like stepping into a world I hadn't known existed. It was as if I'd been color-blind before we started seeing each other. I'd seen the objects surrounding me, but I hadn't been aware that they were so impossibly, beautifully colored. All my senses were heightened – the smell of his body when he lay next to me, the feel of his cheek when he needed a shave, the way his voice sounded when he said something sweet. One late afternoon, we were walking in the woods, and he pulled me up on a large rock. 'Come on,' he said, ignoring my protests and gripping my hands hard. When I stumbled up there with him, he put his arms around my waist and pulled me in. 'You and me,' he said in my ear. 'Together.' He thrilled me; he truly did.

135

I thought nobody knew about us. Or at least that very few people did. Ruth knew. I tried to be nice to her when she came to clean, but she just answered my questions in monosyllables, not stopping her work. 'Why does she hate me so much?' I asked Bobby once. We were in my car, the heater turned up full blast as our hands fumbled under jackets and sweaters and jeans.

He laughed. 'What do you care?'

'I'm just curious.' I pulled away and waited for him to answer.

'You're not like other girls in this town, Sara Lynn,' he replied. 'You're different. She doesn't trust you because you're different.'

'Do you trust me?' I asked teasingly, sliding my hand back into his jeans.

He flinched a little from my cold touch and smiled as he reached up under my sweater. 'Not even a little bit.'

'Not even a little bit?' I asked as I began to move my hand.

He groaned and kissed me. 'Maybe a little bit,' he whispered in my ear.

He didn't come to my father's funeral. I told him it would be better if he stayed away. He didn't argue with me, and I was disappointed. I wished he had insisted on coming, that nothing, not even my words, had kept him away. But he hadn't read the same romantic books I had, and there wasn't going to be any changing him.

A few weeks after the funeral, I tiptoed into the house at two in the morning and found my mother waiting up, marching to the front door to meet me, her eyes wild and her mouth set hard in grief. 'Where've you been?' she asked me as I locked the door behind me and hugged myself to get warm.

'Mama,' I said softly, 'what are you—'

'No,' she said, pulling the belt on her robe tighter. 'No questions for me. I'm absolutely through with your questions, and your insinuations and your . . . your judgment of me.'

'What are you talking about?' I said wearily. I was grieving, tired, and in need of a shower.

'I told you. I'm not answering your questions anymore. Why I did this, why I did that to you growing up . . . I have nothing to apologize for.' Her voice thickened for a moment, but she tossed her head and went on as if it hadn't. 'You' – she pointed at me – 'you failed down in Boston. For the first time, you failed at something, and Lord knows, I wish it had happened earlier. Maybe if you'd failed earlier and more often, you wouldn't be acting so . . . so crazy right now.'

'I didn't fail,' I said hotly.

'Yes, you did,' she said, her eyes blazing. 'You failed, and you're just sick about it.'

'I've got to go up to bed.' I'd had enough. All I wanted was to wash the sex off of me and go to sleep. I brushed by her, and she grabbed my arm.

'No,' she said. 'I'm through pretending I don't see you ruining your life, and all because, for once, you didn't get what you wanted.'

'You have no idea what I want!' I yelled, tears smarting in my eyes.

'Neither do you,' she said, still gripping my arm. 'Unless it's to throw everything in your life – everything – away!'

'Mother!' I cried, jerking away from her and wiping my eyes. 'What are you talking about?'

'What I'm talking about . . . ,' she said almost triumphantly. 'What I'm talking about . . .'

'What is it?' I cried, wanting to just drop to the floor from exhaustion and rage.

'What I'm talking about is your blindness!' she shouted. 'Your blindness! You're supposed to be so smart, so goddamned smart . . . ha! You're the stupidest girl I've ever met!'

My mother never got angry and certainly never swore. I wondered if she'd have a heart attack like Daddy and drop dead right in front of me. She began to sob, folding her arms across her chest as if she were trying to comfort herself.

'Mama . . . ,' I said, touching her arm. She was scaring me.

'Don't you touch me!' she shrieked. 'I know where you've been tonight. I know what you've been doing. You've been giving yourself away to that Teller boy.'

My face crumpled. 'How . . . did you know that?' I whispered, putting my hands to my mouth.

'It's all over the goddamned town! People have eyes, Sara Lynn. Are you so stupid that you don't know how people talk?!' She sank to the floor, putting her head in her hands. Her shoulders jumped up and down with her sobs. 'My God! I just keep picturing you with him in that way. . . .'

'Mama,' I pleaded through my own tears, 'I'm a grown woman. I'm not doing anything wrong. I . . . I think I'm in love with him.'

She jerked her face up to look at me with swollen red eyes. 'In love with him? You think you're in love with him? Oh, God, you aren't, Sara Lynn! You aren't! Do you know what your life would be like if you married him? Do you have any idea?' She got to her feet and took my shoulders in her hands. 'You have nothing in common with him. Nothing. Good Lord – think of your future! Do you really want to have children with someone so . . . so beneath you?'

'You don't even know him,' I said quietly.

'No, *you* don't know him. I know plenty. Mary Teller's been my cleaning lady since before you were born, and I know that you might as well be a different species from anyone in that family. You are asking for a life of misery if you join yourself to him!' She wiped her eyes with the back of her hand. 'Now, I like Mary, but I certainly don't want to share a grandchild with her.'

'Mama,' I said gingerly. I hated seeing her like this. 'Nobody's talking about grandchildren, or getting married, or anything like that.'

'Then shame on you,' she replied, crying fresh tears. 'Shame on you for giving the milk away for free. I thought I'd raised you better than that.'

'These are different times,' I said thickly. 'It's not like when you were growing up.'

'You don't think so?' She laughed bitterly. 'Oh no, there were fast girls around when I was growing up, girls like you! And I know exactly what happened to them! Their reputations were gone forever, just like that' – she snapped her fingers – 'and their lives were ruined.' She looked up at me and laughed again, a hollow, mean laugh. 'You know,' she said, 'I wonder, I truly do, whether your father knew about you, if someone had told him. I wonder if that's what killed him, knowing his daughter was whoring herself to the cleaning lady's son.'

I began to cry myself then, all my sorrow over my father's death pouring out of me. 'I didn't kill Daddy,' I said, and I kept repeating it as if saying it again and again would make it true.

'Stop saying that!' my mother shrieked. 'My God, are you some sort of crazy person, saying the same thing over and over? Please God, may you not be mentally deficient on top of everything else.'

'I'm just . . . I'm just so . . . so . . .' I sobbed, unable to find the words.

She drew herself up. 'Yes.' She nodded. 'Your father's death has broken your heart, and that's understandable. But now it's time to move past that, and past all the bad decisions you made in your grief.'

I saw what she was offering me – a way to end my relationship with Bobby and keep my dignity and her love. It didn't matter that I'd begun seeing Bobby well before my father's death. In my mother's mind, we could tidy up the whole mess and chalk it up to a poor decision made entirely out of grief. We could even push the blame onto Bobby, for who but a monster would take advantage of a grief-stricken young woman? I was so tempted to reach out and grab her excuse, to pretend I was still the good Sara Lynn who'd never once had an independent thought in her entire life.

But then I thought of Bobby and the comforting weight of him on top of me tonight; I thought of how he'd turned me on my stomach, lifted up my hair, and kissed the nape of my neck again and again, murmuring, 'You're so beautiful, Sara Lynn, so beautiful.' In a flash, it was ruined, though. The images of Bobby that I'd hugged to myself night after night weren't mine any longer. I was seeing them through Mama's horrified eyes now, and they just seemed sordid and ugly.

'Why are you doing this?' I asked her softly as my last sweet memory of Bobby faded away.

'For your own good, darling,' she replied, reaching out and touching my cheek. 'For your own good.'

I closed my eyes and reached up to grasp her hand, and I never went to O'Malley's again. She was my mother, and she knew what I should do. Make a clean break of it, she advised, and that's just what I did. To see him again would be too risky, especially now, when I wasn't in my right mind because of my grief.

After that night, I made sure I was gone when Ruth and Mary Teller came to clean, and Ruth must have told him that's when I left the house because he followed me one morning, cut my car off, and motioned me to pull over. I turned onto a side street and stopped. I watched from my rearview mirror as he got out of his car and walked through the snow over to mine.

'What's up?' he asked as he climbed inside my car and shut the door. I smelled his familiar smell, and my mind flashed to him lying over me, looking at me, doing things to me. I closed my eyes for a moment and then opened them.

'I can't do this anymore,' I said.

'Do what?'

'What we've been doing.'

He laughed. 'You mean having a lot of good sex?'

I closed my eyes again to stop the tears from streaming down. I nodded.

'Hey, you can't be serious. Did I do something?'

I shook my head no. 'It's just not going to work out,' I said.

He didn't say anything for a minute; then he banged his gloved hand against the dashboard. 'Who said anything about it working out?' he asked. 'We were just fucking.'

The tears slid down my cheeks then, and I didn't make any motion to stop them.

'Aw, I didn't mean that,' he said, and he clumsily touched my cheek through his heavy glove.

'No,' I said, grabbing his hand and pulling it away from my face. 'Don't touch me.'

'Don't touch you?' he snorted. 'I've done a hell of a lot more than that.' He shook his head. 'Damn! I don't get you.'

I just sat, motionless, and he opened the car door. 'See you around,' he muttered, banging the door shut. And those were the last words I heard from Bobby Teller.

'What're you thinking about?' Sam says in his soft, gravelly voice.

'Me? Nothing,' I say. We're driving home from a wonderful day of walking and eating and talking. And now, on the ride home, we're being silent together, and that feels just fine, too.

'I have to make this turn,' I tell him, sitting forward in the driver's seat and squinting as I try to locate the tiny dirt path on which Sam lives. 'I couldn't find it to save my life this morning.'

He laughs. 'I still can't find it, and I've been living here for a month. Wait.' He touches my arm. 'Slow down . . . here it is.'

'Oh, God,' I say. 'See, I would have missed it without you here.'

I slow down over the dirt road leading back to his house. The soft light of the late afternoon reflects off the rippling waves of the lake. 'It must be lovely living here,' I say. 'It's so peaceful.'

I stop the car to let him out, but he's not moving. He's looking at me with those intense blue eyes, and I turn away from him to stare straight ahead. If I don't look at him, I'll be fine.

'I had a really good time today,' he says.

141

I nod vigorously, still without looking at him. 'Me too,' I say.

'So when can I see you again?'

My insides stop fluttering, and the dreamy feeling I've had all day stops. I wake up, basically, because he can't see me again. 'Look,' I tell him crisply, 'it's not such a good idea that we see each other again. My life is rather . . . complicated.'

'What's complicated about it?' His voice is low and easy, like I have all the time in the world to explain.

'Well . . . things,' I say, wondering how to wrap this up as efficiently as possible. 'I can't really date.'

'Why not?' he asks, touching his hand to mine. Then he laughs and says lightly, 'I know you're not married – you're waiting for the right one.'

'The right . . . pardon me?'

'Hope. She says you'd rather be single than be with the wrong guy.'

I reach up to brush my hair from my eyes, letting his hand slide off mine. 'Oh, Hope. See, that's why I can't date. Hope. My mother. Too many people watching me, wanting me to be . . . well, who I've always been.'

He doesn't say anything to break the silence. Nothing a polite person would say, like 'I understand. See you at the club when you drop Hope off for her next tennis lesson.' He just waits for me to continue, and the quiet between us thickens.

'I have too many responsibilities.' I finally break the silence, annoyed that I have to justify myself to him. 'For all intents and purposes, I'm the mother of a twelve-year-old. I'm also caretaker for my mother, who's getting on in years. Seeing someone doesn't fit into my lifestyle.'

'I'm not asking you to change your lifestyle,' he says, smiling. 'I'm just asking you out on a date.' He nudges me. 'C'mon. We'll have fun.'

I smile back in spite of myself. It's what I've liked about him all day today – his confidence, his optimism, his refusal to take things too seriously. He's young; life hasn't beaten those qualities out of him yet. Oh, if only I were in my twenties, unencumbered by my past and my child. I feel a stab of guilt – of course I don't wish Hope had never come into my life. But at the corners of my mind, there's a whispering 'what if.' What if I were twenty-five right now and just meeting Sam? For a sweet second, I imagine it – I'm twelve years younger and I'm kissing him; I'm giddily free of so many of the things that define me today.

'Well?' he prods.

'Where would we go?' I ask, and I cringe because that's got to be up there as one of the stupidest things I've ever said.

He throws up his hands and laughs. 'I don't know! Where do you want to go?'

To the moon, I think, closing my eyes for a second.

'Listen,' I finally say, my voice coming out in a froglike croak. I clear my throat and lose my nerve, just like that. I shake my head back and forth ruefully. It's time to end this now.

Instead, my words come out in a rush. 'I have to be in Boston next week. To do a piece for the magazine. You could come if you want. Not with me per se, but if you happened to be there, we could meet. See, I just can't . . . it's all too crazy here, and, well, maybe if we weren't here, but there . . . ' My voice trails off, and I know I'm complicating things even more, but surely I'm allowed just one more date with him, one more blissful couple of hours where I'm living in my body instead of in my lonely head.

His eyes brighten, and he says, 'Yeah, I could do that. That would be great. Why don't you give me the date you'll be in town and I'll arrange my schedule to be there at the same time.'

'Okay,' I say, nodding. 'Okay. My interview is next Friday. I . . . I can see you after it's done.'

'Friday night, then?'

I nod. 'But don't . . . don't tell anyone.' I feel my cheeks redden. 'Not that it's on the top of your list of things to talk about,' I add hastily, 'but I just . . . let's just keep it between us, okay? It'll be . . . easier that way.'

He smiles at me, a sort of puzzled, 'whatever you say' smile, and nods. Then he opens his backpack and pulls out his sketch-book and a pencil. He writes something down on a piece of paper and hands it to me. It's one of the sketches he did today of a lavender plant, and there's a number written at the bottom.

'That's the number I'll be at in Boston,' he says. 'Call me when you get in on Friday, okay?'

I smile at the beauty of the sketch, each lavender sprig seemingly alive, and I shake my head and hand it back to him. 'You'll need this,' I say. I reach into my purse and dig out a small notebook. 'Here. You can write it on—'

'No, take it,' he says, handing me back the lavender sketch. 'I've got other sketches.' He smiles at me as he says, 'I want you to have this one.'

Chapter 13

$\mathcal{D}$an is serious about wanting to help me. You'd think he'd just forget about it, but no. Sometimes he rides his bike past my house, and if I'm outside, he asks me when we're going to work on finding my dad. Usually I can't talk long because I'm going off to tennis or something, but since I don't have a lesson today, I'm not going to the club until later. So when Dan comes riding his bike by my house and I just happen to be sitting on the front steps, I give him a wave and walk down the driveway to meet him.

'Hey, Hope,' he says, straddling his bike and twirling a basketball on his finger. 'I'm going to shoot some baskets at that school on the next block. You want to come and we can talk about Operation Padre?'

I squinch up my nose and put my hands on my hips. 'What are you talking about?'

'You know,' he says. 'Finding your dad.'

'Shh!' I glare at him and look over my shoulder. 'It's supposed to be a secret, remember?'

He drops his basketball, and I go into the street to grab it. 'Here,' I say, throwing it back to him. 'Hold on. I'll go get my bike.' I jog up the driveway, hollering, 'Be right back.'

I trot up the steps and into the kitchen, where Sara Lynn is sitting at the table typing on her laptop, her hair pulled off her face in a loose bun. 'Sara Lynn,' I say, panting, 'is it okay if I go bike riding with a friend? We're just going up to Lakewood School.'

'Which friend?' she asks, still typing, her eyes riveted to the screen.

Shoot. I take a deep breath. 'You don't know him. He's new. He'll be going to my school in the fall.'

'He?' Sara Lynn's eyebrows shoot up, and she stops typing. This stupid smile shows up at the corners of her mouth.

Crossing my arms over my chest, I scowl at her. 'Yes. But don't look that way. He's just a friend.'

'How did you meet him?' she asks, cupping her face in her hands. I swear, she looks positively mushy about the whole thing, which is just so completely unlike her.

'At the library. He's going into eighth grade, and his name's Dan Quinn. He lives on Easton Street. And I told you to stop looking like that.' I tap my foot on the floor. 'So can I go?'

'*May* I go,' she corrects. She glances at the clock and says, 'Sure. Just be back in an hour.'

'Why?' I ask, spreading my arms out. 'Why on earth do I need to be back in an hour?'

'Because I don't want you running around town all day with some boy I haven't even met. Why don't you bring him in? Where is he now?'

I groan as I head for the door. 'Fine, fine,' I say. 'I'll be back in an hour.'

I run out the door before she chases after me and reminds me to look both ways before I cross the street or something equally embarrassing. Then I grab my bike from the side yard and ride down the driveway to meet Dan.

We ride pretty fast up to the school. Well, he rides fast, and I just try to keep up with him. I guess he really wants to shoot baskets pretty badly, because right when we get to the playground, he drops his bike and starts dribbling on the court.

'So,' he says, shooting and missing, 'I've been thinking, and I have a plan for finding your dad. It's brilliant.'

I'm skeptical. 'Brilliant?' I say. 'We'll see about that.' I'm sitting on the grass cross-legged, brushing away the occasional ant crawling up my leg.

'Yeah.' He shoots again and – ha! – misses. 'What about Information?'

'What kind of information are you talking about?' Why is he talking in code today? 'Operation Padre.' 'Information.' Maybe it's a guy thing.

'You know, the operator, 411. Information.'

'Oh!' I say, getting what he's talking about. I pluck some grass and let it fall through my hands. 'Well, duh. How am I supposed to call Information if I don't know where he lives?'

'Well, I thought about that.' Bounce, bounce, bounce, shoot. 'What about calling, like, every area code and asking if they have a number for him?'

'Do you know how many area codes there are?' I scoff. This is about the dumbest idea I've ever heard.

'No. Do you?' He finally makes a basket and does that weird dance guys do when they do something good in sports. 'Yah! He shoots! He scores!' he says, prancing around with his arms above his head.

I lie down in the grass. 'Way too many for me to even think about calling.'

'We could split them up,' he says, dribbling between his legs. 'You take some and I take some.'

'The calls will show up on our phone bills,' I point out. 'It'll never work.'

He sighs, grabs the ball, and sinks down on the grass beside me. 'Jeez, you're being so negative about this.'

I sit up, bringing my legs to my chest and squeezing my knees. 'What do you mean, negative?'

'Well, you're shooting down everything I say.'

'No, I'm shooting down your one completely stupid idea.' I

turn my head away from him so I don't have to look at his dumb face.

'Whatever,' he says. Then he shoves the ball at me. 'Here. You want to play?'

'No,' I say, pushing it back at him. I'm not negative. I'm about as positive as a person can be without being an idiot. I mean, the world's not the happy place people like Dumb Dan make it out to be. Hasn't he ever heard of Anne Frank, for example? I get a lump in my throat just thinking about Anne and about how Dumb Dan doesn't understand anything. I wish I hadn't told him about wanting to find my father. I scramble up off the ground. 'I gotta go,' I say, grabbing my bike and hopping on. 'Sara Lynn wanted me back early.'

'Okay,' he says, and he gets up and starts shooting baskets again, like he doesn't even care he hurt my feelings.

I gulp a few times because I'm not going to let some stupid boy with idiot ideas make me cry. No way. I pedal like crazy and say to myself, 'Screw you, Dumb Dan.' That's something Ruth says when she's mad, something I'm not supposed to be saying. I stick up my chin and say it out loud, the whole expression Ruth says under her breath when she's ticked off at someone: 'Screw you and the horse you rode into town on.' Ha! Why don't you just ride that horse right back to New Jersey or wherever the heck you're from? See if I care.

I'm at the top of a hill now, and I take my feet off the pedals as I coast down. I'm practically flying, and I can just hear the fits Ruth and Sara Lynn would have if they saw me. 'Careful, Hope! For goodness' sake, be careful!'

Chapter 14

I haven't been over to Jack's in three days. I just don't have the stomach for it. Literally. I'm queasy as all get-out in the mornings, plus there's the added problem that I don't know what to say to him. I mean, how do you bring something like this up? *Hi, I'm pregnant. I know you're sixty and have grandchildren, but – guess what? – you're going to have another kid!*

Of course, there's always the option not to have the baby. I can nip this problem in the bud tomorrow. Today, if I want to. But I don't want to, goddammit! I'm acting like a fool, but every once in a while I get goose bumps of pleasure, thinking, There's a baby inside me. A baby! *Stop it,* I tell myself. *You can't have this baby.*

But how can I not? I plead with myself. *How can I not?* God! I just want time to stop so I can have a minute to think this through.

'Ruth, how about some more coffee?' It's Ned Torkin from the insurance agency next door. Barking at me like a dog. There goes my minute, goddammit. No time to think! Not in my crazy life! How am I supposed to figure things out if nobody can give me one rotten little minute?

'Hold on a second,' I snap. I stomp behind the counter and grab the coffeepot, then march over to his booth and fill him up. 'There, satisfied?'

'Whew! What's the matter? You get up on the wrong side of the bed today?'

I rub my forehead. Jesus, now I'm yelling at the customers. 'Sorry, Ned. I'm just preoccupied, I guess.'

'Everything all right?' He stirs some sugar into his cup and looks up at me, concerned.

'Yeah, yeah,' I say. 'Just one of those moods, I guess.'

'Well, cheer up, kid. It can't be that bad.'

I go through the motions of laughing as I walk behind the counter to replace the coffeepot. *Oh, yes, it can be that bad,* I say to him in my head. *You have no idea.*

<hr />

I've been trying to sneak out of work before Jack arrives at three. He surprises me today, though, and shows up at two. I'm clearing up after my last lunch customers when I look up and see him walking through the door, and my throat tightens. I quickly bring those dishes back to the kitchen, and there I stand, talking to Chet about anything at all I can think of.

'Jesus, it's hot today, isn't it?'

'Hotter back here at the grill than it is outside,' he replies, scraping off the grill.

'Don't you think it's hotter than normal, though? This summer, I mean. Maybe it's that global warming trend, or whatever it's called.'

Chet raises his spatula and snorts. 'What're you, a goddamn weather girl?'

I laugh, a loud, nervous 'Ha!' and I say, 'Well, the weather's interesting, don't you think? I mean, I just wonder why it's hotter this summer than it has been other years. The winters are different now, too. Not as cold, I don't think, not as much snow.'

I'm babbling on like an idiot when the kitchen door swings open and in comes Jack. He interrupts my little speech on weather patterns, saying, 'Ruth, can I talk to you for a sec?'

I turn and smile as bravely as I don't feel inside. 'Sure thing, Jack. What's up?'

'Alone?'

Chet starts whistling and cleaning his grill again, and I have no choice but to wipe my hands on my apron and nod. I'm so nervous that my lower lip is trembling, and all I can do to make it stop is to start grinning like a foolish circus clown. I'm trying to act like everything's okeydokey as I follow him out front to a corner booth. No one's here, dammit, so I don't have the excuse that I need to wait on someone. I drum my fingers on the table and put my eyes anywhere but on him. He just looks at me, and finally he says in a low voice, 'What's wrong?'

'What do you mean, what's wrong?' I say heartily. 'Everything's great.'

'I don't feel like everything's great,' he says. 'I really miss you.'

I laugh. 'Oh God, don't go getting your feelings hurt. I've just been busy.'

'Busy with what?' He doesn't say it mean; he says it like he really wants to know.

I shrug. 'Stuff. Stuff with Hope. Sara Lynn's been working a lot lately. Trying to meet a deadline for her magazine.'

'Is that why you leave early every day, too?'

I stare at him coldly. 'Dock my pay, Jack.'

He slams his palm on the table, and I jump. I've never seen him angry before. His voice is quiet but strained, like he's trying to keep from yelling. 'Dammit, Ruth, this isn't about the restaurant. This is about you and me.'

I want to cry because there won't be any more him and me after he finds out I'm pregnant. Best to beat him to the punch. 'Maybe I'm tired of you and me.'

He scratches his bald spot like he does when he's trying hard to take something in, and I want to hug him, crying, 'I don't mean what I'm saying. I'm just scared as hell about all of this. Please don't stop loving me.' Stupid fool, that's what I am. I cross my arms over my chest and say, 'Maybe I think we need a break.'

151

He stops scratching and places both hands on the table, palms up, as if he's showing me he's not hiding anything. 'Why?' he asks.

I snort. 'Does there have to be a reason for everything?'

'Yes,' he replies immediately. 'For something like this, you bet there has to be a reason.'

'Well, there's not,' I say, sliding out from the bench. 'So don't bother me about it again.'

I walk back to the kitchen and grab my purse without even saying good-bye to Chet. I march back out to the dining room and try not to look at Jack, still sitting in his booth, looking like I've just kicked him in the stomach. He looks so sad that I can't just leave it like this, and as I pass him I say, 'Listen, I just need time to think, okay?'

He looks at me and says, 'I think I should have a part in any decision you make about our relationship.'

'What relationship?' I hiss. 'It's not like we're a couple, for God's sake.'

'Yes,' he insists, grabbing my hand. 'Yes, we are. It's you who doesn't want to go public. I'd have married you years ago.'

I pull my hand away, and the goddamn tears start coming. 'Well, it's too late for that now,' I say thickly.

'What in God's name do you mean by that?' he says.

I lose it then and run out of there crying to beat the band. Stupid pregnancy hormones. 'Never mind,' I cry. 'Just never mind.'

As I get into my car and start the engine, I wipe away my tears with my arm. This is just so typical. I should have remembered that there wasn't going to be any happy ending here. Not in my goddamn life. See, my track record for relationships isn't so great. Well, let's call a spade a spade – it's pretty much sucked since the beginning.

In April of my senior year, I was coming out of a detention I'd landed for mouthing off to Mr. Dilbert – Mr. Dildo, we called him. It wasn't that big a deal. Hell, it was getting so I was spending more time in the detention room than any other classroom. Too bad they didn't give an award at graduation for 'person with the most detentions.' I would have won for sure, beaten Sara Lynn out of something for once.

Finally, finally, after two hours of sitting at a desk watching the hands of the wall clock creep around the big black numbers, I was free. 'You may go, Ruth,' said Miss Garrison, sighing. I jumped up and walked fast out the door. Turned the corner to get to my locker, and – bam! – ran right into Jeff Barnes.

'Ow!' I rubbed at my head. 'What the hell!'

'Sorry.' Jeff was rubbing his head, too. 'Are you okay?'

'I guess.' I laughed, even though my head still throbbed. 'Man, you've got a hard head.'

He laughed, too. 'Speak for yourself.' He was a rich kid who wore pressed khakis and shirts with a little horse embroidered on the front, so he didn't run with my crowd. But up close, he didn't seem snobby at all. He smiled at me like we were friends, and I realized I liked the way he looked. I liked his short hair and clean-shaven face, his shiny loafer shoes, and the way he stood up straight and looked me in the eye.

'What're you doing here, anyway?' I asked. The halls were deserted. There was only the janitor, pushing a broom down the hallway.

'Yearbook,' he said. 'I'm the editor.'

'Mmm.' I nodded, although I couldn't have told you anything about yearbook. It wasn't the kind of thing that grabbed my interest.

'How about you?' he asked.

'How about me what?'

'Why are you here so late?'

'Guess,' I said, smiling.

'Newspaper?'

I laughed and shook my head.

'Tennis team?'

I laughed some more, still shaking my head no.

He was getting the joke and asked, 'Cheerleading?'

'No way,' I said.

'Future Homemakers of America Club?'

He topped himself there, and I laughed real loud and said, 'No. Future Criminals of America Club. Detention.'

'What did you do?' he asked.

I shrugged. 'Wised off to the Dildo.' He looked sort of impressed, so I bragged on myself a little. 'I'm so sick of his crap. I mean, I'm out of here in two months. I don't have to take his shit.'

'Yeah, no kidding,' he agreed. 'I can't wait to get the hell out of this town.'

'You going to college?'

'Williams,' he said proudly.

'Great,' I replied, because I could tell he thought it was a big deal.

'You?'

'Unclear,' I said. 'Remember, I'm president of the Future Criminals of America Club. We don't exactly go on to stellar college careers.'

He laughed. 'You're funny, Ruth.'

'Yeah, tell it to the Dildo.'

He laughed again and pointed to me. 'See? You're hilarious.'

I was feeling hilarious. I was even feeling pretty, the way Jeff was looking at me. 'You heading home?' I asked.

'Yeah, I was. How about you?'

I shrugged. 'I don't know. I don't really feel like going home. It's not like I have any studying to do or anything.'

'You know what? I'm accepted at college now. I don't have any studying to do, either.'

'That's the spirit,' I told him. 'Better watch it or you'll be a Future Criminal, too.'

154

He was looking at me differently now, like he was sizing me up and thinking. 'You want to ride around a little?' he asked quickly, and I knew pretty well what he was getting at.

I stuck out a hip a little bit and tossed my hair back the way the rich girls did. 'Yeah,' I said. 'Why not?'

'I've got to go to my locker. Don't go anywhere, okay? I'll be right back.'

I stood in the hallway lined with puke-yellow lockers and waited, my mind racing and my heart beating fast. He came back quickly, panting a little, skidding to a stop in front of me. 'Ready?' he asked eagerly. 'Ready to go?'

'I'm just waiting for you,' I said, trying to be cool.

We went out the front door of the high school, a change for me. I used the back door off the gym. I wondered if I became Jeff's girlfriend if I would start marching right in the front door. I saw myself, my frizzy brown hair pulled off my face in a head-band like Sara Lynn Hoffman used, dressed in corduroys and a polo shirt, walking right through that front door.

'Hop in,' Jeff said. He looked a little pale, a little nervous, so I started talking a mile a minute when he started up the car.

'I like your car. I sure wish I had a car. I'm always either walking or depending on other people for rides. You know Gina Logan? She's got a car. I ride with her a lot.'

He just nodded and smiled some, looking preoccupied as he drove us out to the tobacco fields west of town and stopped the car.

'I worked tobacco one summer. I was fourteen and some of my girlfriends were doing it. You know Kathy Lussman and Suzi Morgan? They talked me into it. Man, was it a disgusting job. It's hotter'n hell, for one thing, and your fingers get all gross and brown. You can't get that stuff off your hands. I'm telling you, that was the only summer I could take doing that job. Never again.'

He looked so miserable, squirming in his seat and not even having the courage to look at me, that I finally said, 'Oh, hell,' and leaned over and kissed him myself. Well, that was all I needed to do to break the spell on Mr. Shyness. He started cramming his tongue in my mouth, forcing it past my teeth. Then he reached under my shirt and tried to unhook my bra. It was taking him forever, and I was getting a backache from trying to contort into whatever position would make it easier for him to unhook the damn thing. I finally pulled away from him, saying, 'One sec,' and unhooked it myself. He breathed sort of funny, like he had asthma or something, when he pushed his tongue back in my mouth and grabbed my nonexistent boobs. It flashed through my mind that rich girls always had perfectly perky boobs – not too big, not too small, but just right. Girls like me either had no boobs or disgustingly huge ones. Well, he seemed to be getting along all right. 'Ow,' I muttered as he squeezed a nipple hard. Okay, so there wasn't much for him to feel, but he didn't have to pinch me.

'Sorry,' he said, taking his tongue out of my mouth and then diving it right back in. I was beginning to get the idea of the expression *sucking face.* He started to unzip my pants, and I immediately went for his. Gave me something to do. It wasn't like I hadn't made out with guys before. I'd gone about this far. In fact, I'd gone about this far lots of times. What did I care if some guy felt around my body? I'd always stopped it right about here, though.

'That's it,' I'd say when I'd had my good time, and zipped up my pants and buttoned my shirt.

'But, but . . . ,' the guy would always say, looking at me like his eyes and his private part were going to pop right off his body.

'See ya,' I'd say, and I'd be smiling as I got up and walked away. It always was a good feeling to walk away from a boy right when he wanted me most. Jack yourself off, Jack, I'd think.

So here I was feeling Jeff's little appendage and listening to his breathing get even more fast and wheezy. He was trying and trying to unzip my jeans, and after what seemed like a million years, he finally managed to get them undone. I felt like I was watching a long-distance runner stumble across the finish line. I only

156

had one life to live, and I felt as though I'd soon be turning fifty in this car. Finally, I pulled down my own pants and underpants – with one hand, I might add, as I was still grabbing his puny penis with the other – and I happened to glance at his face and see that it was all red. Little beads of sweat were pouring down his forehead and nose, making his glasses all slippery and crooked. He was so goddamn hopeful, so goddamn excited, I couldn't stop him. Hell, it *wasn't* like watching a long-distance runner, it was like watching a Special Olympics long-distance runner. How do you not give a Special Olympian a medal?

So I didn't pull back when he grabbed me and tried to set me on top of him. I went right along, and I swear, the guy was going to need an inhaler if he kept on the way he was going. My back was jammed into the steering wheel, and I said, 'I can't do this.'

'Oh God, no, please, please,' he cried, wheezing.

I slapped his arm. 'No, silly. I mean, I can't do it right here. Let's get in back.'

So he threw me off him, opened the driver's-side door, shut it again, and got in the backseat through the back door. Me, I just climbed back there. No sense in freezing my ass off.

'Ohgod,' he said, diving his tongue right into me again and pinning me underneath him. Next thing I knew, he was starting to poke himself into me. 'Ohgod, ohgod, ohgod . . . ,' he chanted. 'Wait!' He pulled himself out and leaked his stupid sperm all over my stomach.

Well, if that was sex, you could have it. I liked what came before the act much better, that was for sure. 'Eww,' I said, brushing at my stomach. 'What the hell!'

He was still above me, his eyes closed and his little wheezy breaths coming further apart now. 'Sorry,' he said, panting. 'I wanted to get a condom, but . . .'

But what? I thought. You couldn't hold it, so you sprayed your body fluid all over me? 'Can you get me a tissue?' I asked. 'Look in my bag. On the floor of the front seat.'

He lay there holding himself like he couldn't quite believe his little thing had been inside a girl. His mouth was open, and his glasses were way down his nose. 'Today?' I said. 'Do you mind?'

'Oh, sure. Sorry.' He leaped off me and leaned over the front seat, grabbing for my purse. 'Here you go,' he said, holding the purse by the strap for me to take.

'Um, I kind of *can't move* here,' I told him. If I moved even a little, that gloppy pile of slime lying on my stomach was going to spill everywhere. 'Just go into my purse and get a tissue.'

'Oh, yeah.' He laughed. 'Okay. Sure.' He dug into my purse and handed me a ratty, wrinkled, linty tissue that probably had been at the bottom of my bag since 1978.

I wiped the glob up, but there was still a slimy, shiny layer that didn't seem to want to come off my stomach no matter how hard I rubbed. I sighed again and handed him the tissue while I sat up and rearranged my clothes. When I looked up, he was holding the dirty tissue away from himself and wrinkling his nose.

'What am I supposed to do with this?'

'Sweet Jesus,' I said. I took the tissue, rolled down the window, and threw it into the field. 'Bye-bye.'

'Thanks,' he said. He looked relieved that I had taken care of it, and then he looked sideways at me. 'Thanks for everything,' he said.

'Aw, it's okay,' I said back. I thought it was so nice of him to thank me. He was a real gentleman, I thought. I tried to snuggle into his arms, but those arms didn't seem to want to hug me. Just sort of draped around me limply. I looked up at him and gave him a kiss. He didn't shove his tongue in this time, just sort of let me kiss him without kissing me back.

'What's the matter?' I murmured, cozying myself into his body even more.

'Nothing,' he said. He stiffened and moved away from me. 'It's getting late. We probably should be heading home.'

'Okay,' I said, smiling up at him.

We didn't say much on the ride home. I snuggled in close to

him as he drove, and I kissed him when we got to my house. Poor guy, he was so shell-shocked from what had happened, he could hardly even say good-bye.

'See you tomorrow, okay?' I said as I got out of the car.

He nodded, gripping the wheel and looking straight ahead at the road.

———

They called me 'slut' when I came into school the next morning, all his yearbook buddies and their girlfriends and every snotty rich kid whose house Ma cleaned. It started with a bunch of boys in letter jackets hollering, 'Slut, slut, slut,' when I went to my locker. At first, I wasn't sure what they were saying and who they were saying it to, but as I slammed my locker shut, I looked at them down the hall, and one of them called, 'Does everyone get some, or just Barnes?'

I marched down the hall and got in the guy's face. 'What did you say?'

The group of guys just laughed and jostled me a little bit, and the mouthy guy said, 'We're not afraid of you, slut.'

I pushed him as hard as I could, and the boys roared, 'She wants you; she wants you.'

I stomped down the hall away from them and went into the library, where the smart kids hung out before school. Sara Lynn Hoffman was sitting at a table, twirling a strand of her hair as she looked down at a book. I walked up to her and leaned down, setting my hands on the table's edge. 'Where's Jeff Barnes?' I asked her from between my clenched teeth.

Sara Lynn looked up and twisted her mouth like she was going to laugh. 'Jeff? Oh yeah, your new boyfriend.' She said it real snotty, like she was making fun of me, and I had to restrain myself from reaching across the table and yanking that long blond hair out of her head. 'Room fourteen is his homeroom. Maybe you can find him there.'

I practically ran down the hall to room fourteen, and there he was, sitting at a desk and talking to three other guys. They were giving him high fives when I walked in, and then they started laughing.

'Jeff, your girlfriend's here.'

'Slut,' one of them said as he pretended to cough into his hand. That was all it took for the rest of them to start their fake coughing, too. 'Slut, slut . . .'

'What. The. Fuck,' I said, coming up close to him. 'What the fuck?!'

'Oooh, she's mad,' one of them said.

Jeff sort of smiled at me smugly and shrugged.

'What are you telling people, you asshole?' I said, coming right up to his pimply face. How I ever could have thought he was even a little bit cute yesterday was beyond me.

His smile faded, and then he put on a fake one, like he wasn't so scared he was going to wet his pants.

One of his preppy friends laughed. 'What're you going to do, beat him up?'

Jeff looked at his buddy, then back at me, and said, 'Actually, I like it rough. Cool.'

His friend slapped his hand in a high five.

'Really?' I said. 'Really? Because you weren't liking it rough yesterday. You were just trying to get your little – *little* – penis up. Remember that?'

'Ha! Barnes!' his friends ribbed him, and he flushed, his eyes narrowing at me.

I went on, talking in a mean, baby-talk voice. 'Jeffy was trying so hard to get his itty-bitty penis to work. He was huffing and puffing and working so hard. Jeffy thought sex was like a test in school. If he tried super-duper hard, he'd pass the test.'

'Shut up, you bitch,' he said in a low voice. The boys jeered at him, and he jumped out of his seat toward me. 'You're so ugly, you'd do it with anybody.'

I pointed at him and yelled, 'Yeah? Well, what the hell does that say about you?' I turned on my heel and left that room. Then I marched out of school and walked home. I watched TV all damn day and cried and cried, not so much over that stupid boy, but over who I was and would always be, over my stupid, ugly, pathetic self.

⁓

So here I am in my car, driving through town pregnant without any goddamn air-conditioning, wiping away the tears streaming down my face. God, I wish Ma were here. She'd say, 'Well, well, what have you gone and done now?' She'd sigh and moan and bitch about the trouble I cause just from breathing, but she'd help me. She'd take me by the shoulders and say, 'Okay, Ruth, here's what we're going to do.' That's what I miss about Ma being gone — there's nobody here who will grab my arm and tell me what to do, tell me everything's going to be all right if only I listen to her and do exactly as she says. There's just my own little voice inside, saying it's not sure everything'll be fine, that there aren't any clear answers and all we can do is hope for the best.

I breathe a long sigh as I pull into the driveway. Home at last. Home? Ha! I would have laughed my ass off thirteen years ago if anyone had told me I'd be calling the Hoffman place home. What sort of stuff have you been smoking? I'd have asked them. But here I am, walking up the steps of the big house that's become my home.

'Hi, ladies,' I say, walking into the kitchen and throwing my keys on the counter. Mamie's sitting at the kitchen table with Marge Costa, the woman who comes in to keep her company some afternoons. As usual, they're lost in a game of cards. 'Who's winning?'

'I am,' Mamie brags.

'It's true, Ruth,' Marge says heartily. 'She trounces me every time.'

'Well, you girls finish up your game. I'm going up to take a rest.'

'Don't you feel well?' Mamie asks, widening her eyes and pursing her mouth.

'Oh, I'm just a little under the weather,' I say, brushing her off.

Mamie shakes her head and clucks. 'You poor thing. You get up to bed right now.'

Tears spring to my eyes at the goodness of this little old lady feeling sorry for me. 'Have fun, you two,' I say with a heartiness I don't feel.

As I head up the stairs, I smile through my sadness as I hear Mamie slap her cards down on the table. 'Looks like I win again,' she crows.

Chapter 15

*W*hack! *Whack! Whack!* I'm swinging at ball after ball, as many as Sam keeps hitting to me.

'Good job, Hope,' he calls over the net.

Whack! Boy, it feels good to connect my racket to the ball and slam it hard.

'Nice work,' Sam says, leaping up and catching the last ball I hit. Okay, so I guess I didn't hit it as hard as I thought. 'Take a break?'

I'm panting as I jog up to the net. 'Okay.'

'Hey, you're really flushed,' he says, putting his palm on my hot cheek. 'Sit down and I'll get you some water.'

I park my rear end on the court and try to take some deep breaths. I rub my arm across my sweaty forehead.

'Here.' Sam's back, and he sits beside me as he hands me a cup of water from the cooler that sits beside the courts.

'Thanks,' I gasp, and chug it as fast as I can.

'You want more?' Sam asks. He leans in close to look at me. His eyes look worried, and I have to say it feels as good as that water tasted to have him concerned about me.

I nod. 'Yeah,' I say, starting to scramble up to get some more.

'Whoa, whoa,' Sam cautions, his hands on my shoulders. 'Sit. I'll get it.'

I watch him as he lopes over to the cooler, and I like how he walks – he sort of strides like he's not at all worried about people watching him. Whenever I'm walking, my legs and arms feel stiff, and I never know whether or not to smile. I'm always convinced that there's a big spotlight traveling over me and everyone's watching.

After Sam bends down to fill a paper cup with water, he stands and walks back toward me. He sees me watching him and smiles wide.

'Hey, tiger,' he says, handing me the cup. 'Cheers.'

I take a sip, then wrinkle my nose. 'Tiger?'

'Yeah.' He sits next to me, cross-legged on the court, so close I can see the curly blond hairs on his tanned legs. 'You were pretty vicious out there today.'

'I like hitting the ball hard when I'm mad,' I say, scratching a mosquito bite on my elbow. Oops. There I go again, just saying whatever pops into my mind.

'What are you mad about?' he asks, and doesn't say it the way most grown-ups do, where they sort of chuckle and marvel, 'What on earth do you possibly have to be mad about?' He says it like I have every right to be angry.

'Stuff,' I say with a shrug, looking down at the dark green asphalt.

'You want to talk about it?' he asks, leaning back on his elbows and stretching out his legs in front of him.

Well, yeah, I do, but I'm not sure what to say. See, I don't know if I have words for what I'm mad about. It's everything. I'm mad about everything.

'Anne Frank,' I say, throwing it out there. *I'm mad about a world that killed Anne Frank. How's that?*

'Hmm,' he says, thinking. 'Anne Frank.'

I take a deep breath and say, 'The world. The world is a rotten place when something like that could happen, when Anne Frank could get killed for no reason.' My voice thickens. Shoot. I'm trying to keep my wet eyes from spilling over.

164

'You're absolutely right,' Sam says quietly. 'The world makes me mad, too.'

'It does?' I sneak a quick look at him, and he's looking straight ahead with a sad face.

'Yeah,' he replies, looking at me. 'Who wouldn't be mad?'

'Well, that's exactly it!' I blurt out. 'This kid I know said I was a negative person. And, like, who wouldn't be, right? And Sara Lynn and Ruth – they're always saying, "Smile! Don't be so morbid! Don't read Anne Frank again! Think about good things!"'

'The old "put on a happy face," huh?' Sam says, a smile appearing and then disappearing again in an instant. 'Listen . . .' His eyes are looking straight into mine. 'Life can break your heart, Hope.'

I think about my parents, how I never knew them, and I can't help it, the tears sitting in my eyes spill over onto my cheeks. I wipe them away with my hands real fast.

'But you need to know this, too,' he says, tilting his head back and looking up at the sky. 'Life is also beyond amazing. It'll surprise you, thrill you; it'll knock you over with so much happiness.'

'You mean like being in love?' I say, sniffling.

'Yeah.' He laughs and reaches over to ruffle my hair. 'Or like hanging out with friends. Or like doing something you really enjoy doing.' He smiles at me. 'What do you like to do?'

'Me?' I shrug. 'I don't know.'

'But you'll find out. As you keep living your life. And what an awesome surprise it'll be to discover your passion.'

'What . . . what do you like to do?' I mumble, picking at my fingernail.

'Well, painting, for sure.' He thinks a minute, then continues. 'And playing tennis. And hanging out with my friends. And being in love.'

I put a hand up to my mouth and shake my hair over my face. My heart beats loud as I ask, 'Are you in love?'

He laughs again, clear and loud. 'I believe I'm in the process of falling,' he tells me. He nudges me and whispers, 'Don't tell, though. It'll be our secret.'

'I won't tell,' I whisper back. 'Promise.'

⁓

When Sara Lynn picks me up from the club, she chats with Sam for what seems the longest time. They're just standing there by the pool talking away while I swim with Ginny, and I'm dying to go over there and find out what's so interesting.

I bet anything it's my tennis. Sara Lynn's so fascinated with my tennis these days. What did you learn? What pointers did Sam give you? Blah, blah, blah. I'm sure she's over there boring Sam with strategies about how to make me a better player. He probably thinks she's, like, one of those overbearing stage mothers or something. I come up from underwater and squint at her talking a mile a minute, moving her hands as she talks so the silver bangles she's wearing float up and down her arms. 'How's Hope's backhand?' I can imagine her asking. 'Do you think she should be using two hands, or should we try to break her of that habit?'

I roll my eyes and cringe just to think of it, and I tell Ginny I need to go now, that I'll see her tomorrow. I hop out of the pool and dry off quickly. Then I grab my swim bag and walk over to Sara Lynn and Sam. 'Ready, Sara Lynn?' I say.

Her eyes widen as she looks at me. 'Sure,' she says. 'Of course. Don't you have to change first?'

'I'll shower and change at home.'

'Oh, Hope . . . the leather seats in the car,' she moans. Then she surprises me by laughing. 'Oh, golly, what does it matter? That's fine.' She tosses her hair over her shoulder as she calls, 'See you soon, Sam,' and her eyes are gleaming. She looks . . . giddy or something. Ha! Maybe he told her I was supertalented or something, and she's imagining my professional tennis career.

'Come on,' I mutter, walking away.

166

'See ya,' Sam says, and puts up a hand to wave good-bye. Man, he's probably glad to get rid of her.

The second we hit the parking lot, I hiss, 'What were you talking to Sam about?'

She raises her eyebrows as she looks at me. 'What?'

'Were you all, like, "Oh, how's Hope progressing with her tennis?"' I imitate her snooty voice, the one she uses when she talks to teachers or people she's trying to impress.

She sets her jaw and strides to the car, saying nothing. It's only when I get in and shut the door that she turns to me, two bright spots of red on her cheeks, and says, 'For your information, Hope, my world does not revolve completely around you. I do have other interests, other topics of conversation.'

'Fine, fine,' I protest as she jerks the car backward out of the parking space. 'I was only kidding,' I lie.

She doesn't say anything, just drives looking straight ahead. God, she's so sensitive sometimes. I change the subject so she won't be so mad. 'Listen, Sara Lynn. I have a question for you.'

'What?' she asks, still pouting a little.

'Have you ever been in love?'

'Have I *what*?' She laughs, although I see nothing funny in my question.

'Been in love,' I reply.

'Well . . .' She pauses, then says, 'Y-yes, I suppose I have.'

'Who with?'

'With whom,' she says.

I sigh. Honestly, it's like pulling teeth. 'Okay. With whom?'

She clicks her tongue to the roof of her mouth a few times, like she's thinking. I don't know what she has to think about. If you're in love, you know who it is you're in love with, right? 'Hmm,' she says. 'You know, that's sort of a personal question.'

I just shrug and look out the car window, and in a moment she asks cautiously, 'Have you ever been in love?'

I don't miss a beat. 'That's sort of a personal question,' I say snidely.

She laughs. 'Touché,' she acknowledges.

Since we're (sort of) sharing things here, I decide to ask her another question. 'What was my father like?' My voice comes out all funny, like it's been trapped in my throat.

'Your father,' she says slowly. 'My, you're asking probing questions this afternoon.' She doesn't speak for a minute, then she asks, 'Why do you want to know?'

Oh, for crying out loud. 'Why do I want to know?' I burst out, raising my voice. 'Because he's my father. God, Sara Lynn, you overthink everything. I just want to know what my father was like. What don't you get about that?'

'Calm down,' she snaps. She takes a deep breath. 'Oooh, let's see. Your father was . . . gosh, I don't know how to describe him. He was . . . very irreverent, in the best sort of way.' I can see her lips twist a little, like she wants to smile. 'He saw the absurdities of life.'

Like that makes any kind of sense to me at all. 'What else?' I ask. 'What else do you remember about him?'

'That's . . . all, right now.'

'Well, that's kind of lame,' I say with a snort.

'Yes, Hope,' she retorts sharply. 'I guess I am awfully lame. A real loser.'

Okay, then. So much for a heart-to-heart chat with Sara Lynn. There's no pleasing her. I sigh and roll my eyes, looking out the window. Sometimes I wonder if that woman even has a heart.

Chapter 16

What am I doing? What on earth am I doing? This is the sentence that's been churning through my head since I turned onto the highway leading down to Boston. I'm going to work. That's what I'm doing. Just going to look at a garden. Just going to do my job.

Ha! Doing my job indeed. Does my job involve meeting men . . . no, *boys* – meeting boys for illicit trysts? Illicit trysts . . . good God, I sound like the copy from one of my mother's bodice-ripper books.

I shake my head as I flick my blinker to enter the passing lane. What was I thinking when I agreed to this? No, no – even worse. When I *suggested* this. Because it was absolutely my idea. What must he think of me? My cheeks get warm just imagining. I basically propositioned him. Yes, I did. I as much as said, 'I can't date you, but I'd be happy to meet you secretly in Boston one night next week and have sex with you.'

Oh, for God's sake. I'm not going to do any such thing with him. He can think whatever he likes about how it sounded, but what a person believes and what's the truth are two entirely different matters.

I'm gritting my teeth, and I force myself to stretch my jaw and relax it. My dentist lectured me at my last appointment about the damage one can do from teeth gritting, jaw clenching, and other stress-related behaviors. I take a deep breath – oxygen in, carbon dioxide out. Think about something else. I stretch out my right hand, hit the radio, and flick through the buttons, looking for music that's pleasing. No. No. No. I hit the off button and drum my fingers on the wheel. This drive is boring, a straight line on the map leading from Ridley Falls to Boston. I could do it on autopilot, have done it on autopilot when I used to drive this very highway back and forth and forth and back in my past so long ago that it seems to belong to a different person.

~

In my early twenties, I lived and worked in Boston. I thought I was there to stay until I hit twenty-four and drove back to Ridley Falls for good, having quit my big-time lawyering job and irrevocably ruined the bright future I'd spent my life preparing for.

I was a lawyer at Amos & McAllister, the oldest and most prestigious law firm in Boston. I was lucky, it was said, because Amos & McAllister hired only the best and the brightest. Even my boyfriend, Todd Wilton, hadn't managed to get a job there.

Lucky . . . I thought of the irony of this on a fall afternoon before I brought my life to a full stop as I sat in the law firm's library, working on research for Conrad Dalton, the firm's managing partner. I didn't feel lucky. I felt as if I'd been sentenced to a life made up of equal parts stress and boredom, and there wasn't any way out of the prison I'd diligently constructed for myself.

'How's that research coming?' It was Conrad Dalton, walking through the library. He stood behind my chair and breathed over me, short ugly pants through his nose, as he skimmed the case I was reading.

'Fine,' I said, my heart pounding in my chest.

'Goddammit, I hope so,' he said grimly. 'There better be cases out there on our side.'

As if it were my responsibility to make up the cases that appeared in the law books! As if it were I who had authored the long-winded opinions regarding whether or not the plaintiff truly owned one-half of a racehorse or the defendant should have sanded his sidewalk so the plaintiff didn't fall. As if I cared about any of it!

I sighed and raised my hands from the book. 'I'm not having much luck,' I said. 'I'm trying to find cases that say what you want, but I'm afraid the law comes out the other way.' I cringed inside. Better to disappoint him now than later, I thought. Better to prepare him for the likely scenario that his argument wasn't going to hold up.

He grabbed the open book from the table and, still breathing heavily, began to read. 'What about this?' he said, setting the book on the table and smacking the back of his hand against the page. 'Isn't this exactly what we want?'

'That's a case from 1885,' I said softly. 'The law has changed significantly since then. As I demonstrated to you in my memo of last week.'

'You know, Sara Lynn,' he said, 'I've warned you about this. About your tendency to give up on things. This case might help us. You don't just read it and say, 'Oh, dear, it's too old; the law has changed." He raised his voice to a falsetto to imitate me. 'No! You construct an argument out of it. You use it. You think!'

As he strode away, he said, 'Get working on that argument. And think, Sara Lynn. Show me that you have a brain.'

Have a brain? Have a brain? I fumed inside as I looked down at those dusty law books. I was certain my grades were higher than his had been. Hadn't I been high school valedictorian and summa cum laude out of Wellesley? Hadn't my thesis on the role of nature in Wordsworth's poetry won top honors? But what if he was right? It was a thought that grabbed hold and wouldn't let go. What if I wasn't smart at all? What if my whole life had been

171

a facade and the jig was finally up? What if I really was merely average and not the least bit special?

I toted a pile of books into my office and shut the door. As I sat down to try again, the phone rang.

'Sara Lynn Hoffman,' I said professionally, wondering what hell awaited me on the other end of the line.

'Hi, honey,' trilled my mother. 'I just came in from doing my roses and thought of you.'

'Hi, Mama,' I said.

'You don't sound very perky today.'

'I'm working, Mama. Working.' Mama hadn't worked in donkey's years. She didn't have any idea what it was like to try to please people all day and never measure up to what they wanted out of you.

'I know you are, dear,' she said. 'Oh, I'm so proud of you! My daughter – the lawyer! You're so lucky to be living in today's world, where women are encouraged to have their careers. Now, don't get me wrong – I'm proud to have been a homemaker and mother all these years. But then, I wasn't as smart as you. I didn't have your talents.'

'Oh, Mama,' I said, trying to sound modest.

'How's Todd?' she asked, excited.

'Well,' I said, wanting to please her, 'he invited me to Martha's Vineyard this weekend to stay at his family's house.'

'You're going?'

'Yes,' I said, 'I am. And we're staying in separate rooms, Mama, so don't go hinting around about propriety or anything like that.' I was lying to her, of course, but I couldn't bear for her to think I wasn't her perfect daughter.

'Why, honey,' she exclaimed, 'you're an adult woman. What you do is your business, and I know in my heart I've raised you to be a lady. I know you'll never do anything to shame me. I don't need to ask you personal questions to which I already know the answers.'

My cheeks reddened, and my stomach clenched up.

'He's a nice boy. Any hint of . . . dum dum da dum?' She hummed the first bars of the 'Wedding March.'

'No,' I said hastily. 'No, not at all.'

'You'll be such a lovely bride, Sara Lynn,' she said. 'We'll get you a fairy princess dress that accentuates your tiny waist. And cap sleeves. So demure-looking for a bride, I think. And a long, long veil.'

'I don't even have a ring on my finger yet.'

'Can't start planning too soon,' she retorted.

I sighed. 'No, I guess not.'

'Why don't you bring him home one weekend? We haven't seen you in ages.'

'Mama, I was home last month.'

'Like I said, that was ages ago. And he's never seen your home.'

'I'll ask him,' I said grudgingly, 'but we're both sort of busy right now.'

'You're not too busy to trot off to Martha's Vineyard. It's not too much for me to ask you to bring your fiancé home.'

'He's not my fiancé,' I said from between clenched teeth.

'Oops, got to go, sweetheart. I've got bridge this afternoon. Ta-ta.'

And she hung up in a flurry, convinced I'd be engaged before she took her next breath.

Goose bumps sprang up on my arms. Oh, God. I dialed the number to my parents' house.

'Hello?' she answered expectantly.

'Mama, it's me.'

'What is it, Sara Lynn? I've got to go.'

'Listen,' I said, twisting the phone cord around and around my hand, 'don't go telling anybody I'm engaged or about to be engaged or anything like that.'

She was silent.

'Okay?' I asked.

'I don't know where you got this notion into your head that I haven't any discretion.'

I sighed. 'I'm just asking you to keep it quiet, that's all.'

'What would make you think I'd breathe a word?'

'Nothing, Mama, nothing,' I cried. 'Just see that you don't.'

'All right, Sara Lynn,' she said airily. 'I won't say one word about you. Just in case my discretion fails me. And if anyone asks about you, I'll just say, "I'm sorry. Sara Lynn would prefer that I not speak about her at all, lest I say something I'm not supposed—"'

'Mama,' I snapped, picking up a pen and tapping it like crazy on my desk, 'did I ever say that you weren't to speak about me at all? Did I ever say that?'

'You implied it.'

'I did not. I simply asked that you not share your hopes regarding an engagement with anyone.'

'Fine, Sara Lynn,' she said stiffly. 'Now I really must be going.'

'Fine,' I said, and then I felt guilty for making her feel bad. 'Mama, I'm sorry. I'm under a lot of pressure here at work and I'm taking it out on you. I'm sorry.'

She was waiting for that. 'That's all right, dear. I forgive you. I just wish you'd give your mother a little more credit.'

'I will,' I promised. 'Love you, Mama.'

'Love you, too, sweetheart,' she said, all chipper again. 'Have a good day! Don't work too hard!'

I hung up the phone and opened the top book on my pile. I brought my hands to my eyes and forced my eyelids wide open. I'd fall asleep otherwise, trying to decipher these cases from the days when they drove around in buggies, the days when women couldn't vote.

I had hated law school from day one, when Professor Forrest made Mary Lou Gallant cry because she answered a question in her high, squeaky voice and he kept interrupting her to cup his hand to his ear and say, 'What? What? Speak up, Miss Gallant. The jury members won't be convinced if they can't hear you.'

'Miss Gallant,' he had continued, striding across the room and grinning at her as she piped out a few more words, 'do you not have anything worthwhile to say? Is that why you insist upon whispering, Miss Gallant?'

At this, Mary Lou had stopped completely, and we all could hear the big, round, white-faced classroom clock tick from one minute to the next.

'Can you hear a word she's saying, class?' Professor Forrest threw one arm out from his body to take all of us in, enveloping us in his unquestioned power. We were benevolently welcomed; he would keep us safe. We laughed until Mary Lou ran out of the room with tears streaming down her face. Then we were silent until Professor Forrest shrugged and said mockingly, 'Was it something I said?' He gave us permission to laugh again, and we did, all of us, thanking God we were on the inside instead of the odd person out.

I wasn't a weak person. I understood that we were to shrug off the criticism, the insults, the jeering laughter. So what was it about law school that horrified me so, that made me not even recognize myself in the bathroom mirror when I got up in the morning? I'd blink the sleep crusties out of my eyes and lean in toward the round vanity mirror in my little Cambridge apartment. I'd look and look, and I'd think, Sara Lynn Hoffman, I don't even know who you are.

But they assured us it was to be expected, that we would walk into law school as one person and come out the other end as someone entirely different. We'd reason instead of feel; we'd fight back hard instead of sitting winded in the dust.

There were some people who entered law school longing for transformation. You could see it shining in their eyes. These were the people who, in another time or place, would have been martyrs, would have starved themselves to death for some cause. And the cause wouldn't have been as important to them as the process of starving, the feeling of hunger sliding them into hallucinatory otherness. These were the people who studied ten hours a day, who took down every word of each class as if they were writing a transcript, whose book pages were streaked yellow from highlighting all but a sentence or two. These were the people who wouldn't shower during final exams, who wore their dirt and wild-eyed expressions like badges of pride.

There were other people at law school for whom the transformation was easy because they were already on their way. They – mostly men – were people for whom every social encounter became an excuse to pick, to take issue, to start a fight. Todd Wilton was one of those people. I first met him at lunch with a bunch of other first-year students. He was – as usual – monopolizing the conversation as he discussed whether to continue two-timing his college girlfriend, Miranda, with a third-year law student or tell her the truth and break things off with her.

'What do you think, Sara Lynn?' he asked, pointing at me.

Without thinking, I stopped sipping my soda and said, 'Well, honesty is the best policy.'

He smiled smugly and said, 'Is it really? Is honesty really the best policy all the time?'

'It's just an expression,' I interjected hastily.

Todd looked around the table to be sure he had everyone's attention and then leaned across the table to me. 'You,' he said, 'should think before you speak in generalities like that. Remember, we're being trained at law school to speak precisely. You said, "Honesty is the best policy," but I bet you don't really mean that. For example, Sara Lynn, what if your best friend was wearing an ugly dress and she asked if you liked it? What would you say?'

'Todd,' I protested, 'I was just using an old expression.'

'Answer the question,' he said, crossing his arms across his chest and looking like our law professors, who loved to back us into corners with their extravagant examples designed to show why our answers were as stupid as cow dung.

Hot shame coursed through me; I felt as if I had exposed my ignorance and should never, ever speak again. I took a deep breath and said, 'I'd tell her the dress was ugly only if my words could do some good. Only if she hadn't bought it or could still take it back.'

'Aha!' he said. 'So you'd lie to her if she couldn't take it back.'

'Yes,' I said, 'because I'd be hurting her for no reason if I told the truth.'

'So you were wrong when you said honesty was the best policy?'

'No,' I said stubbornly, because it was the kiss of death ever to admit you were wrong. They trained you to believe that you had to fight on and on, even if it was apparent to everyone in the room that you were banging your head against a brick wall. We were learning it was sheer womanly weakness to give in and say, 'I changed my mind. I see your point. I was in error.'

I should have said no to him when he asked me out during our third year of law school. I should have turned on my heel and run the other way. I should have listened to my instincts instead of being flattered by his interest. It wasn't me he wanted, anyway; it was the girl who got nine job offers, the girl who seemed to have her future spreading out before her.

He broke up with Miranda to go out with me. I wouldn't have it any other way. He'd stop me after class and corner me, asking, 'Why won't you go out with me?'

'Because you're going out with Miranda,' I'd tell him, walking quickly and refusing to stop, clutching my books to my chest.

'I'm not,' he'd say. 'We have an open relationship.'

I'd laugh. 'I know all about your "open relationship." It means you see people on the side and hope she never finds out about it.'

'What'll it take?' he said one day. 'I'll do anything. Do you want me never to see Miranda again? If that's what you want, I'll do it. I'll do anything to go out on a date with you. One date. That's all I'm asking.'

'Fine,' I said, looking up into his eyes. 'Break up with her and ask me out. Then I might say yes.'

He called me that night. 'Done,' he said. 'I broke up with Miranda.'

'How do I know whether to believe you?' I asked, surprised he'd taken such a rash step for me.

'Ask Jody O'Connor,' he said. 'Miranda's probably told her by now.'

'I won't ask her,' I said. 'I don't care that much.'

'Fine,' he said. 'Word will spread. You'll hear about it tomorrow. And I'm going out with you Friday night.'

He showed up at my apartment Friday evening with a dozen roses to take me out for dinner, and he said, 'Pack a bag, Sara Lynn. We're going away for the weekend.'

I buried my nose in the roses, and when I looked up I saw Todd in a different light. 'Where are we going?'

'My folks have a place on Martha's Vineyard. There's an evening flight out of Logan.'

'Well, I can't just take off for the whole weekend,' I said. 'I have things to do. Besides, haven't you ever heard of getting to know someone before you go away for a weekend with them?'

'Come on, Sara Lynn,' he said. 'I've known you all through law school. I broke up with Miranda to be with you. I feel like we're already serious with each other.'

I thought for about one second how romantic it was to have someone just decide, with a snap of his fingers, that he wanted to be serious with me. I thought of how pea green with envy those pasty-looking law school girls would be when it got around that I had been whisked away to an island for my first date with the newly eligible Todd Wilton.

'It's against my better judgment,' I said, 'but I'll go.'

Todd smiled confidently, as if his success in wooing me were all but assured. He liked to win.

We were inseparable after that weekend. I was charmed by his decisiveness in courting me – the flowers that kept coming, the notes that appeared in my locker, the way he'd put his arm around my waist in front of everyone and brag that I was the smartest little thing he'd ever seen. 'She got nine job offers, you know,' he'd say.

When we graduated, we didn't move in together. Mama would have had a fainting spell at that one. 'If he gets the milk for free, he won't buy the cow,' she used to say. That's what I was – a cow to be purchased.

He'd come over for dinner every night, though, and he'd talk, talk, talk about his job – the research he'd done that day, the smartly attired attorney for whom he worked, the way he'd made another new lawyer look bad when he came up with the case that saved the day. It was all I could do to stay awake when he went on about it. I could feel my eyes glaze over as I almost fell forward onto my plate.

But my eyes opened wider than they had in a long time when I walked to Faneuil Hall for lunch the day Conrad told me to prove I had a brain. It was one of those beautiful September days when the sun is high but not hot, the breeze is gentle, and the air smells crisp. I walked from my office without a coat, feeling the sun warm my body and wondering why I believed for a minute that the life I was playacting inside an office building was really living.

As I walked along the cobblestone street, I saw Todd kissing his old girlfriend Miranda on a bench where anyone in the world could see. I turned around, walked back to my office, and opened the law books stacked on my desk. At six-thirty, I put the argument I had written on Conrad's desk and left for my apartment.

Todd and I had it out that night when he came to the door. I told him what I had seen and asked what I was supposed to think.

'Look,' he said, running his hand through his hair and pacing up and down my living room. 'Look . . .'

'I'm looking,' I said pointedly. It was nice to have Todd in the corner, to see him squirm.

'I ran into Miranda on the street a couple of weeks ago and she asked me how my job was going.' He turned to me accusingly and said, 'She was really interested, too.'

'Like I'm not?' I said, arching my eyebrows. 'Like I don't sit and listen to every little stapling of paper you do every day?'

'See?' he said, and pointed at me. 'That's what I mean. Miranda would never say something like that. She's really interested. She's . . . warm.'

'What am I? Cold?' I asked, my arms crossed over my chest.

'Yeah.' He nodded. 'Yeah, you are, actually. Look at you now. You're not even crying or anything.'

'Oh, is that what I'm supposed to do?' I uncrossed my arms and put them on my hips. 'Cry my eyes out for you and beg you to choose me over her? Ha!'

He quickly changed tactics to break up with me before I could break up with him. He hated to lose. 'I've already chosen. I'm marrying her. She's everything I want in a wife.'

'That's about right,' I said. 'You want a little robot to simper at you and tell you how great you are.'

'Don't say such things about Miranda!'

'Oh, please.' I laughed. 'Since I've known you, you've done nothing but cheat on her.'

'I've changed,' he said quietly. 'I know she's who I want.'

'Well, then, you can get out of my apartment.' I marched to the door and threw it open.

'I hope we can still be friends,' he said, looking at me as if I were a client whose case hadn't turned out quite as well as had been hoped for.

'Go to hell!' I said, and slammed the door after him.

Then I started to cry and cry, not because I wouldn't be picking out china patterns and showing off a diamond ring, but because I'd been foolish enough to believe I wanted to marry a man who couldn't even see me.

I quit my job the next day. I hated that job, just like I had hated law school, just like I hadn't found one redeeming quality in Todd Wilton until he convinced me otherwise by sheer force of persuasion.

'I'm leaving,' I told Conrad Dalton. 'I'm going back to New Hampshire to be with my parents.'

'Well, we're sorry to lose you,' he said, but he didn't sound like he'd waste one second before propping up another body to do the work I had done.

I didn't want to set fire to my bridges and watch them burn, didn't have the foolhardy guts to say, 'I hate your goddamn job. It bores me to tears and so do you.' So I minced away, smiling and bowing to the end. 'My parents are aging,' I said by way of explanation. 'They're aging and they need me.'

And then I got into my little red car and tooled up Route 93 back to Ridley Falls, with all my work clothes piled up in the backseat. Beautifully tailored silk blouses and straight skirts and jackets that made me look purposeful and serious and smart. Clothes I vowed I'd never wear again because I was tired of showing everyone I was something I was not.

The truth was, I had no idea who I was on that ride home from Boston. None. My years at law school, my months at my job, my affair with Todd, were a blur already. It was as if I were throwing out the car window onto the highway all those years of being molded into something I never cared to be. I didn't want to be molded anymore; I wanted to be liquid for a while.

I wondered, on that drive back, what my parents would say to me. I pictured my mother's mouth opening into a delicate oval and my father's eyebrows drawing together. I pictured myself tossing my hair back and telling them I wouldn't be marrying Todd, wouldn't be toiling in anybody's law firm, that I was through with Boston and everything that went with it. I pictured myself saying, 'I'm here to stay, Mama,' willing her to see that her daughter was a person in flux, a person altogether different from the precisely defined wonder child she had worked so hard to create.

And who am I now? I can't help but think about it as I park my car in the hotel garage and take the elevator up to the main floor.

Who would I perceive myself to be if I were a stranger watching me approach the front desk?

I would observe my scoop-necked white T-shirt and my pink capri pants. I would note my light-pink-painted toenails in my white leather slide sandals. I would nod approvingly at the Kate Spade bag over my shoulder, the Cartier Tank wristwatch, and the Tiffany pearl earrings. I would imagine that the woman I was watching had everything she could ever want.

⌐

My head clears when I arrive at the garden I'm doing a piece on. It has to. I'm working now. I take all the confusion that's been running around my head all day and put it outside me, outside the me who's interviewing Irene Luger, the garden's owner, and Harold Britton, the garden's designer. We're sitting on the patio enclosed by brick walls on which grow ivy and climbing hydrangea. The beds surrounding the stone patio contain a plethora of shade plants – different varieties of hosta, wild ginger, brunnera, ligularia. It's very peaceful and very ordered. There isn't even a stray blade of grass that's dared to grow up through the spaces between the patio stones. It's absolutely perfect.

Mrs. Luger ('Please, call me Irene') is going on and on about the composition she's created using variegated-leaved plants. 'But, really, the importance of editing, especially in a small urban garden, cannot be overstated,' she says rather self-importantly. Mr. Britton sits next to her, smiling at her every word. He knows who butters his bread.

I don't mean to sound so harsh, but I must admit I have a bit of disdain for these women (and men – I've met one or two in the course of my job) like Mrs. Luger who call themselves gardeners even though they've hired professional landscape designers to create their gardens and an army of worker bees to care for them. It's not that I have anything against using professionals – in fact, I think it's wise. It's just that you don't call yourself a doctor when you have your appendix removed simply because the organ operated on happens to be yours.

'Yes,' I say, smiling brightly. 'You're so wise to understand the importance of editing in the garden. It's really what separates the merely pleasing gardens from the truly breathtaking ones.' Hmm. Guess I'm not the only one aware of who's buttering the bread around here. Flatter the garden's owner and she'll tell all her friends how simply marvelous it was working with you, how you really understood what she was trying to achieve in the garden. Her friends, each with her own plot of land and gifted landscape professional, may well be your next piece for the magazine. You eat what you kill, after all. Have to keep those story ideas coming. I smile even wider at her.

I finish at about five, with Irene waving me out the door after serving me some delicious iced tea. Each ice cube in my heavy crystal glass contained a sprig of mint. I think about this as I walk back to my hotel, imagining the maid painstakingly placing a mint leaf in each ice cube tray slot. I'm not like that. I'm not. I've never even thought of anything as ridiculous as mint sprigs in my ice cubes. And my garden certainly isn't weedless. Sometimes I even leave stray seedlings where they happen to come up, not pulling them because I want to see what will happen when nature is the gardener instead of me. That's spontaneity. Isn't it?

Oh, I'm just cross with myself because I'm meeting Sam in an hour. I instinctively check my watch. Fifty minutes, now. I'm meeting him in fifty minutes. I hurry across the street, picking up the pace. I've got to shower, do my hair and makeup, get my emotions in order. Breathe. Breathe. No time. Not enough time. Should have taken a cab. I'm jogging a little, looking ridiculous, I'm sure. But there's nothing I hate worse than feeling pressed for time. Oh, if only I hadn't accepted Irene Luger's mint-ice-cubed tea. Drat.

I run up the hotel's stone steps, and the doorman nods to me and opens the door. I'm dashing through the lobby when I see Sam, and I'm so surprised that it feels like I've had all the breath knocked out of me. I stop short.

'What are you doing here?' I ask as he stands and walks over to me.

'Hi to you, too,' he says easily. He's so tall, I come up only to his shoulders. His hair is still damp from a shower and parted straight in a way that always make me think of little boys' hair.

'Wasn't I . . . ?' I look up at him, flustered. 'Wasn't I supposed to meet you at six?' It's not like me to confuse times, it truly isn't. Maybe I'm losing my mind. I look at how young he is and smile wryly. Maybe it's Alzheimer's.

'Yeah, you were,' he says. 'I got antsy.'

'Phew,' I say, relaxing my shoulders. 'I thought I'd made a mistake.'

He laughs. 'So what if you had?'

I can feel my annoying blush creep up my cheeks. 'Well, I didn't mean that I never make mistakes. It's just that if I was supposed to meet you at five, I would have been keeping you waiting. And I hate keeping people waiting. It's very rude.' Oh, God. I'm babbling. *Shut up, Sara Lynn.* I remember to breathe. Oxygen in, carbon dioxide out.

He puts his hands on my shoulders. 'Breathe,' he says.

I raise my eyebrows. 'That's just what I was doing.'

'I know. I'm helping you.'

I must be red as a tomato by now. 'It's hard to breathe when someone's watching you.'

He laughs. 'I guess you're right. You just seem out of breath.'

'Well, I was rushing back here to be on time, and then here you were, and . . . Why are you here so early again? You got *antsy*?' I don't mean to sound annoyed, but honestly, I'd planned on showering and changing. I'd planned on looking perfect. Mint-ice-cube perfect. And here he's gone and spoiled it all.

'Yes,' he says lightly. 'I got antsy to see you. It's been a while.'

184

'A while?' I protest. 'I see you at the club practically every day.'

'It's not the same,' he says, shaking his head. 'We have to keep everything' – he leans in to me and whispers in an exaggerated fashion – 'secret.'

'Now, hold on,' I say, putting my hands on my hips. 'There's nothing to keep secret. Nothing. We had an enjoyable time visiting the lavender garden, and now we're . . . we're just going out to dinner. Nothing at all to keep secret.'

'Then why was I instructed not to tell a soul about the "enjoyable time" we had last week or, God forbid, about meeting you here?' His eyes are dancing. He's teasing me, and I don't know that I find it so amusing.

'Because I have Hope,' I hiss. 'Because things at home are a little complicated.'

'Hey,' he says, his eyes softening, 'I'm just kidding around. Listen, everything's cool with me. Really. I'm just happy to be here with you. That's why I came early. Because I like being with you. That's all.'

'Oh,' I say. He likes being with me. Well, that's sweet. And just when I was getting my dander up.

We stand looking at each other for a minute, and then I brush my hand through my hair. 'I really wanted to shower and change,' I say.

'Why?' he asks.

I *tsk* my tongue. 'Because that's generally what people do before they go out on a . . .' I stop myself from calling it a date. 'Before they go out for dinner.'

'No, I mean, why do *you* need to do anything to yourself? You'd look amazing in a paper bag.'

I can feel a corner of my mouth turn up. I shift my bag higher onto my shoulder and check my watch. 'At least let me run upstairs for a minute. Just to freshen up a bit.'

He nods. 'Okay. I'll wait down here.'

I want to tease him the way he's been teasing me, to say something like 'Don't go away, now, you hear?' But, of course, the words stick in my throat, and I just say, 'Bye,' as I turn and stride toward the elevator bank. I sneak a peek back at him as the elevator opens, and he's watching me, smiling. I whip my head forward as I step into the elevator. As the doors shut and the bell rings, I can't help but turn up both corners of my mouth.

The elevator stops at my floor, and I walk down the hall languidly, as if I haven't a care in the world. Well, doesn't that change the second I unlock my room door. I race into my room, throwing off my top and unzipping my pants. I'm going to wear the black sundress I bought for tonight, come hell or high water. I sniff under my arms just before I slide the dress on. I'm fine, really. I don't smell. Not that I ever do. But I still wish there were time for a shower. I zip up the back of my dress and slide into the strappy black sandals I bought to go with it. I stand up straight and take a breath, then trot into the bathroom. A little blush, concealer, mascara, lipstick – no time for anything but a little refresher, a little pick-me-up. I brush my teeth quickly and then study myself in the mirror as I run a brush through my hair. Should I put it up? I twirl it around and pile it on top of my head. No. I shake my head. No time for that. I give myself one last look in the mirror, and then I change my wallet, phone, keys, and tissues from my big purse to my small black satin clutch. I hear Ruth's voice in my head, and I smile. 'How many goddamn purses do you need, Sara Lynn?' she asks whenever I come home with another one. It's always been my belief that a girl can't have too many, and here's proof. I've never had occasion to use this particular bag before tonight, but I'm awfully glad I had it in my closet ready to go.

I leave my room and walk down the hall, my heels clicking on the marble floor at the elevator. As I ride down to the lobby, I smooth the skirt of my dress and wonder what Ruth would say if she knew what I was doing right now. Though we've lived together twelve years, she doesn't really know me. She only sees me the way I was in high school, cocky about the future and so sure of myself that it takes my breath away to recall it. She doesn't see how afraid I am, afraid of everything.

As I walk out of the elevator and across the lobby, I spy Sam, putting down the paper he's reading and rising from his chair. His admiring gaze fills me with so much hope that I feel dizzy for a second, as if I might wobble on my heels. I smile.

'Well, you couldn't resist, could you. You had to change.'

I laugh. 'Yes, that's right. I've been looking for an occasion to wear this dress, and I wasn't going to let you spoil it just because you decided you were "antsy."'

'Fair enough.' He touches my arm and says, 'And you do look beautiful.'

I can feel myself blush, and I instinctively look away from him. 'Let's go, shall we?' I murmur.

'Our dinner reservation's not until seven. Would you like to walk around until then?'

'Sure,' I say. 'I used to live around here, you know. Back when I first got out of law school.'

'Oh yeah.' He smiles. 'Hope told me you used to be a lawyer.'

'In a past life, I always say.' We're walking down the hotel steps into the early evening air. It's cooling off a bit, but the sun is still a hot red ball in the sky, just waiting to set.

'Why'd you quit?'

'How do you know I wasn't fired?' I say half-jokingly.

'Were you?' he asks.

'No.' I shake my head. 'I quit.'

'So . . . why?'

'Because it wasn't right for me.' We're ambling up toward Beacon Hill. 'It made me feel dead inside.'

He chuckles. 'That's a very good reason to quit something.'

'Have you always known you wanted to paint?' I ask.

'Yup. But it took a while to convince my parents. My dad runs a manufacturing business back in Ohio. Since I was little, he wanted me to go into the business with him.'

'What does he manufacture?' I ask.

187

'Safety cones.'

'Safety cones?' I look up at him and laugh; it's such an unexpected answer.

'You know . . . those orange cones you see on the highway when there's roadwork.'

'Oh, I know what they are. It's just that I've never really thought about . . . well, that someone actually makes those things.'

'There's money to be made in safety cones, my friend,' he says in a teasing voice. 'Just ask my dad.'

'So what did he say . . . how did he react when you told him you didn't want to make safety cones?'

'Well, I think my sister had pretty much broken my parents in by that point.' He shakes his head and smiles, as if remembering something funny. 'So it wasn't that tough. Although Dad still takes me aside every Christmas and says, "Son, you know you're always welcome in the business if this art thing doesn't work out."'

I laugh at his imitation of his father and ask, 'What did your sister do that broke them in? Join the circus?'

'Sort of,' he says wryly. 'She was an actress.' He says "actress" in a funny, dramatic way that makes me smile.

'An actress? Would I know her work?'

'Not unless you were a big fan of off-off-off-Broadway plays about six or seven years ago.'

'Oh, she doesn't act anymore?'

'No,' he says, shaking his head. 'Actually, she's dead.'

I stop in my tracks. 'Oh, Sam,' I say. 'I'm so sorry.'

He nods and keeps walking, his head bent toward the ground. 'Yeah. It was a while ago – five years.' Now he stops and looks up. 'God,' he marvels. 'She's been gone five years.'

'What . . . what happened?' I don't know if I should ask, but he seems to want to talk about her.

'Cancer. She got it when she was twenty-eight and made it two years. She died when she was thirty.'

188

'Oh God,' I say, touching his arm. 'What a shame.'

'Yeah,' he says, exhaling. Then he turns and smiles, and he's the Sam I know again, teasing and happy. 'That's why it's a good idea to quit something that makes you feel dead inside – because you may be dead sooner than you think.' He looks up at the sky and points to the sun. 'It's finally setting,' he says. Then he continues, 'Julie was an amazing person.' He lets out a short laugh. 'It sounds goofy, but she taught me so much about how to live.'

'How to live,' I repeat quietly. Then I ask, before I can think better of it, 'How to live? How do you live?'

He flashes me a smile. 'Like there's no tomorrow.' Then he laughs and says, 'That's why I showed up early tonight – I was sitting around looking forward to seeing you, and then I decided it would be more fun to be with you as opposed to just thinking about being with you.'

'So you do things just because you feel like it?'

'I try to,' he says. 'Because what else do I have to go on that's more reliable?'

What he says hurts me with its beauty. It's so pure and guileless, so unafraid, so unlike the way I've lived my life. 'I'm thirty-seven,' I tell him, and I don't know why I choose right now to tell him my age. Perhaps I'm warning him, giving this trusting man information he doesn't yet have. Perhaps I'm warning myself, saying I'm a fool if I think I can change my cautious ways at this late date in my life.

He nods. 'I know.'

'You . . . ? How do you know?' It's certainly not something I've brought up.

'Hope.'

'Hope?' My shoulders stiffen. That little busybody, telling my business all over town.

He must sense my anger, for he explains, 'I asked her. I just wanted to know.'

'Why did you want to know?' I snap. 'To see if I was in an appropriate age range? What if I'd been forty? Would that have been too old?'

'No,' he says gently. 'No. It wouldn't have been too old. I asked her because I couldn't get you out of my head. This was after you and I went to the lavender garden together. I just . . . I wanted to know everything about you. What cereal you eat, what time you go to bed, your favorite season. Everything. So I sort of worked you into my conversations with Hope – general questions like how old you were, how long you'd been working at the magazine, what kinds of things you two do together, stuff like that.'

I'm flabbergasted. Utterly flabbergasted. He wanted to know about me? He actually thought about me all week? But he's so full of life, so sunny, so . . . so young. 'How old are you?' I ask, more shrilly than I mean to sound.

'I'm twenty-nine,' he says calmly.

'Twenty-nine,' I say quietly, shaking my head. I look straight at him. 'Why do you want to be here with me? I'm eight years older than you.'

'What do you mean, why do I want to be here with you?' He sounds frustrated.

'It's not an unreasonable question,' I say huffily.

He sighs, then shrugs. 'I just like you, okay?' he says. 'I get a kick out of you. Since that first day I met you, when you brought Hope to her lesson and you were practically doing cartwheels and wringing your hands at the same time trying to make sure she'd be okay, I just liked you.'

'I wasn't doing cartwheels,' I say haughtily.

He laughs. 'And you're funny. You're a funny person.'

'Funny odd? Or funny ha-ha?' I snap, because if he says I'm funny in an odd way, I'm going back to my hotel and ordering room service.

'Funny ha-ha,' he says.

Well, it's better than funny odd, but I still don't see it. I shake my head and put my hands on my hips. 'I really am not the least bit funny,' I say. 'I can't even tell a joke properly.'

He bursts out laughing and says, 'See? That's funny. You're funny.'

I try not to let him see how pleased I am, so I throw up my hands and act exasperated. 'Okay, I'm funny,' I say. 'So funny that you don't care I'm eight years older than you.'

'God!' he says, grabbing my hand and squeezing. 'Age is just a number! What's eight years when two people feel a connection to each other?' He drops my hand and ducks his head, adding, 'Actually, I don't know that you feel a connection with me. I was being presumptuous.'

No! I want to say. *I do feel it. I feel it for the first time in thirteen years. And why did you have to let go of my hand? I liked it; I liked my hand in yours.* 'Well,' I finally say, 'I . . . I enjoy being with you.' *Stop it, Sara Lynn,* I warn myself. *Just stop it.* 'Look,' I say, putting on my reasonable lawyer's voice, 'let's just enjoy dinner together and leave it at that. I've already told you I don't want my life complicated.'

We stride along together for a moment, and he muses, 'An uncomplicated life. Isn't that an oxymoron?'

⁓

At dinner, we talk and talk and, unfortunately, drink and drink as well. I'm a lightweight to begin with, and I swear these wineglasses are larger than normal. I've had only a glass and a half, and my head feels light while my limbs feel luxuriantly heavy.

'So tell me more about safety cones,' I say jokingly, and then I laugh as if I've uttered the wittiest statement in the world. I think Sam's comment about me being funny has gone to my head as much as the wine.

He puts his elbows on the table and leans across to me. 'You really got a charge out of the whole safety cone thing, didn't you?' he asks, pointing his fork at me and smiling.

'I'm sorry,' I say, still laughing. 'It's just . . . I've never known anyone who makes safety cones.'

'I don't make safety cones,' he replies, bringing his eyebrows together in a mock scowl. 'I make art, remember?'

I laugh a little more loudly than I mean to, and I cover my mouth. 'Oops,' I whisper. 'I forgot to modulate my voice.'

'Modulate your voice?'

I giggle. Giggle? Me? Under normal – that is, nonalcoholic – circumstances, I do not giggle. 'Something my mother used to say.' I clear my throat and imitate my mother's commanding tones. 'A lady must mod-u-late her voice.'

Sam throws back his head and laughs, and I point my finger at him. 'You're not modulating your voice, either.'

He leans in toward me. 'Yes, but I'm not a lady.'

I giggle again and say, 'That's true.' Then I wave my hands and say, 'Listen, you know how you said I was funny? Funny ha-ha?'

'Yes, I remember,' he says, and his eyes are shining.

'Well,' I say, 'I have something funny to tell you. The woman I interviewed for the magazine today . . . she was so perfect. She was so perfect that there weren't any weeds in her garden, and here's the funny part . . .' I'm laughing, and I force myself to stop and clear my throat before I continue. I lean over to look right at Sam. Oh, it's so funny. 'Each ice cube in the iced tea she served me had a perfect sprig of mint frozen in the middle of it!'

He's looking at me a little puzzled, as if he's waiting for the punch line, and I have the uncomfortable sensation that my little anecdote was amusing only to me. I take another sip of wine and keep talking so he doesn't see how foolish I feel. 'You know . . . I am not at all like that woman. Not at all.' Oh, my God. What on earth am I saying? My tongue is tripping along, and the usual censors in my mind aren't working. I put down the glass of wine and push it away slightly. That's enough of that.

'What do you mean?' asks Sam.

He's looking confused, and I can tell I blew it again. I'm not witty or charming or anything except socially impaired. I feel my face going red, and I start to fuss with the teaspoon sitting unused by my plate. 'Well . . .' I don't look at him. 'It's just that some people might *imagine* me to be the kind of person who'd put mint in my ice cubes. You know, because I'm . . . well, I'm a little precise. A little practical. A little . . . unemotional.' I whisper the last word as if I'm confessing something shameful.

Sam puts his hand over mine. 'You're *not* unemotional,' he says, and I blink back the sudden tears that spring to my eyes. It's just such a relief that someone sees this about me, that someone can see beyond the facade I throw up to the world. He leans toward me and says, 'You're beautiful, passionate, feeling, complicated.'

He's taking it a little to the extreme, and I laugh, pulling my hand away from his. 'Are you trying to seduce me?' I joke. Oh, God. Where are these statements that keep blurting out of my mouth coming from? I must never, ever drink again. Not a drop.

'Yes, I am,' he says seriously.

I must look horrified, because he laughs and says, 'Kidding. Well, half kidding, anyway.' His voice turns serious again when he says, 'But I meant what I said about you. You're *not* unemotional.'

'Thank you,' I say, my voice soft.

'Don't thank me,' he says, raising his glass as if he's toasting me. 'I only speak the truth.'

⁓

After dinner, it's cooled down some. The streetlamps glow softly over the brick sidewalks on which we walk, and the evening air is noticeably lighter than the stickiness of this afternoon. It's uncomfortably hot, though, especially after the cool restaurant.

I wave my hand in front of my face. 'Whew! It's still so humid,' I complain.

'That's New England for you,' Sam says. 'In six months we'll be complaining about the cold.'

193

'I'd love to go for a swim right now,' I tell him. 'There's a pool on the rooftop of my hotel, but it closes at eight. Maybe tomorrow morning, before I check out.'

'You want to walk down by the harbor? It'll be cooler there.'

'Sure,' I say. 'Inspired idea.'

'Cab or walk?'

'Hmm?' I ask.

'Do you want to take a cab or walk it from here?'

'Oh, walk,' I say. 'It's not *that* far.'

'My kind of girl,' Sam says, and I feel warm inside to hear him say that. It's just natural, I suppose, to want to be *somebody's* kind of girl.

<hr>

It is cooler by the harbor, and it's romantic, too. I'm a little surprised and, yes, I'll be honest, disappointed that Sam hasn't tried to kiss me. Then he stops and turns to face me, and I catch my breath, my heart fluttering like a schoolgirl's. This is it. This is it.

'Hey,' he says, 'I've been wondering: How did it happen that you're raising Hope?'

Okay. This isn't it. It's something else altogether. 'You really want to know?' I ask, folding my arms over my chest.

'Yeah,' he says. 'I do.'

'Well . . .' I take a deep breath and tell him the truth, the words I've never said out loud. 'She's my ex-lover's child. His and his wife's child, that is. His wife died and he took off – reliability wasn't one of Bobby's strong suits – and he left Hope to me. To me and his sister. It's been twelve years now, and I've never heard from him.'

'So he's not in the CIA?' I look up and see Sam's eyes gleaming.

'What?!' Then I groan. 'Oh God, did Hope tell you that?'

He nods, and I say tartly, 'No. Bobby's most definitely not in

194

the CIA. I can just about guarantee that.' I laugh then, a short bark, and say, 'Although he is a man of mystery, just taking off and leaving me to raise Hope. To this day, I have no idea why he left his daughter to me.'

'I do,' Sam answers. He holds my shoulders and looks down at me, his eyes soft. 'You love Hope, Sara Lynn. I saw it that first day you brought her to her lesson. He must have known you'd love her. He must have seen what I see in you – a goodness. A decency.' He smiles. 'And lots of emotion, too. He must have known he could trust you with Hope.'

'Thank you,' I say briskly, and I turn away because I don't want to be kissed right now, not with Hope standing between us, reminding me I'm hers and not his.

It's almost midnight by the time a cab drops us back at my hotel. We capitulated and took a taxi, but only because of the late hour, not because we weren't hardy enough to walk.

Sam walks me up the stone steps of the hotel and motions to the bar just in the doorway. 'Nightcap?' he suggests.

'No!' I laugh. 'I had quite enough to drink tonight, thank you very much.'

'See, that's your practical side coming out.' His eyes twinkle as he leans in to me. 'Your *unemotional* side.'

I'm used to his teasing by now, and I laugh, hitting his arm gently.

He grabs my hand and whirls me in toward him, kissing me searchingly, like he's drinking me in. It's been thirteen years since a man has kissed me, and I'm moving closer and closer to him, not wanting it to end.

'Want to go swimming?' he murmurs into my hair when the kiss is over and we come up for air.

'We can't,' I say automatically. 'Remember? I told you the hotel pool closed at eight.'

'So what?' he whispers, and that's when an image comes into my mind of me taking caution, crinkling it into a ball, and waving good-bye to it as I throw it to the wind.

I pause for a second, and then I whisper back, 'Yes. I would like to go swimming.'

He kisses me again, a quick kiss this time, a promise of what's ahead. He pulls away from me then and offers me his arm. 'To the roof, Miss Hoffman?' he asks with mock dignity.

I place my hand on his arm and stand up straight. 'To the roof.'

When we get up there, the roof deck is pitch-dark, and I trip over a lounge chair. 'Ow!' I say, grabbing my hurt foot.

'Are you okay?' Sam's voice asks.

'Yes, let me just . . . can I grab on to you?'

'Um, yeah!' He laughs. 'Please do.'

I reach out for him and he pulls me in, kissing me again. 'I can't see a darn thing,' I say between kisses.

'Me neither,' he replies, caressing my back.

'So it's the blind leading the blind, is that it?'

'Pretty much.' He sounds utterly unconcerned. I can't say I'm overly worried myself, not when I'm in Sam's arms like this.

'Now listen,' he says, and I can tell from the sound of his voice that he's teasing me again. 'Never let it be said I'm not a perfect gentleman. You said you'd like a swim and I, well, I aim to please.'

My mouth twists up as I wait for him to continue. This is going to be good.

'It's pretty dark here, and as you yourself said, neither of us can see a thing.'

He pauses, and I say, 'Yes?'

'So, being a perfect gentleman, I'm wondering if I should help you off with that dress. You know, just so you'll be able to take a

196

swim, like you wanted. And since I can't *see* anything, it wouldn't be completely improper.'

I'm laughing and shaking my head. 'Sure,' I say, throwing up my hands. 'Since you can't *see* anything, I guess that would be all right.'

My legs go weak when I feel his hand on my zipper and hear the sound of him unzipping the back of my dress. I step out of my shoes as my dress slides to the floor, and he unhooks my bra and lightly touches my breasts. 'Oh God,' he says, his voice a low moan.

I'm breathing faster now and manage to gasp out, 'Since, um, I can't *see* anything, either, would you like a little help with your clothes? Reciprocity and all that.'

'Reciprocity, huh?' he says. He kisses me hard. 'Yeah. I think reciprocity is a very good thing.'

My hands tremble as I reach out to unbutton his shirt and slide it off him. He pulls my body to his, and he's so warm and good-smelling that I cling to him, kissing his chest again and again and running my hands up and down his smooth, bare back. I can feel his maleness pressing against me, and I want more of him. I want. Two words I haven't allowed myself to feel in some time. I want. I want. I want.

I undo his belt, and he swallows hard as I unzip his pants. Then I pull down his underwear, quickly, in one movement. I want. I want. I want. As I reach for what I want, he tries to step out of his pants and falls backward, pulling me with him. We tumble over lounge chairs and finally hit the cement, me on top of him. Neither of us says anything for a moment.

'Shit,' Sam finally says.

I'm utterly horrified at the entire situation, but then – I can't help it – I laugh and laugh and laugh. This is the absolute an-tithesis of a mint-ice-cube love scene. This would never be hap-pening to Irene Luger.

Sam's laughter joins my own. 'Are you okay?' he asks.

'I'm fine,' I assure him. 'More than fine. How about you?'

'I'll live.' He kisses the top of my head. 'You want to get in the pool, now that I've totally spoiled the mood?'

'You haven't spoiled anything. But, yes, I think taking a swim would be lovely just now.'

I can feel him struggling to get his pants off, and I say, 'Here, let me.' I feel around for his legs, his feet. 'It's your shoes!' I tell him. 'Don't you know you're supposed to take your shoes off so your pants won't get stuck?' I pull them off, then slide off his pants and boxers.

'Thanks,' he says. He moves in to kiss me but hits my eye instead of my lips. I giggle as he moves his lips down to my mouth and cups his hands around my rear end. 'You're not naked yet, Miss Hoffman,' he chides.

'That's because my date hasn't gotten around to taking my underwear off.'

'The guy must be a real idiot,' he says, sliding his hands over my hips and slipping down my panties.

'Well, he may be,' I say, catching my breath. 'The jury's still out on that question.'

He chuckles as he stands up, pulling me up with him. 'You're going in the pool for that one,' he says. We cling to each other as we try to make our way over to the water. Finally, we reach the edge of the pool and he says, 'Ready?'

I know what he's asking, and it's not just about jumping in the water. I nod, even though he can't see me. 'Ready,' I tell him, and he holds my hand as we step off the edge.

Chapter 17

$\mathcal{R}$uth's been barfing her guts out for days now. Barfing. Isn't that a great word? It sounds just like what it is. Barfing. To barf. Barf-o-rama. I'm not allowed to say it, because Sara Lynn thinks it's crude. Ruth goes along with her because she says she doesn't want me growing up like she did, all rough around the edges. But they don't know what I'm thinking, do they? And what I'm thinking is that Ruth's barfing like crazy.

Okay, so I'm exaggerating a little. She's really actually barfed only about three times. But she looks barfy all the time, heaving with nothing coming out. And the heaving's only after a couple of hours of looking miserable, like she's eaten something bad for her.

'You're not doing yourself or us any favors by not going to the doctor,' Sara Lynn keeps telling her.

'Nothing to see a doctor about,' Ruth replies, practically gagging. 'Just a little stomach bug.'

She still goes to work and everything. It's just that when she's home, she sort of lies around looking 'green about the gills,' as Mamie would say.

She's half sitting, half lying on the couch in the den right now, watching TV. I squeeze in beside her. 'Hey,' I say. 'What're you doing?'

199

'Watching the news,' she says with a groan. She reaches for the TV remote on the floor and aims it at the screen, clicking the set off. 'Goddamn depressing,' she says. 'Take it from me – there's never a good reason to watch the news. If the world's ending, we'll all find out about it soon enough without Mr. Anchorman's help.' She leans back on the sofa with a hand on her stomach.

'How're you feeling?' I ask.

'Lousy,' she says. 'My stomach's flipping like a fish. How're you?'

'Me?' I shrug. 'Okay, I guess.'

'Anything new? How's tennis?'

I perk up. 'Awesome! I'm doing so great. Sam says I'm really making a lot of progress. And he . . . he's just nice. He talks to me like I'm a real person, not a kid.'

'Well, you are a real person.' Ruth tries to smile and pulls one of my curls.

I roll my eyes. 'You know what I mean. We talk about stuff. Stuff like life and, you know, falling in love.'

'Falling in love, huh?' She manages a little laugh.

'Have you ever?' I ask. 'Been in love, I mean?'

'Oh yeah,' she answers right away, nodding.

'Who with? I mean, with whom?'

'Father Flanagan,' she says, all serious, and I groan and hit her arm. He's been the priest at the Catholic church for about a hundred years, which would put him at about a hundred and twenty-five years old.

'Be serious,' I tell her.

'I am,' she says, trying not to laugh. 'He's the sexiest thing I've ever laid eyes on. I've longed for him for years. From afar, of course.'

I shake my head and put it in my hands. 'Everyone in this house is crazy,' I say.

'Ha!' Ruth chortles. 'You don't even know the half of it.'

After Ruth goes up to bed – at, like, seven-thirty, for crying out loud – I decide to take a walk around the neighborhood. Not for any reason or anything; not because I'm hoping to run into someone or anything. I just feel like walking.

So here I am just minding my own business when who do you suppose rides his bike up behind me? Yup – Dumb Dan. Mr. Happy. Mr. 'I'm so positive and you're so negative.' I keep my eyes straight ahead, like I don't see him, but he's so clueless that he doesn't even get that I'm trying to ignore him.

'Hey, Hope,' he says.

'Hi.' I keep walking.

'What's going on?'

'Not much.' Walk, walk, walk.

'Any luck on the you-know-what front?'

'Nope.'

'You still trying?'

'I guess.'

He sighs. 'Well, see you around,' he says, and he rides his bike around me.

I shout after him, 'I am not a negative person!'

He brakes and turns around. 'Huh?'

'You said I was a negative person!' I stop walking and cross my arms over my chest. 'When we were up at Lakewood School and you were shooting baskets.'

'I didn't say that,' he says. He's looking at me like I'm nuts.

'You did so! When I didn't jump up and down all excited about your brainiac idea to call Information to find my father.'

'I didn't say you were a negative person. I said you were being negative about finding your father.'

'Same difference.'

'No, it's not. You' – he points to me – 'aren't negative. You have negative feelings about finding your father probably because you're conflicted about it.'

Now it's my turn to look at him like he's crazy. 'What are you talking about?'

He hops off his bike and walks it over to me. 'Look. You want to find your father, right?' I nod. 'Sure you do,' he says. 'That makes sense. But you're also probably pretty scared about it. Wondering about what he'll be like, what he'll say after all this time, whether he'll even like you. You know, things like that.'

I blink a few times. Dan's not so dumb after all. 'How do you know all this stuff?' I ask.

He shrugs and grins, his braces shining. 'My mom. She's a psychologist.'

'She is?' My eyes get wide. 'Like she helps crazy people?'

'Who's not crazy?' he asks. 'That's what my mom says. She says we all have our issues.'

I narrow my eyes. 'So did you tell your mom about me? About me trying to find my father?'

He puts his hands up and says, 'No way! I told you I wouldn't tell, and I haven't.'

'Hmm,' I say.

We walk the rest of the way around the block until we get back to my house, and it's getting dark. The outdoor lights have clicked on, and my house looks like it's waiting for me, like it's saying, *I'm here, Hope, and I'm not going anywhere.*

'I better go in,' I say. 'I'll see you.'

'Okay,' he says. I walk briskly up the driveway, and he calls, 'Hope?'

'Yeah?' I turn around.

'You're not a negative person.'

'I know I'm not,' I call back. I take a few more steps and then turn around again. Dan's still at the bottom of my driveway. 'Hey,' I call, 'thanks for saying that.'

He smiles and hollers back, 'No problem.'

'Bye,' I call.

'Good night, Hope.'

As I walk up the front steps to let myself into the house, I can still hear my name ringing in the twilight.

Chapter 18

I paper-clip the lunch receipts and put them in the far right compartment of the cash register drawer. It's two-thirty, and I walk back to the kitchen and poke my head in. 'Bye, Chet,' I say. 'I'm through for the day.'

He grunts at me. Hasn't said anything about me making a habit of leaving early. Probably knows I'd bite his head off. I just can't risk seeing Jack again. I can't face him. I haven't really thought about how he'll react when my belly gives the game away, but I'll cross that bridge when I get to it. That's the upside of not being a planner. Unlike some people whose names I won't mention, I don't stew over things that haven't happened. I've got a little bit of time yet before anyone knows a baby's coming.

I don't know when I decided I'd have this kid; it just sort of came to me gradually. Every day without making a decision was a day closer to one being made for me. And now I'm headed to the doctor's over in Holliston to confirm what I know to be true.

When I step into the doctor's office, I feel like a duck out of water. Three women with big bellies smile at me as I join them in the waiting room, two of them with small children climbing all over them.

'Why is that lady here, Mom?' a little boy says, pointing to me. 'She doesn't have a baby growing in her tummy.'

'Hush, Tommy.' The woman smiles at me apologetically. 'Mind your own business.'

'But this is the baby doctor. You have to have a baby in your tummy to come here.'

'Shh,' she says, frowning as she bends down to him.

'It's all right,' I say, and wave my hand to let her know I'm not at all sensitive. I tell the little boy, 'I do have a baby in my tummy. You just can't see it yet.'

I think about what I just said, and I shake my head, not quite believing it. A baby! God, it's been twelve years since I've taken care of a baby. Twelve years since Bobby came home with Hope.

⁓

Two weeks after Ma was dead and buried, Bobby called with his news, and it was then that my anger at all these losses rose beyond what I could bear, like a poison corroding my insides.

'Ruth,' he said, his voice sounding dull to me.

'Did the baby come?' I asked. Bobby and Sandra hadn't been able to make it down for Ma's funeral because Sandra was so close to her due date. I could tell that Ma's friends had thought Bobby was disrespectful for staying away, but I knew Ma would have wanted him to be with Sandra while she gave birth. Ma had always resented the fact that while she was doing the laboring, my father had been out getting a jump on the celebrating. She would have been glad to know that Bobby was different.

'Yeah,' Bobby said. 'She came.'

'A girl!' I said, feeling the first glimmer of happiness I had felt in a long time. It took me by surprise; I had forgotten how to feel anything except sorrow or nothing at all.

'Ruth,' Bobby said again, almost like he was warning me about something.

'Aren't you thrilled?' I asked. 'How's Sandra feeling?'

'Ruth, she died.'

'Oh, my God,' I said. My legs gave way and I sank to the floor, panting hard to catch my breath. 'Oh, my God. Oh, my God. Your little baby girl.'

'No, it's Sandra. Not the baby.'

'Sandra?' I moaned. I pressed the phone to my ear, hoping I hadn't heard right. 'Sandra died?'

'Yeah,' he said in a flat voice that sounded too far away from me. 'She died having the baby. Bled to death.'

'Bled to death?' I yelled. 'What do you mean? That doesn't happen anymore.'

There was silence on the other end of the phone, and I forced myself to stop carrying on. 'I'll come up today,' I told Bobby. 'Just let me make a few calls and throw my things together.'

'No,' he said. 'I'm coming home. I buried her already, and I'll be home with the baby.'

'What do you mean, you've buried her already?' The tears wouldn't stop coming.

He paused. 'How can I make it any clearer to you?'

'I would've come,' I cried into the phone. 'I would've come to say good-bye.'

Bobby had married Sandra right around the time Ma got sick. She was a quiet girl from Maine who worked at the bank. She told us she had come to Ridley Falls because she'd wanted a taste of urban life. I recall thinking life in Maine must have been intolerable if Sandra believed that Ridley Falls had something to offer. She was pregnant when they married, and they moved up to Maine. It wasn't that Sandra had family up there – she had been in foster homes during her growing up – it was that she missed it after all. She missed the quiet, she said. She wanted to raise her baby where she could hear herself think.

I knew Bobby had wanted to leave town, too, mostly because of Sara Lynn. He had loved that girl like crazy, and she broke his heart into a million pieces before he'd had enough sense to move on and find Sandra, a girl more like him who loved him back. I knew he hadn't wanted to be in the same town as Sara Lynn, and

I also knew he hadn't wanted to watch my mother die. So they'd moved to Maine.

'Dead!' I said after I hung up the phone. I stood up and walked around my dead mother's house and said, 'She's dead!' Then I got out all our cleaning supplies and cleaned the whole house, top to bottom. I feared I would kill someone or choke myself with my own rage if I didn't make myself do something. 'Keep moving, Ruth,' I advised myself as I scrubbed and rinsed and polished and dusted and cried. 'Whatever you do, don't stop moving.'

Bobby came with the baby, and I fell in love right away. I hugged him first, though, before I even looked at her. He was my brother, after all, and I loved him.

'I'm so sorry,' I said, crying yet again when I reached out and felt him move his big-brother arms around me. 'I am just so sorry.'

'Yeah,' he said, 'me too.' He looked dazed, as if he were an actor in his own life, just barely learning the lines.

'Let me see her,' I said through my tears, and I took Bobby's daughter from her little car seat carrier and held her. 'My Lord,' I whispered. 'She's gorgeous.'

'Yeah,' he said again. He started pacing up and down Ma's little kitchen.

'Can I fix you something to eat?' I asked him. 'Sit down.'

'No, no,' he protested, but he sat at the kitchen table as he said it, and I placed his baby into his arms.

'Grilled cheese okay?' I asked, looking into the refrigerator. He didn't answer, but I made it anyway, served it to him, and poured him a glass of milk.

'Sorry there's no chips to go with it,' I said, shrugging. 'I'm losing my mind lately. I go into the grocery store and stand there scratching my head. "Why am I here?" I say as I look around.

"What did I come here to get?" And then I end up getting things I already have or don't need or don't even like.'

He smiled. He must have seen I was trying to make him laugh, like I'd always done. He was kind to smile. He probably felt like telling me to shut my mouth and give him some peace and quiet.

'When I was at the store the other day, I bought a pint of strawberries, and I don't even like them. Never have. Those little raised bumps on them are creepy – look and feel like a nasty skin disease.'

He didn't smile this time, just gave me the baby, picked up his sandwich, and started eating. I figured I'd keep quiet and let him eat. I had no idea what on earth to say that would make him feel better.

'Got to go out and do an errand,' he said when he had finished his sandwich.

'Drink the rest of your milk.' I motioned to the half-full glass. 'Good for your bones.'

He smiled then, a real smile, and shook his head. He left quietly. I didn't even hear the door shut because his baby girl was cooing in my arms.

When he came home a few hours later, he went right back to his old bedroom.

'What's the baby's name?' I called to him from outside his closed door.

'Doesn't have one,' he said.

'Doesn't have one?' I asked, shocked that this child in my arms didn't even have a name to call her own. 'Do you have a name in mind?'

'Nope,' he replied.

'What about Sandra, or Mary, after Ma?'

'No,' he said, and I could tell he was in there crying. It was all I could do to stay at that door without running away and crying myself.

'Okay,' I said. 'What about Hope?' I didn't know why that name popped into my head. It just struck me as a pretty name, a promise that we could put our troubles behind us and find some bit of happiness in this world.

He didn't answer me, and I said again, 'Hope. Do you like Hope?' Even before he answered, I was kissing Hope's forehead, whispering, 'Hope, Hope.'

'Sure,' he said. 'Hope is fine.'

～◯

He was gone the next morning. I found a note in the bowl of fake fruit on the kitchen table – the place we used to leave messages when we were growing up.

> *Ruth:*
>
>   *Sorry, but I have to go away. It just hurts too damn much to stay here after everything that's happened. I've made you and Sara Lynn Hoffman guardians of the baby. Hope, I guess you're calling her. Mr. Dawes downtown has all the papers you'll need to sign. Thank you for doing this for me, and for understanding why I just can't do it myself.*
>
> *Bob*

I read the note a second and then a third time. 'Sara Lynn Hoffman?' I said aloud. 'Sara fucking Lynn Hoffman?' I glanced down at Hope and said, 'Sorry, honey. I'll try and watch my mouth.'

I read the note again. I knew Bobby had thought he was in love with Sara Lynn, but letting her raise his baby? Was he crazy? I adjusted the blanket around Hope's feet and leaned down to her in her car seat as she sucked her pacifier. 'We'll just see about that,' I whispered.

I hefted Hope out to the car and, after about ten minutes of cursing and fiddling with seat belts, strapped her seat in. Then I drove to Mr. Dawes's office. I didn't call ahead or anything, just barged in on his secretary with my hands full of Hope in her car seat and the diaper bag full of all her baby gear. 'Is he in?' I asked Candy Flores.

'Do you have an appointment?' she asked as if she didn't know me. That was Candy all right. Acting above herself just because she put on heels and a suit to go to work in a lawyer's office.

'Candy,' I said, shifting the damn diaper bag on my arm, 'this is an emergency. Just tell him I'm here.'

She turned her little nose up at me and picked up the phone. 'Ruth Teller is here to see you,' she said. When she hung up the phone, she said, 'Go in.'

I marched into Mr. Dawes's office, and he stood to welcome me. 'Have a seat,' he said. I parked myself in a chair across from his desk and set Hope and the diaper bag down beside me. I fumbled through my jeans pocket, took out Bobby's note, and handed it to him. 'What in hell is going on here? Bobby left me this.'

He glanced at the note and said, 'Mmm-hmm. Your brother came in yesterday and had me draw up papers naming you and Sara Lynn as guardians of the child.' He stood and reached into a file cabinet next to his desk and pulled out a folder. 'Here are the papers you need to sign.' He sat back down and peered across his desk at me. 'Is Miss Hoffman aware of the situation?'

'No,' I said. 'And I don't think she needs to know about it, either. This is my niece we're talking about; she doesn't have any relation to Sara Lynn Hoffman.'

Mr. Dawes sighed and rubbed his nose. 'I told Bobby yesterday it didn't make sense. "Pick one or the other," I told him. 'This arrangement you've proposed will never work.'

'"No, sir," he told me. "I know both of these women will make it work."'

I sat limply, trying to take it all in.

'Well, I should probably call her,' said Mr. Dawes, one hand picking up the phone and the other flipping through his Rolodex.

As he dialed, I stood up and held out my hand for the phone. 'I'll do it,' I said. 'It might as well come from me.'

'Hello?' Sara Lynn answered in her cool, rich-girl voice.

'Hi,' I said. 'This is Ruth Teller. I'm calling you from Mr. Dawes's office. You know, the lawyer? You'd better come on down here. I don't know how to say this, so I'll just spit it right out. It seems Bobby has named both of us guardians of his baby girl.'

She gasped. 'Is he . . . is he dead?'

'No,' I told her. 'Just run off someplace.'

'Oh,' she said calmly, as if we were having a perfectly normal conversation. 'Well, I suppose I'd better come down and meet you at Mr. Dawes's office, then.'

'Fine,' I said. 'I'll see you in a few.'

I hung up the phone and sat back down in my chair. 'She's coming,' I said. 'Hope and I'll wait right here for her, if it's all the same to you.' My tone of voice said it had damn well better be okay with him.

He nodded, shuffling some papers. 'I'll just do a little work while we wait.'

He didn't have to busy himself too long before Miss Sara Lynn herself strutted through the door, wearing a white sleeveless blouse and black pants. She was carrying a black leather shoulder bag and had a pair of sunglasses perched back on her head. Miss Fashion Plate. Well, that was Sara Lynn.

'Hi, Dick,' she said, extending her hand to Mr. Dawes. 'And this must be the baby!' she cooed, bending and putting her face right up to Hope's. 'Hi, sweetie-pie! Hi, little girl!'

'Hi, Sara Lynn,' I said, reminding her I was in the room as well.

'Ruth.' She stood up straight from where she was cooing over Hope. 'Hello. Mama asked after you.'

I nodded curtly. 'Well, I'll see her Wednesday, I guess, when I come to clean.'

As she bent over Hope again, she marveled, 'She's the spitting image of her father.'

'I don't know,' I said, just to be contrary. 'I think she looks like Sandra.'

'No.' Sara Lynn shook her head. 'She's Bobby all over.'

'Suit yourself.' I shrugged. 'Although I think I'd know whether she looks like my own brother.'

'Hmmph-hmmph,' Mr. Dawes cleared his throat. 'Should we get down to business?'

Sara Lynn sat in the chair next to mine and folded her hands on her lap. Mr. Dawes looked back and forth at both of us. 'As you know, Bobby Teller has named you guardians of his child. This' – he held up two packets of paper – 'is the paperwork. It's very general. You two have to work out arrangements for where she'll live, how she'll be raised, et cetera. Bobby made it clear that you two were to have equal authority. Not one or the other of you will have more say than the other. Clear?' He looked at me as he said that last bit, as if I were the one in the room used to bossing everyone around and getting my own way.

'Here you are,' he said, pushing the paper packets and pens to our side of the big desk. I picked up the pen and signed right away. I didn't need to read any papers to know I'd be happy to look after my own niece. Sara Lynn was more deliberate, taking her sweet time to read through all the papers.

'This seems fine,' she said, a questioning tone in her voice. She looked up at Mr. Dawes like she wanted him to reassure her.

'I can't tell you what to do, Sara Lynn,' he said, raising his hands in the air. Mr. Dawes was being nice to her just because her father had been a big-shot lawyer in town. It was making me mad.

She hemmed and hawed some more, flipping through those papers with a line between her eyebrows, and finally I said, 'Sara Lynn, did you ever hear that expression about either shitting or getting off the pot?'

She frowned and said in her high-and-mighty voice, 'This is an important decision. I'll take all the time I need to think it through.'

'That's very wise,' said Mr. Dawes, looking at her as if she'd just come down the mountain with ten more commandments.

I rolled my eyes and sighed. 'Here.' I reached into the car seat and picked Hope up, then shoved her into Sara Lynn's arms. 'If you're having trouble making up your mind, you should at least hold her to see what you're dealing with.'

'Oh, my,' she said, tightening her arms around Hope. 'Oh, my.'

I sat watching, my arms folded against my chest. There was a jealous part of me that didn't want her holding Hope. But there was another part of me that was glad. Glad that Sara Lynn, for once in her life, could see I had something precious, something worth having.

Sara Lynn handed Hope back to me, picked up the pen, and clicked it. 'I'll do it,' she said, signing the papers.

'You're sure?' Mr. Dawes asked her.

'Yes, I am.' She straightened the papers and handed them back across the desk.

'All right, then,' he said. He stood to shake her hand. 'Good luck.'

I put Hope back in her car seat carrier and buckled her in. As I picked up the carrier by its handle, Sara Lynn sidled right over and said, 'Why don't you follow me over to my house so we can discuss this. We'll need to make a solid plan.'

'Let's go to my house,' I said, sticking out my chin and gripping that car seat tightly. I wasn't going to have Sara Lynn Hoffman telling me how things were going to be.

Her face froze for a minute, as if she had to take in the fact that I was telling her what to do, but then it cleared and she said, 'Fine. That's just fine.'

'Ruth Teller,' the nurse calls. Jesus, could she say it any louder? I hop up and walk over to her quickly, so she won't say my name again.

'Hi,' she says. She hands me a cup and some wipes and rattles off her orders in a bored voice. 'We need a clean-catch specimen from you. Instructions are on the door of the bathroom. Give me the urine when you're done, and I'll take you into the examining room.'

I walk into the bathroom she points toward, shutting the door behind me. By the time I read and follow all those directions about how and where to wipe, I'm so nervous that I can't pee. I turn on the sink faucet and make it drip a little. An old trick of Ma's. Come on, come on. I close my eyes and out it comes. Oh, Jesus, put the cup underneath.

I hand the cup to the nurse when I come out, and she takes me into the examining room. 'Gown's on the table. Opening's in the back. Doctor'll be with you in a minute.' When she shuts the door, I take a deep breath, strip, and put on the gown.

I sure as hell am not going to sit on the table with the stirrups while I wait for the doctor, so I hold my gown together in the back with one hand and sit on a chair next to the table. A brisk knock on the door makes me about jump out of my skin.

'Hello, Ruth.' It's a small lady with dark hair and glasses, looking at some papers in a folder. 'I'm Dr. Stearns.'

'Hi,' I say weakly.

'We think we're pregnant?' she says, looking down at the papers and then up at me.

'I don't know about you, but I think I am.' I laugh, but she doesn't even crack a smile.

'Okay,' she says. 'Let's have a look at you.'

I know what that means, and I drag myself over to the table and sit on it. 'Feet in the stirrups, now,' she says. I put my feet in those cold metal contraptions and steel myself while she flicks on a bright light and points it at my private parts.

'All right,' she says, snapping on a glove and then sticking her hand inside me. 'Just a little discomfort . . .'

How in hell does she know how it feels? Maybe to me it's a big discomfort, a big old pain in the ass. Literally.

'Yes,' she says. She takes her hand out and nods at me. 'I'm guessing eight weeks.'

It's hard to have a conversation with someone when your feet are up in stirrups and your private parts are exposed to the world. 'Eight weeks,' I whisper.

'Is this good news or bad news?' she asks briskly.

'Can I . . . ?' I motion to my feet in the stirrups, thinking I can't say another word until I'm sure she's looking at my face instead of my ass.

'Sure,' she says. 'Why don't you get dressed, and I'll come back to talk in a minute.'

I get myself down from the torture table and slip out of the gown and into my clothes. I'm sitting back in the regular chair when she knocks and comes in again.

She sits on her little stool and wheels it closer to me. 'So,' she says, smiling. She actually looks a lot nicer than I originally thought. 'You're pregnant.'

'Yes, I am,' I reply.

'Any questions for me?'

'Nooo, I don't think so.'

'You seem a bit overcome by this,' she says, placing her hand on mine. 'I'm guessing this was not a planned pregnancy.'

'You can say that again,' I tell her.

'Would you like termination information?'

'No!' I say right away. 'No! I . . . you know, what in life is planned? You take what comes, right? Besides, I want this baby.' I test the way that sounds on my tongue, and I like it. 'I want this baby.'

'I'm glad for you, then,' she says, and she smiles at me like I'm a real person, not a vagina she's getting paid to look into. 'Would you like to hear the heartbeat?'

'Can I do that?' I ask in amazement.

'Sure can,' she replies. 'Sit up on the table again.'

I look at her like she's asking the impossible, and she laughs. 'No stirrups this time. No getting undressed. Just pull your top up.'

I do as she says, and she rubs some gel on my belly and puts a wand with a rolling tip to my stomach. She rolls it around a bit and then holds it still. The room fills up with a strong, rapid *thump-thump, thump-thump, thump-thump,* and I don't move a muscle as I listen to the rhythm of a heart inside me that belongs to somebody else.

Chapter 19

*D*ang! I have a humongous zit on my chin. It's the size of Texas, I swear. I tilt my chin up to the bathroom mirror and lean in to look at it real close. *Don't pick it. Don't pick it. Don't pick it.* Oh, rats, I can't help it. I squeeze it, first gently and then hard, and some white stuff comes out. I wipe it off and look again. Great, now instead of a raised white spot, I have a big blotchy red spot. Yuk!

I grab a washcloth and swish it under the hot-water faucet, then put it up to my face. When I remove it, I half expect to see the pimple gone, but it's not. It looks even worse. 'Damn,' I say under my breath. 'Double, triple, quadruple damn.'

'Hope!' Sara Lynn calls from downstairs. 'You'll be late for your lesson.'

'Hold on!' I yell. Man, she's so impatient.

I dab the washcloth on my chin again and take it off. I look in the mirror. No luck. I throw the washcloth in the sink and pull down my shorts to sit on the toilet. I check my underwear as I'm sitting there and, as usual, nothing. I put my head between my knees and sigh. I'll be the oldest girl in school with puny breasts and no period.

When Mamie broke her hip two years ago, she had this nurse who kept telling her to visualize her healing. 'Now, Mrs. Hoff-

216

man,' she'd say, 'I want you to close your eyes and picture your-self walking. Picture yourself putting your right foot in front, now your left, now your right. You're not feeling any pain; you're just walking.'

'If I'm walking, then what the devil am I doing sitting in this foolish chair?' Mamie would snap at her.

The nurse would hold up her hand, her own eyes closed. 'No, no,' she'd say. 'Only positive visualization.'

My head still on my knees, I close my eyes and breathe deeply. I'm imagining blood flowing from my insides to my outsides. From my insides to my outsides. From my insides to my outsides.

'Hope!' It's Sara Lynn, banging on my locked door. 'What are you doing in there?'

I wipe, pull up my shorts, and flush. 'What do you think I'm doing in here?' I shout. 'I'm peeing! Peeing!'

Silence, then: 'You know I don't like that term. It's vulgar.'

I grit my teeth and look in the mirror as I wash my hands. That stupid zit is covering my entire chin. Dammit. I pull open the top drawer under the sink and fish around through the combs and elastics and lip glosses for a Band-Aid.

'You're going to be late,' Sara Lynn warns from outside my door. It's a wonder I don't kill that woman; it really is.

I put the Band-Aid on my chin and take one more look at my-self. Ugly, I think, and I want to throw something at the mirror and smash it into a thousand pieces. I wish I were prettier. I wish I were older. I wish my stupid period would come so I would feel like a normal girl.

⌒

'What happened to your chin?'

At least Sara Lynn didn't ask me right when I came out of my room and stomped downstairs and out the door. At least she had the sense to wait until now, when we're in the car. She's driving, so if I kill her, I'm going down with her. Which, come to think of it, might not be a bad idea.

'Nothing,' I mutter, my hand instinctively going up to cover the Band-Aid.

'Were you picking at a pimple?' she asks, and it's not a question; it's like she knows that's exactly what I was doing.

'Like you'd even know what it's like,' I burst out. 'You probably never had a pimple in your whole perfect life!'

She doesn't speak for a minute, then says quietly, 'Is that what you think? That I've had a perfect life?'

I don't answer, just look out the window.

'Well, I haven't. I don't. I've had my share of 'pimples' – some on the outside and some on the inside, where you can't see them. Maybe I don't . . . I don't know . . . talk about it the way I should, but it's true. My life is far from perfect.'

She sounds a little sad, and her sadness makes my anger disappear. I wish I were little so I could throw my arms around her and cry and cry. Instead, I just kick my foot a little and whine, 'Sara Lynn, when are things going to start happening to me?'

'What kinds of things, honey?' she asks.

What do I say that won't sound stupid? I want my period; I want a real, full-blown romance; I want to find my father; I want to be pretty and self-assured and have a figure like she does; I want to be popular; I want all kinds of things. 'Just things,' I say lamely.

She takes her right hand off the steering wheel and pats my leg. 'Things *are* happening to you, Hope. Every day. You might not see it, but they are.'

'Like what?' I mutter. I'm sounding all sullen, even though there's a part of me that's happy she sees me changing.

'Like . . . well, look how you've taken up tennis this summer. Sam says you've been working hard and improving your game. That's something to be proud of.'

'Big deal,' I say.

'It is a big deal.'

218

I'm silent, then I ask, 'What . . . what else did he say?'

'Sam?'

'Yeah.'

'Oh, that you have natural ability; that he enjoys teaching you. He sees what I see – you're a terrific person.'

'Well, I'm not that terrific,' I say, trying to hide how pleased I am.

'Yes, you are,' she says. 'You're our Hope.'

Turns out I'm not late for my lesson at all. That's the good thing about living with Sara Lynn, who's a freak about being on time – I'm never late for anything. She badgers me to get going way before I actually have to, so even when she thinks I'm running late, I'm really not.

Sam's practicing serves when I walk over to the courts. I'm quiet as I walk behind him, watching him toss the ball high and wind up his body like a spring. Then – bam! – he unwinds and he's over the ball, smashing it hard.

'Hey,' I call as he grabs another ball from the basket.

'Hope!' He drops the ball back in the bucket and grins at me. I can't help but smile back; he just has one of those contagious smiles.

'That was a really good serve,' I tell him.

'It does the job,' he replies. 'Are you ready to start?'

'Yeah,' I say, unzipping my racket case. 'I am.'

'What happened to your chin?'

I shoot him a glare. 'Don't even ask,' I say.

When my lesson's over, Sam sits with me on the bleachers. The sun's hot; it seems we could both use a break.

'I've been thinking . . . ,' he says, twirling his racket between his legs.

'About what?' I ask.

'About you,' he says. 'You and Anne Frank.'

I blush and turn down my mouth, embarrassed. 'Oh, no. Just forget I said anything about that. It's kind of stupid. You know, to get all worked up over a dead person I didn't even know.'

He takes his racket and bops me gently on the head with it. 'No, it's not at all stupid. It shows that you have a heart.'

I shrug and hide my face with my hair.

'Listen,' he says, 'I'm thinking that you're just the kind of person the world needs. Someone who cares about injustice, someone who wants to right wrongs.'

'Well, I'm not Superman,' I say, trying to make a joke out of it so he won't see how much I'm listening, how much I care that he thinks there's a place in the world for a person like me.

He ignores my joke. 'You said last week that you hadn't found your passion; you know, something you like to do that gives your life meaning. I think . . . and it's just a thought . . . but I think you may be on your way to finding it.'

I squinch up my nose. 'What are you talking about?'

'I'm talking about the fact that Anne Frank's story moves you so much. About the fact that you give a damn, and that you're smart and articulate. You know, it's people like you who change the world, Hope. People like Martin Luther King Jr., John and Robert Kennedy, Betty Friedan, Gloria Steinem.'

'Huh?' I know about Martin Luther King and JFK, but not the other names. And what on earth do I have in common with a civil rights guy and a president?

'They're all people passionately committed to ideals. They wanted the world to be different. They were mad about the way things were – like you're mad. So they changed things and made them better.'

I look up at him from underneath my hair. 'So how am I supposed to change things?' I ask skeptically.

He laughs. 'I don't know, my little activist. That's up to you.' He stands up. 'But I have no doubt you'll figure it out. Maybe you'll be a senator. Or the first woman president. Maybe you'll be secretary-general of the UN.' He jumps off the bleachers, turns to me, and smiles. 'But I expect big things from you, Hope.' He puts his racket over his shoulder and calls back, 'You're going to make the world a better place.'

I look at his back as he walks away and put my hands up to my cheeks. He really thinks that about me? I stand up and then sit back down again, laughing. Me – making the world a better place. Ha! But then I stand again and walk down the bleachers, my head held high. Why not me? Why shouldn't I, Hope Teller, change the world?

Chapter 20

𝒯'm kneeling on the ground, cutting back my pansies and pulling off the swollen seed heads, then breaking them so the seeds scatter around the plants. It's close work, requiring time and patience, and I have both today. I'm craving the time by myself, in fact – time to think. Well, not so much time to think as time to feel.

It was just a week ago that I returned from Boston, zipping up Route 93 after kissing Sam good-bye like I'd never see him again. But I am seeing him again – tomorrow, in fact. I'm sneaking out to his lake house to do God knows what, and the hairs on my arms stand up just to anticipate it. It's desire I'm feeling, sweet desire like I haven't felt in years.

He's going back to Boston in a matter of weeks, though. Thud. All that yearning just stops even to think of him going away, and something in my heart hurts. I likely won't see him much once he's gone. There are only so many trips I can say I have to make to Boston for the magazine. But I won't think about that, won't let my deadening pragmatism spoil the lovely feelings buzzing around inside me. He's here now, and that's all that matters.

I'm not used to doing things by my heart, and I laugh out loud at myself – a full and golden sound. The last time I did something just because my heart told me to, it changed my life in ways I couldn't have imagined. The best thing in my life I did by my heart. I got Hope.

I stand up and stretch my arms over my head. I feel like the sixteen-year-old I never was. I feel like dancing through my gardens singing Sam's name. I laugh again and look at the sky. My senses are sharpened today. It's the kind of day where seeing a hummingbird up close would make me cry from happiness; and I'm suddenly still, looking for that hummingbird, for a visible sign that the world is a magical place.

'Sara Lynn,' a male voice says behind me.

'Oh!' I jump, holding my hand to my throat. 'Oh, my goodness! You scared me.'

'Sorry,' he says, and touches my arm to steady me. It's Jack Pignoli, the owner of Ruth's diner.

'My mind was somewhere else,' I say, trying to smile. 'It's all right.'

'I was driving by and I saw you here.'

'Yes?' I'm wondering what in the world he wants and then it hits me – a hard kick in my stomach. 'Is Ruth all right?' I ask. I just know it's Ruth; it's the only reason he'd be here. I stumble backward and raise my hands to my face, as if to shield myself from the pain I know is coming. 'Oh, my God! It's Ruth, isn't it.'

'No, no,' he reassures me. 'No. She's fine. I just came to get some advice.'

'Oh, thank God!' I slowly lower my hands and relax my shoulders.

'Listen, can we talk?' Jack asks.

'Of course.' Goodness, where are my manners? 'Come on, let's go sit on the porch and I'll bring us some lemonade.'

'No, that's not necessary,' he protests.

'Of course it is,' I say firmly, and I start walking up the steps to the house. 'Come on with me now.'

I sit him down at the little table on the porch and tell him to wait just a minute. When I bring out the lemonade and some scones, he's sitting hunched over the table, looking out at the back gardens.

'Here we are,' I say, sitting down with him. 'Now, what did you need to discuss with me?' I smile and wait for an answer. Perhaps he wants my help to plan a party for Ruth or give her an extra-nice birthday present for working so hard.

'I love Ruth,' he tells me without touching the lemonade or scones I've set out. 'I want to marry her.'

I've surely lost my mind. It couldn't be that I just heard him say . . . I set down my lemonade. 'Come again?'

He sighs, picks up one of the scones in the basket, and bites into it. I wait, bug-eyed, I'm sure, for him to chew and swallow. He takes a sip of lemonade and shrugs. 'We've been, well, involved for three years.'

'Three years?' I ask. How did Ruth keep this from me for so long? Where on earth have I been that I haven't seen what was in front of my eyes?

'She didn't want anyone to know,' he says, almost apologizing. 'And she'd kill me if she knew I was telling you right now, but I don't know what else to do.'

I have to remind myself to breathe; that's how shocked I am. 'You and Ruth,' I say weakly. 'Three years.'

He nods, and his eyes are clouded with pain. 'I love her so much, Sara Lynn. I really do.'

I nod back at him because I can't think of a thing to say, and we're like two of those bobble-headed dolls nodding at each other. 'Well,' I finally say. 'Well.'

'She won't see me anymore. Not since last week.'

'Did . . . something happen?' I ask. Oh, they must have had a spat. Probably just a little lovers' quarrel that'll blow over by tomorrow.

'No,' he says. 'Nothing. That's the thing. She just keeps avoiding me.'

Well, she's been avoiding us, too. She's sick, for heaven's sake.

224

'Oh, that's just because she's been under the weather,' I tell him, waving my hand to indicate he's worrying over nothing.

'Under the weather?' He sounds confused, like this is news to him.

'Well, yes. She's got a stomach bug of some sort.' Hasn't he noticed? 'I mean, she has no energy. She just comes home and sleeps. Didn't she tell you she wasn't feeling well?'

He frowns. 'No, she didn't.'

'Oh, my God,' I say. The world is tilting, and there's nothing I can do to keep it upright. 'Oh, my God.'

'What?' he asks, leaning over the table. 'What?'

'Maybe . . . I wonder . . . something might be really wrong with her.' I look down at my hands and see that they're shredding a scone into tiny crumbs. It feels like my fingers aren't part of my body; I can't make them stop. 'She's so stubborn, she'd rather break it off with you than put you through seeing her sick.' Then I remember his wife died some years ago of cancer, and I say, 'Oh, I'm so sorry. I shouldn't be . . .'

'No, no.' He waves his hands. 'It's fine. Diane's death was hard on me; that's for sure. But I was with her, where I needed to be. If there's something the matter with Ruth, I won't be able to stand not being with her, helping her.'

Tears sting my eyes as I picture Ruth's casket being dropped into the ground. 'She's been putting off Hope and me, too,' I say through my clogged throat. 'She's trying to keep us away from her.'

'Do you really think . . . ?'

'I do.' I wipe my eyes and set my jaw. 'If she could keep it from me that she was . . . ah, seeing you for three years, then she's very capable of keeping something like this from all of us.' I'm angry at Ruth, angry at her for being such a stubborn mule all her life. Then I'm ashamed, because it's terribly unbecoming to be angry at a sick person. And then I'm just sad, sad for Ruth because she deserves so much better than this.

I can't bear my own feelings anymore; I can't bear any of this.

225

I finally make myself stop breaking apart the damn scone on my plate and stand up. 'We need to go down to the diner right now to find out what's going on.'

Jack pushes back his chair and says grimly, 'I think that's a good idea. She's too independent – to a fault. She may need us more than ever.'

He offers me his arm as we walk around front to his car, and I think it's the nicest thing. Ruth's lucky to have him, and I'll make her see that she needs us both right now.

And I need her! My shoulders shake as I realize how much I need her, how much she's taught me, how much a part of me she's become since we started raising Hope together.

⁓

I had never set foot in the Tellers' house until the day I followed Ruth home after our meeting at Dick Dawes's office. I looked around closely, trying to picture Bobby growing up here, eating at the rectangular table and sitting on the blue corduroy sofa where Ruth directed me to sit.

'This is lovely,' I trilled, hearing my mother's voice come out of my mouth. It wasn't lovely at all, of course. The rooms were low-ceilinged, small squares, the furniture was worn and mis-matched, and the carpets were cheap remnants. Not to digress, but a good carpet can do wonders for a room. 'It's quite charm-ing, Ruth.'

I waited for the appropriate response. 'Thank you, Sara Lynn' would have done just fine. Instead, she shook her head as if she were trying to get a mosquito out of her ear. 'No, it's not,' she said, holding the baby close and jutting out her pointy Teller chin. Bobby had looked at me with the same expression that snowy day when I'd told him I couldn't see him anymore.

'Well . . .' I whipped out a pad and pen from my purse, busy-ing myself to stop thinking about Bobby. 'Let's get some details sorted out.'

'Don't you even want to know her name?'

'Hmm?' I blushed. Why hadn't I thought to ask that? 'Of course I want to know. Why don't I hold her and you tell me everything about her.'

Ruth hesitated before placing the baby into my arms. 'Her name is Hope. You know Sandra died having her?'

I nodded as I cooed at the baby. Everyone knew everyone else's tragedies in town.

'And you know that's why Bobby took off.'

I didn't nod this time, because everything in me resisted believing that Bobby had left because of Sandra's death. It was ridiculous, I knew, but I didn't want to believe he could hurt that badly over anyone but me. It had stung deeply that he'd found someone so quickly after we broke up, that he had completely moved on from me by the time I was ready to tell him I was sorry, that I wanted him back. It hurt even now, looking at his baby. His baby he'd had with a woman who wasn't me.

'Hope's a good baby. She's not too fussy. She likes to be fed every three hours or so, and she's pretty quiet when she's not hungry.' Ruth shrugged, as if she didn't have anything more to say. 'She's a good baby,' she repeated.

'I can see that,' I said, although I was speaking with no authority whatsoever, never having cared for a baby in my life.

'That's all I know about Hope,' Ruth said. 'The sum total.'

I continued to coo softly at Hope, and Ruth shifted in her seat. 'I suppose we should figure out how we're going to do this together,' she said.

'Yes,' I said. 'Yes.' I handed Hope back to Ruth and picked up my pad and pen. 'First thing is where she should live.'

Ruth scowled. 'That's easy. Right here.'

'Hmmm,' I said, buying myself some time. That wouldn't do. If Hope lived at Ruth's house, I'd never see her. I had Mama to contend with and my job at the magazine. I couldn't be driving over here and back every day. Besides, it wasn't as if I felt particularly welcomed in this house. 'I don't know. I'm so busy with my mother and my job that I'd never see her if she lived here.'

Ruth jiggled Hope in her arms and snapped, 'Well, what about me? God! This is just like you, Sara Lynn. Always thinking about what would be best for you.'

'Just like me?' I laughed in a hard way. 'You don't even know me.'

'I know enough,' she muttered.

'Like what?' My heart was pounding. I wondered what Bobby had told her.

'I was in the same class with you all through school. I listened to enough teachers – my own mother, for God's sake – talk about how wonderful you are. You don't have me fooled, though. You're nothing but a spoiled little brat.'

She was jealous, I thought, closing myself to her words. Jealous because I was pretty and smart and rich and she was none of those things. What could Bobby have been thinking, throwing me together with his bad-tempered sister who hated me? I took a deep breath and tried a different argument. 'Hope will have more advantages living with me. I'll be able to give her nice clothes, ballet lessons, trips, anything she wants.' Every minute I stared at that baby in Ruth's lap, I wanted her more.

Ruth snorted. 'It's just money. Might turn some people's heads, but not mine.'

'Our house is bigger. There's more room for her to play.'

Ruth was silent, and I thought I had her. I was ready to leap across the scuffed-up coffee table, grab Hope from Ruth's arms, and drive her home.

'I'm not living apart from her, Sara Lynn,' Ruth said. 'I think you're a bitch, but I'd sooner have you move in here and live with Hope and me before I'd just hand her over to you.' She paused, then asked, 'Why do you want her so much, anyway? She doesn't have any of your genes. She doesn't have anything to do with you.'

But she did; of course she did. She had everything to do with me because she was part of Bobby. I deeply regretted having broken things off with him – it had been a decision made purely out of fear. This was a chance to . . . to heal, I suppose. I felt as if Bobby were reaching out a hand to me in the guise of his daughter; and I wanted to take it, hold it, and never let it go.

'Well?' Ruth asked. 'Do you or don't you want to come and live with me and Hope? That's my final offer, the best I can do.'

Who did she think she was – talking about final offers and what she could and couldn't do? 'I can take you to court, you know,' I said.

She laughed. 'Your lawyer bullshit doesn't scare me. You quit your big-time lawyering job. You didn't have the teeth for it.'

What had Bobby told her? I smiled through my gritted teeth to prevent her from seeing she'd gotten to me. 'Suit yourself,' I replied, tossing my hair. 'I may have quit practicing law, but I still have the training.'

Hope started to wail, and Ruth jiggled her, saying, 'See what you've done? You've upset her.'

'Oh, that's lovely,' I scoffed. 'Blame me instead of your own stubborn self.'

She strode to the kitchen, where she tried to hold a still screaming Hope and prepare a bottle.

'Here . . .' I followed her and held out my arms. 'I'll take her and you get the bottle.'

'I'm not the maid around here,' she snapped at me over Hope's howls. She shoved the bottle into my hand. 'Why don't you get the bottle and I'll keep a hold of my own niece?'

I looked dumbly at the bottle I was holding. 'I don't know how to do it.'

'Good God,' she said, placing Hope into my arms and snatching back the bottle.

'Well, there's no reason on earth I should know how to do it,' I argued. I hated that Ruth Teller knew how to do something I didn't.

'Stop talking to me and start walking her,' Ruth hollered over Hope's rising screams. 'She likes to be walked.'

'Okay,' I said meekly, scared by Hope's cries into listening to Ruth. I started to walk her and jiggle her a little bit.

'She's not stopping crying, Ruth.' My arms tightened around Hope as I willed her to please, please stop crying. 'It's okay; it's okay,' I murmured frantically.

Ruth came over with the bottle and shook her head. She shoved the bottle into my hand, saying, 'Now, I know you haven't done this before, but sit down over here and I'll talk you through it.'

Ruth sat me in a kitchen chair and positioned Hope's little head so she was poised to take her bottle. She guided my hand so the angle was right, and pretty soon Hope was quietly sucking away.

'Oh, my gosh, she's doing it!' I looked down at Hope's little face, her rosebud lips sucking away, and she snuggled into my arms. 'Thank you, Ruth,' I said humbly. 'Thank you for showing me what to do.'

'Well,' she said gruffly, pulling out the chair next to mine and sitting down, 'I don't think we'll need to go to court to settle our differences if we only work together.'

It was an olive branch she was offering, and I took it gratefully. 'Yes . . . I agree. I agree that we should work together to do right by this child.'

Hope fell asleep in my arms, and I handed her awkwardly back to Ruth, who put her in the car seat. 'No crib,' she said, shrugging.

'I'll buy her one today,' I told her. I had tons of money, more than I needed, anyhow, and I was going to buy Hope the prettiest and best crib a baby could have.

We watched her sleep, the blue veins on her little eyelids visible. She stirred a bit, putting her hand to her mouth, and we held our breath in tandem, breathing again only when it was clear she wasn't going to wake. I glanced at my watch, the Cartier my father had given me when I graduated from law school, and I thought of him with a quick tightening of my throat. Had he looked at me like this when I was a baby? He and Mama?

'I've got to go,' I whispered. 'Mama will be wondering where I am.'

'Okay,' she said. 'We'll talk more later about what arrangements to make.' She walked me to the door and nodded to me curtly, as if I were a traveling salesman who had come by to sell her an encyclopedia she didn't need. But something had opened between us, and when I looked at her and said, 'Good-bye, Ruth,' she grunted and smiled a little as she said, 'Bye, Sara Lynn.'

~⁓

'Ready?' Jack says grimly. He doesn't wait for an answer, just pulls open the door and nods at me to go ahead of him. I see Ruth right away, waiting on the Dolan brothers, wisecracking with them. She sees me and then Jack right behind me, and she rushes over to us, her face twisted in torment.

'Oh Jesus, what's wrong?' she says. She's looking from one of us to the other, and it's my face she fixes on when she says, 'It's Hope, isn't it. Tell me—'

'No, angel, no,' says Jack, putting an arm around her. 'Hope's fine. This is about you.'

'Good Christ.' She leans her head against Jack's chest in relief, then immediately pushes him away. 'What is this – an intervention?' she hisses. 'And what the hell is she doing here?' She jerks her head at me. That's Ruth – the more frightened she is, the tougher she acts.

'Ruth,' I say, putting a hand on her shoulder, 'we need to talk.'

'I'm busy here.' She shrugs my hand away and narrows her eyes at Jack. 'I don't have time to talk.'

'Yeah, you do.' He walks over to the door, puts up the CLOSED sign, and then walks back toward the kitchen.

231

'What the hell is going on?' Ruth demands of me when Jack disappears behind the swinging door.

'Honey, everything's going to be all right,' I tell her, hardly trusting myself to speak without crying.

'"Honey"?' She puts her hands on her hips. 'Since when do you call me "honey"?' She stomps back to the Dolan brothers, snapping over her shoulder, 'Jesus, I feel like I'm on a bad acid trip.'

Jack comes back from the kitchen and motions for me to join him at the Dolan brothers' booth. 'Chet'll take care of you guys,' he tells them. 'We need to talk to Ruth a second.'

'Sure, sure,' they say, 'not a problem.' But their eyes look worried as Jack takes Ruth's arm and steers her along through the kitchen and out the back door, with me following behind.

'What the hell!' Ruth says once the door is closed and we're in the back lot of the restaurant by the big green Dumpster. 'I'm trying to work!'

'Ruth,' I say, 'we have to know something.'

'What?' she asks, tapping her foot on the pavement. 'Spit it out, Sara Lynn.'

Tears well up in my eyes and I shake my head, looking at Jack. He's got to say it, because I can't. I'll fall at her feet crying if I open my mouth, begging her not to leave us.

'Sara Lynn says you're not feeling well,' Jack says. His eyes are moist, too. 'We're worried you're shutting us out.'

'Shutting you out of what?' Ruth says, narrowing her eyes and sticking out her chin.

'Angel, are you sick?' Jack pleads. 'If you're sick, you have to tell me. I can't stand it if you won't let me be with you. I want to take care of you. I want you to be as comfortable and happy as you can be.'

Ruth looks from one to the other of us as though we've lost our minds, and then she bursts out laughing. 'Oh Jesus, you think I'm dying or something, don't you. Ha, ha, ha . . .' She's laughing away, bending over, holding her stomach and howling.

Well, this is simply the limit – having a laughing fit when all our lives are falling apart here. 'I don't think this is at all funny, Ruth,' I say, restraining myself from reaching over and shaking her.

'Oh God . . .' She wipes her eyes and chuckles again. 'This is the best laugh I've had in weeks.'

'Are you sick?' Jack asks insistently, putting his hands on her shoulders and looking her in the eyes.

'No, no.' Ruth waves her hands in the air and laughs again. 'Jesus, no.'

I practically sink to the ground, I'm so relieved, and poor Jack lets out a sob and hugs her close to him, kissing her hair and saying, 'I couldn't stand to lose you, angel. You don't know how scared I was when Sara Lynn told me you were sick. You're everything to me. Oh God, Ruth.'

I expect Ruth to tell him to get a grip, that of course she's fine, but of all things, her shoulders shake and she starts crying in his arms. 'There's still something you don't know,' she wails. 'Something I don't want to tell you.'

'Tell me anything, sweetheart.' Jack pulls away from her and wipes his eyes on his sleeve. 'Tell me anything. As long as you're not sick, I don't care.'

She gets real quiet and looks down at her feet as she half whispers, 'I'm pregnant.'

Well, if I were Mama, I'd faint. That's how many surprises I've had to endure today.

'Pregnant?' Jack asks, the start of a smile playing around his lips. 'You're pregnant?' He hugs her again and lifts her off the ground. 'We're having a baby!'

She's still crying as she says, 'It's not that easy.'

'Sure it is!' he says. 'What's not easy about it?'

'You're sixty; I'm thirty-seven. And that's just for starters. I've also got Hope to think about, my life with her and Sara Lynn and Mamie. Nothing's easy about it.'

Jack waves his hand as if to say there's not a problem in the world. 'We'll work it all out. My God! We're having a baby!'

Ruth starts to smile and says, 'You really want it?'

'Want it? I'm beside myself! I'm going to hand out cigars to everyone in town.'

'But . . . we're both already so set in our ways. You're old, for Christ's sake. . . .'

He just laughs and pats her on the bottom. 'You keep me young,' he says. 'You and our baby'll keep me young.'

He bends down on one knee then, right on the strip of cracked asphalt in front of the Dumpster, and Ruth rolls her eyes and says, 'Oh, for God's sake, Jack. Get up.'

'No way.' He grabs her hand. 'I'm doing this right.' He clears his throat and says, 'Ruth Teller, would you do me the honor of being my wife?'

Her eyes look big and scared, and she's shaking her head slightly. Well, I'm going to kill her if she turns this man down. Three years . . . baby . . . Jack and Ruth . . . It's all swimming around in my brain, making perfect sense even as it's absolutely crazy. Just when I'm beginning to believe she's looking for a way to tell him no, she shrugs and grins. 'Oh, hell. Sure I will.'

Jack gets up and envelops Ruth in a big hug that seems to last for minutes. Then he kisses her, holding her face between his hands. He turns to me and smiles. 'Well, Sara Lynn, you're going to be an auntie. What do you think of that?'

I'm biting my lip, watching them, and I can't say a word. As I open my arms to Ruth and squeeze her bony shoulders, it strikes me that I've been given the sign I was looking for earlier in the garden. I've seen my hummingbird today, and it's Ruth Teller.

Chapter 21

$\mathcal{I}$'m in the pool with Ginny and the KKs, and it's my turn to see how many somersaults I can do in the water. Kelly's leading with two and a half. I think I can do three if I take a huge breath and hold it, and I'm practicing filling my lungs with as much air as they'll hold.

'Will you go already?' Kim says, splashing me.

'I'm going,' I say, splashing her back.

Then Ginny and Kelly start splashing, too, and pretty soon we're shrieking and laughing and the lifeguard has to blow her whistle and tell us to knock it off.

'Hey, isn't that your aunt Ruth?' Ginny asks. Sure enough, Ruth is walking toward us, wearing her usual denim shorts and T-shirt. Uh-oh. She's not in 'appropriate club attire.' Someone will say something to her and she'll fly off the handle at them.

'I gotta go.' I hop out of the pool, grab a towel, and wrap it around myself. I hurry over to meet Ruth, saying, *Damn, damn, damn,* in my head.

'You're not wearing club clothes,' I hiss at Ruth, steering her toward the locker room.

'Oh, excuse me,' she teases. 'Guess I left my white tennis dress at home.'

I dry off and throw on my khaki shorts and red polo shirt. I stuff my wet suit in my swim bag and slide into my sandals. 'Let's go,' I say, figuring I'll comb out my hair in the car.

We walk out to the parking lot and – wouldn't you know it? – run right into Sam getting into his car. I hate myself for feeling this way, but I want to run in the other direction because I don't want him to meet Ruth. She just doesn't fit in here, and I'm afraid he'll think I don't fit, either. 'Hey, Hope!' he says, raising his hand.

'Hi,' I say. I put my head down and keep walking.

'Hold on a sec,' he says. I stop dead in my tracks and close my eyes for a second. 'Where's Sara Lynn today?'

'I don't know,' I say, shrugging. 'She sent someone else to pick me up.'

Ruth is looking at me with hurt, puzzled eyes. She shakes Sam's hand and says, 'I'm Ruth Teller, Hope's aunt.'

Sam grips her hand and flashes his megawatt smile at her. 'Oh, you're Ruth!' he says. 'It's great to meet you finally! I'm Sam Johnson. I teach Hope tennis.'

Ruth looks more relaxed, like she's glad I at least told Sam about her. 'We've heard a lot about you,' she says, and I wish I could pull her away before she says anything really embarrassing. 'Hope talks about you all the time.'

I roll my eyes and tap my foot impatiently on the pavement. 'Let's go, Ruth,' I snap. 'I'm tired.'

'Nice to meet you,' says Ruth.

'Likewise,' Sam calls. 'Bye, Hope. See you tomorrow.'

I wait for Ruth to get in her car, and then I flounce into the passenger seat, do up my seat belt, and cross my arms over my chest.

'What bug's up your ass today?' Ruth asks as she starts the car, pumping the gas.

'Nothing,' I tell her, still pouting.

We drive in silence for the whole way home, and when she shuts off the ignition in our driveway, she says quietly, 'Will you wait a sec? I want to tell you something.'

I undo my seat belt and look up at her, curious. She takes a deep breath and throws her hands up, letting them land on the wheel. 'I don't know how to start,' she says, sort of laughing nervously.

I'm not feeling so good inside. Whatever she has to tell me doesn't sound like it's happy news. 'What?' I demand. 'What is it?'

'I – I'm getting married.' She has this dumb smile on her face, and her eyes are looking at me like they're begging me to approve.

'What? Who?' I sputter.

'Well, brace yourself. Jack Pignoli.'

'Mr. Pignoli?' I shout. 'You're kidding me!'

'No,' she says. 'It's true. We've been dating for quite some time now.'

'Dating? You've been dating him and you never told me?' I turn my head to look straight ahead, because if I have to look at her face one more second, I swear I'll either scream at the top of my lungs or break out crying and never stop.

'I – I guess I was too scared to tell you. Didn't know how you'd react.'

I bang my hand on the dashboard so it stings and yell, 'God! I'm not some little kid! I don't care if you date someone.' I don't care about anything anymore, not anything about her, anyhow. She's such a liar. Such a big, fat liar. How could she say she loved me all my life and then just up and leave like this? Hell, I don't care. I'm glad she's getting married and going away. I'll help her pack. What do I care?

'There's more, too,' she says, her voice timid in a way I've never heard it.

'What?' I ask warily. What could possibly be worse than my aunt leaving me to marry her old-man boss?

'Well, I'm . . . I'm going to have a baby.'

'Oh, gross.' I put my head in my hands. We learned the facts of life a couple of years ago in school, and I have to say, it sounds absolutely disgusting to me. Mr. Pignoli must have made her do that, because he's her boss.

'What's gross about having a new baby around?'

'Well, that's gross, too,' I say, thinking about all the crying, spit-up, and dirty diapers. 'But, you know . . . the thing you had to do to have the baby.'

Ruth chuckles and puts her arm around me. 'Oh, Hope, no. It's not gross. It's something you really enjoy doing with someone you love.'

'Gag,' I say, shrugging off her arm and shifting away from her. 'Gag, gag, gag.'

I keep my head in my hands until Ruth says, 'Well, what do you think? About the getting married part and having a new baby brother or sister?'

Well, this takes the prize. Not only is she springing all this on me with no warning whatsoever, but she's trying to act like it'll be fun. Oooh, a little baby for you to play with, Hope; won't that be just dandy? I raise my face from my hands and spit out the truth. 'It's not going to be my brother or sister. It's going to be *your* baby. Your own baby like you've probably always wanted.' It's hitting me right in the stomach why she's doing this. It's because I'm not really hers. I never was.

Ruth looks confused, and then her eyes mist over. She hugs me as I keep my back ramrod straight. 'No,' she says. 'I already have the baby I've always wanted. This will be another.'

'I'm not your baby,' I say through clenched teeth, and I'm willing the tears not to spill. *Feel mad instead of sad, Hope,* I tell myself. *She never loved you like she said she did, and now she's ditching you for a kid of her own.*

'Oh, yes, you are my baby,' she says, rocking me. 'Oh, yes, you are.'

I blink back my tears as she pats my back, and she says, 'I'll be moving in with Jack, but we want you to stay with us part of every week. You'll have your own room at our house, just like you have here. It'll be like having two houses.'

'Joint custody,' I say, nodding my head into her shirt. I should have guessed this was coming. She just feels too guilty to flat-out leave altogether.

'Huh?'

Doesn't she know anything? I wipe my nose and pull away from her. 'It's what they call it when parents get a divorce and the kid lives sometimes with her mother and sometimes with her father. Kelly Jacobs does that.'

'Yeah, but Sara Lynn and I aren't getting a divorce. Think of it like your family's growing, not splitting apart.'

'That's what Kelly's parents told her, too,' I snap. I fold my arms over my chest and look straight ahead.

She doesn't say anything, and I finally break the silence, asking, 'When's the wedding?' I can't help but wonder if maybe I'll get to be a junior bridesmaid, like Ginny was last summer for her cousin Veronica.

'Soon,' she replies. 'Real soon. And you'll be in it, of course.'

'Can I get a new dress?'

'Absolutely,' she says, and the heavy feeling in my stomach lifts for a second as I imagine myself in a long gown with a twirly skirt. Then all my mad feelings come *whoosh*ing right back because I know just what she's doing. She's trying to bribe me into going along with this whole awful idea. I'll give you a new dress if you don't notice I'm leaving you; that's what she's really saying.

'At least I get a new dress out of the deal. Whoopee,' I say in a snotty voice.

'Hope . . .' Ruth sighs. 'I wish you could be a little bit happy for me.'

'Well, keep wishing,' I snap in my best KK imitation, and I slide out of the car, slam the door behind me, and march into the house without once looking back.

Chapter 22

$\mathscr{I}$'m sitting outside on the terrace bench, just imagining what my little baby will look like. The stars are out and, dammit, I'm happy. I still can't quite believe Jack and I are going to get married and have a baby. But, hell, Sara Lynn and Hope and I were a ragtag bunch at the beginning, and look how far we've come.

Hope's been a little nicer about everything. Poor kid. It was a lot to get used to in one sitting, that was all. I think Sara Lynn might have taken her aside and told her to shape up, because she came up behind me tonight and put her arms around me, whispering that she was sorry for how she's been acting. 'It'll all work out fine,' I told her, and I have to believe it will. That's all a person can do sometimes, just trust that everything'll be okay.

'Ruth?'

'Hey,' I say. It's old Sara Lynn walking down the porch steps, probably about to give me yet another tip on how to care for the bundle of joy growing in my belly. She's already given me a book about how to be pregnant, a book all wrapped up in pretty paper with little blue and pink footprints on it. I smiled and thanked her, but, Jesus H. Christ, women have been having babies for a long time. I likely don't need a book to show me how it's done.

'Sit down.' I move over on the bench and pat the seat beside me. 'Sit with me now because in another few months I'll be a wide load taking up the whole damn bench.'

'In another few months, you'll be married and living with Jack,' she says.

'Won't you be glad to get rid of me?' I joke.

She twists her hands in her lap and gets a pained look in her eyes. 'No, I won't.' She shakes her head. 'I – I don't know how I'll live without you.'

'Well, you won't have to live without me. I'll be just across town, that's all.'

She crosses her arms over her chest like she's cold. 'I'll miss you, Ruth. And I don't know how I'm going to manage my mother without you here.'

'Aah, Sara Lynn, she's harmless.'

'No!' she says, looking at me like I'm climbing over a prison wall to freedom and leaving her on the other side. 'You don't understand.'

'What's not to understand? So you bicker a little bit. Who doesn't, right?'

'I . . .' She looks away from me, hugging herself even tighter. 'There's something I want to tell you.'

I wait for her to spit it out, and finally she says, 'I'm seeing someone. I'm . . . I'm sleeping with him.'

Well, she might as well knock me off the bench and roll me down the hill. 'Who?' I ask.

She clears her throat and turns her face up to the sky and away from my gaze. 'Sam. Sam Johnson.'

'Hope's tennis teacher?' I burst out laughing. 'Jesus, life gets wackier and wackier.'

She nods. 'Mmm-hmm. I know it sounds crazy.' She smiles a little and twists a strand of her hair. 'He's fun, Ruth. I have fun when I'm with him. I just . . . I don't know, I laugh a lot when I'm with him.' She looks at me and says softly, 'He makes me happy.'

Sounds like she's falling for this guy, and I'm glad for her. 'Well, that's great, Sara Lynn.'

She looks straight ahead again and shakes her head. 'Except for the fact that he's twenty-nine.'

I whistle. 'Well, here's to you, Mrs. Robinson.'

'Pardon me?'

Jesus, she's slow on the uptake sometimes. 'You know – *The Graduate*? The Dustin Hoffman character gets seduced by Mrs. Robinson?'

She nods. 'Oh, right, right.' She looks anxious, her eyes blinking and her mouth twisted tight.

'I'm kidding.' I nudge her. 'It's a joke. I mean, I'm marrying Methuselah. I don't really care if your new boyfriend is ten.'

She still doesn't laugh, just puts her face in her hands and starts to cry.

'What's wrong?' I pat her shoulder a little bit, and it feels weird. I mean, I never comfort Sara Lynn. 'Doesn't boy toy make you happy?'

She cries more, and I say, 'I'm sorry. Me and my big mouth. Sometimes I joke when I don't know what to say.'

She lifts her head and wipes her eyes. 'No, no, it's not that. It's just . . . well, he doesn't live here. He's going back to Boston when the summer's over.'

'And . . . ?' I prod. I'm missing her point here.

'Well, that'll be it. I won't be able to see him anymore.'

'Hello?! Cars, telephones? It's a wonderful age we live in, Sara Lynn.'

I'm trying to make her laugh, but she just shakes her head and says sadly, 'It's just a fling; it can't possibly amount to anything.'

'Why not?'

'I'm too old,' she bursts out. 'He makes me feel so young when I'm with him, but I'm not. I'm thirty-seven!'

'Jesus H. Christ, you've got yourself dead and buried. You're not that old, Sara Lynn! Take a look at Jack, why don't you – now that's old.'

She giggles. Phew! Finally. I was beginning to think I was losing my touch.

'And then there's Hope and my mother,' she says, shaking her head. 'How can I be everything they need me to be when I'm running around like a twenty-five-year-old?'

Oh, for Jesus' sake. 'Listen here,' I say, pointing in her face. Someone has to tell her what is what. 'You're afraid. You're afraid of getting your heart hurt, and you're using Hope and Mamie as excuses.' I mimic her soft, rich-girl voice. 'Oh, I couldn't possibly have a love affair. I have too many responsibilities at home. I have a mother and a little girl to care for. I'm going to stay right in my little cocoon because it might hurt too much to take a risk.'

She's sticking her lower lip out at me, like she's not happy to hear the goddamn truth.

'You know how I know that?' I point to myself. 'Because I've been going along doing the same thing. Telling Jack for three years that I didn't want to get serious. Too much to do with Hope, I used to say. How could he ask me to change my way of living? Truth was, I was scared. What if it didn't work out? What if you thought I was the same old idiot Ruth making another mistake with my life?'

She starts to say, 'But I wouldn't think . . .'

I hold up my hand and keep going. 'It took getting pregnant to make me see my life's going on with or without me and I'd better jump on board and live it. Don't you think I'm nervous as a cat about moving in with Jack? About getting married? About having a kid? Good God! When I think about it, I get frozen inside. I think I'm crazy for doing all this. But, you know what? I'm going to be happy! Sure, there'll be days when I wonder what in hell I've gone and done. But that's life. Better to feel that way than to protect yourself from feeling anything at all.'

'My mother won't approve,' she says in this little, timid voice.

'Your mother won't approve,' I say slowly in disgust. 'Jesus Christ, I've just given you this speech that should be in a *Rocky* movie, and that's all you have to say for yourself?' I take her by the shoulders and stop myself from shaking some sense into her. *'What do you care?'*

She looks at me, puzzled.

'What do you care?' I say to her again. I get up and pace a little. 'If she says, "Oh, Sara Lynn, I don't like you having sex with a young stud," you just say, "Well, I hope you're not keeping yourself up nights worrying about it."'

She shakes her head. 'It's the guilt, Ruth. She'll make me feel so guilty and dirty, I won't be able to stand it.'

'Well, you know what? It's time you stop feeling it. It's time you say, "Listen, old lady, this is my life and I'll live it however I want." Sara Lynn, what do you want on your gravestone – 'She pleased her mother"?'

She shakes her head, and I see a hint of a smile. 'No.'

'Do me a favor,' I say. And I haven't even thought this out, but it's exactly what I want.

'What?'

'Be my maid of honor.'

'Really?' she asks. She smiles, and dammit, she's so pretty just now that I feel my old jealousy gnawing at me, just for a second, and then it stops. Because I love Sara Lynn; I truly do. She's not Miss Perfect like I thought she was back in high school. She's Miss Trying to Get Her Shit Together, just like me, just like all of us.

I nudge her. 'See? You love that stuff, wearing a pretty dress and carrying flowers.'

'No, it's just that it's such an honor. I'm, well, thrilled that you'd—'

'Oh, cut the crap, Sara Lynn. Who the hell else am I going to ask? I've been living with you twelve years now. You're like a goddamn sister to me.'

She hugs me, teary, and says, 'I love you, too, Ruth. You know I do even if I never say it.'

I pull away from her and pat her arm. 'That's enough now. If anyone sees, they'll think they were right all these years – we are gay.'

Sara Lynn laughs and wipes her eyes, and then I spring it on her. 'As my maid of honor, you have to do one thing for me.'

'What's that?' Oh, she's probably thinking I'll be asking her to arrange a honeymoon suite or pick out dresses together or some such nonsense.

'You have to bring Sam as your date to my wedding.'

She's quiet, and then she says, 'That's what you really want?'

'Uh-huh.'

'Ha!' she laughs. Her eyes soften as she says, 'I can't very well refuse the bride's request, now, can I?' Then she makes a joke, and it perks me up to hear her sassing. 'Just don't blame me if my mother drops dead at your wedding when she sees Sam and me together.'

'We'll dig a hole in the yard and throw her in,' I say right back. 'I'm not letting little old Mamie spoil my wedding.'

Sara Lynn laughs and looks around the yard. Her eyes have fire in them again, and she points down the hill. 'I was thinking about the ceremony being down in that clearing in front of the meadow garden. What do you think? And cocktails up here on the terrace? And where to put the tent for the reception? Maybe in the side yard. And we have to come up with a color scheme. You know, for the flowers and tablecloths. . . .'

Same old Sara Lynn all right, and I'm more than satisfied, because that's just the way I like her.

Chapter 23

$\mathcal{E}$veryone's in a tizzy because the wedding is in two weeks. Ruth says it has to be that soon because she and Jack are so excited that they don't want to wait. Ha! Does she think I'm stupid? She just wants to tie the knot before her stomach's too fat to fit into a pretty white dress.

We went to the bridal shop today to buy our dresses. Since we didn't have time to special order anything, we had to buy dresses they already had. This was good news for Ruth and Sara Lynn, who *love* their dresses, but bad news for me. My dress isn't anything like what I hoped it would be. It's sort of a girly pink with ruffles at the top and bottom and a skirt that poufs out instead of twirling nicely. I look like a freaky child beauty queen without the beauty.

We're trying on the dresses right now at home so we can double-check to be sure they don't need any alterations. Guess whose idea that was? Not mine, I can tell you that.

'Can you *please* take out the ruffles?' I ask Sara Lynn, scratching at the flouncy folds of fabric at my chest. Sara Lynn is walking around me and positively beaming as she lifts up the skirt of my dumb Shirley Temple dress and puts it back down again.

'Honey, the ruffles are adorable,' she says. 'You'll ruin the dress if you take them out. Besides, it looks so cute on you.'

Sara Lynn is wearing a softer pink; 'blush' is what she keeps calling it. Her dress doesn't have ruffles or bows. It just sort of drapes over her body, clinging a little bit to her curves. I wish I had a dress like hers, instead of this stupid 'adorable' dress she talked me into. She really looks like a knockout. Even Ruth, who can't think about anything these days except the wedding and the baby, notices how fabulous she looks. 'Sara Lynn, that dress was made for you,' she says. 'Turn around.'

Sara Lynn smiles and spins around, her blond hair flying out from her and then settling back over her shoulders.

'Whew! Wait till Sam gets a load of you.'

My ears perk up and the back of my neck tingles. I must have heard wrong, but I don't think so, because I'm getting this awful, sinking feeling in my stomach. 'Sam who?' I ask, my heart beating through my dumb ruffled chest.

They're quiet a minute, and then Sara Lynn says brightly, 'Sam Johnson. He's going to be my date for the wedding.'

'Sam?' I say quietly. Then my voice gets louder because I've had enough of everything, enough of people lying to me and leaving and pretending to care about me when they just plain don't. '*My* Sam? Sam's your date for the wedding?'

'We've been . . . seeing each other,' Sara Lynn says, wringing her hands together and talking all chipper, like she's not totally guilty of stealing him from me. 'I hope that's okay.'

'You hope it's okay?' I feel like a parrot repeating back each unbelievable thing she says. 'You hope it's okay? Well, it's not okay! It's not.' I rip at the ruffle on my dress that's itching me like crazy. 'Are you fucking blind?' It's the first time I've ever said the f-word, and it feels good. 'Are you fucking, fucking, fucking stupid? I hate you!' I grab up my itchy polyester skirt and run from the room. 'I hate you and I'll never forgive you.'

I run downstairs and out to the porch, where Mamie sits rocking. 'What on earth?!' she says as I careen past her and out the porch door. I run down the hill in my bare feet, tripping about halfway down. 'Shit!' I say as I pick myself up and look at the grass stains I've got on my dress. Good! I hope I wreck the damn thing. I'm not going to be in the stupid wedding anyhow.

Then I'm at the bottom of the hill, in Sara Lynn's special gardens, and before this wild idea inside me even has time to settle, I'm doing it. I'm ripping off all of Sara Lynn's flowers. Good-bye, roses. Good-bye, scabiosa. Good-bye, hydrangeas. Good-bye, butterfly bushes. Good-bye, meadow flowers. I'm stomping on the low plants and ripping blooms off the high ones, crying and crying as loud as I can. I don't even care that my hands are getting scraped and cut. It doesn't bother me at all. I wipe some blood on my dress, hoping it stains and won't ever come out.

Sara Lynn and Ruth are here now, and Sara Lynn is screaming, 'Oh, my God, what have you done?'

'I've ruined your garden!' I shout. 'How does it feel? How does it feel to have someone wreck something you love?' I turn to Ruth. 'And I'm not coming to your stupid wedding. You can just find another junior bridesmaid.' My voice catches, and I fall to the ground, wailing. 'It's not fair,' I cry. 'It's just not fair.'

Ruth bends down to hug me. 'No, it sure isn't fair,' she says. 'It sure isn't. Baby doll, we didn't know. You were . . . you were in love with Sam?'

In love? In love? He was my soul mate. I loved him so much, it was something I couldn't say even to myself. He was mine. What about that time he told me he was falling in love and that it was our secret? He was talking about her?! About her?! Oh God! I put my face in my hands and sob. He was going to wait for me, and we were going to change the world together. I think of the way he looked when he called me his little activist, and I realize my stomach's never going to stop feeling this pain that's sharp and hollow at the same time. I'm never going to stop hurting. Never. My whole life is ruined.

I nod, still crying, and say, 'I still do. I'll never stop loving him.'

Ruth hugs me tighter and says, 'Ah, honey, I know. But you'll love someone else someday. Someone right for you.'

'Sam *is* right for me,' I tell her. And it's true, he is. If only Sara Lynn hadn't taken him away with her big boobs and straight blond hair.

'I want to tell you something,' Sara Lynn says. I jerk my head up and see her staring at the trampled meadow garden, her hand at her throat and tears running down her cheeks. 'Something you should know.' She turns to look at me and says, 'A long time ago, before you were born, I was in love with your father. And, Hope, I – I never thought I would love anyone after him.'

I'm sitting on the ground, my mouth open in shock. Sara Lynn was in love with my father? 'Did he love you back?' I ask meanly, because it's pretty clear he liked my mother more than he liked her.

'Mmm-hmm.' She nods, wiping her eyes and smiling through her tears, not at me, but at some memory she's touching with her mind. 'We weren't meant to be together, but we were in love for a brief, wonderful time. And look what he gave me – you, the greatest gift of my life.'

They were in love? But then why . . . ? 'How do you know you weren't meant to be together?' I ask, sniffling. I don't understand any of this.

'You just know, Hope,' says Sara Lynn.

'Are you meant to live your life with Sam?' I say bitterly. I swear, I won't be able to stand it if she says yes.

'I don't know,' Sara Lynn replies. 'I don't know that right now.'

I cry again and say, 'I thought I was meant to live my life with Sam.'

It's Sara Lynn who hugs me now, saying, 'I know, sweet girl, I know.'

I stand up quickly, ripping the skirt of my dress as I jerk my body out of her arms. I start walking up to the house, and she comes after me, calling like she's pleading with me, 'Hope . . .'

'Let her go now,' I hear Ruth say. 'Let her be alone for a little bit.'

I cry even harder because I think about how alone I'll be for the rest of my life. No mother. No father. No Ruth. No Sara Lynn. No Sam. I climb the hill and then run up the porch steps and swing open the porch door.

'What in the world, child!' says Mamie. She's looking at me if I've gone stark, raving crazy, and maybe I have. I walk right by her into the kitchen, and then I race up the back stairs and into my room, slamming the door shut. I strip out of this stupid, itchy, ripped, pink, grass- and bloodstained dress and stamp my feet on it. Then I pick it up and throw it in a ball against my bedroom wall. I slide into shorts and a T-shirt as I watch Sara Lynn and Ruth coming up the hill and onto the terrace below my window, and I hate them. I hate them both. I duck down with my ear to the open window so I can hear what they're saying about me.

'What in heaven was that all about?' Mamie asks from the porch.

'Oh, it's nothing, Mama,' Sara Lynn tells her.

'Nothing, my right foot. Why is Hope screaming and crying and tearing around here like a madwoman?'

'She's . . . upset.'

'Upset? How obtuse do you think I am, Sara Lynn? I could see that with my own eyes.'

Ruth breaks in. 'She's upset because she's had a crush on her tennis teacher, who Sara Lynn just happens to be dating.'

My cheeks get hot, and something in me feels like I want to burst through the window screen. I hop up and race down the stairs and out onto the porch.

'It wasn't a crush,' I say fiercely to Ruth. 'You don't know anything about it.'

Ruth turns to me. 'Baby doll—'

'Good God,' Mamie interrupts, looking in disbelief at Sara Lynn. 'You're dating Hope's tennis teacher?'

'He's also twenty-nine,' Ruth tells Mamie.

'Whose side are you on?' Sara Lynn snaps. She walks away from Ruth and looks out to the backyard, her whole body trembling.

'Yours,' says Ruth, walking over to stand next to her. 'Absolutely yours.' She turns back to Mamie and says firmly, 'Listen, Mamie, Sara Lynn's bringing him to my wedding. She's happy. He makes her happy. And that's all that matters. Isn't it?'

Mamie turns up her nose and looks away from Ruth and Sara Lynn.

Ruth walks over to her and kneels to look her in the face. 'Mamie, I know you love Sara Lynn. I know you love her more than anything.' She puts her hands on Mamie's shoulders and says, 'So you have just got to let her be. Let her be Sara Lynn! She's not you. She's not always going to do what you would do, or what would make you happy. She's her own person.'

Uh-oh. Ruth might as well be jumping up and down and pointing at the wall, the one between Sara Lynn and Mamie that we all pretend isn't there. The air seems still for a second, like we've all sucked in our breath and don't know whether or not to let it out.

Mamie looks straight ahead and blinks her eyes real fast as she twists her hands in her lap. 'I wasn't aware I was making my own daughter so unhappy,' she says.

'Oh, for heaven's sake,' Sara Lynn says with a brittle laugh. 'You're being overly dramatic, Mama.'

Ruth holds up her hand. 'No, Sara Lynn. No, she's not. Just stop pretending you're not . . . suffocating each other. You love each other to death, but you're killing each other, too. Mamie, don't let Sara Lynn lose the chance to be happy—'

'Is that what you think?' Mamie interrupts, looking up at Sara Lynn. 'That I'm stopping you from finding happiness?'

Sara Lynn doesn't speak for a long minute – she just lets the question float out there. Finally, she puts her head down and says quietly, 'Sometimes. Yes, sometimes I do.'

Mamie stands up slowly and says, 'Well.' Then she sets her mouth hard and walks across the porch floor into the house. 'You're free to think whatever you like.'

'Oh, Mama,' Sara Lynn cries, reaching out her arms toward Mamie. It's like telling the truth knocked that wall between them right down, and instead of snarling at each other across it, Mamie's walking away, leaving, just like my father did.

For a second, I want to go to Sara Lynn, so she won't be standing there alone. But then I feel glad that she's sobbing into her hands all by herself. Good! I think. Good!

Ruth pulls Sara Lynn into her and hugs her. It's me she's looking at as she pats Sara Lynn's shoulder, saying, 'No need to worry. Everything will be all right now. Everything will be just fine.'

Chapter 24

$\mathcal{I}$t's raining today – hard – and the house is chillingly quiet. Ruth's at work, and the other two – well, they're not speaking to me. They've decided I'm the devil incarnate. And maybe I am. I won't give up Sam even though I'm hurting Hope and Mama. They think I'm choosing him over them, but I'm not. I'm choosing me.

'You can't make your choices based on what other people want, Sara Lynn.' That's what Ruth told me that awful day last week after Mama huffed her way upstairs and Hope followed her, screaming, 'I'm glad I wrecked your stupid garden!'

'What am I supposed to base them on, then?' I cried. Dear God, hadn't I learned from Bobby? Hadn't I learned that all I do is hurt the people I most love whenever a man is involved? Why, why hadn't I just shaken Sam's hand at the end of our date in Boston? I could have smiled and said, 'Thank you for a lovely evening.' That's what a sensible, mature woman would have done. God, I wanted to tear my hair out and bang my head against the wall to rid myself of my stupidity.

'You have to make your choices based on what you want,' Ruth said, grabbing my hands and squeezing tight. 'On what's good for Sara Lynn. Does Sam make you happy?'

'No,' I said, shaking my head. 'No. Right now he's making me miserable.'

'The truth is, you're making yourself miserable. How do you feel when you're with Sam?'

I bit my lip hard just before I whispered, 'Alive. He makes me feel alive.'

'Then listen here, missy,' Ruth said, and she was saying it roughly, as though I'd better pay attention. 'You get your pretty little ass into your fancy car and you go see him right now. You tell him what's going on. Because, trust me, if he makes you feel alive, that's something. You don't just throw that away because it makes things easier on everyone else.'

'I can't leave here right now,' I practically shouted at her.

'Oh, yes, you can,' she said quietly. Then she looked at me in a hard way, like she was daring me. 'Are you going to give him up, just like you gave up Bobby, because you still don't have any guts?'

I shrugged off her hands and ran into the kitchen to grab my keys. Before I knew it, I was in my car on the way to Sam's. Guts, I fumed; I'll show her guts.

It wasn't until I pulled up to the little cottage on the lake that all my bravado left me, and I got out of the car slowly, half thinking I should just get back in and go away for good. Oh, the monstrous selfishness in me! Who did I think I was to stamp on everybody's feelings just because I might be in love? As I hesitated, standing there in my blush-colored bridesmaid dress and no shoes, the screen door squeaked open, and there was Sam, his eyes opening wide in surprise.

'Sara Lynn?'

I couldn't answer. I could only look at him, my shoulders shaking and tears falling down my cheeks. He bounded down the steps and pulled me close, and I realized that what Ruth had said was the truth: When someone makes you feel alive, you walk toward him, not away.

~~~~~

I sigh and rub the back of my neck. I'm sitting at the kitchen table, trying to edit my piece on Langley's Lovely Lavender Gardens, but my mind keeps wandering. Visiting other places in my mind . . . Oh, Bobby. What would have happened if I hadn't broken things off, if I hadn't let my fear drive him away? I don't know. I shake my head just wondering about it. I don't know.

My cell phone rings, and I jump, startled out of my thoughts. 'Hello?'

'S.L.'

I smile. 'Hi, Sam.' It's his nickname for me – S.L. I've never had a nickname before.

'How are you?'

I sigh. 'Pretty good.'

'Still no peace treaties?'

'Not yet. I'm starting to lose hope.'

'No, no. Don't say that. She'll come around.'

'Which one?' I laugh.

'Well, both of them. But I was thinking about Hope. Are you sure you don't want me to talk to her?'

'I'm positive. She needs time to cool down. Time to hurt, really. She cared about you, Sam.'

'She's a great kid. I care about her, too. I wish . . . I wish there was something I could do.'

'You could stop seeing me,' I say teasingly.

'Not an option,' he replies, and I rest my chin on my hand and smile.

'I'll see you tonight, okay?' I say.

'I'm counting on it.'

'Yeah, me too.'

We don't say anything for a minute, and then he says, 'Well, I just wanted you to know I was thinking about you.'

'Me too.'

'You too what?' he asks.

I laugh. 'I was thinking about you, too.'

His laugh echoes mine, and just before he hangs up, he says, 'See you tonight, S.L. Don't be late.'

Every night after Hope and Mama are in bed, I've been driving out to the lake to see Sam. It was Ruth who insisted.

'I'll watch everyone here. You just go on. Don't worry about anything at home.'

'But Ruth,' I protested, 'what about Jack? You'll want to see him at night now that you're finally out in the open with everything.'

'I'll be seeing his face plenty.' She laughed. 'I'm marrying the guy, remember?'

I shiver a little as I pick up my pen and doodle on my manuscript. I think about my nights with Sam – the sweet shock of his lips as he kisses me tenderly, the slow way he takes off my clothes, and the warmth of his skin as I remove his. And then we're in bed together, his body and mine becoming a beautiful jumble, and he's whispering in my ear that I'm turning him on like crazy, and I moan as I come because there's nobody around for miles and what do I care anyhow if anyone hears us?

Then it's over, and we lie entwined as we talk, our voices meshing like our bodies. We talk about everything – our thoughts, our dreams, our fears, our memories. Last night, as Sam held me and we talked after making love, he said, 'You know, S.L., your body feels absolutely right against mine. It's like we belong together.'

'You think so, huh?' I teased.

'I do.' He turned me around to face him and kissed me hard. 'I am the luckiest guy in the world right now,' he whispered, looking into my eyes.

'I'm feeling awfully lucky myself,' I said, my breath catching in my throat.

I catch my breath now as Hope comes into the kitchen, her eyes not so sullen and a smile poking at the corners of her mouth.

'Sara Lynn?' she says quietly. It's the first time she's said my name since she found out about Sam and me last week.

'Yes?' I ask, dropping my pen.

'I . . . I . . .' She puts her head down and blushes. 'I just got my period.'

'Oh, Hope!' I push my chair back from the table and move to hug her. My eyes mist over as her arms slowly tighten around my neck. 'Congratulations! When did it happen? Just now?'

She nods proudly. 'I went to the bathroom and there it was.'

'Oh, gosh. You'll need pads.'

'I had one in my backpack.' She ducks her head, letting her hair fall in her face. 'I stole it from Ruth a long time ago just in case.'

'Well, you'll need a whole package of them now. Come on; I'm sure I have extras stashed away upstairs.' I start up the stairs, and she follows me silently.

'Hmm . . .' I enter my bathroom and open my cabinet under the sink. 'Aha! Here you go.' I hand her an unopened package of sanitary napkins. 'For you.'

She looks at them, and then she starts to cry. 'Oh, Sara Lynn.' She shakes her head, looking down. 'I'm so sorry I wrecked your garden.'

'It's okay,' I tell her, pulling her into me and kissing her wild hair. God, what do I care about my garden? 'Everything will grow back.'

She sniffles and nods.

'Gardens are surprisingly resilient,' I say softly, and hug her even closer. 'And I'm sorry, too, Hope. I had no idea you had feelings for Sam.'

'Ugh!' She pulls away from me and turns her head. 'Don't even talk about it! It's too embarrassing!'

'No!' I take her shoulders and make her look at me. 'No, it's not embarrassing. It's incredibly brave and, and . . . human. It's human to open your heart to someone. Don't let anyone tell you otherwise.'

'He must think I'm the biggest dork.'

I shake my head. 'No, not at all. He only wishes you weren't hurting so much.'

'Do you . . . You see him every night, right?' She pulls back from me and sets her jaw, challenging me.

'What are you asking me?' I buy myself some time.

'I know you go out every night,' she says. Then she laughs a bit, her face softening. 'That's one thing about not talking to someone. It's quiet enough that you can hear them coming and going.'

'Yes.' I'm not going to lie to her. Not to protect her from a hurt she's already feeling. 'I do see Sam. I'm just sorry it hurts you.'

She shrugs. 'It doesn't hurt so much anymore. At least, it's getting so it doesn't.' Her eyes tell me otherwise, and I want to hug her close again so I don't have to look into them.

I pause, then tell her something I've been thinking about over the last several days, something I wish I'd done differently. 'You know, Hope, sometimes, when you live with someone a long time, you see only what you want to see, or what you're used to seeing. I should have noticed your feelings for Sam. You were right when you told me I was "fucking blind." I was, and I'm sorry.'

'It's okay,' she mutters. She averts her eyes and squeezes the package of pads to her chest.

I want to help her preserve her dignity, so I smile and focus on the good news of today. 'Come on. Let's go put those pads in your bathroom. Find a nice home for them now that you'll be needing them every month.'

As we walk down the hall to her room, I ask, 'Now that you're officially a woman, is there anything you want to ask me? You know, about woman things?'

258

'Yeah,' she says, and takes a deep breath. 'Actually there is.'

'Shoot,' I tell her, plopping on her bed.

'Hold on a sec—' She walks into her bathroom, carrying the pads in front of her like a precious parcel. 'I'm just going to put these away.'

Oh, she's so proud of herself! And she should be – this is the start of something, of lots of things.

When she comes back to the bedroom, she scrambles up on the bed beside me and begins to pick at her nails.

'You wanted to ask me something?' I prompt, brushing my fingers against the hair falling in her face.

She doesn't look up, just says in a low voice, 'You know . . . um, sex?'

'Ye-es,' I say cautiously.

Her words tumble out quickly as she continues to pick at her nails. 'Well, Ruth said it's something you enjoy with someone you love, and I was wondering if that was true.'

'Yes, that's true.' Hmm. This isn't so hard after all. I can handle this. 'When you're with someone you really care about, and you're ready, it's wonderful.'

'So . . . did you have sex with . . .' Or maybe I can't handle this after all. My shoulders stiffen. I simply won't tell her about my sex life with Sam. It's absolutely off-limits. 'With my father?'

My heart leaps into my throat as she continues. 'You said you loved him. That day in the garden. And I was just wondering if . . .' She lifts her head and looks pleadingly at me, like she wants something from me, something like the truth.

'Yes.' I take a running leap and jump off a pier into the waters of my murky past. 'I did.'

She closes her eyes for a moment, and I wonder if I've made a terrible mistake in telling her. 'Oh, wow,' she says softly.

'I loved your father.' I'm surprised to hear my voice break, and I stop a minute to take a deep breath. 'And sex was part of that love.'

'Why did you stop loving each other?'

259

I make a noise somewhere between a laugh and a cry. 'Oh, Hope . . . it's complicated. There's a part of me that'll always love Bobby. And I have to believe he feels the same way about me. He gave me you, after all.'

Hope's mouth twists as if she's in pain. 'But what about my mother? Did he love her?' she asks.

'Oh, my gosh, yes,' I assure her. I wish I'd known Sandra, that I had something to tell Hope about her mother. All I have is what I know about Bobby, though. 'You . . . you can love different people in your life at different times. Nothing that happened with me took away from your father's love for your mother. He was . . . he was absolutely grief-stricken when she died. It's why he left. It just broke his heart.' It's the right thing to say, and it doesn't hurt as I thought it would to acknowledge a fact I've avoided for thirteen years: Of course Bobby loved Sandra.

'Is his heart still broken?' Hope asks in a low voice.

'What do you mean, honey?'

'Is that why he's never come back?' Her eyes are shining with tears, and I see the longing in them.

'I imagine so,' I tell her quietly. 'I imagine so.'

She scrambles up from the bed, goes over to her desk, and pulls a folded piece of paper from the drawer. She hands it to me wordlessly, and I unfold it.

It's a letter Hope wrote to her father, a beautiful, touching, perfect letter. 'Fucking blind again,' I murmur.

'Huh?' Hope asks.

'I . . .' I point at the letter. 'I should have seen this. Should have seen what's been in front of me. You want to see your father.'

Hope's lower lip trembles, and she nods slowly. 'But what if he doesn't want me?' she whispers. A tear leaks out of the corner of one eye and runs down her cheek.

'Doesn't want you? Is that what you think?' Oh, poor Hope. If only she'd known Bobby, she'd realize that couldn't be true. But, of course, if she'd known Bobby, we wouldn't be having this conversation. 'Oh, honey. Trust me when I say he wants you. I'm absolutely sure of that.'

'Then why . . . ?'

'Why hasn't he come back?' I throw my hands in the air. 'Fear. Shame. Pride. Grief. Every reason except that he doesn't want you. That I promise.'

'Really?'

'I'll prove it to you. I will.' I stand up. 'I should have done this a long time ago. Come on with me.'

'Where are we going?' She stands up next to me, looking dazed, following me out of her room.

'I'm calling a detective right now. We're going to find your dad.'

'Just like that?' Hope asks incredulously.

'Just like that. Come on downstairs now. We're making some phone calls.'

She slips her hand into mine as we walk down the stairs. My God, she's growing up so fast that soon she won't need my hand at all. I want to stop and hug her tightly to me, but I just give her hand a quick squeeze, closing my eyes for a second so I'll remember what it feels like as she squeezes back.

Chapter 25

When Ruth comes home, it's still pouring rain. She's soaked as she comes in the front door, patting her wet hair with her hands.

'Ruth!' I've been watching for her car, waiting for her.

'Hmm?' She keeps patting her hair, trying to dry it, I guess. 'Oh, hi, buttercup! How are you?'

'Well, I'm good.' I can't stop smiling at her, and she stops patting and looks at me.

'What's going on?'

'What makes you think something's going on?' I ask, practically dancing around.

She shoots me a suspicious look and says, 'Gee, I don't know. Maybe because you haven't been too happy this past week and today you look like you're ready to burst from joy? Call me crazy, but—'

'You're crazy,' I tell her, laughing.

She laughs with me. 'All right. I set myself up for that one.'

'Guess what?' I ask, hardly holding my news in.

'What?'

'I got my period today.'

'Aaaaaaahhh!!!!' she screams loudly and gives me a big, wet hug.

'And that's not all!'

'Sweet Jesus, be careful what you tell me. Remember I'm carrying a baby here. I'm in a delicate condition.'

'No, it's good news. I'm talking to Sara Lynn again.'

Ruth's face softens. 'I'm so glad. She loves you, Hope.'

'There's more.' I take a deep breath. 'She hired a detective to find my father.'

'O-kay. That I need to sit down for.' She marches to the kitchen and pulls out a chair. I follow her, talking all the way.

'See, I wrote this letter to my father. Only I didn't have an address, so I couldn't send it. And I showed it to Sara Lynn. You know, seeing as how she had sex with my father and all.' Oops. I clap my hand to my mouth.

'What?!' Ruth hoots. 'She told you that?'

'You knew?' I'm a little disappointed. I thought I was the only one to know.

'No, no,' Ruth says hastily, and she sort of twists her lips, like she's trying not to smile.

'It's probably private,' I whisper, 'but I think it's good I told you.'

'Why's that?' Ruth asks.

'Because it makes Sara Lynn more connected to us,' I tell her. 'I mean, you and I are connected by blood, but Sara Lynn's connected too now, on account of, you know . . . her and my father.'

'Oh, she's connected all right,' says Ruth, patting my shoulder. 'I wouldn't worry about that.' She shakes her head and laughs. 'Good God. I'm gone eight hours and the whole house goes flipping mad. Where is Sara Lynn, anyhow?'

'Seeing Sam,' I reply.

Ruth's mouth drops open, and she looks at me hard. I can feel my cheeks get hot as I say, 'It's not a big deal to me anymore. I mean, it is, but I better get over it, right? I told her I was big enough to stay here alone with Mamie until you came home, and that if she had anything she wanted to do or anyone she wanted to see, she could just go on ahead.'

'You know what, Hope?'

'What?'

She nods and smiles at me with her eyes. 'You're all right, kid. You're all right.'

Ruth makes me a really nice dinner – chicken and dumplings with baby peas in the gravy. She sets up a tray for Mamie, who's been taking her meals upstairs lately to avoid Sara Lynn, and I say, 'Can I take that up to her?'

'You sure can,' she says. She gets out a white linen napkin, folds it real pretty, and places it on the tray. 'All set.'

I walk up the stairs slowly and carefully, setting the tray down in front of Mamie's door and knocking.

'Yes?' she says.

'It's me. Hope. I have your dinner.'

'Oh. Come in, then.'

I open the door and then pick the tray back up, carrying it in and setting it on the table by her chair.

'Thank you, dear,' she says.

'Do you want to come downstairs to eat tonight?' I ask.

'No, I think not.'

'I have something to tell you,' I say. She raises her eyebrows expectantly. 'I'm talking to Sara Lynn again. I'm not mad at her anymore.'

Mamie's mouth tightens, and she looks away. I can see she doesn't want to discuss Sara Lynn with me.

'Listen, Sara Lynn's a good person. She couldn't help it if she fell in love with Sam. He's very likable.' I snort out a laugh. 'Trust me.'

'There are things you don't know, Hope.' Mamie picks up the napkin from the tray and shakes it out, placing it on her lap. 'Things you can't possibly understand.'

'Maybe not, but I do know that whenever I fight with my

264

friends at school, Ruth says, "Life's too short to hold grudges, Hope." And I think she's right. I feel so much better since I stopped holding a grudge against Sara Lynn. There's more room inside me for other feelings, better feelings that don't hurt so much.' It strikes me that I'm being exactly the kind of person Sam believed I could be. I'm speaking out about what's right and wrong. I'm taking a stand. And right as he comes into my mind, I know what the word *bittersweet* means; I know how it feels to have something sting your heart and soothe it, all at the same time.

'Thank you for your thoughts, my dear, but I'm afraid it's time for me to have my dinner now.' Mamie picks up her fork and knife.

'Just promise me you'll think about it, Mamie,' I say, walking to the door. Dang, she's stubborn. But at least I've said what's inside me; at least I've spoken up for Sara Lynn. Even if she did cause my heart to get broken, she's still my . . . my what? Sort of mother, I guess. But that's not right, because I already have a mother, even if she did die.

It's okay, my mom's voice says from inside me. It's her spirit again, her spirit that visited me that night I wrote to my father. *I'm glad you have Sara Lynn and Ruth to love you,* she tells me. *It's okay that you love them back.*

'Thanks, Mom,' I whisper, relieved because she understands and I don't have to choose, relieved because I can love everybody.

Chapter 26

When Hope leaves my room, my shoulders start shaking and I sob without making a sound. I push my supper tray away. How am I supposed to even think about eating just now! I could just wring Sara Lynn's neck for putting me through this again. I can forgive her for taking up with that Teller boy. After all, she wasn't in her right mind after her father's death. But she's a grown woman now, a grown woman responsible for raising a child. There aren't any excuses I can think of that would justify her running around town with some young tennis player. What kind of an example is she setting for Hope, for heaven's sake? She needs to let herself be courted by a nice man, a mature man who's in a position to be a father to Hope. In case she's forgotten, that first love of hers abdicated that responsibility.

I put my face in my hands, and as happens sometimes, I'm surprised to feel the slack, wrinkled quality of my skin. *Whose skin is this?* I ask myself, puzzled, and in the same flash of feeling, I realize it's mine.

~

When I was pregnant with Sara Lynn, I was sick to my stomach every day and happier than I'd ever been. 'The nausea is a good sign,' my sister reassured me over the phone. 'It means your hormones are working right this time.'

'You're sure?' I asked her.

'I'm crocheting you a baby blanket as we speak,' she replied firmly. 'I'm sure.'

I'd had four miscarriages during my first three years of marriage, four instances of holding a baby inside me like a secret, a secret told too soon, a secret ruined. 'This just happens sometimes, Aimee,' Eliot said after the first miscarriage. He brought me flowers and warm tea and held my hand while I wept. 'We'll have other babies.' The second time it happened, I screamed while I cried, cursing the God who'd put me through this pain yet again. The third time, I expected nothing good to occur and felt the familiar cramping without emotion, as if I were watching someone else. It was Eliot who cried this time, his head in his hands.

'We can't keep going on like this,' he said in a broken, husky voice.

'We have to,' I snapped, staring straight ahead and willing myself not to think, not to feel. 'There's nothing else we can do.'

I carried my fourth pregnancy for two and a half months, the longest I'd ever managed to keep a baby. And then I lost her — isn't that a ridiculous expression? As if I'd carelessly misplaced my infant and were just waiting for her to turn up.

That fourth baby was a girl. The first was a boy, and the rest were girls. 'Now, you don't know that, Aimee,' Eliot said.

'Yes, I do,' I replied, sitting motionless at the kitchen table. 'A mother knows.'

I'm afraid the pain was too much for me. My mind buckled under it, and I'd wake up every morning earlier and earlier, weeping as if I'd never stop. When it got so that I wasn't sleeping at all, Eliot sent me home to St. Louis, hoping a change of scene would do me good.

Mama and Julia Rae met my train, Julia Rae's wide hazel eyes filling with tears when she saw me. 'You're home now,' my sister whispered, hugging me and stroking my hair. 'You're home now.'

Mama gave me something to make me sleep, for how could I be expected to recover when I couldn't rest? She was indignant about my lack of sleep, as if I were a wayward child who hadn't followed directions. 'For goodness' sake,' she scolded as she fussed with the blankets covering me and plumped the pillow under my head. 'A body needs sleep! It's that simple!' Just before she shut my bedroom door, she said, 'I don't want to hear a word from you until you've slept a good twelve hours.'

I spent a month at home – a month of sleeping late, of Mama's cooking, of Brother and Baby Caroline coming in and out with their noise and their laughter, of Julia Rae coming by the house every day to rub cream into my hands or brush out my hair or massage my shoulders. 'You're getting better, Aimee,' she remarked one day. We were sitting on the porch, rocking and talking, and I had laughed at something she'd said. She put her hand out and touched my arm. 'You'll be going back east soon.'

I didn't know if I was ready to go home. What if I fell into the same despair that had sent me back to Mama's house? What if being at home reminded me of all that sadness, all those babies I didn't have?

'You're ready,' Mama said, brushing a strand of hair from my forehead. 'Eliot misses you, and you need to start living your life again.'

'I'm too scared,' I practically whispered to her.

'No more babies,' she said firmly. She touched my cheek as if to soften her words. 'No more trying. It just isn't meant to be.'

I nodded and went back to my marriage with a new resolve. If babies broke my heart every time, then there would be no more babies. 'I think that's wise,' Eliot said when I told him. 'We're fine as we are.'

And we were fine. Fine for years and years until we got old and thought we didn't need to worry so much about protection anymore. Until I'd missed two cycles and began to wonder. Until I went to the doctor and he confirmed what I'd suspected. Until I burst into tears at the dinner table and told Eliot, 'I'm too old to go through this again! It'll kill me this time!'

But the months passed and this baby stayed with me. I became tired and sick, so sick that I thought I was losing the baby and dying besides. 'No, no,' Julia Rae said, laughing. 'This is how you're supposed to feel.'

I wasn't convinced until I felt the baby kick. I was in my kitchen, going to the refrigerator for some orange juice. 'Oh, my Lord,' I said, my hands instinctively going to my swelling belly. I picked up the phone. 'Julia Rae,' I said, my voice trembling. 'The baby just kicked.'

'Of course it did, silly,' she said. 'Aimee, you're having this baby!'

I didn't let myself think of names. Not yet. Not until she was here. I knew she'd be a girl, the same way I knew the genders of my other children. But it wasn't until the first pains came that I doubled over, clutched my belly, and allowed myself to say the name I'd chosen from a place deep inside myself. 'Hello, Sara Lynn,' I whispered. 'I'm so glad you're coming to me.'

⁓

Oh, my Sara Lynn. My baby girl. I think of her as I sit here alone in my room, wondering how I got to be so old and Sara Lynn grew away from me. Well, I suppose she's been growing away from me ever since that first labor pain I felt, that first time I said her name. I see her so clearly as an infant, with her baby-smelling skin and the blond fuzz covering her soft spot. But I also see her as a toddler, following me around in the garden, dropping seeds and laughing as I tickled her under her chin with a buttercup. 'Who likes butter? Who likes butter?' I teased as she tried to grab the flower, shrieking, 'Mama, you give to Sara Lynn!' I see her getting on the school bus, her two braids bouncing over her shoulders; I see her playing tennis with her father, laughing as

Eliot runs for the ball and misses. I see her as a teenager, reading at her desk as she plays with a strand of her hair; as a college girl, so proud in her Wellesley sweatshirt. I see her as a young woman living in Boston, showing us her first apartment; and I see her with circles under her eyes and thin as a rail when she quit her job and came home to live. I see her showing me Hope for the first time, whispering, 'Mama, this is Hope. Isn't she beautiful?' I see her as she is today, too, her hair piled on her head as she works in the garden. She talks to herself while she's working; I can see her mouth move. My love for Sara Lynn is layered, spread out for all the Sara Lynns I've ever known, all the Sara Lynns she's ever been.

Sometimes I dream about my ghost babies, the ones I never held, the ones I never named. Their chubby little legs kick, their rosebud mouths suck, and their tiny fingers reach up to find me.

All I ever wanted in my life was to be a mother. To love a child and watch her grow. I never could have guessed how it would feel to let her go. Why, it feels like cramping that's come too early, a mass of bloody tissue leaving my body too soon. *Stay,* I want to whisper. *Don't leave me just yet.*

Chapter 27

$\mathcal{J}$ack's bugging the hell out of me, and we're not even married yet. We're lolling around in bed after our usual morning rendezvous, and he just will not stop picking at me. Okay, so it might be a little strange that I want to keep our engagement private. Especially given that the wedding is next week and I'm supposed to be inviting people to come. I've sort of led Sara Lynn to believe that I have invited people, but whenever I see the people I'm supposed to invite, I can't seem to open my goddamn mouth about it. I've sworn Jack to secrecy, too. I'll tell people in my own good time; that's what I keep saying to him. But now it's looking like my own good time has expired, because Jack is wondering just what in hell is up.

'What are we going to do, Ruth?' he's saying, tickling my back. 'Wait till our kid graduates from high school? Say, "Oh, yeah, that's our kid. We got married some years ago. Didn't we tell you?"'

Hmmph! Now he's trying to joke me into saying, 'Okay, Jack. You're right. Let's put up a big sign at the diner. Let's rent a goddamn megaphone and ride through town announcing our wedding so everyone can share the joy.'

'Listen,' he says, 'Sara Lynn couldn't have been happier, could she? And Hope – she's happy, too, now that it's sunk in.' I don't answer, and he adds, 'And Paulie and Donna are thrilled, just thrilled that their old man found someone so great the second time around. Right? So what's the problem? Why not tell everybody else?'

He's waiting for me to say something, but I bury my face in the pillow and pretend I'm not hearing him. Finally I say, my voice all muffled, 'I just don't want anyone to laugh at me.'

'Why would anyone laugh at you? Because you've got the misfortune to be stuck with me?'

I peek my head out and narrow my eyes. 'Don't you ever think that.'

'Then what is it?'

'It's . . .' I sigh and roll over on my back, looking up at the ceiling. 'People at the diner are so used to seeing me one way. They'll just laugh their asses off when they find out I've been carrying on with you. That I'm *in love*.' I say the last phrase in a joking way.

'Are you?'

'Am I what?' I snort.

'In love.'

'What do you think?' I ask, hitting his arm. Damn fool.

'I don't know,' he says, and he sounds a little sad. 'You never say it.'

I feel goddamn tears sting my eyes. I swear, these hormones are going to kill me by the time this kid comes out.

'Say it,' he says, cupping my breast. A plus of pregnancy – I've got some actual, B-cup boobs.

'Say what?' I ask, and push his hand away.

'Say that you love me.'

'Good God, Jack,' I say as I sit up and look at him fiercely. 'Would I be marrying you if I didn't love you? Would I be having your baby?'

He sits up, too, and picks up my chin. 'I love you, Ruth Teller.'

Dammit, I just can't stop the tears from flowing, and I put my hands to my face to catch them. 'I . . . I love you, too, Jack Pignoli.'

'Was that so hard?' he asks, hugging me close.

'Yes . . .' I cry onto his shoulder. 'It was.'

'I know,' he says gently. He kisses me and then pulls away, getting up to go over to his bureau. Jesus, where's he going? Doesn't he know he's supposed to comfort his crying, pregnant, soon-to-be wife?

'Here,' he says, sitting back down on the bed. He takes my left hand and spreads out my fingers to slip on a ring.

'Oh, my God,' I say, and my tears dry right up because I'm in absolute shock looking at the huge diamond I'm now sporting.

'Do you like it?' he asks, and he reminds me of Hope. It's just what she used to say when she'd draw me a picture and give it to me from behind her back, looking up at me with eager eyes.

I can't stop looking at the damn ring. It's likely to blind me, that's how big it is. I can only nod; words seem to be failing me.

Jack pulls me to him and pats my back. 'No one's going to laugh at you for being in love, Ruth,' he whispers. 'And if they do, I'll knock their block off.'

So now I'm at the goddamn diner, wearing a rock as big as Mamie's, a rock that might as well be a huge sign announcing to the world, 'Hello! Somebody's claimed me.'

'More coffee, Tom?' I ask, making my rounds. It's the usual breakfast group, reading their papers and talking local politics before work. I'm just trying to keep out of everyone's way and do my job.

'Jesus, Ruth, what's that?' Tom Cassidy asks as I pour. He's pointing to my ring.

'Oh, that,' I say casually. Here goes nothing. 'I'm getting married.'

He about chokes. 'You're what?'

'Yep.' I can't look at him, just grab a paper napkin and wipe

273

up a tiny drip of coffee on the laminated counter. 'Me and Jack. Next week.'

I steel myself for the laugh, but it doesn't come. Only a happy cheer, and he's up and hugging me. 'I'm happy for you both,' he says, kissing my cheek, and then he bangs his fork against his glass to get everyone's attention.

'Hey, everyone,' he calls to the whole morning crowd. 'Ruth and Jack are getting married!'

Chet's standing in the doorway to the kitchen, shaking his head and beaming with joy. He starts it – puts his hands together and claps – and then everyone else gets on their feet and joins in. They're all clapping and cheering for me, and I swear, I feel like that idiot Sally Field getting her Oscar. You like me, I want to tell them; you really like me.

Chapter 28

When I wake up, it dawns on me that Ruth's getting married in three days. I'm not altogether happy about that because things are going to change big time for me. She's leaving, although I almost believe her now when she says she'll never leave me, not by getting married, not by having a baby, not ever. And Jack *is* pretty nice. I smile, thinking about how he brought me a chocolate sundae from the diner yesterday. Extra cherries on top, too. So I'm okay with Jack, I guess, but I'm still not so sure about the new baby.

Well, worry never stopped life from knocking a person on her ass. That's what Ruth always says anyhow, so I turn off my mind, hop out of bed, and run downstairs.

'Hi, Sara Lynn,' I say as I come into the kitchen. She's sitting at the table, sipping her coffee and reading the paper. I put some bread in the toaster and lean against the counter.

'Good morning.' She smiles at me, looking up from the paper. 'Did you sleep well?'

'Uh-huh,' I say as I wait for my toast to pop up.

'It's going to be hot today,' she says, setting down her coffee cup. 'I'll drive you over to the club to swim if you'd like.'

I shrug. 'Maybe.' I've been avoiding Sam. What am I supposed to say when I run into him – I know you know I totally loved you, but let's play tennis anyway? I don't think so.

When my toast pops up, I butter it and slide into the chair across from Sara Lynn. I look out the bay window and notice all these potted flowers sitting on the lawn. 'You're planting today?' I ask, motioning to the window.

'Well, yes,' she says, bringing her eyebrows together. 'We need a little color down in the gardens for Ruth's wedding.'

'Because I wrecked them, you mean.'

'Oh, Hope.' She waves her hand. 'You didn't wreck them. You just . . .'

'Removed all the flowers?'

She laughs. 'Yes. Temporarily removed all the flowers.'

'I'll help you,' I say, my mouth full of toast.

Sara Lynn tilts her head to the side. 'Help me with what?' she asks.

'Planting. I want to. It'll make me feel better for what I did.'

'Don't be silly; there's no need—'

'I want to,' I say. 'Please let me.'

She looks at me for a moment, like she's thinking about it, then says, 'Well, all right. Thank you. That would be very nice of you.'

Oh, it feels so good to be close to her again. The first few days I wasn't talking to her, it felt great to punish her, to know I was making her feel alone and unloved. But after that, it was lonely for me, too, my stupid pride preventing me from going to her and saying, 'Let's just work this out, because I miss you.'

We hear a shuffling step from the hall, and Sara Lynn pauses in midsip of her coffee. I put my head down over my toast, my heart beating faster. Mamie walks into the kitchen without saying a word. She walks right past the table, opens the porch door, and looks at the herb garden surrounding the terrace – the one garden I didn't get around to wrecking. 'The terrace looks lovely, Sara Lynn,' she proclaims, as if she'd never stopped talking to her daughter. 'You really do have a knack for plants.'

Sara Lynn raises her eyebrows and shrugs her shoulders at me, as if to say, 'Well, that's how it goes. You wait long enough and even the most stubborn person will come around.' Then she smiles her gentle smile. 'Thank you, Mama,' she says. 'I come by it honestly.'

I think I come by some things honestly, too. I get my sense of humor from Ruth, my love of beautiful things from Sara Lynn, and my determination from Mamie. After I find my father, I'll find out what I get from him and my mother. And I think there must be certain things that started with me, special things, things that are just mine alone.

Chapter 29

*I*t's hotter than blazes out here. The air is still and heavy, and my throat already feels parched. I've brought down a jug of water, though, so Hope and I can stay hydrated. That's the most important thing to do in the heat, you know – drink lots of water.

'Are you sure you want to help with the planting, Hope?' I ask. 'It's brutally hot today.'

'Yeah, I'm sure,' she says. 'Just tell me what to do.'

'Okay.' I point to the edge of the meadow garden. 'I'm thinking we'll just plant these annuals right along the edge here. The structure of the garden is still intact. We'll just add some color to pretty it up for Ruth's wedding.'

I kneel down and grab my trowel, but Hope just continues to stand beside me, scratching some bug bites on her arms.

'Ready?' I ask.

'I . . . I don't exactly know how to plant a flower,' she says sheepishly.

Well, my goodness, how can she have lived with me for twelve years and not know how to garden? How is it that we've never worked together like this before? I smile and pat the ground next to me, motioning for her to kneel beside me. 'Of course you don't,' I tell her. 'I've never shown you how.'

As she kneels next to me, I say, 'Look at what I'm doing. First dig a hole. Just like this, see?' I put my trowel in the soil and dig.

'Okay, now you tap the plant out of its pot, gently – watch me.' I pick up a pink petunia and turn it upside down, lightly tapping the bottom of the pot.

'Then you loosen the roots a little at the bottom, see?' I use my fingers to pull out the roots curling in a circle at the bottom of the plant. 'That's so the roots will take in the soil.'

I place the petunia in the hole I dug and use my hands to bridge the gap between the potting soil and the soil of the earth. 'Then you just pop it in the ground. Look how I'm patting the soil around the plant, helping settle it in its new home. And that's it! That's how to plant a flower.'

I smile at her from under my sun hat and see that she's squinting and chewing on the inside of her cheek, looking at me as if I've shown her a complicated mathematical equation. Well, gardening is one of those things you learn best by doing. You can think about it all you like, but there's no substitute for just getting your hands dirty and planting. 'Here,' I tell her, handing her a trowel. 'You try.'

She digs the hole just fine. Everybody knows how to dig a hole. Then she picks up a plant and gingerly taps the bottom of the pot. 'Be a little more forceful,' I tell her. 'You won't hurt it.'

She taps harder and the plant slides out. Then it's in her hands and she says, 'I know you said something about pulling on the roots?'

'Mmm-hmm.' I nod. 'Tip the plant upside down so you can see the bottom. What pattern do the roots make?'

'A circle,' she says. 'The roots are growing in a circle.'

'Right. That's because the plant was growing in a pot. Now, we don't want the roots to keep growing in a circle when we put it in the ground; we want the roots to spread out so they can take in the nutrients and water the plant needs. We want the roots to expand.' I move my fingers apart to show her what I mean. 'So

279

you need to tease those roots on the bottom, to separate them and spread them out.'

She begins to pick at them, then says, 'Uh-oh. I broke some.'

'That's okay. That happens. The plant will thank you for it, because it'll really thrive when it's in the ground. You're setting it up to establish itself well.'

'Okay,' she says, nodding. She hesitantly sets the plant in the ground, then picks up soil with her hands to fill in the rest of the hole.

'Now pat around the plant. You're kind of giving it a little hug to send it on its way.'

Hope firmly tamps down the soil surrounding the plant. 'I did it,' she said.

'You did it,' I agree, putting my arm around her shoulders. 'Now you know how to plant.'

We work side by side, edging the meadow garden with the annuals I was able to scrounge up from the nursery this late in the season. It's pretty, what we're doing. I think it will be lovely for Ruth's wedding.

'Who taught you how to plant?' Hope stands and stretches, then kneels again to continue working.

'My mother,' I tell her, a surprising lump forming in my throat. 'Mamie.'

We cleared the land to make the meadow garden the summer I was ten. Mama just decided one day that she was sick of looking at the ugly overgrown field at the bottom of the hill, and she told me we were going to make a natural garden.

'We'll make a place where the birds will like to come. And the butterflies. And other little creatures.'

I liked the sound of that.

She and I worked in the mornings, when it was relatively cool, clearing the brush and high grasses that had taken root in that field for years and years.

'You're being silly, Aimee,' my father scoffed at her as we waved him off to work in our jeans and T-shirts and scraped arms. 'Why don't you hire someone to do that clearing?'

'Sara Lynn and I are making something, Eliot,' she told him. 'We're doing this ourselves so when we're done, we can say, "That's our garden."'

He just shook his head and got into his car as we headed down the hill for another morning of backbreaking labor.

In the afternoons we rested. Mama put calamine onto my bug bites and said it was a miracle we hadn't got poison ivy yet, and we sat out on the porch and ran the ceiling fan on high as we leafed through her gardening books and decided which plants to put in our meadow garden.

'What about black-eyed Susans, Mama?' I asked, pointing to a picture in the book.

'Oh, yes,' she said, and made a note in her gardening notebook. 'That's a fine idea.' Then she took the book and flipped through the pages. 'And I wanted to ask you about the varieties of butterfly bushes we should have. There.' She pointed to the pictures on the page she had marked. 'What do you think?'

We deliberated over the plants we'd have in our meadow garden more thoroughly, I'm sure, than the jurors down at the courthouse were deliberating over the case Daddy was trying. It was that important to us. We were altering the landscape, after all. We were taking a piece of the earth and saying, 'This is what we will make of it. This is how it will look.'

It took a solid week to clear that land and then another week to bring in soil and spread it. 'Don't you want me to spread that soil for you, Mrs. Hoffman?' Gabe from the nursery asked as Mama showed him where to dump the pile of topsoil.

'No, thank you, Gabe. Sara Lynn and I are quite capable of handling that. This is our summer project, you know.'

I never doubted her, not once. If she said we could do it, well then, we could and we would.

It was Labor Day when we finished planting, and school was to begin the next day. Our garden didn't look like much. Those plants wouldn't come into their own until the next growing season.

'Wait,' Mama said. 'Just wait.'

It was a long winter that year, and snow blanketed the meadow garden from just after Thanksgiving all the way into March. But in April, the forsythias and shads we had planted bloomed their heads off. And in May, the lilacs formed their purple blossoms. Summer brought the butterfly bushes, the echinacea, the phlox, and the black-eyed Susans. The purple asters bloomed in the fall, and in the winter, red winterberries gleamed against the white snow.

It was a late August day of that first growing season that Mama called me from my room where I was reading and told me to walk with her down the hill. The garden was in its glory then – the purple of the butterfly bushes, the rosy pink of the sedum, the lavender of the early meadow asters. 'Look at what we've created, Sara Lynn,' she told me, her hands on my shoulders as we drank in the garden with our eyes. 'Look what we did.'

I didn't say anything; there wasn't a need. The garden said it all. I just nestled back into her strong, firm body and let her wrap her arms around me. I could feel her chest moving up and down with the breaths she took; that's how close we stood. I could feel her heart beating against my ear, and I closed my eyes for a second, a part of me rushing backward through time to the beginning place, when she and I were one.

⌒

'It was my mother,' I tell Hope again, spreading out the roots just like Mama showed me. 'She taught me all I know.'

Chapter 30

Oh, my God, I'm getting married today. It's the first thought that pops into my head when I wake up. As I look up at the ceiling in the room I've occupied for twelve years, I can't believe I've spent my last night here. Then I think about Jack, and I smile. After the rehearsal dinner last night, he drove me home and we sat in his car for a bit. 'Ruth,' he said, taking my hand, 'I won't see you tomorrow until you walk down the aisle, so I want you to know this now: I love you so much, and I'll take good care of you and the baby.'

My first instinct was to say, 'I've done a pretty good job of taking care of myself for thirty-seven years. You won't have to put yourself out much.' But I stopped myself, and I leaned against him, saying, 'I know you will, Jack. I love you, too.'

I kissed him then and said, 'See you tomorrow, I guess.'

He lifted my chin to look in my eyes, and he smiled the smile I've grown to love, where the lines at the sides of his eyes deepen. 'See you tomorrow, kid.'

And now it's tomorrow. My wedding day. I lie in bed and think about Ma for a minute, and I sort of wave to her in my mind. *Hey, Ma, wherever you are.*

Her voice inside me speaks up: *I'm in heaven, you damn fool.*

Where else would God put me after suffering with you and your brothers all those years?

I wish you were here, Ma, I say to myself as I slide out of bed.

I am here, Ruthie, she tells me. *I'm right here where I've always been.*

Still in my nightgown, I pad in my bare feet down to the kitchen. No sense in getting dressed. I'll have to get gussied up in a few hours anyway.

'Oooh . . .' sigh Mamie and Sara Lynn. I swear, they look at me as if I'm a vision floating in the air these days.

'The bride appears,' says Mamie.

'It's just me,' I say, waggling my fingers at them. 'Just old Ruth.'

'You're getting married today,' Sara Lynn says.

'Really?' I joke. 'I forgot.'

Hope says, too casually, 'There's something for you on the dining room table.'

'Is there?' I look at her sharply. Everyone in this house has been acting positively giddy. You'd think *they* were the ones getting married.

As I walk into the dining room, all of them following me like I'm the Pied Piper, I see a vase of red roses on the table. 'Oh, from Jack?' I say. 'That's nice.' They're all looking at those roses like they've never seen flowers before.

'Read the card,' says Sara Lynn.

'Okay,' I say, plucking the tiny envelope stuck in the flowers. I open it and read: 'Thirteen red roses – twelve for you and one for the baby. Look in the driveway and you'll see your real wedding gift.'

I stare at Sara Lynn, then Hope, then Mamie. 'You're all in on this, aren't you.'

Hope jumps up and down and says, 'Come on, before the secret slips out.'

'What is this, a damn treasure hunt?' I grumble, even though I'm about as happy as I can be.

I stomp out to the front hall. 'I suppose you all want to come with me,' I say, standing there and waiting for them. 'Ready or not,' I finally tell them, and I head down the front steps and walk the path to the – *ohmygod* – driveway.

I scream, 'This is for me?' It's a beautiful car with a big red bow on top. I'm jumping around it, looking at it from the front and back and sides. It's silver and shiny, and I shout, 'Come on, we're going for a ride!'

Hope comes running over, yelling, 'Isn't it beautiful? Don't you like it? Mr. Pignoli – I mean Jack – said he couldn't stand the thought of you driving your old junk heap another day. He said he's been wanting to do this for years.'

Sara Lynn is helping Mamie down the walk, and Mamie gives a low whistle. 'My, she's a beauty,' she says, patting the side of the car.

'Hop in,' I say. 'We've got to take this for a spin.'

Sara Lynn helps Mamie into the backseat, where Hope is already sitting, then slides into the passenger seat. 'Come on, Ruth,' she says, tapping her watch. 'We do have a schedule to keep today.'

I take a deep breath and open the driver's door. The car smells new and fresh, and I turn the key that's sitting in the ignition. The engine purrs quietly, and I look at the odometer. 'Ten miles,' I say. 'This car is brand-new.' I back it out of the driveway and say, 'Watch this, ladies.' I crank up the air conditioner as high as it will go, and we all sigh as we take in the cold air.

I drive past downtown and head south until I reach Jack's neighborhood. 'Oh, Ruth, no,' says Sara Lynn. 'You can't let Jack see you before the wedding.'

'I won't, I won't,' I tell her. 'Just watch.' I drive my new car past his house, honking and beeping but not slowing down or stopping. I know he hears me, and I'm laughing and laughing as I careen around the corner with Sara Lynn riding shotgun and Hope and Mamie sitting in the back.

Bobby used to take me driving at night. We'd be at home, just sitting around watching TV or something, and he'd stand up all of a sudden. 'I'm bored,' he'd say. 'Come on, Ruth. Let's go for a drive.'

'At this hour?' Ma would carp, looking up from the TV.

'Come on,' Bobby would urge me. 'Let's go.'

We'd talk on those drives. Something about the darkness and the motion made us surrender the sarcastic, joking tone we usually took with each other. We told each other the truth the gentlest way we knew how.

Once, we drove up into the mountains, taking our chances on the narrow, winding roads that twisted and turned as they took us up, up, and up. This was when Bobby was seeing Sara Lynn. I was furious with him even for looking at her, never mind sleeping with her, and he'd had to strong-arm me into going along with him that night.

'Ruth,' he said, his eyes on the road, 'don't be mad.'

'Who's mad?' I snorted, but then I sighed and said, 'I just don't get why you're wasting your time with Miss Smarty Pants.'

He was silent for a minute, and then he said softly, 'I'm in love with her.'

My God. My heart clenched up like a fist ready to hit. 'At least call a spade a spade,' I snapped. 'You're not in love with her; you just lust after her.'

'No,' he said, still looking straight ahead. 'It's not just that. She's . . . I don't know . . .' He drummed his fingers on the wheel and shook his head. 'I can't explain. It's just . . . she's different.'

'She's different all right,' I said with a snort.

He looked at me then, and I saw a light in his eyes I hadn't seen since we were kids. 'Different in a special way is what I mean,' he said, turning his eyes back to the road. Then he smiled, and I could tell he was thinking about her.

I wanted to be happy for him, I really did. But instead I just felt hollowed out inside. I was losing him to something I didn't understand, and it felt as if I'd never get him back. I turned to

286

look out the window, so he wouldn't be able to see my set jaw and my angry, hurt eyes.

'Ruth?' he finally said.

I took a deep breath. 'My ears are clogged. You're driving too far up.'

He paused, and I could feel the air between us change, almost as if I had thrown up a sign that said, 'We didn't just talk about you and your snotty girlfriend. Everything's just the way it always is between us.'

'So swallow. Pretend like you're chewing gum.'

My shoulders relaxed when I heard his tone. He had read my sign, and he wasn't going to say any more about how that stupid Sara Lynn Hoffman was changing his life. But inside my relief was sorrow, too, because he'd tried to give me something of himself and I had turned it away. I leaned my cheek against the coolness of the car window and watched the headlights sweep over the patch of road ahead.

'Do you remember Dad?' I asked, because the door between Bobby and me was still ajar and because there was something about the pitch black of the night that brought my father to mind.

'Yeah, sure I do,' he said. After a moment, he asked, 'Why, do you?'

'A little.' I stared at the patch of ground the headlights lit up. Wasn't Bobby scared? Didn't he wonder if the headlights were enough to light the way? The road was so twisty. 'Why do you think he left?'

'Jesus Christ, how would I know?' Bobby replied. 'Maybe Ma drove him crazy.'

He laughed, and I joined him. The door between us was closing fast, and I said what I'd never said to anyone. 'I miss him.'

'How do you miss someone you don't even know?' Bobby asked.

'Beats me, but I do.'

I pull into our driveway and stop the car. The brakes work like a dream, and I don't want to shut off the engine. I could just sit in the air-conditioning all day.

'Okay,' Sara Lynn says brightly. I swear, this wedding's brought out her bossy side in spades. 'We have a couple of hours before we need to start getting ready. Ruth, you haven't eaten anything today, so why don't you go inside and have a little toast and a glass of juice. I don't want you running on empty today. I'm going out to the tent and check on things there. I'm sure everything is fine, but you never know. I want everyone to start getting ready at noon. That'll give us a couple of hours, just in case there are any emergencies to deal with.'

'Like what?' I teased. 'A run in our nylons?'

Sara Lynn nods seriously. 'Exactly.'

I roll my eyes, and Hope laughs.

'We don't have time for jokes today,' Sara Lynn says, but she smiles as she slides out of the car.

I take a bagel and a glass of juice out onto the porch, figuring I might just as well obey Miss Bossy.

'Well, well,' says Mamie, rocking in her chair and looking out the screened windows. 'It's your big day today.'

'I guess,' I say, sipping my juice. 'But even if it is my day, Sara Lynn is still the boss. I'd better eat quick, or she'll have my head.'

Mamie chuckles and says, 'Isn't that the truth.'

We're silent for a few minutes, and then I say, 'Mamie, about the other week, with me telling you about Sara Lynn and Sam . . .'

Mamie holds up her hand to stop me. 'I know,' she says firmly. 'Don't let's go into all of that. You're a loyal friend to Sara Lynn. We'll leave it there.'

I take a bite of my bagel and get up and stretch. I want to tell her something before I walk into the house and get ready to be married, something about how she's meant a lot to me all these years, something about how I've grown to love her, too, not just her daughter.

'You'll be okay out here?' I ask her gruffly as I walk to the doorway. It's all I can say. What's in my heart makes it up to my throat and then dies there.

'Oh, I'll be just fine,' she replies, waving me into the house as she pushes the rocking chair back and forth with her feet. 'You don't need to worry about me.'

'Okay, then,' I tell her, and I walk into the house with all the goddamn words I'd like to say trapped inside where no one can hear them.

Chapter 31

$\mathcal{I}$ reapply my lipstick and glance out my bathroom window. Everyone's milling around on the terrace, waiting for the sign to take their seats. I glance down at my watch – it's five minutes to two. Time to get Ruth.

I check the mirror one last time, and I smile, remembering how Sam greeted me downstairs. 'You're even more beautiful than usual,' he said, looking at me in that way he has of making me feel like he's really seeing me.

I pause outside Ruth's bedroom door, then rap lightly. 'Ready to get married?' I ask.

The door opens a crack, and Ruth's pale, scared face peeks out. 'Can you come in for a sec?' she half whispers.

'What's wrong?' I ask as I follow her into her bedroom.

'Oh God,' she moans, sinking to the floor. 'I'm so nervous I'm shaking.'

'What are you nervous about?' I ask. I've never seen her like this. Never. Not easygoing, joke-cracking Ruth.

She puts her head in her hands. 'I don't know if I can do this. Not in front of all these people.'

She's wrinkling her dress by sitting on it like that. 'Why don't you stand up while we talk?' I suggest. 'You'll mess your pretty dress.'

She looks up at me with so much fear in her eyes, she reminds me of a sick animal that wants to be put out of its misery. It appears that wrinkling the dress is the least of our issues here.

I gingerly sit next to her on the floor. 'What's wrong, Ruth?'

She closes her eyes and shakes her head back and forth. 'We should have eloped. I should have known I couldn't do this fancy wedding thing. Traipsing up an aisle in front of people! Can't do it.'

'Of course you can,' I tell her. Oh, she's being ridiculous! I wish I were funny, the way she is. I wish I could be her for just a minute, so I'd know what to say to lighten the air, to make everything all right.

'I'm scared,' she says quietly.

I put an arm around her. 'Oh, Ruth,' I say. I pat her shoulder, at a loss for words. The only thing that comes to mind is the song 'High Hopes.' My mother used to sing it to me when something seemed insurmountable, and it always made me feel better, even though I always wondered if the ant ever managed to move the darn plant. Somehow, I think not. But the sentiment is nice, so I smile and start to warble, just singing 'la la' when I forget the words.

Ruth's eyes get bigger and bigger as I sing, and when I'm finished they look ready to pop out of her head. 'You're pathetic, Sara Lynn,' she says in disbelief. 'Absolutely pathetic.' Then she opens her mouth and howls with laughter, pointing at me and shaking her head.

My forehead crinkles and my cheeks heat up as I realize I've just sung the most ridiculous song ever written as though I were conveying a profound message. But then my mouth twitches, my shoulders shake, and a laugh starts low in my stomach and rises. I'm practically doubled over with hilarity and, just as I catch my breath and start to calm down, Ruth starts in again, setting us both off with fresh shrieks. We're going to sit here together literally dying of laughter, and I can't think of a better way to go. I don't even care that my mascara is running.

I was eight years old and going into third grade when Ruth Teller was my best friend for an August afternoon. It was one of those long summer days when I woke up with nothing to do except play by myself for a million hours. I went outside to make my dolls a little tea party when I spied Mrs. Teller's old brown Ford coming up our driveway.

I started waving away, excited that I wouldn't be alone today after all. Mrs. Teller didn't mind if I followed her around the house, showing off to her how smart and gifted I was. 'Geesh, Sara Lynn,' she'd tell me after I'd recited a poem for her or done a tap dance, 'you certainly are talented.'

Mama liked for me to be nice to Mrs. Teller, because she was less fortunate than we were. She didn't have a husband who supported her nicely the way my daddy did us. Her husband hadn't died, either; I wasn't sure what had happened to him. Nothing good, I knew, from Mama's stern, hushed voice.

'Hi, Mrs. Teller,' I called. I picked up my jump rope and started skipping rope so Mrs. Teller would be sure to say, 'My, you're good at that. So graceful and quick. Is there anything you can't do?'

My rope and my face fell when I saw all four doors of Mrs. Teller's car open.

'Look who's here to play today,' Mrs. Teller said with a tight smile as she popped open the trunk and pulled out her buckets and rags. 'Ruth and her brothers!'

Ruth glared at me as she slammed the door of her mother's car. I narrowed my eyes right back at her.

'Do you like Ruth Teller, Sara Lynn?' my mother would ask me occasionally as she combed out my wet hair after my evening bath. I knew she wanted me to like Ruth Teller just enough so it could never be said I was unkind to her, just enough so the teacher would say quietly to my mother, 'Sara Lynn is kind to her classmates who are less fortunate than she.'

Not that Ruth needed me to be friends with her. She was tall for our age, and she wore Sears Toughskin jeans and basketball sneakers. My mother dressed me in fancy dresses and patent-leather buckle shoes from Boston, and Ruth called me Miss Priss and got the other girls to do the same. They were followers, those girls. Lord knows I tried to boss them myself, but Ruth Teller had them under her thumb through her sheer bullying.

'Let's play house,' I'd say to the girls at recess. 'I'll be the mother.'

'That's dumb,' Ruth would scoff, standing on her hands just to show off. 'That's the dumbest game I ever heard of. My brothers and all their friends would die laughing if they saw us playing that game. Let's play horsie instead.' She'd break from her hand-stand and get down on all fours, kicking up her legs and shouting, 'Neigh, neigh!' All the other girls would follow her, and I would stalk off to sit on the school steps, waiting for the bell to ring.

I finally broke my eyes from Ruth's mean stare and turned to run into the house. 'Excuse me, Mrs. Teller,' I called.

My feet pounded on the marble floor of the front hall, and I raced into the living room, where Mama sat sipping an iced tea and listening to the record player.

'Mama,' I hissed, 'Mrs. Teller brought her children today.'

Mama looked startled and put her glass on the side table. Before she could say anything to me, Mrs. Teller was at the living room doorway, asking, 'Mrs. Hoffman, could I talk to you a minute?'

'Run along, Sara Lynn.' Mama gave me a kiss on the cheek, then she smiled at Mrs. Teller and motioned her to come in. 'Sit down,' she said. 'And how many times do I have to tell you to call me Aimee?'

I perched myself just outside the living room doorway so I could hear every word.

'My sitter's gone,' Mrs. Teller said. 'My ex-husband's sister Maria. She ran off last night and just didn't show up to watch the kids today. Can I keep them here with me today? I'll find another sitter as soon as I can. It'll only be today. I've told them to play in your backyard quietly and not disturb you.'

'Why, Mary,' my mother said, and I guessed that she was patting Mrs. Teller's arm in that comforting way she had about her, 'of course that's just fine. Sara Lynn will adore having Ruth for company this morning.'

'Really?' Mrs. Teller said. 'Thank you so much. Sara Lynn's a little doll. Maybe she can teach my kids some manners.'

They laughed together, and I could hear them get up to leave the room, so I hightailed it out of the hallway and ran through the kitchen and out the back porch door. I stood on our terrace, taking in the view of my beautiful backyard being trampled by the Teller children.

There was bossy Ruth, down on all fours like a horse and kicking as usual, pawing up the grass. She probably loved my big backyard that sloped gently down a hill. Had it not been for the presence of her brothers, I would have marched down there and told her to stop rolling in my grass. But those Teller boys scared me to death.

There were two of them, Tim and Bobby, and everyone in school knew exactly who they were. They were always fighting in the school yard or showing up tardy with no excuse or being sent to the principal's office for doing disgusting things like passing gas loudly during music class. They were big for their ages, and I'd heard rumors that they smoked cigarettes in the woods behind school.

I saw them on my swing, hanging from the ropes and fighting for the seat. I wanted to screech, 'Get off my swing!' in a tone Mama would refer to as tacky.

'Hey!' Bobby Teller, the oldest and baddest, was shouting up at me.

I walked to the edge of the terrace and called, 'What?'

'You want to go on the swing? I'll push you, if you want.'

Before I could answer, Ruth yelled, 'Sara Lynn is stuck-up. She's the most stuck-up girl in my class.'

'Am not!' I yelled back, stamping my foot. My face burned as she laughed at me, and I turned and walked into the coolness of my house, letting the porch's screen door slap behind me.

'Are my kids behaving themselves?' Mrs. Teller asked. She was down on her knees, scrubbing the kitchen floor.

'Yes, ma'am,' I said. 'The heat's just a little too much for me. I believe I'd best run upstairs and have a little lie-down.' I fanned myself and sighed as I walked past her and up the stairs to my room with the pink-flowered wallpaper.

I slammed my bedroom door shut, turned up my window-unit air conditioner, and stood in front of it until my dress blew up and I felt goose-bumpy all over. Once Mama had caught me doing this. 'Stop that, Sara Lynn,' she'd scolded. 'That's the tackiest thing of all.' I couldn't help myself, though. I liked that goose-bumpy feeling where my private area was.

'Sara Lynn . . .' Mama rapped on my door, and I jerked myself away from the air conditioner just as she poked her head inside. 'What are you doing up here when you have guests?'

'I'm suffering heat exhaustion, Mama,' I said, and I tried to make my voice sound trembly and sick.

Mama pursed her lips together and shook her head slightly. 'A lady is always gracious to her guests,' she said, 'no matter who those guests happen to be.'

'I know, Mama,' I said innocently. 'I was just feeling a little dizzy from the heat.'

'I think you're better,' she said tartly, holding the door wide open for me.

I flounced past her and started down the stairs. 'That's my good girl,' she said.

I went out the front door so I wouldn't have to pass Mrs. Teller again, and I stood motionless for a moment on the bluestone path that led from the front steps around to the back of the house. A slight breeze lifted the skirt of the light green sleeveless summer dress I wore, and I lifted my chin. I wasn't going to be afraid of those Tellers. This was my house, after all. My house and my yard. I ran around to the back before I lost my nerve.

Ruth was on my swing, standing on it, of all things, putting her dirty bare feet on the seat. Her brothers stood on either side of her, jiggling the ropes that held the swing.

'Sara Lynn, why don't you come down here?' Ruth jeered when she spotted me. 'Are you afraid of my brothers?'

I tossed my head. 'No, I'm not.'

'Prove it,' she yelled.

'Fine,' I said, and I walked with my head high down into the grass. When I reached the swing, I crossed my arms over my chest and said, 'Here I am.'

'You want me to push you on the swing?' asked Bobby. His voice was softer than I would have imagined it to be, and I tilted my head to one side and looked at him.

'I'm on the swing,' said Ruth, stamping her foot on the narrow wooden seat and holding on tightly to the ropes. She wore blue jogging shorts with three orange stripes down each side. Standing on the ground as I was, I was eye level with her legs rather than her face.

'What's that?' I asked, pointing to an ugly red raised splotch just below her kneecap. It wasn't like any cut or scab I had ever seen. It was a living thing, growing and angry and throbbing.

'Nothing,' Ruth snapped at the same time Tim said loudly:

'It's im-pe-ti-go. Don't touch it or you'll get it, too.'

I snatched my hand back and looked at Bobby for confirmation. He nodded. 'It is contagious,' he said.

Tim grinned. 'We call her impetigo girl.'

'Cut it out,' Ruth said from between her set teeth. 'Cut it out if you know what's good for you.'

'Impetigo girl,' I whispered, thrilled with the secret I had learned, as if I had walked in on Ruth while she was on the toilet going to the bathroom. 'Impetigo girl,' I said louder.

'Impetigo girl,' Tim chanted with me, and then Bobby, and

pretty soon we three were running around the swing shouting it. My throat was getting sore from screaming, 'Impetigo girl! Impetigo girl!'

'Stop it! Stop it!' shouted Ruth, stomping on the swing. Finally, she jumped right into me, knocking me to the ground and pinning my shoulders. She rubbed her knee on my legs.

'There,' she said as she got off me. 'Now you'll be impetigo girl, too. I just gave it to you.'

She stood over me, glaring fiercely, while I lay still and tried to catch my breath.

'See what you've done, you bitch,' said Tim. 'She's gonna tell.'

'If I'm a bitch, then you're an asshole,' Ruth retorted.

Although I'd never heard such words, I knew instinctively they were bad. I knew I wouldn't be the same Sara Lynn just for hearing those words, and the thought of that made me shaky inside, as if I wanted to cry. I sat up in the grass and held my knees to my chest. I was breathing hiccupy breaths, and my face was turning red.

'Sara Lynn, it's okay.' Bobby knelt in the grass beside me. 'She didn't really give you her impetigo. Ma's been putting ointment on it, and it's not catching anymore. I swear.'

It was his kindness that made me cry soft little sobs with my head buried in my knees.

'Oh, gosh. Oh, gosh,' Ruth kept saying. She sank down to sit in the grass, too, and said, 'Please don't cry. I'm really, really sorry.'

My tears dried up in a minute, and, embarrassed, I busily plucked grass from the ground where I sat.

'Are you okay now?' Bobby said. He touched my shoulder with his boy hand, and I had to catch my breath. I thought of the goose-bumpy feeling I got when I stood in front of the air conditioner; I thought of the way my father touched my mother's arm when he wanted her attention, the way he pronounced her name as a statement of fact. 'Aimee,' he'd say to her, 'Aimee.'

'I'm fine,' I said softly, still plucking grass strands.

'Well, good,' he said, and took his hand away from my shoulder.

'Don't tell on me,' Ruth babbled. 'I swear I was just joking around. Ma says I have a mean streak in me, but I really don't. I just get a little carried away sometimes. Can you not tell?'

'I won't tell,' I said, feeling generous toward her because of Bobby.

'You want to play some more?' asked Tim.

'Sure.' I scrambled up and wiped off the back of my dress. 'I'll play.'

'Horses!' cried Ruth. 'Let's play horses!'

'Something else,' I said, feeling like my old self again. 'I don't want to play horses.'

'Well, what do you want to play?' Bobby asked.

'House,' I replied.

They groaned.

'Okay,' Ruth said grudgingly. 'We'll play house. What do you want us to do?'

'I'm the mother,' I said immediately. 'And you can be the father,' I said, pointing to Bobby. 'You two' – I pointed to Ruth and Tim – 'can be the kids.'

'How come you get to be the mother?' asked Ruth, narrowing her eyes. 'That's not fair. I don't even want to play this stupid game, and you're making me be the kid.'

'Wait!' I clapped my hands and jumped up and down. 'I've got it! You can be the horse!'

'The horse?' said Bobby, looking at me skeptically.

'Mmm-hmm.' I nodded. 'The family can have a pet horsie.'

'Yay!' yelled Ruth. She jumped down on all fours and began neighing.

'Good horsie,' I said, patting her back.

'Can it be my horse?' asked Tim. 'I'm the kid, so it should be my pet.'

'Yeah, but don't ride me,' Ruth warned him. 'You're too heavy.'

'Okay, I'll be fixing supper in the house, and then the husband comes home. That's you, Bobby. And you ask what's for dinner. And then we call in our son, who's outside playing with his horse.'

They did it. They didn't like it, but they did it. And when they couldn't do it anymore, when I pushed the Tellers to their very limit and saw I was going to have a mutiny on my hands, I twirled around so my dress flared out and said to Bobby, 'You know, you never did push me on the swing like you said you would.'

'Race you there,' he said, relieved to be set free from playing house. He punched me lightly on the arm as he ran by me.

'Wait!' I hiked up my skirt and raced after him, but Ruth beat me to the swing. I looked at Bobby pleadingly.

'Off,' he told Ruth, jerking his thumb away from his body. 'Off now.'

'I was here first,' she whined.

'I let you be the horsie in house,' I reminded her.

She swung a little and then jumped off. 'Fine,' she said. She plopped down on the grass and watched me hop on.

Bobby swung me higher and higher so that my stomach kept lurching into my throat. As I wondered if I'd throw up, I laughed and laughed, shrieking, 'Higher! Higher!'

'Let me push her,' Tim said. 'I can go even higher.'

'No,' I said, looking back in alarm. 'I only want Bobby to push me.'

'Sara Lynn has a crush on Bobby,' Ruth said from the ground, smiling evilly.

'She does not,' said Tim, pulling at one of the swing's ropes. 'She has a crush on me. I'm going to kiss her.'

'Yeew!' I said. I was going crooked now, and I jumped off the swing, screaming, falling on my knees and dirtying my dress.

'Get away from me!' I screeched as Tim began to chase me. 'I have impetigo! Ruth gave it to me, and I'll give it to you. I swear I will!'

'Yeah!' Ruth hopped up from the grass and chased Tim. 'I'll help you, Sara Lynn. Us impetigo girls have to stick together.' She caught up to him easily and wrestled him to the ground. 'Impetigo girl to the rescue!' she hollered.

Bobby came over to help Tim up and warned, 'Cut it out. She doesn't want you to kiss her.'

'Fine,' said Tim, brushing off his pants. 'I didn't really want to, anyway.'

'Yay!' Ruth grabbed my hands and spun around with me. 'We won!'

'Hooray for the impetigo girls!' I screeched, my voice getting hoarse. I glanced sideways at Bobby to see him looking at me, and I jumped higher and yelled louder, dancing around and holding Ruth Teller's warm hands.

⁓

I reach for her hand now. 'You ready, impetigo girl?'

'Oh God,' she says, laughing. 'I remember that day.'

'It was one of the happiest days of my childhood,' I tell her.

'Why weren't we friends after that?' she wonders.

I shake my head quickly and say, 'I wish I knew. But we're friends, more than friends, now.' Her hand feels cold in mine, and I give it a squeeze.

'Sara Lynn, give me away,' she says.

'What?'

'You know,' she says. 'Give me away. I can't walk down that damn aisle myself. Not in front of all those people. Let Hope lead the way, and you walk me down the aisle. Okay?'

'Sweetie,' I say, 'of course I will. But I hate to think of giving you away. This is hard enough already.' My vision blurs, and I sniffle. 'I can't imagine you not being here.'

'Listen,' she warns, 'if you start bawling, I'll never do it. I'll never go down there and walk that damn aisle.'

'Okay.' I blink back my tears and nod. 'Okay. You're right.

Impetigo girl, you're getting married today and I'm dragging you down to your groom. Ready?' I stand up and offer her my arm.

'I guess,' she says, gripping my arm tightly. As we head down the stairs, she says, 'Jesus, I feel like the bride of Frankenstein in this confection of a dress.' And I laugh and laugh because she'll always be with me, even when she's not living here anymore.

Chapter 32

*M*y stars, Ruth looks beautiful. She's standing up front with Jack, holding his hands as they say their vows. I nod, watching her. I knew she had it in her.

Now, I won't say I was thrilled to pieces when she first moved in with us. Oh, that took some persuasion on Sara Lynn's part. Indeed. But I love that girl. I love my cleaning lady's daughter.

Ah, poor Mary. I surprise myself with the tears I'm blinking back. Someone cleans your house for so many years, though, and you get to know her. She'd be proud of her daughter. Proud of Ruth.

Has it been twelve years? Twelve years since Ruth and Hope came to this house and filled it with the life I hadn't known it needed. I turn my eyes to see Hope, standing up under the bower by Sara Lynn. She's my granddaughter, just as sure as if she were my own flesh and blood. And Ruth's baby . . . well, I suppose that'll be my grandchild, too.

I put my hand into my purse and reach my fingers around the ruby pendant I'm meaning to give Ruth today. Marge Costa leans over to me and says, 'Can I get you something, Aimee? Are you looking for a handkerchief in your purse?' She holds a tissue up to me, and I shake my head.

The bride and groom are kissing now. Oh, it does make me cry. I tap Marge's arm and say, 'I think I will take that tissue.'

'Here you are,' she says.

I dab at my eyes as Ruth and Jack walk down the aisle. Ruth is leaving us, and I cry into my cheap little tissue even as I'm overjoyed for this girl I've grown to love.

~~~~

Julia Rae married Harrison on the hottest day of an August many years ago, and I left home the very next week. I'd been wanting to get away since Julia Rae's engagement, for it seemed that her life was moving forward at a rapid pace and mine was stuck where it had always been.

My family came to see me off, of course, all dressed in their best clothes. Mama stood crying silent tears, even though she kept smiling and saying, 'I'm fine. Don't worry about me.' Papa was gruff, wishing me luck at my new teaching job and telling me to make the family proud. Baby Caroline kept looking at the train's large engine, saying, 'I sure wish I was going somewhere.' Brother had been made to be there; he stood in his suit, rolling his eyes and whistling impatiently, as if he were missing the important business of his life due to my going away. Julia Rae came with Harrison, standing close to him in her new pink suit.

'Well, this is it,' Papa said heartily as the final whistle blew. 'You call right when you arrive, now.'

'I will, Papa,' I told him automatically, but it was Mama I was looking at, standing straight with her red-rimmed eyes. I wanted to throw down my suitcase and say, 'I can't do this. I can't leave you. How am I supposed to be able to manage without you?' But everyone was counting on me, and I'd look like a weak little fool if I went home instead of getting on that train.

I hugged everyone again, all except Harrison, leaving Mama to the last. 'Bye, Mama,' I whispered, and I ached at the thought of leaving those arms that had buoyed me up forever.

'Go on now,' she said, giving me a little push. 'Time for you to go.'

I boarded the train and found my seat, next to a gentleman as old as Papa, no doubt traveling for his business. I tried to arrange my mouth in a smile as I sat beside him and said, 'Good morning.' I fiddled with my hands on my lap for a moment, and then I asked my seatmate, 'Do you mind if I take the window just until we're out of the station? I want to wave good-bye to my family.'

'Certainly,' the man said, and he closed the newspaper he had been reading and changed seats with me. 'Keep the window for the trip. I don't care.'

I looked for my family standing together on the pavement outside. I rapped at the window hard to get their attention, and it was Baby Caroline who spotted me and shouted to the others, pointing me out. Mama gently pulled down Baby Caroline's finger and said something to her, and I knew she was admonishing my sister for pointing. I waved to them frantically, and they all waved back. Julia Rae was smiling, and she blew me a kiss. The whistle blew, and the train jerked forward as it pulled slowly out of the station. I put my clenched fists against my cheeks and was surprised to feel wetness on my hands. I was crying without effort as the train moved faster and faster and I watched my family recede into the distance. The man next to me cleared his throat and nudged me, and I turned to see him silently offer me his handkerchief. His kindness touched me, and I cried even harder as I took the handkerchief and buried my face in it. As I wiped my eyes, I had to press my arms against my fluttering heart to make it stay inside of my body, to keep it from flying back to the only people in the world who knew its rocky terrain.

I wouldn't have met Eliot if I hadn't gone away. Wouldn't have had Sara Lynn. Wouldn't have grown to love Ruth and Hope. Life has a strange way of surprising a person. There isn't any way of telling how it will all work out.

I laugh out loud to think of myself, an old lady — yes, it's true; I'm not afraid to speak the truth — with ties that bind me here, ties I dearly love. But I'm still that shy, awkward girl, boarding a train, scared to death of leaving my mama behind.

'Are you all right, dear?' Marge puts her hand on my shoulder, and I pat it briskly.

'Oh, I am,' I tell her, my heart full with the past and the future melding together to make . . . well, to make right now, of course; to make the present moment.

Chapter 33

We all held our breath together as Ruth married Jack. I walked down the aisle first, and I was surprised to hear people in the crowd murmuring, 'Oh, she looks so pretty.' It took me a minute to realize they were talking about me.

When I got to the end of the aisle, Jack winked at me. I smiled at him and took my place on the other side of the justice of the peace. Then Ruth came down, holding Sara Lynn's arm. Well, that was my family for you. Couldn't have a normal wedding, with Ruth holding the arm of a guy standing in for her father. No. Ruth had to walk down with Sara Lynn. I scanned the faces of the crowd, but nobody seemed to think it looked weird. Everyone's face just looked happy and soft. There was Chet, handsome in his suit with his hair parted precisely and neatly combed. There was Mrs. Costa, her head tilted to one side as she patted Mamie's arm. And there was everyone from the diner, all those people Ruth served day after day, beaming like they'd never seen a wedding take place before. I loved them all, every single person looking up at Ruth and Jack. If my arms had been big enough, I would have held them out right then to hug everyone at the wedding.

And now the music is starting, and I'm in the reception tent sitting next to Mamie and Mrs. Costa, eating my third chocolate party favor.

'You'll make yourself sick,' Mamie scolds, but I just shrug because I've already popped the candy into my mouth.

Ruth is dancing with Jack, and I have to say they look really good together. He holds her firmly, like he's not going to let her go. She's laughing up at him, and I see how happy she is. A pang of jealousy stabs my heart, because I want to be the only one who makes her that happy. But it's time to share her, whether I like it or not.

'Dance?' It's Sam, standing behind me and offering me his arm. My heart does a little skip, but then it stops and goes back to normal. It's the first time I've seen him since all hell broke loose.

'Sure,' I say, and I get up from where I'm sitting and let him lead me to the square wooden floor.

We start to dance a halfhearted waltz, and he says, 'Hope . . . ,' like he wants to tell me something.

'Hmm?' I say.

'I'm sorry.'

'Sorry about what?' I ask, my heart pounding again.

'Sorry about you and me. I think the world of you. You're a wonderful girl who will make some man very happy someday.'

'But not you,' I say.

'Not in that way, no,' he says gently. 'But it would make me very happy if we could still be friends. I don't say that lightly, either. I want to keep getting to know you, because I like you. I think you're an interesting person.'

'Well, I guess you'll have to keep getting to know me if you're going to be dating Sara Lynn.' I sound like Ruth when I say this, and it makes me proud.

He stops dancing for a minute and looks down at me. 'This doesn't have anything to do with Sara Lynn,' he says. 'I'd think you were a person worth knowing even if there was nothing between Sara Lynn and me. I'd still want to keep in contact with you.'

'You would?' I say.

He nods and starts circling around with me again. 'Don't sell yourself short, Hope. I like you for you, not because you're related to Sara Lynn.'

'Well, I'm not really related—' I stop myself. 'Thank you,' I say, lifting my chin and looking in his eyes. 'Thank you.'

He hugs me for a minute and says, 'I'm glad to know you, Hope.'

I blink back tears that are happy and sad at the same time, and I nod into his shirt.

⌒

'You look beautiful, you know,' says Sara Lynn, smoothing my hair as we leave the dance floor after a funny fast polka we did together.

'No, I didn't know,' I reply shyly, twirling the skirt of my dress. It's my purple dress, the one I got for my birthday.

'You were right,' Sara Lynn tells me. 'That ruffled pink dress didn't suit you. Too little-girlish. You really look like a beautiful young lady in this dress.'

I blush with happiness and say softly, 'Thanks for telling me I'm pretty.'

She looks surprised. 'You didn't know?'

I shake my head, and she takes me by the shoulders. 'You're the most beautiful girl I know,' she says, her eyes looking at me proudly. 'You're absolutely lovely.'

⌒

Ruth and I are dancing together to an Elvis song, and she's crooning along.

'I'm glad Jack makes you happy, Ruth,' I say, interrupting her singing.

Her eyes get big, like she's surprised. 'Thanks, Hope.' She sounds sort of shy, and I can tell my words mean a lot to her.

'Promise I'll still be your baby even when your real baby comes?' I ask.

'You are my real baby,' she says without missing a beat. 'And

I swear I'll ground you for a month if you say otherwise. Got it?'
She glares at me.

I smile. 'Got it.'

She grabs my hands and whirls me around so my head spins.

Jack dances a slow dance with me, and I'm sort of tongue-tied with him. I've known him forever, but now that he's Ruth's husband, I can't think of a thing in the world to say to him.

'When we get back from our honeymoon, I want you to come over and decorate your room, okay?'

I shrug. 'Okay.'

'You can do it however you want it. You and Ruth figure it out. But it's going to be your home, too. I want you to know that.' He pauses, then says, 'You know, I'm a lucky man to be married to your aunt.'

'Yes, you are,' I tell him.

'I'm also lucky because I'm getting you as part of the deal. You're the icing on the cake, Hope,' he says. 'I know you have a lot of people who care about you already, but I hope you'll let me be part of that group.'

I let him lead me around the dance floor – he's of that generation, Ruth jokes; he can't not lead – and I look up at him and smile. 'Thanks, Jack,' I say, and I squeeze my arms awkwardly around his neck to let him know I mean it.

I dance all afternoon with everyone. I'm dancing to celebrate Ruth's marriage, but also to celebrate something about myself. A lot of things have happened to me recently. I got my period, I fell in love, and I'm on my way to finding my father. Sara Lynn says she expects the detective to call any day now.

You know, he might not want me – no matter what Sara Lynn

thinks, that's the truth. And that'll hurt real bad. But then again, he just might hold out his arms and hug me in close. He just might whisper, 'Hope, I've been waiting for you for twelve whole years.' See, I don't know what's going to happen. But I can't let not knowing stop me from finding out.

———⌒———

Ruth goes upstairs to change into what Sara Lynn calls 'her going-away outfit' and what Ruth herself calls 'my Sara Lynn priss-ass dress.' It's taking her forever, and we're all waiting for her in the front yard. Jack is joking with his grown-up kids, and he sees me watching him. 'C'mere,' he says, motioning me over. He gives me a big hug and says, 'It's a great day, isn't it, kid?'

I hear someone yell, 'Here she comes!' and I twist out of Jack's arms to look. It's Ruth, and she looks so pretty in her new red dress. 'It's not everyone who can carry off red, Ruth,' Sara Lynn told Ruth when we all went dress shopping together. 'With your coloring, this'll be lovely.'

Jack walks forward to meet her and says in a nice loud voice, 'Here comes my wife! Isn't she a looker?'

We all step back a little to give them room as they walk hand in hand down the stone path and over to Jack's car. 'What're you all staring at?' Ruth laughs, looking around at us.

'You've still got your bouquet, Ruth,' calls Mrs. Costa. 'Throw it.'

'Oh, God,' Ruth says, looking down at the small bouquet of white roses in her hand. 'Sara Lynn, will you take these foolish things? I can't take them with me to the Cape.'

'Throw it,' Mrs. Costa urges. 'Throw the bouquet.'

'I'm not throwing it,' says Ruth. 'I'd probably bonk someone on the head.' Everyone laughs because it's true. 'Besides, I want Sara Lynn to have it, her being such a flower freak.'

Sara Lynn walks up to Ruth and takes her bouquet from her. She hugs Ruth and whispers something, and they both laugh in a way that sounds happy and sad at the same time. Then Mamie totters up to them and says, her voice clear as a bell, 'I want you to have this,' and she's holding out something in her hand. Oh, my gosh, Mamie's giving her Julia Rae's pendant. It's the teardrop ruby necklace that belonged to Mamie's sister, the one who was so pretty that all the boys in town were just crazy about her.

'Oh no,' Ruth gasps. 'I couldn't take something like that.'

'Yes,' Mamie insists, grabbing Ruth's hand with her own trembly one and placing the necklace into it.

Ruth puts her hand up to her mouth and looks at the jewel in her other hand. 'But this is Julia Rae's pendant.' That's the thing about an old person repeating her stories all the time – everyone knows which piece of jewelry comes from which dead person.

'Yes, it is. And you remind me so of her. You have her spirit, her big heart.'

'Mamie, it's too much,' Ruth argues, trying to give the necklace back.

'Nonsense,' says Mamie, scowling. 'It's my way of telling you—' Her voice breaks. 'I love you.'

Ruth gets all pale and wide-eyed, like she's scared she made Mamie cry, but before she can say anything, Mamie looks at Sara Lynn. 'And let's get something else straight. I love you, too. My lovely, sweet, strong daughter. I always have, and I always will.' She touches Sara Lynn's cheek and says, 'I want you never to doubt that. Do you understand me?'

Sara Lynn's forehead puckers as she nods slowly, and the three of them awkwardly pull together in a hug. 'The end of an era,' jokes Ruth.

'The beginning of a new one,' Mamie adds firmly.

'Where's Hope?' they all seem to ask at once, turning their heads from one another to look for me. The circle of women opens, and I hike up the skirt of my dress and run toward them, my feet beating a rhythm on the asphalt of the driveway.

'Here I am,' I call. 'I'm right here.'

Acknowledgments

I owe tremendous thanks to the following people for helping make one of my oldest and dearest dreams come true: Jamie Raab, thank you for your warmth, intelligence, and guidance. Lisa Bankoff, thanks for taking a chance on me and watching my back with such finesse and good humor. Risa Miller, your kindness and generosity to a fellow writer are much appreciated. Thanks to Kate Swanson, efficient assistant with a smile, and to Mark Fischer and Jon Burr for sharing their legal and business expertise. Thanks to all my family and friends for love and laughter along the way. I especially appreciate the feedback I received from early readers Liz Flaherty and Judy Willard, and the good conversation and girl power I get monthly from my hilarious and ultra-supportive book club. Last, but never least, I send my gratitude and love to the memory of Arthur Edelstein: writer, teacher, mentor, and friend to so many.

SPECIAL MESSAGE TO READERS

THE ULVERSCROFT FOUNDATION
(registered UK charity number 264873)
was established in 1972 to provide funds for
research, diagnosis and treatment of eye diseases.
Examples of major projects funded by
the Ulverscroft Foundation are:-

- The Children's Eye Unit at Moorfields Eye Hospital, London
- The Ulverscroft Children's Eye Unit at Great Ormond Street Hospital for Sick Children
- Funding research into eye diseases and treatment at the Department of Ophthalmology, University of Leicester
- The Ulverscroft Vision Research Group, Institute of Child Health
- Twin operating theatres at the Western Ophthalmic Hospital, London
- The Chair of Ophthalmology at the Royal Australian College of Ophthalmologists

You can help further the work of the Foundation
by making a donation or leaving a legacy.
Every contribution is gratefully received. If you
would like to help support the Foundation or
require further information, please contact:

**THE ULVERSCROFT FOUNDATION
The Green, Bradgate Road, Anstey
Leicester LE7 7FU, England
Tel: (0116) 236 4325**

website: www.foundation.ulverscroft.com

Brian McGilloway was born in Derry, Northern Ireland, in 1974, and teaches English at St Columb's College, Derry. He lives near the Irish Borderlands with his wife and four children.

You can discover more about the author at www.brianmcgilloway.com

HURT

In mid-December, a fifteen-year-old girl is found dead on a train line near Derry, and Detective Sergeant Lucy Black is called to identify the body. The only clues to the dead teenager's last movements are stored in her mobile phone and on social media — and it soon becomes clear that her 'friends' were not as trustworthy as she thought. Lucy is no stranger to death: she is still haunted by the memory of the child she failed to save, and the killer she failed to put behind bars. And with a new boss scrutinizing her every move, she is determined that — this time — she will leave no margin for error.

BRIAN McGILLOWAY

◆

HURT

Complete and Unabridged

CHARNWOOD
Leicester

First published in Great Britain in 2013 by
Constable & Robinson Ltd
London

First Charnwood Edition
published 2016
by arrangement with
Little, Brown Book Group
London

A catalogue record for this book is available
from the British Library.

ISBN 978–1–4448–2782–8

Published by
F. A. Thorpe (Publishing)
Anstey, Leicestershire

Set by Words & Graphics Ltd.
Anstey, Leicestershire
Printed and bound in Great Britain by
T. J. International Ltd., Padstow, Cornwall

This book is printed on acid-free paper

Friday 9 November

Prologue

The one benefit with getting a school picture taken was that it took so long you missed an entire lesson. Especially when all the other girls in the class were taking forever, fixing their hair, nipping out to the toilet to put on make-up they weren't even meant to have in school. Her mother forbid her using it. 'Fourteen is too young for make-up,' she'd said. Not that make-up would have made much difference, Annie thought.

Annie Marsden stood, watching the group in front of her, their conversation soundtracked by the music leaking from her headphones. If they were aware of her standing behind them, none showed it.

A flash to their left. Up on the stage an old guy, white-haired, slightly stooped, was standing at the camera while Nuala Dean preened herself, angling a little in front of the canvas image of a library of leather-bound books, their spines mixtures of red and blue and green. Showing her good side. At least she had a good side, Annie thought.

The line in front of her shuffled forward a space and she moved to fill the gap.

She glanced up only to catch the eye of her physics teacher. He was standing, his arms folded, watching her. Without unfolding his arms, he gestured towards his own ear then

3

waggled his finger at her.

She obligingly pulled out her earphones and pocketed them. The group ahead of her had moved onto the steps of the stage now, their conversation reduced to a murmur as each prepared themselves for their shot.

'Move up, will you!' someone behind her said, and Annie shuffled forward again, pulling her cardigan sleeves further down, gripping their cuffs in her hands. The floor was yellow, she noticed. Assembly hall floors always are. Yellow because that's the only colour of light they can't absorb. Or it's the only one they can absorb. She couldn't remember which.

'Give me a beautiful smile,' she heard the old man say. The girl on the stool in front of him obliged.

'Button up your top button, Annie,' someone said. The physics teacher was standing next to her now. 'Look like you have some pride in your uniform.'

Annie blushed slightly, murmured an apology as the girls behind her tittered at the comment. She struggled to bring the collars close enough together to clasp, in the end gave up and tightened the knot of her tie nearer her throat. She'd told her mum she needed a new shirt in September. Four months later and she was still waiting. Either that or she'd put on too much weight.

'Aren't you just lovely?' the old man said, earning the reward of a smile from Sally McLaughlin.

Annie made her way up the steps, stood, next

in line, for the shot, her stomach churning. Sally got up, flicked her hair over her shoulder and strode across and down the set of steps on the other end of the stage.

'Sit yourself down, love,' the old man said.

Annie came across to the stool, edged herself onto it, picked a spot above the photographer's head to look at, waited. He was busying himself with the flash, adjusting the angle.

Hurry up, Annie thought. She was aware that her skirt was pulled up on her thighs a little, revealing the whitened scar of the ladder in her black school tights. She shifted in the seat, pulling at the hem.

'Right, look at the camera, please,' the old man said.

Annie, despite herself, did. She saw a distorted version of herself reflected in the concave of the lens.

'Haven't you the prettiest eyes?' the old man said.

Annie instinctively glanced at the floor, just as the flash brightened the stage.

The wood was yellow.

Sunday 16 December

1

He'd just got a pint in when the aura started. A quick flickering of iridescence on the periphery of his vision that already made his stomach turn. He shut his eyes in the hope that perhaps it was a trick of the light, overtiredness from the night before. The last thing Harry needed was another late evening, but then he'd promised the missus this for months. A bit of dinner, a few glasses of wine, then down to the pub after for an hour. The tentative re-beginnings of a relationship which had sprung leaks years earlier, but whose gaping holes only became apparent with the departure of their only son to university.

'Empty nest syndrome,' one of the drivers had told him that day as he'd mentioned during break that he had to go out. They'd all been out the night before on a work do; John-Joe Carlin's leaving party. He'd been driving the Belfast-Derry train for thirty-three years, through all kinds of shit. And now, this evening, he was bringing his last train home.

Harry glanced at his watch, could just make out the time beyond the growing intensity of the flickering, his whole field of vision now haloed with shifting ripples of light. John-Joe would be on the final stretch of his final drive, passing Bellarena.

He stumbled back to the table where his wife,

Marie, sat, glancing around her, smiling mildly at the other drinkers.

'I need to go home,' Harry said. 'I've another bloody migraine starting.'

Marie tried to hide her disappointment, a little. 'Have you none of those tablets?'

Harry shook his head. 'They're in my work uniform. I left them in the station.'

She tutted, turning and picking up her coat, the fizzing soda water untouched on the table where Harry had set it fifteen minutes earlier. 'Come on, then. I knew it was too good to be true.'

The shimmering had thickened now into a perfect circle of tightly packed strands of light that seemed to encircle his pupil. Harry felt his stomach lurch, swallowed hard to keep down his meal. It really would be a wasted night if he brought that back up.

His phone started vibrating a second before he heard the opening notes of 'The Gypsy Rover', his ringtone. He stared at the screen, trying to make out the caller ID.

'John-Joe,' he said, answering the phone. 'You're done early.'

'Earlier than I'd planned. Something's happened. The train's just died.'

'Where are you?'

'Just past Gransha. Coming in on the final stretch.'

That was less than two kilometres from the station. The train would already have been slowing, rounding the curve at St Columb's Park, then the last few hundred metres in past the Peace Bridge.

'What happened?' Harry asked, shifting the phone to his other ear.

'I don't know. We just lost power. Everything. Can you check it out?'

Harry glanced up at where Marie stood, the keys in her hand, the hoop of the key ring hanging off her wedding finger.

'I'll be right down,' he said.

★   ★   ★

As he moved onto the tracks, away from the brightness of the station, Harry was grateful for the silence after all he'd listened to in the car. The darkness actually helped ease his building headache a little. The aura had stopped as they'd pulled into the station, though that was perhaps because his attention was diverted into trying to placate Marie. After all, he was well enough, she suggested, to work, but not to take her out for the night. How could he explain that it was John-Joe's final night? That the man needed to get his train home, one last time? She wouldn't understand it. He could see her now, sitting in the car, the heater turned up full, arms folded, tight-lipped, her expression pinched.

He could feel the migraine proper begin to build. He tried focusing on the bobbing of the torch he held as he walked the line. He glanced ahead a distance, to his right, at the looming shapes of the trees separating the train line from St Columb's Park.

Power cables ran along the track side, heavy copper, sheathed in plastic. It was to these that

Harry turned his attention, for undoubtedly that was the reason for the train stopping. Sure enough, only ten yards ahead, just beneath the Peace Bridge, the lines had been cut.

He dialled through to the train.

'John-Joe? Sorry, man. You're not going to be bringing this one in for a while. The lines have been cut just outside of the station. We'll need to get the passengers bused out. Have you many on board?'

'One. And he's sleeping off a session.'

It wasn't unusual. The Belfast to Derry train was so slow a journey most people took the bus. The line had been promised an upgrade for years. They were still waiting. Maybe, Harry reflected, the cost of replacing the broken lines would be the latest excuse for not doing it.

'Maybe just a taxi, then.'

'How much cable is missing?' John-Joe asked.

'I'm still walking it,' Harry said. 'It's gone until at least St Columb's Park,' he added, shining his torch along the side of the tracks, noting the absence of the thick cabling.

He was moving away from the light thrown off from the street lamps of estates up to his right now, and heading below St Columb's Park itself. The moon hung low over the tops of the thick-limbed sycamores above him. To his left, the lights of the city seemed to wink at their own reflection off the river's surface. Harry could smell the sharpness of the mudflats he knew to be just a few feet away from him, a sudden drop down from the tracks to the river's edge.

Suddenly, ahead of him, he saw something.

'Shit, I think one of them is still here,' he whispered, lifting the mobile to his mouth again.

'Get out of there. Call the cops,' John-Joe said.

Harry squinted up ahead. His headache had gathered now behind his right eye. He felt a wave of nausea, felt the sweat pop on his forehead. He could make out a figure who seemed to be lying on the ground, as if hiding, perhaps hoping that, in so doing, he wouldn't have noticed them.

'Oi! You!' Harry shouted. He tried training the torch beam on the spot where the figure was lying, but even so, his headache had grown in intensity to the point that he found it hard to make out what exactly he was looking at.

'Get up off the tracks,' he shouted as he stumbled up the tracks, his foot catching on one of the sleepers beneath, his hands taking the main force of the impact on the sharp-edged grey gravel between the tracks as he fell.

Cursing, he stood again, retrieved his torch and stumbled onwards. It was clear now that the figure was lying on the train line. It looked like a girl, for the hair was long, brown, hanging over her face. She was lying face down on the tracks, her throat resting on the side closest to the river, her legs supported by the other side, her body sagging into the space between them.

'Jesus, get up,' he shouted. 'You'll be killed.'

It seemed a pointless thing to say. The train wasn't going anywhere because of the cables. Besides, lying where she was, she was obviously trying to kill herself anyway. Not brave enough to throw herself in front of the train, she was lying on the tracks, waiting for it to come. She'd

13

picked a spot on the curve so the driver wouldn't have time to brake by the time he'd seen her. In fact, he might not even realize he'd hit anyone at all, until the body was found.

'Come on! Get up, love,' Harry shouted, as he covered the last hundred yards. He wondered if she'd be pleased or sad to find out that the train wouldn't have made it as far as her. Maybe God was looking out for the girl when he sent whoever out to steal the cabling. Mysterious ways and all that.

'Are you all right?' he asked, approaching the girl now. He couldn't tell her age, but she was dressed young: flowered leggings and a hoodie. He noticed one of her baseball boots was lying on the gravel off to one side.

He crouched down beside her, placed a hand on her shoulder. 'You need to get up, love.'

No response.

He left the torch on the ground and, using both hands, gripped her shoulders harder, struggled to turn her over. Finally, she fell onto her back, though in doing so, he knocked the torch onto its side, its beam spilling out onto the river.

At first, he couldn't quite comprehend what had happened. Her head lay unnaturally tilted back, though in the weakening gradations of light thrown from the torch, he couldn't quite see why. It was only when he shifted the torchlight towards her that he saw the gaping wound severing her throat.

Harry struggled to his feet but only managed a few yards before he finally brought his meal back up.

2

A flash of lightning bloomed inside the thunderheads far to the east as DS Lucy Black, trailing a step behind her boss, DI Tom Fleming, picked her way along the train tracks towards the arc of light thrown off from the crime scene beyond. A sharp, earthy smell carried off the River Foyle, which was slate grey and choppy in the rising breeze. From the canopy of the trees bordering St Columb's Park, to their right, the crows shifted uneasily on the branches, curious as to the disruption to their night roost.

As they approached the crime scene tape, Fleming flashed his badge at the uniformed sergeant standing at the cordon.

'And Sergeant Lucy Black, also Public Protection Unit,' Fleming added as the man wrote the names on the clipboard he held.

Lucy glanced to her left; the lights of Derry City winked in the shivering water of the river next to the train line as a breeze shuddered down the Foyle valley. The embankment across the water had been pedestrianized and newly refurbished. The increased street lighting meant Lucy could make out the figures gathered across there, watching over at them.

Fleming stood back, holding up the tape for Lucy to duck under it.

'It's a mess up there, Sergeant,' the officer at the tape said.

15

'I'll manage,' Lucy commented, noting that he had not offered the same advice to Fleming.

As they made their way along the edge of the train tracks, the first thick drops of rain raised dusty plops from the wooden sleepers the tracks dissected. Lucy recognized the figure coming towards them as Tara Gallagher, a DS from CID.

'Hey you,' Tara said, smiling warmly when she saw her. 'I didn't know you'd been called.'

'DI Fleming suggested we should ID Karen. Is it her?'

Tara nodded. 'We think so. She fits the description, anyway. I'll get the boss down.'

Tara lifted her radio. 'Inspector Fleming and DS Black from the Public Protection Unit are here, sir,' she said.

Lucy glanced up to the scene, saw one of the suited figures put away his radio and turn towards them. He lumbered down the tracks. Lucy assumed this to be the new CID Superintendent, Mark Burns, who had been recently appointed as the replacement for the late Chief Superintendent Travers.

Burns had been fast-tracked up through the ranks though and was a very different creature from the late Chief Super, by all accounts. He'd only taken up the post a week or two earlier, following the last round of promotions.

'What's he like?' Lucy asked Tara, nodding towards the approaching figure.

The girl shrugged. 'All right, so far. *Thorough*,' she added, in a manner that meant Lucy couldn't tell if it was intended as a compliment or a pejorative.

16

'Chief Superintendent Burns,' the man said, approaching them, gloved hand outstretched. 'Tom, I've met before. You must be Lucy Black. I've heard a lot about you.' His eyes twinkled above the paper mouth mask he wore. Lucy wondered just how much he could have heard in a fortnight.

'Lucy can ID the body,' Fleming said. 'She'd been heading up the search for the girl. She knew her a bit.'

'Great,' Burns said. 'Of course. Come with me.'

He held out his hand, gesturing that Lucy should lead the way. 'I'm sorry for the loss. Did you know her well?'

'I'd met her in one of the care homes a few times,' Lucy said. 'Her mother's an alcoholic; Karen would be taken in anytime her mother went on a particularly long bender. She was a nice girl.' Lucy's placement with the Public Protection Unit of the PSNI meant that she primarily worked cases involving vulnerable persons and children. As a result, she spent quite a bit of time in the city's Social Services residential units, in one of which Karen Hughes had been an occasional inhabitant.

'How do you like the PPU?' he asked, as they walked. 'It's a strange posting for a young DS. I'd have thought CID would have been the obvious place for someone like you.'

What did he mean, *someone like me?* Lucy thought. Young? Female? Catholic? All of the above?

'I'd rather work with the living than the dead,'

17

Lucy said a little tritely, though she knew it was not entirely true even as she said it. The dead motivated her as much as the quick. More perhaps.

Burns nodded. 'I'm afraid in this case that will prove a little difficult. There's no doubting which she is.'

They had reached the body now, which lay across the tracks so that the girl's neck was supported by one of the metal rails. It could easily have been mistaken for a suicide attempt, had it not been for the knife wound that had severed her windpipe. A handful of SOCO officers continued to work the immediate scene. One documented the area with a hand-held video, while a second used a digital camera to take still shots.

The girl lay on her back. Her clothes were as described in the Missing Person's alert that Lucy had released just three days earlier. She wore a white hooded top, too long for her, over flower-patterned leggings. The top was soaked in blood now, but the material near the hem still retained the original white.

Lucy couldn't really see the face too clearly. Part of it was smeared in the girl's own blood, the rest covered by the loose straggles of her hair. She could make out, on one side, the soft swell of her cheek, still carrying puppy fat. A smattering of freckles was more vivid now, against the pallor of her skin.

Her hair had also become stuck to the blood that was already congealing at the edges of the wound at her throat. Lucy didn't look too closely at it. No doubt she'd be treated to all manner of post-mortem pictures over the coming days without having to look at it here, too. She resisted an urge to push Karen's hair back from her face, instead gently touched it with the tips of her gloved fingers. 'Jesus,' she said, softly.

She tried to dissociate the memories of Karen alive from the scene before her as she examined the body. 'She used to wear a cross and chain around her neck,' Lucy said. 'It might have been lost when her throat was cut.'

'Any other identifying features?' Burns asked. 'Or do you want to wait until she's cleaned up?'

Lucy lifted the girl's left hand. She noticed that the tips of each of her fingers were scored with deep gashes.

'Defence wounds,' Burns said, watching her. 'She must have tried to grab the knife as he was slitting her throat.'

'He?'

'Most likely,' Burns said.

Lucy turned the dead girl's arm. She wore a number of leather wristbands and friendship bracelets. Lucy recognized them. She pushed them up the girl's arm, exposing the skin of the wrist, finding what she was looking for: a series of criss-crossing scars in broken lines traversed the girl's lower arm.

'That's Karen Hughes, all right,' Lucy said, tenderly laying the girl's hand back onto the grey gravel.

3

Burns walked back up the tracks with them to Lucy's car. The breeze off the river had risen now, bringing with it further flecks of rain and a sudden chill that heralded the first grumble of thunder overhead.

'We'll need to get her covered before the rain hits,' Burns said. 'So, what's the story with the girl, then?'

'She's been in and out of care for years now,' Lucy said. 'She'd be in the residential unit for a few months at a time, then out home again.'

'What are the home circumstances?'

'As I said, the mother is an alcoholic. Every time she'd be taken in to dry out, Karen ended up in care. Plus, occasionally, Karen would be hospitalized for self-harming and would be kept in care until her mood stabilized.'

Burns nodded. 'And I don't need to ask about the father.'

The element of the story the media had focused on, despite Lucy's best attempts to keep it all about the girl, was the fact that her father was Eoghan Harkin, a man coming to the end of a twelve-year stretch for murder. He'd been part of an armed gang that had robbed a local bank in a tiger kidnapping which had left the bank's manager dead.

He'd done his time in Magherberry, in Antrim, only to get moved closer to home a few

20

months earlier, to Magilligan Prison in Coleraine. He currently resided in the Foyleview unit there, which prepared offenders for release. As the girl had used her mother's surname, it hadn't been an issue when Lucy had drafted the first press release on Friday expressing concern for Karen. By Sunday, one of the trashier papers had somehow made the connection and ran a front-page story under the heading 'Killer's Girl Goes Missing'.

'Who found her?'

'A poor sod working for the railways,' Burns said. 'He was called in because someone stole cabling. The late train is stuck down at Gransha. Lucky really. The bend she was on, the train would have been straight into her before the driver would have seen her.'

'Was that the point? Lay her on the tracks so that, when she gets hit by the train, the damage it'd do would hide the wound to the throat?'

'Make it look like suicide,' Burns agreed. 'We'd have thought nothing of it with her having been in care and that.'

'Whoever did it knew she was in care then,' Lucy ventured.

His face mask down now, Lucy could get a better look at Burns. He was stocky, his features soft, his jawline a little lacking in definition. But his eyes still shone in the flickering blue of the ambulance lights.

'Maybe.' He huffed out his cheeks. 'Look, I appreciate you coming to ID the remains, folks. We'll be another few hours here at least and we'll have the PM in the morning. Maybe you could call to the CID suite about noon and we'll take it from there.'

'Of course, sir,' she said.

Burns pantomimed a winch. 'And a second favour. Seeing as how you already know them, perhaps you'd inform the next of kin.'

★ ★ ★

They stopped first at Gransha, the local psychiatric hospital, where Karen's mother, Marian, was being held while she dried out after her latest two-week session. She'd be in no fit state to talk to them for some time. At that moment, they were informed, she was insensible.

As they left the ward to return to the car, Lucy glanced across to the secure accommodation where her own father was a permanent resident. The block was in darkness now, low and squat. Her father had once been a policeman too, but had been suffering from Alzheimer's disease for the past few years. Lucy's estranged mother, the ACC of the division, had sanctioned the man's incarceration in the secure unit following the events in Prehen woods a year earlier.

'Will we get the prison officers to break the news to the grieving father? Or do you fancy a drive to Magilligan?' Fleming asked.

'We'd best tell him ourselves, sir,' Lucy said, deliberately turning up the heat in the car.

It had the desired effect. By the time they were passing the road off for Maydown station, on their way to Coleraine, Fleming was already swaying gently asleep in the front seat. Lucy

22

flicked on a CD of the Low Anthem, turned it up enough to hear without wakening the DI beside her, and let her mind wander.

4

Their voices echoed in the emptiness of the visiting room. Eoghan Harkin had been brought in, dressed in his own clothes, evidence of the relaxed regime in Foyleview wing. As he took his seat opposite Lucy and Fleming, he'd already guessed the nature of their visit.

'She's dead, isn't she?'

'I'm afraid so, Mr Harkin,' Lucy said. 'I've just left her.'

He wiped at his nose with his hand, sniffing once as he did so, glancing at Tom Fleming. He raised his chin interrogatively. 'Who's he?'

'This is DI Fleming, Mr Harkin,' Lucy said. 'He's my superior officer.'

Fleming stared at him steadily. 'I'm sorry for your loss, Mr Harkin.'

Harkin accepted the sympathies with a curt nod. 'Where's her mother? Has she been told yet?'

'Not yet. She's in Gransha at the moment. They felt she might not be receptive to the news until morning.'

Harkin accepted this, likewise, with a terse nod. 'So what happened to her? Did she cut herself again?'

'No. We believe she was murdered,' Lucy said.

Harkin initially seemed unaffected by the news then, at once, reached out to grip the back of the chair nearest him. He missed and the prison

24

guard, Lucy and Fleming had to grapple with him to pull him back onto the chair from the floor.

'I'll get him a drink,' the guard said and, crossing to the wall, lifted the receiver of the phone attached there and passed the request along. A moment later, someone knocked at the door and, opening it, the guard accepted a clear plastic cup of water and brought it across.

Harkin accepted it and sipped. 'Sorry, George,' he said to the man, his head bowed. His back curved as he inhaled deeply, then he straightened himself, puffing out his cheeks as he released the breath. Finally, he looked up to Lucy. 'How?'

Lucy moved and sat in the seat next to him. 'The postmortem won't be till the morning, sir, but it appears she died from a knife wound.'

'A stabbing?'

'Not quite,' Lucy said.

Harkin processed this piece of information, considering all the alternatives. Finally, he settled on the right one, for his face darkened.

'Who did it?'

'It's a little early — ' Fleming began.

'You must have some fucking ideas,' Harkin spat, rising from his seat in a manner which caused George to immediately stand to attention again. Aware of his reaction, Harkin raised a placatory hand then slowly lowered himself into his seat again. 'You've been looking for her since Thursday. Where did you find her?'

'On the railway line. At St Columb's Park.'

Harkin stared at the tabletop, his breath heavy

and nasal. 'Was it me?' he asked finally.

'What?'

'Was it because of me?'

Lucy shook her head. 'We've no reason to believe so, Mr Harkin. Your daughter hasn't shared your name since she was a child.'

'She still was a child,' he retorted, though without rancour. He sat a moment in silence, before speaking again. 'That trash rag ran the story about her today. About her and me. If I thought it was done because of me, I'd . . . You read all this shit in here, educating you. *Sophocles* and that. You know, the daughters die because of who the father was. You start . . . you know, you can't help . . . ' He stared at them, his mouth working dryly, though producing no sound.

Lucy shook her head, but did not express her own thoughts. The girl was missing until the papers ran with the connection to Harkin. Suddenly, she turned up with her throat cut, set up to look like she killed herself on the train line. Except the train never came. They couldn't discount the idea that her death was connected with her father, even if she didn't believe the two things to be related.

'Can you think of anyone who *might* want to get back at you, Mr Harkin?'

'You mean apart from the family of the poor sod I shot?'

'Anyone else?' Lucy continued, silently considering the possibility as one she'd need to mention to Burns.

If there was, Harkin wasn't going to share the

26

information with them.

'When did you last see Karen, Mr Harkin?' Fleming asked.

Harkin looked up at him, then dipped his head again. 'About a fortnight ago. She'd started visiting after I wrote to her a while back. She was here three times, I think.'

'Did she mention anything to you during any of her visits? Anything that suggested she might have been in trouble?'

'She barely knew me. She was four when I went inside.'

His expression darkened suddenly, his eyes hooded by his brows where they gathered. Lucy felt Fleming's hand rest on her arm on the desk. She glanced at him and he shook his head lightly. They would get nothing further of use from Harkin.

'Is there any thing we can do for you, Mr Harkin?' Lucy asked, standing to indicate to the prison officer that they were concluding their visit.

'I'm out of here next Saturday. If you find out who it was, give me half an hour with whoever killed her.'

'Careful, Eoghan,' George called from the corner. 'I'm sorry for your news, but we don't want you back in here again too soon, now do we?'

'Half an hour,' Harkin repeated to Lucy.

*   *   *

The prison officer, George, walked them back out to the main reception area where they

27

returned their visitors' badges, crunching on an apple as he walked with them.

'You found her on the train line?' he asked, clearly having overheard.

'Just at St Columb's Park. There's a dark bend on the line.'

'Oh, I know it surely,' the man said. 'I'm from Londonderry myself. I get that train in the evenings if I'm doing the day shift. When did you find her?'

'Sometime before midnight,' Lucy said. 'A little before that, maybe.'

'The body can't have been there too long then.'

'Why?'

'There's a train that leaves Coleraine about 9.10 p.m. I aim to make that if my shift finishes on time. It gets into the city for just shy of 10. If I miss that, I have to get the late train, hanging around Coleraine till 10.40. It makes it in for 11.30. If the body had been lying for a bit, the 10 o' clock train would have run over it. Whoever put it there must have done so between 10 and 11.30.'

'What about trains coming out of Derry?' Lucy asked.

'The last Londonderry train is at 8.30,' the man replied. 'There's none after that.'

He took another chunk off the apple, chewing happily as he said, 'If you need me to solve the whole case for you, just let me know.'

Monday 17 December

5

The smoke was so dense, Lucy could barely see in front of her. She felt the burning in her lungs, the need to take a breath, but she knew she had to resist. Somewhere, below her, the heat was rising, its presence marked by a vague yellow glow from the living room, the splintering of wood as the door cracked.

To her left she saw Catherine Quigg's closed door. The woman bolted it from the inside; Lucy remembered that. She reached for the door, tried to open it. Locked. Raising her boot, she kicked at the spot below the handle where she knew the sliding bolt inside had been screwed. Once, twice, a third boot at it before it too splintered and she tumbled through the doorway into the room. Empty. She didn't stop to think how an empty room might be locked from the inside; didn't find it strange.

Where was Mary's room? Ahead of her, at the end of the corridor. She looked up. Cunningham had fitted a brass bolt on Mary's door too, but on the outside so he could lock her and her brother Joseph into the room when he stayed over with their mother. She fumbled with the bolt. It wouldn't shift. She felt across its length with her fingers, then found the heavy padlock attached to it.

From inside the room, she could hear the muffled cries of the baby, the sounds indistinct.

She knew this was because Mary had wrapped towels around the child's head to protect him. She'd used all the towels on him, left none for herself. Lucy hammered on the door.

'Mary? Mary? Can you hear me?'

She heard a reciprocal light thumping from the other side.

'Mary?' she screamed.

She heard the alarm ringing. Finally, she thought. After all this smoke and it's only starting to ring. Maybe help would come.

The thumping from the other side seemed to intensify in frequency, though not strength.

'Mary, I'm here,' Lucy cried, tears streaming down her face now.

Suddenly, the thumping stopped.

'Help me,' Mary whispered in her ear.

Lucy looked down to her arms, where she held the baby, Joseph, his swaddling clothes frayed towels, singed and black with soot.

The alarm grew louder, pulling her away from the door.

'Help me,' the child repeated.

★ ★ ★

Lucy jolted awake, almost falling off the sofa where she'd lain down when she finally got home after 4 a.m. She put her hands to her face, felt the wetness of her cheeks. The tears, at least, were real.

She sat up, glanced across at the clock on the mantelpiece; it was already gone 7 a.m. The sky beyond was beginning to lighten behind the miasma of rain misting the windows.

The house was quiet, save for the creaking of the floorboards upstairs and the occasional rattling cough of the water pipes when the timer switched on the central heating at 7.45. Lucy had yet to redecorate, had yet to see this as her own home, rather than her father's home in which she was staying. She showered, then clattered about in the kitchen, pouring herself out cereal, eating it in front of the TV, watching the news.

She thought again on what Harkin had said, about Sophocles and his being to blame for Karen's death. It seemed unlikely somehow. The man had not been a feature of the girl's life. Indeed, she had jettisoned his surname at the first opportunity, just as Lucy had retained her father's name after her mother reverted to her maiden name, Wilson. Even when Lucy had met Karen, in the months before when she was still in care, she'd never once named her father. It had struck Lucy more than once that they had that disowning of a parent in common. It was, perhaps, why Lucy had been drawn to the girl. That coupled with the fact that, as her mother had quite correctly commented, Lucy had an affinity for the vulnerable, for all the little lost girls she encountered. None more so than Mary Quigg, the girl about whom she had recurrent dreams who had died along with her mother the year previous.

The mother's partner, Alan Cunningham, had been a low-level recidivist who the PSNI had arrested erroneously for child abduction. Lucy had managed to prove the man innocent. Upon release, however, Cunningham had gone on the run, but not before ransacking his partner's home, stealing all he could sell from it, then setting the house alight with his partner and her children still sleeping inside. The only survivor was the baby of the family, Joe.

★ ★ ★

Lucy was at the City Cemetery as the gates opened at nine o'clock. The council worker in the high-visibility jacket who unlocked them waved her in, before opening the second gate back.

Lucy drove up the incline to the very top of the cemetery. She knew where the plot was, knew well enough the handiest place to park. She got out of the car, stood and stared down at the river below and across to Prehen, the houses of the estate emerging from the ancient woodland which surrounded them. It was a breathtaking view, even on so bracing a morning.

Locking up the car, she climbed the last hundred yards of the incline to the row where Mary Quigg was buried. Even before she reached the grave she could tell something was wrong. The graveside railings that Lucy had had set around the grave were missing, the only evidence of their absence a thin trench in the soil, a few centimetres wide. The gravestone itself was still intact, fine black marble, with the names of the mother and daughter. However, the bunch of flowers that Lucy had laid there a week earlier were crushed, as if underfoot. The small teddy bear she'd placed on the grave for Mary lay dirtied now, its face pressed against the clay. Lucy could see the muddied ridges of a boot mark on the sodden fur.

She must have been visibly upset by the time she found the man who had opened the gates for her, for his first instinct was to place his arm awkwardly on her shoulder.

'We didn't know who to contact, love. I'm sorry,' he said. 'We found it like that yesterday. They came in the night before and took the wee railings off a couple of graves.'

'Who did?'

The man shrugged. 'God knows. They took the lead flashing off the roof of the church that same night. It was probably the same people. The cops told us there's a gang going about, lifting metal. Its price has rocketed with the recession and that. It's being investigated, but you know the police; God knows if they'll ever get them.'

Lucy shuddered with a mixture of anger and the effort she needed to suppress her tears.

'Look, love. I'll get the grave tidied up for you,' the man said, his hand still on her shoulder. 'Don't be upsetting yourself. I know it seems it, but it's not personal. These things never are.'

Lucy stared at him.

'Of course it's personal,' she said.

6

The Public Protection Unit, in which Lucy was a sergeant, had a wide remit, taking responsibility for cases involving domestic abuse, children, missing persons and vulnerable adults, frequently working closely with Social Services. It operated from Maydown PSNI station in the Waterside of Derry City. Maydown was actually a compound rather than a simple station: a range of buildings stretched across a site of about ten acres, housing many of the PSNI units for the city, as well as a branch of the training college. It was surrounded by twelve-inch-thick corrugated metal fencing, a vestige of the Troubles that had yet to be replaced. This was not the only visible impact the Troubles had had on the design of the place. Rather than consisting of one large building, which would have proved an easy target for potential rocket attacks, even those requiring a degree of pot luck in the targeting due to the height of the perimeter fencing, the compound was divided up into a number of small blocks, squatting at various points around the station area.

The PPU was Block 5. Lucy parked just outside and went up to the front door of the block to punch in her access code. As she did so, she regarded herself in the reflective foil coating on the door itself. She had cut her hair a few weeks earlier and was still undecided. She'd worn her hair in a ponytail for as long as she could remember until recently; during an altercation with a drunken father whose wife had had enough and locked him out of the house, the man had grabbed Lucy by the hair, pulling her down to the ground and managing a kick that glanced off the side of her head before the uniforms accompanying her had managed to subdue him with pepper spray. She'd lost weight and that, combined with the haircut, made her features thinner than she realized. For a moment, she saw her mother reflected back at her. She turned away quickly, pulling open the door.

Once inside, she headed up to Fleming's office first, but it was empty; having not got home himself until 3.30, Lucy figured he'd slept in. She crossed the corridor to the open area where interviews were conducted. Generally, the people interviewed here were children, so the room was spacious, with plastic crates of toys and a worn red cloth sofa. Two mismatched bookcases sat against the wall, holding a variety of kids' books of all shapes and sizes. To the immediate left of the bookcases sat a video camera on a tripod, which was used for recording the interviews as unobtrusively as possible.

Her own office was on the first floor. She hung her coat over the back of her chair and, standing on tiptoe, peered out of the small window high on the wall behind her desk to where the last of the previous night's raindrops glistened off the barbed wire curling along the top of the compound fence.

As she turned her attention to the room again, she noticed the small red flashing light on her desk phone indicating that she had a message. She dialled in her code then listened to the various options available to access her voicemail. As she did, she glanced up to where the picture of Mary Quigg remained pinned to her noticeboard. Lucy had sworn to herself that it would remain there until she had found Mary's killer, Alan Cunningham.

The message was from a man who introduced himself as David Cooper. He was with the Information and Communication Services Branch, a team specially developed to support operations that involved analysis of computer equipment. Lucy guessed that he'd been tasked with examining Karen Hughes's phone. Karen had been reported missing from the residential unit on Thursday night. Lucy had called at the unit to find that Karen's phone had been left in her room. When she still hadn't turned up on Friday, she'd released the first press appeal and sent the phone to ICS to be examined.

Lucy dialled the number he had left on the message and, when he answered, introduced herself.

'DS Black. Thanks for getting back to me. I've taken a look at this phone and I'm pretty sure I've found something. I'm over here in Block 10. Can you come across?'

7

Designed during the North's Troubles, the various blocks in Maydown Station had not been geographically placed in sequential order; Lucy suspected that, as with the small, high windows, it was an attempt to reduce the likelihood of an attack from outside. If someone wanted to target Block 3, for instance, they couldn't be sure that the third block from the entrance was indeed Block 3. Of course, those attacking the compound probably wouldn't have realized that, so rather than preventing an attack, it would simply mean that the wrong block would be targeted. Someone would still get hurt — just not the intended victim. This thought offered her scant comfort.

Block 10 was at the opposite end of the compound from the PPU, so it took Lucy a few minutes to get across. The man who buzzed her in was tall, carrying a little extra weight around the gut, but not much. His hair was wavy brown, his features even. He wore a black suit over a white cotton shirt.

'DS Black? I'm Dave Cooper. Come in.'

She followed him into an office which sat to the left of the main corridor. Once inside, she realized that, in fact, the room spanned the entire left-hand side of the corridor. His desk, which had been visible from the doorway, sat at the top of a huge room. Along one wall, on a worktop, over a dozen computers and laptops hummed quietly as lists of operating system information ran up the screens.

'I'm afraid I've only started a few weeks ago here, so I don't really know anyone yet,' Cooper said as he led her across to his desk on which sat a large iMac.

'I'm here over a year and I still feel that way,' Lucy said, gaining his smile in reciprocation.

'I'm not sure if that's comforting or not,' he said. 'I've hacked into this phone. Look at this.'

Lucy moved in closer as Cooper leaned in towards the screen, bringing up on the iMac an image of what was showing on the phone's screen. She felt the pressure of him beside her, but didn't move.

When he spoke again, his voice was deeper, quieter, as if in accommodation of her proximity. 'Up until about eight weeks ago, she was using this phone for everything. Texting, calls, the lot. Then she stopped. The only calls she made to and from there are to four different numbers. Here.'

He pointed on screen to the listed numbers. Lucy immediately recognized one as the number for the residential unit in the Waterside run by Social Services where Karen had been resident, and the second as Robbie's work mobile number. Robbie had been Karen Hughes's key worker. He was also Lucy's former boyfriend. Lucy told Cooper the first of these pieces of information.

'The other two numbers are also to mobiles registered with Social Services,' he said.

40

'But she didn't make *any* other calls?'

Cooper shook his head.

'She must have got a new phone and didn't tell them,' Lucy said.

'That's what it looks like. She also stopped using this one for internet access. But I was still able to trace her history from before she changed. I also managed to access her Facebook account. She has about a hundred friends,' Cooper said. 'I managed to trace a lot of them back to the contacts listed on the SIM card of the phone.'

'You've only had this since Friday afternoon,' Lucy commented, impressed.

'The case has changed from missing person to murder. I assumed that took priority over checking bankers' accounts for fraud.'

'I'm not complaining, trust me,' Lucy said.

Cooper smiled as he turned to the screen again. In the wake of the movement, Lucy could still smell the citrus scent of his aftershave.

'She has a number of friends who she's not really in contact with — pop groups and that. And a few fellas who obviously know friends of hers in real life, based on their messages to her on Facebook.'

He scrolled through the friends list and stopped at someone called Paul Bradley. 'Then we have him.'

'Paul Bradley?'

'They became friends three months ago. I've printed out the status comments between them. Here.'

He handed her a list of messages which she

read through quickly. The first was dated 18 September. Karen and Bradley had become friends and he had thanked her for adding him, which suggested he had made the first approach. The same day, Karen had posted a comment about a band she was listening to, and Bradley had liked her comment. This continued until Karen had, according to her news feed, updated her profile picture two months previous. In the picture, her eyes were not quite meeting the lens, her smile embarrassed. Her hands were clasped in front of her as though crossing one arm over the other.

The message from Paul Bradley simply said, '*Cute pic.*'

Karen's reply had been simply '*LOL.*'

'Laugh out loud,' Cooper said. 'It's one of those — '

'I am younger than you,' Lucy said.

'Do you think?' Cooper laughed gently.

Lucy smiled as she read Bradley's reply. '*Seriously. Cute pic. U R gorgeous.*'

'*HaHaHa,*' was Karen's response.

'That's a standard expression of amusement, both for the younger generation and indeed for my own,' Cooper said.

'That's useful to know, Officer Cooper.'

'David,' he said.

Lucy scrolled on through the wall posts, but no more came from Bradley.

'Is that his only contact with her?'

'Oh no,' Cooper said. 'From then on in, he contacted her through her messages rather than her wall. More privacy.'

He opened her message account and opened the first message. It was posted the same day as the comments about her picture.

Hey Karen, Don't put yourself down. Too many people will do that to you. U look lovely. Don't let anyone tell you different. Friends, family, whoever. WTF do they know anyway? Don't take any shit from anybody. Paul x

'He knows how to impress a fifteen-year-old girl,' Lucy said. She read through the rest of his messages. Many of them commented on music or books he had read, with Karen replying that she loved the same song, or the same author. 'They're remarkably well matched, too,' she added.

'Everything he mentioned there, she had listed as her Likes. It's like he's tailor-made for her.'

About eight weeks earlier, Paul had suggested they should meet. They agreed to do so in the Foyleside Shopping Centre, at his suggestion, at 3.30 on the following Saturday afternoon.

'He chose a public place to meet,' Lucy commented. 'To make her feel safe.'

'Every update she made thereafter to her page is made via iPhone,' Cooper said. 'That seems to have been when she got her new phone. And her messages to him stop completely. So, either they fell out on their first date . . . '

'Or they found an alternative method of communication.'

'I assume her iPhone hasn't been found, or I'd

43

have been examining that too.'

Lucy shook her head. 'You can't trace it, can you?'

'I can try reverse tracking it through her account for a number, then try the mobile networks to get access to the records but it'll take weeks, probably.'

Lucy nodded. 'Can we trace Paul Bradley?'

'That might be a little quicker. He says in some of his messages that his mobile is broken, so there's no number recorded for him here. Presumably after Karen got her phone, he gave her a number that she was able to use. I could get a warrant and ask Facebook to give me the ISP address for his activities.'

'And for the younger generation that means?'

'Where he used the internet. His home Wi-Fi or that. We can trace back to the phone line that he was attached to each time he logged on. It'll take a day or two to get, but it is one way.'

'That would be great, David.'

'You're very welcome, DS Black,' Cooper said.

'Call me Lucy.'

'Lucy,' he agreed.

8

Burns was standing with the CID team investigating Karen's death in the incident room when Lucy arrived just before noon. Two smaller desks had been pushed together in the centre of the room, around which were placed ten chairs. The two main walls were covered with corkboards onto which already a variety of crime scene pictures had been pinned, including ones depicting Karen's remains in situ. A timeline ran along the top of the noticeboard, marked from Thursday, when she had first gone missing, until Sunday night, when she had been found. A few markers had already been placed along its spectrum.

DS Tara Gallagher was standing at the coffee urn with a newly promoted DS whom Lucy had met before called Mickey Sinclair, a thin-faced, handsome man. When they saw Lucy, Tara raised a polystyrene coffee cup interrogatively, to which Lucy nodded.

'Inspector Fleming's not joining us?' Burns asked, approaching her. Now, out of the forensics suit he'd been wearing the previous night, Lucy could see that Burns's hair — loose, sandy curls — was already thinning. His face was a little shapeless, as if a little extra weight had robbed him of his definition, his features soft, his cheeks fleshy. But his eyes were still sharp and bright and Lucy realized with a little embarrassment that while she was studying him, he'd been doing the same with her. Instinctively, she put her hand up to cover her mouth.

'I've not seen him yet, sir,' Lucy said. Then added, 'I know he had some stuff to follow up this morning.'

'I see,' Burns said. 'In that case, we'll get started, shall we?' He turned to address the room. 'Grab your coffees, people, and take a seat.'

Tara brought Lucy over her cup. 'Milk and one,' she said. Lucy nodded, a little flattered that Tara knew how she took her drink.

Burns took his place at the top of the table and introduced Lucy to the team, then quickly introduced each of them in turn.

'Mickey, perhaps you'd start us off with the results of the PM?'

Tara nudged Lucy as Mickey stood up. 'Cause of death was the cut to the throat. Time of death was sometime on Sunday between eight in the morning and lunchtime, despite her body not being left on the train tracks until that evening.'

'Which means the killer held on to the body until dark before moving her,' a DC commented unnecessarily.

'The stomach contents included peanuts,' Mickey continued. 'But little else. She didn't seem to have eaten much. There were signs of sexual contact in the hours before death. Significant signs, the pathologist said. He'd taken samples for testing, along with toxicology samples for drugs and drink.'

'Was she raped then?'

'He wouldn't rule out consensual,' he said.

'Not that that means anything,' Burns commented. 'Anything else?'

'That's all he had to start with. The full report will be sent on when it's done.'

'What about SOCO, Tara?'

Unlike Mickey, Tara stayed in her seat, clearing her throat before addressing them. 'Blood smearing on her clothes suggested she'd been wrapped in plastic sheeting for the transport of her remains. And they pulled dog hairs from her boots. Black dog hairs.'

'DS Black, maybe you can update us on the work you'd done, to put it in context for the team.'

Lucy nodded. 'I'm afraid there's not a huge amount to tell, sir. She went missing last Thursday. She didn't come back to the unit from school but that wasn't entirely unusual.'

'She was in residential care?'

'Yes. Social Services contacted us and we started looking for her in the usual haunts: shopping centres, the Walls, places like that.'

'Had she run away before?'

'A number of times,' Lucy said, nodding. 'Initially we assumed it was more of the same. She usually came back the next day — often she'd spent the night with friends, boyfriends maybe.'

'Did she have a boyfriend?'

'Nobody serious. Not that we know of so far.'

'But she *was* sexually active?'

'She was fifteen, sir,' Lucy said.

Burns nodded, jotting down notes as Lucy spoke.

'So you put out the press appeal?'

'After she went missing, the social workers in the residential unit found her phone in her room which panicked them. They alerted us and we did the press release,' Lucy said. 'Then someone found out about the connection with her father yesterday and the papers ran with it.'

'Any idea who told them? Could it have been one of us?' He glanced around the room as he spoke. 'One of you' was actually what he meant, and Lucy knew it. PPU had been handling the case — herself and Tom Fleming essentially.

'I wouldn't think so, sir,' she replied. 'Derry's a small city. Everyone knows everyone else here. You'll find that once you're here a while.'

'Do you think she was targeted because of who she was?' Mickey asked.

'The father asked the same thing,' Lucy said. 'It seems unlikely. She wasn't using his name. He did suggest the family of the bank man he shot in the robbery might have cause for revenge, but I'm not convinced.'

'We'll follow up on it,' Burns commented. 'Was anything useful found on the phone?'

'Actually, I spoke with someone in ICS just before coming up here. She was befriended on Facebook by someone called Paul Bradley. He made first contact in September. About eight weeks ago they met and she seems to have managed to get an iPhone that she's since kept hidden from the residential unit. ICS are trying to track Bradley through his internet address.'

'Brilliant,' Burns said. 'I'll need the details of the officer in ICS. Is Bradley known to PPU?'

'Well, I ran him through the system based on the personal information on his Facebook page, but no luck,' Lucy said. 'It could be a cover name.'

'He could be a known offender then,' Burns said. 'We'd best speak to the usual suspects first.'

Burns flicked through his notes, words forming silently on his lips as he read through what he'd written. 'Was she using drugs?'

Lucy shook her head. 'Maybe a little — it wasn't something we ever investigated. It didn't seem relevant.'

Burns nodded. 'Everything can be relevant,' he said. 'Toxicology will show if she was using prior to her death. How long had she been self-harming?'

'It was first noticed when she was nine. She went into care about then after her mother was locked up to dry out for the first time. Karen had been looking after her for four years by that stage. The social workers asked Karen about when she'd started cutting herself, but she wouldn't tell them. Still, she continued with it until . . . well until she died, I suppose.'

Burns nodded. 'Was she ever considered a suicide risk?'

'Not to my mind,' Lucy said. 'Or Social Services.'

'Despite the cutting?' Mickey asked incredulously.

'Self-harming, especially the type of cutting that Karen did on herself, is a way of coping with life, a way of surviving. She did it to make life tolerable, not to end it.'

'Why?'

Lucy shrugged. 'How else could she deal with adolescence and babysitting her alcoholic forty-year-old mother?'

'Was there any history of alcohol abuse in the girl?'

'The usual,' Lucy said.

'How did you come to know her so well?' Burns asked.

'I didn't know her that well. I just met Karen at the residential unit a few times when I had to call up there about some of the other kids. We got on OK.'

'Why?'

Lucy considered the question. 'I just got her.'

Burns considered the response. 'OK then, so who was she? Describe Karen Hughes to us. Help us better understand her.'

Lucy shrugged. 'She was nice. She was caring, looking after her mother. She was patient, putting up with all the crap that she dealt with. She had a weird sense of humour. But she was troubled. She had . . . she had very low self-esteem.'

'There's a reason the ACC wanted you in PPU, obviously,' Burns commented.

Lucy silently reflected that there was more than one reason her mother had pushed her into the PPU, but she did not speak.

'These hairs Forensics pulled from Karen's clothes. I don't suppose Social Services have a dog in the residential unit?' Burns said.

'No, sir.'

'What about known sex offenders? Have you

followed up on those?'

'Inspector Fleming and I had already begun interviewing known sex offenders in the area as part of the search for Karen.'

'How many are there?'

'In the Foyle Command area alone we have sixty-six. We'd seen most.'

'Any black dog owners?' Burns asked, with a laugh.

'Actually one of the offenders we've yet to see has,' Lucy said.

'Maybe make him a priority for a visit. What's he called?'

'Eugene Kay. He prefers Gene.'

'Does he, now?' Burns asked, noting the name. 'If you and Tom could follow up on it and let me know your thoughts, I'd appreciate it. The ACC has already approved your working alongside us on this.'

Lucy stood to leave, then stopped. 'There's something about the timing of the trains last night,' she said. 'The previous train passed there at ten, so the body would have been — '

Burns raised a hand to stop her. 'We're already on top of that.'

'There's also the metal theft,' she added. 'There's every chance that whoever was cutting those cables may have seen who brought Karen down to the tracks. Considering the timing of the trains. The previous train ran — '

'We're on that too,' Burns commented, smiling. 'We're following it up.'

'A gang robbed the cemetery the night before, too,' Lucy said. 'They could be the same people.'

Burns looked at her. '*That* I didn't know,' he said. 'But it could be useful. Tara, maybe you'd contact the local scrapyards and see if anyone's been selling stuff they shouldn't. Mickey, I want you to contact the school and see what you can find out about the girl from there. Ian, check if the CCTV system in the city centre picked up any activity around St Columb's Park last night. OK?'

There were general murmurs of agreement as the team got up to leave. Lucy could sense Tara's annoyance as she shoved her seat under the table and left the room.

Before leaving, Lucy approached Burns. 'I'll update Inspector Fleming, sir,' she said.

Burns smiled. 'That's fine.'

Still she stood and did not leave.

Burns's smile faltered a little. 'Is there something you want to ask me?' he said, uncertainly.

'I was wondering about the state of the Alan Cunningham investigation, sir,' she said, finally.

'Remind me,' he said, his fingers interlinking, his joined hands resting on the notebook in front of him on the desk.

'He set fire to his partner's house in Foyle Springs last year. The parent, Catherine Quigg, and her daughter Mary were killed. The baby, Joe, survived.'

'I remember reviewing the file before I started here,' Burns said. 'My recollection is that it hit the three-month flag without progress and was relegated. This Cunningham character went over the border, is that right?'

Lucy nodded. 'To Donegal initially.'

'I've a feeling I read there was intelligence on the ground that he'd settled in Limerick, but we asked the Guards to follow it up and they got nothing. The inquiries here hit a dead end, too. There was a suggestion that Cunningham was being protected. His family were well known Republicans.'

'I see.'

'Why?'

'I knew the girl who died. She'd come to our attention in the days before her death. She called me on the night she died, but I didn't get the call until . . . until after.'

'I see,' Burns repeated.

'I was just wondering if any progress had been made.'

'None, I'm afraid,' Burns said. 'Nor will there be any until Cunningham comes back over the border, or makes a public appearance in the south so that the Guards can get to him. But I'll double check for you. As I say, I just reviewed the more recent open files. I might have missed something.'

Somehow, Lucy doubted it.

9

Tara was waiting for her in the corridor outside the room when Lucy came out.

'Schmoozing with the boss?' she asked, a little petulantly.

'He's not *my* boss,' Lucy commented. 'I wanted to check up on something.'

Tara waved away the explanation. 'Sorry. It's bloody Mickey Sinclair. He's the blue-eyed boy since he got DS. He gets to run down leads in the school, and I'm struck tracing thieved metal. This whole bloody unit is all politics. You're lucky you ended up in PPU.'

Lucy grunted by way of offering sympathies for Tara's complaint. 'If you do find anything, I'd be interested in knowing,' she said. 'About the stolen metal.'

Tara frowned. 'Why?'

'Someone stole the metal railings off the grave of a friend.'

'Scumbags. I'll let you know what I hear. We've targeted a scrap merchant called Finn out in Ballyarnet. Apparently he'd been shipping metal with Smart dye on it from electric cabling. Whoever's stealing is selling through him. He's going to let us know when they bring the next load down to him to sell.' She considered a moment, then added, 'He's a fence.'

Lucy smiled at the joke. 'So you don't like Burns then?'

'He's OK. Hard to impress. Mind you, do you know why he got where he got?' she added, warming to her gossip.

Being based in the centre of town, Tara seemed to glean all the station gossip. Lucy, on the other hand, sharing a unit with Tom Fleming out at Maydown, heard nothing.

'Why?

'The ACC!'

'What?'

Tara nodded, smiling. 'Apparently. The two of them were spotted out having dinner in Eglinton.'

'Said who?'

'The community team was doing a drink-driving campaign, going around the local pubs. I know one of the fellas who spotted them.'

Lucy smiled, trying to remember the name of the man she'd met the one time she'd visited her mother's house. Peter? Paul? She'd obviously moved on.

'At least that explains his meteoric rise to the top,' Tara said. 'Eh?'

'Mmm,' Lucy agreed. Not for the first time, she felt awkward with Tara. By rights she should have told her about the ACC being her mother. But each time they discussed her, it was generally Tara being critical. To admit to the relationship would just make things awkward. Lucy knew though that whatever time the information became common knowledge, Tara's seeming proximity to the grapevine would result in her being one of the first to know. How that would change their friendship remained to be seen.

'That's not all they saw,' Tara went on. 'Your man was spotted too.'

'*My* man?'

'Tom Fleming. He's back on the sauce. Not that I blame him, mind you, the shit you have to deal with. Being an alco seems to be a survival technique.'

Like self-harming, Lucy reflected.

★ ★ ★

After stopping to pick up lunch of a sandwich and a packet of crisps from the supermarket along the Strand Road, Lucy headed back to Maydown to see if Tom Fleming had arrived in. At first, his office looked empty. Then Lucy noticed his keys lying on the desk and heard, a moment later, the flushing of the toilet behind the kitchenette. Because of the nature of their work, theirs was one of the few blocks in the station to have access to their own kitchen where juice and biscuits were kept for interviewees.

Lucy headed across to the kitchenette, just as Fleming came out of the toilet. He looked as though he had just arrived indoors, his face flushed, his breathing quick and shallow.

'Afternoon,' she said.

Fleming grunted. 'I missed your calls.'

'We had a meeting with Superintendent Burns earlier,' Lucy explained.

'Was he asking for me?'

'I told him you had a few things to follow up.'

'I was at the dentist,' he explained. 'How did

the meeting go? Anything useful?'

'They've found black dog hairs on Karen's clothes, apparently. He asked about known offenders with black dogs. I mentioned we'd yet to see Gene Kay and he suggested that we make him a priority.'

'Did he indeed? Giving orders to all divisions now? He's really being groomed for greatness, isn't he?'

Lucy thought again of what Tara had said about Burns and her mother. She also recalled the comments about Fleming himself, standing now, florid-faced, his breath sweet with the Polo mints he was cracking between his teeth.

'He said we were to work alongside CID on Karen's case. The ACC approved it.'

Fleming allowed himself the briefest flicker of a smile. 'Of course she did.'

'Should we do it, then?'

'Have we a choice?' Fleming said. 'I'll get my coat.'

10

Kay lived in Gobnascale, in the Waterside. A staunchly Nationalist area, it abutted the equally hard-line Unionist area of Irish Street, the interface between the two marked by the point where the alternating red, white and blue paint on the kerbstones changed to green, white and orange ones. Kay's terrace house was the end one of four. The front garden was small, the scrap of land thick with grass, trodden down in narrow lines by his dog, presumably.

As they stood at the front door, Fleming nudged Lucy and nodded towards the end of the street. 'We're being watched,' he said.

Lucy followed his gaze to where a half-dozen youths stood at the corner, staring across at them. 'They'll hardly start anything,' Lucy commented. 'It's still early.'

They heard the dead bolt click and the door opened. Gene Kay was short, not much taller than Lucy herself, but stocky, broad-shouldered. His face was jowly, his hair and moustache white. He glanced past them at the group of boys.

'You may come in,' he said, without looking at either of his visitors, then turned and moved back inside the house.

Kay led them into the lounge. Two brown tweed armchairs faced a small TV jabbering away in the corner, tuned to a daytime chat show. In the other corner, a glass cabinet stood, its shelves empty of anything but dust. Behind the furthest armchair was a small drop-leaf table with two wooden seats placed either side of it. A computer sat on the table, the screen black.

'What do you want then?' Kay wore jeans and a red sweater. He was barefooted. His hand shook as he pulled a hand-rolled cigarette from a tin on the mantelpiece and lit it. Flakes of flaming tobacco fluttered to the ground and he stepped on them with his bare foot.

'We'd like to ask you a few questions, Gene. As part of an ongoing inquiry,' Fleming began.

'Do I need a lawyer?' Kay said, sitting on the armchair in front of the table. On the wall behind him was a painting of a child, a single tear perfectly formed on his face, his doe eyes, huge and brown, staring down beneath a ragged blond fringe. He held a cap in his hand. Lucy had seen similar pictures before, remembered in fact a newspaper story that suggested they were cursed in some way.

'That's your right, Gene,' Lucy said. 'But at the moment, we're just hoping to eliminate you from our inquiries. Do you know this girl?'

She handed Kay a picture of Karen, which Social Services had provided, taken from her care plan. He studied the face, before handing the picture back.

'I think I saw her picture on TV earlier. Didn't catch her name. She's missing or something, is that right?'

'She's dead, Gene,' Fleming said. 'She was found last night.'

Kay nodded. 'Well, it had naught to do with me. I'm sorry for the wee girl.'

'Where were you yesterday morning, Gene?' Lucy asked.

Kay considered the question. 'I was at church at eleven,' he said. 'Then I went straight to my sister's for Sunday lunch. I took a taxi to church, so I left here just after half ten. I didn't come back until about six.'

'Did you go back out again last night?'

'I don't go out at night,' Kay said. 'That group of thugs out there hang around the streets drinking every night. It's not safe. Not that the police do anything about it.'

'You didn't have anyone here with you, who could confirm that you were at home?'

'What do you think?' Kay snapped. 'Of course I didn't.'

'What about last Thursday? Do you remember where you were on Thursday?'

'I was in bed sick most of last week,' Kay added. 'I've a prescription from the chemist's to prove it. I can get it if you want.'

Fleming nodded. 'That would be helpful. Nothing serious, I trust.'

Kay hoisted himself out of the armchair and padded out to the kitchen. He returned with a small bottle of cough mixture, dated the previous Thursday.

'Does your pharmacist deliver?'

'No. I had to go out with a dose to get it.'

Fleming glanced at the bottle. 'Of course, that doesn't prove you were in your bed sick.'

'Well I was,' Kay said. 'You people are

torturing me, you know that? That gang out there, seeing you coming here. They'll be attacking me while I sleep.'

Lucy had to stop herself from commenting on the irony of such a comment. Kay had been arrested in Limavady after several years of abusing one of his neighbour's sons. He had first assaulted the child while babysitting for the couple when the wife went into labour. The abuse had continued for eight years. Kay had served less than half that in prison as punishment.

'Karen Hughes was murdered, Gene,' Lucy said. 'Black dog hairs were found on her clothing. You have a black dog, don't you?'

'Half the town has black dogs.'

'But not a record for sexual assault as well,' Lucy retorted.

Kay straightened himself, regarded Lucy coolly. 'You're a smart one, aren't you? I'd nothing to do with whoever was killed. I never killed no one. The only person I'll ever be hurting is myself someday if you people don't leave me in peace.'

'It would be really helpful if we could maybe get a strand of your dog's hair,' Lucy said. 'To compare with the strands we found.'

'Don't you need a warrant for something like that?' Kay asked.

'We could get one,' Lucy agreed.

'Although, making us go for a warrant suggests you're reluctant to help with our inquiries,' Fleming added. 'It might look like you have something to hide.'

'I don't want her hurt,' Kay said. 'I won't have anyone hurt Mollie.'

Lucy said nothing.

At Kay's mention of her name though, the dog itself appeared at the door of the kitchen, yawning lazily, its tongue lolling to one side. Mollie crossed to Lucy and sniffed at her legs, the dog's tail offering a desultory wag, then falling limp.

Lucy reached into her pockets and pulled on a glove. Bending down, she held out her hand. Mollie approached tentatively, sniffing at the latex of the glove before tasting it with a quick lather of her tongue. She moved closer to Lucy, allowing Lucy first to rub her hand across the dome of the animal's head, then to bury her hand among the thicker fur at the top of her spine. Lucy rubbed vigorously at the fur, as if petting the dog, then checked her hand. A few black strands of hair clung to the glove.

'Do you consent to our taking these for testing?' Lucy asked.

Kay nodded, once, curtly. He took a last drag from his cigarette then threw the butt into the hearth, before dropping down and calling the dog to him. As he kissed its snout, Mollie licked at the tobacco rich air of his breath.

'Thank you,' Lucy said. She pulled off the glove inside out to trap the hairs, then placed it in an evidence bag.

'We'll be in touch,' Fleming said. 'And of course, if you think of anything else, do let us know.'

Lucy opened the front door and stepped out.

The group of youths had grown larger now and had moved directly across the road. They stood beneath the street lamp opposite, without words. One of the youths, at the centre of the group, regarded her coldly. He was tall, wearing a black T-shirt beneath a badly worn leather jacket. 'All right, love?' he called, winking at her, to the amusement of the rest who stood around him.

As she reached the car, Lucy recognized another of the youths, standing at the outer edge of the group. He wore a grey woollen hat pulled down low over his head, covering his scalp completely. He had thick black eyebrows, both of which had a stripe shaved down their centre. Lucy started to raise her hand, then thought better of it and stopped.

'Someone you know,' Fleming asked, when she closed the door.

'Gavin Duffy,' Lucy said. 'He's in the residential care unit. His father was Gary Duffy. He hung himself about a month ago. Gavin's grandparents asked he be moved closer to them.'

'Gary Duffy? The Louisa Gant guy?'

Lucy nodded. Louisa Gant had been a nine-year-old girl who vanished in 1998. The girl herself had never been found. Lucy and her father had moved out of Derry by that stage, though she recalled the case for the child had gone missing the day the Good Friday Agreement had been finally signed, her vanishing a coda to news reports filled with images of bleary-eyed politicians heralding the beginning of a new future for Northern Ireland and Blair's sound bite about the 'hand of history'. Lucy remembered sitting with her father, watching events unfolding. Then, at the end, Louisa Gant was mentioned.

Her remains had never been found, but, within a few days, the police investigation changed from missing persons to murder. The reason Lucy remembered it so clearly was because during one of the press conferences covered by the TV news on the case in subsequent weeks, it was her mother who read a statement about the investigation in her newly appointed role as Chief Superintendent. It was the first time Lucy had seen her in months.

Despite not recovering the child, police charged local man, Gary Duffy, with her murder in 1999. Following a tip-off from an informant, police had discovered one of the girl's chunky black shoes in Duffy's garage, the pirate motif decorating its strap distinctive. The shoe had been badged with the girl's blood. Though he claimed innocence, Duffy had been tried, found guilty and imprisoned. He had been released on parole only a few months previously. And had committed suicide soon after.

'The young lad's found himself some new friends already,' Fleming said.

'So it seems,' Lucy said, glancing out again at the group, her stare being held by Gavin's all the way to the corner of the street.

11

Before finishing for the day, Lucy drove back to Gransha Hospital to see Karen's mother, Marian Hughes.

She'd met her once before when Karen had been taken to hospital eight months earlier after cutting her wrists too deeply. Lucy had been visiting Robbie on her evening off when the girl cut herself while having a bath. Lucy had helped dress her while waiting for an ambulance to take her to hospital.

Karen had apologized over and over for spoiling their evening. Her face had paled, her lips bloodless beneath her small teeth.

'What were you thinking?' Lucy had asked.

Karen had shrugged, her head tilted to one side.

'You could have killed yourself,' Lucy said. 'Or is that what you wanted to do?'

Karen shook her head, her hair falling across her face as she did so. Lucy pushed it back with one hand, her other helping Karen keep the pressure on the towel they had wrapped around the wound. The broken pieces of a safety razor lay on the floor, the blade she'd removed from it glinting darkly beneath the sink.

'I can usually control it,' Karen said. 'My hand slipped is all.'

Lucy knew girls from school who'd hurt themselves, understood only too well the impulses that drove them to it. So, she'd said nothing more, but simply put her arm around the girl, pulled her closer to her, stayed like that until the ambulance arrived.

Marian Hughes had turned up at the hospital later that evening. She'd already been drinking before she got there, her breath warm and ketonic in the closeness of the room in which Karen sat while her arm was stitched.

'Should someone not have been watching her?' the woman had asked.

'Karen was having a bath, Mrs Hughes,' Robbie explained.

The woman shook her head, muttering to herself, as she sat by the girl. 'Someday you'll do it for real,' she said to Karen; her first words to the girl since her arrival. 'Some day you'll actually manage it and give us all peace.'

Karen had stared at her arm, watching the doctor as he worked, never once lifting her head to look at the woman.

'Someone should have been watching her,' the woman repeated to the room, looking from face to face in hope that one of them would agree with her. The doctor coughed embarrassedly and kept working.

* * *

Marian Hughes looked considerably older now, the drinking having taken its toll. Her hair, brown though streaked with grey, was tied back from her face accentuating the sharpness of her features. The skin of her cheeks, taut against the

66

bone, was waxy in appearance save for threads of burst veins. She sat in the chair next to her bed, wearing a hospital gown and pink slippers, while Lucy and a doctor spoke to her about Karen's death. She was sober now, but clearly the days of drying out seemed to have left her in a daze of sorts, for if she understood what Lucy had told her, Hughes showed little sign of it until Lucy stood to leave.

'So, did she kill herself or not?' she asked, looking up at her with vacant eyes.

'No, Marian,' Lucy said. 'Someone killed her.'

The woman nodded her head. 'That's what I thought.'

'Can you think of anyone who might have had reason to hurt your daughter, Marian?' Lucy asked.

The woman pursed her lips, her brow knotting briefly as she considered the question. Finally she shook her head.

'Were those Social Service people not watching her?' she asked.

'They were,' Lucy said. 'She'd been missing for a few days now.'

'Why wasn't I told?'

Lucy glanced at the doctor. 'You were here, Marian. You weren't really in a fit state to receive the news.'

'I should have been told,' Marian said. 'She never told me nothing.'

Lucy glanced again at the doctor who shook his head lightly. She laid her hand on Marian's arm. 'If you do think of anything, Marian, will you let someone know? They'll get word to me.'

As Lucy left the room, she heard the woman address the doctor who had remained with her. 'I told her that would happen. She was always cutting at herself. I warned her about that.'

★ ★ ★

Before leaving Gransha, Lucy walked across to the low block where her father was resident. She hadn't seen him in a few weeks and was shocked to see how frail he looked. He lay in the bed, his wrists strapped to the side bars. His pyjama jacket had pulled open revealing the curve of his chest, his hair white and tangled as it rose and fell with each breath. He smacked his lips as he slept, his eyelids not quite closed, his breath wheezing in his throat.

The skin below his left eye carried a yellowed bruise, while a small stitch bulged on his lip. The wooden chair next to his bed creaked as she sat, causing him to open his eyes.

'Who's that?' he asked.

'It's Lucy, Daddy.' She stood and leaned across him to kiss him on the forehead, his skin clammy beneath her lips, the air between them foul with the funk of his breath. 'What happened to your eye?'

The man shook his head, then lifted his right arm ineffectually pulling at the limits of the strap. 'I can't remember.'

Lucy nodded, sitting again next to him, her hand resting on his.

'I was thinking of the fountain. In Prehen,' he said suddenly.

'There was no fountain in Prehen, Daddy,' Lucy said softly.

His eyes flicked across to stare at her. 'On the lane. The cottage on the lane. You used to climb onto my shoulders so you could see it.'

'Jesus.' Lucy remembered now. A lane ran along the back of the housing estate, between it and the woodland. It had been the coach track from the big house at the top of the park, once owned by the Knox family. Legend had it that their daughter's lover had shot the girl as she passed in their coach driving along this lane in the seventeenth century. He'd intended to kill her father.

Near the bottom of the lane was a cottage, surrounded on all sides by a dense laurel hedge. The owners had a fountain in the middle of their garden. When Lucy was a child, she'd been unable to see above the hedge. Her father used to lift her, swinging her up onto his shoulders, holding her fast by the ankles as she craned up to see the fountain. That achieved, she would cling to him, resting her chin against the thickness of his hair.

For a second, she felt a rush of warmth towards him that was instantly dispelled by the memory of what her father had done. Had he, even then, already embarked on an affair with a teenaged girl? She pulled her hand quickly from his and sat back in the seat, recoiling at the thought of what she had learnt about him the previous year.

'I was thinking of the fountain,' he said. 'Is it still there?'

'I'm not sure,' Lucy managed, barely trusting herself to speak.

'Will you help me to see it? If I can't see over the hedge any more?'

'I need to go,' Lucy said, swallowing down the tears and the bile that burned at her throat. 'I'll see you before Christmas.'

12

She joined a tailback on the roundabout at the end of the Foyle Bridge, just outside Gransha and could see, by the flashing blue lights on the Limavady Road, that a road traffic accident had happened that would see the road closed for a while. She considered driving across to offer help, but she'd had a long day and the last thing she wanted was to get caught up in something on her way home. Instead, she drove up the dual carriageway, into the heart of the Waterside, planning on cutting through Gobnascale and down the Old Strabane Road to Prehen along the back road bordering the old woodland.

She was just reaching the junction of Bann Drive with Irish Street when a youth thudded onto the bonnet of her car as he careened across the road in front of her. He righted himself quickly, glancing into the car, long enough for Lucy to see his face. Then he set off, eight other youths in pursuit.

Lucy grabbed her phone and speed-dialled the residential care unit as she pulled out onto the road, steering one-handed. It was Robbie who answered.

'Lucy, it's g — '

'Robbie, is Gavin there?' She spoke over him.

'What? No, he's out. What's wrong?'

'I think I've just seen him being chased by a

gang. I'm going after him.' She cut the call immediately.

She could still see the gang running after him along Irish Street. Suddenly, Gavin, about twenty yards in front, sprinted across the road, weaving his way around cars coming in the other direction. The gang in pursuit split, some continuing on the same side of the road, others following him across to the opposite pavement. Lucy sped up, angry that being in her own car, she didn't have a siren that might help scare the gang away.

Up ahead, Gavin darted off the pavement, slipping through a gap in the wooden fencing to his right and into the car park area at the front of the River City Apostolic Church. The building itself was a basic single-storey affair, with a set of steps to the front and little other external ornamentation that would mark it out as a place of worship. By the time Lucy pulled to a stop opposite it, the youths who had been pursuing Gavin had gathered in a scrum at the front steps of the building. Gavin was lying on the ground at the centre of it taking a beating from a dozen Nike-shod feet.

Ignoring the oncoming cars, Lucy sprinted across the street, calling out to the gang to stop. Some pack instinct, though, seemed to compel them for none paid her any heed. She reached the outer edge of the scrum and pulled the youth nearest to her backwards, away from the melee. He spun, raised his fist and slashed at her, but she'd anticipated it and slipped to the side. Quickly, she gripped his flailing arm and twisted it sharply back, against the joint. The youth screeched, following the direction his arm was being tugged to alleviate the pain. Lucy tucked her leg behind his and pulled him off balance, onto the ground.

'Police,' she shouted. 'Disperse, now.'

One of the others had turned to see what had happened to his friend and swung a kick wildly in Lucy's direction. It glanced off her side. He lifted his boot a second time, aiming to stamp rather than kick. Lucy deflected the kick, bringing herself in close enough to him that she could grab his jacket and pull him away from Gavin.

'I'm the police,' she shouted at him.

The boy stared stupidly at her for a moment then helped his mate to his feet and ran.

Lucy turned to face the rest of the gang, but the numbers were winnowing out. Two boys continued to kick and stomp on Gavin, who had curled himself almost into a foetal ball by this stage, his hands up over his head, the blood marking his face black under the street lights. They took a final kick, then both turned and ran. One spat at Lucy as he did so.

'Fenian bitch,' he shouted.

Lucy followed them a step or two as they ran, then gave up. Several cars had stopped on Irish Street now, the occupants staring at her. One man was standing out of his car, a mobile phone raised, recording what had happened.

A second man was just getting out of his car. 'Are you all right?' he called, coming across to her. The mobile phone man continued to film even this.

Lucy grunted thanks for his help and they both went across to Gavin. The boy still lay on the ground, but had brought his hand down from his face. His head was closely shaven, just as Lucy had remembered it from when she had last seen him. In addition to assorted grazes and cuts, a bruise was forming on his cheek. His mouth was slick with blood when he looked up at her. She could tell that he was dazed and was trying to work out how he knew her.

'Gavin. It's Lucy. Robbie's . . . friend. Can you hear me OK?'

He looked around him, staring wildly at the man who had come to help. 'Who's he?' he said, then tried to turn and lift himself up a little. Lucy and the other man gripped him around the trunk to help him up, earning only a shriek of pain from him as they did so.

'His ribs could be broken,' the man said. 'He seemed to be taking quite a beating.'

'What happened, Gavin?'

'I don't know. I never seen them before. I was just walking home and they chased me,' Gavin said. 'I never said nothing to them.'

'That wasn't the crowd I saw you with earlier?'

Gavin shook his head. 'Nah. The ones you saw me with are my friends. I don't know who *that* crowd were.'

'They maybe saw this,' the man said, pulling the lapels of Gavin's jacket back to reveal the blood-spattered green and white hoops of a Celtic football top. 'Not the right colours for this part of the town, son.'

'I can wear what I want,' Gavin snapped, then

turned and spat a bloody globule of saliva onto the ground.

'This man is only trying to help, Gavin,' Lucy said.

'I don't need help,' the boy replied. 'I need to go, or your boyfriend will be looking for me. He'll probably phone the cops.'

'Maybe we should phone them,' the man muttered to Lucy.

'I am one,' she replied. 'I'll take him up to the hospital for a check-up, then get him home.'

'I'm not going to the hospital,' Gavin said, limping away from them. 'I'll walk home myself.'

'I'll drive you back at least, Gavin,' Lucy said.

The boy turned to look at her, then looked around him, as if to see who was watching. 'Me in a cop's car? Not a fucking chance.'

13

In the end, after walking almost half a mile towards the residential unit with Lucy trailing him slowly in her car, Gavin gave in and agreed to be taken to Casualty. Lucy called Robbie, who was nearing the end of his shift in the unit and was waiting for his replacement for the evening shift. He suggested that if Lucy could take Gavin to A & E, he would come across and relieve her as soon as he was done.

The waiting area in Casualty was busy, though it was early enough in the evening that the habitual drunken injured hadn't yet begun to seep in. A few obvious fracture injuries were waiting. A young man who had fallen through a pane-glass doorway was rushed through, the blood trailing behind him all the way in, despite his best efforts to stymie its flow from his arm.

Gavin sat sullenly next to Lucy, playing a game on his phone. He slouched low in the seat, his hood pulled up over his head.

Lucy glanced at the phone. 'Do you play Angry Birds?'

Gavin answered without looking at her. 'That's ancient,' he said.

'That's a nice phone. Is it new?'

His head twisted within the hood so she could only see his left eye, squinting suspiciously. 'I didn't steal it if that's what you think.'

'I didn't think anything,' Lucy said, though

she was immediately reminded of the new phone Karen Hughes had been given.

'Anyway, it's not a phone. It's an iPod Touch. My granda bought it for me.'

'It's nice.'

Gavin grunted in response, then resumed playing.

'I was sorry about Karen.'

'It's shit,' Gavin muttered. 'She was nice. When I moved into care, like, she was good to me.'

'Between your dad's death and now Karen. I know she wasn't family or that, but, you know . . . it must have been a difficult few weeks for you.'

'Me da was a useless bastard. No loss that he topped himself.'

Lucy said nothing, glancing across at the couple opposite who were watching them, perhaps attempting to work out how Lucy, in her late twenties, could have a son Gavin's age.

'He had issues,' Gavin offered suddenly, making speech marks in the air with his fingers. 'So the shrink told me.'

'The shrink?'

'They made me see one — a thingie. To talk about it.'

'How's that going?'

'It's a load of bollocks. She says that loads of men from the Troubles and that are killing themselves now. She says they have inter-somethinged their guilt and anger.'

'Internalized.'

'Aye, that's it.'

The fingers stopped sliding over the screen. 'What does that mean?' he asked quietly. 'I didn't want to ask her in case she thought I was stupid.'

'You're not stupid.'

'I didn't say I was. I said I didn't want to look it. There's a difference, you know.'

Lucy ignored the comment. 'It means when the Troubles were happening, people had places to direct their anger, to get rid of it. When it all ended, that anger didn't go away too. It was still there, except a lot of people couldn't get rid of it the way they used to.'

'Like in riots and that.'

'Aye. Or even just quietly supporting what was happening. Turning a blind eye to things. People can be complicit without doing anything.'

The boy didn't speak and she knew she had lost him, though he wouldn't admit such after the previous comment.

'Anyway, whatever. It means that, because they can't get rid of their anger — or guilt in your dad's case — the way they used to, they turn it inward, on themselves.'

'Like hurting themselves. Like Karen.'

Lucy was momentarily surprised that Karen had confided in Gavin about her self-harming. They'd not known one another long. Then again, they had been in the residential unit together, both let down by their families. The same boat.

'Yes,' Lucy said. 'Like Karen.'

Gavin nodded.

'Did Karen ever mention any boys to you? Anyone called Paul Bradley, maybe?' Lucy asked. If she'd confided her harming to Gavin during the period when they had been in the care unit together, she might have mentioned the new boyfriend, if that was what Bradley had been to her.

The boy considered the name then shook his head. 'I saw her once or twice with a fella. A bit older than her, short dark hair. That was it. She never mentioned him though. Never mentioned any names anyway. Is he a suspect?'

'She met someone on Facebook. We're not sure if the name's real or not. It's something we're following up,' Lucy said. 'Speaking of following, why were that crew following you tonight?'

'Maybe they had anger issues too.' Gavin chuckled darkly to himself, then resumed the game again.

By the time Robbie arrived, Gavin was already being assessed by the doctor on duty. He'd removed his top to reveal a series of vivid bruises forming along his back and ribcage, a mixture of reds and purples. There were other, yellowed bruises too, healing already from earlier beatings.

'It's just scars on top of scars,' the doctor said to them disgustedly after the assessment. 'He has bruised his ribs, so I'm going to get some X-rays done. He has taken a few blows to the head, too, but no concussion. Maybe keep an eye on him tonight. Wake him a few times during the night to make sure he's OK. We'll get him back from the X-rays as soon as we can.'

Robbie and Lucy went back out to the waiting area again and Robbie bought them two coffees from the vending machine humming in the corner.

It was the first time they had been alone together since Lucy had broken off their relationship a month earlier after hearing from one of the kids in the residential unit that Robbie had been seen kissing one of the other social workers at a Hallowe'en party. Robbie had tried to explain to her that the kiss had gone no further than that. To Lucy's mind, a kiss was already too far. As she watched him approach, bearing two steaming polystyrene cups, she wondered, not for the first time, whether she had overreacted.

The first drunk had arrived and was declaiming to all those still waiting as to just why Christmas was so shite. He waited for fifteen minutes before announcing that he'd been kept too long, and so left. It was never clear to anyone else there what the nature of the injury that had brought him to A & E in the first place had been.

'Thanks for the coffee,' Lucy said, sipping at it.

They sat for a moment, drinking in silence.

'You don't need to stay if you have somewhere to go,' Robbie said.

'I know,' Lucy said.

Robbie nodded. 'So, any plans for Christmas?'

'Not yet. You?'

'I'll cover the day shift so that the workers with families can be at home with their own kids. Then in the evening I'll probably head home to Omagh. My parents still like us all to come home for Christmas. We all muck in and make dinner. It's always good fun. For an hour. Then you remember why you moved out.'

Lucy laughed lightly. 'I don't remember family

Christmases,' she said. 'I've vague recollections of Santa and that, but the one I remember clearly was when I was eight, just after Mum left. Dad decided I was old enough to be told the truth after he read my Santa letter that year.'

'Why?'

'I'd asked him to bring my mother back.' Lucy glanced at Robbie, the expression of concern on his face, and smiled. 'That was the last time I wanted that, mind you.'

'Santa's a bastard that way,' Robbie said. 'I always wanted Mousetrap, and he never brought that to me. That and a James Bond attaché case.'

Lucy laughed, then turned her attention to the polystyrene cup in her hands, tearing the rim and folding down the top of the cup.

Robbie nudged her and handed her a folded piece of paper.

'What's that?' she asked. She took it, unfolded the page and found an address written on it.

'You'd asked me where Mary Quigg's baby brother, Joe, ended up. Before we . . . you know. Before.'

Lucy nodded. 'Thanks, Robbie,' she said, refolding the page slowly and slipping it into her back pocket.

'A token of my regret,' Robbie said. 'Over all that happened.'

'And mine,' Lucy added, though she suspected not referring to the same events as Robbie.

'Nothing broken,' Gavin said, interrupting them. They looked up to where he stood. 'No bones at least,' he added, looking from one of them to the other.

81

Tuesday 18 December

14

The following morning, Lucy drove into work via the Culmore Road. The note Robbie had given her sat open on the passenger seat. The address listed was in Petrie Way, a fairly affluent area of the city. Joe Quigg had been the only survivor of the fire that had killed Mary and her mother. With no family left, he would be placed with foster parents in the hope that someone might adopt him. Lucy had asked Robbie, while they had still been together, for details of the family with whom the baby had been placed. He'd refused then; it said something about the guilt he felt that he should give it to her now, she reflected.

The house in question was detached, two storeys, with a faux Tudor facade. A silver 4 x 4 was parked in the driveway, and, behind it, a smaller Ford. Lucy had intended to drive past, but when she reached the house, she found herself parking up on the kerb a little down the street from it, then twisting in her seat to better examine the place.

Just then, the front door opened and a man stepped out, dressed in a suit, clutching a plastic shopping bag which looked to contain his lunch. He was perhaps mid-thirties, Lucy thought. His wife appeared at the doorway, dressed in jeans and a white T-shirt. In her arms, she held an infant. Lucy felt her throat constrict as Joe lifted a small fist and reached out to the man, looking to be held. Joe had only been a baby the last time Lucy had seen him. He'd grown in a year. The man moved quickly towards him and embraced him, then turned away and climbed into the 4 x 4 while Joe cried and the woman shushed him, bouncing him lightly in her embrace.

As Lucy watched the woman and child retreat back inside their house, the husband passed her in his 4 x 4, staring in at her, as if realizing that she'd been watching his home.

★ ★ ★

Tom Fleming wasn't in his office when she arrived nor had he left a note to say where he was. However, the phone was ringing in the main office and Lucy went in and answered it.

'Can I speak to Tom Fleming, please?' a young, female, English voice asked.

'I'm afraid not,' Lucy said. 'He's not here.'

'Do you know where he is?'

'I'm afraid not,' Lucy repeated. 'Can I help?'

'This is Euro Security. Mr Fleming's burglar alarm has registered an intruder. Are you a key holder?'

'I'll check on it,' Lucy said, hanging up.

★ ★ ★

She was already on the dual carriageway towards Fleming's house in Kilfennan when she reflected that she should, perhaps, have asked someone to accompany her, in case there actually were intruders in the house. She comforted herself with the thought that, if Fleming himself had been there, he'd have used his panic button. She decided to get as far as his address. If it appeared that there was a need for backup, she'd call for it then.

As she pulled into the street, her stomach constricted. Fleming's car, still owned from his disqualification for drink driving, sat in the driveway, as she'd expected. The curtains in the windows of the house, however, were closed. She pulled up outside and went up the drive. The alarm continued to blare, the blue light on the box attached to the front of the house winking, as if against the morning breeze.

None of the windows or door to the front seemed disturbed, though all were curtained, including one across the front door. Lucy skirted the side of the house, climbing the low gate into the back yard. Again, the windows were shut and the back door locked. She peered in through the kitchen window, using her gloved hand to shield her eyes from the glared reflection on the glass.

The kitchen gave way onto the hallway to the immediate right of which climbed an open staircase. As Lucy squinted to see better, she thought she could make out something, at the far end of the hall, at the foot of the stairway. Shifting her position slightly for a better view, she caught clearer sight of it. Someone was lying at the foot of the stairs.

Taking out her phone, she called for an ambulance immediately. She hammered on the back door a number of times, leaning against the window and calling Fleming's name, but the body did not move.

Finally, she hunted through the overgrown flowerbeds bordering the garden until she found a rock. Using it, she smashed the pane of glass in the back door and, reaching in, grateful for the protection of her work gloves, she unbolted the door and ran into the kitchen.

Tom Fleming was lying face down in the hallway, the lower half of his body still stretched up the staircase from where he had fallen. A pool of vomit haloed his head, sticking to his hair and skin. Lucy pulled off her gloves and placed her hand against his cheek. His skin was pale and clammy, his breath rank with sickness and alcohol.

'Inspector Fleming,' she said, shaking him. 'Tom.'

He moaned, but did not rouse from his torpor. The ringing bell of the outer alarm had been replaced in here by an intense electronic tone that was pitched at such a level it made Lucy wince.

She slapped Fleming's face lightly, all the time calling his name. Eventually, unable to rouse him that way, she went into the kitchen, filled a kettle with cold water, brought it back to the hallway and poured it on his face.

The effect was instantaneous. He jerked awake, staring around him blindly. He caught sight of Lucy standing above him and seemed to struggle to focus on her or place her in the context of his own home. He smacked his lips together dryly and looked as if he might speak. Then he twisted and vomited again onto the carpet, his back arching with each retch.

Lucy heard the wailing siren of the ambulance cut through the white noise of the alarm.

'What's the code for the alarm?' she asked.

Fleming looked up at her, then turned to the floor once more as he dry-heaved. Finally he struggled to stand, seemingly not realizing that his feet were still on the stairs.

'The alarm, sir,' Lucy said. 'What's the code?'

'One, two, three, four,' he managed hoarsely.

So much for police officers being security conscious, Lucy thought.

Lucy had just managed to get the code entered and the alarm silenced when the blaring of the siren outside crescendoed, then stopped abruptly. She could see the flickering of the blue lights through the chink in the curtain over the front door. She pulled the curtain back, turned the key left in the lock and opened the door, flooding the stultifying atmosphere of the hallway both with light and fresh air.

'Is there an officer down?' the paramedic asked, stepping into the hallway and catching sight of Fleming at once.

'I thought he was injured when I looked in from outside,' Lucy explained. 'I don't think it's quite as serious as I thought.'

The paramedic approached him. 'Sir?' he said. 'Can you hear me?'

Fleming groaned and tried to shift himself again.

'Is he pissed?' the paramedic asked incredulously.

Lucy nodded, the gesture greeted by Fleming's grumbles of disagreement.

'I'm sorry,' she said. 'I thought it was . . . you know. I looked in and saw him lying there.'

'We'll give him a quick check over,' the man said. 'He might have injured himself in the fall.' He shifted across to Fleming again. 'We're going to lift you, mate, all right?'

Fleming muttered something, but the man moved in and, gripping the drunk man under the armpits, hefted him to his feet.

'Sit there a moment and I'll get some help,' he said as he helped Fleming to sit on the bottom step of the staircase.

Fleming slumped on the step, then leant sideways, against the wall. His face was pale, his stubble grey against his skin, flecked with his vomit.

'Are you OK, Tom?' Lucy said, stepping past the pool on the floor and laying one hand on his shoulder.

He stared at her accusingly. 'What the hell did you call them for?' he said.

15

She was making coffee for them both in Fleming's kitchen when Tara Gallagher called. They'd had a hit on the metal thefts. Finn's scrap metal yard had called to say that a team was offloading cabling at that moment. Finn, keen to avoid charges of handling stolen goods, had said that if the police were quick enough, they might catch them in the act.

★ ★ ★

Finn's yard was on the outskirts of the city, past Ballyarnett, where Amelia Earhart had landed following her cross-Atlantic flight in 1932. The yard itself was a half-acre compound, enclosed on all sides by a metal palisade fence. A small portable unit from which the owner operated his business sat behind the front section of the fence, at the single gateway into the yard.

The PSNI teams had parked some distance away and were watching the gang as they moved to and fro, shifting metal from the rear of their white Transit van, which was parked on the roadway that bisected the yard.

To the left-hand side of the road, the skeletal remains of crushed cars sat atop each other, three high, six piles deep, against the palisade fence. The other half of the yard, to the right of the gang's van, was comprised of piles of scrap

91

metal and skips, some already filled, as best Lucy could tell. She could see four men moving backwards and forwards, removing scrap from the back of the van and depositing it in different piles and skips, perhaps in an attempt to mix the stolen metal more thoroughly with the legitimate scrap.

Lucy approached Tara. 'What's the plan?'

Tara smiled. 'There's only the one roadway, with the entrance next to the Portakabin,' she pointed out. 'We'll block it with the Land Rover and move in and arrest them. Simple.'

They climbed into the Land Rover, alongside the four Tactical Support Unit officers who had accompanied Tara and the driver down. They wore blue cargo pants and fleeces over their shirts. They all carried guns with them.

The Land Rover's doors slammed shut and the vehicle's engine roared into life as the driver accelerated it up the roadway towards where the van was parked. Leaning forward, Lucy could see through the reinforced windscreen over the driver's shoulder. The four gang members outside heard their approach and instantly dropped what they were doing. One's instinct was to run for the white van, possibly too shocked to realize that he was already blocked in by the police. The other three, however, scattered in different directions across the yard. One made for the area of scrap to the right, scrambling over the pile nearest to him, failing to find purchase on the metal, which slid away beneath his feet with each step he tried to take. The other two cut left towards the carcasses of the cars.

Lucy felt the Land Rover brake suddenly then one of the uniforms flung open the back doors and the four men jumped out and set off in pursuit of the gang members. Lucy and Tara followed, Tara heading straight for the man struggling through the piles of scrap, accompanied by a TSU officer.

The other three TSU men made for the piled cars, in pursuit of the two who had run, leaving Lucy to approach the white Transit van. She pulled her own gun from its holster and, holding it in front of her, both hands to steady it, banged on the side of the van three times in quick succession.

'PSNI,' she shouted. 'Show me your hands.'

Behind her, she heard the thud of the police Land Rover door as the driver got out to support her.

She could see the face of the man in the white van reflected in the side mirror as he tried to gauge the likelihood of his escape. Then, incrementally, she saw the side window begin to lower. Instinctively she pressed herself against the side of the van, gun ready.

'Show me your hands,' she shouted again. 'Now.'

The window cranked down faster now and, slowly, the man's two hands appeared through the gap.

With the PSNI driver approaching from the passenger side of the van, Lucy stepped up and pointed her gun into the van cabin. A single man, in his late teens at most, sat in the driver seat. His face was swarthy, a raw black beard on his chin. His eyes focused on the tip of Lucy's gun and did not waver. Then he heard the passenger door of the van open behind him and turned to face a second PSNI gun.

'Please,' he whimpered, turning to look at the other officer.

Lucy pulled the cable ties from her belt and quickly looped them around his hands, then pulled the plastic tight, cuffing him. Then she opened the door and gripping the man by his shirt front, pulled him out of his seat and onto the ground.

He lay on his face while she sat astride his back, frisking him quickly to check for any weapons. Satisfied that he had none, she twisted him round, onto his back. The PSNI driver had approached them now and stood above them.

'What's your name?' he asked.

'Marcus,' the man said, wide-eyed.

As the officer cautioned the man, Lucy moved to the back of the van and climbed inside to see what the men had been shifting. Coils of copper wiring were stacked to one side of the van, while against the back wall wads of folded lead flashing were piled to the height of the seats in the cab beyond. To the left-hand side were various bits of scrap metal, among which Lucy spotted one section of the cast metal fencing she'd had placed on Mary Quigg's grave.

She climbed back down from the van, just as Tara approached with the second man in cuffs.

'Well?'

'It's the right team for the churches and graveyards anyway,' Lucy said. Over to her left,

94

Lucy could see the other three uniforms tracking their way through the rows of piled cars, still searching for the two men who were presumably hiding inside some of the wrecks.

Lucy grabbed Marcus and, pulling him to his feet, brought him round to the rear of the van.

'Is this cabling from the train line?'

The boy nodded. 'It wasn't us,' he said.

'This wasn't you?'

'No. The girl. She was there when we arrived. We'd only cut a bit and we came round the bend and saw her. She was just lying there. She was dead already.'

The boy was clearly terrified, perhaps believing that the police suspected the gang of Karen's killing.

'So you say,' Lucy snapped.

'I swear,' the boy managed. 'We saw someone leaving when we arrived. An old guy, grey hair. He was getting into a car. It was red, I think. I didn't see what make. But it was small. Like a Fiesta or something.'

'What about the stuff from the graveyard?' she demanded. 'Did you take that?'

Marcus glanced at the officers standing around and nodded.

'We'd best leave this till we get to the station,' Tara cautioned.

Ignoring the comments, Lucy pointed to the fencing from Mary's grave. 'This was taken from a child's grave. Who stole it?'

The man shook his head. 'Not me. That was Shaun. In the red T-shirt. He did the graveyard while we did the church roof.'

95

He nodded towards the piled cars. Shaun was evidently one of the two men still hiding there.

As they glanced across towards where the man had indicated, they suddenly saw that one of the columns of cars, close to the fencing, was beginning to sway. Below it, in the small pathway between the carcasses, they could see the uniforms moving, searching for the two missing men.

'Jesus,' Tara shouted, as the uppermost car of the moving pile, a red Skoda missing a door and bonnet, seemed to teeter at the edge, then fell forwards, knocking into the adjacent pile in the next row. In a moment, in a domino effect, the piles of scrapped cars began tumbling one into the next, bits of the car bodies dropping into the gaps between the rows where the three uniforms were, trapping them beneath the debris.

With the uppermost car now fallen, Lucy could see Shaun, the man in the red T-shirt, his back pressed against the far fence, using his legs as leverage to the uppermost car in the next pile over, recreating the effect again. Then he turned and began scrambling up the metal fence, using the barbs at the top as a grip to pull himself up.

As Tara and the two uniforms ran towards the fallen cars to look for their colleagues, Lucy sprinted down the roadway out of the scrapyard, trying to keep an eye on Shaun's progress. As she reached the main gateway, she saw him swing over the top of the fence, as if to drop to the ground beyond.

Puffing furiously, she sprinted the circumference of the fence, aware now that at least one other TSU officer was following some distance behind her, realizing that she needed support.

As she neared the spot where Shaun had been climbing, she realized that he'd not made it down, as she'd expected. His trousers had become entangled in the barbs and he was caught at the top of the fence, tugging at the material, trying to tear himself free. Just as Lucy approached, she heard the rip of fabric and he fell onto the ground in front of her. He struggled to get to his feet, but Lucy covered the final few yards and fell onto him, pinning him back down.

He writhed beneath her, trying to buck her off his back as Lucy laid her full weight against him. Finally, the TSU officer arrived and, dropping beside her, laid his weight on Shaun's legs, effectively pinning him to the ground.

'You're under arrest for theft,' Lucy managed. 'Put your hands in front of you.'

Shaun tried to kick and shifted his weight, but he was overpowered. Finally, Lucy felt him slump, and he extended his two hands out in front of his head, his face pressed into the dirt of the ground where he'd fallen.

Lucy moved quickly, looping the cable ties around his outstretched hands, pinching them tight against the skin of his arm. His hands lay flat on the ground, the wrists bound together, his arms outstretched above his head.

The TSU man stood up, dusting himself as he did so, then turned quickly to look into the yard through the gaps in the fence to where one of his colleagues lay on the ground beneath the scrapped Skoda.

'Are you OK, Danny?' he called.

Lucy leaned down close to Shaun's ear. 'You stole from graves, is that right?' she said.

Shaun looked up at her, his face smeared with mud. 'No comment.' He smiled.

Rising, Lucy stepped on his hand with her steel-capped boot, pressing down until she heard the fingers' crack behind the screaming of the man and the shouts of the TSU officer as he tried to pull her away.

16

A fire tender was at the scene within minutes, with cutting equipment, lest it should be needed. They shifted the remains of the cars as carefully as possible in order to create sufficient space for the PSNI men trapped beneath to crawl out. In addition, it became apparent that in pushing over the cars, Shaun had trapped one of his own gang members beneath a badly rusted Scenic. He cried out periodically in rage as the officers worked first to rescue their own colleagues before coming to his aid.

* * *

The metal gang members were brought back to Strand Road station, where Tara, preening herself on having overseen the operation to arrest them, briefed Burns. Lucy was called into his office after he had spoken with Tara.

'I understand you questioned one of the suspects?' he said, without preamble.

Lucy nodded. 'I wanted to be sure we had the right people,' she said. 'I'm sorry. I should have waited.'

'You should indeed,' Burns said. 'You got a description apparently. What did he say?'

'As they arrived, they saw an older man, grey-haired, getting into a red car in the parking bay. He drove off and they started harvesting the

99

metal. As they moved down the line, they came across Karen's remains. He said they didn't touch the body. They scarpered when they found it.'

'You should have left it until he was brought back here.'

'We have a description now, at least, sir.'

'Though there's no guarantee that the man they saw had anything to do with Karen's disappearance.'

'It seems a little odd that a man would be in the park at that time of night for any legitimate reason.'

Burns accepted this with a curt nod. 'Regardless, we needed him to make a proper statement.'

'Sorry, sir,' Lucy said.

'I understand you also broke another suspect's fingers.'

'That was an accident. I didn't feel his hand beneath my boot until he cried out.'

'You were asking the first suspect you arrested about taking fences off a child's grave, apparently. I hope the two things aren't connected.'

'No sir,' Lucy said, thinking back, trying to remember who had heard her asking Marcus about Mary's grave. Then she remembered.

As she left Burns's office, Tara sat at her desk in the incident room, watching her. When she saw Lucy, she raised her hand meekly. Lucy nodded curtly and left without speaking.

★ ★ ★

100

After leaving Strand Road station, Lucy had headed back to Maydown. Fleming was in his office at least, though with the door closed. Lucy considered knocking to ask how he was feeling, but decided against.

She'd just made it into her own office when her phone rang.

'Dave Cooper here, Lucy. I think Bradley is about to go online.'

'Is this some sixth sense, ESP thing?'

Cooper laughed. 'No. He's online already. Just not as himself. Come across and I'll show you.'

★   ★   ★

Cooper's office was as cluttered as it had been the day previous. The large iMac sitting on the main desk displayed Karen Hughes's Facebook account profile.

'I checked out Bradley's account yesterday, tracing through all of the friends that he had, in case there were other girls there he was targeting,' Cooper explained. 'I have a feeling that a number of these friends are sock puppet accounts.'

Lucy shrugged. 'What's that mean?'

'I think Bradley created a whole load of accounts, all in different names, which he then befriended.'

'He made friends with himself? Why?'

'To make him seem more normal.'

Lucy raised a sceptical eyebrow.

'Look,' Cooper said. 'If he sent you a friend request, and he only had one or two other online mates, you'd think it a bit strange. If instead he has loads of friends, all your age, all with similar interests, he looks less suspicious.'

'How do you know they're sock puppets?'

'A lot of the accounts either aren't fully developed, or their content is repetitive, where the same message is being posted in fourteen or fifteen accounts almost in rotation. Look.'

He showed her Paul Bradley's page. He'd posted a status update the previous Saturday saying 'Saturday lie-in =)'.

'See this,' Cooper said. 'Watch.'

He opened a second Facebook profile, this time for someone called 'Liam Tyler'. 'Look.'

On the previous Saturday, 'Tyler' had posted the same status update. A girl named Annie Marsden had attached a comment with a smiley face of her own.

'You think 'Tyler' is actually Paul Bradley?'

Cooper nodded. 'If Paul Bradley is even his real name. That could simply be another alias.'

'But one of his aliases has gone online?'

Cooper nodded. ''Simon Harris' went on about ten minutes ago. Watch.'

He pointed to a small pane in the lower half of the page, which listed online friends of Bradley's. A green circle marked the name 'Harris'. Suddenly the name vanished.

'We've lost him again?' Lucy asked.

'Wait,' Cooper said. 'If I'm right, you'll see one of these other names go live.'

Sure enough, a moment later, a green dot appeared next to the name 'Tom Gallagher'. Cooper pointed to the screen. 'That's another of them.'

'How many does he have in total?'

'I think about twenty,' Cooper said. 'We need him to log in as Paul Bradley though; I've got Facebook to agree to give us Bradley's ISP address when he next logs in. But we can't ask for that for all of these accounts too unless we can prove they're all the same person.'

'I'll update Burns anyway,' Lucy said, going out of the unit and phoning through to CID. As she was explaining to Burns what Cooper had told her, Cooper himself appeared, barely able to contain his excitement.

'They've been in touch. Bradley's just gone online. I've reverse-checked the ISP address they've given us. It's a restaurant in the Foyleside shopping centre.'

17

The Foyleside Centre was built in the early nineties, covering four floors and housing almost fifty different stores. Level four was little more than a central concourse with shops lining both sides. The two middle floors, however, were more open-plan, meaning that there were a variety of approaches and escape routes, should Bradley try to make a run for it. Fortunately for them, the Wi-Fi address they had been given belonged to the fast-food outlet on the uppermost floor.

The difficulty was that, although they had a picture of Bradley from his account page, there was no guarantee that the man in question would even look like his picture. They did, though, have the description from the metal theft gang, who'd seen a man with grey hair in the area where Karen's body had been found.

All of this was explained to the team by Burns who briefed them in the back of the Land Rover on their way to the Foyleside. The rear of the Land Rover was stuffy, the benches on each side lined with members of one of the two Tactical Support Units accompanying the investigating team. The proximity of the bodies, and the vague smell of sweat generated by the boiler-suit type uniforms the officers wore made it difficult for Lucy to concentrate on what Burns was saying. She wanted to get out and get moving.

'Lucy and Tara go in together first. Get

104

something to eat, scope the place out. We're probably looking for a man, on his own, using a phone. Grey-haired particularly. Obviously if you recognize anyone on the Offenders Register let us know immediately. We'll hold back on a full entrance until we have a target,' Burns said, before turning to Mickey and the DC sitting next to him. 'You two hang around outside; be ready in case anything goes down. We'll post one TS Unit outside the main entrance and a second at the bottom of the stairs to the fourth floor. If he makes a run for it within the centre, they can close in on him from top and bottom floors.'

'How come they get food and we have to window-shop?' Mickey complained.

'How many women only window-shop?' Burns asked. 'Besides, you've had a few too many dinners recently by the looks of you.'

The team erupted into laughter, the loudest of which belonged to Mickey himself, keen to ingratiate himself with the boss.

Lucy and Tara stepped out into the light mizzle of rain that seemed to hang perpetually over the city. Lucy glanced at the shoppers passing, arms laden with bags, looking forward to Christmas, blithely unaware that a possible child killer was sitting in their midst.

'What do you fancy?' Tara asked as they entered the Foyleside. 'I'll get the grub, you have a look around; you've a better idea of some of the weirdos out there through the PPU anyway.'

Lucy grunted, already scanning the area as they entered the central concourse. If the Wi-Fi signal was strong enough, there would be no need for Bradley even to sit inside the restaurant.

'I'll have a cheeseburger and Diet Coke,' Lucy said. 'I'll grab a table near the door. That'll give us a good chance to look around.'

As it transpired, that would prove difficult. The centre was heaving with people, burdened down with shopping, presumably trying to complete Christmas shopping. They could already see a queue for the fast-food place stretching out through the main doors.

'We've another week to go and I'm sick of bloody carols already,' Tara said as a piped version of 'In the Bleak Midwinter' began playing over the centre's speakers.

There were two doors into the restaurant; the main one where the queue had formed and a second exit to the left, nearer the front entrance of the Foyleside itself.

'You take the main entrance and join the queue,' Lucy said, 'I'll take a look around the place, like I'm looking for seats.'

Lucy moved to the nearest door and pushed her way in. As she did, she phoned Cooper.

'Is he still online?' she asked quietly.

'He's switched accounts again,' Cooper said. 'I think he's currently 'Steven Burke'.'

Lucy ended the call and began weaving between the packed tables, looking for any single men. To her left was a harried family, four kids climbing on the seats while their father and mother tried to distribute their boxes of food. The youngest, a girl with tight curled hair, smiled up at Lucy who winked at her in return. Her three brothers, meanwhile, were fighting

106

over who was getting the first strawberry milkshake.

Over to the right, a number of tables were filled with young girls, out shopping together, five of them crowded around one bag of chips and a drink. All had phones, probably sending texts to one another as they sat there, Lucy reflected. Then a little further ahead, she saw the actual recipients of their messages: a table of teenage boys, similarly clumped around food for one, watching across at the girls.

A man banged into Lucy, his tray held in front of him defensively.

'Sorry,' he managed. Lucy glanced at him, middle-aged, grey-haired, then checked his tray, three drinks, enough food for a family. Across to the right, at the window, she saw a man, mid-twenties, black hair, sitting alone. He had a phone in his hand, the crumpled wrapper of his burger lying on the table in front of him. As she moved towards him, she got a clear view of the table and saw a woman and child also sitting at it.

Suddenly, Tara's voice crackled through her earpiece. 'In the corner. The grey coat.'

Lucy glanced across to where Tara had indicated. A grey-haired man sat alone, staring intently across the restaurant. He had a coffee cup in front of him and the remains of a doughnut. He was holding his phone, raised off the table, glancing occasionally at the screen. He seemed to be holding it steady. Lucy followed the direction of the phone and realized it was pointing at the table of teenage girls.

The man looked up and, for a moment, caught Lucy's gaze. He recognized her at the same moment she recognized him.

'Gene Kay,' she said. 'It's Gene Kay.'

As she spoke, Kay got to his feet, pushed his way through the gathered queue and made for the exit.

'He's moving,' Tara said. 'Middle-aged, grey coat. Can we pick him up?'

'Mickey, pick him as he comes out,' Burns ordered.

Kay had started to move towards the main door, then seemed to realize that the two men moving towards it from the outside were coming for him. He cut quickly towards Lucy, pushing past a young man, knocking over his tray.

'Mr Kay, stop,' she shouted.

Lucy reached out to stop him as he approached, but he rushed her, pushing through, shouldering her off balance and knocking her to the ground, then bolted for the second exit, the doorway Lucy had just entered.

There he must have seen the Tactical Support officers coming in through the Foyleside entrance for he turned and ran back down the concourse towards the escalators leading to the lower floors. Lucy glanced across to see that Mickey and the DC had come into the restaurant after him through the other door and were now trying to get back out again, having become caught in the middle of a crowd of school children being herded in through the main doors by their teacher.

Lucy pushed through towards the exit Kay

108

had taken and, once on the main concourse, turned to see his retreating back as he reached the top of the escalators. He hesitated, then took the stairs instead. At least the second TS Unit would pick him up, she thought. But, if Kay had seen them on the lower floor down there, why had he willingly gone down?

'Are the TSU in place on level three?' Lucy breathed into the earpiece.

'Can I get a location?' she heard Burns snap.

'Floor two, sir. We've been held up with three shoplifters coming out of Boots. We're on our way up.'

Lucy weaved through the crowd, travelling seemingly against the direction of foot flow, as the rest of the team finally appeared through the other door.

'Fucking pantomime trips,' Mickey spat, rounding the last of the school children.

They took the stairs, two at a time, and reached the third floor, which opened out in four directions from the bottom of the stairs.

'I'll take straight ahead,' Mickey said, taking control. 'You go left, Tommy; Tara go right; Lucy check the shops. TSU will catch up.' Then he set off before anyone could argue.

The first shop to her left was the book store, Eason. Lucy ran in then stood on tiptoe to better scan the shoppers. She couldn't see Kay and left, moving towards the next shop. The neighbouring units were all similarly clear. The last store was a larger department store, and Tommy had headed in there. She cut across and began checking the shops along the opposite wall. She was just coming out of a clothes shop when she spotted Kay, his coat off now and hanging over his arm, as he walked out of the O_2 shop. The central portion of level three had actually been cut away, allowing those on the level to look down to the one beneath. The shop from which Kay had come was on the opposite side of the gap from where she stood, meaning Lucy would need to move around it to get to Kay. He would undoubtedly see her approach. In fact, even now, he was glancing around, obviously looking to see where the police were.

'He's here,' Lucy said.

'TSU are on the level now. What's your location?' Burns snapped.

'He's outside the O_2 shop,' Lucy said, 'moving towards the lower escalator.'

Kay must have spotted the two uniforms coming up the escalator he was about to take for he turned suddenly. Then he saw Lucy too, stood, holding her gaze, the space between them the ten-foot opening in the floor, surrounded by guard rails, giving way to a drop of about twenty feet down to level two. At the centre of the space below, a small water feature twinkled beneath the fluorescent centre lights.

Kay glanced to his left, where the two TSU officers were approaching, then to his right, where a team from above was likewise fanning out as they approached him.

He stared across at Lucy, placing both his hands on the rail, as if to brace himself for a jump.

Lucy shook her head. *Don't*, she mouthed.

Kay paused a second, then lifted his leg and began clambering over the guard rail.

'He's going to jump,' Lucy shouted. Glancing down, she saw Mickey and Tommy arrive beneath them.

Instead, the man pulled his phone from his pocket and flung it to the floor below. Looking down, Lucy could only watch as it shattered off the side of the tiled water feature below and slid beneath the water to rest on a bed of winking good luck pennies.

18

Lucy and Tom Fleming were sent to Kay's house first to search for evidence that might connect him with Karen Hughes. There was no doubt that, like all abusers, Kay would have a collection of material somewhere in the house, most likely stored on his PC. The difficulty with abusers' collections, however, was that they were not always obviously related to the abuse that had been carried out. Any officer would pick up a box containing obscene photographs straight away; a box of seemingly innocuous souvenirs might not be noticed. Burns reasoned that Fleming and Lucy would have a better sense of what to look for than CID.

When they entered the living room, however, the first thing Lucy noticed was the space on the table where the computer had been.

'PC's gone,' she said to Fleming.

'We'll keep an eye out for it,' Fleming commented. 'You do the upstairs rooms, I'll do down here.'

There were three rooms upstairs. The first, a bathroom, was almost bare. The walls were blue, the paint bubbling and blistered in places behind the sink. A scum-ringed glass on the windowsill. Toothbrush, razor, a rolled tube of paste. A few bottles of cheap aftershave on the windowsill next to that, and a bottle of talc. There were no obvious hiding places. Lucy pulled the plastic front off the bath and peered underneath, illuminating the space with her torch beam, but there was nothing there.

The second room was a spare bedroom. The wardrobe was empty save for an old suit jacket, which, judging by the musty smell coming from it, had not been worn in some time. Lucy checked the room, under the bed, the dresser in the corner, but there was nothing of interest.

Finally, in Kay's own bedroom, she found what she'd been looking for: a box on the top shelf of his wardrobe. She quickly checked the rest of the room then, when she was sure there was nothing else of interest, she took the box down to the living room to catalogue with Fleming present.

Fleming came struggling in through the back door carrying a black rubbish bag.

'In the bin,' Fleming explained, dumping the bag on the ground. 'What did you find?'

Lucy laid the box on the table, opened it and began sifting through the contents. It contained mostly objects rather than pictures. Among them was a teddy bear, several pairs of ticket stubs, some to a local cinema, two pairs to the circus, though dated on different years, and a dried-out daffodil. At the bottom of the box were a handful of sea shells, a single glove, a doll. With each object, Lucy reflected on the child whom it represented to Kay. Trips to the circus and cinema suggested the family of the child had trusted him, known him well, had allowed him to inveigle his way into their home.

'A bit careless of him keeping these in the

house,' Fleming said.

'They don't prove he did anything wrong,' Lucy muttered. 'He's probably hidden his other collection much more carefully.'

She knew that there would be another collection, the one which, despite her time in the police, she knew would still make her stomach twist with revulsion when she saw it. But, strangely, she found these collections — the objects — to be equally disturbing, reflecting as these did the innocence of the ones Kay had clearly been grooming. In the bottom corner, beneath the glove, she found a bar of hotel soap and pointed it out to Fleming, who groaned.

'Some of these stubs are years old,' Lucy commented.

Fleming shook his head. 'Anything you see there connect him to Karen Hughes?'

'No,' Lucy said. 'If anything, if all this stuff is connected to his victims, they're a little young in comparison with Karen. She was mid-teens, this stuff suggests that might have been too old for Kay.' She gestured towards the black bag. 'What was he dumping?'

Fleming lifted the black bag and emptied it. Pictures cut from newspapers and magazines spilled out onto the floor. One by one, they picked through them, examining each. While each image was of a child, none were of a sexual nature. The children pictured were predominantly pre-teen.

They worked through each image, but again, none related to Karen Hughes.

'He must have other stuff somewhere,'

Fleming said. 'Presumably on his computer. He's stashed it somewhere after we called for the dog hairs.'

'Would he have destroyed it?' Lucy asked. 'Or hidden it in the garden?'

Fleming shook his head, his breath sweet as he exhaled. 'If Kay's been building these collections for years, his real one will be massive. He'll not just get rid of it. Someone's keeping it for him or he's hidden it somewhere. It's not out back. I searched the shed, checked the lawn for signs of recent disturbance. Nothing.'

They had just finished bagging the collections to be transferred back to the Strand Road when Fleming took a call from one of the district teams to say that another fifteen-year-old girl, called Sarah Finn, had been reported missing.

19

Sarah Finn's mother, Sinead, sat on the sofa in the living room of their family home in Fallowfield Gardens, in Gobnascale. She was in her mid-thirties, at most, dressed in a heavy white dressing gown over her pyjamas. She wore thick grey bed socks into which she had tucked the legs of her pink pyjama bottoms. Her legs were crossed, the foot of the upper leg jittering as she spoke.

'The school phoned just after lunch to say she's been off all day. I thought maybe she'd bunked off with friends.'

'Had she bunked off before?' Lucy asked.

Finn shrugged lightly. 'A few times, maybe.'

'And she's not been in touch since?'

The woman shook her head. 'I checked when I got in from the shops but she weren't in her room. She normally gets herself back in from school and that.'

'So when was the last time you saw her?'

The woman reached across to the pack of cigarettes on the table next to the sofa and withdrew one, shaking it free of the pack. She lit it, dragged deeply, then held it between the fingers of the hand resting on her knee. Lucy couldn't help but notice that her nails looked freshly painted. She glanced across to where the cigarette box sat and, sure enough, a bottle of nail polish stood behind them. If she'd been concerned by the news of her daughter's absence from school, it hadn't affected her cosmetics routine.

'Last night some time.'

'Last night?' Fleming asked, glancing at his watch. It was almost three. 'What time?'

'Before seven, maybe. She were going out with her friends.'

'You didn't see her come home last night?'

'I went to bed early.'

'And this morning? Was she home this morning?'

The woman shrugged. 'I don't know. She normally sorts herself out in the morning.'

'Was her bed made or unmade?' Lucy asked. 'Had she slept in it?'

Again a shrug. 'I don't know. It was made, I think. But she always makes it.'

'Has she ever run away before?' Lucy asked.

'Never.'

'So you last saw her before seven last night. Almost twenty hours ago,' Fleming said.

The woman laughed embarrassedly. 'It sounds bad when you say it like that. She went out to the local youth club. I went to bed early last night.'

'Did she?'

'Did she what?'

'Go to the club?'

'I don't know,' the woman said, blankly.

Fleming moved from the window, finally, and sat on the armchair against the opposite wall. 'You might be best to check,' he said.

Sinead Finn dragged again on her cigarette,

then folded it into the ashtray balancing on the arm of the sofa. She rooted through the pocket of her gown until she produced a mobile phone.

While she rang Sarah's friend, Lucy glanced around the room. It was cramped, the three-piece suite on which she sat much too big for the room. An electric fire flickered on the hearth. Above it, on the mantelpiece, a small gold carriage clock squatted, the lower works spinning back and forth. It was framed on either side by two small pictures. One was of Sinead Finn herself and a man.

Lucy struggled out of the seat, went across to the mantelpiece and lifted the photograph. It looked fairly recent, judging by the appearance of Sinead Finn. The man was small, little taller than Sinead, his head shaved, though the shadow of stubble across his skull carried a reddish sheen. The buzz cut accentuated his ears, which seemed to protrude a little. His eyes were narrowed, his mouth frozen open in a laugh. He stood slightly behind Sinead, his right arm reaching around her neck and across her chest, the bicep flexed protectively in front of her, the hand lightly clasping her left breast.

Lucy put the photograph down and lifted the second. It was, presumably, Sarah Finn, for the person in the picture wore a school uniform. She sat in front of a bookcase, laden with red-spined leather volumes. Lucy guessed it was a screen backdrop used by the school photographer. Sarah was brown-haired, her features soft, still carrying a little puppy fat on her face. She looked up at the camera from below her fringe,

118

her mouth frozen in an embarrassed smile.

Lucy turned and handed the picture to Fleming, then returned to her own seat.

'Linda? Sinead Finn again. Was Sarah at the club with you last night?'

Lucy sat, clasped her hands between her knees. Instinctively she stretched them out towards the fire, then realized it was electric and returned them to between her legs. She could hear the raised murmur of the other speaker for a second as Sinead adjusted the phone against her ear, reaching for another smoke.

'Well she said she was going with you,' Sinead said.

Linda obviously took exception to this last comment for her voice became loud enough for them to hear.

'She said she was with you,' Sinead countered, raising her voice too, as if in so doing, she could convince Linda that she was mistaken and that Sarah had indeed been at the club.

Sinead snapped the phone shut and, lifting her lighter, lit the cigarette.

'She weren't there at all,' she explained, unnecessarily.

'Has Sarah a phone? Have you tried calling her?' Lucy asked.

'I'm not bloody thick,' the woman snapped. 'Of course I tried. There's no answer. I've left her a message to call me, but nothing yet.'

Fleming nodded. 'So you didn't notice that she hadn't come home last night?'

Sinead Finn stared at him a moment, teasing out the implied criticism of his question.

119

'Sometimes she's home late,' she explained. 'The friends she runs around with and that.'

Fleming rose from the seat a little sullenly, crossed to the window and turned his attention again to the road outside.

'Is this Sarah?' Lucy asked, lifting the picture from the arm of the chair where Fleming had left it.

Sinead smiled. 'That's her. She looks so pretty.'

Lucy nodded in agreement. 'She's lovely,' she said. 'Is it a recent picture?'

'A few months ago just. The start of the new term.'

'Can we hold on to this, to show people if we need to ask around?'

Sinead nodded. 'Seamy, my partner, was heading off early this morning, so we had a few drinks and an early night. That's how I didn't notice she was gone.' She folded her arms against her chest, staring at Fleming.

'Where's he gone?' Fleming asked, turning back to the woman again.

'Manchester. He's a lorry driver. He had to leave at five this morning to get the early ferry across.'

'This would be Mr Finn, would it?' Lucy asked, pointing to the picture on the mantelpiece.

'No,' Sinead said, with a confused laugh. 'That's Seamy.'

'What's his full name, Mrs Finn?'

'Sinead, Jesus,' the woman replied. 'Seamus Doherty.'

'Who does he work for?'

'H. M. Haulage. Harry Martin's his boss. He's H. M.'

'I see,' Lucy said, jotting down the name. 'Sarah wouldn't be with Mr Doherty, would she? Maybe went to keep him company?'

Sinead shook her head. 'No. They don't really get on. Sarah's dad left a few years back and it's still raw, like. You know?'

'How long have you been with Mr Doherty?'

'A year or two.'

'Does he live here?'

Finn nodded. 'When he's not working. He drives a lot.'

'Have you checked with him that Sarah's not with him at the moment?'

'His phone's switched off,' Sinead said. 'Besides, he'd have phoned to let me know if she was with him.'

'And what about Sarah's father? Would she be with him?'

'I doubt it,' Sinead said. 'He lives in Australia. He headed out for work and never came back.'

'How did Sarah take to you having Mr Doherty staying here?' Fleming asked.

'It's my house, isn't it?' Sinead said.

She lifted another cigarette, lit it off the butt of the smouldering one she held, then flicked the dead one into the fireplace. She folded her arms again, facing Lucy and Fleming, as if challenging them to disagree.

'Of course,' Fleming said. 'Look, before we start a full search for Sarah, DS Black is going to take a quick look through the house. Just to double-check that she's not here. Is that OK?'

She bristled a little, perhaps at the implication that she may not have looked for her own daughter. Before she could speak, though, Fleming raised a placatory hand.

'I'm sure you checked already, but sometimes we get called out to houses and the child in question is hiding somewhere inside. Sometimes they enjoy all the fuss and attention of people searching for them. It won't take long.'

'Please yourself,' Sinead Finn said. 'I've looked for her already.'

'I understand,' Fleming said, attempting a smile. Not quite managing it. 'A fresh pair of eyes and that. How about you sit and tell me a bit more about Sarah? Give us a sense of who she is.'

20

Lucy went to the rear of the ground floor first and worked her way up. The back room was a small toilet, plain. A raft of coats hung on coat pegs screwed to the wall. She patted through the coats; just to be sure Sarah wasn't in there. The kitchen and dinette were next. There were precious few places where a fifteen-year-old girl could hide.

The kitchen itself was small, something accentuated by the amount of stuff cluttering the worktops. The remains of a Chinese takeaway from the previous evening congealed to two plates. The tinfoil trays remained, half filled, among the torn scraps of a brown paper bag. Two wine bottles sat next to them; one empty, the other perhaps a quarter full. Two glasses sat beside it. The sink was filled with older dishes again: a pan with spaghetti sauce hardened to the surface, a scattering of plates and cups beneath it, forming a pyramid of crockery that spilled over onto the draining board.

The next room was the sitting room where Fleming and Sinead Finn sat. Lucy could hear a snippet of the conversation as she passed the room and headed up the stairs to check the first floor.

The upper floor had two bedrooms and a bathroom. The bathroom was to her left. She took a quick look in; nothing out of the ordinary.

A white T-shirt and a pair of boxer shorts lay discarded behind the door, nestled on top of a sodden bath towel.

Lucy stepped across to the glass above the sink which held toothbrushes and paste. Three brushes. Assorted pieces of make-up were scattered across the windowsill.

Moving back out to the landing, she glanced into the next room, knocking on the door as she did so. It was, presumably, Sinead Finn's bedroom. A double bed with the clothes spilling onto the floor. A pint glass of water sat on the bedside cabinet on one side, a crowded ashtray on the other. The face of the old-style alarm clock behind it was magnified through the glass. Lucy picked her way across and, lifting the clock, checked the alarm time: 4.30 a.m. As she replaced the clock on the cabinet, she noticed a number of small oval scorch marks blackening the cabinet surface.

Two built-in wardrobes faced the bed. Lucy checked the first. A smattering of shirts and jeans, all male. Two pairs of sneakers sat on the floor.

The dressing table between the wardrobes held more cosmetics and a large pine jewellery case, so full that the lid did not close properly. The second wardrobe contained Sinead Finn's clothes, crammed tightly together in the space; Lucy struggled to make room to check that Sarah was not hiding behind them.

Finally, Lucy dropped to the floor and checked under the bed. Another pair of trainers, a used condom folded on itself, a spoon, lying face down, the curve of its back blackened with soot. Quickly she got up again, wiped her hands on her trouser leg.

The room next door was clearly Sarah's. It was simply furnished. A single bed, white wooden frame. A desk and a wooden chair. A single standing wardrobe. A small cabinet beside the bed on which sat another alarm clock with a space on top for docking an iPod. Instinctively, Lucy checked the alarm time on this: 7.30 a.m. The alarm was turned off.

The bed was neatly made, the pink duvet something Lucy would have expected in the room of a child many years younger than Sarah Finn. Again, she glanced under the bed, but the space was empty.

She opened the wardrobe. Fewer clothes hung in this compared to Sinead's. But what was there was hung neatly, first tops, then jumpers, then jeans. No dresses or skirts, Lucy noticed. Mind you, she didn't wear either that often herself.

'Are you lost up there?'

Lucy looked out to see Sinead Finn mounting the final steps onto the landing.

'I'm almost done. Is there anything missing from her room? Anything obvious?'

The woman stepped into the bedroom and glanced around, mouthing quietly to herself as if counting off items on a list. 'She's an old rabbit sits on her bed,' she said finally. 'That's about all.'

'An old rabbit. A toy?'

The woman snorted lightly. 'Aye. An ole white thing her father gave her. She'd taken it down from the attic a few weeks ago and started sleeping with it.'

'Any reason why?' Fleming asked.

'Why what?'

'Why she started sleeping again with a childhood toy?'

The woman looked at him, then shrugged, pulling her dressing gown around her as she did. 'I dunno,' she said.

21

Fleming stood at the door of the car, waiting for Lucy to unlock it. 'What's your feeling?'

'Hard to say,' Lucy commented. 'She could have run away if she's taken the rabbit toy with her.'

'Though we need to get to the bottom of what made her start sleeping with it.'

'Maybe she missed her dad,' Lucy offered.

'Maybe,' Fleming agreed, though he sounded unconvinced. Lucy was well aware what he was thinking; older children regressing to childhood toys in that manner could be an indicator of something more sinister.

'So, we know the mother started up with the new fella,' Lucy said. 'Maybe the girl was struggling with it a little.'

Fleming nodded. 'Follow up on the partner, Seamus Doherty. See if his work has a way of contacting him.'

'He has another place,' Lucy commented. 'The clothes in the wardrobe upstairs look like spares he keeps for when he stays over. He's living somewhere else.'

'Check again with Sinead Finn, see if she knows where else he might live.'

'And one of them is using heroin. I found works in their bedroom.'

'Of course you did,' Fleming said, shaking his head. 'That might explain why she didn't even notice if the wee girl hadn't come back last night. We'll do a sweep around of the local shops, see what people have to say. And try to find out whereabouts on the road to Manchester Mr Doherty is at the moment.'

* * *

They drove across to the small shopping area to the left of the local primary school. The block comprised a hairdresser's, post office, supermarket and chip shop. They decided Lucy might have best luck in the hairdresser's. Fleming volunteered to take the chippie.

As she approached the shops, she noticed a gang of teenagers standing on the corner of the block. She thought she recognized some of them as having been with Gavin Duffy when she saw him standing opposite Gene Kay's, but she couldn't be sure.

As she approached them, she realized that one of them was slightly older than the rest. The group fanned out behind him in a semicircle.

He raised his chin slightly at her approach and she recognized him as the one who had shouted and winked at her when she and Fleming had left Kay's house.

Lucy scanned the group behind him for Gavin but could not see him.

'I need some help,' she said.

The boy at the head of the gang smirked. 'Do you now?'

Lucy produced the picture of Sarah Finn and showed it to him. 'Do any of you know this girl?

She's a local lass. She's missing.'

The youth shook his head.

'That's Sarah, Tony,' one of those behind him said, earning a scowl for the comment from the youth whom Lucy now took to be Tony.

'You do know her?'

Tony nodded. 'I know of her. She goes to the youth club times. That's all. We've not seen her in a while though.'

'We?'

Tony nodded towards those behind him. 'If they'd seen her, I'd have seen her.'

'Will you let someone know if you hear anything of her whereabouts?' Lucy asked. She pulled out her card, which Tony looked at but did not touch.

He nodded. 'We hear anything, we'll pass it on,' he said, then turned from her, indicating that, for him at least, their discussion was concluded.

As it turned out, Lucy was finished much sooner than she expected in the hairdresser's too. There were only two customers in there, neither of whom knew Sarah Finn. Like Tony and his gang, the girls working in the place knew her, but hadn't seen her in a few days. They did promise to keep an eye out for her. Similarly, the post office next door was quiet, with only two people in the queue ahead of Lucy.

The man behind the counter knew Sarah well, he said. She often came in on messages for her mum. She was a very sensible girl, he said. A little awkward, maybe. A little shy.

'Have you see her today?'

'No,' the man said. 'Not since yesterday afternoon. Why?'

'She's not come home,' Lucy said. 'Her mum's asked us to look out for her. If she comes in at all, can you give me a call?' Lucy handed the man the card Tony had refused to take through the gap at the bottom of the glass partition between them.

'Of course,' he said. 'You know the mother then?'

Lucy nodded. 'Mrs Finn contacted us about Sarah. She's very worried.'

'Mmm,' the man replied.

Lucy waited a beat to see if he would elaborate, but to no avail. 'What was Sarah in for yesterday?'

'She was taking money out for her mother,' he said. 'Her card account. She withdrew two hundred pounds from her child benefit account.'

'You've a good memory,' Lucy said. 'A police officer's best friend.'

'I remember that,' he said. 'Normally you wouldn't let a child withdraw that kind of money, but Sarah did a lot of that type of stuff for her mother.'

'I see,' Lucy said.

The man leaned closer to the glass. Lucy noticed his name tag resting against the partition. Ian Ross.

'Have you met the partner?'

'Seamus Doherty?'

Ross nodded. 'He's a strange one. Quiet. He's away a lot.'

Lucy nodded, leaning closer in the hope that

130

Ross might elucidate, but the man simply nodded knowingly.

'Thank you, Mr Ross. That's very helpful.'

The man sank back to his stool. 'I'll call if I see Sarah,' he promised. 'I'll ask about too, with the customers.'

'That would be very helpful, Mr Ross,' Lucy said.

She headed back out to the car again, but there was no sign of Tom Fleming. The people in the corner shop must have been more talkative than he expected, she thought.

Ian Ross's comments had reminded her, however, that she was to follow up on Seamus Doherty.

She took out her phone and googled H. M. Haulage. The first result gave the contact details and a Google map of the office location in Coleraine.

A friendly-sounding girl with a broad Ballymena accent answered the call almost immediately.

'Can I speak with Mr Martin, please?' Lucy asked, having introduced herself.

'With what is it in connection?' the girl asked.

'With a missing person inquiry,' Lucy replied tersely.

She was put on hold without further comment and for almost two minutes Lucy listened to an electronic version of 'Greensleeves'. Given the choice, she'd rather have listened to silence while she waited.

Finally she heard a click and Harry Martin introduced himself. His voice was deep, gruff, his accent a little closer to home, as best Lucy could tell.

'Yes, Inspector Black,' Martin said. 'You needed to speak to me.'

'It's Sergeant,' Lucy said. 'Thanks for your time. I'm trying to contact one of your drivers, Seamus Doherty. His mobile phone is out of network apparently. I was wondering if you might have some kind of system where I could contact him in his lorry.'

'We do,' Martin said. 'But I'm not sure how much use it will be. Seamus isn't out today.'

'His partner told us he left at five this morning for a trip to Manchester.'

'Not for me, he didn't,' Martin said. 'We don't have any contracts in Manchester.'

22

Fleming appeared out of the chip shop a few minutes later, carrying two small brown bags in his hand.

'Lunch,' he said, tossing one of them to Lucy.

'It's gone three, sir.'

'Dinner, then,' Fleming said.

'Bit early for chippie grub, sir,' she commented, opening the bag. A floury bap sandwiched sausage, bacon, egg and potato bread. 'Mind you, I did have an early start.'

Fleming had already started into his own, chewing happily, his cheeks dimpled with dollops of tomato ketchup.

'Seamus Doherty's not in Manchester,' Lucy said, opening her own bap and peeling the rind of fat off the bacon, before replacing the upper part of the bread and taking a tentative bite.

'Where is he then?' Fleming managed through a mouthful of food.

Lucy shrugged as she chewed. 'Not where he said he would be.'

'And not answering his phone. Get the details of his lorry and organize a Be On Look Out.'

Lucy nodded. 'I'll have to ask Mrs Finn.'

'What did the boss say about Doherty? Anything useful?'

Lucy shrugged. 'Not much. Just they don't have contracts in Manchester. He said if he was going there, it wasn't for his company.'

'So either he's driving for someone else, or he's been lying to Finn every time he's told her he's doing a Manchester run. Sound her out on that too.'

'Yes, sir,' Lucy said. 'I spoke to the fella in the post office too. Sarah withdrew £200 from her mother's child benefit account yesterday afternoon.'

Fleming slowed in his chewing. 'Check if the mother knew. If not, the wee girl's run away.'

Lucy nodded agreement.

'The shop was useless,' Fleming added. 'But the chippie proved more useful. And not just for these. The owner's daughter was working in the place. She's a friend of Sarah's.'

Lucy understood why Fleming had bought food now. It gave him an excuse to stand longer, encouraging the girl to talk while the food was prepared.

'Sarah wasn't at the youth club last night. She had to go out with her mother and Seamus Doherty for dinner. Because he was headed away for the week today.'

'A week to go to Manchester?'

Fleming raised his eyebrows as he popped the final mouthful of his bap into his mouth. 'So she lied to both her mother and her friends. Plus she got herself a new phone a few weeks back. The girl has given me the number. Compare with the one the mother has and see if she knew about the phone,' he added, handing her a torn corner of a brown paper bag on which the number was written.

Lucy's mobile phone rang. It was the desk

sergeant in Maydown, confirming that a team of uniforms had been dispatched to Finn's house to begin house-to-house inquiries.

'Best head back and meet the team,' Lucy said.

*   *   *

They met the team outside Sinead Finn's house. Fleming split the uniforms into pairs and divided up the local housing estates around Fallowfield Gardens into six blocks, one for each pair. One of the men had brought copies of the picture Lucy had sent into the station.

'Meet back here at 5.30,' Fleming said. 'And call either myself or DS Black if you find anything. I'm going to call down to the youth club just to double-check Sarah definitely wasn't there last night.'

As the pairs dispersed, Lucy called back in with Sinead Finn. The woman opened the door, then hobbled back into the living room. She still had on the white dressing gown she'd worn earlier.

Lucy closed the door and followed her in. 'Any word?' she asked Sinead Finn's retreating back.

'Nothing,' the woman said. 'I've called all her friends. And her mobile, too,' she added. 'Nothing. No one's seen her. Her friends said she wasn't with them last night.'

'Can I check what number you're calling her on? Only one of her friends said she got a new phone a while back.'

'Not that I knew of,' Finn answered, opening

135

her phone and checking the listing, before reading out the number. It did not match the one Lucy had been given by Fleming.

'I need a second,' Lucy said, calling ICS. She recognized Dave Cooper's voice when he answered, felt a little surprised at the pleasure it brought her.

'We've a second missing person,' she explained after introducing herself. 'The girl has a new phone . . . '

'Like Karen Hughes?' Cooper asked.

'Maybe,' Lucy began. 'If I gave you the number, could you try tracing it?'

'No problem. I'll be quick as I can.'

Lucy thanked him after reading the number off the scrap of paper, then hung up. 'I've a few more questions,' she said, addressing Sinead Finn. 'Has anything like this ever happened before?'

Finn shook her head as she lowered herself into her seat. She pulled a pouffe across and raised her feet onto it. Lucy noticed balls of cotton wool between each of her toes. Her nails were freshly painted, having progressed on from doing her fingers.

'Never. She stayed out late at times, but she's a good girl. I never have no bother with her.'

'She went to the post office for you yesterday, is that right?'

Sinead struggled to remember. 'She might have. She ran jobs for me all the time. I've problems with my legs, you see.'

'I see. Sarah withdrew money from a child benefit account using your card yesterday,' Lucy said.

'Did she?' Finn looked towards the ceiling, trying to remember. 'I didn't ask her to do that.'

'A significant amount, Mrs Finn. Two hundred pounds. You're sure that wasn't for you?'

'Two hundred pounds?' Finn snapped. 'The wee bitch.'

Lucy bowed her head. 'You didn't — ?'

'The post office shouldn't have given it to her. It's my account.'

'Apparently she did this for you a lot,' Lucy said.

Sinead gave a non-committal grunt.

'She told her friends she was going out with you and your partner for dinner last night, too,' Lucy added.

'We weren't going for dinner. I told you already — we ate here.'

'I know,' Lucy said. 'I'm just trying to be certain we have all the facts.'

'Well, where the hell is she then?' Sinead Finn said, her eyes glistening, as if, for the first time, she had begun to realize the seriousness of her daughter's absence.

'Did she have a boyfriend or anything?'

'She was fifteen for Christ's sake!'

Lucy wasn't sure how she was meant to interpret that and rephrased the question. 'Was there anyone she might have run off with? Taking the money and that suggests she might have had plans to go somewhere.'

'She'd mentioned the odd boy or two at the youth club, but no one special. Not that I remember.'

Lucy nodded. 'What about Facebook or

Twitter? Did she have any friends on there?'

Finn shrugged. 'I don't know.' She leaned forward and picked up her cigarettes. Her dressing gown sleeve drooped over her hand and she slid it quickly up her arm with her free hand. For a second, Lucy caught sight of a network of small red scars on her inner forearm, then the sleeve slipped down and covered it again. Finn followed her line of sight, sniffed loudly, then wiped her sleeve across her nose.

'Do you have a computer that Sarah used?'

Finn shook her head. 'No. She used the ones in school or the club for school work and that.'

Lucy nodded. 'Have you had any luck with contacting your partner? Mr Doherty?'

Sinead Finn shook her head. 'He's going to message. And I've texted him. Maybe he doesn't want to answer when he's driving.'

'Maybe,' Lucy repeated. 'Does he go to Manchester often?'

Finn shrugged. 'Every few weeks. Sometimes he has other runs to do too — Dublin, Cork or that. But he'd do Manchester once or twice a month.'

'Always for a week?'

Finn raised her left shoulder. 'I guess. Why? What's that to do with Sarah?'

'Probably nothing,' Lucy said.

★ ★ ★

By five it had already become clear that Sarah Finn was not in the immediate vicinity. All her friends had been contacted; none had seen her since the previous day. The youth club leader, Jackie Logue, confirmed she had been absent the previous evening, which was, by his account, quite unusual.

'It's a bit of a family here,' he had told Fleming. 'I think Sarah loved coming and seeing everyone. She didn't get involved so much, mind you. But she liked having people around her, even if she didn't chat too much.'

The neighbours had not seen her, though all concurred with the general consensus, which was that she was a quiet girl. Friendly, but shy.

Fleming ordered for the search to be widened. Press releases were drawn up and distributed to the local radio and news stations ahead of a press conference the following day if Sarah had not returned.

Hospitals and doctors' clinics were already being contacted by uniforms in the Strand Road, though as yet had yielded no results.

Lucy and Fleming had just met back at Finn's when Lucy's mobile rang. It was Cooper.

'Lucy. The phone number you gave is ringing out. But I've been able to trace its position from the GPS in it. It's along the Glenshane Road. It seems to be in a picnic area, just opposite the turn-in for the Old Foreglen Road.'

'I know it,' Lucy said. 'Thanks, Dave.'

'Lucy,' Cooper added grimly, 'the phone isn't moving.'

23

The lay-by in question was a popular one with long-distance lorry drivers. A small burger van squatted at one end, the owner seated in front of a portable TV, the fryers behind him empty.

He stood up when he saw the police cars pull in, reaching for the bag of cut chips and pouring them into the fryer basket in the expectation of business.

Three teams poured out into the lay-by. Fleming directed them to different sections of the space. They moved off to work quietly, all expecting to find not just Sarah's phone, but possibly the child herself.

Beyond them, the mass of the Ness Woods loomed, the dying light already darkening between the trees. To the west, three huge wind turbines stood on the hill to their left, where a mist had already begun rolling down into the Ness valley. Behind them, the dying light of the sun, already passed below the horizon, scorched the top of the hill, the shape of the turbine arms standing above it, piercing the mist, itself like molten gold inside the sunset, the whole image like Golgotha ablaze.

'It's beautiful,' Fleming commented, standing beside her, watching the scene.

'It is,' Lucy agreed.

'Why is every nice place you see tainted with the shit of what happens there?' he asked.

140

'Inspector,' a voice shouted. They looked across to where one of the officers stood, having emptied out the contents of one of the litter bins spotted around the area. He held, in his gloved hand, a black iPhone.

Lucy reached the man first, already pulling on her own gloves. She pressed the home button and saw that there were twelve missed calls. She unlocked the screen. The main wallpaper image was of a small cat. Clicking on the photo icon, she scrolled through the assorted images. Sure enough, there was picture of Sinead Finn and, in one, reflected in a mirror due to the angle of the shot, Sarah Finn herself could be seen.

She moved back to the home screen. A red numeral 1 over the message icon showed she'd an unread message. Lucy opened it. The name Simon H appeared at the top of the screen. 'We still OK for 8?' the most recent message read. It had been sent at 2.30 p.m.

'Get it down to ICS straight away,' Fleming said. 'See if someone there can't get something from it.'

'Wait,' Lucy said. 'Let me check something.' She scrolled up to the top of the page and clicked on the contact details for Simon. The next page listed his name, picture, email and number. The email address was a Facebook one. The name on the account was 'Simon Harris'.

Lucy opened her own phone and called Cooper.

'We got the phone,' Lucy said, without introduction. 'But I need you to do me a favour. 'Simon Harris' — the one on Facebook this

141

morning. Can you get up his picture and send it to me?'

'Give me a minute,' Cooper said.

It took less than that for a text message with the picture attached, photographed from the screen of Cooper's computer, to beep on Lucy's phone. She opened the message and compared the image to the picture Sarah had assigned to Simon H. It was the same picture.

'Shit,' Lucy muttered. 'It's one of the sock-puppet accounts belonging to Paul Bradley.'

Fleming took the phone and scrolled through the messages again. 'He's asked her to meet him tonight five times today. If he's doing that . . . '

'She's not with him,' Lucy concluded.

'And he doesn't know she's vanished,' Fleming said.

Lucy thought for a moment. 'He wants to meet her tonight,' she said. 'So why don't we arrange it?'

24

'It's too dangerous,' Burns said, stooping to lean on the table at which the rest of the Hughes Inquiry team, along with Lucy and Fleming, sat. Lucy glanced at Fleming, who stifled a yawn, earning a dirty look from Burns. 'We're working on the theory that 'Harris' doesn't know she's vanished. For all we know, he could have picked her up somewhere since that last message was sent.'

Lucy accepted the point with a nod. 'But if he doesn't realize that she's gone, we could set up a sting and catch him. If 'Harris' *is* Paul Bradley, we'll have Karen's killer, too.'

'It's a big if,' Mickey commented.

'Not according to ICS,' Fleming countered. 'The scrap metal thieves reported seeing someone in a red car leaving the scene where Karen was left. So, we make contact with 'Harris', arrange a pick-up point, then watch from a safe distance. If someone does turn up in a red car, we tail them and see what we get.'

'This is all based on the belief that Gene Kay is not Karen's killer,' Burns said. 'Kay who is still sitting in one of our holding cells.'

'Has he said anything to make you think he is guilty?' Fleming asked.

Burns shook his head. 'The phone was unusable, so we don't know whether he was on Facebook or not. He claims he was taking snaps of a group of girls sitting at the table opposite.'

'Can we not do him for that?'

The door opened suddenly and Lucy felt her stomach sink as she recognized the slim figure of her mother stride into the room.

'ACC Wilson,' Burns said, straightening. 'Good evening, ma'am.'

'Mark,' Wilson said. 'Good evening folks,' she added, glancing around the table. Her gaze lingered a moment on Lucy, or, at least, so it seemed to her. 'Any progress on the Hughes killing?'

Burns exhaled sharply. 'We've a bit of a breakthrough. But a second girl has gone missing in Gobnascale.'

'Sarah Finn,' Wilson said, nodding. 'Are they connected?'

'The PPU team managed to locate her phone in a lay-by near the Ness Woods. She appears to have been receiving text messages from a 'Simon Harris', which ICS believes is one of the sock puppet accounts owned by Paul Bradley, our suspect in the Hughes case.'

'How far back do the messages go?'

'A few months,' Burns said. 'Classic grooming pattern. They seem to have arranged to meet with some regularity for the past eight weeks, one night a week.'

'So?'

''Harris' has texted several times today asking the Finn girl to meet him tonight.'

'So he doesn't know she's gone missing?'

'Possibly,' Burns said.

'I think Sarah has left with her mother's

partner,' Lucy said, then realized that the others at the table had turned to stare at her. 'Ma'am,' she added.

Wilson nodded again. 'By force or choice?'

'We don't know yet, ma'am,' Fleming said. 'DS Black is trying to locate the partner. He's told the girl's mother he's in Manchester with work, but the work says he's not.'

'So are you going to agree to meet with 'Harris'?' Wilson asked. 'I assume that's the topic of discussion here.'

Burns nodded. 'It does run the risk of alerting the suspect to the fact we have his alias.'

'The debacle in the Foyleside today has probably already done so,' Wilson said. 'Very publicly. My feeling is that it's worth the risk. The worst that will happen is that he doesn't turn up. What time was the last message sent to Sarah's phone?'

'Two thirty, ma'am,' Burns said.

'Was that before or after we lifted Kay?'

'Around about the same time,' he admitted. 'But we've not been able to connect Kay to Karen Hughes's killing yet.'

'I think the decision's clear then,' Wilson said. 'I'll see you when you're finished, Mark. Maybe I could have a quick word with DS Black,' she added, standing up to leave.

'Of course, ma'am,' Burns said.

Lucy pushed back her chair to stand while Tara, sitting next to her, leaned closer to her. 'Good luck,' she whispered.

Wilson was standing in the corridor when Lucy left the room. She nodded across to

Burns's office which lay empty and led Lucy in.

'So how are things, Lucy?'

'Fine, ma'am.'

Wilson nodded, as if this was the response she'd expected. 'How's the PPU treating you?'

Again. 'Fine.'

'Have you seen your father recently? How was he?'

Lucy was unsure what to say, aware that both of them knew of her father's troubled past. 'He's fine. Considering what he did.'

Wilson nodded lightly. 'Yet you still visit him?'

Lucy folded her arms. 'Someone has to. Or he'd be completely on his own.'

'I see,' Wilson replied.

'If you're that interested, he's getting worse actually.'

'I'm sorry to hear that,' Wilson said.

'Really?'

Wilson sighed. 'Must every exchange we have be adversarial, Lucy? It's getting a little tiring.'

Lucy shrugged, aware that any further comment would seem petulant. She waited for her mother to speak, studying her face. She'd cropped her hair again, in a manner that accentuated the sharpness of her features. Instinctively, Lucy touched the ends of her own hair, aware, again, that the gamine cut had actually made her look more like her mother. She was more concerned that the similarity between them might run deeper than simply how they looked.

'What did you want to see me about?' she asked, keen to dismiss that last thought.

'I understand you assaulted a suspect during the arrest of the metal theft gang this morning. Is that right?'

'I inadvertently stepped on his hand,' Lucy said, not quite meeting her mother's stare. 'It was an accident.'

'Nothing to do with the theft of railings off a grave then?'

'Who told you that?'

'Never mind. Did you assault a suspect for stealing railings off a grave? Yes or no?'

'Dad was asking about the fountain in the house down the lane the last time I saw him,' Lucy said, using a trick of her mother's, shifting the conversation from the professional to the personal without warning. 'That place is a prison.'

'Then he deserves it,' Wilson countered, unfazed by the attempted distraction. 'You've not answered my question.'

'It was an accident,' Lucy said.

'I hope so,' her mother said. Her expression softened a little and she sat in Burns's chair. 'Close the door and sit down.'

Lucy shut the door, but contrarily remained standing. Her mother looked up at her, waiting for her to sit, then continued regardless. 'How is Tom Fleming? I understand there was an incident at his house this morning, too?'

'He seems fine. You'd be best to ask him about anything that happened at his house.'

'I will. I thought I'd ask you first, since you were the officer who called it in,' Wilson said. 'So what happened to him?'

'He overslept,' Lucy said. 'Didn't hear the alarm.'

Wilson shook her head. 'I see. Nothing's easy with you, Lucy, is it? How's the boyfriend then? Are you still doing a line?'

Lucy suppressed a cringe at the twee comment. 'Broken off,' she said.

'I'm sorry to hear that. What happened?'

'We had a difference of opinion.'

'About?'

'Monogamy,' Lucy said, refusing to explain any further.

'I see,' Wilson replied. 'That's a pity.'

'What about you?' Lucy countered, reflecting on the gossip Tara had shared about her mother and the new Chief Super. 'Still seeing Mark?' Her mother stared at her quizzically. 'The night I stayed with you, you said your partner's name was Mark.'

'Ah. Same name, different man.'

'Is it Chief Super Burns by any chance?'

Wilson took off her glasses. 'That's a dangerous rumour to be spreading,' she said.

'I'm not spreading anything. I just asked. You asked about my love life, I asked about yours. You don't have to explain yourself to me. God knows, that was never a consideration before.'

Wilson allowed herself a brief, brittle smile. 'It's always a pleasure catching up with you, Lucy,' she said.

25

The team was dispersing by the time Lucy made it back into the room. A few of them glanced at her as she entered, and she guessed from their expression, half pitying and half elated, that they thought she'd been called out by the ACC to be chastised.

'If you don't want anyone to know she's your mother, maybe you oughtn't to talk to her in public as if she is,' Fleming commented when she moved across to him.

'I'll bear that in mind,' Lucy muttered brusquely.

Tara approached them a little diffidently, her papers clasped against her chest by her crossed arms. 'Everything all right?' she asked. 'With the ACC?'

'Fine,' Lucy said, still angry that Tara had told Burns about her questioning a suspect over the stolen railings.

It was clearly on Tara's mind too. 'Was it about this morning?'

Fleming glanced up at the two of them sharply. Lucy suspected he'd guessed at the real topic of the conversation.

'I stood on a suspect's fingers during an arrest,' Lucy explained quickly, not wishing her boss to think that she'd been discussing him with her mother.

'I didn't think Burns would say anything, you

know?' Tara said, touching Lucy lightly on the arm with one outstretched hand.

'It's fine,' Lucy repeated. 'I know you need to impress the new Super,' she added dryly.

'It wasn't like that,' Tara said. 'We don't all get private audiences with the ACC, you know.'

The comment caught Lucy off guard. Did Tara know that Wilson was Lucy's mother? Maybe Fleming was right about her attitude to the woman.

'We're together on this tonight,' Fleming said quickly, providing a diversion for which Lucy felt most grateful. 'DI Burns has replied to the text message as Sarah, telling 'Harris' that she'll meet him. 'Harris''s messages in the past suggested several times that they meet at the entrance to Glenaden Industrial Estate. Burns reckons that's their usual pickup spot. We're to be parked down at the Northern Bank opposite the hospital to pick up 'Harris''s tail if he goes that way.'

Lucy knew the spot. It wasn't far from the residential unit where Karen had been. It also afforded 'Harris' a choice of directions to go. Along the Belt Road, he could go west back into Gobnascale, or east towards the hospital, with smaller roadways leading off into the Waterside or out towards Ardmore. There were potentially four different directions he could take. Added to that, they didn't have a great description of the car save for that it was red and small, like a Fiesta.

'We'd best grab something to eat,' Fleming said. 'Before we take up our positions.'

★   ★   ★

Tara joined them for food — burger and chips from the chippie across from the station — clearly in the hope that Lucy would eventually forgive her for having betrayed her to Burns. It meant that Lucy and Fleming were not alone again until they climbed into her car to head up to the spot to which they'd been assigned to wait for 'Harris'.

'So how was ACC Wilson?' Fleming asked for the second time as they pulled out onto the roadway past the thick metal gates which had rolled back to allow them exit.

'Fine,' Lucy said, reflecting that she really needed to find an alternative statement of non-comment. 'Good.'

'Anything wrong?'

'Nothing,' Lucy replied. Though Fleming knew that Wilson was her mother, he'd never asked before when she'd spoken to her. Lucy wasn't sure whether to tell him that her mother knew about the incident in his house, or whether to leave it lest he react badly.

'Personal stuff, or . . . work related?'

'Personal stuff,' Lucy agreed.

'Not the suspect's hand then?'

'No,' Lucy said.

'I take it she knows about this morning then?' he said finally.

Lucy looked across at him. 'I'm sorry, Tom. I didn't say anything, I — '

Fleming held up his hand in placation. 'It was bound to get back to her. An ambulance being

151

called for an officer. Especially one in the state I was in.'

'If I'd known, I wouldn't have called them,' Lucy said. 'I panicked.'

'It's done now,' Fleming said. 'You did what you thought was right. I'll give you a key the next time.'

'Will there be a next time?' Lucy ventured.

'Probably not,' Fleming said.

Lucy nodded, though she realized he couldn't see the movement, staring as he was out the side window now.

'Is everything all right?' Lucy asked. 'Is there anything I can do?'

He glanced across at her, as if evaluating the sincerity of the question.

'My ex-wife has moved away,' he said. 'She and her new husband. They've emigrated to Australia for a few years. Part of his job.'

'I'm sorry to hear that,' Lucy said. Fleming had mentioned his wife once before, when telling Lucy about his losing his licence. It was the only time he'd ever spoken about his family.

'Oh, I don't give a monkey's about her going,' he said, smiling sadly. 'She's taken our daughter with her.'

'I didn't know you had a daughter, Tom,' Lucy said.

'Megan,' Fleming said. 'She's fifteen.' He obviously read the expression on Lucy's face, for he added, 'I married late.'

'I didn't say a word.' Fleming had been a colleague of both Lucy's parents, which suggested he was in his fifties by now.

152

'Nor did you need to, Sergeant,' Fleming said with a brief laugh, stressing Lucy's rank.

'I'm sorry to hear that though.'

Fleming nodded, dragged his hand down his face, as if wiping sleep from his eyes.

'They won't be here for Christmas then?'

Fleming shook his head. 'No. The tickets are cheapest in November, because no one wants to travel then apparently. They had to leave last month or it would have cost them an extra three grand.'

'I'm sorry,' Lucy repeated.

'What about you, Lucy? Any plans for Christmas?'

Lucy shook her head. 'I'll visit my dad. Eat crap and watch TV.'

'We're doing a soup kitchen,' Fleming said. 'My church. We're doing Christmas dinner for the homeless and that. You'd be welcome to come along if you wanted some company.' Lucy had forgotten about Fleming's conversion. He'd mentioned to her before that he'd found God after he swore off drink. It appeared that the two were not mutually exclusive.

'Thank you, Tom. I might,' Lucy said, quietly thinking that the last thing she felt like at Christmas was company.

'Bear it in mind, Lucy,' he added. 'If you're stuck.'

26

The car park at the Northern Bank was deserted, the area afforded some shade from the street lights lining the roadway by the overhanging branches of the fir trees bordering the garden to the rear of the building. Lucy and Fleming were parked off the eastern side of a crossroads, along any arm of which the car might approach. The cold had already begun to sharpen, the bonnet of the car sparkling with the first frost fall. Fleming turned up the heat, wrapped his coat around him and sat back in his seat.

'I *am* sorry about this morning,' Lucy said, finally.

'Forget it. I'd have done the same,' he admitted.

They sat in silence for a few moments, watching the clock's display flicker towards eight. Finally, Lucy clicked on the CD player but there was nothing in it, being an unmarked squad car and not her own.

Just then, the radio buzzed into life.

'Movement at the estate,' Burns said. 'We've a red car passing. Looks like two people inside. Can someone pick up their tail?'

A click responded in the affirmative, then Lucy heard Tara's voice. 'They're turning in towards the Waterside. We have them, sir,' she said.

A moment later, Tara spoke again. 'They've

turned in at Next, sir. An elderly man and woman.'

'Get their names,' Burns said. 'The guy at the park had grey hair apparently.'

'This one has *no* hair, sir. He's bald.'

Fleming snorted quietly.

'Get the car details, at least. We'll follow up on that.'

'Another vehicle.' Mickey's voice crackled through the speaker. 'Red Corsa. Old model. Approaching from Ardmore.'

This meant the car was coming up the southern approach to the crossroads, running just behind the bank where Lucy sat. Mickey's team was placed in the car park of a pub halfway up that roadway.

'He's indicating to turn left.' Towards Glenaden. 'Should we follow?'

'Hold your place,' Burns said. 'If he sees the girl's not there, he may head back the way he came and you can pick him up then.'

Lucy found herself craning to try to see past the tree line, which was obscuring her view of the entrance to the industrial park a few hundred yards further along the western arm of the crossroads.

'It's slowing,' Burns said. 'He's approaching the entrance. He's moved off again, towards Gobnascale. Someone get ready to pick him up.'

'He's turning,' another voice cut in. 'I think he's heading back for a second look.'

Lucy, unable to wait, opened the door of the car and stepped out, then moved across to the pavement, past the tree line, where she could better see what was happening. In the distance she could see the lights of the car as it completed a U-turn and came back towards the industrial estate. Towards her.

'If he cuts back down towards Ardmore, pick him up Mickey. PPU, be ready to assist.'

Fleming leaned out of the door. 'Get in. We're to pick up with the Ardmore team.'

Lucy watched the car speeding up as it drove away from the estate. 'He's not turning in,' she muttered, slipping as she turned to get back into the car. Sure enough, a second later, Mickey's voice. 'He's passed our turn-off,' he said. 'He's on his way towards the bank.'

'PPU, pick up; Mickey assist.'

Lucy started the engine and pulled out to the entrance of the car park, just as the red car pulled up at the junction next to where they sat. The driver, an older man, jowly, looked both ways to see if the path was clear. For a second, he caught Lucy's eye, held her stare, then he pulled out quickly into the traffic, without waiting for a gap, causing an ambulance, coming out of the entrance to the hospital on the other side of the junction, to have to swerve to avoid him.

'He's running,' Lucy said, pulling out herself into the middle of the traffic in pursuit, the blur of wailing horns in her wake.

Fleming, meanwhile, lifted the radio. 'Red Corsa. NHZ 4635. Can we get details on the owner?'

The car in question accelerated towards the roundabout at the hospital. A left turn would

156

take him back towards where Tara's team would be approaching. Straight ahead would take him into the Waterside. Turning right would take him onto the dual carriageway, which would lead, eventually, to the Foyle Bridge. Without indicating, it was this path that he chose.

Lucy floored the accelerator, pulling onto the oncoming lane to get past a car struggling towards the roundabout, the L driver inside gripping the wheel with both hands as she stared out at them.

'He's on the Crescent Link,' Lucy reported. 'In pursuit.'

The Corsa swerved in and out of the traffic, which was moving its way slowly towards the Tesco store a mile or so further along the carriageway. Lucy followed suit, trying to keep visual contact.

'The car belongs to Peter Carlin,' Burns said. 'The address we have for him is 144 Foreglen Road. Where is he?'

Carlin was, at that moment, cutting across the two lanes of a roundabout at a shopping complex, shearing off the bumper of a car in front of him. For a moment, the drag of the impact seemed to slow him, then he accelerated again, the bumper bouncing in the roadway, effectively blocking one of the lanes, while the car to which it had been attached blocked the other.

'Go the other way,' Fleming shouted.

Lucy pulled onto the roundabout, cutting right, following the lane clockwise as the oncoming traffic pulled to a stop.

'Police,' Fleming shouted as he wound down

157

the window. 'Move.' He leaned forward and flicked on the blue lights and siren. The cars slowly inched forward, allowing just enough room for Lucy to squeeze through and complete the circuit back onto the correct lane again. Carlin had made some distance on them now, though Lucy could see the blinking of his brake lights on the curve of the road in the distance as she slowed to avoid colliding with someone.

'He's heading towards the Foyle Bridge,' Lucy shouted. Again, the roundabout here would offer him a number of choices: left towards the Waterside, straight through onto the bridge and into the city, or right, out towards Strathfoyle and Maydown, where the PPU was based.

As Lucy passed a car on the inside, beneath the overhang of trees bordering one side of the carriageway, she felt the car shift slightly on the roadway. Ahead of them, Carlin pulled across onto the outer lane.

'He's not going into the Waterside,' Fleming said, pointing at the car. 'City or Strathfoyle, then.'

Lucy slowed as they approached the round-about, its centre island so heavily planted with trees they could not see which direction Carlin had taken. A few seconds later, they saw the red Corsa appear around the other side of the curve and cut down right, towards Maydown. Lucy glanced in the mirror, saw the flickering blue of the other police cars appear behind her, then she accelerated again, pulling onto the roundabout.

She took the curve at speed, the car again sliding a little in the angle, leaving her having to overcompensate as she straightened up again to continue on the carriageway the Corsa had taken. This road was quieter at least, so it was easier to spot the Corsa ahead.

'We've teams coming up from Maydown,' Burns said. 'They'll get him along the road.'

Sure enough, a moment later, Lucy could see the strobing blue lights ahead. So too could Carlin, for all of a sudden he swerved to the left off the carriageway, pulling down Judge's Road, alongside the rugby club.

Fleming relayed this information through the radio.

'Keep on him,' Burns shouted.

'Really? I was planning on letting him go now,' Lucy muttered to herself.

Lucy followed Carlin, taking the turn sharply then having to correct her position quickly as the road curved again. To their left now, the dark mass of Enagh Lough, reflecting the clear sky above, was visible past the boughs of the massive trees lining the road's edge. Ahead, the red tail lights of Carlin's car disappeared around another bend.

Lucy slowed a little, taking the corner more gently than the last. As she did so, she and Fleming caught sight of the red Corsa, which was now careening along the straight stretch of road. Suddenly, the car swerved and mounted the narrow pavement bordering the roadway before breaking through the tree line at the edge of the road. It seemed to sit suspended for a second then fell forwards into the lough.

'Jesus,' Lucy screamed, slamming on her brakes, the car sliding towards the gap in the trees now.

As her car screeched to a halt, Lucy undid her seat belt and jumped out, Fleming following her.

Carlin's car was already beginning to sink. She could see Carlin winding at the window, trying to open it in order to escape the vehicle.

Without thinking, Lucy peeled off her coat and launched herself into the water. The cold winded her, causing her muscles to spasm. She breathed through it, her teeth gritted. She'd swum every morning for years while she'd been working as a fitness instructor before joining the police.

She pounded against the water, aware as she neared the car that it was slipping deeper into the water. Carlin had the window down now, and was fumbling with his seat belt, the cold presumably making it hard for his numbed fingers to release the clasp.

She neared the vehicle, reaching in and gripping Carlin's jumper, while she held on to the roof of the car. Too much of the vehicle was submerged now for her to try pulling open the door against the weight of water pressing against it. Dragging Carlin out through the window was the best option.

'Get out,' she shouted, as the front of the car dipped under completely, the boot rising slightly in the water.

'Peter, get out,' she repeated, pulling at his jumper.

The water was past his chest now, his chin breaking the surface as he tried to look down at the seat belt.

He looked at Lucy, his eyes wide, his mouth

open. 'I can't free the belt.'

'Keep trying,' Lucy shouted. She let go of him and tried pulling at the door, but knew already that the water pressure would make it impossible to open.

Carlin was screaming now as he tried to pull at the seat belt The water filled his mouth, causing him to spit it out again, angling his head back to try to keep his mouth clear of the surface. But already the level was rising.

'I'm sorry,' he cried. 'The girls. I'm sorry for them all. But I didn't do the killing. I didn't kill anybody. Jesus, forgive me.'

'Any of who?' Lucy shouted. 'How many girls?'

Carlin had stopped fumbling with the seat belt now and had begun winding up the window as the car slipped further below the surface. He turned to look at Lucy as the glass slid up between them, catching her hand, trapping it between the glass and the rubber of the frame. His face was drawn with terror as he opened his mouth.

The car dipped further, the water lapping the roof now, as Lucy pulled to free her hand from the window.

Beside her, a figure appeared, his baton raised. Mickey beat at the glass until it shattered, freeing Lucy's hand. Then he gripped her around the chest from behind as he pulled her away from the bubbles that surfaced as the car finally slipped below the water, even as she fought to get back to Carlin.

27

Burns, Fleming and the ACC were in discussion in the CID suite when Lucy arrived back in the incident room. She'd been brought straight back to the station, dismissing suggestions she attend A & E and instead opting for a hot shower in the station's locker room and changing into a spare uniform someone had managed to find, her own clothes still soaked through from the lough. Tara, along with a few other members of the team, sat in the main incident room, sharing tea and sandwiches.

'Are you all right?' Tara asked when Lucy came in. 'Do you want tea?' she added, not waiting for a response to the first question.

'Please,' Lucy said. 'I'm grand,' she added.

'You're nuts jumping in after him,' Tara said.

'Nearly cost you and Mickey both your lives,' someone commented.

Lucy glanced around; it was Mickey's partner, the DC from Foyleside. She sensed from his tone that only one of those outcomes caused him concern. She was acutely aware all of a sudden that she was not one of them, not CID.

'It was instinct,' Lucy offered by way of explanation.

'Your instinct should be to stay alive,' he countered.

The door of Burns's office opened and he

peered out. 'You're back,' he said, nodding at Lucy. 'All OK?'

'Fine,' she said, taking the tea which Tara was offering her.

'Bring it in here for a quick chat if you're feeling up to it,' Burns said.

Tara raised her eyebrows quickly at Lucy then moved away towards her seat again.

Burns held open the door for Lucy and, as she passed him, she caught the faint scent of his aftershave. When she entered his room, she saw her mother sitting behind his desk, while he and Fleming had clearly been sitting on the opposite side. There was only one spare seat.

'You sit,' Burns said. 'I'm good standing.'

Lucy thanked him and sat down, sipping from her tea. Tara had added extra sugar to it, its sweetness too sharp.

'DI Fleming has filled us in on what happened up to Carlin going in the water,' her mother began without preamble. 'Maybe you'd help fill in the rest of it for us.'

Lucy nodded, took a second mouthful of tea, then set the cup on the edge of the desk. She glanced at Fleming who smiled briefly.

'After I saw the car going in, I went in after it. It all happened very quickly. At first Carlin was trying to get out. His seat belt must have been stuck or something, because he'd wound down the window, but seemed to be fumbling with the belt. I tried dragging him out, but the belt prevented it. When he realized he was going down, he said he was sorry.'

'Sorry?'

163

Lucy nodded. ''I'm sorry for them all,' he said. 'But I didn't do the killing.''

'You're sure of that?' Wilson asked.

Lucy nodded, glancing at both Burns and Fleming, neither of whom had spoken. 'He said 'them all' and that he hadn't killed them.'

''Them' plural,' Burns commented. 'We know of Karen Hughes. Who is the rest of 'them'?'

'And how many?' Fleming added.

Lucy watched Wilson. Her face, always sharp, had thinned. When she removed her glasses, two red ridges marked the sides of the bridge of her nose. She was still attractive, Lucy conceded, but she was beginning to show her age. Either that, or her position as ACC was beginning to tell on her.

'And, of course, if Carlin didn't kill 'them', then who did?' she added.

'What's happening at the site?' Fleming asked.

'The car's being removed from the lough,' Wilson said. 'But it'll be morning before it's out. The underwater team has recovered Carlin's body and any obvious belongings. We've sent a team out to start searching the house on the Foreglen Road to see what they can find.'

'That's on the way to the Ness Woods, where the Finn girl's phone was found, isn't it?' Burns said.

'Yes. Though we have to work on the assumption that, if Carlin was trying to make contact with her, then he probably isn't the one who took her.'

'Nor was Kay,' Fleming said. 'Unless he took her in the middle of the night, disposed of her,

164

and then went for coffee to photograph groups of girls.'

'Have we anything connecting Kay to Karen Hughes?' Wilson asked.

Burns shook his head.

'So, in fact, he might have nothing to do with Karen Hughes at all. His being in the centre might have been sheer coincidence.'

'I don't believe in coincidences,' said Burns defensively.

'Why not?' Wilson snapped. 'They happen all the time. Cut Kay loose then, pending a file on the images he's admitted to taking. If we can ever recover them,' Wilson added.

'What about Carlin?' Lucy asked. 'Does he have a record?'

Fleming shook his head. 'All low-level stuff. He was questioned about flashing at a school girl in the bus depot a few years back.'

'What happened?'

'He was warned off. Told to stay clear of the depot. He was occasionally visiting the community mental health team. He was deemed a vulnerable person.'

'Not that that necessarily makes him a predator,' Wilson said.

Fleming nodded in agreement.

'We'll see what the searches of the car and house throw up,' Wilson decided. 'As for the events of this evening, the Ombudsman will have to investigate Carlin's death. You'll need to make statements about the events. Best get it out of the way tonight, while it's fresh in your mind. I've already contacted their office to get someone down here to take initial statements.'

Lucy nodded. It was standard practice that the Ombudsman would investigate the death of an individual who'd had immediate prior contact with the police.

'If it turns out that Carlin was abducting and killing young girls, no one's going to mourn his death,' Burns said.

'Least of all Eoghan Harkin,' Lucy reflected. He'd asked for half an hour with the person who'd killed Karen. If Carlin had told the truth, that person was still walking free.

Wednesday 19 December

28

It was pitch black in her room when the phone woke her at 6.30 the next morning. She'd only been asleep for two hours, yet had dreamed again of Mary Quigg and the fire. It meant that it took her a moment to realize she was awake when, upon answering, she was told that Gene Kay's house was burning down. And that he was still inside it.

★   ★   ★

When Lucy arrived, a number of Land Rovers lined the roadway leading to the junction of the Trench Road. At first, Lucy couldn't understand what was preventing them moving closer to where Kay lived. Then, as she got out of her own car, she noticed the flaming carcass of a car, angled across the junction, illuminating the pre-dawn scene. Behind it, their features covered with scarves, their figures seeming to ripple and shimmer in the heated air that rose from the burning vehicle, Lucy spotted a crowd of a hundred or more youths, already dressed for battle. Occasional bottles and stones arched over the burning car, breaking through the thick plumes of black smoke and skittering impotently along the tarmac of the roadway. Only once did one explode with a hollow thud against the side of a Land Rover, the sound being greeted with cheers by those beyond the smoke. Despite the attempts to provoke a response from the PSNI officers, Lucy knew why her colleagues were holding back. Any heavy-handed attempt by the PSNI to break through the line of youths would be immediately politicized and could undo years of painstakingly developed cooperation between the residents in the area and the community policing teams.

'The fire service can't get in near it,' Fleming told Lucy after he spotted her among the gathered officers. 'They've gone up the other way and are coming down the Trench Road from the upper end. We're going to try to push through here when they arrive. Hopefully, the kids will be so focused on what's happened at this end as we come at them, they'll miss the fire crews coming from behind.'

'Any word on Kay?'

Fleming shook his head. 'A case of bad timing. He was released before midnight. The first word of the fire came from a neighbour about half an hour ago. The crew who did it probably didn't even realize that he was back in the house.'

As they spoke, Lucy noticed teams of officers, in Tactical Support gear, moving quickly into formation behind the Land Rovers. They heard the heavy clunk of the doors on the vehicles closing and the familiar roar of the engines as they came to life. The kids on the other side of the burning car must have heard it too, their ears well tuned through experience to the sounds of a gathering force. Lucy could make out, through the smoke, as they fixed their scarves around their lower faces, some passing round bottles and stones. She noticed a few of them huddling together, their backs turned to the officers, then saw the blooming of light between them as they ignited the first of the petrol bombs.

There was a thud as the first Land Rover pulled off the kerb, where it had been parked, and, revving its engine, it began moving towards the car, inching its way forward. It was clearly hoping to push the vehicle to one side, thereby allowing those vehicles and officers behind enough space to move towards the gathered crowd.

'The plan is to push the kids back down the Old Strabane Road and free up the junction so we can get to Kay. Tactical Support will hold them in bay once we get them shifted,' Fleming explained.

Stones began clattering against the armoured sides of the Land Rover now, a bottle shattering against the reinforced windscreen. Then the first of the petrol bombs was thrown. It had been sloppily packed, and the flaming rag became dislodged as it turned in the air, a horsetail of flame in its wake as its contents spilled, so that, by the time it hit, the flames it produced on the Land Rover's bonnet spluttered and quickly died.

The Land Rover pushed forward, its front grille now making contact with the burning car. The driver had approached at an angle so that, as he moved, the car shifted down to the right, into the junction.

Lucy glanced up to the left. She could see the

171

flickering blue of the Fire Service vehicle lights intensify as it seemed to bounce off the gable walls of the houses beyond.

A sharp pop, followed by a cheer, brought her attention back to the scene in front of her. A petrol bomb had broken across the windscreen of the first Land Rover, leaving it ablaze. The driver turned on his wipers, scattering the fluid in flaming drops, to right and left.

She heard a faint whistle, then the body of officers moving silently behind the vehicles suddenly split, scattering in all directions. A moment later, a firework exploded on the tarmac where they had stood, in a ball of magnesium white. Another cheer from the crowd.

At a signal, several of the support vehicles drove around the front one and cut sharply towards the assembled kids, forcing them backwards, herding them down towards the Old Strabane Road, away from Kay's house, effectively hemming the crowd of youngsters in.

'Let's go,' Fleming said.

He and Lucy moved up quickly through the gap towards Kay's house. The Fire Service had already reached the street and was pumping water into the house. Another crowd had gathered here; spectators this time, watching with macabre fascination as, one by one, the windows at the front of Kay's house exploded with the pressure of heat ballooning from within. Some, though, were clearly neighbours driven from their own homes due to their proximity to the fire.

On the front of the house, sprayed in paint,

blood red in the blue wash of light thrown off the fire tenders, were the words 'Paedos out!'

Kay's black dog, its fur soaked by the overspill from the flumes of water splashing against the window frames as the fire crew aimed their hoses, whimpered as it gingerly approached the front door of the house, then hastily withdrew before trying to approach again.

'The poor wee dog,' Lucy heard someone near her say as she passed. 'Someone should lift it.'

* * *

It was almost eight thirty before the blaze had been controlled to the point that the first fire crew struggled in through the remnants of the front door, the charred remains hanging off the still bright brass hinges.

The crowd had thickened now, including younger children stopping on their way to school gawping at the scene, necks craned to see past their parents who stood, in groups, commenting on the events, some in condemnation, many in quiet agreement with what had happened. Only the man who owned the house next to Kay's was receiving any sympathy from those around him.

After the first of the fire crew re-emerged from the remnants of Kay's house Lucy and Fleming moved across to where the men spoke with their District Commander, a man who Lucy had met once before outside the charred remains of Mary Quigg's home. If the man recognized her, he didn't show it. She, on the other hand, would never forget him.

'Well?' Fleming asked.

The man shook his head. 'One dead inside,' he said. 'Looks like a male.'

'That would be right,' Lucy said. 'Any sign of how it started?'

The man nodded towards the front of the house. 'Judging by the damage done to the door, it started there. I'd hazard we'll find it was petrol through the letterbox. The fire seems to have been most intense at the front of the house. We'll need to do a proper investigation once the whole place is clear, obviously, so this is just an educated guess.'

'But definitely started deliberately?' Fleming asked again.

The Commander nodded. 'Looks like you can add another murder case to your workload.' He pointed to the writing on the wall before adding, 'You'll not have far to look for motive, though, judging by the graffiti.'

*　*　*

As she was making her way back to her car, Lucy noticed a heavy-bodied man, his hair thick and white, standing speaking with two of the officers on duty at the cordon, which had been set up near the junction to keep the rioters contained. He moved away as she approached.

'Concerned resident?' Lucy asked one of the officers.

'Community leader,' he replied. 'That's Jackie Logue.'

Lucy shrugged. She'd heard the name

174

recently, but couldn't place it.

'He runs the community up here. He's been talking to the kids since we pushed them back. Most of the wee shits have buggered off home thanks to him.'

'Ah,' Lucy said, remembering now that he was the one with whom Fleming had spoken about Sarah Finn in the youth club.

'Oh, Jackie's a legend up here. Voice of moderation. He's the reason why we can usually come in and out of here without what happened this morning happening.'

'So what was different this time?'

The uniform shrugged as he stepped away to speak to the driver of a car that had approached the tape, clearly hoping to be allowed access.

29

After nine, Lucy and Fleming returned to Sarah Finn's house. The mood in the house seemed to have changed from the previous day. Sinead Finn sat at the edge of the seat now, her knee jiggling up and down, one hand clutching her dressing gown shut, the other holding her cigarette.

'Was that pervert involved? The one they burned out down the road?' she asked, after Fleming had updated her on the previous day's events.

Fleming glanced at Lucy before answering. 'We don't believe so, Mrs Finn. No.'

'Well, where is she?' she asked, her hand extended, palm up, the cigarette clenched between her fingers. 'What are you doing to find her?'

'We believe she may be with your partner, Mr Doherty,' Lucy said. 'We've followed up with his work and they tell us that he isn't in Manchester.'

'What do you mean? Where is he then?'

'We hoped you might be able to help us,' Fleming said. 'Have you had any luck contacting him?'

The woman shook her head. 'I'd have said if I had, wouldn't I?'

'I noticed yesterday, when I was looking for Sarah, that Mr Doherty doesn't keep many

176

clothes here,' Lucy began. 'Does he have somewhere else he stays when he's not here with you?'

'He's at work when he's not here with me.'

'Not according to his employer. Can you give us the dates of his most recent trips?'

'Did he take my Sarah?' she asked, one eye weeping against the smoke that twisted in the air off her cigarette.

Lucy sat, while Fleming moved across to the window again, glancing out. Lucy suspected he was a little on edge following the riot; two officers split from the rest of their team were easy targets.

'We know Sarah went to the post office and withdrew £200. We know she lied to both you and her friends about where she was going the previous night. Both of those things would suggest that she was planning on going somewhere. Then your partner ups and leaves in the middle of the night, saying he's going to Manchester, but we know he's not. The lack of his possessions here suggests he has somewhere else where he stays. Either he has taken her, or else his leaving is purely coincidental.'

'Experience suggests that generally these things aren't coincidence,' Fleming commented. 'You must have some idea where else Mr Doherty might be. Where is he from? We have no records for him.'

'He grew up in Donegal, I think,' Finn said. 'I think he said he had a house in Foyle Springs, but I'm nearly sure he sold it.'

'Do you know his date of birth, Mrs Finn? We

177

have over four hundred Seamus Dohertys on the system.'

Finn angled her head in thought, then finally shook it. 'He never told me.'

'Even his age,' Fleming said. 'That would be a start.'

Finn shrugged. 'In his forties, maybe.'

★　★　★

As they left Finn's house, Lucy phoned through to H. M. Haulage again. The secretary who answered told her that she couldn't speak to Mr Martin as he had meetings all morning.

'This is part of a child abduction investigation,' Lucy explained.

'Mr Martin was very clear that he wasn't to be disturbed,' the girl explained, stuttering slightly. Lucy guessed she was young, afraid to annoy the boss, not confident enough to use her common sense.

'I spoke with Mr Martin yesterday about one of your employees, Seamus Doherty. We're having trouble locating an address for Mr Doherty and we really need to find him. Would you have an address for him?'

'I really think you need to speak to Mr Martin,' the girl said. 'I'm not sure I can give that information out. How do I know you're a police officer?'

'You can call my station if you want,' Lucy offered. 'Look, tell you what, how about you give me his driving licence number? If I'm not police, there's nothing much I can do with that, is there?'

'Wait a moment,' the girl said, and 'Green-sleeves' clicked into action. After a dozen renditions, the girl's voice cracked on the line.

'There's no one else here,' she explained. 'I'm not sure if . . . '

'Look, it's fine,' Lucy said. 'All I need is the number.'

She glanced at Fleming who rolled his eyes exasperatedly.

'We have GB5786345 on record if that's any good.'

'That's perfect,' Lucy said, repeating it while Fleming copied it down. 'Thank you.'

Within minutes, they had called the number through to the station and been contacted to be told that Doherty's last recorded address was in Norburgh Park. They were also told that he had a record for assault following a bar brawl in Belfast in the late eighties. Beyond that, and a few speeding tickets in the mid-nineties, Doherty had stayed off the system.

* * *

They pulled up outside the house twenty minutes later. Initially, they believed the place to be empty. Lucy banged on the door several times while Fleming skirted the perimeter of the house.

'All the ground floor curtains are drawn,' he observed as he joined her at the front step.

'One window up the stairs is the same,' Lucy said, nodding up.

'So someone's probably home.'

Lucy nodded. 'I've knocked a few times.'

'Maybe he can't hear very well,' Fleming commented, hammering his fist against the door three times, so sharply it rattled in the frame.

'I think the people in the next street overheard that,' she said.

'And success,' Fleming added, nodding to where a figure could be seen moving down the hallway towards the door.

They heard the click of the dead bolt being drawn back, then the door opened slightly. The man who peered out through the opening allowed by the security chain between door and frame had black hair. He pulled a blanket around his shoulders as he hunched over, clasping the gathered corners at his throat.

'Yes?' he asked, nasally, before sniffing audibly.

'Mr Doherty?'

'Yes?'

'Seamus Doherty?'

The man shook his head. 'No. Ian,' he said, straightening slightly. 'What's wrong?'

'You're not Seamus Doherty,' Lucy stated, though the young man misread the tone and responded.

'No, I'm not. Why?'

'We're sorry to have bothered you,' Fleming said. 'We're looking for Seamus Doherty. We were given this address as his last known residence.'

'You've the wrong Doherty,' the man said, standing taller now, his voice noticeably clearer.

'Do you know the other Mr Doherty?' Lucy asked.

'I bought the house last year,' he replied. 'I know the last owner was called Doherty. There's some of his post lying in here. I gathered it up in case he ever called to collect it, but he never did. Junk mostly, I imagine.'

'Can we see it?'

The man glanced backwards, hesitating, then finally closed the door, undid the security chain and allowed them in.

As Lucy followed him down the hallway towards the kitchen, she caught a glimpse of a second figure, female, turning quickly from the top of the stairs. She too had been wrapped in a blanket.

'Your cold's improved,' Fleming commented, glancing around the kitchen as the man padded across to a black unit in the corner and began flicking through the piles of paper shoved into it.

'I've thrown a sickie to be honest,' the man said. 'I thought you were someone from my work.'

The creaking from the room upstairs as the man's partner climbed back into bed made it fairly obvious why he'd thrown a sickie. He blushed slightly as he handed them a pile of white and brown envelopes.

As he did so, Fleming's phone rang. He glanced at the screen and, excusing himself, moved into the hall. Lucy heard him begin the conversation with 'Yes, ma'am.'

'Can you remember who sold you the house?' Lucy asked as she glanced at the envelopes. The name on the address labels was Mr S. Doherty. 'Was it an estate agent?'

'It might have been,' he commented at last. 'O'
Day, or something like that.'

'If you could try to remember, maybe you'd
give me a ring,' Lucy added, handing the man
her card with the PPU number on it.

Fleming reappeared in the doorway. 'We're
wanted back in the station, DS Black,' he said.
'Thanks for your help, Mr Doherty.'

'Bad news?' Lucy asked, as they made their
way back to the car.

'When your mother phones it's always bad
news. They've been in Kay's house. They found
his collection.'

30

The CID team was gathered in the incident room in the Strand Road when Lucy and Fleming arrived. A black bin bag lay on the table, on top of which sat a large metal security file box with a lock to the front. It had already been opened and some of the contents removed.

The vast bulk of the images already arranged on the table were Category 9 or 10. The young people pictured in the ones Lucy saw as she glanced across the collection were girls, all teenagers. They were engaged in a variety of activities, the men in all cases unidentifiable due to the angles at which the images had been taken.

'I take it they survived the fire because of the metal box,' Fleming said, as he leaned over, scanning the images.

'They survived the fire because they were in the shed,' a voice said. Lucy turned to where her mother had entered the room. 'I'd like to see you for a moment, Inspector Fleming.'

Fleming glanced at Lucy and raised his eyebrows. She guessed why her mother wanted to speak to Fleming. The box was so big, Lucy wondered how he could have missed it when he'd claimed he'd searched Kay's shed. She suspected her mother would want to know the same thing.

She worked with the rest of the CID team,

sorting through the images, attempting as best they could to organize them into piles, each one assigned to a different girl.

Within minutes, Lucy had found a picture of Karen Hughes. Shortly after, someone handed her an image that, they believed, was of Sarah Finn. Lucy studied the picture, blanking out the background, the position in which the youth was pictured, focusing only on the girl's face. She was pretty certain that it was indeed an image of Sarah. A second was handed to her; this time, it was a closer shot of the girl and there was no doubting her identity. Yet, while she was facing the camera, her eyes were downcast, as if unable to meet the stare of the one photographing her, his hand just visible under her chin as he tried to raise her head to take the picture.

'DS Black. The ACC wants to see you,' Burns called.

Lucy put the picture down, nodding to confirm that it was Sarah Finn, then moved gratefully away from the images and in to her mother.

'Sit down,' her mother said as Lucy entered Burns's office. 'Everything OK?'

'The collection out there. It's a little . . . disturbing.'

'We're lucky we got it finally. We can catalogue Kay's lists of abuse.'

'It's a little late,' Lucy said. 'Considering the bastard died.'

'I agree,' her mother replied. 'In fact that's what I wanted to ask you. We found the collection in the shed. Who searched there the day you were at the house?'

Lucy held her mother's stare. 'I don't remember. It could have been either of us.'

'Was it you?'

'I don't recall.'

The ACC nodded. 'DI Fleming has already confirmed that he was the one who checked.'

'Then why did you ask me?'

Wilson ignored the question. 'He's also already accepted that he missed it.'

'We all make mistakes.'

'Indeed. Though had we found this yesterday, Kay would be in a cell and facing justice. Instead we have to deal with what he did, the fallout from his being torched alive in his house, and a second Ombudsman inquiry in so many days.'

Lucy's phone began to ring. She pulled it out and saw Robbie's name on the caller ID. Apologizing, she switched it to silent and put it away again.

'I'd like to know again what happened yesterday morning in DI Fleming's house.'

'I'm not sure that's relevant to what we're talking about,' Lucy said quickly.

Her mother retorted, 'I decide what's relevant, Lucy. And I think it's completely fucking relevant that Tom Fleming was so insensible with drink yesterday morning that you called an ambulance for him. So drunk he didn't even hear his own burglar alarm going off. Yet he then comes into work and misses one of the biggest paedophile collections we've managed to find in years. Gene Kay is dead today because Tom Fleming was drunk yesterday.'

185

'That's a little unfair,' Lucy countered.

'It's very unfair,' Wilson agreed. 'On you, and me, and the rest of the teams working these cases.'

Lucy looked down at her hands folded in her lap. 'Looking at the images out there, I'd say Kay got what he deserved.'

'That's not our call to make,' Wilson snapped. Lucy shrugged.

'Inspector Fleming will be suspended pending an investigation,' her mother said.

Lucy glanced up sharply. '*That's* not fair. He needs help.'

'You're not the only one who cares for Tom Fleming, Lucy.'

'You've a funny way of showing it.'

'I remember the *first* time he went through all this,' her mother snapped. 'I saw what it did to him. He needs time to go and get himself sorted out. That's what he'll get. Do you think sitting out there looking at that filth is going to help him dry out? It's no wonder he drinks.'

'Yet you put me in the PPU when I asked to go to CID,' Lucy retorted. 'So it's OK for me to look at them, is it?'

'Don't make everything about yourself, Lucy.'

Lucy swallowed her immediate response, not trusting that her mother wouldn't have her punished for insubordination. 'So what do I do while he's off?'

'The Finn case dovetails with the Hughes murder,' the ACC said. 'Continue to work the case and report to Chief Superintendent Burns.'

Lucy stood, saying nothing.

'I admire your loyalty, Lucy. In this case, though, Tom needs more than loyalty.'

'I wouldn't expect you to understand,' Lucy replied. 'After all, loyalty was never one of your strong suits, was it?'

31

Burns was waiting when Lucy came out of the office.

'You've heard about Inspector Fleming, I assume,' he said.

Lucy nodded.

'Look, I'm sure you know what you're doing. I'd appreciate your help with following up on Carlin. Was he known to PPU?'

Before I drove him into a lough, Lucy thought, bitterly. 'I'd not come across him before last night, sir,' she said. 'Inspector Fleming is the obvious person to ask though.'

'We already have,' Burns said. 'He'd not heard the name before either.'

Lucy folded her arms across her chest, then, being suddenly aware of the defensiveness of the gesture, unfolded them, before finally clasping her hands behind her back.

'We know he was being supported by the Community Mental Health team. I'd like you to speak to his care worker there and see what you can find out. To fill in the background, you know.'

'What about the house, sir? Has anyone found anything there yet?'

'Forensics are doing a full sweep. It'll take a while before we get any results.'

★ ★ ★

The Community Mental Health team worked out of Rossdowney House in the Waterside. Lucy knew most of those who worked there, not least because many of the children in the residential unit had been referred to them at one time or another. When she arrived, she was told that she'd best speak with the unit psychiatrist, Noleen Fagan.

'Good to see you, Lucy. Long time,' Fagan said as she brought Lucy into her office. 'Grab a seat.'

The room was small, the walls lined with bookcases, the desk — a modern beech affair — overloaded with green and red files, many of them bulging to the point that elastic bands wrapped around them had been knotted together.

'How're things?' Lucy asked. 'I've not seen you in a while.'

'The Trust took all the older kids' cases off us,' Fagan said. 'A few years back, they widened the remit of the children's team to take up to eighteen. We're adult only now.'

Lucy nodded. 'That must make things easier.'

'No change ever makes things easier,' Fagan laughed. 'You must know that. How's the PPU treating you?'

Lucy thought of the images she had been examining half an hour earlier. 'The same as always,' she said. 'I've been dispatched to find out about Peter Carlin.'

Fagan nodded. 'I heard this morning. He drove into Enagh Lough, is that right?'

'By accident. We were pursuing him and he

189

lost control, I think.'

'You think?'

'His car swerved. The road was a little slippy . . . '

'But?'

'He was on a straight stretch.'

'You think he drove off deliberately?'

Lucy shrugged. She'd not mentioned it to anyone; there seemed little point. Still, she had wondered how he could have lost control on a straight road.

'Why were you chasing him? What had he done?'

'We think he was grooming teenagers online. Someone online who had created a range of sock puppet accounts groomed Karen Hughes, the girl found dead on the railway tracks. That same person arranged to meet another girl last night at eight o' clock. Carlin turned up at the meeting, then did a runner when he spotted us.'

Fagan listened, threading the pen in her hand from between one finger to the next as she did so. 'How many accounts?'

'We don't know for sure. Certainly more than a dozen.'

'Are you sure it was Peter Carlin who arranged all this?'

'It looks that way. We think he was working with Gene Kay.'

'The fire in Gobnascale? I heard that this morning, too.'

'They unearthed a collection of images in his house. Including some of both Karen and the girl Carlin had arranged to meet.'

190

'That might make more sense,' Fagan commented. 'Carlin had paedophiliac proclivities, certainly. But Peter Carlin couldn't have arranged a dozen fake identities, let alone have been able to manipulate a child through a process of grooming. Carlin had a fairly extreme dependent personality disorder.'

'A personality disorder? Would that not predispose him to something like this?'

Fagan shook her head. 'Carlin was intellectually limited, to put it mildly. More importantly, though, he displayed almost all the defining features of dependency: extreme passivity, tolerating abusive relationships in order to feel wanted; not trusting his own judgement on anything. He was pathologically indecisive, unless someone told him what to do. He'd come in here some days with two pairs of socks and ask me which I thought he should wear for the day. He'd never be able to start something off his own bat. He'd need to be told what to do, to the letter.'

'And he'd follow the direction because . . . ?'

'Because he had a need to be accepted. If Carlin was involved in what you're saying — and I've no reason to doubt you — then someone was telling him what to do. Someone powerful in his eyes, someone whom he trusted and whose approbation he needed. If anything, Peter Carlin would have been just another puppet.'

'Could it have been Gene Kay?'

'Maybe. I spoke with him a few times to do a psychiatric evaluation after his release from prison a few years back. He wasn't the most

191

charismatic or trusting. He didn't strike me as the type to work with others. They'd make an unlikely pairing. That said, stranger things have happened.'

'So it's possible that Kay controlled Carlin?'

'It's possible,' Fagan conceded. 'Anything is possible. But I'd be fairly certain that the idea of Carlin grooming someone is a non-starter. Though if he did deliberately drive his car off the road, it would have been because someone told him to. There was no one in the car with him?'

Lucy shook her head.

'He wasn't on the phone with anyone? Perhaps he'd tried to contact someone if he was being pursued. He'd have needed someone to tell him to run.'

'And if they told him to drive his car into a lake?'

'If he admired them enough — was controlled enough by them — he'd do it.'

'Jesus,' Lucy said, standing. 'I almost feel sorry for him now. Almost,' she added.

Fagan smiled lightly. 'I was sorry to hear about Karen Hughes. I worked with her over the self-harming before she was transferred to the children's team. She was a lovely girl,' Fagan added, standing to see her out.

Lucy nodded, not trusting herself to speak. 'She was,' she managed finally.

*　*　*

After leaving the block, she phoned through to the Incident Room to speak with Burns. She wondered if she should mention her doubts about whether Carlin going off the road was an accident. If he'd been on the phone, it would have been recovered when the car was pulled out of the lough. Unless he had been told to toss it out the window. It might explain why he'd had the driver's window down when he hit the water, despite the cold of the night. If that was the case, it would never be found.

'The team are out,' the officer who answered the call told her. 'They've gone to the Carlin house. Forensics have found a body. A young girl.'

'Is it Sarah Finn?' Lucy asked quickly, hoping that it would not be and yet aware that, even if it wasn't, it would still be someone's daughter. Another lost girl.

Lucy saw again, unbidden, in her mind, the image of Sarah Finn she had seen earlier, the girl's gaze not meeting that of the camera, her eyes downcast; a child already broken.

'I don't know,' he replied.

32

The Foreglen, along which Carlin's house was situated, was one of the main routes out of the city, heading first to Dungiven, then on over the Glenshane Pass and down towards Belfast. It was the same route along which Sarah Finn's phone had been found.

Carlin's house was a two-storey block affair, the yellowed paint weathered, blistering and crumbling off the walls. To the rear were a number of dilapidated farm buildings, dominated over by a rusted barn, the roof jousts visible through the wide gaps worn through the corrugated metal front sections. A wooden door slanted off its hinges, exposing the insides.

Lucy parked up behind a marked car whose lights still soundlessly flashed. Its driver was on the phone and waved a single gloved hand salute out at her as she passed.

Lucy looked around for someone from CID. Despite her best efforts, the whole way from Derry, she'd been unable to contact anyone who might be able to tell her for certain that the dead body that had been found was Sarah Finn. There was a uniformed officer standing at the main door of the house while Forensics officers moved in and out wordlessly. Despite the activity, Lucy was struck by how quiet the scene was. Those who passed did so without speech, their heads lowered, as if in show of respect to the one dead.

It was always so when the crime involved children.

'Is the Chief Super about?' she asked the uniform, flashing her warrant card.

'He's at the scene.'

'Is it inside?' Lucy asked, nodding past the man towards the hallway of the house beyond.

The uniform shook his head. 'There's a pond up at the top of the next field across. They found a pit there where he'd been dumping stuff for years. She was in there.'

'Is it Sarah Finn?'

The uniform shook his head. 'I've no idea, Sergeant; I've not been up.'

Lucy thanked him, then cut round the side of the house in the direction the man had suggested. To the rear of the house, standing on bricks, was the wheelless chassis of a car, the frame exposed and, like the barn, brown with rust. Lucy glanced over her shoulder, observing the back of the house. She could barely make out any movement in the rooms, the film of dirt on the windows being so thick.

The uniform had told her that the site was in the second field across. The first through which she trudged was water-logged, her boots sinking into the ground, the beer-brown water pooling around her feet with each step she took. Eventually, she worked out to walk the circumference, the earth being a little firmer near the hedge bordering the field. The sky above was clear, the sun low, the shadows of the trees stretching across the grass towards her.

She glanced around, attempting to gauge the

distance to Carlin's nearest neighbour, but there were none immediately visible.

She reached the top of the first field and, cutting across to the left through a gap in the hedging, saw in the distance a crime scene tape already tied between two trees. Beyond it, a team of people in forensic suits were moving about. Using the edge of the field again, she was halfway across when she met Tara coming in the opposite direction.

'Is it Sarah Finn?' Lucy asked as she drew near.

'I don't know,' Tara said. 'I don't think so. Apparently it looks like it's been there for some time. Years, like.' Without stopping, Tara trudged past. 'I've to get food in,' she offered.

Lucy felt immediate relief at the news, then felt instantly guilty at having done so. That the dead girl was not Sarah Finn did not mean that there was not still a dead girl.

When she reached the crime tape, she saw Burns and Mickey standing to one side, watching the Forensics team working. She understood now Tara's shortness; Mickey seemed to be constantly at Burns's side, while Tara herself was being dispatched on minor tasks. Lucy reflected that at least with Fleming she had never felt under-appreciated.

Lucy flashed her card again at the officer standing at the scene tape and ducked under. 'You'll need one of these,' the officer said, handing her a face mask.

'You're back,' Burns said, unnecessarily, from behind his own mask as she approached him.

196

'It's not Sarah Finn?' Lucy answered.

'Seems not,' he said. 'This one is old. Could have been in there ten years, they think. They've found all kinds of stuff. The place was full of asbestos. You'll need your mask.'

Lucy quickly pulled it on, pulling the straps taut against her scalp.

The pit, beyond where they stood, was about twenty feet wide, though she could not from this angle tell its depth. A few of the CSIs, dressed in industrial protection gear, were already removing the asbestos, sealed in plastic, shifting it to one side to allow the officers access to what lay beneath.

'They found a black dog in the house,' Burns said. 'We're checking the hairs against those found on Karen.'

Lucy nodded.

'They've found all kinds of stuff in the house,' Burns continued. 'Traces of fluids all over the place.'

'Blood?'

'And the rest,' Burns added. 'It looks like Carlin was doing all kinds of things to all kinds of people in there. An orgy site, one of the SOCOs said.'

'I spoke with Noleen Fagan,' Lucy said. 'Carlin's psychiatrist in the Mental Health team. She reckons it's unlikely he would be our groomer.'

'How had he not come to our attention before?' Mickey asked. 'Surely he should have been flagged up.'

'He had dependent personality disorder,' Lucy

said. 'It doesn't mean he's likely to be a criminal. In fact, Fagan reckoned he probably wouldn't have been capable of grooming anyone.'

'Is she sure?' Burns asked. 'The evidence is pretty compelling at this stage.'

'He needed to be told what to do, by people whose approval he sought. He may even have been told to drive off the road the other night.'

'What?' Burns asked, exasperated.

'He looked like he swerved off the road deliberately,' Lucy said. 'Fagan suggested he might have been instructed to do so by someone. Maybe someone he was speaking to on the phone.'

Mickey scoffed. 'Or maybe he was on his phone and lost control. Nothing complicated about it.'

Lucy ignored him, addressing Burns. 'Fagan reckons he'd be more a puppet than a manipulator.'

'More puppets,' Burns said. 'This bloody case is built on puppets.'

Lucy shrugged and relayed the rest of what Fagan had said.

'Then he must have been in cahoots with Kay. He does the arranging, Carlin does the dirty work. Then they used this place as their spot for carrying out the abuse,' Mickey said.

'I thought that too. However, Fagan reckoned Kay wouldn't have been the type to work with others.'

Burns considered the comment, though Lucy could already sense without conviction.

'We'll wait to see what Forensics pull from the

two houses. If we can connect one with the other, we're sorted.'

One of the suited men approached them, a camera held in his hand.

'This is what we've got, sir,' he said, handing Burns the camera. 'It's the best I can get for you at the moment, until we get all the asbestos moved. She's down near the bottom.'

Burns held one hand over the viewing screen at the back of the camera as he flicked through the images the man had taken. Mickey craned his head to see too. Lucy waited until he was done, then asked to see the images. Since she had started in the PPU, over a year earlier, four children in the area under the age of eighteen had gone missing who had never been found. That was low; she knew that there had been twenty-two missing across the North in a previous year alone. If this child had been in the ground for ten years, based on those figures, it could be any one of forty or fifty children in the Foyle district area who had been reported missing within that time period. That was assuming that the child had been reported missing in the Foyle district to start with.

Burns scanned through the images for a few moments, then handed the camera to Lucy. 'See if anything stands out.'

The body was small, clearly a child, though the legs carried a good length. 'What height is she?'

'We think about five foot,' the SOCO said. 'She's measuring four foot ten, so allowing for some curvature and that.'

She wore a T-shirt, yellowed and grubby with dirt, but originally white, Lucy guessed. She wore baggy jeans. Her hair seemed blonde. Her face, though wizened, was not decayed as Lucy had expected.

'He buried her in quicklime, we think,' the man said. 'It helped preserve her.'

Lucy nodded. Contrary to popular belief, quicklime didn't accelerate decomposition. Indeed, it was quite the reverse. She could understand why Carlin might have used it. If the farm on which he lived had been functioning at one stage, he'd have had to cover any of the animals that had died and been buried to kill the smell of the bodies.

'I can follow up on the clothes,' Lucy said. 'See if it matches any Missing Persons investigations.'

'And the shoe,' the SOCO said. 'I've a close-up of it further on.'

Lucy scrolled through the images. One of the last was indeed close up on the girl's shoe. She wore a chunky black shoe, whose sole was almost three inches thick. At the strap, Lucy could make out an off-white skull and crossbones motif.

'Just the one shoe?'

'So far,' the man replied.

'I'll run both through the older cases.'

'Do that,' Burns said. 'What about the Finn girl? Any luck tracing the stepfather?'

'He's not . . . ' Lucy began, then decided better of it. 'The last address we had for him was sold a while back. He didn't leave a forwarding address, but I'm going to try the estate agent who handled the sale to see if we can track him down through them.'

'What about the phone we found yesterday? Have ICS found anything on it?'

'I'm not sure, sir. I've not had time to check.'

'Get a press release out this evening asking for the stepfather to do the right thing and hand himself in. Then organize for the mother to do an appeal tomorrow morning for the news.' He held out his hand, looking for the camera to be returned. 'You need to stay on top of it, Lucy. Let me know if the techies find anything.'

Lucy demurred from pointing out that she and Fleming had been following it up when Burns had had them called back to the station to see the collection found in Kay's shed. For the foreseeable future, he would be her superior and she saw little value in unnecessarily antagonizing him. Instead she handed him back the camera with a simple, 'Yes, sir,' then ducked back under the tape and began picking her way back to the farmhouse.

'Sergeant?' the uniform called after her.

Lucy turned expectantly.

'Your face mask? I need it back,' the man said, smiling.

Lucy handed him the mask, then stopped, glancing back up to where Burns stood. Something struck her about the clothes of the child. Not the clothes. The shoe. She remembered again the shoe found in Gary Duffy's garage, which had provided the evidence that led to his imprisonment. The distinctive skull and crossbones motif.

'Sir,' she called, moving past the uniform. 'Sir!'

Burns turned towards her.

'It's the shoes. I think I know who the girl is.'

Mickey glanced at her, his face sharp.

'I think she's Louisa Gant.'

Burns angled his head slightly. 'We'll check it up. Thank you, Sergeant,' he added, turning from her again.

33

After pulling up in front of the PPU block, Lucy thought better of it and drove across to the ICS block. She buzzed at the door and waited, studying her reflection in the foiled glass of the door, fixing a stray hair behind her ear.

Cooper opened the door. He wore a black shirt, open at the collar, and jeans.

'Lucy, come in,' he said, holding the door open so that she could pass.

'I've been sent to find out if you got anything on the phone we recovered yesterday.'

'Not even a good morning?' Cooper smiled, leading her towards his workroom.

'Sorry,' Lucy said. 'It's not been good. More a fairly shitty one, to be honest. But good morning,' she said, then glanced at her watch. 'In fact, good afternoon. I didn't realize the time.'

'You've not had lunch then,' Cooper said. 'I'll make tea. Milk? Sugar?'

'Both,' Lucy said, sitting down heavily on the stool by the workbench where she stood.

'So what's happened?' Cooper asked.

'My boss has been suspended,' Lucy said. 'Both suspects in our case have died so far, we've not found the one girl we lost and I think we've found a girl that went missing years ago and whose killer is also dead.'

'That is fairly shitty,' Cooper agreed.

'Actually, it's probably business as usual, if I'm

203

honest,' Lucy conceded. 'I just feel bad for Tom Fleming.'

Cooper carried across two mugs of pale liquid and handed one to Lucy.

'When you asked about milk and sugar, I assumed I'd not need to specify I wanted actual tea in my tea too,' she said, peering doubtfully at the mug.

'The bag's in there,' Cooper said. 'You can stir yourself.'

He pulled a Twix out of his coat pocket, opened the packet and handed Lucy one of the two fingers.

'I couldn't work out if you liked it weak or strong,' he added. 'You strike me as strong.'

Lucy pulled the bag up with her spoon and squeezed out the tea. 'So, any luck with the phone?' she asked, before lifting the finger of Twix and taking a bite.

'The same as with Karen Hughes,' Cooper said. 'Almost an identical pattern. 'Harris' started contact with her on Facebook. She befriended him the same as Karen, they batted some comments back and forwards. She mentioned her favourite band was Florence and the Machine. Then when she changed her profile picture from a puppy to a shot she took of her garden, he posted a comment 'Dog Days are Over'.'

'One of her songs,' Lucy said, nodding.

'I had to google it,' Cooper admitted. 'Sarah got the joke though. She agreed to meet him not long after.'

'How long ago was this?'

'Ten weeks ago,' he said. 'Their first contact was on 9 October. Their first meeting was in early November. They seemed to meet up for drinks or coffee a few times, then he suggested they go to a party. It quietened down a bit after that, then they seemed to make contact more frequently, another party, now she's vanished.'

'Can you find out who 'Harris' is? Assuming it's not his real name.'

'I thought 'Harris' was lying in a morgue with two lungs full of Enagh Lough.'

'Regardless,' Lucy said. 'Has there been any activity on the accounts since?'

Cooper shook his head. 'Not a peep. Certainly none of the identities that I'd traced.'

Lucy supped at her tea, washing down the last of the chocolate, the taste cloying at her throat.

'Thanks for that,' she said.

'The first contact with Sarah Finn was on 9 October, right?' Cooper said. 'The first contact with Karen Hughes was on 18 September. We know that Bradley or 'Harris' or whatever his name is selected these girls for a reason, groomed them online to meet them in the real world. Assuming that something made Bradley target these specific girls online, then he must have encountered them in some way in the real world prior to that first online contact. It might be worth looking at where the girls were or who they met in the days prior to the two first contacts. If you find something the two had in common, you'll not have far to look for Bradley, I'd have thought.'

Lucy felt her phone vibrate in her pocket and,

pulling it out, saw Robbie's name on the caller ID. She realized that he had left her a message earlier which she hadn't listened to yet. She hesitated answering, feeling absurdly guilty, then excused herself and, moving out of the office, answered the call.

'Hey, Lucy,' Robbie said when he answered. 'I've been trying you and Tom all morning.'

'We've been busy,' Lucy said quickly, despite the fact there had been nothing accusatory in his comment.

'Sorry,' he said. 'It's about Gavin. He skipped out in the middle of the night. He didn't arrive back here until just after seven this morning. I got him out to school. He signed out of school at eleven to attend a Mass for his father with his grandparents. He's not come back to the school yet and I can't get in contact with the grandparents.'

Lucy exhaled deeply.

'I'm sorry to land this on you,' Robbie said. 'You know the protocol, though.' If a child in care didn't return to the residential unit when expected, Social Services were required to inform the PPU.

'It's no problem,' Lucy said. 'Why didn't you contact us last night when he went out?'

'I didn't know,' Robbie replied sheepishly. 'I fell asleep on the sofa in the common room. He'd already gone to bed and I'd the place locked up for the evening. I got up to wake him this morning and saw he was gone. I was about to call when he arrived at the front door.'

If Gavin had been missing during the night

there was every chance that he, and his new gang of friends, had been part of the recreational rioting that Lucy had witnessed in Gobnascale earlier. 'I'll get onto it as soon as I can,' Lucy said. Despite her caseload, she would have to follow up on it, especially without Fleming to handle it.

'There's something else,' Robbie said. 'I stuck on a washing load after he went to school. When I gathered up his clothes, they were stinking of petrol. Especially the sleeves of his hoodie.'

'He was probably part of the crew rioting at the top of the hill this morning,' Lucy said. 'I spotted him with them the other day.'

'Great!' Robbie said, sarcastically. 'He's only here a matter of weeks and he's already found himself a gang.'

It was as she was hanging up that Lucy realized that if Gavin had been back at the unit just after seven the riot had not even started by that stage. In fact, the only petrol they knew of as having been used at that stage was the stuff that had been poured through Gene Kay's letterbox before being set alight.

34

Gavin Duffy's grandparents' house was in Holymount Park, in Gobnascale. Lucy rang at the door and waited, but no one answered. She peered in the windows, smearing away the misting of rainwater that had gathered there, a result of the fine miasma which had swept up over the city from along the Foyle Valley. She angled her head to see through the cracks in the blinds, but the place seemed empty, the darkened outline of a small Christmas tree visible in the corner. Lucy considered that the couple would hardly feel like celebrating Christmas, having lost their son only a month earlier.

She was turning to leave when a couple came shuffling up the street under a black umbrella towards the house. The woman looked to be in her sixties, brown hair streaked with grey, her eyes rheumy. The man seemed older, balding with a grey moustache. He blinked at Lucy from behind rain-streaked glasses.

'Yes?'

'I'm looking for the Duffys,' she explained.

'That's us,' the woman answered, smiling uncertainly.

'I'm Detective Sergeant Black of the Public Protection Unit. I'm looking for your grandson, Gavin. He's not turned up at school. They've been trying to contact you.'

'We were at Mass, over in the chapel.'

They pointed towards the outline of the Immaculate Conception Church, across the road from the estate where they lived. 'We went to the cemetery afterwards.'

'It's our son's Month's Mind,' the man said. He shuffled past, pulling out his keys, and opened the door. 'You may come in, so,' he added.

The house was compact, three rooms downstairs — a living room, kitchen and cloakroom. The living room was cosy, the small fire smouldering in the grate surprisingly warming. The old man grunted as he bent and flicked on a switch at the wall, bringing the thin Christmas tree in the corner alight, throwing kaleidoscopic shadows on the wall.

'You'll have tea,' Mr Duffy said, a statement not a question.

'I was sorry to hear about your son,' Lucy said, a little insincerely, to the woman, who sat next to the fire now. She twisted slightly to address the husband who stood in the adjacent room, filling the kettle. 'It must be very hard. Especially at this time of the year.'

'We wouldn't have been celebrating it at all were it not for Gavin being here.'

Lucy heard a grunt of derision from the kitchen. 'When he's here. He was to be at the Mass this morning. His own father's Month's Mind.'

'It's a Mass for when — ' the woman began.

'I know,' said Lucy. Catholic families celebrated Mass one month after the death of a loved one in their memory. Lucy had attended a number herself over the years.

'Oh,' Mrs Duffy replied, understanding the implication. 'He'd wanted Gavin to come. The wee boy didn't know his father at all.'

'Only his bitch of a mother,' her husband said, passing Lucy a cup of black tea and handing a second cup to his wife.

'Don't say that,' his wife commented, though without conviction.

The man reappeared a moment later with a small tray, a cloth doily on it, on top of which sat a milk jug, a sugar bowl and a plate of biscuits. Lucy took milk and sugar, declined the Bourbon creams, then regretted having done so having managed only a single finger of a Twix bar since breakfast.

'She ran off the first time Gary went inside. Then she remarried. Do you know what the new one did to the wee boy?'

Lucy had heard when he'd first been transferred in. His stepfather, in order to teach him a lesson for accidentally breaking the wing mirror of his car with his bike, had beaten him with the flex of a games console. His PE teacher had noticed the shape of the bruises the following day when Gavin was changing for football, his T-shirt riding too high up his trunk as he pulled his shirt over his head. The doctor who examined him said there were injuries consistent with punches around the boy's ribcage, in addition to repeated bruising from an electric flex.

The officers who had questioned his mother

and stepfather, separately, said that the mother had accused the boy of injuring himself because he didn't like her husband. It was only after she read the extent of the injuries that she admitted what had happened. She claimed that the boy was uncontrollable, and that she could no longer look after him. At the age of twelve, Gavin had entered residential care and there remained, until his grandparents had asked to have him brought nearer their home after his father's death.

'What's he done then?' Mr Duffy asked.

'Nothing that I know of,' Lucy said. 'He's just not in school.'

'We hardly see him,' the man commented.

'We need to give him space,' his wife countered. 'It's been difficult for him.'

'He should have been there this morning,' the man repeated, earning a roll of her eyes from his wife.

'He wasn't at the Mass?' Lucy asked.

The woman shook her head. 'He's like his father. Wayward. Gary was the same. Even after he got out. He was so angry all the time when he was younger. Then they lifted him for that wee girl's killing — all the people who'd been his friends would have nothing to do with him. They wouldn't let him onto their wing in the prison. For his own safety. Then he became withdrawn, wouldn't talk about anything. We couldn't get through to him. We asked him to say where the wee girl's body was, to admit if he'd done it.'

'Did he?' Lucy asked, having debated whether to mention the body that had been found on

Carlin's farm. There was no point. She'd still not heard whether she was right in believing it to be Louisa Gant.

The woman shook her head. 'He said he was innocent of it.'

'But you didn't believe him?'

The woman's eyes filled. 'That's a terrible thing for a mother to say. That she didn't believe her own son. But he was a bad boy. From he was a teenager, it was like something was broken inside him.'

'He'd his mother's heart broken before he ever went inside. Then, when he did, they all abandoned him. All the ones he ran with. He'd no one left in the end. Nowhere to go.'

'He even moved back here; we made him, to be near us,' Mrs Duffy added.

'For all the difference it made in the end,' her husband muttered.

'He went down to the river,' Mrs Duffy said. 'To spare us finding him. His father always brought him up his breakfast in the morning. He didn't want him to see him . . . you know.'

They sat in silence, watching the flames curl round the briquette the woman had thrown on the fire when they'd arrived in.

'I'm sorry,' Lucy repeated again.

'We thought having Gavin around would help,' Mr Duffy said. 'But he's out with that crew more often than not.'

'The street gang?'

'Local lads is all,' Mrs Duffy said, quickly. 'He'll be out running around somewhere.'

Lucy drained her tea then placed the cup back

212

on the tray. 'I'd best take a drive around and see if I can find him. Would they be anywhere in particular?

'I'd try the back of the shops,' the man said. 'That's where they normally be.'

The couple saw her to the door, where Lucy thanked them for the tea and offered her condolences once more.

'Gavin's very lucky he has you,' she said. 'He showed me the iPod you got him. You're very good to him.'

'What's an iPod?' Mr Duffy said, his face creased in bewilderment.

35

Lucy drove across to the parking bays outside the shops where she and Fleming had gone looking for Sarah Finn. She jumped out of the car, the air heavy with the smell of hot grease from the local chip shop reminding her she should eat. She had no time, for now, she decided.

Lucy had considered whether it might be best to call for backup, but if there was a gang of fellas standing, bored, in the rain, a Land Rover-load of PSNI officers pulling up would be the perfect entertainment to keep them occupied after the events at Kay's house. She thought she would try to get Gavin's attention and take him away quietly, rather than having to take a heavy-handed approach.

As she opened the boot to take out her coat, she caught a glimpse of a red car parked at the outer edge of the bays. A stocky man wearing a brown overcoat and a black beanie hat sat in the driver's seat while, at the open door, two younger boys, in their late teens at most, leaned in. She recognized one of the boys as Tony, the leader of the gang with whom she had spoken about Sarah Finn. For a moment, Lucy thought they were robbing him, until the three of them started laughing. The man seemed to sense her watching, for he stared across at her. It took her a moment to place him as Jackie Logue, the community worker who'd helped calm the riot during Kay's burning.

After pulling her hood up enough to cover her face, she slammed the boot shut and headed across to the shops. Aware that she was still being watched, she instead went into the shop to buy a bar of chocolate, rather than heading directly around the back.

Two women served in the shop; one looked to be in her early twenties. She was loading the display in front of the tills with bags of crisps, while the older woman behind the counter chatted to a customer.

It was the younger girl that Lucy approached first.

'Can I have a packet of those?' she asked, only realizing after she'd done so that they were Worcester sauce flavour. 'I'm looking for my nephew. I'm told he hangs around with a crowd of boys around here.'

The girl looked up at her, blinking against the strip lights above Lucy's head. 'What's he called? I'll know if he's been in.'

'Gavin,' Lucy said, aware that the conversation at the counter had stopped.

'He's round the back, I think,' the girl said.

'They're not doing any harm,' a voice said.

Lucy turned. Both the woman behind the counter, and the older man to whom she had been talking, were now looking at her.

'They're all right out there. The back's covered over, so they stand in there out of the rain. Besides, Jackie keeps tabs on them.'

'Jackie?' Lucy asked. 'Jackie Logue?'

'Gavin's your nephew, is he?' the woman said.

'Gavin who?' the old man asked in response.

'Gary Duffy's boy,' she replied, as if Lucy wasn't there.

'The Duffys only had the one,' the man commented.

'That's right,' agreed his co-conspirator. 'You're no aunt. Police, is it?'

'His grandparents are wondering where he is,' Lucy lied. 'I'll take a Bounty too.'

'He's doing no harm out there. Leave him alone.'

Lucy said nothing further about the boys, thanking the woman and leaving, pulling her hood up again.

The area to the side of the shops was covered by sheets of corrugated metal, providing a smoking area along the entirety of the row, presumably for the staff of the various shop units who were being forced to smoke outside in the wake of the ban on smoking indoors. A group of around twenty youths were congregated there, a mixture of boys and girls, in half shadow, their faces faintly illuminated by the green emergency exit lights above the rear doors of each unit.

Four plastic dumpsters sat to one side, and it was against one of these that Gavin was standing, a cigarette in his hand, talking to a boy and girl of about the same age as him.

One of the kids shouted, 'Five oh,' quickly killing the conversation. They all turned to look where Lucy stood. She knew there was no way they could have made her out as a police officer so quickly, so guessed the Five-O reference

216

covered all adults. It was hard not to find it more than a little absurd that the kids who used the designation probably had no idea where it came from. Unless they'd caught the remake or *The Wire*, she reflected.

The gathered kids stared from one to the other, as if trying to work out who Lucy was looking for, before turning defiantly towards her again. Gavin was standing with his arm around a thin girl, mid-teens, perhaps, her face sharp-featured, accentuated by the glow of the lights above them. He waited a moment, then pushed himself away from the dumpster and moved towards Lucy, drawing on his cigarette as he did so. The blackness around his eye shone beneath the green exit lights.

'Is something wrong?'

Lucy turned to see Jackie Logue standing a few feet from her, Tony behind him.

'It's fine, thank you,' Lucy said, turning towards the gathered group again. 'Come on, Gavin.'

'Are you a relative?' Logue asked.

'I know Gavin,' Lucy commented. 'Thanks for your concern.'

'These kids have nowhere else to go, Officer,' the man said.

'Apart from school?' Lucy countered.

'We're too old for school now,' Tony muttered, earning a glance of rebuke from Logue.

'They're not doing any harm here, as you were told,' Logue himself said, turning his attention again to Lucy.

So the woman from the shop had gone out

and told him Lucy was police. She could also hear the kids passing along word that she was a cop.

'What do you want?' Gavin said, standing a few feet from her, defiantly refusing to take the final steps towards her.

'Robbie's looking for you. Let's go.'

Logue moved a step closer. 'That's not very helpful. You don't have to go if you don't want to, Gavin.'

'Yes, he does,' Lucy said, turning to the man. 'Mr Logue, is it?'

Logue raised his chin slightly but did not answer.

'Gavin is still young enough that he should be in school.'

'He told me he was allowed off to go to Mass for his father.'

'He didn't turn up at that either. His grandparents are worried about him.'

'I am standing here, you know,' Gavin snapped. 'Stop talking about me like I'm not here.'

'Let's go, Gavin,' Lucy said.

Gavin hesitated, as if considering returning to his friends. Lucy shook her head lightly. If he didn't come with her now, it would be worse when a response team arrived for him.

'Later,' Gavin said, turning to the other kids. He winked at the girl with whom he'd been standing. 'See you, Jackie,' he added to the stocky man.

'Mr Logue,' Lucy said, as she passed the man, walking behind Gavin to stop him changing his

218

mind and turning back.

Gavin barely spoke the whole way back to the residential unit, even when Lucy asked how he felt after the beating he had taken.

He shrugged his shoulders. 'It was nothing,' he said.

'Your grandparents seem very nice,' Lucy said. 'They seem really keen to have you in their family.'

Again, the boy shrugged.

'They didn't give you the iPod though,' she added. 'Did they?'

The boy twisted and glared at her. 'Are you checking up on me?'

'I want to make sure you're OK,' Lucy said. 'Everyone just wants to help.'

'You can help by not coming for me in front of my friends again. OK?' With that he got out of the car and slammed the door, storming past Robbie where he stood at the unit entrance waiting for him.

36

The night had already thickened across the city by the time Lucy made it back to Maydown again. She'd called in with Sinead Finn after leaving Gavin at the unit, but there was still no word from either the girl or Seamus Doherty. The woman had agreed to do an appeal the following morning, wondering what she should wear.

'Anything,' Lucy had replied.

The Tactical Support Units had been doing further checks in the area, but it seemed likely that, by this stage, the girl had either been taken by Doherty, or had used his leaving as an opportunity to get away herself, having taken the money from her mother's post office account the day before.

Lucy went up to her office and began typing up the press release for the late evening news. She mentioned both Doherty and Sarah Finn as being missing and encouraged either to contact home or the police as soon as possible. She also included a description of both Sarah Finn and Seamus Doherty and added that they could be travelling together or separately.

She called Communications to tell them the release was on its way and to book a press conference for the morning in the Strand Road should Sarah Finn not be located before then. She'd just emailed it through when she heard a thud from the office below. She went out to the top of the stairs and, looking down, shouted, 'Hello.'

A moment later, Tom Fleming's face appeared from the gloom of the corridor below. 'I didn't know you were in,' he said. 'I've called to collect some stuff.'

Lucy came down to him. 'I'm sorry about the whole . . . thing,' she offered.

Fleming accepted the comment with a light nod. 'It's fine,' he said. 'I could maybe be doing with a breather from all this.'

Lucy nodded, unconvinced. 'What are you planning on doing?'

'Dry out,' he said, without humour. 'Then, I'm not sure. Bits and pieces.'

Lucy nodded again. She forced her hands into her pockets, wondering why she was struggling to find something to say to this man with whom she had worked for over a year.

'I hear they found Louisa Gant,' Fleming added.

'Is it confirmed?' Lucy asked, trying to hide her annoyance that Burns hadn't come back to her to tell her she'd been right.

'It's on the news so it must be,' Fleming said. 'On Carlin's farm.'

Lucy nodded. 'I was there,' she said. 'We can include Gary Duffy in our list of suspects then,' she added. 'Along with Kay and Carlin.'

Fleming nodded. 'All dead.'

'And I suspect all incapable of having actually groomed either Karen Hughes or Sarah Finn.'

Fleming shook his head. 'I'll not miss any of

this for the next few weeks,' he said. 'All this grimness and . . . and nastiness. All these broken families.'

Lucy nodded. 'I can imagine.'

'No, you can't,' Fleming said, smiling sadly. 'Give it another few years. I've had a lifetime of this. Abused kids and abusive parents. Broken families, dead children. It changes you, you know?'

Lucy nodded again but did not speak.

'All this shit and filth,' Fleming continued. 'When did you last deal with a normal family? Apart from your own?'

'My own family are the least normal I know,' Lucy retorted, laughing.

Fleming smiled again, briefly. 'I began checking up on estate agents this afternoon,' he said. 'Before my suspension sunk in. I've not found who handled the sale of Seamus Doherty's house yet, but I can give you a list of all who didn't. You'll need to check the remaining local ones tomorrow.'

'I know,' Lucy said. 'The Chief Super has already told me I need to stay on top of things.'

Fleming snorted derisively. 'Clark in Forensics also came back to us this morning to say that the dog hairs we took from Kay's house didn't match those found on Karen Hughes's body. Apparently they're checking some mongrel they found wandering around Carlin's now.'

'So Kay might not have been involved at all.'

'Apart from the collection of pictures featuring Karen found in his shed. Eventually.'

'There weren't there the first day we searched it, were they?'

Fleming swallowed dryly. 'I honestly don't know,' he managed after a pause. 'I didn't see them when I checked, but I wasn't in the best of shape. We both know that.'

'It seems odd. All of the evidence suggests Kay, but nothing sticks. He was in the restaurant in the shopping centre where we know the groomer was, but we couldn't find anything on his phone to prove he was the one sending the messages. The dog hairs now are a non-starter. And the collection appears after he dies.'

'Have they found anything connecting him to Carlin's farm yet?'

Lucy shook her head. 'The first I'll hear about it will be on the news. I spoke with Carlin's shrink. She reckoned that he wouldn't have had it in him to groom anyone. That he was easily led.'

'Could Kay not have led him?'

'She said it was possible, but, in her opinion, it was unlikely.'

Fleming shrugged. 'They're both dead now anyway, so we'll maybe never know for sure.'

'Burns wants Sarah Finn's mother to speak at a press thing tomorrow. Make an appeal for the girl to contact her.'

'If you have luck with some of the estate agents and find Doherty with the girl, you might not need her to.'

Lucy nodded. 'And now Louisa Gant is thrown into the mix.'

Fleming straightened up. 'Well, any help you need with that one, your mother's the place to start. She led the original investigation.'

37

It was nearing nine by the time Lucy left Fleming in the car park, having locked up the Unit with his help. They embraced quickly, awkwardly, as she wished him good luck.

Once she was on the road, though, she did not feel like going home to the silence. When her father had been there, while it had been difficult on account of his condition, she had, at least, been so occupied with looking after him that she had little time to think. Now though the silence of the house was oppressive.

Instead of driving home, she cut across the Foyle Bridge at the roundabout, and drove across onto the Culmore Road and up into Petrie Way. She parked up on the pavement, a few houses down from where Joe Quigg now lived and, turning the engine off, sat in the darkness, watching the house. Through the uncurtained windows, she could see the couple who had fostered him moving about. At one stage, the mother came into view, Joe hoisted on her hip, her arm cradling his rump, his arms wrapped around her neck.

Lucy recalled Catherine Quigg, his actual mother. The last time she'd seen her alive had been when Lucy had had to break down the woman's bedroom door and try to get her to sober up and get dressed for her children.

Her mobile rang, and Lucy recognized the

number as being the CID suite in the Strand Road.

'Black? Burns here. I was expecting you to call in with an update.'

'Sorry, sir,' Lucy said. 'I'm out on a call. I've the press release sent out and we've followed up on most of the local estate agents. We've not located who handled the sale of Doherty's house yet, but I should get it finished in the morning.'

'I've rescheduled the press conference for eleven,' Burns said. 'Karen Hughes's funeral is in the morning. Maybe some of the people who knew her might know Sarah Finn too, so I want bodies at the funeral to chat to the younger girls there. Discreetly, obviously.'

'Yes, sir,' Lucy said. 'I'd planned on going anyway.'

'Fine. We've been following up on Carlin,' he said. 'The black dog hairs that were found on Hughes appear to match a black collie Carlin had around the farm.'

'So we know she was in contact with *him* at least, if not Kay,' Lucy commented.

'Indeed,' Burns agreed. 'We've also spoken to the metal theft crew and shown them Carlin's image. Two of them have confirmed he was the figure they saw at the railway tracks.'

Lucy considered the comment. It had been dark, under tree cover. Their identification of him would be shaky at best if it went to court. Not that it would be going to court. Not now.

'Plus we managed to pull CCTV footage from along the Limavady Road that picked up Carlin's car on the way to St Columb's Park

225

around the time Hughes was dumped.'

'Any clear pictures of the driver?'

'Certainly the figure driving looks like Carlin.'

Lucy said nothing, her breath fuzzing against the receiver.

'It'll never see court, but we got him, Lucy. And you were instrumental in that.'

'Thank you, sir,' she said.

'We've ID'd the remains found at the farm, too, as Louisa Gant.'

'I heard, sir. On the news.'

'Well, it looks like Carlin and Kay were in on things together. One of them must have been 'Bradley' or 'Harris' or whatever he was calling himself. Gary Duffy must have been part of their little group at one stage. Once we can establish that the case is closed. We're looking for the connections now.'

'I'd thought of contacting the schools of the two girls to see if there were any events or visitors common to both in the week or two before 'Bradley's' first contact with them. That might help us find the connection between Kay and Carlin and we can work back,' Lucy added.

'Of course, what would be really useful would be to find Sarah Finn,' he stated. 'That's your priority.'

'Of course, sir,' she said.

'There is something else, Lucy. I checked up on the Cunningham case, as you asked.'

Lucy straightened. 'Yes?'

'Intelligence on the ground in Limerick is saying Cunningham is either home or planning on coming home soon. His mother is dying by

226

all accounts. Maybe keep your ear to the ground. If we get a credible lead we'll get a team organized to see if we can't pick him up for the Quigg killings.'

'Thank you, sir,' Lucy said.

'We'll see what we can do.'

'Yes, sir.'

Lucy ended the call and looked up. Joe Quigg's foster father was standing at the end of his drive, a parcel in one hand, the boot of the car yawning open, his face turned towards her.

She started the engine and drove away quickly, avoiding his gaze as she passed.

38

'Keep an ear to the ground,' Burns had said.

Lucy reflected on the comment as she drove. She'd been doing just that from the moment Cunningham had vanished, keeping her ear to the ground. But no one was talking. While none of those who knew Cunningham necessarily agreed with what he had done, nevertheless they had not been prepared to help the police to find him. She'd called at homes of his family and friends, asked local informers and petty criminals who might have known him, had called round the various divisions both of An Garda and PSNI where he was rumoured to be hiding, asking if they'd seen him. No one would help.

Lucy knew then that if Cunningham was back in Derry, there was only one other place for her to look. She didn't even need to check the system for Cunningham's home address. Like Joe Quigg's new family home, she had spent more than one evening sitting parked outside it on the off chance she might catch a glimpse of the man himself. She had not yet satisfactorily considered what exactly she would do with him when she found him.

* * *

The house was the middle one of three in a row of terraced houses. It comprised of two storeys, the front windows in each room curtained, lights visible through the thinness of the fabric. The door was heavy mahogany, with a single frosted glass pane set in the wood.

Lucy pulled up opposite the house and turned off the engine, leaving the key in the ignition to allow her to run the heater. She questioned whether she should call at the house, but knew that not only would she be refused entry, but it would alert Cunningham himself to her presence. Instead, she would sit in her car to watch and wait. Being in her own unmarked vehicle, she would not be recognized as a PSNI officer.

As she sat, a middle-aged couple shuffled past, barely glancing at her, then crossed over and moved up the Cunninghams' driveway. Lucy leaned forward to get a better view of the house. She saw the door opening, recognized the man answering it as Peter Cunningham, the younger brother of Alan. Peter was a low-level dealer who'd been in and out for drugs offences. Strangely, despite the claims by dissident Republicans that they were targeting all known drug dealers in the area, Peter had continued his trade unaffected by the shootings which had claimed a number of his peers. In fact, if anything, he had benefited from their punishments, their hasty retreat from the scene leaving a vacuum that he had quickly filled. The popular view in the Drugs Squad, she'd heard, was that Peter was paying off the right people.

The older couple stepped into the house, the

man proffering a hand to Peter, and, for a moment, Lucy wondered whether the mother had already died and that her wake had started. She felt shame at the hope this thought engendered, for it meant Alan Cunningham would almost certainly come home. However, the two men began to laugh and she guessed not.

Lucy lowered herself back in her seat and fiddled with the radio presets until she found a station playing Villagers, singing about a new-found land. Then she leaned back, resting her eyes for a few moments.

She jumped when she heard the sharp tapping at the window. Glancing across, she realized there was a child, perhaps little more than ten, standing by the passenger side door of her car. He tapped on the glass a second time.

Lucy tried to stretch across to open the door, but her seat belt restricted her. Instead she reached down and depressed the electric window button. The glass slid down and the boy stepped gingerly closer to the car, his chin almost resting on the lower edge of the window frame.

'Do you have a ciggie?' he asked.

'I don't smoke, I'm afraid,' Lucy said. 'Nor should you. It's not good for you.'

'My teacher says that, too.'

'Your teacher's right,' Lucy said. 'What's your name?'

'Why?' the boy asked, angling his head.

Lucy shrugged. 'Just being friendly.'

The boy raised his chin a little. 'I'm not meant to talk to strangers.'

'That's very true,' Lucy said. 'Did your teacher tell you that too?'

'Nah,' the boy said, spitting on the ground next to the car. 'Your lot did.' He smiled quickly then ran.

Lucy felt a sudden rush of cold air as the driver's side door next to her was wrenched open. She turned just as Peter Cunningham's punch connected with her, the movement meaning the punch glanced off her forehead rather than connecting with her temple as he had intended.

He leaned into the car, reaching for her. She felt his hands grapple with her, tugging at her jumper, trying to pull her out of the car. Her seat belt, still connected, prevented him from doing so.

She began to fumble with the keys in the ignition, trying to control her feet sufficiently to press the right pedals to shift the car into gear.

Cunningham continued to pull at her. 'Bitch,' he shouted. 'My mother's dying.' He gave a final tug, then, realizing the futility of it, leaned in and tried landing more punches instead. The first caught Lucy on the mouth, the second catching her below the eye as her head shifted sideways with the earlier impact.

'Bitch,' he spat again. Frustrated by the ineffectual nature of his blows, he moved backwards and, lifting his leg, attempted to stomp in at her, holding on to the door of the car to give himself sufficient leverage to do so.

Lucy finally felt the gear stick shunt into place, heard the engine rev as the ignition caught. She didn't even try to close the door, didn't check to see if anyone was coming. Instead the car jerked forward into the road. Cunningham, still using the door for balance, shifted suddenly sideways, falling backwards onto his rump. Lucy sped forward a few hundred yards, then slowed just long enough to pull the door shut and engage the central locking. She could taste blood in her mouth, like old pennies, could feel the building heat as the skin around her eye began to swell and tighten.

Rounding the corner at the end of the street, she saw the young boy who had stopped at her car standing with a group of kids. They watched her as she passed, each raising their middle finger in a silent salute.

Thursday 20 December

39

The following morning, the cut above her lip had sealed and thickened, swelling the skin of her upper lip into what appeared a parody of a pout. Though her eye had not swollen it was encircled by a bruise, which was sore to the touch when she tried applying foundation to it to cover it up. There was little she could do to conceal the injury to her mouth.

The first thing she did when she arrived in her office was to contact the two schools that Karen and Sarah had attended. Knowing the dates of first contact by 'Bradley'/'Harris', Lucy asked both if they could think of any events that had happened in the school, particularly involving outside visitors, during the week or two prior to that first contact.

The first contact between Karen Hughes and 'Paul Bradley' was made on 18 September. Lucy called Karen's school and spoke to the secretary.

'I'm looking specifically at the week running up to the eighteenth,' Lucy explained. 'Was Karen involved in anything that week? We need to know if she encountered anybody new, maybe through a club or something?'

'Give me a moment, please.'

Lucy listened to an electronic version of 'Ode to Joy' three times before the voice came back on the line. 'We had geography field trips on the Monday, a theatre company visit on the

Wednesday, the school photographer on the Thursday and a Young Enterprise day on the Friday.'

'Can I get details of each of the events, please?' Lucy asked. 'Especially where outside visitors were involved.'

'I'll send them through.'

Sarah Finn's school was a little less organized. The secretary to whom she spoke, who appeared to be dealing with two phone calls at the same time, promised her she would fax through anything she found.

★ ★ ★

Before Karen Hughes's funeral, Lucy called on the remaining estate agents that Fleming had mentioned to her to check if any of them had been responsible for the sale of Seamus Doherty's house and might have a forwarding address for him. She got lucky on the second visit.

The man with whom she spoke, who introduced himself only as Richard, was from a different era. He was a heavy man, white-haired, ruddy-faced, wearing a three-piece tweed suit, the waistcoat straining at the buttons when he sat.

'I can't interest you in a place while you're here?' he asked, smiling as he lowered himself into his seat.

'Maybe later,' Lucy said.

'Now's the time to buy while prices are rock bottom. Someone with a bit of cash could make some canny purchases.'

'The 'bit of cash' part is the problem.' Lucy smiled.

'For all of us,' Richard agreed, though his appearance suggested that the downturn in the market had not had quite the same impact on him as it had on everyone else.

'So, Seamus Doherty. He had a house in Foyle Springs.'

Robert nodded. 'I remember it well. It was one of the last things we sold to be honest. People can't get mortgages you see. We've had stuff on the books for a few years now.'

'Would you have a forwarding address for Mr Doherty? We're looking for him in connection with a missing persons case,' she added. It would be public knowledge after the press conference anyway, she reasoned.

'I see,' Richard said. 'Let me check.'

He turned his attention to the PC on the desk in front of him, his chin almost touching his chest.

Lucy glanced around the office. A secretary sat at the front desk, busily tapping at the keyboard of the computer in front of her. From this angle, Lucy could see that, in fact, she was surfing the net.

'Nothing, I'm afraid,' Richard said. 'I can give you the name of the solicitor who handled the deal for him, but I've no address recorded for him.' He grimaced, as if imparting this news caused him physical pain.

'That's fine,' Lucy said, trying to hide her disappointment. 'Thanks anyway.'

She stood to leave, but Richard remained in his seat, staring at the screen in front of him.

'Wait a bit,' he said. 'Now I think about it, I did price his parents' house for him too.'

'What?'

'After he sold his own house, he asked me to value his parents' house. I think his mother had died a few months earlier and he couldn't decide what to do with the house. He asked me to give him a valuation for it.'

'Did he sell it?'

'No. I don't think he thought the money he'd have got was worth it. The house was in a bit of a state from what I remember. It needed new windows, central heating, roof fixed, the whole bit. In the good days he'd have managed ninety plus for it, I thought, but with the crash, he'd have been lucky to have passed thirty-five.'

'Do you remember where the house was?'

Richard shook his head. 'I'm trying to think. It was past Dungiven. Up on the Glenshane. There was a circle of trees round it. I remember that. Bleak, like.'

'Would you have the address?'

'I should have somewhere. I have a diary I keep valuation stuff in, in case someone comes back to you. I'll need to dig out the old ones and take a check through it. It was a few weeks after we finalized sale of the one in the city, so it should be easy enough found.'

'Could you check now?' Lucy said, a little more impatiently than she intended.

Richard shook his head again, the skin beneath his chin wobbling with the effort. 'I've my old diaries in my office at home. I can take a run out and get it for you. I'll call you as soon as I find it.'

'Is home close?' Lucy asked. 'I could run you there.' She glanced at her watch. Karen Hughes's funeral was in three quarters of an hour.

'Ballybofey,' Richard said. 'I'll head up myself in a bit. I've a light morning anyway.'

Lucy knew that the journey there would take the guts of an hour. 'I have a funeral at ten,' she said. 'Would you be able to call me with the address when you find it?'

Richard nodded.

'The missing person case we're investigating?' Lucy added. 'The missing person in question is a child.'

The comment had the desired effect.

'I'll go now, then, so,' Richard said, pushing back his seat and standing.

40

A guard of honour, comprising a group of Karen's classmates, lined the pathway up to the church. Lucy passed along them, nodding at one or two as she did so. At the top of the walkway, Karen Hughes's mother, Marian, stood, supported by two older men, both bearing a strong familial resemblance to her. They held an arm each, as if the woman was physically unable to remain upright unaided. Her face was slick with tears as she nodded her head in acknowledgement of the condolences offered to her by two passing mourners.

Lucy approached her, her hand extended. 'Ms Hughes,' she said. 'I'm sorry for your loss.'

The woman stared at her, trying to place her perhaps, and Lucy could see in the glaze of her eyes that she had obviously taken something to help her make it through the morning.

'Thank you,' she said, having failed to recognize her. 'These are my brothers.'

Lucy smiled grimly as she took the hand of each, one after the other, and offered her sympathies on their loss. She reflected that, in the entire time she had known Karen, she had not once seen or heard of either man.

Across from where they stood, she caught a glimpse of Robbie and moved over to him. They hugged briefly, Lucy breaking away from the embrace first.

'What the hell happened to your face?' Robbie asked, holding her at arm's length as he examined her injuries.

Lucy moved out of his grasp. 'Nothing. They look worse than they are.'

'They look pretty bad. Who hurt you?'

'How are you?' she asked in reply.

'OK,' Robbie commented, reluctant to allow the subject to be changed. 'Considering.'

Lucy nodded.

'You?'

'OK,' she returned. 'Considering.'

It was Robbie's turn to nod. 'Apart from someone having beaten you up,' he added, a little bitterly.

'I wasn't beaten up,' Lucy remarked. 'How's Gavin?'

Robbie hesitated, clearly aware that Lucy didn't want to discuss her injuries further, but reluctant to let the topic drop. Finally he said, 'Not so good. He's inside already. He's hurting.'

'For Karen or his dad?' Lucy asked.

'Both,' Robbie said.

At that moment, a blue, unmarked car pulled up at the foot of the pathway and Eoghan Harkin stepped out, before the car drove away again. So close to his release, he would be allowed to attend the funeral unaccompanied. Still, Lucy could tell by the bulge around his ankle that he was wearing a tracing bracelet, just in case he had thoughts of not returning to finish the final days of his sentence. Having made it this far, it seemed unlikely he would risk his early release for the sake of a matter of days.

As he approached her, Lucy could see he recognized her from the night she had broken the news of Karen's death. He barely glanced in his wife's direction, save for a curt nod to the two brothers, never raising his head enough to make eye contact with either. No love lost there, Lucy guessed.

'Inspector,' he said, as he drew level with Lucy.

'Sergeant,' she corrected him. 'I'm sorry again for your loss, Mr Harkin.'

The man acknowledged the comment with a slight raising of his chin. 'How are you doing?' he added, addressing Robbie.

'I'm sorry for your loss, Mr Harkin,' Robbie echoed.

'This is Robbie McManus,' Lucy explained. 'Karen's key social worker.'

'Thanks for all you did for her,' Harkin said. Lucy could see that Robbie was looking for any hidden meaning in the comment. 'What happened to you?' This time, he was addressing Lucy herself. He lifted one nicotine-yellowed finger and rubbed at the side of his mouth.

'Nothing,' Lucy said, then, realizing the response did not satisfactorily explain the injuries she bore, 'I had an incident with a suspect,' she lied.

'I thought maybe it was that Cunningham boy. I heard on the jungle drums that he hit a copper a few smacks last night for staking out his house.'

Lucy reddened enough for Harkin to know he'd hit a nerve. He smiled wryly. Lucy turned her head slightly, keen to avoid Robbie's gaze.

'Had Cunningham anything to do with Karen?' Harkin said quietly.

Lucy shook her head. 'His brother killed a child and her mother a while back, then did a runner. I'd heard he might be back in Derry. You didn't happen to hear anything about that did you? On your jungle drums?'

Harkin shook his head. 'Alan? He's a horrible wee bastard. That would be his form all right, killing women and kids.'

'It's a pity no one else shares your assessment. I can't get anything concrete on his whereabouts. No one will talk.'

'Somebody must be protecting him then. Someone with a bit of clout in the community,' Harkin reasoned. 'By the way, I heard you were there when the guy that killed Karen got it.'

'Gene Kay or Peter Carlin?'

'I was told Carlin,' Harkin said. 'Who's Kay?'

'He may have been involved too,' Lucy nodded. 'Did you know Peter Carlin?'

Harkin shook his head. 'Not until I heard about it inside. One of the guards told me.'

'But you knew Gary Duffy?'

'The guy who killed the Gant girl?'

Lucy nodded. 'They appear to have been working together.'

'I remember Duffy all right from years back,' Harkin commented. 'He was bad news. A real hawk. Jackie Logue is the one who could tell you about him. Jackie took over from Duffy after he went inside. Except Jackie wasn't as hard line.'

'Did he and Duffy know each other?'

Harkin shrugged. 'I'm not too sure. I never

243

heard of this guy Carlin before all this though.'

Lucy gazed down towards the roadway, long enough to see Chief Superintendent Burns arrive. He made straight for Karen's mother, his hand outstretched.

'Did he suffer?' Harkin hissed suddenly. 'Carlin?'

Lucy glanced at him. 'He drowned. Make of that what you will.'

Harkin snorted derisively. 'It's a pity you let him die. If you'd kept him for me, I'd have made sure the world became a much lonelier place for Alan Cunningham as a thank you.'

'You know where Cunningham is?' Lucy said, quickly turning to face him.

Harkin shrugged. 'Not necessarily. But, as I said, someone with clout in the community could do all kinds of things. I'd have made sure he wasn't protected no more. You'd have had to find him yourself, of course.'

Lucy felt her breath catch in her chest, felt herself unsteady on her feet.

''Course, it's a moot point now, isn't it?' Harkin added, then moved on into the church, where his daughter lay.

'You went after Cunningham,' Robbie said suddenly, gripping Lucy by the arm. 'Jesus Christ, Lucy! You're going to get yourself killed, you know that?'

Lucy pulled her arm away. 'What should I do? Forget about her?'

'You don't need to forget her, but . . . '

'But what?' Lucy demanded.

'But you need to let it go, Lucy.'

'I don't let things go,' she snapped.

Robbie swallowed dryly. 'You let me go,' he muttered.

Lucy was caught by surprise by the tenderness in his voice. The regret. She struggled to respond.

'Is that why you wanted the child's address? To reopen your wounds?'

'I wanted to make sure he's OK.'

'You know, he'll not even remember what happened, Lucy. Nor should you want him to. You're the only one still carrying that with you.'

Lucy nodded. 'That suits me fine. Someone has to give a shit.'

'People do give a shit,' Robbie whispered urgently, as the people around them began moving inside the church for the funeral service. 'We just don't forget to live, too. I'm sorry I ever gave you that address.'

Lucy felt a vibration in her pocket. 'Don't worry about it,' she said, pulling out her phone. 'I'll not tell anyone where I got it from.'

'That's not what I'm worried about,' Robbie managed, before she stepped away from him, putting the mobile to her ear. It was the estate agent.

'DS Black? Richard O'Dowd here. I've got that address for you.'

Lucy made her apologies to no one in particular and ran to her car.

41

The Glenshane Pass, cutting through the Sperrin mountain range, was named after the eighteenth-century highwayman, Shane Crosagh O'Maolain, who had operated there before being caught and hanged with his brothers in the Diamond in Derry. His name, Crosagh, referred to the pock-marks on his face which were a feature of his family. Ironically, the name applied equally well to the topography of area where he had lived, the thick bogland of which undulated along the valley.

The house that O'Dowd had valued was situated on the outer edge of the Glenshane Forest, just under ten miles beyond Dungiven. The Pass itself was heavy with traffic heading from Derry towards Belfast. The mountain area around it, though, was sparsely inhabited. The land was primarily peatland, the grass and scrub being grazed upon by a few hardy sheep, yellowed and wiry. The soil beneath, however, was black, meaning the run-off water from it was like stout as it cascaded down the rock face bordering the roadway on one side. To the other, Lucy could look down over the valley of the Pass beneath, where the River Roe began to gather strength as it cut down through the mountains.

Lucy had entered the address of the property in Google Maps, but it had not been recognized. Instead, she had taken a series of directions over the phone from O'Dowd. She had passed the entrance way to the abandoned quarry, which had carved into the sides of the mountain, its rusting equipment seeming to breathe dust with each gust of wind carrying up the valley. Further along the road, she passed the Ponderosa bar, a sign outside proclaiming it the highest public house in the country.

Finally, as the road began to flatten after the climb from Dungiven, she saw the roadway to her right that O'Dowd had said she should take. She pulled off the main Glenshane Road onto this narrower one and drove parallel to the main flow of traffic for a few hundred yards, before the road cut sharply to the right and took her down, into the valley, towards the dark mass of the forest.

O'Dowd had warned her to look out for a further turning, this time onto a laneway. In fact, she had already passed it by the time she registered its presence and had to reverse several hundred yards in order to take the turn.

The laneway was narrow, the hedging on both sides scratching against the doors of her car as she progressed along it. Up the centre of the lane, the tarmac had risen in a central ridge from which thick tussocks of grass had grown.

After a few minutes on the laneway, Lucy finally saw the house that O'Dowd had visited, standing enshadowed by a circle of trees surrounding it. While the building was not as ramshackle as Lucy had expected, it was, without doubt, in need of repair.

Still, as she pulled into the driveway, she noticed the two-tone effect of the roof slates where the newer red ones stood out against the moss-thick russet ones with which the roof had originally been tiled. There was no doubt that someone had been at the house more recently than O'Dowd's valuation visit. That didn't necessarily mean that Doherty hadn't managed to sell it to someone else, without O'Dowd's help, since then.

She drew up outside the house and, reaching across, unlocked the glove compartment and removed her service gun. Fitting it inside her coat pocket, she got out, leaving the car unlocked lest she needed to make a quick getaway. She realized that she should have brought support but, with Fleming suspended, there were few alternatives. Besides, there was no guarantee that the house was even occupied.

She moved across to the door, passing the main window that carried a single thick crack running across the width of its pane. The glass itself was coated with dust so she was unable to see anything in the gloom beyond.

She tapped on the door twice and, stepping back, regarded the front of the house. Despite her first impressions, she could see curtains hanging down the sides of the window of the small room to the left. She thought she saw something shift quickly from her sight and, moving across, she leaned against the window, using her glove to smear away the dust and allow her a view inside. She tensed as she now saw a small fire burning in the hearth. She stepped back and, glancing up, realized she had missed the thin skeins of smoke drifting against the cloud-grey sky above the chimney of the house.

She heard a click and the front door opened. She shifted quickly back to come face to face with Seamus Doherty. He stared at her, clearly waiting for her to speak.

'Mr Doherty?'

'Yes?'

'My name is Detective Sergeant Lucy Black. I'm with the Public Protection Unit. Can I come in?'

She motioned as if to step into the house, but Doherty held his ground, moving more fully into the doorway to block the entrance.

'Why? Is something wrong?'

'I'm looking for Sarah Finn, the daughter of your partner. I'd like to search your property. Please let me in.'

Doherty licked dryly at his lip, glancing past Lucy, clearly trying to gauge whether she was on her own. His eyes flitted across her face, his thoughts racing.

Lucy moved her hand towards her pocket, feeling for the weight of the gun she had placed there. Doherty saw the motion and, in an instant, had slammed the door on her.

'Shit,' Lucy snapped, pulling her gun free of her coat pocket and, raising her boot, kicking at the door. Its state belied its sturdiness, for though it rattled in its frame, it did not move.

Lucy stepped back, allowing herself more room, and kicked a second time, harder. She heard the crack as the wood around the catch splintered. A third kick and the door swung open. She moved into the room quickly, her back against the wall, her gun held in front of her.

'Mr Doherty. My colleagues are on their way. Please surrender yourself.' She moved into the room proper, scanning for hiding places. A bookcase against one wall, a heavy unit in the centre of the floor, on which sat two cereal bowls. A threadbare sofa pulled forward to meet it.

'Sarah?' Lucy shouted. 'Sarah Finn?'

To the rear of the house, she heard a crash, as if a piece of furniture had been knocked over. Lucy moved quickly, still scanning the room, trying to keep her back to the areas she knew to be clear of potential hiding spots.

The room she was in opened out into the kitchen, where a chair lay on the floor. To her right was a hallway opening onto three further rooms. She moved up the darkened corridor, swinging quickly into the first room to the left. A bedroom, the bed unmade, a tangle of clothes on the floor. Jeans, a jumper, men's boots. A paperback book steepled on the bedside unit. The bed was old, cast iron, high-legged enough to offer Lucy an unrestricted view through to the far wall.

Satisfied, she turned to the second room, just a little further up the hallway, on the opposite side. A bathroom. Untidy. The toilet seat down.

The last room was to her right again. Lucy pushed open the door with her foot, then moved quickly in. A second bedroom, bigger than the first, the lower half of the walls panelled in dark wood. The bed was made here. A bag sat on a chair in the corner. On the bed, its head resting against the pillow, sat a tattered child's toy, a white rabbit with one ear hanging loose over the eye, the stuffing showing at the stitching.

'Sarah?' Lucy shouted. 'I'm with the police. Don't be afraid.'

Lucy was turning to leave the room when she noticed a smaller door seemingly cut into the wood panelling in the corner opposite where the chair sat. She moved across and banged it with her foot. Gripping the small handle, she twisted it and pulled the door open. Beyond lay a set of wooden steps leading downwards, beneath the house.

'Sarah?' Lucy shouted.

She went down the steps towards the darkened room below. As she moved beneath the upper floor level, she realised that there was some natural light leaking into the cellar from a small window high up on the back walls.

Lucy moved down, surveying the area beneath as the objects scattered about began to take form in the gloom. She realized that at one end of the space, under the window, stood a heavy wooden table. Above it, hanging from small hooks in the wall, hung a set of meat cleavers.

Gasping, Lucy moved quickly across. The knives were clean, one or two badged with spots of rust.

'Jesus,' she muttered.

Suddenly she heard a movement behind her and turned. At first she thought Doherty was running at her, but as she raised her gun to shoot, she saw him grab at the handrail of the steps as if to pull himself up the steps again, as if

251

to escape from where he had been hiding in the cellar.

'Stop,' Lucy shouted. 'I *will* shoot you.'

Doherty paused, his foot on the bottom step, then slowly raised his hands.

'On the floor,' Lucy shouted. 'Now! Face down.'

'You've got it wrong,' Doherty began.

'Shut up,' Lucy snapped, pushing him onto the floor, kneeling on his back as she pulled two plastic cable ties from her coat pocket and tightened them around Doherty's wrists.

Just then, something in the periphery of her vision moved and she saw a figure rush down the steps towards her. Sarah Finn.

She stood to embrace the girl she had rescued. Instead, Finn lashed out at her with her fists, battering at Lucy as she struggled to contain the child.

'Leave him alone,' the girl screamed. 'Don't hurt him.'

42

A response team soon arrived from Dungiven station after Lucy had phoned through for support. They had brought with them a local doctor who examined Sarah Finn in the large bedroom in which she had been sleeping. The girl had wept uncontrollably as Doherty had been led away to be taken into Dungiven where he would be held for questioning. Sinead Finn had been called and was being brought to her daughter by Chief Superintendent Burns himself. A forensics team was on the way from Derry as was a social worker, after Lucy had called Robbie. Sarah would not be allowed back with her mother until she had been assessed by Social Services.

Lucy, meanwhile, sat in front of the fire, warming herself. The girl's reaction was not unusual, she reasoned. Often, vulnerable children became attached to those who had exploited them, believing the abuse they had suffered to be a form of love. But Lucy found the use of the two bedrooms unusual. They clearly had been sleeping in different rooms. Doherty had told her she had got it wrong. Only when the doctor had finished, would Lucy be able to ask the girl herself directly.

* * *

The interview room into which they were led in Dungiven was old-fashioned, the ceilings high, the pipework of the heating system running along the base of the walls, the pipes painted the same puce shade as the walls. They could hear water gurgling through the pipes while they spoke, as the heating system shuddered into life.

Sarah Finn sat in the seat opposite Lucy. Ideally, Lucy would have preferred there to be no desk between them lest it create an adversarial atmosphere that she did not want.

Finn looked a little different from the school picture that Lucy had been using in the search for the girl. The brown hair of the image was actually sandy in reality. Perhaps as a result of the past few days, the puppy fat she had carried in the image had gone from her face, even if the top she wore seemed swollen a little around the softness of her stomach.

Robbie sat down, but not before pulling his chair around so that he was positioned midway between Lucy and the girl. Sarah wiped at the tears that had gathered around her eyes as she waited for Lucy to begin. She'd met her mother, Sinead, half an hour previous; their conversation had been little more than muffled cries from the girl and promises from the mother that she'd never let her go again.

Sinead Finn had protested when she was told that she could not be present when her daughter would be interviewed. Lucy explained to her that the girl was more likely to tell them the full truth without the mother's presence distracting her. Especially when her statement might implicate

254

Finn's own partner.

The man himself, having been already taken to another interview room in the station, had not said a word following his protestation to Lucy that she had got it wrong.

'It's good to finally meet you, Sarah,' Lucy began. 'I'm DS Lucy Black. I work for the Public Protection Unit. I deal with cases involving vulnerable people and especially young people.'

Finn swallowed nervously and nodded, though Lucy had not asked a question.

'This is Robbie. He's a social worker who will be sitting in on the interview. Obviously, you can tell us anything at all that you want. Nothing you can tell us will shock us or make us think any less of you. I can't promise that what you tell us will be confidential; we might need to use some of the things you say, if we decide to prosecute someone because of your abduction.'

The girl muttered something, her head lowered, her fingers playing with a strip of laminate peeling off the edge of the table.

'Sorry?' Lucy said. 'We didn't catch that, Sarah. You need to speak as clearly as you can, because this is being recorded so that we can be sure we don't miss anything you tell us.'

The girl looked up through the loose strands of her fringe. 'I weren't abducted. I went with Seamus.'

Lucy nodded. 'Maybe you'd tell us in your own words what happened over the past few days? Yeah?'

'I knew Seamus was going away for a bit and decided to go with him.'

'Why?'

The girl paused. She picked off the laminate strip, then muttered an apology and tried to reapply it to the table's edge.

'I wanted to get away. I thought Seamus was going to Manchester. That's what he'd told Mum. But he weren't. I didn't know until I heard the van stop. I thought we were at the boat. When I got out, we were in the middle of the countryside. I'd nowhere else to go.'

'Did Mr Doherty know you were in his van?'

She shook her head. 'I took some money from the post office and packed my bag. I thought if I got to the boat, I'd hide out and get a lift somewhere else.'

'Why?' Lucy asked.

'I wanted to get away.'

'Did this have anything to do with 'Simon Harris', Sarah?' Lucy asked.

The girl glanced up quickly, tears swelling in her eyes. Just as quickly she looked down at her lap again, sniffing. A tear dripped onto the floor from her bowed head. 'I don't know who that is.'

'We found your phone, Sarah,' Lucy said. 'We know who 'Harris' was.'

If Sarah realized the significance of the past tense she didn't show it. Meanwhile, Lucy realized an incongruity in her story.

'You said you didn't get out of the van until Mr Doherty stopped at the house on the Glenshane?'

Finn nodded.

'But we found your phone in a lay-by along the Glenshane Road.'

The girl nodded again. 'Seamus took it off me the next day and dumped it somewhere. He didn't tell me where.'

'Why?

'The messages.'

''Harris''s messages?'

Finn nodded again, the tears coming more freely now.

'Did you not want to get any more messages from him?'

Finn shook her head, sniffing loudly. She raised her head, her hair sticking to the dampness of her cheeks.

'I told Seamus that he'd given me the phone in the first place. He'd 'Find a Friend' set up on it.'

'What?'

'It's a thing where you can see on a map on your phone where all your friends are. It meant he knew where I was if he wanted to find me. I told Seamus. We switched it off, but I didn't think it was enough. So he took the phone away.'

'You don't have to be afraid of 'Simon Harris', Sarah,' Lucy said. 'He's dead.'

The girl momentarily brightened, then at once, her expression seemed to darken and she began twisting one hand around the other. 'That wasn't his real name,' she said.

'We know,' Lucy said. 'He'd loads of names he used on Facebook. We know he targeted other girls, too.'

The girl straightened a little. 'You're sure he's dead?'

Lucy nodded. 'I watched him drown myself.'

She managed a smile, which was reciprocated by Sarah Finn. 'So you don't need to be afraid any more,' Lucy said. 'You can tell us everything.'

'Can I get a drink?' Finn said. 'And can you let Seamus out, too? He's been looking after me.'

Lucy glanced quickly at Robbie who raised his eyebrows sceptically.

'We'll certainly manage a drink,' Lucy said. 'Let's see what you have to say first before we worry about the other thing, eh?'

43

'It started out OK,' Finn said, sipping from the can of Diet Coke she'd been brought from the Mace across the street from the station.

'We'd meet in town sometimes. I knew the first time I met him that he was older than he'd said in his profile. He said he preferred the company of teenagers 'cause we always told the truth. We weren't phonies, he said.'

She glanced up at Lucy, then quickly to Robbie. 'I tried to stay away from him, but he seemed harmless. He'd talk about music and that. But he had some really cool bands I'd never heard of. He'd let me listen to some. And we always met in the town where there was people about, so it was never weird or anything.'

She paused, sipping again at the Coke. A little dribbled as she lowered the can and she lifted her hand and wiped at her mouth with the back of her wrist.

'There was this one band I'd never even heard of. A singer. Jessica Hoop. He let me hear some of her songs. He said he thought I'd like it.'

She paused again, staring down at her hands. 'I bet if you asked my mum what music I liked, *she* wouldn't be able to tell you,' she snapped. 'She'd not have a notion. She'd not care.'

'But he did,' Lucy said softly. The girl needed to justify what had happened as a result of her trusting 'Harris'. She needed to know that Lucy

259

understood. And she did.

She nodded. 'He told me he'd put it on a disc for me. Then, when we met the next time, he gave me a phone with a whole load of stuff on it. I didn't want to take it, but he said it was an old one he didn't need any more; he'd got a new one on contract and was just going to dump it anyway, he said. He'd put all this music on it for me. I didn't want him to think I wasn't grateful. He'd gone to all that effort.'

She finished her Coke, pressing on the two sides of the can, pinching with her fingers until it bent double in her hands.

'He phoned me and said he was going to a party. Did I want to come with him? They'd be loads of people — girls my own age and that, so I'd not to be worrying.

'I told my mum I was going out with my friends. She didn't give a shit anyway. Half the time I was there she didn't know it anyhow. She'd not care. Her and Seamus were out all the time when he was here.'

She placed the can on the table, moved it slightly until it sat just in the position she wanted it, a small act of control to compensate for the fact that the events she was describing would soon involve those over which she had had none.

'He picked me up at the bus depot. Me and another girl. I didn't know her. He said he would drop us off then he had to collect a friend. The other girl seemed to know him really well. He handed her a bottle of cider. She took some and gave it to me. I wasn't going to drink it, but she looked at me like I was just a kid, like I was too young to drink. I'd had some before, at parties and that. So I took it.'

She swallowed. 'When we'd finished that bottle he handed us back another one.'

'Where was the party?' Lucy asked.

Sarah shook her head. 'I don't know. It was dark outside of the car. And the cider was making everything weird. It was in the country somewhere because I asked him to stop. I thought I was going to be sick and he pulled in along the road. There were no street lights or anything. I could see cows watching me from the field beside where we stopped. They were just staring at me. I thought I'd be sick, but I wasn't. Not then anyway. Later.

'We arrived at this old house. It smelt bad, like it wasn't being used all the time. There were loads of men in the house, all older than us. And a few girls sitting in the living room. I knew one of them to see, from about town. They were all drinking cider and beers. We went in with them and starting drinking.'

She paused again, moved the can again.

'I didn't notice that they were being taken out of the room. One at a time. Then 'Simon' appeared. He was smiling. Said he had something to give me. A present. He didn't want the other girls to see, in case they were jealous. We went into one of the rooms by ourselves. He took out something in a packet. Said it would give my drink a kick. He put it in the drink, gave it a swish around and then took some, to show it was OK. Except . . . except I don't think he took any at all.

'I drank it because I knew he wanted me to. Then he started kissing me. I felt like I had to — he'd been so kind to me.'

The girl lowered her head, her tears coming freely now.

'I don't remember what happened after that. Only what had happened when I woke up again.'

She glanced at Lucy, scouring her face to see if she was being judged. She ignored Robbie completely.

'What he had done. What he done to me.'

She shuddered now and she spluttered into sobs. Lucy moved from her seat, round to where Sarah sat, put her arms around the girl and held her while she cried.

'Ssh,' she said finally. 'He can't do anything to you anymore.'

She looked up at Robbie, who was sitting, his hands folded in his lap, his expression studiously neutral. 'Let's take a break, shall we?'

44

As they sat again after a toilet break for Sarah, Lucy sensed that something had changed about the girl, that in the telling of what had happened, and perhaps in the knowledge that 'Simon Harris' — as she knew him — was dead, the girl had found some degree of comfort, a modicum of solace in knowing she had been heard and believed.

'Will I start where I left off?' the girl asked, sitting.

'Please,' Lucy said.

She brushed her hair from her face. Her cheeks were dry now, but the skin still flushed, the eyes red-rimmed with crying, the whites of her eyes threaded with veins. She looked somehow younger than her fifteen years.

'It happened a few times after that,' the girl said. Lucy realized that far from Sarah feeling relieved at what had passed, she had instead simply been steeling herself for the rest of the story. 'He'd invite me to a party. He'd pick me up with some other girls and we'd get drunk. Most of the time it was in the same house. A couple of times it was somewhere different. A bit nicer. Further away, though. Near the sea, I think. There was a room with an old pool table in it. We'd all hang around in there until he came back with more drink and . . . whatever it was.'

'Did he always rape you?'

The girl hesitated a moment before answering. 'I didn't know if it was rape or not. Because I'd had the cider and that. He said I'd agreed.'

'You can't agree, Sarah,' Lucy said. 'You're too young. He knew that.'

The girl flushed, her eyes brimming again. She inhaled, held the breath a moment, then let it go. 'Sometimes others did it. I woke one time and there was someone leaving the room that I didn't know. It wasn't 'Simon'. But I knew what he'd done.'

Lucy pulled a handful of tissues from the box on the table. Sarah took them and rubbed at her nose. She raised her head a little, as if to stymie her tears.

'How often did this happen?' Lucy asked.

'Every week,' Sarah said. 'We'd go every week.'

'Always to the same house?'

She shook her head. 'Two different places. It was like taking turns week about week; one week in the smelly house, the other in the place with the pool table.'

'Were the men there always the same?'

She shook her head. 'Some.'

'And what about your mum? Did she not wonder where you were all night?'

Sarah shrugged. 'She'd be out of it when I got home. She'd not even know I'd been out to start with.'

Lucy paused as she considered how best to word the next question without sounding accusatory. 'I don't want you to take this the wrong way, Sarah, but I need to know. Why did you meet with him again, after the first time he raped you, Sarah?'

'He said if I didn't, he'd hurt my mum.'

'Did you ever try telling your mother about what was happening?'

The girl shook her head. 'He said if I told her, they'd kill her. He said he knew who she was. They'd . . . he said he'd . . . shoot her.' Though the girl paused as she spoke as if to give the impression that she was too upset to speak freely, Lucy wasn't wholly convinced.

'What did he really say, Sarah?'

The girl stared at her, her mouth hanging a little open. 'He said he knew who sold her stash to her. That they'd put something in it if I told. She'd just not wake up again, he said.'

'But you told Seamus? Your mum said you didn't get on.'

'We didn't,' the girl conceded quietly. 'I didn't mean for him to find out. I just wanted to hide in the van. But I'd no choice. He wanted to take me back to my mum, but I knew Simon'd think I'd told her when I hadn't answered his messages and that.'

Lucy considered what the girl had said. 'Did Seamus ever try anything on with you?'

'God, no,' she replied. 'He made me up my own room. I didn't know he'd another house.'

'Did he tell you why he lied about going to Manchester?'

Sarah shrugged. 'He said Mum's using got to him. She was fun to be about for a while, then she started all that shit and he needed to get a breather from her for a few days. I know how he felt.'

'Why now?'

Sarah rubbed at her nose, balled the tissues in her hand and buried it deep in the pocket of the hooded top she wore. 'What?'

'Why leave now? What happened? Why not run away weeks ago?'

Immediately, she saw the girl glance at the doorway, as if to reassure herself that there was a way out. She licked at her lips. 'Can I get another Coke?' she asked.

'Why now?' Lucy persisted. 'Tell me that and we can take another breather if you need to.'

Sarah Finn seemed to consider the offer. 'The girl the first night. The one with the cider. I saw her a few times after that. At the parties. She was a nice girl. She looked after some of the others when they were hurting after . . . you know. She took care of them. Even when she was being hurt herself.'

Lucy could feel something gnawing at her insides, sensing already where the conversation was headed.

'There was a party at the weekend. All weekend. I was there just on Saturday night. But she was there. She'd been there for a few days. She was out of it, completely. It was like she didn't know where she was or what was happening. Well, I saw her again after the party.'

'Where?'

'She was the girl they found dead on the train tracks. Karen was her name, I think.'

They left Sarah to have her Coke while Lucy went to the main office and called through for the Strand Road to fax through pictures of both Karen Hughes and Carlin himself. Though the quality of the faxes wasn't ideal, both were still recognizable. 'Is this the girl you met?' Lucy asked, handing Sarah the image of Karen Hughes as she re-entered the room.

The girl looked at the image, her eyes flushing once more. She nodded. 'That's her.'

'One more question, Sarah,' Lucy said. 'This man.' She handed Sarah the page with Carlin's picture on it.

'I know him,' the girl said, dropping the page on the desk as if it had scalded her simply to hold it. 'He was one of them. He was at the parties.'

'One of them?' Lucy said. 'He was 'Simon Harris'.'

Sarah Finn's eyes widened, her face paling under the harsh fluorescent glare of the strip lighting in the room.

'That's not 'Simon Harris'. That's nothing like him. Is he the man who died? This man?'

Lucy glanced at Robbie, before nodding lightly.

'Jesus Christ,' Sarah Finn keened, backing into the corner, balling in on herself, wrapping her arms around her knees. 'Jesus. He's going to kill me.'

'No one's going to kill you, Sarah,' Lucy said, moving to the girl. 'I promise.'

The girl looked up at her from where she sat, her face a mask of disbelief. Lucy could think of nothing to say that might convince her otherwise.

45

Despite their best efforts, neither Lucy nor Robbie could convince Sarah Finn that she was safe from 'Harris'. Eventually Robbie agreed that her mother be allowed to spend some time with her in the interview room, though under his supervision, in the hope that her presence might help settle the girl a little. Lucy took Sinead Finn's arrival as an opportunity to check how the interview with Seamus Doherty was developing.

Burns was leading the interview with Doherty in Interview Room 2. He glanced round with some irritation when Lucy first tapped on the door, but upon seeing who it was, rose and came out to her.

'Has she said anything we can use on him?' he asked. '*He*'s saying nothing.'

Lucy shook her head. 'She claims that she hid away in his lorry. She got out when she felt it stop, thinking she was on the ferry. Instead, he was parked up at the house. She was at a party with Karen Hughes the night before she died, during the time Karen was missing.'

'Does she know if Carlin killed her?'

Lucy shook her head. 'She says Carlin wasn't 'Harris'. He was one of the others.'

'What others? Maybe she's confused. Give her a breather and try again.'

Lucy raised a hand to silence him, then

realized the inappropriateness of the gesture to her superior.

'She was groomed by 'Harris'. They met up a few times in town. He eventually gave her the phone with some music on it, made a show of saying it was nothing too big. After a while he invited her to a party. He got her drunk, slipped her something in a drink and raped her. She says it happened several times after that, at other parties. Then, when she was passed out, she thinks other men raped her too. She recalls seeing at least one leaving her room as she came round from whatever 'Harris' had given her.'

'Was Carlin one of the ones who raped her?'

Lucy nodded. 'He was at the parties. We can assume if he was there, he was involved in some way. I need to get pictures of Gene Kay, too, to see if he was there. But she says 'Harris' definitely isn't Carlin. I think we're looking for someone younger.'

Burns swore softly under his breath. 'We *need* to connect Kay. After the prick burning to death over it.'

Lucy said nothing for a moment, guessing that his need to connect Kay had more to do with expediency than justice. 'She says Karen had been at the last party for most of the weekend. She saw her there on the Saturday. I think she went missing on the Thursday because she was taken away to a house party for the weekend.'

'Why did they kill her?'

'Maybe she recognized someone she shouldn't have,' Lucy suggested. 'But if she'd been there all weekend — been at the parties before — she'd presumably have encountered whoever it was before that.'

'She was seen alive on the day before her death? On the Saturday?'

Lucy nodded.

'Then what happened on the Sunday that would have caused someone to kill her?'

Lucy thought about it. She had done the press releases about her being missing, but that had been on Friday and had been in the Saturday press.

'Her father,' she said suddenly. 'The Sunday papers — one of them ran a story about her father. They'd connected her with Eoghan Harkin somehow.'

'Whoever had her knew her father then?' Burns offered.

'Maybe,' Lucy said. 'Or maybe they were just afraid of what he'd do if he found out. Sarah said that 'Harris' said he'd kill her mother if she told. That threat might have been a little harder to use about Eoghan Harkin.'

'It couldn't have been a message to him? Retaliation in some way?'

Lucy shook her head. 'The body was set up to look like she'd killed herself on the train tracks. If someone wanted to send a message they'd want him to know she'd been murdered. In this case, they wanted to kill her and cover it up. Make it look like suicide.'

'Which would only be believable if she was the type to kill herself.'

'She was depressed,' Lucy said. 'She was struggling with self-esteem issues. She was the perfect candidate for it. And the perfect candidate for grooming, too. Lacking in confidence, open to flattery, unstable home life.'

All of which applied equally to Sarah Finn, Lucy reflected. 'The question is, how did the groomer know that they were perfect candidates for it?'

'Ask the girl, see if she knows. See if he gave her any hints about where he first saw her. And get a description.'

★ ★ ★

Lucy stopped at the main office again to phone through for a picture of Gene Kay. It took all of thirty seconds for Sarah Finn to confirm for her that Kay was not 'Simon Harris' either, nor indeed had she ever seen him at any of the parties.

'You're sure?' Lucy asked. 'Look again at the image. He might have been dressed differently.'

The girl studied the image, examining the eyes and mouth, covering part of the face with the flat of her hand to better focus on particular features. Finally she shook her head. 'I've never seen him before. I'd remember any of the people there if I saw them again. He wasn't there.'

'And the other man I showed you earlier, he was there but wasn't 'Simon Harris'?'

Finn nodded her head. 'I remember his face. Simon was younger than them, in his twenties maybe. Thin-faced. Short dark hair. He wasn't an old man.'

'But this guy was definitely not involved?' she

272

asked, pointing to Kay's picture.

'I never saw him. Not once.'

If that was the case, Lucy realized, then how had the collection of images, taken from the parties, ended up in Kay's house, after Fleming had checked it and found nothing there the day before?

46

Robbie eventually agreed that Sarah Finn be allowed home with her mother, though only with the understanding that they would be visited daily and that Sinead Finn was to agree to enter an addiction programme. The woman announced that Seamus Doherty was no longer welcome in her home, having lied to her and kept her daughter from her for so long. Having been the only person Sarah felt able to confide in, Doherty now found himself excluded from the girl's life.

Lucy drove back to the PPU struggling to make sense of all that had happened. Gene Kay had clearly been used as a distraction, a scapegoat on whom could be pinned the killing of Karen Hughes. The fact that he had died in the house fire prevented him being able to argue his innocence.

When she reached the unit, instead of going into her own office, she cut across to Cooper in Block 10. He was working on a laptop, scrolling through a series of spreadsheets, when she came in, one of his colleagues having allowed Lucy into the block as he was leaving.

'That looks interesting,' Lucy said.

'Serious or sarcastic?' Cooper asked, leaning backwards to see who was talking to him. 'Oh, hi, Lucy,' he said, when he saw her. 'Sarcastic then.'

'That's very cynical,' she commented, pretending to be offended.

'But probably very accurate,' he countered. 'I hear you found the girl. It's been on the news. How is she?'

'Useful,' Lucy said.

'Well, I'm sure that'll be a relief to her parents.'

'After 'Harris' had won the girls' trust, he took them to a house party and got them either drunk or high. They were raped while they were out of it.'

'This is why I work with numbers,' Cooper said. 'Tax fraud doesn't make you want to kill someone.'

'The important thing is she saw 'Harris'. And 'Harris' is not Carlin.'

'Really?' Cooper asked, sitting up. 'What about Kay?'

Lucy shook her head. 'She'd never even seen him before. Carlin, at least, she'd seen at the parties. She thought he might have been one of the men who raped her. Kay, though, drew a complete blank.'

'That doesn't mean he wasn't involved.'

'Perhaps. But it does mean he wasn't 'Simon Harris' and, therefore, not 'Paul Bradley' or any of the other sock puppet identities.'

Cooper pushed back from the desk he was working at and rolled his seat across to the opposite bench, propelling himself with his feet. He reached the large iMac and began clicking through folders.

'What are you after?' Lucy asked, joining him.

275

'"Bradley' or 'Harris' or whatever he was called was definitely using the free Wi-Fi in the Foyleside the day you went in. Kay was there obviously, but if he wasn't 'Harris', then someone else in the restaurant must have been.'

'What, and it was just a coincidence that Kay was there too and we went after him?'

'Maybe,' Cooper said. 'Or maybe not. Maybe Kay was set up. Maybe 'Bradley' got wind that we were on to his account after Karen's death and made a point of going on the accounts somewhere public, where we would find Kay. Regardless, we do know that whoever was on the accounts was in the restaurant, right?'

'OK,' Lucy said, pulling over a chair and sitting.

'I had the CCTV footage for the day sent across after I couldn't retrieve anything off Kay's phone. I wanted to satisfy myself that he had been online. If Sarah Finn has seen 'Harris', or 'Bradley', then she might recognize him as one of the other customers.'

'She might,' Lucy said, approvingly.

Cooper finally found the folder he wanted and opened up the footage. He played it through at half-speed, allowing them time to examine it in more detail, looking for possible candidates.

'Do you remember anyone standing out, apart from Kay?' Cooper asked.

Lucy shook her head, but, as she considered it, she recalled a man she'd put in his twenties sitting by the window. He'd been with a woman and child though. She assumed that the perpetrator would be alone. She told Cooper as much.

'If he was at the window, this camera angle will be no good,' Cooper commented. He closed the image he was looking at and picked another from the folder. This time, the view was of the seating area, the main concourse of the Foyleside visible through the window beyond.

Cooper forwarded the footage until the time counter in the corner read twelve, then continued at half-speed. Sure enough, some time later, a young man with thinning black hair appeared in the image, bearing a tray with a burger and drink on it. He sat alone at the window and, taking out his phone, spent some time seemingly texting on it. After ten minutes a woman and child arrived. Though there was no sound, Lucy could tell that the woman was asking if they might share his table. He agreed without even looking at them, his attention focused on the phone he held in front of him.

Some minutes later, those in the seats all around him stood quickly, their attention directed off screen to where Lucy knew Kay had been. Sure enough, in the subsequent images, Kay could be seen running down the concourse outside the window, pursued by several officers, Lucy included.

Those inside watched as the events unfolded. Rather than following the events unfolding outside the restaurant, the man quickly put away his phone and continued eating. A few minutes later, a uniformed officer appeared at the table, paused for a few moments, clearly taking the names of all those there, then moved on. After a further minute, the man balled up the wrapping of his food, gathered his stuff and left, pulling the hood of his top over his head as he did.

'Can you run me off the best picture of him you can find?'

'The best? It's all relative,' Cooper offered apologetically. 'I could try sourcing footage from outside, but with the hood up, he'll be even more difficult to identify.'

He moved back through the footage slowly until he found the best image he could. He was right about it being relative; the image was grainy, the man's features blurred. Still, it would hopefully be enough for Sarah Finn to at least be able to confirm whether or not he was 'Simon Harris'.

★ ★ ★

Lucy drove straight up to the Finn house, having thanked Cooper for his work. Sinead opened the door, the action soundtracked by raucous laughter from the living room beyond. Sinead wore a black dress, low-cut enough to provide Lucy with a view of her cleavage.

'Is Sarah free for a moment?' Lucy asked, stepping inside. In the confines of the hallway, she could smell the spirits off Sinead's breath, sweet and sharp.

'We're having a party, celebrating her safe return,' Sinead explained. 'Sarah?' she shouted.

A moment later, Sarah appeared from upstairs. It seemed she was the only one not attending the party being held in her honour.

'All right, love,' Sinead said, rubbing her

daughter's arm a little too vigorously, smiling through the haze of her drink, a rictus that lacked all warmth. 'Come in for a drink if you want one,' she added to Lucy. 'Or are you on duty?'

Lucy wondered at the mentality of the woman, inviting an officer in for a drink hours after being told she would need to enter an addiction programme if she wanted to keep her daughter at home.

When the door to the living room closed, Sarah seemed to slump against the wall.

'Are you OK?' Lucy asked.

'I . . . I don't want to be here any more. Being away with Seamus, even for those few days, was so easy. There was no shit, no drugs or drinking or parties. It was like a normal life.'

Lucy nodded. 'That's understandable,' she said.

'But how do you come back to this shit? At least before I didn't know any different. I thought this was normal.'

'I can ask them to leave if you'd like,' Lucy offered.

Sarah shook her head. 'They'll leave in a bit anyway, once the carry-out is finished.'

Lucy nodded, the folded picture in her hand, suddenly reluctant to ask the girl to look at it.

Sarah, though, had already worked out the purpose of the visit. 'Is this another picture to look at?' she asked, gesturing towards the sheet.

Lucy nodded. 'Do you mind?'

The girl shook her head, taking the page and opening it. She hissed a sharp intake of breath as she looked at it, then, handing it back quickly to Lucy, said, 'That's him. That's 'Harris'.'

'You're sure?' Lucy asked.

Sarah Finn nodded her head. 'I think that's him.'

47

'This is 'Simon Harris'?' the ACC asked. She was sitting in Burns's office, having been called by the Chief Super.

'According to Sarah Finn,' Lucy said. 'He was in the Foyleside at the time we picked up Kay. He was using his phone.'

'He could be anyone,' Burns said. 'The image is so grainy, it doesn't really help us move forward.'

'It at least necessitates that we do move forward,' Lucy said. 'We know Carlin was involved in this ring, but we don't have the ringleader. I think this is him.'

Her mother held the picture at arm's length, lowering her glasses to see if doing so aided her examination of the image. Finally she nodded, laying the picture on the desk.

'So, what's your next move, Superintendent?' she asked.

Burns was leaning against a filing cabinet to her right, biting on the skin around his finger, angling his hand to facilitate the process. He spat the small bit of skin he had removed from the tip of his tongue. Lucy watched the exchange between her mother and her lover with distaste.

'If the girl says he was the one who groomed her, then we need to follow it up. I still think Kay is involved, though, regardless of what the girl said. Why would he have had pictures of her?'

'Why would she not remember having seen him take them if he had?' Lucy asked.

'You said yourself she was drugged,' Burns retorted. 'Even she's not sure if she said she *thinks* it's him.'

'What if he played us?' Lucy said, pointing towards the picture lying before her mother. 'What if he knew Kay would be a suspect with his history and he set him up, going online somewhere public where we'd find Kay? He's been offline since, as far as we know. Maybe he saw Kay as the perfect fall guy. Then planted the pictures in his house after he'd been lifted.'

'What? Do you think he set the house alight too?' Burns scoffed.

'It's possible,' Wilson said.

'I don't think so,' Lucy began. After all, she suspected she knew who had been involved in lighting the fire. Gavin Duffy. 'I think Kay's burning was in retaliation for Karen Hughes's death. But we do know that uniforms took the names of all those who were in the restaurant at the time. Maybe we could follow up on any single men listed in that.'

'That's all been done already,' Burns said. 'Nothing showed up from it.'

'If whoever was interviewing thought Kay was our man, they may not have been too thorough,' Lucy objected.

'Careful, Sergeant,' Burns said. 'I seem to remember it was PPU who missed Kay's paedophile collection when you searched his house.'

'Maybe we didn't miss anything. If this is how

it went down, maybe there was nothing to find when we searched the house,' Lucy argued. 'In which case what about Inspector Fleming?'

The comment was greeting initially with silence, her mother glaring at her as she lifted her glasses and put them on, the skin around her mouth tightening. Finally she spoke. 'That's not your concern, Sergeant. Leave it at that.'

'But the stuff in Kay's might have been a set-up, to put Kay in the frame for Karen Hughes,' Lucy began. 'It's not fair if Tom — '

'That's enough, Lucy,' her mother warned. Then she turned to Burns. 'Would you give me a moment, Mark?'

Burns lingered a second, as if in protest at yet again being ask to leave his own office, before pushing himself off the cabinet with his rump and padding out of the room.

Wilson stared at Lucy a moment before speaking. When she did speak, it was not what Lucy had expected.

'What happened to your face?'

'I was hit.'

'By whom?'

'A suspect.'

'I see.' She rubbed at the bridge of her nose, then removed her glasses again. 'These bloody things are new and they're leaving me with sores on my nose. I should have stayed with the old ones.'

Lucy watched her, aware of the tactic, the circling around small talk as she worked out the best angle for attack.

'I heard there was an incident at Alan

283

Cunningham's family home last night.'

'Really?'

Wilson stared without speaking this time.

'If you heard that,' Lucy queried, straightening herself up in the seat, 'then why are you asking what happened to my face?'

'I just wondered if you were really so stupid as to go to that house alone.'

'No one else is interested.'

Wilson shook her head, smiling ruefully. 'The martyr role doesn't suit you, Lucy. Is that what you think? You're the only one who cares? That we should take every case personally, make it our mission?' She widened her eyes on the final word to emphasize its grandness.

Lucy shrugged. 'I think we should at least give a shit.'

'But no one feels as deeply as you do, isn't that right?' Wilson replied, sitting back now. 'Because that's what we should do. Invest everything in our work. Care so deeply that we forget about everything around us.'

'Well, I learnt from the master,' Lucy commented, holding her mother's stare.

Wilson accepted the comment with a light laugh. 'Always the answer, Lucy.'

Lucy folded her arms, waiting to see what the next angle would be. Again, it was not what she had expected.

'The Kellys in Petrie Way. How do they fit into this case you're working?'

Lucy shook her head, once, briefly. 'I don't know who you're talking about.'

'The Kelly family. You've been parked outside

their house, watching them three or four times now.'

'Twice,' Lucy corrected, then regretted speaking.

'My mistake,' Wilson replied. 'And they connect to Karen Hughes, how?'

'They don't,' Lucy said, softly. Then she straightened herself again and, clearing her throat, repeated the comment. 'They're connected to something else.'

'They are the family who have adopted the Quigg child, is that right?'

'Again, if you already know that, why ask?'

'How did you find out?'

'How did you?' Lucy retorted.

'Officially,' Wilson snapped. 'Not through the back door. Not off a cheating ex-boyfriend.'

'He's not a cheat,' Lucy said.

'You told me he cheated on you.'

'I said we disagreed on monogamy. I didn't say he was the one who cheated.'

'Of course he was the one who cheated; you're not the type, Lucy,' Wilson said.

'So says the expert on commitment,' Lucy replied.

Wilson shook her head, as if appraising her daughter anew. 'I've had my fill of the cheek, Lucy. And the chip on your shoulder.'

Lucy blushed in spite of herself, but did not respond.

'If you really cared as much as you say, you wouldn't be putting other people at risk. If this comes out, about you stalking that family, what would happen to your boyfriend? Giving out details of foster families? Is that you caring deeply?'

'He can fend for himself,' Lucy snapped. 'I didn't ask for it.'

'I'm sure you didn't have to.'

'I wanted to make sure he was OK. Joe Quigg.'

'And when you did? The first time you went you must have seen that he's in a good home. A home vetted by people who actually know what they're doing. What took you back the second time?' she added scornfully.

'I don't know,' Lucy muttered.

'They've reported your car registration number,' Wilson said.

'How did it come to you?'

'Never mind,' Wilson said, glancing at her desk. Lucy knew that such a small matter wouldn't make it to the ACC unless she was keeping tabs on Lucy.

'Are you checking up on me?' Lucy asked suddenly.

'I'm your mother, Lucy. I've a right to be interested in how you're getting on. God knows, talking to you gets me nowhere. I worry about you.'

The baldness of the comment caught Lucy off guard. She shifted in her seat uncomfortably. 'Well, you don't have to. I'm just doing my job. You were the one who put me in the PPU because of my 'affinity for the vulnerable', wasn't that what you said?'

'Having an affinity with them doesn't mean becoming one of them,' her mother said. 'I know how you feel. I used to — look, Lucy, you can't take every case personally. Because some things don't get solved. Killers walk the streets every day — even ones we caught and jailed. We have to see them back on the streets because an agreement was made. Should we all *feel* that?'

'At least you'd know you could feel.'

'Don't be so melodramatic, Lucy,' her mother snapped. 'Look at where feelings got Tom Fleming.'

'He's a good man.'

'He's responsible for you!' Wilson said suddenly, standing now. 'He should be looking out for you. If he's drinking, he can't do that. His drinking puts you at risk and I won't tolerate that.'

'Don't pretend you're looking out for me,' Lucy said, standing, feeling suddenly unsteady, the room seeming to shift beneath her. She could feel her face flush with heat.

'Of course I am, Lucy,' Wilson said. 'I worry about you.'

'Like you did when you walked out on me? Left me with a father who liked teenage girls? I preferred you when you didn't give a shit. At least then we knew where we stood.'

Her mother opened her mouth to speak, then seemed to swallow back her words. Instead she moved back behind her desk and sat, putting on her glasses again. 'You have one chance left, Lucy,' she said finally. 'You're making mistakes, putting yourself and others at risk. Your stalking the Cunningham house could be used against us if we ever do get him and try to convict. Police victimization. You should be taken off the case immediately. I'm giving you one last chance. Do the job you're expected to do. That's all. No personal vendettas. Before someone gets hurt.'

Lucy remained standing, struggling to find something to say.

'And leave that family in peace.'

'Alan Cunningham's or Joe Quigg's?'

'Both,' her mother said.

48

Tara Gallagher was sitting in the incident room working on a report at her PC. The remains of her dinner sat on the desk next to her: an empty crisp packet and an opened can of Diet Coke. She leaned close to the screen as she typed, stabbing one-fingered at the keyboard.

'Thinking of someone?' Lucy asked.

Tara glanced up. 'Oh, hey,' she managed, then turned her attention to the screen, swore softly and deleted the mistake she had just made.

Lucy pulled across a seat and sat next to her. 'Everything all right, you?'

'I'm stuck with bloody witness reports,' Tara said. 'Everyone else is working on other things and I'm stuck writing up this crap. I can hardly read half of the notes.'

'Where's the rest of the team?'

'Reassigned. There's been a spate of beatings in the town. A young lad got a battering this evening on his way to his work do.'

'Christmas parties week,' Lucy said. She realized that she'd not given it much thought.

Tara nodded. 'You know. I thought you'd made the wrong choice, going with PPU. But at least you're working stuff. This is mind numbing.'

'Burns?'

Tara nodded again, lowering her voice as she spoke, glancing furtively towards his office door lest she be heard. 'It's like an old boys' network. Your face needs to fit. And mine doesn't.'

'That's 'cos you're too good-looking,' Lucy said, laughing. 'How could this face be fitted in a frame?'

Tara laughed, thumping Lucy lightly on the leg. 'Bitch,' she said.

'You know I mean it,' Lucy replied, glad that whatever uneasiness she'd felt over Tara reporting her to Burns following the scrapyard had been passed. She knew Tara was finding it hard to make her mark in CID. There was little point in holding a grudge. 'So what are you working?'

'Door-to-door statements from the Finn abduction.'

'Sure we've got her back now,' Lucy protested.

'Tell that to him,' Tara said, sulkily. 'All Ts need to be crossed apparently.'

Lucy began sifting through the paperwork piled on the desk. 'The day we got Kay in Foyleside. Someone went round taking the names of everyone else in the restaurant afterwards. Do you have that here?'

'You're messing it up,' Tara said, slapping Lucy's hand away. 'It's in reverse order.'

'Reverse order? Do you want to feel challenged?'

Tara laughed. 'I lifted it out of the box like that. The newest stuff went on top. The Kay arrest was before the house-to-house.' She sorted through the pages, eventually pulling out handwritten lists of names and contact details stapled to handwritten statement sheets.

'Bingo,' she said. She laid them on the desk and began leafing through each page. 'Mickey did the checks,' she said. She read through the first brief statement, then flicked to the next. 'Jesus,' she muttered. 'Look at the state of this.'

Lucy leaned across and began reading the statement. The first was taken from a fifty-five-year-old school teacher who had been in the restaurant with his wife and children for lunch.

The interviewee reported first being aware of the suspect's presence when the suspect assaulted an officer and fled the scene. The interviewee saw officers pursue the suspect along the central concourse of the shopping centre.

When Lucy turned the page to the next statement, she understood Tara's reaction, for that statement was exactly the same.

'Look at the time he recorded for each statement,' Tara said. Lucy glanced at the details on the bottom of the page. Each statement was separated by at most ten minutes.

'He interviewed them by phone,' Lucy said. 'And copied the same statement over and over.'

Tara beamed. 'The lazy bastard! Wait till I tell Burns,' she added, gathering the sheets.

Lucy raised a placatory hand. 'Would it not be even better if we could show that the actual perpetrator had been interviewed by Mickey and he'd not picked up on it?'

She knew it was a low shot at Mickey, with whom she had no particular gripe. Nevertheless, having got this close to the list of names, the last thing she needed was for Tara to hand them over to Burns before she had a chance to look at them.

Tara hesitated, clearly torn between her desire to land Mickey in it straight away and the possible increased kudos she'd gain if she could only delay gratification for a few hours.

'Let's just take a look at the men he spoke with, eh? See if anything stands out,' Lucy suggested.

A little reluctantly, Tara sat again, laying the pages down flat.

'Have you the list of names first? We know that the possible suspect was sitting with a woman and child. Let's see if we have any groupings of three, with the man having a different surname from the woman and child accompanying him.'

It was not quite so simple, for the names were listed continuously, so that the size of each group could not be determined. Still, there were, in the end, only eight men listed who did not share surnames with any of the family groups.

'Have we statements for these eight?' Lucy asked. 'We can check their dates of birth, see if that helps eliminate some of them.'

Comparing names against statements, they were able to identify two of the men as being over forty-five. While it didn't exclude them completely, Sarah Finn had suggested that 'Simon Harris', as she knew him, was in his twenties. Four of the men listed were, in fact, teenagers, ranging in age from fourteen to eighteen. The elder ones certainly would have to be considered. Of the final two — Peter Bell and Gordon Fallon — Fallon's date of birth put him at twenty-nine, while the other, Bell, did not have a date of birth listed.

'He didn't speak to him,' Lucy said. 'He filled out the statement sheet without talking to him.'

Lucy could understand entirely. Kay had been caught, a paedophile with history. Why waste time taking witness statements from people who were all saying the same thing?

'Let's check the driving licences,' Lucy suggested. 'See if their pictures match the image ICS pulled from the CCTV footage.'

Tara contacted Licensing while Lucy made them both tea. By the time she'd come back, the images had been emailed through. Both men were in their twenties; Bell was twenty-five. Both were relatively slim in their picture, both had dark hair, though the shadows on the images made it impossible to tell whether this was natural or a trick of the light.

According to the addresses on the licences, Fallon was a local, born and bred in the Creggan, while Bell's address was actually listed for Belfast. Despite this, he had given the officer in Foyleside an address in the Waterside.

'Do you fancy a run out?' Lucy asked. 'We'll try Mr Fallon first, shall we?'

49

Fallon's driving licence details placed him in Westway, in Creggan. They took an unmarked car, planning on speaking to Fallon simply to ascertain whether he had remembered anything further following his initial interview with Mickey.

Fallon lived in a row of houses opposite the local boys' school.

Tara nodded across at the building as they pulled up in front of Fallon's house.

'Significant?' she asked.

'All the victims we know of were girls,' Lucy said. 'That doesn't mean we should dismiss it entirely.'

They knocked at the door of the house, aware that in both houses abutting Fallon's, neighbours had appeared at the living room windows, watching their approach, one more surreptitiously than the other.

The door opened to reveal a girl, in her late teens, standing in the hallway, a baby nestled against her hip.

'Yes?' the girl asked.

'Can we speak with Gordon Fallon, please?'

'Who are you?' the girl demanded, hoisting the child from one hip to the other. The child watched them both with wide-eyed wonder, a baby's bottle of orange cordial clenched in her tiny fist.

'We're with the PSNI,' Tara said. 'We'd like to speak to him about an incident he witnessed last week.'

'The paedo in the Foyleside?' the girl commented. 'Come on in, then.'

The house was small, the lower floor constituting a living area, giving way to a kitchen. The wall separating them carried a breakfast bar and a hatch in the wall through which food could be handed between one room and the next. The girl led them into the living area, then opened the hatch.

'There's two cops to see you,' she called. 'About the paedo.'

'What age is your child?' Lucy asked.

'Fourteen months,' the girl replied. 'She should be walking by now but she's too lazy. She wants to be carried everywhere.'

Fallon appeared at the doorway, looking in. 'All right?' he asked. 'Do youse want a drink of something before I sit down?' he added to Lucy and Tara.

'I'll have a can,' his partner said.

'I'm already in,' Fallon replied. 'I was asking them.'

'I'll take some of yours, then,' the girl commented.

Fallon scowled, moving into the room, handing the girl his beer can and taking position in the armchair opposite the TV. 'What's up? I already talked to the guy on the phone about this. I told him I didn't see anything.'

'Maybe you'd talk us through it again,' Lucy offered. 'Just in case something had bubbled to the surface of your memory between then and now.'

Tara glanced at her, incredulously. For his part, affecting an air of boredom, Fallon ran through a description of the incident that was, in fairness to Mickey, very close to the cut and paste job he'd done on all the witness statements.

'Do you drive?' Lucy asked, when Fallon was finished.

'What's that to do with anything?'

'I'm just wondering,' she offered, nonchalantly. 'I noticed there's no car outside, even though you have a licence.'

'Got repossessed, didn't it,' Fallon said, glancing across at the girl who stood watching proceedings, sipping from the beer can while the child hefted against her side reached out to try to take it from her.

'I told him not to buy it. It was too dear for us. Now I have to take the bus everywhere, wi' a pram and everything.'

'We'd have kept it if you'd stayed working,' Fallon snapped.

'I had to have me baby, didn't I?' the girl retorted.

Aware that long-simmering tensions had been brought quickly to air by the comment, Lucy changed the topic. 'Who were you with when you saw Kay's arrest?' she asked.

'A couple of people from work,' Fallon replied, glancing quickly at his partner again.

'Can you give us their names?' Lucy asked.

'Fiona Doherty, Sharon McMenamin, Kayley Gallagher.'

Though he said nothing further, Lucy could see from the looks they exchanged, that at least one of those named was not someone Fallon's partner was happy to have sharing lunch with him.

'Did any of them have their children with them?' The man in the image had been sitting at a table with a woman and child.

'They've not got kids. Any of them,' Fallon replied.

'Yet,' came the muttered comment from the corner.

★　★　★

'No car,' Lucy said as she and Tara climbed back into their own, having left the couple to whatever fight was brewing between them.

'No hope either,' Tara commented. 'That poor kid.'

They drove down through the town to head across to the Waterside. The streets were busy, people heading to staff parties, some already stumbling along in a manner which suggested that the party, for them at least, had started some hours earlier. Part of Bishop Street was closed off by a police cordon.

'That must be where the beating happened,' Tara said.

They cut down Shipquay Street and waited, halfway down the hill, while a girl tottered across the road, her arms stretched outwards to help her maintain balance on a pair of shoes several inches too high for her own safety. Her dress, meanwhile, was both several sizes too small and several inches too short for her not inconsiderable frame. She held, in one hand, a tiny clutch purse, in the other a bottle of WKD. Despite the cold, and the paucity of material on her dress, she did not carry a coat.

'Jesus, there's someone who got dressed without the three Ms,' Tara said, watching her cross. 'No mother, no mates, no mirror.'

Lucy tried unsuccessfully not to laugh. The girl, glancing up mid-crossing, saw them doing so and loosened the grip on her clutch bag enough to offer them a one-fingered salute.

'Pure class,' Tara commented.

★ ★ ★

They reached the address listed for Bell a few minutes later. He lived on Bond's Hill, a steep incline running towards the railway station in the Waterside. While most of the buildings along it were businesses, the lower few were residential. The house they stopped at was in darkness. They knocked several times, without response. Finally, Lucy knocked at the door of the neighbouring property.

'We can come back,' Tara said.

'He clearly didn't answer Mickey's call, nor is he answering his door. We don't even know if this is his real address.'

'In that case, we don't even know if Peter Bell is his real name.'

'I think it is,' Lucy began, but was interrupted by the shunting of a dead bolt of the door at

298

which she now stood. The neighbour who answered was an elderly woman. She opened the door a fraction, a thick security chain obscuring a clear view of her face.

'Yes?' she asked.

Lucy held up her warrant card for the woman to see. 'My name is DS Black with the PSNI's Public Protection Unit. We're looking for your neighbour, Mr Bell. Have you seen him lately?'

'What's he done?' the lady asked, the door not moving, Lucy's warrant card clearly not sufficient to engender trust.

'Nothing. He witnessed an incident a few days back and we wanted to check some details on his statement.'

The woman nodded, the gesture clear only through the slight rise and fall of the wisps of grey hair Lucy could make out.

'He keeps strange hours,' the woman said. 'I never know when he's coming. Sometimes I hear him playing music, but that's about it.'

'Do you know what he does?' Lucy asked. 'Does he work locally? We could maybe call with him at work tomorrow?'

'I don't know,' the woman said. 'I think he works with computers.'

Lucy rummaged in her pocket, pulled out the sheet taken from the CCTV footage. 'Mrs . . . ?'

'Sinclair.'

'Mrs Sinclair. If I hand you in a picture, would you mind looking at it and telling me if it's Mr Bell? In case we've got the wrong person.'

'What was your name again?'

'DS Black,' Lucy said. 'Lucy.'

A thin hand emerged through the gap, the fingers impatiently flicking at the page, taking it and withdrawing back through. Lucy watched as the small figure, her back hunched over, shuffled to beneath the meagre light being thrown off by the ceiling lamp in the hallway. Lucy could understand the woman's reluctance to open the door even to two girls. She was less than five feet tall, her arms narrow, her calf muscles carrying little flesh. Lucy imagined the fear that each knock on the door at night must produce in the woman.

Finally, she shuffled back towards the door. The page was pushed through the gap.

'It could be him,' the woman said. 'It's hard to tell. It could be.'

50

'If it is our guy, what makes you think it's his real name?' Tara asked, as they pulled away from the front of the house.

'When we raided the restaurant, he was online. He'd been using each of his accounts, updating things. When we arrived, if he did think we were after him, he couldn't be sure which identity we'd uncovered. Working on the assumption that the only identity he hasn't used online is his real one, it would make sense that that would be the only one he'd give to police. Besides, that was the only name he had an ID for, if it was needed: his driving licence.'

'I think that's logical,' Tara said. 'You lost me at 'online'.'

Lucy raised an eyebrow and smiled. 'I've one other stop I want to make,' she said. 'There's a young lad in care, he was with Karen and saw her with someone in the weeks before she died. I want to check this picture with him. Are you in a rush to get back?'

Tara looked at the clock on the dashboard. 'I'm on shift till ten,' she said. 'You have me for another hour and a half.'

'You're a star,' Lucy said, patting her leg. She took out her phone and called through to the unit.

'Robbie,' she said when he answered. 'Is Gavin

301

there? I wanted to call up and see him for a moment.'

'Sorry, Lucy,' Robbie said. 'Gavin's not come back to the unit yet. The grandparents don't know where he is either.'

'We're in the Waterside,' Lucy said. 'I'll take a quick check around the shops, see if he's hanging around there again. I'll let you know.

'Is that OK?' she asked Tara, who had overheard the conversation. 'It'll only take a few minutes.'

'Is that the boyfriend?'

'Ex,' said Lucy.

'What happened?'

'He snogged one of his co-workers on Hallowe'en night.'

'You broke up with him for that? That's a bit harsh,' Tara said. 'Mind you, he must be a dick, cheating on you,' she added, glancing across at Lucy, holding her gaze.

'I don't take well to people messing me around,' Lucy said.

★ ★ ★

They pulled up in front of the block of shops, looking around for Gavin or the gang of kids who seemed to habitually congregate there. Tara stayed in the car while Lucy moved around to the rear of the block, but the place was deserted. Finally, she went into the shop. A different assistant was working, a young girl, a student, Lucy guessed, by virtue of the fact she sat behind the till, a lined notebook on her lap, filled with neat blue copperplate script, a copy of 'The Pardoner's Tale' in her hand.

She placed the books on the stool and stood as Lucy approached.

'Sorry,' Lucy said. 'I'm just . . . ' She scanned the sweet selection in front of her, lifted a bar and offered it to the girl, hunting through her pockets for money. 'No youngsters hanging around tonight,' she asked, handing the girl a pound.

'You get three for one fifty,' she replied. 'The bars. They're eighty pence each, but you get three for one fifty.'

Lucy glanced down to the sign, which stated this, hanging off the shelf. 'Of course. Great. I'll do that, then.' She lifted the other two bars and handed them to the girl. 'Thanks.'

The girl waited while she hunted again for fifty pence. 'No kids . . . ' she repeated.

'They're all in the local youth club tonight. It closes at ten.'

The girl stood patiently, waiting for Lucy to continue. Something in her features, the sharpness of her nose, thin and aquiline, made Lucy think she had seen her before.

'Are you looking for Gavin again?' the girl asked and Lucy realized why she recognized her: she had been standing with Gavin the night she had first picked him up from behind the shops.

'Yes.'

'Is he in trouble?'

Lucy shook her head. She glanced at the girl's name badge, which read 'Elena'. 'I needed to ask him something, Elena. Are you and he . . . ?' She

303

left the question open-ended.

Despite this, the girl blushed. 'Kind of,' she said.

'You're not at the club, then? Too busy working?'

Elena nodded. 'I miss all the *craic*. They all went away paint-balling a few weeks ago to Magilligan for the weekend and I had to work then, too. They stayed over and had a party and everything.'

'It'll be worth it in the long run,' Lucy said, suddenly aware as she said it that it was the typical platitude that an adult might come out with. 'Though it's crap missing stuff like that. Where did they stay?' she added, for she did not remember Gavin being away. Of course, she reasoned, she and Robbie had broken up by then; there was no reason for her to know.

'Jackie has an old house there. They all stayed there, in sleeping bags and that. The youth club supervisors went too, but they were sound about them partying.'

'I'll take a run down to the club and see if Gavin's about,' Lucy said, taking the bars and turning to leave. She turned back and handed one of the bars to the girl. 'For when you're having your break,' she said.

The girl flashed her a smile. 'Thank you,' she said. 'Exam tomorrow,' she added as explanation for the books.

'Good luck,' Lucy offered.

★ ★ ★

Tara agreed to take her to the Oaks Youth Club in return for the other chocolate bar. The youth club was actually an annex off one of the local factories, a low, stucco block, flat-roofed, with metal grilles on the walls. While the grilles were marked with dried splatters of various colours of paint, the walls of the building, though not freshly painted, were clean of all graffiti.

Two younger lads stood in the entrance way, one trying to strike a match to light their cigarettes while the other sheltered him, his coat a makeshift windbreaker.

Beyond them, Lucy saw a figure appear and advance towards the double doors in front of which they stood.

Jackie Logue pushed open the door. 'Not in front of the door, lads,' he said. 'Go on off the grounds if you're going to insist on smoking.'

One of the lads straightened and, for a second, Lucy expected him to challenge Logue. Instead, hiding the cigarette behind his back, he said, 'Sorry, Jackie. We can't get a light out in the wind.'

Logue nodded, signalling that they could continue. 'You shouldn't be smoking at all, you know that. It stunts your growth.'

The boy, now successfully puffing on his cigarette, standing almost a head higher than Logue, laughed good-naturedly. 'Is that what happened you, Jackie?' he asked.

'Bugger off, you cheeky git,' Logue laughed. Then, he must have seen Lucy standing on the pathway to the club. 'Let the lady through, lads.

305

And no smoking on the grounds. Off you go now.'

Logue stepped back, holding open the door, which Lucy took as an invitation to come in. To do so, she had to pass by the two smokers who stood, almost as a guard of honour, on either side of the doorway. Lucy passed so close to one she could smell the stale sweat off his football top, ripe beneath the cigarette smoke.

'Mr Logue?'

'DS Black, isn't it,' Logue said. 'Gavin told me about you. What's he done now?'

'Vanished. He wouldn't be in here, would he?'

'I don't think so,' Logue said. 'Come on in. We'll go through to the office.'

The city had a number of such youth clubs, set up in community centres by the local people to keep the youths off the streets and out of trouble. Lucy followed Logue through the building, which was mostly a single open-plan area. The centre of the room was dominated by two snooker tables. A handful of fellas stood around them, stacks of twenty-pence pieces sitting on the cushioned ledge of one showing that they would be playing for some time. The crack of the balls carried in its wake a collective groan at a missed pocket.

In the far corner was an old-style TV. Another group sat around it, two at their centre gripping the controls of a games console as they steered the two cars racing each other on screen.

As she passed through, Lucy saw a small tuck shop, being staffed by one of the teenagers and, against the back wall, a row of PCs, all of which were in use. At the furthest end of the block was a small room partitioned from the rest of the building. Though it was this that Logue had called his office, it was, in fact, a small kitchen, leading off to a toilet.

'How's Gavin getting on?' Logue asked, as they came into the room. 'Tea? Coffee?'

'No, thanks,' Lucy said. 'He's doing OK. Apart from the gang he's running with.'

'They'll keep him out of trouble,' Logue said, lifting a mug down from the cupboard above his head. 'And I keep them out of trouble. You sure you don't want a brew?'

'I think he was involved in the burning of Gene Kay's house,' Lucy said, studying Logue's face for any flicker of reaction.

He set down the mug and turned to face her. 'Have you any reason for thinking that?'

'He arrived back in the residential unit smelling of petrol.'

Logue shrugged. 'He was probably part of the petrol bombing.' He raised his hands, as if anticipating argument. 'I'm not justifying it. But we both know that they all engage in a bit of recreational rioting on occasions.'

'He was back before the rioting started.'

Logue leaned back against the counter. 'I'm assuming that you've kept this to yourself for now. Or else he would've been lifted long ago for it.'

'He's had his problems,' Lucy said. 'I'm not keen on complicating things for him.'

'He's very lucky then,' Logue said. 'I knew his father. The apple's not fallen too far from the tree there.'

'Was he a killer?' Lucy asked.

'Apart from serving time for the murder of Louisa Gant,' Logue said, confused.

'Of course,' Lucy said. 'But before that, I mean. Did he strike you as a killer? As capable of killing a child.'

'You never really know someone,' Logue said. 'But he was troubled. He was part of the old guard. Hated your crowd for a start. He ruled this area with an iron fist. Had kids kneecapped for thieving, drugs, the whole bit.'

'Whereas you offer them snooker and games consoles?'

'I offer them a roof over their heads and a bit of respect. There's always one or two who are beyond the pale, but most of them are just looking to test the boundaries. That's all. You see this place — no litter, no scrawls on the walls. Set high expectations, and they'll meet them. Bully them and they become bullies.'

'You know a lot about teenagers,' Lucy said. 'Experience?'

Logue shook his head. 'I lost my own boy when he was a teenager,' he said.

'I'm very sorry,' Lucy said, caught off guard by the comment.

Logue shrugged. 'These things happen.'

'How do you find Gavin? Like his father, obviously,' Lucy said, steering the conversation to safer topics.

'He's troubled like Gary. They both struggled with anger. Like they're angry inside and can't deal with it. Gavin might learn from the other kids here how to handle things better.'

'Or those in the residential unit,' Lucy suggested.

Logue nodded. 'Though they've all got their own problems, too, haven't they?' he said.

'Do you think he did burn Kay's house?'

Logue shrugged. 'He was angry about the Hughes girl. He might have, to be honest. I'd hope not. Still, if Kay did kill her, he got what was coming to him. I make no apology for saying that.'

'If,' Lucy agreed.

'You think Kay didn't kill Karen?' Logue asked. 'I assumed it was him. From what was said on the news and that.'

Logue's use of her Christian name struck Lucy as odd, though she did not comment on it. 'The investigation is ongoing.'

'I see,' Logue said. 'I'll ask some of the lads where Gavin is.'

Logue moved out of the office and whistled sharply through his teeth. 'Jimmy, lad. Come 'ere.'

The boy in question slouched into the kitchen, his shoulders hunched, his hair hanging over his face.

'Gavin's missing,' Logue said. 'Any ideas where he's at?'

Jimmy shook his head, the hair flicking across his brow with the movement.

'You don't know who he'd be with? Tony?'

'Tony's here,' the young lad said. 'He's playing 'G. T. A'.'

Logue repeated the call, this time for Tony.

'Any ideas where Gavin is this evening?' Logue asked.

Tony looked at him, then at Lucy, then back to Logue.

'It's OK. He's done nothing wrong,' Logue reassured him.

'I don't know,' Tony said. 'He had class earlier.'

'School?' Lucy asked.

'Nah. Here.'

'There are after-school classes run for the kids here,' Logue said. 'Homework clubs, first aid, basic IT, literacy and numeracy skills, the like of that.'

'Was Gavin here for that?'

Tony nodded. 'He left after six. He's going out with a girl over in the Bogside. He might be away to her.'

'What about Elena?' Lucy asked. 'Is he not going out with her?'

Tony smirked, lowering his head and wiping at his nose with the back of his hand. 'Off and on,' he said. 'Know what I mean?'

Lucy thanked him. Eventually, she figured, Gavin would return to the residential unit. She could drop Tara back, then head to the unit to wait for him there. It might also, she reasoned, give her a chance to talk with Robbie.

As Logue walked her out of the centre, Lucy asked, 'Just as a matter of interest, did Louisa Gant live around here too?'

'Just a few streets across,' Logue said, indicating the direction with the half-empty mug he carried. 'Her father's still there. The mother died a few years after the wee girl. Hanged herself. He found her in the garden. They'd planted a tree with the wee girl in the yard. She hanged herself off it.'

'Jesus,' Lucy whispered. 'I'd not heard that. I remember the case, but I didn't hear what happened afterwards.'

'That's always the way, though,' Logue said. 'All the attention at the time. It's them that have to live with what's happened that have to go on in secret. Knowing what they know. What they can't forget.'

51

After leaving Tara off at the Strand Road, Lucy collected her car and headed back to the unit. Before doing so, though, she took a detour via her own house in Prehen for a quick shower. She'd bought Robbie a shirt and a bottle of aftershave for Christmas a few weeks earlier, the two gifts hanging in a plastic bag over the ornamental carving at the bottom of the banisters, mocking her for having thought of him. Still, she wrapped them now, figuring that it might be the last time she would see him before Christmas. Besides, it was the week before Christmas and she was alone. Not that that was good enough reason to reconcile. But it was, she decided, a reason.

Robbie looked pleased to see her when he answered the door to her an hour later. 'Come in. You look great. Off on a night out?'

Lucy shook her head. 'I wanted to see Gavin,' she said. 'I just freshened up. Am I normally so bad-looking?'

Robbie smiled. 'You know that's not what I meant. Come on in. Gavin's just back. He's in his room.'

Lucy sat on the sofa and placed the plastic bag containing the present on the floor, pushing it slightly beneath the seat so that it wasn't immediately obvious. She realized with some embarrassment that Robbie may not have ought her anything, that he would be embarrassed himself if she gave him a gift without anything to offer in return.

Gavin arrived down a moment later, dropping onto the end of the sofa sullenly, folding his arms across his chest. 'What?'

'I was looking for you,' Lucy said. 'Where have you been?'

'Out.'

'Out where?'

'Just out. What do you want?'

Lucy knew better than to push it. If Gavin felt he was being compelled into telling her where he had been, it could make him more uncooperative as a result. 'I need you to look at something,' Lucy said, taking out the folded sheet on which was printed the image of the young man from Foyleside. 'The guy you saw Karen with a few times? Remember? Was that him?'

Gavin took the sheet from her, studying the page. His mouth seemed to move, as if he were silently forming words to speak, but lacked the ability to do so. Finally, he handed the sheet back.

'I don't know him,' he said.

'Is he the man you saw with Karen?'

'Jesus,' he snapped. 'I said I don't know him. All right?'

'Fine,' Lucy said, putting the page away. 'If you remember anything, let me know.'

Gavin pushed himself up from the seat again and made as if to head back to his room. He stopped, though, and turned to face her.

'I thought Kay killed her,' he said at last.

Lucy shook her head. 'I don't think he did,' she said. 'I think he was set up.'

Gavin stared at her, his shoulders curving into a slight crouch, his hands balling into fists, which he lodged in his trouser pockets. He raised his head interrogatively. 'By who?'

'Possibly by this man,' Lucy said. 'You're sure you don't know who he is?'

'I told you already,' he said. 'I'm going to bed.'

He slouched back towards the rooms, his hands still in his pockets, his gait like one defeated.

'He'll be all right,' Robbie said, though Lucy had not commented.

'If the petrol on his clothes didn't come from petrol bombs, he's probably struggling with whatever it was he did the morning Gene Kay died now he knows Kay didn't kill Karen.'

Robbie moved across to the kitchen. 'Do you want a cuppa?' he asked.

Lucy followed him, leaving her bag on the sofa, Robbie's gift still sitting beneath the seat. 'Have you nothing stronger?' she asked.

Robbie opened the top cupboards, using the small key from his key ring to undo the lock. Inside were bottles of red wine, which a grateful parent had left to the unit months earlier. Lucy remembered it well; Lorna, another member of staff, had told her all about it, proudly showing her the bottles that same evening.

'We don't often get those,' Lorna had commented.

'Bottles of wine?' Lucy had asked.

'No. Grateful clients.'

Robbie lifted down a bottle now. 'Do you fancy a glass?' he asked. 'I've only red.'

'Red's fine,' Lucy said. 'I'll have just the one.'

'I'll maybe join you,' Robbie said. 'A very small one, though.'

They moved back to the sofa, the TV playing soundlessly in the corner. Robbie sat at one end of the sofa, Lucy at the other. He tapped at the bag lying on the floor with his foot. 'Is this mine?' he asked.

'That's very presumptuous,' Lucy smiled. 'It could be for Gavin.'

'Is it?'

She shook her head. 'Happy Christmas.'

Robbie leaned down and, lifting the parcel, weighed it in his hands, as if that might give him some hints as to the contents. 'Clothes?'

'Duh.'

'Can I open it now?'

Lucy shrugged. 'It's up to you.'

Robbie stood and moved back across to the locked cupboard. This time, though, he lifted down a small box, gift wrapped, and carried it across to Lucy.

'And Happy Christmas to you too,' he said, handing the box to her.

Lucy took it sceptically. 'Is that another present from a grateful client you've just given to me?'

Robbie pantomimed offence. 'I bought it before, you, know, it all . . . you know.'

Lucy shook the box lightly, heard the rattle of a chain against the inside of the box.

'Not clothes,' she guessed.

'You'll have to open it to find out.'

She peeled back the tape from the folds c paper at the bottom of the box, pulling off the ribbon tied around it, which had clearly been applied by the woman in the shop who had sold the gift to Robbie, for such wrapping skills were well beyond his abilities. Or Lucy's if she was honest, as she glanced at the sloppily wrapped gift Robbie was tearing open.

She opened the small jeweller's box. Inside was a fine gold chain, at the end of which was a small gold square framing a golden heart.

'It's beautiful,' Lucy managed, unclipping it from the fitting in the box and putting it on.

'I'm glad you like it,' Robbie said, pulling out the shirt, atop which sat a bottle of aftershave. 'Lovely,' he said, nodding with approval to emphasize his apparent satisfaction.

'It's a bit crap now I see it,' Lucy said. 'Sorry. The aftershave's nice, though.'

Robbie opened it, sprayed some onto his neck.

'How do I smell?' he asked, leaning across, offering her neck to sniff.

Lucy smiled. 'Thank you for the necklace. It is beautiful. Happy Christmas.'

'And you,' Robbie said, angling his head, moving closer, until they kissed.

★　★　★

When she woke, just after five the following morning, it took Lucy a moment to realize that she was not in her own bed. She was in the spare room of the residential unit, her clothes lying in

316

pile on the floor next to the bed. Her mouth felt thick and heavy. One glass of wine had segued into one bottle, the kiss had developed to more than just a kiss. Now though, the duvet was flicked up on the other side of the bed, Robbie was nowhere to be seen.

She heard the thudding of his footfalls, then the door opened and he was standing in the doorway, half blocking the hallway light beyond, dressed in his underwear and T-shirt.

'Gavin's gone,' he said.

Lucy pulled the sheet around her, aware of her nakedness. 'Shit! How long's he been gone?'

'I was sleeping,' Robbie said, shrugging sheepishly. 'He's done a runner.'

Lucy sat up in the bed, too quickly, the room starting to spin with the movement. She swung her legs out of the bed, hoped the solidity of the floor beneath her bare feet might provide her with some semblance of stability.

'I'll head out and see if I can spot him about,' she said. 'He might have headed back up to where those kids hang around.'

'You've drunk too much,' Robbie said. 'I only had two glasses. I'll drive you.'

Lucy pulled on her clothes, suddenly aware of the coldness in the room. 'It's bloody freezing,' she said.

'Gavin left the back door open,' Robbie explained.

'Where did he get the key?' Lucy asked. The children in the unit had to be locked in at night.

Robbie reddened. 'I left it hanging in the cupboard door last night when I got your present

317

out. I meant to take it out, but I got distracted,' he added.

Lucy rubbed her face, lightly slapping her cheeks to wake herself up. 'Have we time for coffee?' she asked.

Robbie lifted his jeans and shirt off the floor. 'I'll stick some on,' he said.

Lucy heard him rattling about the kitchen as she padded down to the toilet. She threw some water on her face to freshen herself up a little, but could do nothing to take the taste of red wine from her mouth.

When she came into the kitchen area, the fluorescent lights seemed unnaturally harsh. Robbie was finishing his own mug of coffee. He handed her a steaming cup. 'Give me your keys,' he said. 'I'll start the engine up and get the car heated. There was fairly heavy frost last night and the windows'll need cleared.'

Lucy rooted through her bag, handed him the keys, then began drinking the coffee, after blowing on it to cool it down. Finally, to speed up the drinking of it, she moved across to the sink, turned on the tap and poured in cold water to cool it, then drained the cup.

She was just at the door when the windows shivered. She heard the dull thud of the explosion outside, saw the blast of light from the car, felt the thick buffet of air from the blast, as the glass rained around her.

Friday 21 December

52

It took Lucy a moment to regain her balance. The room filled with a high-pitched whining and she tugged at her ear, as if to loosen whatever obstruction she felt was there.

Finally, recognizing the noise as an after effect of the explosion, she hauled herself through the doorway, struggling to pull her phone from her pocket. She could see flames ballooning in the darkness beyond.

Her car sat in the driveway, though had shifted several feet sideways from where it had been parked. The side panel around the wheelbase of the driver's side was shorn open, the under carriage of the car exposed. The tyre of the front wheel, deflated now, was alight, the metal wheel itself sitting askew. The driver's door hung at an angle from its upper hinge, the glass of the window shattered in pieces on the ground beneath. The windscreen, while still intact, was a mesh of cracks and fractures, which made it impossible for her to see in to Robbie. All she could tell, through the black smoke of the burning rubber and the thick cloud of dust in the air, thrown up by the blast, was that he was no longer sitting upright.

She managed to key in 999, screaming as she did for Robbie, hoping that, perhaps, he had not been in the car at all, scanning the shrubbery bordering the driveway lest the force of the blast had blown him onto it. She heard the emergenc operator respond to the call and managed the salient details, before dropping the phone, still connected to the operator, onto the ground.

As she approached the car, the flames from the burning tyre were building now, licking across the side panels, scorching the metal. Grabbing at the handle to pull the door open, she could see now, through the shattered window, that Robbie lay across the two front seats. She could see blood on his shirt and face.

She tugged at the door, but the twisted metal of the frame had caught somehow and, try as she might, she could not pull it free. She suddenly realized that the flames had caught her jacket, the bottom of which was now alight. She shrugged it off, pushing her way around to the passenger side of the car.

She tugged open the door and clambered into the car, reaching for Robbie's head, desperate to check if he was, at least, still breathing. She leaned in as close as she could, shaking him by the shoulder, calling his name. Finally, a soft moan formed on his lips. She noticed that his face carried a deep gash on the side that had faced the blast, perhaps a result of the flying glass from the window. She also knew that, as the fire spread on the other side, there was a much greater chance that the petrol tank, which had not yet seemingly been affected by the blast, could ignite. She needed to get Robbie out quickly.

She reached across his body, spidering her way along his trunk until she felt the hard edge of the eat belt. Tracing along its length, she finally was able to stretch far enough to feel the metal clasp. She fumbled in the half-light of the flames beyond, trying to find the release latch which would loosen the belt. As she did so, she was acutely aware that she did not know the extent of Robbie's injuries. Leaning any weight on him might only exacerbate any internal damage already done. Still, leaving him here was not an option.

At last, the clasp gave and the seat belt recoiled across his body. Lucy pushed it out of the way, then, gripping him beneath his armpits, she hefted him across, away from the building flames.

A groan escaped his lips as she pulled, though he himself did not seem conscious. 'Robbie,' she cried, as she tugged at him, dragging him towards her. Her left hand slipped, causing her to lose her grip and, looking down, she saw it was slick with blood from the right-hand side of his face. Wiping it on her own top, she tugged at him again, but he would not move, as if caught on something. She shifted over the top of his body, pulling at his legs, but they seemed free of obstacles. Then she realized that the handbrake had caught his belt, preventing movement. She had to angle herself in order to push him back towards the flames in the hope that, in doing so, it might free him from the lever. As she did so, she heard the metal frame of the car keening as it warped beneath the heat.

In the end, she had to twist him slightly before pulling once more, finally hefting him across onto the passenger seat and out of the car. Sh dragged him away from the car, back towards the unit, managing as far as the doorstep before she lost balance and fell back into the hallway. She scrambled back to the step, pulling Robbie towards her, cradling his head in her hands as his blood seeped onto her jeans.

The air popped as the petrol tank caught, the force of the subsequent blast throwing Lucy and Robbie onto their backs on the step, scattering flame onto the trees at the edge of the garden from whose branches now dripped flame onto the frosted grass below.

Then, through the thickening smoke, Lucy noticed the flickering blue of the ambulance lights in the distance, dancing along the fronts of the houses opposite where, one by one, lights were coming on.

53

Lucy was examined in one of the ambulances while Robbie was receiving attention in the other. The closeness of the hospital to the residential unit meant that they had been on the scene within minutes. After the paramedic had checked her over and offered her a foil blanket against the pre-dawn chill, she moved across to where Robbie lay, still inert.

'Is he going to be OK?' she managed.

'He's alive,' the man tending him commented. 'He's not awake yet, but he's alive. He has a fairly deep leg wound. We need to get him into surgery. Do you want to come with?'

Lucy nodded. For a moment she thought she had blood on her face, for her skin felt suddenly chilled. She smeared her hand across her cheek and was a little surprised to find that she had been crying.

'Climb in,' the man said, offering her a hand.

She steadied herself. 'I'd best wait here. They'll want to know what happened,' she said. 'I'll be straight up then.'

★ ★ ★

In fact, it was almost an hour before Lucy was even able to leave the scene. Soon after the first patrol cars arrived, her mother appeared, her face drawn, her mouth a pale line.

'What happened?'

Lucy nodded towards the wreckage of the car 'A bomb by the looks of it. Robbie went out to defrost it and it went off.'

'Your car was here all night then?' her mother asked.

Absurdly, Lucy could not discern if she was asking in a maternal or professional capacity. 'Yes. It was here all night. As was I.'

'Who would have known that?'

'Gavin Duffy,' Lucy said. 'The kid in the unit. Gary Duffy's boy. I came up last night to see him, to see if he recognized the man from the Foyleside CCTV image. He'd told me before that he saw someone with Karen Hughes matching the description Sarah Finn gave me.'

'Did he recognize him?'

'He said he didn't,' Lucy replied. 'But he's done a runner.'

Her mother pantomimed bewilderment.

'I think Gavin was part of the gang that torched Kay's house. I think when he found out that Kay might not have been responsible for Karen's death, it pushed him over the edge. He helped kill the wrong man.'

'You think he knows who the man in the picture is?'

Lucy nodded.

'And Duffy told him that you were here?'

Again Lucy nodded.

'How's Robbie?'

'I don't know,' she said. 'I'm not — '

She felt her eyes fill, felt the tears brimming. Her mother stood, looking at her a moment,

326

en leaned in towards her and put her arms around her, hugging her lightly, shushing in her ear. Lucy accepted the embrace.

'You can say I told you so,' Lucy managed. 'It's my fault he was hurt.'

Her mother shook her head sadly. 'You know that's not what I meant,' she said.

'But it *is* my fault,' Lucy said.

One of the technical officers who had been examining the now smouldering car came across to them. They moved apart. Lucy daubed her eyes dry with the sleeve of her top. Her mother held her other hand, clasped tightly.

'Ma'am,' he said, nodding lightly to the ACC. 'Sergeant.'

'Did you find anything?' Wilson asked, glancing quickly at the wreckage.

'He was very lucky,' the man began.

'Lucky?' Wilson repeated, incredulously.

The man blushed, aware of the insensitivity in the statement. 'It was a rushed job, ma'am. They placed it under the engine block, which absorbed most of the blast. If they'd had it a foot to the other side of the wheel bay, it would have taken a fair chunk out of the whole side of the car. They'd not have stretchered him away from it.'

★　★　★

Robbie was still in surgery when Lucy reached the hospital. Her own hands having been scorched while she'd tried to open the driver's door, she was sent to A & E where they applied salve to the already blistered skin and dressed it

327

with light gauze. She returned again to th̶
theatre ward to see how Robbie was, but was
told instead to wait at the café for word.

She sat alone, drinking a cup of hot chocolate
from the vending machine, so tepid and watery
that neither part of its name seemed wholly
accurate. The foyer was in semi-darkness, the
only illumination coming from the padlocked
fridge which, during the day, would hold
sandwiches and plastic dishes of salad. In the
half-light, she stared at her reflection in the
windows. The sky beyond was still dark.

She reflected back on all that had happened.
On Kay. Carlin. Louisa Gant. Karen Hughes.
Sarah Finn. All of them featuring in Kay's
collection. A collection that, she believed, had
been planted by whoever was actually responsible.

Louisa Gant. She had planned to go back to
the start, to see where the groomer had crossed
paths with Karen and Sarah. She remembered
that the information she had requested from the
schools would be in her office in the Public
Protection Unit in Maydown. However, perhaps
she needed to go back further, she reasoned.
Louisa Gant was actually where it started; she
was, in reality, the first victim who had found
their way to Carlin's house.

She took out her mobile and called Tara. The
phone rang out three times before she eventually
answered, her voice little more than a whisper.

'Lucy, is everything all right?' she managed.

'Did I wake you?' Lucy asked.

'It's fine. Is everything all right?'

'The Louisa Gant murder. Has anyone been looking back at the files?'

'We all have,' Tara said. 'Why? What's wrong?' She sounded a little angrier now and Lucy realized that she had woken her without explanation.

'Someone put a bomb under my car this morning,' she said.

'Jesus. Are you okay?'

'Fine,' Lucy said, her mouth dry. 'Robbie was the one in the car. He's in surgery.'

'Is he . . . ? Will he be . . . ?'

'He was alive when I pulled him from the car. I think his leg is injured. They've not told me.'

'Do you want me to come up to you? Are you in the hospital?'

Lucy was touched by the offer. Her own mother had asked an officer to bring her across while she went back to the station. While Lucy could understand that, had the ACC accompanied her, it might have drawn attention to the fact that she was taking a personal interest in Lucy, at the same time she couldn't help but feel a little annoyed that she'd been left on her own.

'I'm OK, thanks,' Lucy said. 'I wanted to know about the Gant killing though. Was it definitely Gary Duffy? Was there any suggestion that someone else might have been involved?'

'Why?'

'Louisa Gant's body was buried at Carlin's farm, supposedly by Gary Duffy. Except Duffy's dead now and yet the house is still being used, by Karen's abductor for his house parties. Maybe Duffy didn't kill Louisa Gant. Or maybe he had help and the person who helped him then is the one grooming these girls now. Was there any suggestion of other people being involved in Duffy's file?'

'I don't know,' Tara said. 'The file was full of gaps.'

'Why?'

'Because Duffy was who he was. His being connected with the paramilitaries, it seems that Special Branch took over the case. A lot of the files contained intelligence material apparently. Names of informants that couldn't be revealed.'

'Said who?'

'Burns. He said the ACC told him herself.'

'Mr Gant lives locally, doesn't he?' Lucy asked. If the files couldn't offer new light on the girl's killing, perhaps her father might still recall something from that time. Whether he'd thank Lucy for reopening old scars was a different matter. Though, Lucy reflected, if her feelings over Mary Quigg's death were any indicator, those old scars might not have healed anyway.

'I don't know. I'm not sure,' Tara said. 'Look, maybe you should take — '

'He does,' Lucy said. 'Thanks.' She hung up. Leaving her cup, she crossed to the main desk where a night porter was playing Temple Run on his phone.

'Can I borrow your phone book?' Lucy asked.

54

Just after nine, a doctor came down to tell her that Robbie was out of surgery. He'd lost a significant amount of tissue and muscle from his right leg and had required stitching to his side and face. That said, he was, she argued, lucky to not have been more badly hurt.

'Is he awake?'

'He's coming round,' she said. 'He'll be on morphine for the day though, so he'll be out of it. You can see him briefly if you want to.'

She stood by his bedside, watching him drifting in and out of consciousness. At one stage she thought he recognized her, for he smiled lightly, his lips moving as if he were trying to say something.

Before she left, she leant over and kissed his cheek, wiping away the tears that dripped from hers onto his. She noticed, where he lay, that he had a small scar on his neck she'd never noticed before. She traced its outline with the tips of the fingers of her bandaged hand.

* * *

She took a taxi to Gant's house. The phone book had only listed one in the immediate area and Logue had told her the previous night that the man still lived in the vicinity, so she took a chance that it was the right address.

The house was neat and clean-looking from the front, the small lawn trim and tidy. Lucy knocked on the door and waited. The man who answered was in his fifties. He wore brown corduroy trousers and a loose-fitting white shirt, which did little to disguise the fact that he stooped slightly as he walked.

'Yes?' he asked.

'Mr Gant?'

'Yes.'

'I'm Lucy Black from the PSNI's Public Protection Unit.'

The man attempted to straighten himself a little. 'Yes?' he repeated, more slowly this time.

'I'd like to talk to you about Louisa,' she said.

He raised his head, glancing up and down the street. Finally he nodded lightly and stepped back. 'You may come in, so.'

She followed him down the darkened hallway.

'Do you want something?' he asked. 'I'm making breakfast.'

'I'm fine,' Lucy said. 'Thanks.'

'You'll have an egg,' he said, shuffling into the kitchen.

He moved across to the fridge and removed two eggs from the shelf. A saucepan of water was already coming to the boil on the cooker. He placed the eggs in the water then, reaching up, opened a cupboard above his head and lifted down two egg cups. As he did so, Lucy saw a small plastic mug with the image of Ariel from *The Little Mermaid* on it. Beneath the image, the name 'Louisa' was written in multicoloured lettering.

'You found her then?' he asked suddenly, not
.acing her. 'They told me they think they found
her.'

'It's not confirmed yet,' Lucy said. 'I'm sure
someone will be in touch as soon as they know
for sure.'

He nodded. 'So why are you here?'

'I don't know,' Lucy said. 'I wondered if,
maybe, the right man had been caught.'

Gant nodded lightly. 'I heard he died.'

'That's right.'

He nodded again. 'I hope he suffered.'

Lucy cleared her throat, beginning to regret
having called with the man. She feared that, far
from helping her, the visit would only serve to
reopen old wounds for Louisa's father.

'*She* suffered,' he said. 'Louisa's mother. She
suffered every day for eight months after Louisa
went.' He raised the spoon he held and pointed
out through the window to where a single
hawthorn tree stood in the centre of his back
garden. 'I found her hanging off that.'

Lucy felt sudden shame for having intruded
on the man's grief.

'Do you want to see Louisa? She was a
beautiful child. I've pictures here.'

He turned, leaving the saucepan bubbling, and
led her into the front room. Against one wall
stood a dark wooden bookcase. A range of
pictures, each in small silver frames, sat on the
shelves. With a pang, Lucy realized that the
images were not photographs of Louisa as a
child. They were the police mock-ups of how she
might look, released each year after her

disappearance in the vain hope than she might still be alive.

'That's how I watched her grow up,' Gant said. 'Just like that. In pretend photographs.'

Lucy remembered vaguely some of the images being released. Despite Duffy being charged with her murder, in the absence of a body, the family had issued a picture each year, in hope. Lucy realized now that it was Mr Gant himself who had done it, for when Louisa had been taken from him, so too had the rest of his family. Only he had remained, to carry the hurt alone. It was no wonder, she reflected, that he had bent beneath its weight.

'That was taken the day she went,' he said, pointing to a picture sitting on the mantelpiece.

Lucy moved across to lift it. 'May I?' she asked.

'Please,' he said.

In the photograph Louisa Gant wore the same clothes in which Lucy had seen her remains pictured. The girl was not smiling in the picture, but looked past the camera, as if ignoring its presence. Around her neck, she wore a leather necklace on which hung a round, green decoration.

'What is that?' Lucy asked.

'One of those hologram things that were all the rage back then,' Gant said. 'An eye. One of her friends bought it for her. She never took it off.'

Lucy tried to remember if she had been wearing it in the images she had been shown at Carlin's farm, but could not recall its presence.

'You never thought of leaving here,' Lucy asked, replacing the photograph exactly where it had been. Despite this, Gant moved past her and shifted it a fraction. Lucy suspected that he simply wanted to touch it, to maintain his connection with the child who never came home.

'No,' he said. 'I couldn't have done that. What if she'd made her way back and we were gone? What if she thought she'd been forgotten?'

Lucy nodded. 'Of course,' she said.

'Even if she had . . . if she wasn't coming back . . . wherever she is, she needs to know that I have not forgotten her.' He spoke so earnestly that, for a moment, Lucy could not reply.

'That sounds stupid, perhaps,' he said.

Lucy shook her head. 'I understand completely. While we remember, they are never truly lost.'

Gant smiled at the comment and nodded, once, satisfied that Lucy shared his belief. 'I'll show you her room,' he said. 'I never changed it either. Whatever time they tell me for definite that it's her, I'll maybe need to redecorate then.'

He moved up the stairs. Lucy could hear the sizzling as the pan spat water onto the cooker. She went into the kitchen and removed it from the hot ring before following the man up the stairs.

As he had claimed, Louisa's room remained unchanged since her disappearance. The walls were painted a shade of pink, but the girl had perhaps felt the colour too babyish for the bedclothes on her bed were a paisley pattern.

On a chair next to the bed, a small black top

335

had been placed. Lucy moved across, afraid touch anything in the room, as if in the presenc of relics. Gant followed her, lifting the garmen from the chair, holding it to his face, breathing in.

'You can still smell her off her clothes,' he said. 'Sometimes. Sometimes I can't catch it any more.'

Lucy nodded, not trusting herself to speak. On the bookcase, a small photo album sat, its spine decorated in pink feathers. 'Can I — ' She cleared her throat, tried again. 'Do you mind if I take a look?'

'Go ahead,' the man said, smiling gently. 'We bought her a camera for Christmas that year. She loved taking pictures. She said she'd be a photographer when she grew up.'

Lucy lifted the book and opened it gently, so as not to disturb its contents.

'You look like her,' the man said.

Lucy felt a shiver wash through her. 'Excuse me?'

Gant smiled mildly in a manner that made Lucy wonder whether his survival technique all these years had been drug-enhanced.

'The first officer. When Louisa went. There was a woman officer too. She stood where you're standing. Looked at that book too. You look like her. You remind me of her.'

Lucy felt something tickle at the back of her throat, had to cough several times to clear it. The photographs in the book had been taped in. In some cases, the tape had dried, leaving a brown line on the page, the picture itself lying in the

.ds of the book at the spine. Most were of ouisa and her parents. Lucy was surprised to ee how young Mr Gant appeared in them, how significantly he'd aged in the intervening years.

One set of photographs, towards the end, was taken on a beach. Louisa was pictured sitting on the sand. Her head was bowed slightly, her eyes lowered, as if embarrassed by the picture.

'She didn't like getting her picture taken as she got older,' Gant said, moving closer to Lucy to point to the photograph in question. Lucy could smell something, almost like infection, off his breath in such close proximity. His stomach rattled with wind.

'Excuse me,' he said. He moved away from her, rifting lightly to clear the wind from his gut. 'Pardon me.'

Lucy flicked through the album. Towards the end she saw a picture of a young boy, perhaps a year or two older than Louisa. He wore a black T-shirt, emblazoned with a Guns N' Roses logo. His black hair hung over his eyes. His dress seemed out of place for a trip to the beach.

'Was this your son?' Lucy asked. There had been no other pictures in the house, so Lucy could not be sure if Gant even had a son.

'God, no. He was a friend of Louisa's,' Gant said. 'Peter. He was a bit old for her. Not age wise — I think he was only a year older than her — but in other ways. She insisted on him coming with us that day.'

'What happened to him?'

'He moved away after she died. With his

337

mother. I think the family broke up. He went Belfast, I think.'

Lucy nodded.

'He was the one bought her that necklace you'd asked about. The eye. The eggs should be done,' he added. 'Will you come down?'

Lucy nodded, placing the album back on the shelf where it had been, then followed him out of the room.

'I'm sorry if my calling has been difficult for you — ' she began.

Gant stopped on the steps and turned, snapping his fingers, his face alight with remembrance. 'Bell,' he said.

'Excuse me?'

'I've been trying to remember his name. It's Peter Bell,' he said.

'Who?'

'The boy at the beach. Peter Bell.'

55

A team was already at Bell's house by the time Lucy managed to get a squad car to pick her up from Gant's. A uniform was banging on the door, but without response from inside. Despite this, Lucy noticed that the curtains had now been pulled closed.

Lucy introduced herself to the Senior Officer.

'Chief Superintendent Burns will be here shortly,' the man said. 'Must be important for the Super to come out.'

Lucy nodded then glanced next door to where the lace curtains hanging on the windows shifted incrementally at her gaze.

She knocked on the door. A moment later, she heard the light click of the lock and the door opened fractionally. The elderly neighbour, with whom she had spoken the previous night, peered out at her through the gap. She wore a thin net over her hair, her cheeks sunken in a manner that suggested she had not yet put in her teeth.

'Good morning, Mrs Sinclair. I'm sorry we've bothered you. Do you remember me? From last night?'

The woman tutted as if the question had offended her.

'We're looking for Mr Bell now, Mrs Sinclair. A bit more urgently. Has he been home since I called last night?'

The woman nodded.

339

'Can I come in, Mrs Sinclair?'

'No,' the woman said.

Lucy tried to glance behind her, wondering if perhaps Bell had hidden out in his neighbour's house.

'Is everything OK?' Lucy asked. 'Is there someone in the house with you?'

The woman glanced across at where other officers had gathered on the roadway. She said something, her voice faint and dry.

'I'm sorry?' Lucy said.

'I'm not dressed,' the woman replied. As she spoke, she pointed towards where the male officers stood.

'I understand. Of course. Has Mr Bell been home since I spoke with you?'

The woman nodded lightly. 'He came back late. I didn't get a chance to speak with him about you calling.'

'That's fine,' Lucy said. 'Is he still in his house, Mrs Sinclair?'

'I don't know. I heard shouting though. It woke me up. Around four o'clock.'

'Shouting?'

A brief nod. 'Thudding and shouting. Then I heard his front door slam. It makes my windows rattle. I've asked him not to do it. He normally doesn't.'

'But you heard signs of fighting in the middle of the night?' Lucy repeated, loudly enough for the Response Team officers standing around to hear her.

The woman rolled her eyes, repeating it louder herself lest Lucy was hard of hearing.

'Thank you, Mrs Sinclair. Keep your door closed. We're going to check on Mr Bell.'

Lucy called over the man who had been banging on Bell's door. 'The neighbour says she heard a fight in there at four in the morning, then someone leaving. For all we know, Bell could be lying dead in there.'

'We should wait for the Chief Super,' he replied. 'To be sure.'

'We can't wait,' Lucy said. 'She said she heard a violent struggle.' She moved across and pushed at the door, shoving it with her shoulder. The man with whom she had spoken took out his radio and contacted the station. The other three officers stood watching her as she tried to force the door, without success. Two of them began to laugh at her efforts. The third however, a younger uniform, came across to her. 'Do you need a hand, Sergeant?' he asked.

'A shoulder would be more useful,' she said, smiling.

Between them, on the second shove, they managed to crack the frame of the door jamb sufficiently to push the door open.

'Mr Bell?' Lucy called, entering the house. 'PSNI. Are you here, Mr Bell?'

The man who had helped her moved in behind, the others following them in through the open doorway.

'Mr Bell?' Lucy called. 'We've had reports of a fight, Mr Bell. Are you here?'

The house was silent. Lucy moved in through the living room. 'Check upstairs,' she said to the man behind her. 'I'll check the kitchen.'

She moved through into the kitchen area. A scattering of dishes lay on the worktop. Beyond that, nothing seemed disturbed. She checked the back door into the yard, which was locked.

'Sergeant,' she heard one of the men shout from above.

Taking the stairs two at a time, she came into the room from which the call had come. The young uniform stood in what had presumably been a bedroom that Bell had converted into a workroom. An old piece of kitchen worktop had been screwed into the wall. Along it sat three different computers. A tangle of cables snaked beneath the worktop and down to a wall socket.

Lucy took out her phone and called through to ICS. The call went to answering machine, though the recorded message listed a mobile number for emergencies. Lucy scribbled it onto her hand as she listened, then redialled the new number. David Cooper answered.

'Are you free?' she asked.

'Now there's a question I don't get every day,' he replied. 'What's up?'

'I followed up on the names from Foyleside when Kay was lifted. I think I've found something. One of them works with computers. Can you come across?'

'What's the address?' Cooper said. 'Give me ten minutes.'

★ ★ ★

Burns arrived before that. His initial anger at the fact that the team had entered Bell's house was

342

...mpered somewhat by learning that the ...eighbour had provided them with a cause for concern regarding the health of the person inside.

'I heard about this morning,' he said to Lucy when he saw her. 'Are you sure you should be working today?'

'I wasn't the one hurt,' Lucy replied, disingenuously.

'Regardless,' he said. 'No one would think less of you for needing a break.'

Lucy shook her head. 'Gavin Duffy has vanished,' she said. 'I showed him the image of the young guy from the Foyleside and, a few hours later, he'd gone. I think he knew who the man in the picture was. I think he's gone after him, because of Karen.'

'I see,' Burns said. 'Do you think the Duffy boy was involved in placing the device under your car?'

Lucy shook her head. Gavin could be difficult, but she'd sensed that they had got on well. She didn't believe that the youth would want to kill her, or, more particularly, Robbie. She told Burns as much, adding, 'Maybe he caught up with Karen's killer and revealed that he'd identified him from an image I had. Peter Bell, if he is the groomer, might have panicked.'

'If that's the case,' Burns said, 'we need to find Gavin, in case Bell has hurt him too.'

'I've asked David Cooper from ICS to come across and look at the machines here to see what he can find. It might help us locate Bell.'

Burns shook his head. 'Not without cause, he

343

won't be examining them. You broke in becau
you heard there had been a disturbance. Ther
being no sign of anyone injured, we have no
excuse to start searching the man's computers.'

'He was in the Foyleside when Kay was
arrested. He was best friends with Louisa Gant
before she died. It can't be just coincidence that
he crosses both cases.'

'Possibly not,' Burns said. 'But you can't check
his computer. You'll need to call ICS off. We'll
set officers outside. If Bell returns, we can bring
in him for questioning. But we can't start
checking his PCs. Without a warrant.'

'That's — ' Lucy began.

'The law, Sergeant,' Burns snapped. 'What
would you do? Fuck up a prosecution because
you stormed ahead and ignored procedures.
Let's say he is the one who killed Karen Hughes.
Will it help us if he gets off because we didn't
follow procedures? We arrest him, get cause, then
we get a warrant. OK?'

Lucy grudgingly nodded assent.

'I suggest you either return to the PPU or go
home, Sergeant,' Burns said. 'But either way,
you're not staying here.'

The officers from the Response Team, who
were standing in the living room below, watched
silently as Lucy passed them and moved back
out of the house. She knew they had heard
everything, knew that it would be the station
gossip for the next day or two.

As she stepped out into the weak mid-morning
light, she remembered she didn't have a car. She
was damned too, though, if she was going to go

ck inside and ask for a lift now. She was taking ut her phone to call for a taxi when a black wensis pulled to a stop outside the house and Dave Cooper waved out.

'Where do I start?' he asked, climbing out of the car.

'Giving me a lift back to the PPU would be a great place,' Lucy said.

56

'I know it's him,' Lucy said, after explaining to Cooper why he was no longer needed at the scene.

He was driving back down the Limavady Road, slowing as they approached the roundabout at the Foyle Bridge. 'Burns is right, you know,' he said.

'That doesn't make me feel any better,' Lucy grunted. 'We're this close to catching him. We just need something to fall into place.'

'Take a step back from it,' Cooper said. 'Forget about it for a while. It'll sort itself out in your head when you're not trying so hard. Have a night off.'

Lucy scoffed, assuming he was joking. 'Gavin went after him,' she said. 'I'd bet money that's what the fight was. He went and faced him down.'

'How did he know who he was?' Cooper asked.

'What?'

'How did Gavin know who he was?'

Lucy shrugged. 'I dunno,' she said. 'He knew Karen was with someone in the weeks before she died. Maybe she told him Bell's name.'

Cooper nodded. They passed Gransha Hospital to their right as they drove. Lucy glanced back, feeling a pang of guilt that she had yet to go back and see her father again.

What happened to you?' Cooper asked. He ~ed his own hand off the gear stick and gently ~ouched Lucy's bandaged hand to indicate what ~e meant.

'I had an accident,' Lucy said, flushing as she wondered why she hadn't told him the truth. Told him about Robbie. She felt a further pang of guilt that she hadn't contacted the hospital since to see how he was doing.

'You're pushing yourself too hard,' Cooper said, his hand remaining lightly on top of hers a second longer, before he had to change gears again. 'You need to take a breather.'

'I need a cup of tea,' Lucy said.

'I have no milk,' Cooper said. 'Unless you have some in PPU?'

'Possibly,' Lucy said. Fleming was the one who usually bought the milk and biscuits. Lucy didn't even know if he did so out of his own pocket. Had never thought to ask.

'Then tea you shall have,' Cooper said, pulling in through the main gates, waving to the officer on duty at the entrance checkpoint.

★ ★ ★

The Unit seemed cold, less inviting without Fleming's presence. The lights were off, the rooms gloomy. Lucy turned on the main light and directed Cooper towards the kitchen.

'I'm expecting a fax,' she said, remembering that the schools had said they would send through a list of events prior to Karen and Sarah's first contact with 'Bradley'. Or 'Harris'. Or Bell.

347

When she went up to her room, Mary Qu____ stared at her silently from her space on the wa____ The fax machine in her room was still on, sever____ pages of text lying on the tray at its base. She flicked through them. A number were Missing Persons posters from other districts: most were children who had run away from care, foster parents, or their own homes. Requests to be on the lookout. While many of the notices were from England or Scotland, one was from An Garda Sciochanna, in the Republic. A fifteen-year-old, Annie Marsden, had gone missing from the care home in which she was placed in Stranorlar. Something about the girl's name seemed familiar, though Lucy could not place it. Regardless, she marked the fax to remind herself to send out a BOLO to all local cars, considering the proximity to their own jurisdiction.

Lucy eventually found the lists from the two schools. Karen's had already given her a list of the events of the week prior to 'Bradley' contacting her, but had now sent through details of each event and the people involved. The secretary had noted at the bottom that all appropriate background checks had been done on anyone coming into contact with the children. Besides, Lucy knew that someone in CID had done checks on Karen's school and would have checked such vetting had been completed.

She flicked through to Sarah Finn's school's list next. It was significantly longer, seemingly a calendar of events for the entire term rather than just the week before she'd first been contacted online. As Lucy scanned through it, one name stood out. A name that had also appeared on the list from Karen's school: Country Photographers.

Lucy sat at her desk and phoned through to the school, asking to speak to the secretary. If schools were anything like police stations, the people in the front office would have a better sense of what was happening in the school on any given day than anyone else.

After Lucy introduced herself the woman on the other end, who'd called herself Rose, interrupted her. 'I sent you through the list already.'

'I know. Thank you,' Lucy said. 'I wanted to ask you about Country Photographers.'

'Yes?' the woman replied slowly.

'Are they a new company to the school?'

'God, no. They've been coming into us for years. Why?'

'And they'd have done vetting and background checks, presumably.'

'Of course,' Rose replied. 'What's this about?'

'Where could I find them?' Lucy asked.

'Have you not got a phone book?' Rose snapped. 'Or a computer.'

'I've got a pen,' Lucy asked. 'Ready to write down the address which I'm betting you know by heart.'

There was silence for a moment, then the woman rattled off the address once, before hanging up.

Cooper was sitting in the Interview Room on the sofa, drinking his tea. A second mug sat on the table, blobs of cream gathering on its surface.

'I'm not sure about your milk,' he offered when she came down the stairs.

'Do you fancy giving me another lift?' Lucy asked, handing him the faxes. 'My car's out of action.'

57

Country Photographers was operated by a man named Niall Hines, out of the ground-floor unit of a block on Spencer Road. The shop itself was small; the walls cluttered with wedding and graduation pictures, displayed to show the range of Hines's craft. In fact, Lucy thought, they all looked remarkably similar. What scope there was for originality in an image of someone in a cloak holding a scroll, Hines seemed not to have explored it.

An older blonde woman was sitting at the reception desk when they came in. She looked up and smiled at them. 'How are you? Wedding photos is it?' she asked.

'No,' Lucy said, glancing at Cooper to see him struggling to conceal his smile. 'We're a little past that, I'm afraid. We were hoping to speak with Mr Hines. I'm DS Black of the Public Protection Unit. This is Officer Cooper.'

The woman's smile faltered. 'Oh. I'll see if he's available.' She stepped in through the gap in a curtained partition. Cooper moved across to where she had gone and peered through.

'The master's at work,' he said.

Lucy followed him and they stood looking into a small studio space. The back wall had been painted white. Three coloured beanbags of varying sizes were placed in the middle of the floor. On one a young boy sat cross-legged. Next

351

to him, on a bigger red bag, lay a girl who Lucy took to be the boy's sister. She was lying flat on her stomach, propping herself up on her arms. Hines himself was standing next to a camera on a tripod. He was a small man, thin-framed, with wiry grey hair. Despite standing erect, his back seemed to arch outwards, as if he was so used to hunching that even when he stood straight, his back retained the shape.

'Give me a smile, young man,' he said. The boy obliged, smiling brightly, in doing so revealing the gap where his two front teeth had once been.

'And now, you my pretty? Can you give me a smile, like your brother?'

The girl nodded with such vigour, her pigtails wagged wildly on either side of her head.

'Haven't you the prettiest eyes?' he said.

The girl beamed at the compliment and, in that instant, a flash illuminated the ceiling as the camera shutter clicked.

'And now one of the two of you. Nathan, can you lie next to your sister and both of you look at me?'

Lucy looked across and saw the clearly proud mother of the two children standing at the far wall, absurdly using her phone to take pictures of the pictures being taken.

The boy did as he was directed and, after a few minor adjustments to positions, the final few shots were taken in quick succession, each image preceded by a compliment from Hines to the children.

After the children had been led out by their

other, Hines came across to them.

'Wedding photographs, is it?' he asked, smiling. 'Such a beautiful couple.'

'I'm afraid not,' Lucy said, glancing at Cooper who, again, couldn't resist grinning. 'I'm with the PSNI Public Protection Unit. I'm investigating a case involving two school children.'

Hines's expression darkened. 'I've been completely vetted,' he said.

Lucy raised a placatory hand. 'I'm simply following up on connections between the two girls,' she said. 'You visited the schools of both in the days before they were first targeted.'

'What schools?'

Lucy told him. The man muttered to himself, his hand to his mouth, his eyes downcast, as if searching the studio floor for an explanation. 'Are you sure I even took pictures of the children?'

'I'm not,' Lucy admitted.

'What were the dates of the shots?' he asked, moving across to a small anteroom set off the studio. In it a single computer hummed on the desk.

Lucy offered him the date of the visit to Karen's school. The man scrolled through folders, finally hitting on one for that date. He opened the folder and a series of images of girls, numbered from 001, all seated in front of faux bookcases, appeared.

He began scrolling down through the images. 'Tell me if you see her. I have no names with the images here.'

As he scrolled, Lucy scanned the pictures.

Eventually, at image 098, she saw the picture Karen Hughes.

'That's her,' she said, pointing.

'Where are images 96 and 97?' Cooper asked. He pointed to the screen. Lucy noticed now that the image of a child before Karen was number 095 and yet Karen was 098.

Hines peered closely at the screen. 'Those shots were spoiled. She might have blinked, or looked at the floor, or something. What was the second date?'

As Lucy told him, he closed one folder and opened another. Again he scrolled through the images. This time, when Lucy saw the picture of Sarah Finn, a copy of the one she had seen in Finn's house the day she vanished, she noticed that there were three shots of the child. In the first two, she was glancing downwards.

'You see,' Hines said, pointing to the picture. 'This folder hasn't been cleared yet. She kept looking at the floor.'

'Why? The flash?'

Hines shook his head. 'The flash doesn't hit them directly. I angle it to the ceiling. I always tell the girls that they have pretty eyes. It makes most of them smile. A handful can't take the compliment and they look away. When that happens, I usually just have to get them to say 'Cheese'. They get embarrassed by it.'

'Why?' Cooper asked.

'Low self-esteem,' Lucy said, reflecting on how she had described Karen Hughes to Burns on the day she had been found.

'You can spot them a mile off,' Hines

mitted. 'But what can you do? They hear me
iling the others how pretty they look. I can't
ery well not say it to them.'

'Maybe not say it at all,' Lucy suggested.

The man shrugged, unconvinced. 'I've been
doing it twenty-five years,' he said.

'How many people work here?' Lucy asked.

'Just me and my daughter, Julie,' Hines said.
'You met her at the front desk.'

'And you've both been vetted?'

Hines nodded. 'Of course. I've been in schools
for twenty-five years doing this,' he repeated.
'Whatever happened to these girls, my being in
the school is coincidence.'

'No one else would have access to these
images?'

Hines shook his head, though a little slower
now, less certain.

'Who?'

Hines scratched the side of his head. 'I have
someone who handles my online stuff. Orders
and that. He designed the website and keeps it
updated. He would see them. He helps me out at
times if we're busy. The start of the school year
and that, it can get a bit hectic.'

Lucy felt the hairs on her arms rise. 'Who is
he?'

'He's a good fella.'

'Who is he?' Lucy repeated.

'Peter Bell's his name,' Hines said.

58

On the way back to the Strand Road, Lucy called through to the Press Office and asked them to send out details of the child from Donegal, Annie Marsden. She had called through to the incident room to be told that Burns was in a meeting, but would be free shortly. Lucy hoped that if she could convince him about the need to examine Bell's PCs they might get a warrant quickly and Cooper could get started straight away.

When she came into the incident room, Tara immediately ran across to her and hugged her, quickly. 'Are you OK?' she asked.

Cooper looked at Lucy quizzically.

'Fine,' Lucy said, a little flustered.

'Why are you in work? You should have gone home.'

'I'm OK,' Lucy said, quietly, hoping Tara might take the hint.

'You were in a bomb,' Tara said. 'That's not OK.'

'You were in a bomb?' Cooper repeated, turning to Lucy.

Lucy shrugged. 'I was *near* a bomb. This is Dave Cooper from ICS Branch, Tara.'

'Hi.' Cooper smiled. Then to Lucy: 'How near?'

'Her boyfriend was in the car,' Tara said to Cooper, then she asked Lucy, 'Any word?'

'Your boyfriend?' Cooper repeated. 'Was he injured?'

Lucy nodded. 'Leg injuries,' she said. 'I've not had a chance to find out how he is since,' she added to Tara. It wasn't entirely true. She could easily have phoned from Cooper's car, but had been reluctant to do so in front of him. 'Is Burns here?'

'In his office,' Tara said. 'Just.'

'Can I borrow a computer?' Cooper asked. 'While I'm waiting?'

★ ★ ★

Burns was fixing his tie when he called Lucy into the office. 'I thought you were going home,' he said, watching her in the mirror as he straightened his collar.

'I went back to the Unit,' she said. 'I discovered the connection between Sarah Finn and Karen Hughes. Both had their photographs taken by Country Photographers in the weeks before they were first contacted online.'

Burns nodded curtly, angling his head to examine that his tie was sitting right. 'We did all the background checks on them,' he said. 'They'd been vetted.'

'Peter Bell was their web designer. At times he helped out with processing the photographs when they were in a busy period; like the first weeks of school term for example.'

Burns turned and stared at her a moment, before sitting behind his desk. 'Was he vetted?'

Lucy shrugged. 'Possibly not. He never came

357

into actual contact with any of the kids. But his name keeps cropping up in connection with these girls. I think I know how he picked them too. Sarah and Karen. When they were having their pictures taken, Hines the photographer told the students that they had pretty eyes or smiles or whatever. To get a reaction. Both Karen and Sarah reacted in the same way.'

Burns shrugged. 'How?'

'By staring at the floor. Embarrassed.'

'So?'

'I think that as Bell worked through the images from the schools, he realized that the kids who stared at the floor were shy, lacking in self-esteem. That they were vulnerable.'

'How would he have got their contact details? To find them online?'

'Bell processed orders for Hines through his website but, during busy periods, helped out with the ones coming in through schools, too. Maybe they thought because he wasn't in direct contact with the kids, it didn't matter. But he had access to their images and their names.'

Burns considered what she had said. 'I'll need to speak with the ACC before we do anything,' he said. 'Though this might be enough to get a warrant to examine his house.'

There was a brief knock at the door and, as it opened, Tara peered around. 'Sir, there's something you need to see.'

They moved out into the incident room where Cooper was working at one of the PCs. 'I've found something,' he said.

He clicked on the mouse and a website for

358

ountry Photographers appeared on the screen. A range of images decorated the main page, including wedding shots, children posing on the beanbags they had seen on their visit to Hines's studio and staged portraits. One of the images was a close-up picture of a daisy. The individual stamens of its head could be seen, encircled by a white crown of petals.

'I've found a tiny key here,' he said. 'On the fifteenth petal around.'

He moved the mouse in a slow circular motion. They could see the arrow on screen moving across each petal. Sure enough, as it reached the fifteenth petal, the arrow changed to a pointing finger, suggesting that it was hovering over a web link. Cooper clicked on it and the screen changed to a plain black screen with a single white text box at the centre.

'What's that?'

'A password,' Cooper said. 'The rest of the site is word protected. This part of the site is hosted in a different place from the rest, too,' he added. 'We've been taken to a different website.'

'How do you know?'

'There's no IP address as such,' Cooper said. He typed a few keys and pointed to a piece of text at the bottom of the screen: a series of numbers ending with the word 'onion'. 'It's a darknet site.'

Lucy shrugged. 'And that means?'

Cooper sighed, then raised his hands, laid flat one above the other. 'This,' he said, moving his upper hand, 'is the ordinary internet that we all use. Google and Yahoo and that. OK?'

'If you say so,' Lucy said.

Then, moving the lower hand, he said, 'This ⌐ the darknet. Instead of a range of servers hosting sites, which can be traced, it's created by file sharing between users. It means it's completely untraceable.'

'Why is that allowed?'

'No one can prevent it,' Cooper said. 'Besides, it does have advantages in, say, a dictatorship where people can't express political views openly. It just also is used for all kinds of online criminal activity. And paedophiliac websites, obviously.'

'How would users know how to enter this site?' Lucy asked.

'They'd get the address through a forum or personal recommendation,' Cooper said. 'I'm guessing too that there's a common password for getting through this level of the site to whatever's behind this. You'd have to be given the password to go beyond here, in case anyone stumbled on it by accident. You'd probably find that there's then a second level of password protection to go beyond the next page, probably personalized from then on in.'

'Can you break the password?' Burns asked.

Cooper shook his head. 'No. But, if it is a common password, there's a chance that we might find it on some of Bell's PCs in his house. My guess is that it will be something obvious, something significant to the type of people attracted to that type of site. Humbert, Lolita, Wonderland, something along those lines.'

'Get across to Bell's house,' Burns said. 'I'll have a warrant sorted by the time you get there.'

59

Cooper told Lucy that he wanted to return to the unit first to collect some of his equipment, which might make working through any encryption on the machines easier.

While she had waited in the car, she reflected on what they had found. Peter Bell had been a childhood friend of Louisa Gant when she died. Now he appeared to be involved in, or running, a paedophile website and was grooming teenage girls to be used for sex at house parties he organized in Peter Carlin's house, next to where Louisa Gant's body had been buried. Somehow, Gavin had recognized Bell in the picture and had clearly gone after him. He must have told Bell that Lucy had his picture and that she was in the unit, allowing Bell an opportunity to plant the device in her car. She had to assume that Gavin had been coerced into giving this information. Unless he had been involved in Karen's death himself. Lucy found that hard to believe, based on her experience with the boy. Still, she could not fully dismiss the thought, even after Cooper got back in the car and began speaking to her.

On the way from the unit to the house, Cooper finally raised the subject of the car bombing. 'So, you didn't think it was worth mentioning then?'

'It was nothing.'

'It left your boyfriend hospitalized.'

'He's not . . . ' she began. 'It's complicate⸎ she managed finally.

'I assumed as much, considering you're still at work and he's lying in hospital,' Cooper commented. 'In fact, I'd say 'complicated' is an understatement.'

'I need to borrow your car,' Lucy said. 'The kid from the residential unit vanished after the attack. I need to see if I can find him.'

'I'd also say that was a neat change of subject, but it wasn't,' Cooper commented. 'Can you drive with a bandaged hand?'

Lucy smiled. 'Is that concern for me or for your car?' she asked.

'Are you mad? My car, obviously.'

* * *

By the time they reached Bell's, the house was cordoned off and teams were already beginning to conduct a search of the rooms.

Cooper went straight upstairs and booted up the three PCs. Lucy, for her part, drove on up to Gobnascale. She phoned the school first, already guessing that Gavin would not have turned up. The person she spoke to explained that they had closed early for the Christmas holidays and that attendance had been very poor.

She continued round to the youth club. Jackie Logue was standing in the middle of the hall, directing several of the kids where to pin up Christmas decorations.

'DS Black. We're having a party tonight. A Christmas disco. Do you want to come?'

'I'm looking for Gavin,' Lucy said, without
:eamble.

Logue shrugged. 'He's not here. I've not seen him all day.' He called to the kids. 'Anyone seen Gavin?'

There were murmurs from the kids as they worked, all in the negative.

'Will you contact me if he appears?' Lucy asked.

Logue nodded. 'I hope you weren't badly hurt,' he said.

Lucy stared at him. 'What?'

He pointed towards her hand, thick in bandages. 'Your hand,' he said. 'I hope it wasn't anything serious.'

'No,' Lucy said. 'Not serious.'

As she was leaving, she met Elena coming up the path to the hall.

'Hi,' she said, though did not raise her head to look at Lucy.

'You haven't seen Gavin have you?' Lucy asked.

Elena shook her head. 'He was meant to meet me after my exam this morning. He never showed up. Not even a text.'

'How did it go?' Lucy asked.

The girl glanced up briefly. 'Shit,' she said.

'I know how that feels,' Lucy commented.

* * *

She stopped at the hospital on her way back to Bell's. Robbie was in a room of his own, dozing quietly. She came across and lifted the chart at

the end of his bed, scanning it, while all the ti.
aware of the futility in so doing for it mea.
nothing to her. When she glanced up, she saw h
was awake and watching her.

'Hey, you,' she said.

He smiled, his lips dry, and winced as if the
slight movement had hurt the stitches in his
cheek.

'I wondered where you were,' he said. 'When I
woke. I thought you'd be here.'

'Sorry,' Lucy said, putting the chart back. 'I
think Gavin went after whoever killed Karen.
And I think he told them I was with you.'

'Why?' Robbie managed.

'Maybe he was forced into telling. If that's the
case, he may be in trouble. I hoped if I could
find Gavin, I could find the person who did this.'

'That's not what I was thinking about when I
woke,' he managed, pushing himself up in the
bed. Lucy moved across and, lightly gripping
beneath his armpits, helped him shift. In doing
so, she was reminded of having done something
similar to pull him out of the burning car hours
earlier.

'What?'

'I wasn't thinking about catching the person
who tried to blow you up. I was thinking about
you.'

Lucy nodded. 'I'm sorry,' she said. 'How are
you feeling?'

'Like I've just been in a bomb,' Robbie
commented, smiling wryly.

Lucy smiled. 'That sounds about right,' she
said. She moved closer to him, laid her hand

ınst his face. 'I'm sorry it was you in the car, ᵒbbie. I'm so sorry.'

'I'm not,' Robbie said, placing his own hand ᵒver hers.

Lucy leaned down and kissed his lips. They felt dry and cracked, his breath stale behind the kiss.

She felt her phone vibrating in her pocket. Embarrassed, she straightened and took the call. It was Cooper calling from Bell's house.

'You need to come back here. Now.'

★ ★ ★

'I was able to bypass the password,' Cooper said, when Lucy arrived. He was standing at the front door of Bell's, waiting for her return.

'All in one piece,' Lucy said, handing him the keys. The parking ticket she'd been given for not paying and displaying at the hospital car park, she kept in her pocket.

'Thanks,' Cooper said, looking at the keys but seeming not to realize the import of her comment. 'I was right.'

'I thought you said you couldn't break the password,' Lucy said, following him up the stairs.

'I didn't. I traced his history on one of the PCs. He had used it to access the site. The computer had automatically remembered the password through to the next level. You need to see it.'

They went into the small room. Lucy could see one of the PCs displaying a web page very similar to the main Country Photographers'

website. On it were a number of pictures, al_
school children, all taken by Hines. In each, t_
girl, for they were all girls, was sitting in front c
the faux library of books that Hines used as his
backdrop.

Lucy leaned in and examined the screen. She
felt her throat tighten as she recognized one of
the pictures as that of Karen Hughes. The next
one was the image of Sarah Finn that she had
seen before.

'That's not quite what I was expecting,' she
said.

'It's like a stud wall into the site,' Cooper said.
'Let's just say someone does accidentally make it
through the first level, they reach this, it's
innocuous-looking. Click on one of the individual pictures, though, and you get this.'

He clicked on the image of Karen Hughes and
a pop-up box appeared requesting a username
and password.

'You register for membership here,' Cooper
said, pointing to a small text box at the bottom
of the page he had shown her, where viewers
could sign up for a newsletter. 'Again, it looks
innocuous. Presumably, though, once you
request a newsletter, Bell has your details and
sends you a password and username. Then you
get to whatever he's hiding back there.'

'It's definitely him,' Lucy said.

'Look at this,' Cooper said, pointing to the
bottom picture of a schoolgirl. Lucy stared at the
girl's face a moment before she realized where
she had seen her before. Immediately she also
realized why the name had seemed familiar. The

ently reported missing Annie Marsden had ommented on a Facebook posting by one of the uspected sock puppet accounts, 'Liam Tyler'.

'The girl from the Missing Persons fax,' Cooper said. 'Annie Marsden. I think he's got her.'

60

Lucy contacted An Garda to tell them about her concerns regarding Annie Marsden's safety. The Inspector with whom she spoke, a softly spoken man, promised that he would visit the Marsden house and check whether Liam Tyler was a real friend of Annie's, or whether the account was simply another sock puppet.

Cooper had been busy working at Bell's PC with a black external hard drive which he'd connected through a USB. He muttered to himself as he worked.

'What are you doing?' Lucy asked.

'Deciphering Bell's password,' Cooper said. 'The website will have a memory of his password, so that, when he logs in, it knows it's him. I can access the database of the site for his password. It brings up the text as a series of hashes. This device tries to decode them by cycling through every possible letter, number or symbol for each hash.'

'Like breaking a safe?'

'Pretty much. It guesses each letter at high speed. Because we're using his own computer, it will automatically complete his username.'

'Impressive,' Lucy said.

'But slow,' Cooper countered. 'How's your boyfriend?'

Lucy nodded. 'He's OK,' she said, feeling her face flush. She couldn't understand if it was at

368

the thought of Robbie or because it was Cooper asking about him.

On the device, the series of six hashes flickered as the first one converted to the letter L.

'It's a start,' Cooper said.

A few seconds later it flickered again and the second hash converted to 'o'.

'Now we're moving,' Cooper said. 'Anyone any good at crosswords?'

Lucy stared at the word: Lo ####. Some of the other officers had moved across and were standing behind Cooper, watching.

'Lovers,' one suggested. Cooper tried typing it in, but the screen simply returned to the empty password box.

'Louisa,' Lucy said.

Cooper glanced at her and nodded. He typed in the word. For a second, nothing happened, then the screen changed and a series of folders appeared on the screen. Each folder had a different name. One was marked 'Karen'.

'Open that one,' Lucy said.

She recognized some of the images that the folder contained as being part of the collection that had been found in Gene Kay's house. There were others, though, where the perpetrator was clearly visible. Lucy wanted to reach out and cover Karen in each image, cover her from the watching eyes of the officers who stood in silence as Cooper quickly scrolled through the images.

'Do we need to look at these?' she asked.

'There were two houses, you said,' Cooper replied. 'I'm trying to see if there's anything to help us find the second one.'

Lucy nodded. 'Try Sarah,' she said. 'She told us that she remembered being in two different houses.'

Cooper went back and opened the second folder. The images contained in there were of similar quality and content to those featuring Karen. In one, Lucy recognized the man with her as Carlin. Any possible misgivings she'd had about his drowning in Enagh Lough were swiftly dispelled.

'There,' Cooper said, quickly.

He stopped at one image in particular and, double-clicking, enlarged it. It was clearly taken in a different room from the bulk of the other images. It was brighter, the bed on which Sarah Finn lay placed next to a window. What Cooper was pointing to was something visible through the window, in the middle distance.

At the far right of the window frame, almost moving out of sight, was a silver four-by-four.

'It's facing onto a road,' one of the uniforms said.

'No,' Cooper commented. 'Look beside it.'

Sure enough, the rest of the surrounding space was the slate grey of water, the white heads of waves just visible.

'So how would a four-by-four go on water?' Cooper asked.

'On a car ferry,' Lucy said. 'And there's only one car ferry within driving distance of here.'

'Magilligan Point,' Cooper said.

61

The light was beginning to fail by the time the Response Teams were on their way. Magilligan lay about twenty-five miles away from the city, along the Sea Coast Road that skirted Lough Foyle. At its narrowest point, between Magilligan and Greencastle in County Donegal, the Foyle was only 2 kilometres wide and it was at this point that the ferry crossed, taking cars between the Republic and Northern Ireland.

Having studied the maps that they had, which, due to the location there of Magilligan Prison were fairly detailed, they had worked out approximately where the house must be, based on the angle at which the ferry had been viewed through the window.

The wind that carried up the lough buffeted the sides of the cars as they travelled the coast road, the cold draughts of air pushing through the gaps in the doors at the rear of the Land Rover.

Lucy glanced out through the viewing slits along the side of the vehicle. To her left, bright against the starless December night, the illuminated shape of Magilligan Prison stood out. Somewhere inside, she realized, Eoghan Harkin would be passing his final night in prison. She wondered, in fact, if his daughter, Karen, had ever been in the Magilligan house where Sarah Finn had been photographed, whether she had realized her proximity to father.

They trundled along the roadway until, after few moments, Lucy heard Burns speaking from the front where he was sitting. She looked up to see him pointing out to the right. Moving across, she looked out through the opposite side of the vehicle and saw, set against the darkness, the squat shape of a small house about a mile down a laneway. By its angle, its rear would have looked out onto the lough, facing the path of the ferry.

Burns twisted in his seat, his face pressed against the mesh that separated them from the front seats. 'This is us, folks,' he said. 'Our priority is to get any children out first. We can round up any adults in the place. And obviously, Peter Bell is our target.'

They felt the Land Rover turn sharply to the left, Lucy almost losing her balance with the suddenness of the movement. A moment or two later, they pulled to a halt and the back doors were flung open. In addition to the CID team, there were several uniforms to assist. Further Land Rovers, behind, had been brought to carry any suspects lifted in the raid.

The house was a low-set dormer style. Lights shone from almost all windows, their glare deadened by the thin scraps of curtains that hung over the windows themselves. Even from out here, above the sharp whistling of the wind against the visors of their helmets, they could hear the raised voices inside, the sounds of laughter.

The uniforms approached the front of the house and positioned themselves with the small blue metal battering ram. Two swings were sufficient to force in the front door. Lucy thought of Cooper, brute-forcing his way through the website, as she watched them work.

Then, at a word, they poured in through the open doorway, immediately splitting in all directions, moving into the body of the house. Almost at once, the noise inside increased, people shouting and screaming. Lucy filed in through the door, the clumsiness of the riot gear helmet she wore obscuring her view. She glanced across and saw, in one room, several men sitting, cans of beer in their hands. She saw at least two young girls sitting among them, fully dressed at least, their faces drawn in bewilderment at the source of the intrusion, their eyes glassy. Whoever they were, neither looked like Annie Marsden.

Across to the other side was a smaller room, with a pool table sitting in the middle of it, just as Sarah Finn had described. A number of younger people stood around in here, boys and girls. Some of them were loudly remonstrating with the officers who had entered the room, shouting in their belligerence that the raid was an invasion of privacy. Lucy scanned the group for either Annie Marsden or Gavin Duffy but could see neither.

Instead of entering either room, she quickly pushed her way upstairs, using the banisters to help her pull her way upwards. Mickey shoved past her on his way up, immediately cutting left at the top of the stairs and pushing open the door of a bedroom. Lucy glanced across to an older man standing, naked, twisting to see t. source of the intrusion. A thin pale figure la prone on the bed in front of him. Mickey shovec his way into the room and Lucy saw him grab the man and shove him face down onto the floor.

The door of the room facing Lucy was closed. She turned the handle and pushed it open. In the half-gloom, she could make out two figures lying on the bed, both in a state of undress. Lucy reached across and clicked on the light. Gavin Duffy, stripped to the waist, turned to look at her, his eyes wide and red-rimmed. Beneath him lay a young girl, still in her underwear. She too stared up at Lucy, her face drawn in terror. The side of her face, and the hair which clung to it, seemed matted with vomit.

Lucy pulled off her helmet. 'Gavin?' she said.

'Lucy?' Gavin asked, his face draining of colour. He stumbled off the bed, struggling to keep his footing. 'Lucy?' He moved across to her, his hand extended, touching her arm. 'Are you OK?'

At such close proximity, Lucy could smell the haze of alcohol that surrounded him. His eyes were wide, the whites threaded with burst blood vessels, the pupils little more than pinpricks of black at the centre of each iris.

'Are you OK?' he slurred. The words bubbled into sobs which broke from him.

'I'm so sorry,' he said. 'I didn't know he'd do it.'

'Where's Peter Bell?' Lucy managed, struggling to control her anger.

'Not Peter. Tony. I didn't know he'd do it. The
r.'

'Tony?' Lucy asked. She remembered the tall
youth who had seemed to run the gang in
Gobnascale. 'Tony who?'

'I don't know. I told him you'd shown me
Peter's picture. He asked where you were. I
didn't know he'd do that.' Gavin nodded, then
straightened, as if aware that he was drunk and
trying very hard to appear sober. Lucy suspected
he'd taken more than just alcohol.

'Tony planted the device in my car?'

Gavin nodded. 'I didn't know,' he said. 'I
swear. But you're all right.' He gripped her arm,
forcefully. 'You're all right,' he repeated.

'Robbie was in the car,' Lucy said. 'He was the
one who caused it to blow. He is in hospital.'

'Jesus,' Gavin said, the tears streaming now,
bubbling round his lips as he spoke.

'You set him up, Gavin,' Lucy said, shoving
him roughly backwards, towards the bed. The
girl who had been lying there was trying with
difficulty to sit up, pulling at the bedclothes,
searching for her top.

'I didn't,' Gavin said. 'The picture you showed
me. I knew who it was. I went and told him and
he said he'd take care of it. He asked where you
were and I told him.'

'You told Tony?'

Gavin shook his head. 'Jackie. I told Jackie.'

'Jackie Logue? Why?'

'Peter took a computer class run by the youth
club. I went and told Jackie that he had killed
Karen. Jackie said he'd take care of it.'

'Bell taught in the youth club? Did Kar
know him?'

Gavin shook his head. 'No. He didn't teach i
the club. He worked in a place across the town.
Jackie only allowed some of us to go. Karen
didn't do the class.'

'What about Sarah Finn?' If Sarah had known
Bell already, Lucy wondered why she hadn't told
them his name when they'd interviewed her.

'I don't think so. It was just me and a few
other fellas.'

'Where is Bell now?' Lucy asked.

'He went to get drink,' Gavin said. 'Him and
Tony. And the new girl.'

'Annie?'

Gavin nodded. 'I think so. Maybe. They said
we needed more drink. I came up for a sleep.'

Lucy pointed at the girl sitting up now. She
looked little more than fourteen.

'A sleep?' she asked.

Gavin glanced at the girl, then back at Lucy,
his mouth hanging open. 'I don't . . . I can't
remember if — '

He did not finish the sentence for Lucy struck
him across the face with such force, he lost his
balance and stumbled, having to put out his
hand to arrest his fall.

'You better hope you didn't,' she said, moving
past him to reach for the girl. 'Are you OK?'
Lucy asked her, putting out her hand to help the
girl up off the bed.

62

As they came downstairs, Burns was standing in the hallway, his hands on his hips, glancing between the two rooms as officers in both dealt with those who had been arrested. He smiled when he saw Lucy.

'Is this Annie?' he asked. 'Is she all right?'

Lucy shook her head. 'Annie's been taken out with Bell and a youth called Tony. He runs a gang in Gobnascale. Under Jackie Logue's watch. Bell taught a computer class apparently that some of the youths attended.'

'We'll put out descriptions,' Burns said. 'Someone will spot them. This is a great result.'

'They've gone for drink,' Lucy said. 'They'll have to come back this way. If they see the Land Rovers outside they'll either turn back or drive on round the point. We should send a car up as far as the prison. It can close in behind them when they pass. They'll not see the activity here until after that anyway and we can maybe sandwich them in.'

Burns considered the suggestion a moment, then nodded. 'Take a team with you,' he said. 'A few uniforms in case Bell gets heavy-handed. Eh?'

★   ★   ★

377

In the end, they sat at the entrance to the pri:
for almost an hour before they saw t
headlights of a car bouncing along the roadwɛ
towards them. They had parked about two mile:
from the house, on the verge at the prison gates;
no one would think a police car outside a prison
odd, even at that time of night, Lucy reasoned.

As the car passed, Lucy glanced across, keen
not to be too obvious lest Tony recognize her,
even through the tint of the police car windows.
She was fairly sure that the vehicle that passed
had three people in it. Certainly, there were two
men in the front and a further figure sitting in
the back seat.

Once the car had rounded the bend past the
prison, they pulled off the verge and followed
them along the road, keeping their own
headlights off, using the overspill of light from
the prison to help make their way. The last thing
they wanted was Bell to spot them and take off
around the point.

Instead, after a few hundred yards, they saw
the bright red blinking of the brake lights on
Bell's car as he realized that there were Land
Rovers parked outside the house. Instantly the
lights on the car went out, save, however, for the
reversing light to the rear of the vehicle as Bell
tried reversing back along the roadway he had
just driven down.

Lucy radioed through to the waiting Land
Rover sitting outside the house to move up the
road towards them, effectively sandwiching Bell's
car between them.

When Bell's car appeared at the end of the

tch of roadway on which they now sat, Lucy
ned across and switched on their headlights
d told the uniform driving to speed up.

The car ahead of them stopped abruptly. For a moment, nothing happened. Then the two front doors flung open and Bell and Tony spilled out onto the road and set off, one in each direction, down the incline into the fields bordering the road.

'Get after them,' Lucy snapped, already opening her own door. She sprinted the distance to Bell's car, pulled open the rear door and reached it. A young-looking girl sat in the back seat, her expression one of shock.

'Annie Marsden?' Lucy asked.

The girl nodded.

'I'm DS Black of the PSNI. You're safe. OK?'

The girl glanced around her, then nodded.

'Have they hurt you in any way?' Lucy asked.

'No,' Annie replied quietly.

'They haven't tried to make you do anything?'

The girl shook her head.

'Stay here,' Lucy said. 'I'll be back in a moment. Don't get out of the car until I come back, do you understand?'

Annie Marsden nodded. She wore a light vest top and a denim skirt, her legs bare, save for streaks of fake tan. Lucy shrugged off her coat and handed it into the girl. 'Wrap that around you,' she said.

Standing, she looked across to the field where Tony had run. She could see the bobbing of torch beams as the two uniforms pursued him as he zigzagged in and out of the edge of the light from Magilligan. Finally, he seemed to lose footing as he turned, and instead he slid, hitti. the ground an instant before the uniforms we. on him.

Lucy turned towards the opposite field where Bell had run and began the descent down the incline from the road. The ground was little more than marshland, and she could feel it seep around her feet as she stepped onto it. As she moved she could feel the mild tension of the mud sucking at her boots, the squelch as each foot was lifted.

To her left, she could see the uniform scouring the gorse that bordered the field, moving along it slowly, his torch angled at a height, the beam focused down to offer as wide an illumination as possible, searching for Bell.

Lucy pulled her own torch off her belt and, flicking it on, ran it along the length of the field. She could hear, beyond the shouting of Tony in the field opposite and the terrified lowing of cattle, the gentle rushing of water and she realized why the uniform had stopped where he had: the field abutted a stream, running down towards the lough. The edge of the field ended in a slight rise, where the stream, when it had burst its banks over the years, had pushed the earth along its edges upwards, creating a natural levee. She assumed that either Bell was hiding along it, or indeed had crossed the stream beyond in making his escape.

She slowly shone her torch along the length of the earthen levee, even as she moved closer to it. At its far end, away from where the uniform was ving, it merged with a thin copse of trees and w-lying bushes. It was for here that Lucy set f, assuming that Bell would have headed for over.

She tried to increase her pace, constantly slowed by the sucking mud of the field, her feet sinking deeper as she moved closer to the stream itself, the land now water-logged, the surface reflecting the bounce of her torch beam.

As she approached the tree line, she could see a thin mist gather in loose clouds just beyond the levee, as if someone's breath was condensing in the chilled night air. She assumed that Bell was lying just on the other side, panting hard from his own exertions, his breath condensing above his head, marking out his spot. She tried to step more carefully as she approached, aware that the dull sucking of mud around her feet would alert him to her proximity.

Gun in one hand, torch in the other, she crested the earthen embankment, moving over the top quickly, expecting to see Bell on the other side. Instead, the wide eyes of a cow rolled towards her as it struggled to raise its heft off the sodden ground in which it was trapped. The sudden movement of the creature caused Lucy to start and she lost her footing a little, sliding down the embankment towards the stream.

Suddenly, from among the trees to her right, Bell appeared, launching himself at her. He made to grab at her hair, managing only a loose grip. It was enough to pull her off balance, though not enough for him to retain hold of her as she fell.

She scrabbled along the ground, reaching his feet, even as he kicked out at her to shake h loose. She grabbed one leg and tugged as hard a she could, effectively pulling Bell over the top o her and forcing the two of them to roll into the freezing water of the stream.

Lucy fell awkwardly, the motion of the roll resulting in Bell lying above her, pinning her down beneath the surface. She could taste mud in her mouth, her ears filled with the rush of the water, her hands grappling with the slimed stones of the stream bed in an attempt to gain purchase enough for her to push upwards and dislodge Bell from where he lay on top of her.

She could feel again his hands gripping at her hair, the back of her neck, trying to force her head downwards, further into the water. Bell, shifting his position now, straddled her, his knees either side of her body as he tried to drown her, leaning his weight onto her. She managed to shift a little, onto her side, moving her head enough to manage a gasp of air, before Bell pressed harder, scraping the side of her face against the rocky stream bed.

By angling herself, however, she'd freed her hand a little. Scrabbling along the ground, she managed to find a solid enough surface to press against to lever herself. She pushed as hard as she could, her lungs feeling as if they would burst, her body suddenly aware of the chill. She bucked her body upwards, unseating Bell sufficiently for her to repeat the manoeuvre a second time, more forcibly. Bell, reaching out to arrest his fall, lost his balance sufficiently that

382

cy was able to drag herself from under him. ripping a rock from beneath her, she turned arply in the water and swung upwards. The ock connected with the side of Bell's face, stunning him enough momentarily for Lucy to push herself away from him and struggle to her feet.

Bell, too, was rising to his feet, cursing in the dark. He lunged for Lucy now, but she sidestepped him, swinging the rock a second time, connecting with his temple.

The lunge, combined with his weight and the slippery surface on which he stood, conspired against him and he fell into the water. In an instant, Lucy was on him, straddling him now, holding his head into the water. She gripped the back of his hair, pulled his head upwards sharply then slammed it downwards, his face connecting with the stones beneath the water with each strike.

She felt something rising inside her, felt a rage she had not felt since the night Mary Quigg died. She tightened her grip, holding his head under now with both hands as he thrashed in the water beneath her.

Suddenly, she was being lifted up and away from him. She felt arms constricting across her chest and she realized that the uniform had arrived and was pulling her away from Bell.

'I'm all right,' she said, twisting to look at the man. Only when she saw his expression did she understand that he had dragged her away for Bell's protection, not for hers.

She stepped quickly away from him, holding

her hands aloft to indicate she would not to
Bell again.

For his part, Bell rolled onto his back. H
struggled to pull himself out of the stream and
lay on the embankment, retching as he brought
up the water Lucy had forced him to swallow.
His hair was plastered to his scalp, his face
smeared with dirt, his nose and lips oozing fresh
blood and saliva down over his mouth and chin.
He lay back finally, his breaths coming in
laboured pants in between fits of laughter.

Lucy leaned over him, the movement causing
the uniform to step towards her. Around Bell's
neck he wore a leather necklace on which hung a
green holographic pendant. Shining her torch on
it, Lucy saw, at its centre, an eye.

'Get up,' she said, pulling him by the shoulder.

'I want to speak to my father,' he said, not to
Lucy, but to the uniform, twisting his head to
look past her at the man. 'Call my father. Call
Jackie Logue.'

Saturday 22 December

63

Bell and Tony were bundled into the back of the police car, the other uniform and Lucy taking Bell's car, still blocking the roadway, in which sat Annie Marsden.

When she sat next to her, the girl offered Lucy back her coat.

'You're soaked,' she explained.

Lucy smiled, taking it and wrapping it around herself. After the initial buzz she had felt, first in overpowering Bell, then in his arrest and the revelation that Jackie Logue was his father, Lucy now began to feel the chill, the sodden clothing clinging to her with a damp heat that she knew would eventually sap her energy. She rifled through her coat pocket and took out her phone.

Handing it to the girl, she said, 'You should phone your parents. Tell them you're with us.'

The girl hesitated, her hand stretching out towards but not touching the phone. 'What should I tell them?' she asked, unconsciously pulling at the hem of the skirt she wore.

Lucy looked across at her, smiling a little sadly. 'Tell them you're safe. That's all that they'll care about for now.'

★   ★   ★

An hour later, Lucy sat before her own mother. A Response Team had brought with them a

387

change of clothing and Lucy now wore one c the unit's boiler suits.

'I'm fine,' Lucy reassured her, as her mother asked for the third time how she felt.

'That'll need stitched,' Wilson said, touching the gash on her face with the tips of her fingers.

Lucy shifted her head away sharply from her touch. 'You knew about Bell, didn't you?'

Her mother raised an eyebrow quizzically. 'How would I have known? You only made the connection yourself today.'

'Not about now. About Louisa Gant. He killed her, didn't he?'

Wilson stared at her a moment. They were sitting in one of the upper bedrooms, the one in which she had found Gavin Duffy. She moved across and closed the door softly, then turned and leaned her back against it. Lucy, sitting on the edge of the bed, stared at her, waiting for her to speak, determined to stay silent, determined not to allow her a way out.

Her mother coughed to fill the silence, then pushed herself off the door with her rump and moved towards her daughter. She sat next to her, their bodies not touching, both staring straight ahead.

'He never admitted to it, but I knew Bell had been with her on the day she died,' her mother said, finally. 'I found a picture of him with her in an album she kept.'

'I saw it,' Lucy said.

Her mother turned. 'You visited Gant's? How is he?'

'Broken,' Lucy said. 'How would you expect

to be? So you knew?'

'I started investigating. Bell was only fourteen at the time. His mother was still with Logue at that stage. Once I connected his name to Bell, Special Branch took over.'

'Why?'

Wilson shrugged.

'Don't pretend to be stupid. Why?'

Wilson took a deep breath, held it a moment, then released it slowly. 'It was the new age of policing. They needed to be sure they had some support in those communities that hadn't backed the RUC before the change. Gary Duffy was set against the Peace Process and especially against the police, even with the changes. He was threatening to target Catholics who joined, the whole bit. Logue was known to be more sympathetic to policing change.'

'By the police covering up the fact that his son had killed a child, he became even more sympathetic, I'd imagine.' Lucy had been told Gary Duffy had been a hawk. He'd never have supported the newly formed PSNI and, as a community leader, would have ensured that the residents in the area would not cooperate with them either. From her searches for Cunningham, Lucy knew just how damaging that lack of cooperation could be to an investigation. If Duffy could be discredited in the community's eyes, and a more sympathetic community leader, like Jackie Logue, put in his place, the PSNI would find policing the area much easier. By covering up for Jackie Logue's son, the PSNI had managed to make Logue a puppet himself, she reflected.

Wilson nodded. 'I'd assume so.'

'And Gary Duffy was put in the frame to tak him off the picture?'

'Arresting him for terrorist activity would simply have strengthened his reputation, strengthened his position in the community.'

'Label him a paedophile, though, and he'll be ostracized,' Lucy said.

'Presumably.'

'Why not give Gant back his daughter's body?' Lucy asked.

Her mother remained silent. Lucy studied the circling floral pattern of the carpet beneath her feet, piecing it together. 'Because then there'd have been forensics that Gary Duffy could have challenged in court, that would have implicated Logue's son,' she said, turning to look at her mother.

If the woman heard the comment, she did not react.

'So what role did you play in all this? Was this how you were groomed for success? Turning a blind eye?'

'No,' Wilson said, looking at Lucy directly for the first time. 'The case was taken off me. I was a young officer, told to hand over what I had. I simply did as I was told.'

'And what happened to Bell? Jackie Logue told me he'd had a son that he'd lost when the boy was a teenager. I assumed he meant the child had died.'

Wilson shook her head. 'He and his mother were forced to move away and change their nes to Bell. In the hope that he wouldn't offend.'

'Because that's worked so well in the past,' Lucy spat. 'You knew — '

'I knew nothing for certain, Lucy,' Wilson said sharply. 'Nor do you.'

'You. You and your . . . secrets.'

Wilson's mouth tightened as she sat more erect. 'We all have secrets, Lucy. That's what happened. Doing deals with bad people to try to do some good. On all sides.'

'And that justifies it?'

'That Finn girl went missing and you could go into that community to investigate it, without fear of being shot. Because of those deals. That's the price we pay for peace.'

'So what will happen to Jackie Logue now?'

'If he was involved in this ring, he'll face charges,' Wilson said. 'If he wasn't, he won't.'

'About Louisa Gant, I mean?'

'Nothing. He didn't do it. Peter Bell will face charges if any forensics taken from her remains implicate him.'

'Jackie Logue's an accessory.'

Wilson dismissed the statement. 'So too is Special Branch then. And every officer who benefited from our having Logue on the ground, arguing on our behalf.'

'That's rubbish,' Lucy muttered.

'Don't you judge me. Not until you're able to make the hard decisions too.'

'John Gant deserved to know the truth about his daughter. That's not a hard decision. The man's living in a museum,' Lucy said, aware as she said it that Gant was not the only ⸱ refusing to let go of past grief. Was the picture Mary Quigg, pinned to her office wall, an different from Gant looking at E-FIT images of the girl his daughter might have grown up to be? 'He deserves the truth,' Lucy repeated.

'Well now he'll get it. Some of it at least,' Wilson said.

'A father deserves to know who killed his child,' Lucy stated. 'It doesn't matter the cost.'

Wilson shook her head and stood. 'Go back to Derry and get changed. Get that wound on your face checked.'

⋆ ⋆ ⋆

Lucy borrowed one of the squad cars that had come down from Derry. It was after ten in the morning by the time she left the house. She reached the front of Magilligan and parked up on the verge where she had sat the night before when they had waited for Bell.

Just after 10.45 a.m., the front gates swung slowly backwards and a single figure stepped out into the watery sunlight, his hand raised above his eyes as he glanced up and down the roadway. A little distance down the road, there was a bus stop and he started walking towards it, hefting his bag onto his shoulder.

As he drew abreast the car, Lucy leaned across and opened the door. Eoghan Harkin leaned down.

'Officer,' he said. 'Whatever it was, I didn't do it. I've only just got out.'

392

I thought I should give you a lift,' Lucy said. Ve should talk.'

Harkin looked up and down, as if judging whether there were any potentially better offers, then nodded and, pushing his bag over the shoulder rest onto the floor of the back seat, got in.

Tuesday 25 December

★ ★ ★

Lucy went to first Mass on Christmas morning. The air was sharp with the promise of coming snow, despite the sky being clear of cloud. The other parishioners smiled at her and offered her a Happy Christmas. She returned the wishes, even as she struggled to feel the joy they should have carried with them.

After Mass, she drove to see her father. She had dug out a picture of the garden with the fountain from the laneway behind Prehen and had it framed. When he unwrapped it, he smiled and thanked her, but she could tell from the blankness in his expression that he did not recognize the place. Another of his memories had passed beyond him forever, the wisps of her childhood diminishing one by one with each day his illness progressed.

'What's this for?' he asked.

'It's Christmas, Daddy,' she said.

'I've not got you anything,' he said, his eyes rheumy.

'That's OK,' she said.

She sat next to him, her hand on the arm of her chair, his hand, soft and warm, lightly balanced on top of hers.

'Are we having dinner?' her father asked suddenly.

'No, Daddy,' Lucy said. 'I've got to go soon.'

'Where to?'

'The cemetery,' Lucy said.

The man snorted, derisively. 'What's a young girl like you doing going to visit the dead?'

Lucy stared at him, surprised by the lucidit[y]
the comment.

'You want to take Lucy somewhere nice tod[ay]
love,' he said, winking against the light coming i[n]
through the window of his room.

'I am Lucy, Daddy.'

He squinted at her, then patted her hand
lightly. 'Isn't that funny? I thought you were your
mother for a minute,' he said.

★   ★   ★

As she was leaving, Lucy was surprised to see
her mother's car pull into the small car park in
front of the block where her father was being
held. In truth, she had assumed that the woman
did not visit her father. She moved quickly across
to the squad car that she was using until her own
was replaced, but struggled to get the door open,
her movements clumsy because of the bandage
on her hand. By the time she'd managed to pull
it open, she had no choice but to speak to her.

Her mother approached, walking crisply
across the scattered leaves that blew around their
feet.

'Happy Christmas, Lucy,' she said.

'And you,' Lucy said. They leaned awkwardly
towards one another, briefly pressing their
cheeks lightly together.

'I didn't know you visited him,' Lucy said.

'Well, I do.'

'He's not well,' she said, unnecessarily.

Her mother nodded absently. She glanced
around, pulling her coat tighter around her

_nst the bracing wind. 'So, what are your _ns for the day?'

'I'll see Robbie. Then Tom Fleming asked me _o help out with a soup kitchen he works in for the homeless and that. Part of his Christian group.'

'You could call for some dinner later with me, if you wanted,' her mother said. 'I'm having some friends around. But you'd still be welcome.'

Lucy smiled. 'Thanks, but I'm OK.'

'You'd rather eat with the homeless?'

'I've things to do,' Lucy said, suddenly pained that she had inadvertently offended the woman.

'On Christmas Day?'

Lucy shrugged. 'It's just a day,' she said, feeling her eyes fill. The gash on her cheek, stitched up a few nights previous, throbbed angrily.

'I see,' her mother said. 'I'll go on.'

Lucy nodded and turned to fumble with her car keys again.

'Oh, we found Jackie Logue last night,' her mother said, turning on her step.

'Really?' Lucy asked. Logue had vanished soon after his son, Peter Bell, had been arrested in Magilligan. They'd assumed someone had tipped him off that the PSNI would be coming for him. 'Where's he being held?'

'The morgue. He'd been stripped naked and shot in the head. His body was laid out on the train tracks where they found Karen Hughes.'

'That's . . . terrible,' Lucy said, aware of how insincere the words sounded.

'Yes. Eoghan Harkin gets out of prison, Logue goes missing, then he's murdered on the spot where Harkin's daughter was found. You'd s~~ someone had told Harkin that Logue ~~ involved in Karen's death.'

Lucy felt the wound in her face throb again.

'And you were so moralistic,' her mother said.

'I don't know what you mean,' Lucy mumbled, her face flushing.

'You were spotted picking up Harkin outside the prison. What did you tell him?'

Lucy shook her head but said nothing.

Her mother stepped closer to her again. 'I put you in PPU because I didn't think you'd be able to handle the politics of CID. I thought you were better than that. It seems I was wrong.' She regarded Lucy a moment coldly, as if appraising her anew. 'You're more like than me than you want to admit.'

With that, she turned and strode off. Lucy stood watching her, her face so hot and sore, she felt as though she had been slapped.

* * *

Robbie was eating his own dinner when Lucy went in. He smiled as she entered the room, leaning towards her to accept her kiss.

'Merry Christmas,' he said.

Lucy smiled, sitting on the bed next to him. 'How are you feeling?'

'Sore,' he said. 'But I'll recover.'

Lucy took his hand in hers, was reminded in the gesture of the feeling of her father's hand earlier.

'I am sorry, Robbie. For this. And for us, too.'

e smiled sadly. 'I know, Lucy.'

'd rather it had been me,' she said. 'You
ln't deserve all this.'

He shrugged. 'I'm glad it wasn't you,' he said.

'When do you get out?' Lucy asked,
embarrassed by his comment.

'The next day or two,' he said. 'I'm going to go
home for a while. To my folks.'

'Do you want me to give you a lift up? I'll
check under the car before you get into it this
time,' Lucy said.

'And so you should,' Robbie joked. 'No. My
dad's going to collect me.'

Lucy swallowed, shifting on the bed. 'Will I
see you over the holidays at all?'

Robbie looked at her, his eyes soft in their
kindness. 'I don't know,' he said. 'I'm not sure
what's happening.'

'With the holidays or with us?' Lucy said,
trying to smile, pretending indifference.

'Both,' he said. 'Either. I'm not sure.'

Lucy patted his hand with hers, then lifted it
again and, clasping it between both hers, drew it
to her lips and kissed the skin between his finger
and thumb.

'I am sorry,' she repeated.

★　★　★

She didn't go to the cemetery in the end. Instead
she found herself once more on Petrie Way,
glancing in the mirror at the wrapped gift that
sat on the back seat of the car as she pulled up
outside the house.

She sat, watching the house, wonde
whether she should leave the gift at all. Perh
wait until the sky darkened and then leave it
the doorstep. But she knew they would nev
give it to the child, not knowing whence it came

Finally, she got out, clutching the gift in her
hand. She made it as far as the driveway of the
house before stopping. Through the large front
window she could see, in the lounge, the Kelly
family sitting on the floor. Joe sat at the centre of
a scattered collection of new toys, his foster
mother helping him play with a truck while her
husband recorded it.

Lucy could see, for the first time, how happy
the child looked, how content was the whole
family. She knew that, if she knocked at the
door, left her gift, she would have to explain how
she knew the child and why she felt responsible
for him. She would have to share Mary's
sacrifice with them. She knew that the
knowledge of what had happened to him would
profit none of them. In the end, she turned to
leave.

Across the street, a neighbour was standing at
his car, watching her. 'Are you looking for
someone?' he called over.

'No,' Lucy said. 'I've the wrong house,' she
explained, moving back to her car.

★ ★ ★

Around four she went to the soup kitchen where
Tom Fleming was working. She helped them to
prepare the meals for the homeless. As she

402

ed laying the tables, she watched out for
..et, the girl who had featured so prominently
Lucy's own father's past. The last time Lucy
..ad seen her she had been living on the street, an
alcoholic, abandoned by her own family. Lucy
hoped and feared, in equal measure, that Janet
might appear at the soup kitchen for food, but
she did not.

After the dinner, she and Fleming stood in the
kitchen of the church hall, drinking coffee.

'Pudding?' Fleming asked, offering her a dish.

Lucy shook her head. 'I'm stuffed.'

'I'm not allowed it,' Fleming said, putting the
dish down a little ruefully. 'Because of the
brandy. In case it sets me off on another bender,'
he added with a smirk.

'How is it going?' Lucy asked.

'I'm OK,' he said, smiling lightly. 'I had to dry
out for a few days. It was a little hairy, but
. . . it's done now.'

Lucy nodded. 'I did tell them you didn't miss
that stuff in Kay's. I told them it was planted.'

Fleming patted her arm. 'I know,' he said.
'Your mother told me. But she was right, Lucy. I
needed a break, to sort myself out. I wasn't
doing anyone any favours, the state I was in.'

'Are you OK now?'

He nodded. 'I will be,' he said. 'I heard about
the attack on your car. Are *you* OK?'

Lucy nodded, busying herself with rinsing her
cup. 'Robbie was the one who was hurt.'

'You're not having dinner with your mum
today?'

Lucy shook her head. 'No. I must feel more at

home here, I guess,' she said, looking aroun the ragged dinner guests sitting before her.

'You and me both,' Fleming said, putting l arm around her shoulders and briefly pulling he close. 'Happy Christmas, Lucy.'

'And you, Tom.'

* * *

She drove down through the Waterside on her way home. As she passed the shops at Gobnascale, she glanced across. They were closed for the day, their shutters pulled. Despite that, a group of kids still gathered outside them, standing in a loose circle.

As she slowed to glance across, Lucy saw a car sitting in the parking bay opposite, the door open, the owner sitting half out of the car, watching over the group, a cigarette in his hand.

When he saw her, Eoghan Harkin stood and moved across to the fence between the shops and the road.

Lucy rolled down the window as she pulled abreast where he stood.

'Have you no home to go to?' Harkin asked. 'It's Christmas.'

'I could say the same,' Lucy said.

'Someone needs to keep an eye on this crowd. Give them some direction. Now that there's a vacancy in the area, what with Jackie Logue in the wind.'

'Not any more. They found his body on the railway tracks last night.'

'Did they now?' Harkin asked. 'Imagine that.'

e smiled at her, his grin feral. Lucy tried to ore the sickness gnawing at her guts.

'So what about Alan Cunningham? Any amours on his whereabouts?' Lucy asked.

Harkin straightened, looking across the top of her car a second, drawing a final pull on his cigarette. 'I wouldn't know anything about that, now,' he said. 'Though wherever he tries to go from here onwards, he'll be getting a cold reception. He'll have no more bolt-holes. He'll have to resurface eventually. When he does, you'll need to be ready to grab him, Sergeant.'

Suddenly, two figures stepped out onto the road from the pavement opposite and passed in front of her. Gavin, his arm wrapped protectively around Elena's shoulder, his head held high, crossed in front of Lucy's car while she waited, staring in at her as he did so. Lucy held his stare until finally the boy had to turn away to step up onto the pavement where Harkin stood. At his arrival, the group of youths, who had been at the shop, moved towards him, their voices raised in greeting, as if to welcome a returning conqueror, encircling him the way they had once done for Tony.

Harkin smiled and raised his voice to be heard above the noise of the youths. 'That's the thing about your bad deeds. They'll always resurface eventually,' he added. 'You take care for now, Lucy Black. I'll be seeing you again.'

Lucy watched as he turned to lead the gang back to the shops, Gavin by his side, the youths trailing in his wake.

'I can promise you that,' she said.

Acknowledgements

Thanks to Finbar Madden and all my friends and colleagues in St Columb's College for their continuing support, and to Bob McKimm and James Johnston for their invaluable advice.

Thanks to all the team at Constable & Robinson, particularly James Gurbutt, Lucy Zilberkweit, Clive Hebard, Sandra Ferguson and Martin Palmer, and to Jenny Hewson of RCW and Emily Hickman of The Agency.

Continued thanks to the McGilloways, Dohertys, O'Neills and Kerlins for their support, especially Carmel, Joe and Dermot, and my parents, Laurence and Katrina, to whom this book is dedicated.

Finally, my love and thanks to my wife, Tanya, and our children, Ben, Tom, David and Lucy.

We do hope that you have enjoyed reading this large print book.

Did you know that all of our titles are available for purchase?

We publish a wide range of high quality large print books including:
Romances, Mysteries, Classics
General Fiction
Non Fiction and Westerns

Special interest titles available in large print are:
The Little Oxford Dictionary
Music Book
Song Book
Hymn Book
Service Book

Also available from us courtesy of Oxford University Press:
Young Readers' Dictionary
(large print edition)
Young Readers' Thesaurus
(large print edition)

For further information or a free brochure, please contact us at:
Ulverscroft Large Print Books Ltd.,
The Green, Bradgate Road, Anstey,
Leicester, LE7 7FU, England.
Tel: (00 44) 0116 236 4325
Fax: (00 44) 0116 234 0205

Other titles published by Ulverscroft.

THE NAMELESS DEAD

Brian McGilloway

Declan Cleary's body has never been found, but everyone believes he was killed for informing on a friend over thirty years ago. Now the Commission for the Location of Victims' Remains is following a tip-off that he was buried on the small isle of Islandmore, in the middle of the River Foyle. Instead, the dig uncovers a baby's skeleton, and it doesn't look like death by natural causes. But evidence revealed by the Commission's activities cannot lead to prosecution. Inspector Devlin is torn. He has no desire to resurrect the violent divisions of the recent past. Neither can he let a suspected murderer go unpunished. He must trust his conscience — even when that puts those closest to him at terrible risk . . .

LITTLE GIRL LOST

Brian McGilloway

Midwinter. A child is found wandering in woodland, her hands covered in blood. Unwilling, or unable to speak, the only person she trusts is the officer who rescued her, Detective Sergeant Lucy Black. Then, DS Black is baffled when she's suddenly moved from a high-profile case involving the kidnapping of another girl, a prominent businessman's teenage daughter. Black's problems are not only professional: she's caring for her increasingly unstable father, and trying to avoid conflict with her frosty mother: the Assistant Chief Constable. As she struggles to identify the unclaimed child, Black begins to realize that her case and the kidnapping may be linked by events that occurred during the grimmest days of the country's recent history — events that also defined her own troubled childhood.

THE RISING

Brian McGilloway

Garda Inspector Benedict Devlin is summoned to a burning barn and finds the remains of a local drug dealer. And when it becomes clear that his death was no accident, suspicion falls on a local vigilante group: former paramilitaries called The Rising. Meanwhile, Devlin's former colleague's teenage son has gone missing during a seaside camping trip. Devlin is relieved when the boy's mother, Caroline Williams, receives a text message from her son's phone, but is mystified when a body is washed up on a nearby beach. When another drug dealer is killed, Devlin realizes this is not just civic-minded vigilantism. But a personal crisis strikes at the heart of Ben's own family, and he's forced to confront the compromises his career has forced upon him . . .